maKers

maKers

CORY DOCTOROW

HARPER
Voyager

HarperCollins*Publishers*
77–85 Fulham Palace Road,
Hammersmith, London W6 8JB

www.harpercollins.co.uk

Published by Harper*Voyager*
An imprint of HarperCollins*Publishers* 2009

1

A catalogue record for this book
is available from the British Library

ISBN-13: 978 0 00 732522 1

Printed and bound in Great Britain by
Clays Ltd, St Ives plc

For "the risk-takers, the doers, the makers of things"

PART I

Suzanne Church almost never had to bother with the blue blazer these days. Back at the height of the dot-boom, she'd put on her business-journalist drag—blazer, blue sailcloth shirt, khaki trousers, loafers—just about every day, putting in her obligatory appearances at splashy press conferences for high-flying IPOs and mergers. These days, it was mostly work at home or one day a week at the *San Jose Mercury*'s office, in comfortable light sweaters with loose necks and loose cotton pants that she could wear straight to yoga after shutting her computer's lid.

Blue blazer today, and she wasn't the only one. There was Grimes from the *NYT*'s Silicon Valley office, and Gomes from the *WSJ*, and that despicable rat-toothed jumped-up gossip columnist from one of the U.K. tech-rags, and many others besides. Old home week, blue blazers fresh from the dry-cleaning bags that had guarded them since the last time the NASDAQ broke five thousand.

The man of the hour was Landon Kettlewell—the kind of outlandish prep-school name that always seemed a little made up to her—the new CEO and front for the majority owners of Kodak/Duracell. The despicable Brit had already started calling them Kodacell. Buying the company was pure Kettlewell: shrewd, weird, and ethical in a twisted way.

"Why the hell have you done this, Landon?" Kettlewell asked himself into his tie-mic. Ties and suits for the new Kodacell execs in the room, like surfers playing dress-up. "Why buy two dinosaurs and stick 'em together? Will they mate and give birth to a new generation of less-endangered dinosaurs?"

He shook his head and walked to a different part of the stage, thumbing a PowerPoint remote that advanced his slide on the JumboTron to a picture of a couple of unhappy cartoon brontos staring desolately at an empty nest. "Probably not. But there is a good case for what we've just done, and with your indulgence, I'm going to lay it out for you now."

"Let's hope he sticks to the cartoons," Rat-Toothed hissed beside her. His breath smelled like he'd been gargling turds. He had a not-so-secret crush on her and liked to demonstrate his alpha-maleness by making half-witticisms into her ear. "They're about his speed."

She twisted in her seat and pointedly hunched over her computer's screen, to which she'd taped a thin sheet of polarized plastic that made it opaque to anyone shoulder-surfing her. Being a halfway-attractive woman in Silicon Valley was more of a pain in the ass than she'd expected, back when she'd been covering rust belt shenanigans in Detroit, back when there was an auto industry in Detroit. California was full of pretty girls, right? But that was the *other* California, south of San Luis Obispo, the part of the state where the women shaved their pits and straightened their hair. The women of Silicon Valley were only barely more attractive than their male counterparts.

The worst part was that the Brit's reportage was just spleen-filled editorializing on the lack of ethics in the valley's boardrooms (a favorite subject of hers, which no doubt accounted for his fellow-feeling), and it was also the crux of Kettlewell's schtick. The spectacle of an exec who talked ethics enraged Rat-Toothed more than the vilest baby killers. He was the kind of revolutionary who liked his firing squads arranged in a circle.

"I'm not that dumb, folks," Kettlewell said, provoking a stagy laugh from Mr. Rat-Tooth. "Here's the thing: the market had valued these companies at less than their cash on hand. They have twenty billion in the bank and a sixteen-billion-dollar market cap. We just made four billion dollars, just by buying up the stock and taking control of the company. We could shut the doors, stick the money in our pockets, and retire."

Suzanne took notes. She knew all this, but Kettlewell gave good sound bite, and talked slow in deference to the kind of reporter who preferred a notebook to a recorder. "But we're not gonna do that." He hunkered down on his haunches at the edge of the stage, letting his tie dangle, staring spacily at the journalists and analysts. "Kodacell is bigger than that." He'd read his email that morning, then, and seen Rat-Toothed's new moniker. "Kodacell has goodwill. It has infrastructure. Administrators. Physical plant. Supplier relationships. Distribution and logistics. These companies have a lot of useful plumbing and a lot of priceless reputation.

"What we don't have is a product. There aren't enough buyers for batteries or film—or any of the other stuff we make—to occupy or support all that infrastructure. These companies slept through the dot-boom and the dot-bust, trundling along as though none of it mattered. There are parts of these businesses that haven't changed since the fifties.

"We're not the only ones. Technology has challenged and killed businesses from every sector. Hell, IBM *doesn't make computers anymore*! The very idea of a travel agent is inconceivably weird today! And the record labels, oy, the poor, crazy, suicidal, stupid record labels. Don't get me started.

"Capitalism is eating itself. The market works, and when it works, it commodifies or obsoletes everything. That's not to say that there's no money out there to be had, but the money won't come from a single, monolithic product line. The days of companies with names like General Electric and General Mills and General Motors are over. The money on the table is like krill: a billion little entrepreneurial opportunities that can be discovered and exploited by smart, creative people.

"We will brute-force the problem-space of capitalism in the twenty-first century. Our business plan is simple: we will hire the smartest people we can find and put them in small teams. They will go into the field with funding and communications infrastructure—all that stuff we have left over from the era of batteries and film—behind them, capitalized to find a place to live and work, and a job to do. A business to start. Our company isn't a project that we pull together on, it's a *network* of like-minded, cooperating autonomous teams, all of which are empowered to do whatever they want, provided that it returns something to our coffers. We will explore and exhaust the realm of commercial opportunities, and seek constantly to refine our tactics to mine those opportunities, and the krill will strain through our mighty maw and fill our hungry belly. This company isn't a company anymore: this company is a network, an approach, a sensibility."

Suzanne's fingers clattered over her keyboard. The Brit chuckled nastily. "Nice talk, considering he just made a hundred thousand people redundant," he said. Suzanne tried to shut him out: yes, Kettlewell was firing a company's worth full of people, but he was also saving the company itself. The prospectus had a decent severance for all those departing workers, and the ones who'd taken advantage of the company stock-buying plan would find their pensions augmented by whatever this new scheme could rake in. If it worked.

"Mr. Kettlewell?" Rat-Toothed had clambered to his hind legs.

"Yes, Freddy?" Freddy was Rat-Toothed's given name, though Suzanne was hard-pressed to ever retain it for more than a few minutes at a time. Kettlewell knew every business journalist in the Valley by name, though. It was a CEO thing.

"Where will you recruit this new workforce from? And what kind of entrepreneurial things will they be doing to 'exhaust the realm of commercial opportunities'?"

"Freddy, we don't have to recruit anyone. They're beating a path to our door. *This* is a nation of manic entrepreneurs, the kind of people who've been inventing businesses from video arcades to photomats for centuries." Freddy scowled skeptically, his jumble of gray tombstone teeth protruding. "Come on, Freddy, you ever hear of the Grameen Bank?"

Freddy nodded slowly. "In India, right?"

"Bangladesh. Bankers travel from village to village on foot and by bus, finding small co-ops who need tiny amounts of credit to buy a cellphone or a goat or a loom in order to grow. The bankers make the loans and advise the entrepreneurs, and the payback rate is fifty times higher than the rate at a regular lending institution. They don't even have a written lending agreement: entrepreneurs—real, hard-working entrepreneurs—you can trust on a handshake."

"You're going to help Americans who lost their jobs in your factories buy goats and cellphones?"

"We're going to give them loans and coordination to start businesses that use information, materials science, commodified software and hardware designs, and creativity to wring a profit from the air around us. Here, catch!" He dug into his suit jacket and flung a small object toward Freddy, who fumbled it. It fell onto Suzanne's keyboard.

She picked it up. It looked like a key-chain laser pointer, or maybe a novelty lightsaber.

"Switch it on, Suzanne, please, and shine it, oh, on that wall there." Kettlewell pointed at the upholstered retractable wall that divided the hotel ballroom into two functional spaces.

Suzanne twisted the end and pointed it. A crisp rectangle of green laser-light lit up the wall.

"Now, watch this," Kettlewell said.

NOW WATCH THIS

The words materialized in the middle of the rectangle on the distant wall.

"Testing one two three," Kettlewell said.

TESTING ONE TWO THREE

"Donde está el baño?"

WHERE IS THE BATHROOM

"What is it?" said Suzanne. Her hand wobbled a little and the distant letters danced.

WHAT IS IT

"This is a new artifact designed and executed by five previously out-of-work engineers in Athens, Georgia. They've mated a tiny Linux box with some speaker-independent continuous speech recognition software, a free software translation engine that can translate between any of twelve languages, and an extremely high-resolution LCD that blocks out words in the path of the laser pointer.

"Turn this on, point it at a wall, and start talking. Everything said shows up on the wall, in the language of your choosing, regardless of what language the speaker was speaking."

All the while, Kettlewell's words were scrolling by in black block caps on that distant wall: crisp, laser-edged letters.

"This thing wasn't invented. All the parts necessary to make this go were just lying around. It was *assembled*. A gal in a garage, her brother the marketing guy, her husband overseeing manufacturing in Belgrade. They needed a couple grand to get it all going, and they'll need some life support while they find their natural market.

"They got twenty grand from Kodacell this week. Half of it a loan, half of it equity. And we put them on the payroll, with benefits. They're part freelancer, part employee, in a team with backing and advice from across the whole business.

"It was easy to do once. We're going to do it ten thousand times this year. We're sending out talent scouts, like the artists and representation people the record labels used to use, and they're going to sign up a lot of these bands for us, and help them to cut records, to start businesses that push out to the edges of business.

"So, Freddy, to answer your question, no, we're not giving them loans to buy cellphones and goats."

Kettlewell beamed. Suzanne twisted the laser pointer off and made ready to toss it back to the stage, but Kettlewell waved her off.

"Keep it," he said. It was suddenly odd to hear him speak without the text crawl on that distant wall. She put the laser pointer in her pocket and reflected that it had the authentic feel of cool, disposable technology: the kind of thing on its way from a start-up's distant supplier to the schwag bags at high-end technology conferences to blister packs of six hanging in the impulse aisle at Fry's.

She tried to imagine the technology conferences she'd been to with the addition of the subtitling and translation and couldn't do it. Not conferences. Something else. A kids' toy? A tool for use by Starbucks-smashing anti-globalists planning strategy before a WTO riot? She patted her pocket.

Freddy hissed and bubbled like a teakettle beside her, fuming. "What a cock," he muttered. "Thinks he's going to hire ten thousand teams to replace his workforce, doesn't say a word about what *that* lot is meant to be doing now he's shitcanned them all. Utter bullshit. Irrational exuberance gone berserk."

Suzanne had a perverse impulse to turn the wand back on and splash Freddy's bilious words across the ceiling, and the thought made her giggle. She suppressed it and kept on piling up notes, thinking about the structure of the story she'd file that day.

Kettlewell pulled out some charts, and another surfer in a suit came forward to talk money, walking them through the financials. She'd read them already and decided that they were a pretty credible bit of fiction, so she let her mind wander.

She was a hundred miles away when the ballroom doors burst open and the unionized laborers of the former Kodak and the former Duracell poured in on them, tossing literature into the air so that it snowed angry leaflets. They had a big drum and a bugle, and they shook tambourines. The hotel rent-a-cops occasionally darted forward and grabbed a protestor by the arm, but her colleagues would immediately swarm them and pry her loose and drag her back into the body of the demonstration. Freddy grinned and shouted something at Kettlewell, but it was lost in the din. The journalists took a lot of pictures.

Suzanne closed her computer's lid and snatched a leaflet out of the air. WHAT ABOUT US? it began, and talked about the workers who'd been at Kodak and Duracell for twenty, thirty, even forty years, who had been conspicuously absent from Kettlewell's stated plans to date.

She twisted the laser pointer to life and pointed it back at the wall. Leaning in very close, she said, "What are your plans for your existing workforce, Mr. Kettlewell?"

WHAT ARE YOUR PLANS FOR YOUR EXISTING WORKFORCE MR KETTLEWELL

She repeated the question several times, refreshing the text so that it scrolled like a stock ticker across that upholstered wall, an illuminated focus that gradually drew all the attention in the room. The protestors saw it and began to laugh, then they read it aloud in ragged unison, until it became a chant: WHAT ARE YOUR PLANS—*thump* of the big drum—FOR YOUR EXISTING WORKFORCE *thump* MR. *thump* KETTLEWELL?

Suzanne felt her cheeks warm. Kettlewell was looking at her with something like a smile. She liked him, but that was a personal thing and this was a truth thing. She was a little embarrassed that she had let him finish his spiel without calling him on that obvious question. She felt tricked, somehow. Well, she was making up for it now.

On the stage, the surfer boys in suits were confabbing, holding their thumbs over their tie-mics. Finally, Kettlewell stepped up and held up his own laser pointer, painting another rectangle of light beside Suzanne's.

"I'm glad you asked that, Suzanne," he said, his voice barely audible.

I'M GLAD YOU ASKED THAT SUZANNE

The journalists chuckled. Even the chanters laughed a little. They quieted down.

"I'll tell you, there's a downside to living in this age of wonders: we are moving too fast and outstripping the ability of our institutions to keep pace with the changes in the world."

Freddy leaned over her shoulder, blowing shit-breath in her ear. "Translation: you're ass-fucked, the lot of you."

TRANSLATION YOUR ASS FUCKED THE LOT OF YOU

Suzanne yelped as the words appeared on the wall and reflexively swung the pointer around, painting them on the ceiling, the opposite wall, and then, finally, in miniature, on her computer's lid. She twisted the pointer off.

Freddy had the decency to look slightly embarrassed, and he slunk away to the very end of the row of seats, scooting from chair to chair on his narrow butt. On stage, Kettlewell was pretending very hard that he hadn't seen the profanity, and that he couldn't hear the jeering from the protestors now, even though it had grown so loud that he could no longer be heard over it. He kept on talking, and the words scrolled over the far wall.

THERE IS NO WORLD IN WHICH KODAK AND DURACELL GO ON MAKING FILM AND BATTERIES

THE COMPANIES HAVE MONEY IN THE BANK BUT IT HEMORRHAGES OUT THE DOOR EVERY DAY

WE ARE MAKING THINGS THAT NO ONE WANTS TO BUY

THIS PLAN INCLUDES A GENEROUS SEVERANCE FOR THOSE STAFFERS WORKING IN THE PARTS OF THE BUSINESS THAT WILL CLOSE DOWN

Suzanne admired the twisted, long-way-around way of saying "the people we're firing." Pure CEO passive voice. She couldn't type notes and read off the wall at the same time. She whipped out her little snapshot and monkeyed with it until it was in video mode and then started shooting the ticker.

BUT IF WE ARE TO MAKE GOOD ON THAT SEVERANCE WE NEED TO BE IN BUSINESS

WE NEED TO BE BRINGING IN A PROFIT SO THAT WE CAN MEET OUR OBLIGATIONS TO ALL OUR STAKEHOLDERS SHAREHOLDERS AND WORKFORCE ALIKE

WE CAN'T PAY A PENNY IN SEVERANCE IF WE'RE BANKRUPT

WE ARE HIRING 50000 NEW EMPLOYEES THIS YEAR AND THERE'S NOTHING THAT SAYS THAT THOSE NEW PEOPLE CAN'T COME FROM WITHIN

CURRENT EMPLOYEES WILL BE GIVEN CONSIDERATION BY OUR SCOUTS

ENTREPRENEURSHIP IS A DEEPLY AMERICAN PRACTICE AND OUR WORKERS ARE AS CAPABLE OF ENTREPRENEURIAL ACTION AS ANYONE

I AM CONFIDENT WE WILL FIND MANY OF OUR NEW HIRES FROM WITHIN OUR EXISTING WORKFORCE

I SAY THIS TO OUR EMPLOYEES

IF YOU HAVE EVER DREAMED OF STRIKING OUT ON YOUR OWN EXECUTING ON SOME AMAZING IDEA AND NEVER FOUND THE MEANS TO DO IT NOW IS THE TIME AND WE ARE THE PEOPLE TO HELP

Suzanne couldn't help but admire the pluck it took to keep speaking into the pointer, despite the howls and bangs.

"C'mon, I'm gonna grab some bagels before the protestors get to them," Freddy said, plucking at her arm—apparently, this was his version of a charming pickup line. She shook him off authoritatively, with a whip-crack of her elbow.

Freddy stood there for a minute and then moved off. She waited to see if Kettlewell would say anything more, but he twisted the pointer off, shrugged, and waved at the hooting protestors and the analysts and the journalists and walked offstage with the rest of the surfers in suits.

She got some comments from a few of the protestors, some details. Worked for Kodak or Duracell all their lives. Gave everything to the company. Took voluntary pay cuts under the old management five times in ten years to keep the business afloat, now facing layoffs as a big fat thank-you-suckers. So many kids. Such and such a mortgage.

She knew these stories from Detroit: she'd filed enough copy with varying renditions of it to last a lifetime. Silicon Valley was supposed to be different. Growth and entrepreneurship—a failed company was just a stepping-stone to a successful one, can't win them all, dust yourself off and get back to the garage and start inventing. There's a whole world waiting out there!

Mother of three. Dad whose bright daughter's university fund was raided to make ends meet during the "temporary" austerity measures. This one has a Down's syndrome kid and that one worked through three back surgeries to help meet production deadlines.

Half an hour before, she'd been full of that old Silicon Valley optimism, the sense that there was a better world aborning around her. Now she was back in that old rustbelt funk, with the feeling that she was witness not to a beginning, but to a perpetual ending, a cycle of destruction that would tear down everything solid and reliable in the world.

She packed up her laptop and stepped out into the parking lot. Across the freeway, she could make out the bones of the Great America fun-park roller coasters whipping around and around in the warm California sun.

These little tech-hamlets down the 101 were deceptively utopian. All the homeless people were miles north on the streets of San Francisco, where pedestrian marks for panhandling could be had, where the crack was sold on corners instead of out of the trunks of fresh-faced, friendly coke dealers' cars. Down here it was giant malls, purpose-built dot-com buildings, and the occasional fun-park. Palo Alto was a university-town theme park, provided you steered clear of the wrong side of the tracks, the East Palo Alto slums that were practically shanties.

Christ, she was getting melancholy. She didn't want to go into the office—not today. Not when she was in this kind of mood. She would go home and put her blazer back in the closet and change into yoga togs and write her column and have some good coffee.

She nailed up the copy in an hour and emailed it to her editor and poured herself a glass of Napa red (the local vintages in Michigan likewise left something to be desired) and settled onto her porch, overlooking the big reservoir off 280 near San Mateo.

The house had been worth a small fortune at the start of the dot-boom, but now, in the resurgent property boom, it was worth a large fortune and then some. She could conceivably sell this badly built little shack with its leaky hot tub for enough money to retire on, if she wanted to live out the rest of her days in Sri Lanka or Nebraska.

"You've got no business feeling poorly, young lady," she said to herself. "You are as well set up as you could have dreamed, and you are right in the thick of the weirdest and best time the world has yet seen. And Landon Kettlewell knows your name."

She finished the wine and opened her computer. It was dark enough now with the sun set behind the hills that she could read the screen. The Web was full of interesting things, her email full of challenging notes from her readers, and her editor had already signed off on her column.

She was getting ready to shut the lid and head for bed, so she pulled her mail once more.

From: kettlewell-l@skunkworks.kodacell.com
To: schurch@sjmercury.com
Subject: Embedded journalist?

Thanks for keeping me honest today, Suzanne. It's the hardest question we're facing today: what happens when all the things you're good at are no good to anyone anymore? I hope we're going to answer that with the new model.

You do good work, madam. I'd be honored if you'd consider joining one of our little teams for a couple months and chronicling what they do. I feel like we're making history here and we need someone to chronicle it.

I don't know if you can square this with the *Merc,* and I suppose that we should be doing this through my PR people and your editor, but there comes a time about this time every night when I'm just too goddamned hyper to bother with all that stuff and I want to just DO SOMETHING instead of ask someone else to start a process to investigate the possibility of someday possibly maybe doing something.

Will you do something with us, if we can make it work? 100 percent access, no oversight? Say you will.
Please.

Your pal,
Kettlebelly

She stared at her screen. It was like a work of art; just look at that return address, "kettlewell-l@skunkworks.kodacell.com"—for kodacell.com to be live and accepting mail, it had to have been registered the day before. She had a vision of Kettlewell checking his email at midnight before his big press conference, catching Freddy's column, and registering kodacell.com on the spot, then waking up some sysadmin to get a mail server answering at skunkworks.kodacell.com. Last she'd heard, Lockheed Martin was threatening to sue anyone who used their trademarked term "Skunk Works" to describe a generic R&D department. That meant that Kettlewell had moved so fast that he hadn't even run this project by legal. She was willing to bet that he'd already ordered new business cards with the address on them.

There was a guy she knew, an editor at a mag who'd assigned himself a plum article that he'd run on his own cover. He'd gotten a book deal out of it. A half-million-dollar book deal. If Kettlewell was right, then the exclusive book on the inside of the first year at Kodacell could easily make that advance. And the props would be mad, as the kids said.

Kettlebelly! It was such a stupid frat-boy nickname, but it made her smile. He wasn't taking himself seriously, or maybe he was, but he wasn't being a pompous ass about it. He was serious about changing the world and frivolous about everything else. She'd have a hard time being an objective reporter if she said yes to this.

She couldn't possibly decide at this hour. She needed a night's sleep and she had to talk this over with the *Merc.* If she had a boyfriend, she'd have to talk it over with him, but that wasn't a problem in her life these days.

She spread on some expensive duty-free French wrinkle cream and brushed her teeth and put on her nightie and double-checked the door locks and did all the normal things she did of an evening. Then she folded back her sheets, plumped her pillows and stared at them.

She turned on her heel and stalked back to her computer and thumped the spacebar until the thing woke from sleep.

From: schurch@sjmercury.com
To: kettlewell-l@skunkworks.kodacell.com
Subject: Re: Embedded journalist?

Kettlebelly: that is one dumb nickname. I couldn't possibly associate myself with a grown man who calls himself Kettlebelly.

So stop calling yourself Kettlebelly, immediately. If you can do that, we've got a deal.

Suzanne

There had come a day when her readers acquired email and the paper ran her address with her byline, and her readers had begun to write her and write her and write her. Some were amazing, informative, thoughtful notes. Some were the vilest, most bilious trolling. In order to deal with these notes, she had taught herself to pause, breathe, and reread any email message before clicking send.

The reflex kicked in now and she reread her note to Kettlebelly—Kettlewell!—and felt a crimp in her guts. Then she hit send.

She needed to pee, and apparently had for some time, without realizing it. She was on the toilet when she heard the *ping* of new incoming mail.

From: kettlewell-l@skunkworks.kodacell.com
To: schurch@sjmercury.com
Subject: Re: Embedded journalist?

I will never call myself Kettlebelly again.

Your pal,
Kettledrum

Oh-shit-oh-shit-oh-shit. She did a little two-step at her bed's edge. Tomorrow she'd go see her editor about this, but it just felt *right,* and exciting, like she was on the brink of an event that would change her life forever.

It took her three hours of mindless Web-surfing, including a truly dreary Hot or Not clicktrance and an hour's worth of fiddling with tweets from the press conference, before she was able to lull herself to sleep. As she nodded off, she thought that Kettlewell's insomnia was as contagious as his excitement.

Hollywood, Florida's biggest junkyard was situated in the rubble of a half-built ghost mall off Taft Street. Suzanne's Miami-airport rental car came with a GPS, but the little box hadn't ever heard of the mall; it was off the map. So she took a moment in the sweltering parking lot of her coffin hotel to call her interview subject again and get better coordinates.

"Yeah, it's 'cause they never finished building the mall, so the address hasn't been included in the USGS maps. The open GPSs all have these better maps made by geohackers, but the rental car companies have got a real hard-on for official map data. Morons. Hang on, lemme get my GPS out and I'll get you some decent lat-long."

His voice had a pleasant, youthful, midwestern sound, like a Canadian newscaster: friendly and enthusiastic as a puppy. His name was Perry Gibbons, and if Kettlewell was to be believed, he was the most promising prospect identified by Kodacell's talent scouts.

The ghost mall was just one of many along Taft Street, ranging in size from little corner plazas to gigantic palaces with broken-in atria and cracked parking lots. A lot of the malls in California had crashed, but they'd been turned into flea markets or day cares, or, if they'd been abandoned, they hadn't been abandoned like this, left to go to ruin. This reminded her of Detroit before she'd left, whole swaths of the inner city emptied of people, neighborhoods condemned and bulldozed and, in a couple of weird cases, actually *farmed* by enterprising city dwellers who planted crops, kept livestock, and rode their mini-tractors beneath the beam of the defunct white-elephant monorail.

The other commonality this stretch of road shared with Detroit was the obesity of the people she passed. She'd felt a little self-conscious that morning, dressing in a light short-sleeved blouse and a pair of shorts—nothing else would do, the weather was so hot and drippy that even closed-toe shoes would have been intolerable. At forty-five, her legs had slight cellulite saddlebags and her tummy wasn't the washboard it had been when she was twenty-five. But here, on this stretch of road populated by people so fat they could barely walk, so fat that they were desexed marshmallows with faces like inflatable toys, she felt like a toothpick.

The GPS queeped when she came up on the junkyard, a sprawling, half-built discount mall whose waist-high walls had been used to parcel out different kinds of sorted waste. The mall had been planned with wide indoor boulevards between the shops, wide enough for two lanes of traffic, and she cruised those lanes now in the Hertzmobile, looking for a human. Once she reached the center of the mall—a dry fountain filled with dusty Christmas-tree ornaments— she stopped and leaned on the horn.

She got out of the car and called, "Hello? Perry?" She could have phoned him, but it always seemed so wasteful spending money on airtime when you were trying to talk to someone within shouting range.

"Suzanne!" The voice came from her left. She shielded her eyes from the sun's glare and peered down a spoke of mall lane and caught her first glimpse of Perry Gibbons. He was standing in the basket of a tall cherry picker, bare-chested and brown. He wore a sun visor and big work gloves, and big, baggy shorts whose pockets jangled as he shinnied down the crane's neck.

She started toward him tentatively. Not a lot of business-reporting assignments involved spending time with half-naked, sun-baked dudes in remote southern junkyards. Still, he sounded nice.

"Hello!" she called. He was young, twenty-two or twenty-three, and already had squint creases at the corners of his eyes. He had a brace on one wrist and his steel-toed boots were the mottled gray of a grease puddle on the floor of a muffler and brake shop.

He grinned and tugged off a glove, stuck out his hand. "A pleasure. Sorry for the trouble finding this place. It's not easy to get to, but it's cheap as hell."

"I believe it." She looked around again—the heaps of interesting trash, the fountain dish filled with thousands of shining ornaments. The smell was a mixture of machine oil and salt, jungle air, Florida swamp and Detroit steel. "So, this place is pretty cool. Looks like you've got pretty much everything you could imagine."

"And then some." This was spoken by another man, one who puffed heavily up from behind her. He was enormous, not just tall but fat, as big around as a barrel. His green T-shirt read IT'S FUN TO USE LEARNING FOR EVIL! in blocky, pixilated letters. He took her hand and shook it. "I love your blog," he said. "I read it all the time." He had three chins, and eyes that were nearly lost in his apple cheeks.

"Meet Lester," Perry said. "My partner."

"Sidekick," Lester said with a huge wink. "Sysadmin slash hardware hacker slash dogsbody slashdot org."

She chuckled. Nerd humor. Ar ar ar.

"Right, let's get started. You wanna see what I do, right?" Perry said.

"That's right," Suzanne said.

"Lead the way, Lester," Perry said, and gestured with an arm, deep into the center of the junk pile. "All right, check this stuff out as we go." He stuck his hand through the unglazed window of a never-built shop and plucked out a toy in a battered box. "I love these things," he said, handing it to her.

She took it. It was a Sesame Street Elmo doll, labeled BOOGIE WOOGIE ELMO.

"That's from the great Elmo Crash," Perry said, taking back the box and expertly extracting the Elmo like he was shelling a nut. "The last and greatest generation of Elmoid technology, cast into an uncaring world that bought millions of Li'l Tagger washable graffiti kits instead after Rosie gave them two thumbs up in her Christmas shopping guide.

"Poor Elmo was an orphan, and every junkyard in the world has mountains of mint-in-package BWEs, getting rained on, waiting to start their long, half-million-year decomposition.

"But check this out." He flicked a multitool off his belt and extracted a short, sharp scalpel blade. He slit the grinning, disco-suited Elmo open from chin to groin and shucked its furry exterior and the foam tissue that overlaid its skeleton. He slid the blade under the plastic cover on its ass and revealed a little printed circuit board.

"That's an entire Atom processor on a chip there," he said. "Each limb and the head have their own subcontrollers. There's a high-powered digital-to-analog rig for letting him sing and dance to new songs, and an analog-to-digital converter array for converting spoken and danced commands to motions. Basically, you dance and sing for Elmo and he'll dance and sing back for you."

Suzanne nodded. She'd missed that toy, which was a pity. She had a five-year-old goddaughter in Minneapolis who would have loved a Boogie Woogie Elmo.

They had come to a giant barn, set at the edge of a story and a half's worth of anchor store. "This used to be where the contractors kept their heavy equipment," Lester rumbled, aiming a car door remote at the door, which queeped and opened.

Inside, it was cool and bright, the chugging air conditioners efficiently blasting purified air over the many work surfaces. The barn was a good twenty-five feet tall, with a loft and a catwalk circling it halfway up. It was lined with metallic shelves stacked neatly with labeled boxes of parts scrounged from the junkyard.

Perry set Elmo down on a workbench and worked a miniature USB cable into his chest cavity. The other end terminated with a PDA with a small rubberized photovoltaic cell on the front.

"This thing is running InstallParty—it can recognize any hardware and build and install a Linux distro on it without human intervention. They used a ton of different suppliers for the BWE, so every one is a little different, depending on who was offering the cheapest parts the day it was built. InstallParty doesn't care, though: one click and away it goes." The PDA was doing all kinds of funny dances on its screen, montages of playful photoshopping of public figures matted into historical fine art.

"All done. Now, have a look—this is a Linux computer with some of the most advanced robotics ever engineered. No sweatshop stuff, either, see this? The solder is too precise to be done by hand—that's because it's from India. If it was from Cambodia, you'd see all kinds of wobble in the solder: that means that tiny, clever hands were used to create it, which means that somewhere in the device's karmic history, there's a sweatshop full of crippled children inhaling solder fumes until they keel over and are dumped in a ditch. This is the good stuff.

"So we have this karmically clean robot with infinitely malleable computation and a bunch of robotic capabilities. I've turned these things into wall-climbing monkeys; I've modded them for a woman from the University of Miami at the Jackson Memorial who used their capability to ape human motions in physiotherapy programs with nerve-damage cases. But the best thing I've done with them so far is the Distributed Boogie Woogie Elmo Motor Vehicle Operation Cluster. Come on," he said, and took off deeper into the barn's depths.

They came to a dusty, stripped-down Smart car, one of those tiny two-seat electric cars you could literally buy out of a vending machine in Europe. It was barely recognizable, having been reduced to its roll cage, drivetrain, and control panel. A gang of naked robot Elmos were piled into it.

"Wake up, boys; time for a demo!" Perry shouted, and they sat up and made canned, tinny Elmo "oh boy" noises, climbing into position on the pedals, around the wheel, and on the gear tree.

"I got the idea when I was teaching an Elmo to play Mario Brothers. I thought it'd get a decent diggdotting. I could get it to speedrun all of the first level using an old paddle I'd found and rehabilitated, and I was trying to figure out what to do next. The dead mall across the way is a drive-in theater, and I was out front watching the silent movies, and one of them showed all these cute little furry animated whatevers collectively driving a car. It's a really old sight gag, I mean, like racial memory old. I'd seen the Little Rascals do the same bit, with Alfalfa on the wheel and Buckwheat and Spanky on the brake and clutch and the doggy working the gearshift.

"And I thought, 'Shit, I could do that with Elmos. They don't have any networking capability, but they can talk and they can parse spoken commands, so all I need is to designate one for left and one for right and one for fast and one for slow and one to be the eyes, barking orders, and they should be able to do this.' And it works! They even adjust their balance and centers of gravity when the car swerves, to stay upright at their posts. Check it out." He turned to the car. "Driving Elmos, ten-HUT!" They snapped upright and ticked salutes off their naked plastic noggins. "In circles, DRIVE," he called. The Elmos scrambled into position and fired up the car and in short order they were doing doughnuts in the car's little indoor pasture.

"Elmos, HALT," Perry shouted and the car stopped silently, rocking gently. "Stand DOWN." The Elmos sat down with a series of tiny thumps.

Suzanne found herself applauding. "That was amazing," she said. "Really impressive. So that's what you're going to do for Kodacell, make these things out of recycled toys?"

Lester chuckled. "Nope, not quite. That's just for starters. The Elmos are all about the universal availability of cycles and apparatus. Everywhere you look, there's devices for free that have everything you need to make anything do anything.

"But have a look at part two—c'mere." He lumbered off in another direction, and Suzanne and Perry trailed along behind him.

"This is Lester's workshop," Perry said as they passed through a set of swinging double doors and into a cluttered wonderland. Where Perry's domain had been clean and neatly organized, Lester's area was a happy shambles. His shelves weren't orderly, but rather, crammed with looming piles of amazing junk: thrift-store wedding dresses, plaster statues of bowling monkeys, box kites, knee-high tin knights in armor, seashells painted with American flags, presidential action figures, paste jewelry, and antique cough-drop tins.

"You know how they say a sculptor starts with a block of marble and chips away everything that doesn't look like a statue? Like he can *see* the statue in the block? I get like that with garbage: I see the pieces on the heaps and in roadside trash and I can just *see* how it can go together, like this."

He reached down below a worktable and hoisted up a huge triptych made out of three hinged car doors stood on end. Carefully, he unfolded it and stood it like a screen on the cracked concrete floor.

The inside of the car doors had been stripped clean and polished to a high metal gleam that glowed like sterling silver. Spot-welded to it were all manner of soda tins, pounded flat and cut into gears, chutes, springs, and other mechanical apparatus.

"It's a mechanical calculator," he said proudly. "About half as powerful as Univac. I milled all the parts using a laser cutter. What you do is, fill this hopper with GI Joe heads, and this hopper with Barbie heads. Crank this wheel and it will drop a number of M&M's equal to the product of the two values into this hopper, here." He put three scuffed GI Joe heads in one hopper and four scrofulous Barbies in the other and began to crank, slowly. A music box beside the crank played a slow, irregular rendition of "Pop Goes the Weasel" while the hundreds of little coin-sized gears turned, flipping switches and adding and removing tension to springs. After the weasel popped a few times, twelve brown M&M's fell into an outstretched rubber hand. He picked them out carefully and offered them to her. "It's OK. They're not from the trash," he said. "I buy them in bulk." He turned his broad back to her and heaved a huge galvanized tin washtub full of brown M&M's in her direction. "See, it's a bit bucket!" he said.

Suzanne giggled in spite of herself. "You guys are hilarious," she said. "This is really good, exciting nerdy stuff." The gears on the mechanical computer were really sharp and precise; they looked like you could cut yourself on them. When they ground over the polished surfaces of the car doors, they made a sound like a box of toothpicks falling to the floor: *click-click, clickclickclick, click*. She turned the crank until twelve more brown M&M's fell out.

"Who's the Van Halen fan?"

Lester beamed. "Might as well jump—JUMP!" He mimed heavy-metal air guitar and thrashed his shorn head up and down as though he were headbanging with a mighty mane of hair-band locks. "You're the first one to get the joke!" he said. "Even Perry didn't get it!"

"Get what?" Perry said, also grinning.

"Van Halen had this thing where if there were any brown M&M's in their dressing room they'd trash it and refuse to play. When I was a kid, I used to *dream* about being so famous that I could act like that much of a prick. Ever since, I've afforded a great personal significance to brown M&M's."

She laughed again. Then she frowned a little. "Look, I hate to break this party up, but I came here because Kettlebelly—crap, Kettle*well*—said that you guys exemplified everything that he wanted to do with Kodacell. This stuff you've done is all very interesting—it's killer art—but I don't see the business angle. So, can you help me out here?"

"That's step three," Perry said. "C'mere." He led her back to his workspace, to a platform surrounded by articulated arms terminating in webcams, like a grocery scale in the embrace of a metal spider. "Three-D scanner," he said, producing a Barbie head from Lester's machine and dropping it on the scale. He prodded a button and a nearby screen filled with a three-dimensional model of the head, flattened on the side where it touched the surface. He turned the head over and scanned it again and now there were two digital versions of the head on the screen. He moused one over the other until they lined up, right-clicked a drop-down menu, selected an option, and then they were merged, rotating.

"Once we've got the three-D scan, it's basically plasticine." He distorted the barbie head, stretching it and squeezing it with the mouse. "So we can take a real object and make this kind of protean hyper-object out of it, or drop it down to a wireframe and skin it with any bitmap, like this." More fast mousing—barbie's head turned into a gridded mesh, fine filaments stretching off along each mussed strand of plastic hair. Then a Campbell's Cream of Mushroom Soup label wrapped around her like a stocking being pulled over her head. There was something stupendously weird and simultaneously very comic about the sight, the kind of inherent comedy in a cartoon stretched out on a blob of Silly Putty.

"So we can build anything out of interesting junk, with any shape, and then we can digitize the shape. Then we can do anything we like with the shape. Then we can output the shape." He typed quickly and another machine, sealed and mammoth like an outsized photocopier, started to grunt and churn. The air filled with a smell like Saran Wrap in a microwave.

"The goop we use in this thing is epoxy-based. You wouldn't want to build a car out of it, but it makes a mean dollhouse. The last stage of the output switches to inks, so you get whatever bitmap you've skinned your object with baked right in. It does about one cubic inch per minute, so this job should be almost done now."

He drummed his fingers on top of the machine for a moment and then it stopped chunking and something inside it went *clunk*. He lifted a lid and reached inside and plucked out the barbie head, stretched and distorted, skinned with a Campbell's Soup label. He handed it to Suzanne. She expected it to be warm, like a squashed penny from a machine on Fisherman's Wharf, but it was cool and had the seamless texture of a plastic margarine tub and the heft of a paperweight.

"So, that's the business," Lester said. "Or so we're told. We've been making cool stuff and selling it to collectors on the Web for, you know, gigantic bucks. We move one or two pieces a month at about ten grand per. But Kettlebelly says he's going to industrialize us, alienate us from the product of our labor, and turn us into an assembly line."

"He didn't say any such thing," Perry said. Suzanne was aware that her ears had grown points. Perry gave Lester an affectionate slug in the shoulder. "Lester's only kidding. What we need is a couple of dogsbodies and some bigger printers and we'll be able to turn out more-modest devices by the hundred or possibly the thousand. We can tweak the designs really easily because nothing is coming off a mold, so there's no setup charge, so we can do limited runs of a hundred, redesign, do another hundred. We can make 'em to order."

"And we need an MBA," Lester said. "Kodacell's sending us a business manager to help us turn junk into pesos."

"Yeah," Perry said, with a worried flick of his eyes. "Yeah, a business manager."

"So, I've known some business geeks who aren't total assholes," Lester said. "Who care about what they're doing and the people they're doing it with.

Respectful and mindful. It's like lawyers—they're not all scumbags. Some of them are totally awesome and save your ass."

Suzanne took all this in, jotting notes on an old-fashioned spiral-bound shirt-pocket notebook. "When's he arriving?"

"Next week," Lester said. "We've cleared him a space to work and everything. He's someone that Kettlewell's people recruited up in Ithaca and he's going to move here to work with us, sight unseen. Crazy, huh?"

"Crazy," Suzanne agreed.

"Right," Perry said. "That's next week, and this aft we've got some work to do, but now I'm ready for lunch. You guys ready for lunch?"

Something about food and really fat guys—it seemed like an awkward question to Suzanne, like asking someone who'd been horribly disfigured by burns if he wanted to toast a marshmallow. But Lester didn't react to the question—of course not; he had to eat; everyone had to eat.

"Yeah, let's do the IHOP." Lester trundled back to his half of the workspace, then came back with a cane in one hand. "There's like three places to eat within walking distance of here if you don't count the mobile Mexican burrito wagon, which I don't, since it's a rolling advertisement for dysentery. The IHOP is the least objectionable of those."

"We could drive somewhere," Suzanne said. It was coming up on noon and the heat once they got outside into the mall's ruins was like the steam off a dishwasher. She plucked at her blouse a couple of times.

"It's the only chance to exercise we get," Perry said. "It's pretty much impossible to live or work within walking distance of anything down here. You end up living in your car."

And so they hiked along the side of the road. The sidewalk was a curious mix of old and new, the concrete unworn but still overgrown by tall saw grass thriving in the Florida heat. It brushed up against her ankles, hard and sharp, unlike the grass back home.

They were walking parallel to a ditch filled with sluggish, brackish water and populated by singing frogs, ducks, ibises, and mosquitoes in great number. Across the way were empty lots, ghost plazas, dead filling stations. Behind one of the filling stations, a cluster of tents and shacks.

"Squatters?" she asked, pointing to the shantytown.

"Yeah," Perry said. "Lots of that down here. Some of them are the paramilitary wing of the AARP, old trailer-home retirees who've run out of money and just set up camp here. Some are bums and junkies; some are runaways. It's not as bad as it looks—they're pretty comfy in there. We bring 'em furniture and other good pickings that show up at the junkyard. The homeless with the wherewithal to build shantytowns, they haven't gone all animal like the shopping-cart people and the scary beachcombers." He waved across the malarial ditch to an old man in a pair of pressed khaki shorts and a crisp Bermuda shirt. "Hey, Francis!" he called. The old man waved back. "We'll have some IHOP for you 'bout an hour!" The old man ticked a salute off his creased forehead.

"Francis is a good guy. Used to be an aerospace engineer, if you can believe it. Wife had medical problems and he went bust taking care of her. When she died, he ended up here in his double-wide and never left. Kind of the unofficial mayor of this little patch."

Suzanne stared after Francis. He had a bit of a gimpy leg, a limp she could spot even from here. Beside her, Lester was puffing. No one was comfortable walking in Florida, it seemed.

It took another half hour to reach the IHOP, the International House of Pancakes, which sat opposite a mini-mall with only one still-breathing store, a place that advertised ninety-nine-cent T-shirts, which struck Suzanne as profoundly depressing. There was a junkie out front of 99-Cent Tees, a woman with a leathery tan and a tiny tank top and shorts that made her look a little like a Tenderloin hooker, but not with that rat's-nest hair, not even in the 'Loin. She wobbled uncertainly across the parking lot to them.

"Excuse me," she said, with an improbable Valley Girl accent. "Excuse me? I'm hoping to get something to eat. It's for my kid; she's nursing. Gotta keep my strength up." Her naked arms and legs were badly tracked out, and Suzanne had a horrified realization that among the stains on her tank top were a pair of spreading pools of breast milk, dampening old white, crusted patches over her sagging breasts. "For my baby. A dollar would help, a dollar."

There were homeless like this in San Francisco, too. In San Jose as well, she supposed, but she didn't know where they hid. But something about this woman, cracked out and tracked out, it freaked her out. She dug into her purse and got out a five-dollar bill and handed it to the homeless woman. The woman smiled a snaggletoothed, stumpy grin and reached for it, then, abruptly grabbed hold of Suzanne's wrist. Her grip was damp and weak.

"Don't you fucking look at me like that. You're not better than me, bitch!" Suzanne tugged free and stepped back quickly. "That's right, run away! Bitch! Fuck you! Enjoy your lunch!"

She was shaking. Perry and Lester closed ranks around her. Lester moved to confront the homeless woman.

"The fuck you want lard ass? You wanna fuck with me? I got a knife, you know—cut your ears off and feed 'em to ya."

Lester cocked his head like the RCA Victor dog. He towered over the skinny junkie, and was five or six times wider than her.

"You all right?" he said gently.

"Oh yeah, I'm just fine," she said. "Why, you looking for a party?"

He laughed. "You're joking—I'd crush you!"

She laughed, too, a less crazy, more relaxed sound. Lester's voice was a low, soothing rumble. "I don't think my friend thinks she's any better than you. I think she just wanted to help you out."

The junkie flicked her eyes back and forth. "Listen can you spare a dollar for my baby?"

"I think she just wanted to help you. Can I get you some lunch?"

"Fuckers won't let me in—won't let me use the toilet even. It's not humane. Don't want to go in the bushes. Not dignified to go in the bushes."

"That's true," he said. "What if I get you some takeout? You got a shady place you could eat it? Nursing's hungry work."

The junkie cocked her head. Then she laughed. "Yeah, OK, yeah. Sure—thanks, thanks a lot!"

Lester motioned her over to the menu in the IHOP window and waited with her while she picked out a helping of caramel-apple waffles, sausage links, fried eggs, hash browns, coffee, orange juice, and a chocolate malted. "Is that all?" he said, laughing, laughing, both of them laughing, all of them laughing at the incredible, outrageous meal.

They went in and waited by the podium. The greeter, a black guy with cornrows, nodded at Lester and Perry like an old friend. "Hey, Tony," Lester said. "Can you get us a go-bag with some takeout for the lady outside before we sit down?" He recited the astounding order.

Tony shook his head and ducked it. "OK, be right up," he said. "You want to sit while you're waiting?"

"We'll wait here, thanks," Lester said. "Don't want her to think we're bailing on her." He turned and waved at her.

"She's mean, you know—be careful."

"Thanks, Tony," Lester said.

Suzanne marveled at Lester's equanimity. Nothing got his goat. The doggy bag arrived. "I put some extra napkins and a couple of wet-naps in there," Tony said, handing it to him.

"Great!" Lester said. "You guys sit down, I'll be back in a second."

Perry motioned for Suzanne to follow him to a booth. He laughed. "Lester's a good guy," he said. "The best guy I know, you know?"

"How do you know him?" she asked, taking out her notepad.

"He was the sysadmin at a company that was making three-D printers, and I was a tech at a company that was buying them, and the products didn't work, and I spent a lot of time on the phone with him troubleshooting them.

We'd get together in our off-hours and hack around with neat little work-bench projects, stuff we'd come up with at work. When both companies went under, we got a bunch of their equipment at bankruptcy auctions. Lester's uncle owned the junkyard and he offered us space to set up our workshops, and the rest is history."

Lester joined them again. He was laughing. "She is *funny*," he said. "Kept hefting the sack and saying, 'Christ, what those bastards put on a plate, no wonder this country's so goddamned fat!'" Perry laughed, too. Suzanne chuckled nervously and looked away.

Lester slid into the booth next to her and put a hand on her shoulder. "It's OK. I'm a guy who weighs nearly four hundred pounds. I know I'm a big, fat guy. If I was sensitive about it, I couldn't last ten minutes. I'm not proud of being as big as I am, but I'm not ashamed, either. I'm OK with it."

"You wouldn't lose weight if you could?"

"Sure, why not? But I've concluded it's not an option anymore. I was always a fat kid, and so I never got good at sports, never got that habit. Now I've got this huge deficit when I sit down to exercise, because I'm lugging around all this lard. Can't run more than a few steps. Walking's about it. Couldn't join a pickup game of baseball or get out on the tennis court. I never learned to cook, either, though I suppose I could. But mostly I eat out, and I try to order sensibly, but just look at the crap they feed us at the places we can get to—there aren't any health food restaurants in the strip malls. Look at this menu," he said, tapping a pornographic glossy picture of a stack of glistening waffles oozing with some kind of high-fructose lube. "Caramel pancakes with whipped cream, maple syrup, and canned strawberries. When I was a kid, we called that *candy*. These people will sell you an eight-dollar, eighteen-ounce plate of candy with a side of sausage, eggs, biscuits, bacon, and a pint of orange juice. Even if you order this stuff and eat a third of it, a quarter of it, that's probably too much, and when you've got a lot of food in front of you, it's pretty hard to know when to stop."

Suzanne couldn't help it; she blurted out: "But willpower—"

"Sure, willpower. Willpower *nothing*. The thing is, when three quarters of America are obese, when half are dangerously obese, like me, years off our lives from all the fat—that tells you that this isn't a willpower problem. We didn't get less willful in the last fifty years. Might as well say that all those people who died of the plague lacked the willpower to keep their houses free of rats. Fat isn't moral, it's *epidemiological*. There are a small number of people, a tiny minority, whose genes are short-circuited in a way that makes them less prone to retaining nutrients. That's a maladaptive trait through most of human history—burning unnecessary calories when you've got to chase down an antelope to get more, that's no way to live long enough to pass on your genes! So you and Perry over here with your little skinny selves, able to pack away trans fats and high-fructose corn syrup and a pound of candy for breakfast at the IHOP, you're not doing this on willpower—you're doing it by expressing the somatotype of a recessive, counter-survival gene.

"Would I like to be thinner? Sure. But I'm not gonna let the fact that I'm genetically better suited to famine than feast get to me. Speaking of, let's eat. Tony, c'mere, buddy. I want a plate of candy!" He was smiling, and brave, and at that moment, Suzanne thought that she could get a crush on this guy, this big, smart, talented, funny, lovable guy. Then reality snapped back and she saw him as he was, sexless, lumpy, almost grotesque. The overlay of his—what?— his *inner beauty* on that exterior, it disoriented her. She looked back over her notes.

"So, you say that there's a third coming out to work with you?"

"To *live* with us," Perry said. "That's part of the deal. Geek houses, like in the old college days. We're going to be a power trio: two geeks and a suit, lean and mean. The suit's name is Tjan, and he's Singaporean by way of London by way of Ithaca, where Kettlebelly found him. We've talked on the phone a couple times and he's moving down next week."

"He's moving down without ever having met you?"

"Yeah, that's the way it goes. It's like the army or something for us: once you're in you get dispatched here or there. It was in the contract. We already had a place down here with room for Tjan, so we put some fresh linen on the guest bed and laid in an extra toothbrush."

"It's a little nervous-making," Lester said. "Perry and I get along great, but I haven't had such good luck with business types. It's not that I'm some kind of idealist who doesn't get the need to make money, but they can be so condescending, you know?"

Suzanne nodded. "That's a two-way street, you know. Suits don't like being talked down to by engineers."

Lester raised a hand. "Guilty as charged."

"So what're you planning to do for the rest of the week?" It was Wednesday, and she'd counted on getting this part of the story by Saturday, but she was going to have to wait, clearly, until this Tjan arrived.

"Same stuff as we always do. We build crazy stuff out of junk, sell it to collectors, and have fun. We could go to the Thunderbird Drive-in tonight if you want; it's a real classic, flea market by day and drive-in by night, practically the last one standing."

Perry cut in. "Or we could go to South Beach and get a good meal, if that's more your speed."

"Naw," Suzanne said. "Drive-in sounds great, especially if it's such a dying breed. Better get a visit in while there's still time."

They tried to treat her but she wouldn't let them. She never let anyone buy her so much as a cup of coffee. It was an old journalism-school drill, and she was practically the only scribbler she knew who hewed to it: some of the whores on the Silicon Valley papers took in free computers, trips, even spa days!—but she had never wavered.

The afternoon passed quickly and enchantingly. Perry was working on a knee-high, articulated Frankenstein monster built out of hand-painted seashells from a beachside kitsch market. They said GOD BLESS AMERICA and SOUVENIR OF FLORIDA and CONCH REPUBLIC and each had to be fitted out for a motor custom built to conform to its contours.

"When it's done, it will make toast."

"Make toast?"

"Yeah, separate a single slice off a loaf, load it into a top-loading slice toaster, depress the lever, time the toast cycle, retrieve the toast, and butter it. I got the idea from old-time backup-tape loaders. This plus a toaster will function as a loosely coupled single system."

"OK, that's really cool, but I have to ask the boring question, Perry. Why? Why build a toast robot?"

Perry stopped working and dusted his hands off. He was really built, and his shaggy hair made him look younger than his crow's-feet suggested. He turned a seashell with a half-built motor in it over and spun it like a top on the hand-painted WEATHER IS HERE/WISH YOU WERE BEAUTIFUL legend.

"Well, that's the question, isn't it? The simple answer: people buy them. Collectors. So it's a good hobby business, but that's not really it.

"It's like this: engineering is all about constraint. Given a span of foo feet and materials of tensile strength of bar, build a bridge that doesn't go all fubared. Write a fun video game for an eight-bit console that'll fit in thirty-two K. Build the fastest airplane, or the one with the largest carrying capacity. . . . But these days, there's not much traditional constraint. I've got the engineer's most dangerous luxury: plenty. All the computational cycles I'll ever need. Easy and rapid prototyping. Precision tools.

"Now, it may be that there is a suite of tasks lurking *in potentia* that demand all this resource and more—maybe I'm like some locomotive engineer declaring that sixty miles per hour is the pinnacle of machine velocity, that speed is cracked. But I don't see many of those problems—none that interest me.

"What I've got here are my own constraints. I'm challenging myself, using found objects and making stuff that throws all this computational capacity at, you know, these *trivial* problems, like car-driving Elmo clusters and seashell toaster-robots. We have so much capacity that the trivia expands to fill it. And all that capacity is junk capacity, it's leftovers. There's enough computational capacity in a junkyard to launch a space program, and that's by design. Remember the ipod? Why do you think it was so prone to scratching and going all gunky after a year in your pocket? Why would Apple build a handheld technology out of materials that turned to shit if you looked at them cross-eyed? It's because the ipod was only meant to last a year!

"It's like tail fins—they were cool in the Tail-fin Cretaceous, but wouldn't it have been better if they could have disappeared from view when they became aesthetically obsolete, when the space age withered up and blew away? Oh, not really, obviously, because it's nice to see a well-maintained land-yacht on the highway every now and again, if only for variety's sake, but if you're going to design something that is meant to be au fait then presumably you should have some planned obsolescence in there, some end-of-lifing strategy for the aesthetic crash that follows any couture movement. Here, check this out."

He handed her a white brick the size of a deck of cards. It took her a moment to recognize it as an ipod. "Christ, it's *huge*," she said.

"Yeah, isn't it just. Remember how small and shiny this thing was when it shipped? 'A thousand songs in your pocket!' "

That made her actually laugh out loud. She fished in her pocket for her earbuds and dropped them on the table, where they clattered like M&M's. "I *think* I've got about forty thousand songs on those. Haven't run out of space yet, either."

He rolled the buds around in his palm like a pair of dice. "You won't—I stopped keeping track of mine after I added my hundred-thousandth audiobook. I've got a bunch of the Library of Congress in mine as high-rez scans, too. A copy of the Internet Archive, every post ever made on Usenet . . . Basically, these things are infinitely capacious, given the size of the media we work with today." He rolled the buds out on the workbench and laughed. "And that's just the point! Tomorrow, we'll have some new extra-fat kind of media and some new task to perform with it and some new storage medium that will make these things look like an old ipod. Before that happens, you want this to wear out and scuff up or get lost—"

"I lose those things all the time, like a set a month."

"There you go then! The iPods were too big to lose like that, but just *look at them*." The ipod's chrome was scratched to the point of being fogged, like the mirror in a gas-station toilet. The screen was almost unreadable for all the scratches. "They had scratch-proof materials and hard plastics back then.

They *chose* to build these things out of Saran Wrap and tinfoil so that by the time they doubled in capacity next year, you'd have already worn yours out and wouldn't feel bad about junking them.

"So I'm building a tape-loading seashell toaster-robot out of discarded obsolete technology because the world is full of capacious, capable, disposable junk and it cries out to be used again. It's a potlatch: I have so much material and computational wealth that I can afford to waste it on frivolous junk. I think that's why the collectors buy it, anyway."

"That brings us back to the question of your relationship with Kodacell. They want to do what, exactly, with you?"

"Well, we've been playing with some mass-production techniques, the three-D printer and so on. When Kettlebelly called me, he said that he wanted to see about using the scanner and so on to make a lot of these things, at a low price point. It's pretty perverse when you think about it: using modern technology to build replicas of obsolete technology rescued from the dump, when these replicas are bound to end up back here at the dump!" He laughed. He had nice laugh lines around his eyes. "Anyway, it's something that Lester and I had talked about for a long time, but never really got around to. Too much like retail. It's bad enough dealing with a couple dozen collectors who'll pay ten grand for a sculpture: who wants to deal with ten thousand customers who'll go a dollar each for the same thing?"

"But you figure that this Tjan character will handle all the customer stuff?"

"That's the idea: he'll run the business side; we'll get more time to hack; everyone gets paid. Kodacell's got some micro-sized marketing agencies, specialized PR firms, creative shippers, all kinds of little three-person outfits that they've promised to hook us up with. Tjan interfaces with them, we do our thing, enrich the shareholders, get stock ourselves. It's supposed to be all upside. Hell, if it doesn't work we can just walk away and find another dump and go back into the collectors' market."

He picked up his half-finished shell and swung a lamp with a magnifying lens built into it over his workspace. "Hey, just a sec, OK? I've just figured out what I was doing wrong before." He took up a little tweezers and a plastic rod and probed for a moment, then daubed some solder down inside the shell's guts. He tweezed a wire to a contact and the shell made a motorized sound; a peg sticking out of it began to move rhythmically.

"Got it," he said. He set it down. "I don't expect I'm going to be doing many more of these projects after next week. This kind of design, we could never mass-produce it." He looked a little wistful, and Suzanne suppressed a smile. What a tortured artiste this Florida junkyard engineer was!

As the long day drew to a close, they went out for a walk in the twilight's cool in the yard. The sopping humidity of the day settled around them as the sun set in a long summer blaze that turned the dry fountain full of Christmas ornaments into a luminescent bowl of jewels.

"I got some real progress today," Lester said. He had a cane with him and he was limping heavily. "Got the printer to output complete mechanical logical gates, all in one piece, almost no assembly, just daisy-chain them on a board. And I've been working on a standard snap-on system for lego-bricking each gate to the next. It's going to make it a lot easier to ramp up production."

"Yeah?" Perry said. He asked a technical question about the printer, something about the goop's tensile strength that Suzanne couldn't follow. They went at it, hammer and tongs, talking through the abstruse details faster than she could follow, walking more and more quickly past the vast heaps of dead technology and half-built mall stores.

She let them get ahead of her and stopped to gather her thoughts. She turned around to take it all in and that's when she caught sight of the kids sneaking into Perry and Lester's lab.

"Hey!" she shouted in her loudest Detroit voice. "What are you doing there?" There were three of them, in Miami Dolphins jerseys and shiny bald-shaved heads and little shorts, the latest inexplicable rapper style, which made them look more like drag queens in mufti than tough guys.

They rounded on her. They were heavyset and their eyebrows were bleached blond. They had been sneaking into the lab's side door, looking about as inconspicuous as a trio of nuns.

"Get lost!" she shouted. "Get out of here! Perry, Lester!"

They were coming closer now. They didn't move so well, puffing in the heat, but they clearly had mayhem on their minds. She reached into her purse for her pepper spray and held it before her dramatically, but they didn't stop coming.

Suddenly, the air was rent by the loudest sound she'd ever heard, like she'd put her head inside a foghorn. She flinched and misted a cloud of aerosol capsicum ahead of her. She had the presence of mind to step back quickly, before catching a blowback, but she wasn't quick enough, for her eyes and nose started to burn and water. The sound wouldn't stop; it just kept going on, a sound like her head was too small to contain her brain, a sound that made her teeth ache. The three kids had stopped and staggered off.

"You OK?" The voice sounded like it was coming from far, far away, though Lester was right in front of her. She found that she'd dropped to her knees in the teeth of that astonishing noise.

She let him help her to her feet. "Jesus," she said, putting a hand to her ears. They rang like she'd been at a rave all night. "What the hell?"

"Antipersonnel sonic device," Lester said. She realized that he was shouting, but she could barely hear it. "It doesn't do any permanent damage, but it'll scare off most anyone. Those kids probably live in the shantytown we passed this morning. More and more of them are joining gangs. They're our neighbors, so we don't want to shoot them or anything."

She nodded. The ringing in her ears was subsiding a little. Lester steadied her. She leaned on him. He was big and solid. He wore the same cologne as her father had, she realized.

She moved away from him and smoothed out her shorts, dusting off her knees. "Did you invent that?"

"Made it using a HOWTO I found online," he said. "Lot of kids around here up to no good. It's pretty much a homebrew civil defense siren—rugged and cheap."

She put a finger in each ear and scratched at the itchy buzzing. When she removed them, her hearing was almost back to normal. "I once had an upstairs neighbor in Cambridge who had a stereo system that loud—never thought I'd hear it again."

Perry came and joined them. "I followed them a bit, they're way gone now. I think I recognized one of them from the campsite. I'll talk to Francis about it and see if he can set them right."

"Have you been broken into before?"

"A few times. Mostly what we worry about is someone trashing the printers. Everything else is easy to replace, but when Lester's old employer went bust we bought up about fifty of these things at the auction and I don't know where we'd lay hands on them again. Computers are cheap and it's not like anyone could really *steal* all this junk." He flashed her his good-looking, confident smile again.

"What time do the movies start?"

Lester checked his watch. "About an hour after sunset. If we leave now we can get a real dinner at a Haitian place I know and then head over to the Thunderbird. I'll hide under a blanket in the backseat so that we can save on admission!"

She'd done that many times as a kid, her father shushing her and her brother as they giggled beneath the blankets. The thought of giant Lester doing it made her chuckle. "I think we can afford to pay for you," she said.

The dinner was good—fiery, spicy fish and good music in an old tiki bar with peeling grass wallpaper that managed to look vaguely Haitian. The waiters spoke Spanish, not French, though. She let herself be talked into two bottles of beer—about one and a half more than she would normally take—but she didn't get light-headed. The heat and humidity seemed to rinse the alcohol right out of her bloodstream.

They got to the movies just at dusk. It was just like she remembered from being a little girl and coming with her parents. Children in pajamas climbed over a jungle gym to one side of the lot. Ranked rows of cars faced the huge, grubby white projection walls. They even showed one of those scratchy old "Let's all go to the lobby to get ourselves a treat" cartoon shorts with the dancing hot dogs before the movie.

The nostalgia filled her up like a balloon expanding in her chest. She hadn't ever seen a computer until she was ten years old, and that had been the size of a chest freezer, with less capability than one of the active printed computer cards that came in glossy fashion magazines with come-ons for perfume and weight loss.

The world had been stood on its head so many times in the intervening thirty-plus years that it was literally dizzying—or was that the beer having a de-layed effect? Suddenly all the certainties she rested on—her 401(k), her house, her ability to navigate the professional world in a competent manner—seemed to be built on shifting sands.

They'd come in Lester's car, a homemade auto built around two electric Smart cars joined together to form a kind of mini-sedan with room enough for Lester to slide into the driver's perch with room to spare. Once they arrived, they unpacked clever folding chairs and sat them beside the car, rolled down the windows, and turned up the speakers. It was a warm night, but not sticky the way it had been that day, and the kiss of the wind that rustled the leaves of the tall palms ringing the theater was like balm.

The movie was something forgettable about bumbling detectives on the moon, one of those trendy new things acted entirely by animated dead actors who combined the virtues of box-office draw and cheap labor. There might have been a couple of fictional actors in there, too, it was hard to say; she'd never really followed the movies except as a place to escape to. There was real magic and escape in a drive-in, though, with the palpable evidence of all those other breathing humans in the darkened night watching the magic story flicker past on the screen, something that went right into her hindbrain. Before she knew it, her eyelids were drooping and then she found herself jerking awake. This happened a couple times before Lester slipped a pillow under her head and she sank into it and fell into sleep.

She woke at the closing credits and realized that she'd managed to prop the pillow on Lester's barrel chest. She snapped her head up and then smiled embarrassedly at him. "Hey, sleepyhead," he said. "You snore like a band saw, you know it?"

She blushed. "I don't!"

"You do," he said.

"I do?"

Perry, on her other side, nodded. "You do."

"God," she said.

"Don't worry, you haven't got anything on Lester," Perry said. "I've gone into his room some mornings and found all the pictures lying on the floor, vibrated off their hooks."

It seemed to her that Lester was blushing now.

"I'm sorry if I spoiled the movie," she said.

"Don't sweat it," Lester said, clearly grateful for the change of subject. "It was a lousy movie anyway. You drowned out some truly foul dialogue."

"Well, there's that."

"C'mon, let's go back to the office and get you your car. It's an hour to Miami from here."

She was wide awake by the time she parked the rent-a-car in the coffin hotel's parking lot and crawled into her room, slapping the air-con buttons up to full to clear out the stifling air that had baked into the interior during the day.

She lay on her back in the dark coffin for a long time, eyes open and slowly adjusting to the idiot lights on the control panel, until it seemed that she was lying in a space capsule hurtling through the universe at relativistic speeds, leaving behind history, the world, everything she knew. She sat up, wide awake, on West Coast time suddenly, and there was no way she would fall asleep now, but she lay back down and then she did, finally.

The alarm woke her seemingly five minutes later. She did a couple laps around the parking lot, padding around, stretching her legs, trying to clear her head—her internal clock thought that it was 4 AM, but at 7 AM on the East Coast, the sun was up and the heat had begun to sizzle all the available moisture into the air. She left the hotel and drove around Miami for a while. She needed to find some toiletries and then a café where she could sit down and file some copy. She'd tweeted a bunch of working notes and posted a few things to her blog the day before, but her editor expected something more coherent for those who preferred their news a little more digested.

By the time she arrived at Perry's junkyard, the day had tipped for afternoon, the sun no longer straight overhead, the heat a little softer than it had been the day before. She settled in for another day of watching the guys work, asking the occasional question. The column she'd ended up filing had been a kind of wait-and-see piece, describing the cool culture these two had going between them, and asking if it could survive scaling up to mass production. Now she experimented with their works-in-progress, sculptures and machines that almost worked, or didn't work at all, but that showed the scope of their creativity. Kettlewell thought that there were a thousand, ten thousand people as creative as these two out there, waiting to be discovered. Could it be true?

"Sure," Perry said, "why not? We're just here because someone dropped the barrier to entry, made it possible for a couple of tinkerers to get a lot of materials and to assemble them without knowing a whole lot about advanced materials science. Wasn't it like this when the Internet was starting out?"

"Woah," Suzanne said. "I just realized that you wouldn't really remember those days, back in the early nineties."

"Sure I remember them. I was a kid, but I remember them fine!"

She felt very old. "The thing was that no one really suspected that there were so many liberal-arts majors lurking in the nation's universities, dying to drop out and learn perl and HTML."

Perry cocked his head. "Yeah, I guess that's analogous. The legacy of the dotcom years for me is all this free infrastructure, very cheap network connections, and hosting companies and so on. That, I guess, combined with people willing to use it. I never really thought of it, but there must have been a lot of people hanging around in the old days who thought email and the Net were pretty sketchy, right?"

She waved her hands at him. "Perry, lad, you don't know the half of it. There are *still* executives in the rust belt who spend bailout money on secretaries to print out their email and then dictate replies into tape recorders to be typed and sent."

He furrowed his thick eyebrows. "You're joking," he said.

She put her hand on her heart. "I kid you not. I knew people in the newsroom at the *Detroit Free Press*. There are whole industries in this country that are living in the last century."

"Well, for me, all that dotcommy stuff was like putting down a good base, making it easy for people like me to get parts and build logs and to find hardware hackers to jam with."

Perry got engrossed in a tricky bit of engine-in-seashell then and she wandered over to Lester, who was printing out more Barbie heads for a much larger version of his mechanical computer. "It'll be able to add, subtract, and multiply any two numbers up to ninety-nine," he said. "It took decades to build a vacuum-tube machine that could do that much—I'm doing it with *switches* in just three revs. In your face, Univac!"

She laughed. He had a huge bag of laser-cut soda-can switches that he was soldering onto a variety of substrates from polished car doors to a bamboo tiki bar. She looked closely at the solder. "Is this what sweatshop solder looks like?"

He looked confused, then said, "Oh! Right, Perry's thing. Yeah, anything not done by a robot has this artisanal quality of blobbiness, which I quite like; it's aesthetic, like a painting with visible brushstrokes. But Perry's right: if you see solder like this on anything that there are a million of, then you know that it was laid down by kids and women working for slave wages. There's no way it's cheaper to make a million solders by hand than by robot unless your labor force is locked in, force-fed amphetamine, and destroyed for anything except prostitution inside of five years. But here, in something like this, so handmade and one of a kind, I think it gives it a nice cargo-cult neo-primitive feel. Like a field of hand-tilled furrows."

She nodded. Today she was keeping her computer out, writing down quotes and tweeting thoughts as they came. They worked side by side in companionable silence for a while as she killed a couple thousand spams and he laid down a couple dozen blobs of solder.

"How do you like Florida?" he said after straightening up and cracking his back.

She barely stopped typing, deep into some email: "It's all right, I suppose."

"There's great stuff here if you know where to look. Want me to show you around a little tonight? It's Friday, after all."

"Sounds good. Is Perry free?"

It took her a second to register that he hadn't answered. She looked up and saw he was blushing to the tips of his ears. "I thought we could go out just the two of us. Dinner and a walk around the deco stuff on Miami Beach?"

"Oh," she said. And the weird thing was, she took it seriously for a second. She hadn't been on a date in something like a year, and he was a really nice guy and so forth. But professional ethics made that impossible, and besides.

And besides. He was huge. He'd told her he weighed nearly four hundred pounds. So fat, he was, essentially, sexless. Round and unshaped, doughy.

All of these thoughts in an instant and then she said, "Oh, well. Listen, Lester, it's about professional ethics. I'm here on a story and you guys are really swell, but I'm here to be objective. That means no dating. Sorry." She said it in the same firm tones as she'd used to turn down their offer to treat her at the IHOP: a fact of life, something she just didn't do. Like turning down a glass of beer by saying, "No thanks, I don't drink." No value judgment.

But she could see that she had let her thinking show on her face, if only for the briefest moment. Lester stiffened and his nostrils flared. He wiped his hands on his thighs, then said, in a light tone, "Sure, no problem. I understand completely. Should have thought of that. Sorry!"

"No problem," she said. She pretended to work on her email a while longer, then said, "Well, I think I'll call it a day. See you Monday for Tjan's arrival, right?"

"Right!" he said, too brightly, and she slunk away to her car.

She spent the weekend blogging and seeing the beach. The people on the beach seemed to be of another species from the ones she saw walking the streets of Hollywood and Miami and Lauderdale. They had freakishly perfect bodies, the kind of thing you saw in an anatomical drawing or a comic book—so much muscular definition that they were practically crosshatched. She even tried out the nude beach, intrigued to see these perfect specimens in the altogether, but she chickened out when she realized that she'd need a substantial wax job before her body hair was brought down to norms for that strip of sand.

She did get an eyeful of several anatomically correct drawings before taking off again. It made her uncomfortably horny and aware of how long it had been since her last date. That got her thinking of poor Lester, buried underneath all that flesh, and that got her thinking about the life she'd chosen for herself, covering the weird world of tech, where the ground never stood still long enough for her to get her balance.

So she retreated to blog in a café, posting snippets and impressions from her days with the boys, along with photos. Her readers were all over it, commenting like mad. Half of them thought it was disgusting—so much suffering and waste in the world and these guys were inventing ten-thousand-dollar toys out of garbage. The other half wanted to know where to go to buy one for themselves. Halfway through Sunday, her laptop battery finally died, needing a fresh weekly charge, so she retreated again, to the coffin, to wait for Monday and the new day that would dawn for Perry and Lester and Kodacell—and her.

Tjan turned out to be a lot older than she'd expected. She'd pictured him as about twenty-eight, smart and preppy like they all were when they were fresh out of B-school and full of Management Wisdom. Instead, he was about forty, balding, with a little potbelly and thinning hair. He dressed like an English professor, blue jeans and a checked shirt and a tweedy sports coat that he'd shucked within seconds of leaving the terminal at Miami airport and stepping into the blast-furnace heat.

They'd all come in Lester's big, crazy car, and squishing back in with Tjan's suitcases was like a geometry trick. She found herself half on Perry's lap, hugging half a big duffel bag that seemed to be full of bricks.

"Books," Tjan said. "Just a little personal library. It's a bad habit, moving the physical objects around, but I'm addicted." He had a calm voice that might in fact be a little dull, a prof's monotone.

They brought him to Perry and Lester's place, which was three condos with the dividing walls knocked out, in a complex that had long rust streaks down its sides and rickety balconies that had been eaten away by salt air. There was a guardhouse at the front of the complex, but it was shuttered, abandoned, and graffiti-tagged.

Tjan stepped out of the car and put his hands on his hips and considered the building. "It could use a coat of paint," he said. Suzanne looked closely at him—he was so deadpan, it was hard to tell what was on his mind. But he slipped her a wink.

"Yeah," Perry said. "It could at that. On the bright side: spacious, cheap, and there's a pool. There's a lot of this down here since the housing market crashed. The condo association here dissolved about four years ago, so there's not really anyone who's in charge of all the common spaces and stuff, just a few condo owners and speculators who own the apartments. Suckers, I'm thinking. Our rent has gone down twice this year, just for asking. I'm thinking we could probably get them to pay us to live here and just keep out the bums and stuff."

The living quarters were nearly indistinguishable from the workshop at the junkyard: strewn with cool devices in various stages of disassembly, detritus, and art. The plates and dishes and glasses all had IHOP and Cracker Barrel logos on them. "From thrift shops," Lester explained. "Old people steal them when they get their early bird specials, and then when they die their kids give them to Goodwill. Cheapest way to get a matched set around here."

Tjan circled the three adjoined cracker-box condos like a dog circling his basket. Finally, he picked an unoccupied master bedroom with moldy lace curtains and a motel-art painting of an abstract landscape over the head-board. He set his suitcase down on the faux-Chinoise chest of drawers and said, "Right, I'm done. Let's get to work."

They took him to the workshop next and his expression hardly changed as they showed him around, showed them their cabinets of wonders. When they were done, he let them walk him to the IHOP and he ordered the most austere thing on the menu, a peanut butter and jelly sandwich that was technically on the kids' menu—a kids' menu at a place where the grown-ups could order a plate of candy!

"So," Perry said. "So, Tjan, come on buddy, give it to me straight—you hate it? Love it? Can't understand it?"

Tjan set down his sandwich. "You boys are very talented," he said. "They're very good inventions. There are lots of opportunities for synergy within Koda-cell: marketing, logistics, even packing materials. There's a little aerogel start-up in Oregon that Kodacell is underwriting that you could use for padding when you ship."

Perry and Lester looked at him expectantly. Suzanne broke the silence. "Tjan, did you have any artistic or design ideas about the things that these guys are making?"

Tjan took another bite of sandwich and sipped at his milk. "Well, you'll have to come up with a name for them, something that identifies them. Also, I think you should be careful with trademarked objects. Any time you need to bring in an IP lawyer, you're going to run into huge costs and time delays."

They waited again. "That's it?" Perry said. "Nothing about the designs themselves?"

"I'm the business manager. That's editorial. I'm artistically autistic. Not my job to help you design things. It's my job to sell the things you design."

"Would it matter what it was we were making? Would you feel the same if it was toothbrushes or staplers?"

Tjan smiled. "If you were making staplers I wouldn't be here, because there's no profit in staplers. Too many competitors. Toothbrushes are a possibility, if you were making something really revolutionary. People buy about 1.6 toothbrushes a year, so there's lots of opportunity to come up with an innovative design that sells at a good profit over marginal cost for a couple seasons before it gets cloned or out-innovated. What you people are making has an edge because it's you making it, very bespoke and distinctive. I think it will take some time for the world to emerge an effective competitor to these goods, provided that you can build an initial marketplace mass-interest in them. There aren't enough people out there who know how to combine all the things you've combined here. The system makes it hard to sell anything above the marginal cost of goods, unless you have a really innovative idea, which can't stay innovative for long, so you need continuous invention and reinvention, too. You two fellows appear to be doing that. I don't know anything definitive about the aesthetic qualities of your gadgets, nor how useful they'll be, but I *do* understand their distinctiveness, so that's why I'm here."

It was longer than all the speeches he'd delivered since arriving—put together. Suzanne nodded and made some notes. Perry looked him up and down.

"You're, what, an ex-B-school prof from Cornell, right?"

"Yes, for a few years. And I ran a company for a while, doing import-export from emerging-economy states in the former Soviet bloc."

"I see," Perry said. "So you're into what, a new company every eighteen months or something?"

"Oh no," Tjan said, and he had a little twinkle in his eye and the tiniest hint of a smile. "Oh no. Every six months. A year at the outside. That's my deal. I'm the business guy with the short attention span."

"I see," Perry said. "Kettlewell didn't mention this."

At the junkyard, Tjan wandered around the Elmo-propelled Smart car and peered at its innards, watched the Elmos negotiate their balance and position with minute movements and acoustic signals. "I wouldn't worry about it if I were you," he said. "You guys aren't temperamentally suited to doing just one thing."

Lester laughed. "He's got you there, dude," he said, slapping Perry on the shoulder.

Suzanne got Tjan out for dinner that night. "My dad was in import-export and we traveled a lot, all over Asia and then the former Soviets. He sent me away when I was sixteen to finish school in the States, and there was no question but that I would go to Stanford for business school."

"Nice to meet a fellow Californian," she said, and sipped her wine. They'd gone to one of the famed Miami deco restaurants and the fish in front of her was practically a sculpture, so thoroughly plated it was.

"Well, I'm as Californian as . . ."

". . . as possible, under the circumstances," she said, and laughed. "It's a Canadian joke, but it applies equally well to Californians. So you were in B-school when?"

"Ninety-eight to 2001. Interesting times to be in the Valley. I read your column, you know."

She looked down at her plate. A lot of people had read the column back then. Women columnists were rare in tech, and she supposed she was good at it, too. "I hope I get remembered as more than the chronicler of the dot-com boom, though," she said.

"Oh, you will," he said. "You'll be remembered as the chronicler of this— what Kettlewell and Perry and Lester are doing."

"What you're doing, too, right?"

"Oh, yes, what I'm doing, too."

A robot rollerbladed past on the boardwalk, turning the occasional somersault. "I should have them build some of those," Tjan said, watching the crowd turn to regard it. It hopped onto and off of the curb, expertly steered around the wandering couples and the occasional homeless person. It had a banner that streamed out behind it: CAP'N JACKS PAINTBALL AND FANBOAT TOURS GET SHOT AND GET WET MIAMI KEY WEST LAUDERDALE.

"You think they can?"

"Sure," Tjan said. "Those two can build anything. That's the point: any moderately skilled practitioner can build anything these days, for practically nothing. Back in the old days, the blacksmith just made every bit of ironmongery everyone needed, one piece at a time, at his forge. That's where we're at.

Every industry that required a factory yesterday only needs a garage today. It's a real return to fundamentals. What no one ever could do was join up all the smithies and all the smiths and make them into a single logical network with a single set of objectives. That's new and it's what I plan on making hay out of. This will be much bigger than dotcom. It will be much harder, too—bigger crests, deeper troughs. This is something to chronicle all right: it will make dotcom look like a warm-up for the main show.

"We're going to create a new class of artisans who can change careers every ten months, inventing new jobs that hadn't been imagined a year before."

"That's a pretty unstable market," Suzanne said, and ate some fish.

"That's a *functional* market. Here's what I think the point of a good market is. In a good market, you invent something and you charge all the market will bear for it. Someone else figures out how to do it cheaper, or decides they can do it for a slimmer margin—not the same thing, you know; in the first case someone is more efficient and in the second they're just less greedy or less ambitious. They do it and so you have to drop your prices to compete. Then someone comes along who's less greedy or more efficient than both of you and undercuts you again, and again, and again, until eventually you get down to a kind of firmament, a baseline that you can't go lower than, the cheapest you can produce a good and stay in business. That's why straight pins, machine screws, and reams of paper all cost basically nothing, and make damned little profit for their manufacturers.

"So if you want to make a big profit, you've got to start over again, invent something new, and milk it for all you can before the first imitator shows up. The more this happens, the cheaper and better everything gets. It's how we got here, you see. It's what the system is *for*. We're approaching a kind of pure and perfect state now, with competition and invention getting easier and easier—it's producing a kind of superabundance that's amazing to watch. My kids just surf it, make themselves over every six months, learn a new interface, a new entertainment, you name it. Change-surfers . . ." He trailed off.

"You have kids?"

"In St. Petersburg, with their mother."

She could tell by his tone that it had been the wrong question to ask. He was looking hangdog. "Well, it must be nice to be so much closer to them than you were in Ithaca."

"What? No, no. The St. Petersburg in *Russia*."

"Oh," she said.

They concentrated on their food for a while.

"You know," he said, after they'd ordered coffee and dessert, "it's all about abundance. I want my kids to grow up with abundance, and whatever is going

on right now, it's providing abundance in abundance. The self-storage industry is bigger than the recording industry, did you know that? All they do is
provide a place to put stuff that we own that we can't find room for—that's
superabundance."

"I have a locker in Milpitas," she said.

"There you go. It's a growth industry." He drank his coffee. On the way
back to their cars, he said, "My daughter, Lyenitchka, is four, and my son,
Sasha, is one. I haven't lived with their mother in three years." He made a face.
"Sasha's circumstances were complicated. They're good kids, though. It just
couldn't work with their mother. She's Russian, and connected—that's how
we met; I was hustling for my import-export business and she had some good
connections—so after the divorce there was no question of my taking the kids
with me. But they're good kids."

"Do you see them?"

"We videoconference. Who knew that long-distance divorce was the
killer app for videoconferencing?"

"Yeah."

That week, Suzanne tweeted constantly, filed two columns, and blogged ten
or more items a day: photos, bits of discussion between Lester, Perry, and Tjan,
a couple videos of the Boogie Woogie Elmos doing improbable things. Turned
out that there was quite a cult following for the BWE, and the news that there
was a trove of some thousands of them in a Hollywood dump sent a half-dozen
pilgrims winging their way across the nation to score some for the collectors'
market. Perry wouldn't even take their money: "Fella," he told one persistent
dealer, "I got forty *thousand* of these things. I won't miss a couple dozen. Just call
it good karma."

When Tjan found out about it he pursed his lips for a moment, then said,
"Let me know if someone wants to pay us money, please. I think you were
right, but I'd like to have a say, all right?"

Perry looked at Suzanne, who was videoing this exchange with her key
chain. Then he looked back at Tjan, "Yeah, of course. Sorry—force of habit.
No harm done, though, right?"

That footage got downloaded a couple hundred times that night, but once it
got slashdotted by a couple of high-profile headline aggregators, she found her
server hammered with a hundred thousand requests. The *Merc* had the horse-
power to serve them all, but you never knew: every once in a while, the Web hit
another tipping point and grew by an order of magnitude or so, and then all the
server-provisioning—calculated to survive the old slashdottings—shredded like
wet kleenex.

From: kettlewell-l@skunkworks.kodacell.com
To: schurch@sjmercury.com
Subject: Re: Embedded journalist?

This stuff is amazing. Amazing! Christ, I should put you on the payroll. Forget I wrote that. But I should. You've got a fantastic eye. I have never felt as in touch with my own business as I do at this moment. Not to mention proud! Proud— you've made me so proud of the work these guys are doing, proud to have some role in it.

Kettlebelly

She read it sitting up in her coffin, just one of several hundred emails from that day's blog posts and column. She laughed and dropped it in her folder of correspondence to answer. It was nearly midnight, too late to get into it with Kettlewell.

Then her computer rang—the Net phone she forwarded her cellphone to when her computer was live and connected. She'd started doing that a couple years back, when soft phones really stabilized, and her phone bills had dropped to less than twenty bucks a month, down from several hundred. It wasn't that she spent a lot of time within arm's reach of a live computer, but given that calls routed through the laptop were free, she was perfectly willing to defer her calls until she was.

"Hi, Jimmy," she said—her editor, back in San Jose. Nine PM Pacific time on a weeknight was still working hours for him.

"Suzanne," he said.

She waited. She'd half expected him to call with a little shower of praise, an echo of Kettlewell's note. Jimmy wasn't the most effusive editor she'd had, but it made his little moments of praise more valuable for their rarity.

"Suzanne," he said again.

"Jimmy," she said. "It's late here. What's up?"

"So, it's like this. I love your reports but it's not Silicon Valley news. It's Miami news. McClatchy handed me a thirty percent cut this morning and I'm going to the bone. I am firing a third of the newsroom today. Now, you are a stupendous writer and so I said to myself, 'I can fire her or I can bring her home and have her write about Silicon Valley again,' and I knew what the answer had to be. So I need you to come home, just wrap it up and come home."

He finished speaking and she found herself staring at her computer's screen. Her hands were gripping the laptop's edges so tightly it hurt, and the machine made a plasticky squeak as it began to bend.

"I can't do that, Jimmy. This is stuff that Silicon Valley needs to know about.

This may not be what's happening *in* Silicon Valley, but it sure as shit is what's happening *to* Silicon Valley." She hated that she'd cussed—she hadn't meant to. "I know you're in a hard spot, but this is the story I need to cover right now."

"Suzanne, I'm cutting a third of the newsroom. We're going to be covering stories within driving distance of this office for the foreseeable future, and that's it. I don't disagree with a single thing you just said, but it doesn't matter: if I leave you where you are, I'll have to cut the guy who covers the school boards and the city councils. I can't do that, not if I want to remain a daily newspaper editor."

"I see," she said. "Can I think about it?"

"Think about what, Suzanne? This has not been the best day for me, I have to tell you, but I don't see what there is to think about. This newspaper no longer has correspondents who work in Miami and London and Paris and New York. As of today, that stuff comes from bloggers, or off the wire, or whatever—but not from our payroll. You work for this newspaper, so you need to come back here, because the job you're doing does not exist any longer. The job you have with us is here. You've missed the night flight, but there's a direct flight tomorrow morning that'll have you back by lunchtime tomorrow, and we can sit down together then and talk about it, all right?"

"I think—" She felt that oh-shit-oh-shit feeling again, that needing-to-pee feeling, that tension from her toes to her nose. "Jimmy," she said. "I need a leave of absence, OK?"

"What? Suzanne, I'm sure we owe you some vacation but now isn't the time—"

"Not a vacation, Jimmy. Six months' leave of absence, without pay." Her savings could cover it. She could put some banner ads on her blog. Florida was cheap. She could rent out her place in California. She was six steps into the plan and it had only taken ten seconds and she had no doubts whatsoever. She could talk to that book agent who'd pinged her last year, see about getting an advance on a book about Kodacell.

"Are you quitting?"

"No, Jimmy—well, not unless you make me. But I need to stay here."

"The work you're doing there is fine, Suzanne, but I worked really hard to protect your job here and this isn't going to help make that happen."

"What are you saying?"

"If you want to work for the *Merc,* you need to fly back to San Jose, where the *Merc* is published. I can't make it any clearer than that."

No, he couldn't. She sympathized with him. She was really well paid by the *Merc.* Keeping her on would mean firing two junior writers. He'd cut her a lot of breaks along the way, too—let her feel out the Valley in her own way.

It had paid off for both of them, but he'd taken the risk when a lot of people wouldn't have. She'd be a fool to walk away from all that.

She opened her mouth to tell him that she'd be on the plane in the morning, and what came out was, "Jimmy, I really appreciate all the work you've done for me, but this is the story I need to write. I'm sorry about that."

"Suzanne," he said.

"Thank you, Jimmy," she said. "I'll get back to California when I get a lull and sort out the details—my employee card and stuff."

"You know what you're doing, right?"

"Yeah," she said. "I do."

When she unscrewed her earpiece, she discovered that her neck was killing her. That made her realize that she was a forty-five-year-old woman in America without health insurance. Or regular income. She was a journalist without a journalistic organ.

She'd have to tell Kettlewell, who would no doubt offer to put her on the payroll. She couldn't do that, of course. Neutrality was hard enough to maintain, never mind being financially compromised.

She stepped out of the coffin and sniffed the salty air. Living in the coffin was expensive. She'd need to get a condo or something. A place with a kitchen where she could prep meals. She figured that Perry's building would probably have a vacancy or two.

The second business that Tjan took Perry into was even more successful than the first, and that was saying something. It only took a week for Tjan to get Perry and Lester cranking on a Kitchen Gnome design that mashed together some Homeland Security gait-recognition software with a big solid-state hard disk and a microphone and a little camera, all packaged together in one of a couple hundred designs of a garden-gnome figurine that stood six inches tall. It could recognize every member of a household by the way they walked and play back voice memos for each. It turned out to be a killer tool for context-sensitive reminders to kids to do the dishes, and for husbands, wives, and roommates to nag each other without getting on each other's nerves. Tjan was really jazzed about it, as it tied in with some theories he had about the changing U.S. demographic, trending toward blended households in urban centers, with three or more adults cohabitating.

"This is a rich vein," he said, rubbing his hands together. "Living communally is hard, and technology can make it easier. Roommate ware. It's the wave of the future."

There was another Kodacell group in San Francisco, a design outfit with a bunch of stringers who could design the gnomes for them, and they did great work. The gnomes were slightly lewd-looking, and they were the product of a generative algorithm that varied each one. Some of the designs that fell out of the algorithm were jaw-droppingly weird—Perry kept a three-eyed, six-armed version on his desk. They tooled up to make them by the hundred, then the thousand, then the tens of thousand. The fact that each one was different kept their margins up, but as the gnomes gained popularity their sales were steadily eroded by knockoffs, mostly from Eastern Europe.

The knockoffs weren't as cool-looking—though they were certainly weirder looking, like the offspring of a Norwegian troll and an anime robot—but they were more feature-rich. Some smart hacker in Russia was packing all kinds of functionality onto a single chip, so that their trolls cost less and did more: burglar alarms, baby monitors, streaming Internet radio source, and low-reliability medical diagnostics that relied on quack analysis of eye pigment, tongue coating, and other newage (rhymes with *sewage*) indicators.

Lester came back from the Dollar Store with a big bag of trolls, a dozen different models, and dumped them out on Tjan's desk, up in old foreman's offices on the catwalk above the workspaces. "Christ, would you look at these? They're selling them for less than our cost to manufacture. How do we compete with this?"

"We don't," Tjan said, and rubbed his belly. "Now we do the next thing."

"What's the next thing?" Perry said.

"Well, the first one delivered a return on investment at about twenty times the rate of any Kodak or Duracell business unit in the history of either company. But I'd like to shoot for thirty to forty times next, if that's all right with you. So let's go see what you've invented this week and how we can commercialize it."

Perry and Lester just looked at each other. Finally, Lester said, "Can you repeat that?"

"The typical ROI for a Kodacell unit in the old days was about four percent. If you put a hundred dollars in, you'd get a hundred and four dollars out, and it would take about a year to realize. Of course, in the old days, they wouldn't have touched a new business unless they could put a hundred million in and get a hundred and four million out. Four million bucks is four million bucks.

"But here, the company put fifty thousand into these dolls and three months later, they took seventy thousand out, after paying our salaries and bonuses. That's a forty percent ROI. Seventy thousand bucks isn't four million bucks, but forty percent is forty percent. Not to mention that our business drove similar margins in three other business units."

"I thought we'd screwed up by letting these guys eat our lunch," Lester said, indicating the Dollar Store trolls.

"Nope, we got in while the margins were high, made a good return, and now we'll get out as the margins drop. That's not screwing up, that's doing the right thing. The next time around, we'll do something more capital intensive and we'll take out an even higher margin: so show me something that'll cost two hundred grand to get going and that we can pull a hundred and sixty thou's worth of profit out of for Kodacell in three months. Let's do something ambitious this time around."

Suzanne took copious notes. There'd been a couple weeks' awkwardness early on about her scribbling as they talked, or videoing with her key chain. But once she'd moved into the building with the guys, taking a condo on the next floor up, she'd become just a member of the team, albeit a member who tweeted nearly every word they uttered to a feed that was adding new subscribers by the tens of thousands.

"So, Perry, what have you got for Tjan?" she asked.

"I came up with the last one," he said, grinning—they always ended up grinning when Tjan ran down economics for them. "Let Lester take this one."

Lester looked shy—he'd never fully recovered from Suzanne's turning him down, and when she was in the room, he always looked like he'd rather be somewhere else. He participated in the message boards on her blog, though, the most prolific poster in a field with thousands of very prolific posters. When he posted, others listened: he was witty, charming, and always right.

"Well, I've been thinking a lot about roommate ware, 'cause I know that Tjan's just crazy for that stuff. I've been handicapped by the fact that you guys are such excellent roomies, so I have to think back to my college days to remember what a bad roommate is like, where the friction is. Mostly, it comes down to resource contention, though: I wanna cook, but your dishes are in the sink; I wanna do laundry, but your boxers are in the dryer; I wanna watch TV, but your crap is all over the living room sofa."

Living upstairs from the guys gave her fresh insight into how the Kodacell philosophy would work out. Kettlewell was really big on communal living, putting these people into each other's pockets like the old-time geek houses of pizza-eating hackers, getting that in-the-trenches camaraderie. It had taken a weekend to put the most precious stuff in her California house into storage and then turn over the keys to a realtor who'd sort out leasing it for her. The monthly check from the realtor left more than enough for her to pay the rent in Florida and then some, and once the UPS man dropped off the five boxes of personal effects she'd chosen, she was practically at home.

She sat alone over the guys' apartments in the evenings, windows open so that their muffled conversations could drift in and form the soundtrack as she wrote her columns. It made her feel curiously with, but not of, their movement—a reasonable proxy for journalistic objectivity in this age of relativism.

"Resource contention readily decomposes into a bunch of smaller problems, with distinctive solutions. Take dishes: every dishwasher should be designed with a 'clean' and a 'dirty' compartment—basically, two logical dishwashers. You take clean dishes out of the clean side, use them, and put them into the dirty side. When the dirty side is full, the clean side is empty, so you cycle the dishwasher and the clean side becomes dirty and vice versa. I had some sketches for designs that would make this happen, but it didn't feel right: making dishwashers is too industrial for us. I either like making big chunks of art or little silver things you can carry in your pocket."

She smiled despite herself. She was drawing a half-million readers a day by doing near to nothing besides repeating the mind-blowing conversations around her. It had taken her a month to consider putting ads on the site—lots of feelers from blog "micro-labels" who wanted to get her under management and into their banner networks, and she broke down when one of them showed her a little spreadsheet detailing the kind of long green she could expect to bring in from a couple of little banners, with her getting the right to personally approve every advertiser in the network. The first month, she'd made more money than all but the most senior writers on the *Merc.* The next month, she'd outstripped her own old salary. She'd covered commercial blogs, the flamboyant attention-whores who'd bought stupid cars and ridiculous bimbos with the money, but she'd always assumed they were in a different league from a newspaper scribbler. Now she supposed all the money meant that she should make it official and phone in a resignation to Jimmy, but they'd left it pretty ambiguous as to whether she was retiring or taking a leave of absence, and she was reluctant to collapse that waveform into the certainty of saying goodbye to her old life.

"So I got to thinking about snitch-tags, radio-frequency ID gizmos. Remember those? When we started talking about them a decade ago, all the privacy people went crazy, totally sure that these things would be bad news. The geeks dismissed them as not understanding the technology. Supposedly, an RFID can only be read from a couple inches away—if someone wanted to find out what RFIDs you had on your person, they'd have to wand you, and you'd know about it."

"Yeah, that was bull," Perry said. "I mean, sure you can't read an RFID unless it's been excited with electromagnetic radiation, and *sure* you can't do that from a hundred yards without frying everything between you and the target. But if you had a subway turnstile with an exciter built into it, you could snipe all the tag numbers from a distant roof with a directional antenna. If those things had caught on, there'd be exciters everywhere and you'd be able to track anyone you wanted—Christ, they even put RFIDs in the hundred-dollar bill for a while! Pickpockets could have figured out whose purse was worth snatching from half a mile a way!"

"All true," Lester said. "But that didn't stop these guys. There are still a couple of them around, limping along without many customers. They print the tags with ink-jets, sized down to about a third the size of a grain of rice. Mostly used in supply-chain management and such. They can supply them on the cheap.

"Which brings me to my idea: why not tag everything in a group household, and use the tags to figure out who left the dishes in the sink, who took the hammer out and didn't put it back, who put the empty milk carton back in the fridge, and who's got the TV remote? It won't solve resource contention, but it will limit the social factors that contribute to it." He looked around at them. "We can make it fun, you know, make cool RFID sticker designs, mod the little gnome dolls to act as terminals for getting reports."

Suzanne found herself nodding along. She could use this kind of thing, even though she lived alone, just to help her find out where she left her glasses and the TV remote.

Perry shook his head, though. "When I was a kid, I had a really bad relationship with my mom. She was really smart, but she didn't have a lot of time to reason things out with me, so often as not she'd get out of arguing with me by just changing her story. So I'd say, 'Ma, can I go to the mall this aft?' and she'd say, 'Sure, no problem.' Then when I was getting ready to leave the house, she'd ask me where I thought I was going. I'd say, 'To the mall, you said!' and she'd just deny it. Just deny it, point-blank.

"I don't think she even knew she was doing it. I think when I asked her if I could go, she'd just absentmindedly say yes, but when it actually came time to go out, she'd suddenly remember all my unfinished chores, my homework, all the reasons I should stay home. I think every kid gets this from their folks, but it made me fucking crazy. So I got a mini tape recorder and I started to *tape* her when she gave me permission. I thought I'd really nail her the next time she changed her tune, play her own words back in her ear.

"So I tried it, and you know what happened? She gave me nine kinds of holy hell for wearing a wire and then she said it didn't matter what she'd said that morning, she was my mother and I had chores to do and no *how* was I going *anywhere* now that I'd started sneaking around the house with a hidden recorder. She took it away and threw it in the trash. And to top it off, she called me 'J. Edgar' for a month.

"So here's my question: how would you feel if the next time you left the dishes in the sink, I showed up with the audit trail for the dishes and waved it in your face? How would we get from that point to a happy, harmonious household? I think you've mistaken the cause for the effect. The problem with dishes in the sink isn't just that it's a pain when I want to cook a meal: it's that when you leave them in the sink, you're being inconsiderate. And the *reason* you've left them in the sink, as you've pointed out, is that putting dishes in the dishwasher is a pain in the ass: you have to bend over, you have to empty it out, and so on. If we moved the dishwasher into the kitchen cupboards and turned half of them into a dirty side and half into a clean side, then disposing of dishes would be as easy as getting them out."

Lester laughed, and so did Tjan. "Yeah, yeah—OK. Point taken. But these RFID things, they're so frigging cheap and potentially useful. I just can't believe that they've never found a single really compelling use in all this time. It just seems like an opportunity that's going to waste."

"Maybe it's a dead end. Maybe it's an ornithopter. Inventors spent hundreds of years trying to build an airplane that flew by flapping its wings, and it was all a rat hole."

"I guess," Lester said. "But I don't like the idea."

"Like it or don't," Perry said. "Doesn't affect whether it's true or not."

But Lester had a sparkle in his eye, and he disappeared into his workshop for a week and wouldn't let them in, which was unheard of for the big, gregarious giant. He liked to drag the others in whenever he accomplished anything of note, show it off to them like a big kid.

That was Sunday. Monday, Suzanne got a call from her realtor. "Your tenants have vanished," she said.

"Vanished?" The couple who'd rented her place had been as reliable as anyone she'd ever met in the Valley. He worked at a PR agency, she worked in marketing at Google. Or maybe he worked in marketing and she was in PR at Google—whatever, they were affluent, well-spoken, and had paid the extortionate rent she'd charged, without batting an eye.

"They normally paypal the rent to me on the first, but not this month. I called and left voicemail the next day, then followed up with an email. Yesterday I went by the house and it was empty. All their stuff was gone. No food in the fridge. I think they might have taken your home theater stuff, too."

"You're fucking kidding me," Suzanne said. It was 11 AM in Florida and she was into her second glass of lemonade as the sun began to superheat the air. Back in California, it was 8 AM. Her realtor was pulling long hours, and it wasn't her fault. "Sorry. Right. OK, what about the deposit?"

"You waived it."

She had. It hadn't seemed like a big deal at the time. The distant owner of the condo she was renting in Florida hadn't asked for one. "So I did. Now what?"

"You want to swear out a complaint against them?"

"With the police?"

"Yeah. Breach of contract. Theft, if they took the home theater. We can take them to collections, too."

Goddamned marketing people had the collective morals of a snake. All of them useless, conniving, shallow—she never should have . . .

"Yeah, OK. And what about the house?"

"We can find you another tenant by the end of the month, I'm sure. Maybe a little earlier. Have you thought any more about selling it?"

She hadn't, though the realtor brought it up every time they spoke. "Is now a good time?"

"Lot of new millionaires in the Valley shopping for houses, Suzanne. More than I've seen in years." She named a sum that was a third higher than the last time they'd talked it over.

"Is it peaking?"

"Who knows? It might go up, it might collapse again. But now is the best time to sell in the past ten years. You'd be smart to do it."

She took a deep breath. The Valley was dead, full of venal marketing people and buck-chasers. Here in Florida, she was on the cusp of the next thing, and it wasn't happening in the Valley: it was happening everywhere *except* the Valley, in the cheap places where innovation could happen at low rents. Leaky hot tub, incredible property taxes, and the crazy roller-coaster ride—up 20 percent this month, down 40 next. The bubble was going to burst someday and she should sell out now.

"Sell it," she said.

"You're going to be a wealthy lady," the realtor said.

"Right," Suzanne said.

"I have a buyer, Suzanne. I didn't want to pressure you. But I can sell it by Friday. Close escrow next week. Cash in hand by the fifteenth."

"Jesus," she said. "You're joking."

"No joke," the realtor said. "I've got a waiting list for houses on your block."

And so Suzanne got on an airplane that night and flew back to San Jose and took a pricey taxi back to her place. The marketdroids had left it in pretty good shape, clean and tidy, clean sheets in the linen cupboard. She made up her bed and reflected that this would be the last time she made this bed—the next time she stripped the sheets, they'd go into a long-term storage box. She'd done this before, on her way out of Detroit, packing up a life into boxes and shoving it into storage. What had Tjan said? "The self-storage industry is bigger than the recording industry, did you know that? All they do is provide a place to put stuff that we own that we can't find room for—that's super-abundance."

Before bed she posted a classified on Craigslist for a couple helpers to work on boxing stuff, emailed Jimmy to see if he wanted lunch, and looked up the address for the central police station to swear out her complaint. The amp, speakers, and A/V switcher were all missing from her home theater.

She had a dozen helpers to choose from the next morning. She picked two who came with decent references, marveling that it was suddenly possible in Silicon Valley to get anyone to show up anywhere for ten bucks an hour. The police sergeant who took the complaint was sympathetic and agreed with her choice to get out of town. "I've had it with this place, too. Soon as my kids are out of high school I'm moving back to Montana. I miss the weather."

She didn't think of the marketdroids again until the next day, when she and her helpers were boxing up the last of her things and loading them into her U-Haul. Then a BMW convertible screeched around the corner and burned rubber up to her door.

The woman marketdroid was driving, looking crazy and disheveled, eyes red-rimmed, one heel broken off of her shoes.

"What the FUCK is your problem, lady?" she said, as she leapt out of her car and stalked toward Suzanne.

Instinctively, Suzanne shrank back and dropped the box of books she was holding. It spilled out over her lawn.

"Fiona?" she said. "What's happened?"

"I was *arrested*. They came to my workplace and led me out in handcuffs. I had to make *bail*."

Suzanne's stomach shrank to a little pebble, impossibly heavy. "What was I supposed to do? You two took off with my home theater!"

"What home theater? Everything was right where you left it when I went. I haven't lived here in *weeks*. Tom left me last month and I moved out."

"You moved out?"

"Yeah, bitch, I *moved out*. Tom was your tenant, not me. If he ripped something off, that's between you and him."

"Look, Fiona, wait, hold up a second. I tried to call you, I sent you email. No one was paying the rent, no one told me that you'd moved out, and no one answered when I tried to find out what had happened."

"That sounds like an *explanation*," she said, hissing. "I'm waiting for a fucking *apology*. They took me to *prison*."

Suzanne knew that the local lockup was a long way from prison. "I apolo-gize," she said. "Can I get you a cup of coffee? Would you like to use the shower or anything?"

The woman glared at her a moment longer, then slowly folded in on her-self, collapsing, coughing, and sobbing on the lawn.

Suzanne stood with her arms at her sides for a moment. Her Craigslist helpers had gone home, so she was all alone, and this woman, whom she'd met only once before, in passing, was clearly having some real problems. Not the kind of thing she dealt with a lot—her life didn't include much person-to-person hand-holding.

But what can you do? She knelt beside Fiona in the grass and took her hand. "Let's get you inside, OK?"

At first it was as though she hadn't heard, but slowly she straightened up and let Suzanne lead her into the house. She was twenty-two, twenty-three, young enough to be Suzanne's daughter if Suzanne had gone in for that sort of thing. Suzanne helped her to the sofa and sat her down amid the boxes still waiting to go into the U-Haul. The kitchen was packed up, but she had a couple bottles of Diet Coke in the cooler and she handed one to the girl.

"I'm really sorry, Fiona. Why didn't you answer my calls or email?"

She looked at Suzanne, her eyes lost in streaks of mascara. "I don't know. I didn't want to talk about it. He lost his job last month and kind of went crazy, told me he didn't want the responsibility anymore. What responsibil-ity? But he told me to go, told me it would be best for both of us if we were apart. I thought it was another girl, but I don't know. Maybe it was just crazi-ness. Everyone I know out here is crazy. They all work a hundred hours a week, they get fired or quit their jobs every five months. Everything is so expensive. My rent is three quarters of my salary."

"It's really hard," Suzanne said, thinking of the easy, lazy days in Florida, the hackers' idyll that Perry and Lester enjoyed in their workshops.

"Tom was on antidepressants, but he didn't like taking them. When he was on them, he was pretty good, but when he went off, he turned into . . . I don't know. He'd cry a lot, and shout. It wasn't a good relationship, but we moved out here from Oregon together, and I'd known him all my life. He was a little moody before, but not like he was here."

"When did you speak to him last?" Suzanne had found a couple of blister packs of antidepressants in the medicine chest. She hoped that wasn't Tom's only supply.

"We haven't spoken since I moved out."

An hour later, the mystery was solved. The police went to Tom's work-place and discovered that he'd been fired the week before. They tried the GPS in his car and it finked him out as being in a ghost mall's parking lot near his old office. He was dead behind the wheel, a gun in his hand, shot through the heart.

Suzanne took the call, and though she tried to keep her end of the conversation quiet and neutral, Fiona—still on the sofa, drinking the warm, flat Coke—knew. She let out a moan like a dog that's been kicked, and then a scream. For Suzanne, it was all unreal, senseless. The cops told her that her home theater components were found in the trunk of the car. No note.

"God, oh God, Jesus, you selfish shit fucking bastard," Fiona sobbed. Awkwardly, Suzanne sat down beside her and took her into a one-armed hug. Her helpers were meeting her at the self-storage the next day to help her unload the U-Haul.

"Do you have someone who can stay with you tonight?" Suzanne asked, praying the answer was yes. She had a house to move out of. Christ, she felt so cold-blooded, but she was on a goddamned schedule.

"Yes, I guess." Fiona scrubbed at her eyes with her fists. "Sure."

Suzanne sighed. The lie was plain. "Who?"

Fiona stood up and smoothed out her skirt. "I'm sorry," she said, and started for the door.

Groaning inwardly, Suzanne blocked her. "You'll stay on the sofa," she said. "You're not driving in this state. I'll order in pizza. Pepperoni mushroom OK?"

Looking defeated, Fiona turned on her heel and went back to the sofa.

Over pizza, Suzanne pulled a few details out of her. Tom had fallen into a funk when the layoffs had started in his office—they were endemic across the Valley, another bust was upon them. His behavior had grown worse and worse, and she'd finally left, or been thrown out, it wasn't clear. She was on thin ice at Google, and they were laying people off too, and she was convinced that being led out in handcuffs would be the straw that broke the camel's back.

"I should move back to Oregon," she said, dropping her slice back on the box top.

Suzanne had heard a lot of people talk about giving up on the Valley since she'd moved there. It was a common thing, being beaten down by life in the Bay Area. You were supposed to insert a pep talk here, something about hanging in, about the opportunities here.

"Yes," she said, "that's a good idea. You're young, and there's a life for you there. You can start something up, or go to work for someone else's startup." It felt weird coming out of her mouth, like a betrayal of the Valley, of some tribal loyalty to this tech mecca. But after all, wasn't she selling up and moving east?

"There's nothing in Oregon," Fiona said, snuffling.

"There's something everywhere. Let me tell you about some friends of mine in Florida," and she told her, and as she told her, she told herself. Hearing it spoken aloud, even after having written about it and written about it, and been there and DONE it, it was different. She came to understand how fucking *cool* it all was, this new, entrepreneurial, inventive, amazing thing she was engaged in. She'd loved the contrast of nimble software companies compared with gigantic, brutal auto companies, but what her boys were doing, it made the software companies look like lumbering lummoxes, crashing around with their fifty employees and their big purpose-built offices.

Fiona was disbelieving, then interested, then excited. "They just make this stuff, do it, then make something else?"

"Exactly—no permanence except for the team, and they support each other, live and work together. You'd think that because they live and work together that they don't have any balance, but it's the opposite: they book off work at four or sometimes earlier, go to movies, go out and have fun, read books, play catch. It's amazing. I'm never coming back here."

And she never would.

She told her editor about this. She told her friends who came to a send-off party at a bar she used to go to when she went into the office a lot. She told her cab driver who picked her up to take her to the airport and she told the bemused engineer who sat next to her all the way back to Miami. She had the presence of mind not to tell the couple who bought her house for a sum of money that seemed to have at least one extra zero at the end—maybe two.

And so when she got back to Miami, she hardly noticed the incredible obesity of the man who took the money for the gas in her leased car—now that she was here for the long haul she'd have to look into getting Lester to help her buy a used Smart car from a junker lot—and the tin roofs of the shantytowns she passed looked tropical and quaint. The smell of swamp and salt, the pea-soup humidity, the bass thunder of the boom cars in the traffic around her—it was like some kind of sweet homecoming for her.

Tjan was in the condo when she got home and he spotted her from the balcony, where he'd been sunning himself, and helped her bring up her suitcases of things she couldn't bear to put in storage.

"Come down to our place for a cup of coffee once you're settled in," he said, leaving her. She sluiced off the airplane grease that had filled her pores on the long flight from San Jose to Miami and changed into a cheap sundress and a pair of flip-flops that she'd bought at the Thunderbird Flea Market and headed down to their place.

Tjan opened the door with a flourish and she stepped in and stopped short. When she'd left, the place had been a reflection of their jumbled lives: gizmos, dishes, parts, tools, and clothes strewn everywhere in a kind of joyful, eye-watering hyper-mess, like an enormous kitchen junk-drawer.

Now the place was *spotless*—and what's more, it was *minimalist*. The floor was not only clean, it was visible. Lining the walls were translucent white plastic tubs stacked to the ceiling.

"You like it?"

"It's amazing," she said. "Like Ikea meets *Barbarella*. What happened here?"

Tjan did a little two-step. "It was Lester's idea. Have a look in the boxes."

She pulled a couple of the tubs out. They were jam-packed with books, tools, cruft, and crud—all the crap that had previously cluttered the shelves and the floor and the sofa and the coffee table.

"Watch this," he said. He unvelcroed a wireless keyboard from the side of the TV and began to type: T-H-E C-O . . . The field auto-completed itself— THE COUNT OF MONTE CRISTO—and brought up a picture of a beaten-up paperback along with links to Web stores, reviews, and the full text. Tjan gestured with his chin and she saw that the front of one of the tubs was pulsing with a soft blue glow. Tjan went and pulled open the tub and fished for a second before producing the book.

"Try it," he said, handing her the keyboard. She began to type experimentally: U-N and up came UNDERWEAR (14). "No way," she said.

"Way," Tjan said, and hit return, bringing up a thumbnail gallery of fourteen pairs of underwear. He tabbed over each, picked out a pair of Simpsons boxers, and hit return. A different tub started glowing.

"Lester finally found a socially beneficial use for RFIDs. We're going to get rich!"

"I don't think I understand," she said.

"Come on," he said. "Let's get to the junkyard. Lester explains this really well."

He did, too, losing all of the shyness she remembered, his eyes glowing, his sausage-thick fingers dancing.

"Have you ever alphabetized your hard drive? I mean, have you ever spent any time concerning yourself with where on your hard drive your files are stored, which sectors contain which files? Computers abstract away the tedious, physical properties of files and leave us with handles that we use to persistently refer to them, regardless of which part of the hard drive currently holds those particular bits. So I thought, with RFIDs, you could do this with the real world, just tag everything and have your furniture keep track of where it is.

"One of the big barriers to roommate harmony is the correct disposition of stuff. When you leave your book on the sofa, I have to move it before I can sit down and watch TV. Then you come after me and ask me where I put your book. Then we have a fight. There's stuff that you don't know where it goes, and stuff that you don't know where it's been put, and stuff that has nowhere to put it. But with tags and a smart chest of drawers, you can just put your stuff wherever there's room and ask the physical space to keep track of what's where from moment to moment.

"There's still the problem of getting everything tagged and described, but that's a service business opportunity, and where you've got other shared identifiers like ISBNs you could use a camera phone to snap the bar codes and look them up against public databases. The whole thing could be coordinated around 'spring-cleaning' events where you go through your stuff and photograph it, tag it, describe it—good for your insurance and for forensics if you get robbed, too."

He stopped and beamed, folding his fingers over his belly. "So, that's it, basically."

Perry slapped him on the shoulder and Tjan drummed his forefingers like a heavy-metal drummer on the side of the workbench they were gathered around.

They were all waiting for her. "Well, it's very cool," she said, at last. "But, the whole white-plastic-tub thing. It makes your apartment look like an Ikea showroom. Kind of inhumanly minimalist. We're Americans, we like celebrating our stuff."

"Well, OK, fair enough," Lester said, nodding. "You don't have to put everything away, of course. And you can still have all the decor you want. This is about clutter control."

"Exactly," Perry said. "Come check out Lester's lab."

"OK, this is pretty perfect," Suzanne said. The clutter was gone, disappeared into the white tubs that were stacked high on every shelf, leaving the work surfaces clear. But Lester's works-in-progress, his keepsakes, his sculptures and triptychs were still out, looking like venerated museum pieces in the stark tidiness that prevailed otherwise.

Tjan took her through the spreadsheets. "There are ten teams that do closet organizing in the network, and a bunch of shippers, packers, movers, and storage experts. A few furniture companies. We adopted the interface from some free software inventory-management apps that were built for illiterate service employees. Lots of big pictures and autocompletion. And we've bought a hundred RFID printers from a company that was so grateful for a new customer that they're shipping us a hundred and fifty of them, so we can print these things at about a million per hour. The plan is to start our sales through the consultants at the same time as we start showing at trade shows for furniture companies. We've already got a huge order from a couple of local old-folks' homes."

They walked to the IHOP to have a celebratory lunch. Being back in Florida felt just right to her. Francis, the leader of the paramilitary wing of the AARP, threw them a salute and blew her a kiss, and even Lester's nursing junkie friend seemed to be in a good mood.

When they were done, they brought takeout bags for the junkie and Francis in the shantytown.

"I want to make some technology for those guys," Perry said as they sat in front of Francis's RV drinking cowboy coffee cooked over a banked wood-stove off to one side. "Roommate ware for homeless people."

Francis uncrossed his bony ankles and scratched at his mosquito bites. "A lot of people think that we don't buy stuff, but it's not true," he said. "I shop hard for bargains, but there's lots of stuff I spend more on because of my lifestyle than I would if I had a real house and steady electricity. When I had a chest freezer, I could bulk-buy ground round for about a tenth of what I pay now when I go to the grocery store and get enough for one night's dinner. The alternative is using propane to keep the fridge going overnight, and that's not cheap, either. So I'm a kind of premium customer. Back at Boeing, we loved the people who made small orders, because we could charge them such a premium for custom work, while the big airlines wanted stuff done so cheap that half the time we lost money on the deal."

Perry nodded. "There you have it—roommate ware for homeless people, a great and untapped market."

Suzanne cocked her head and looked at him. "You're sounding awfully commerce-oriented for a pure and unsullied engineer, you know?"

He ducked his head and grinned and looked about twelve years old. "It's infectious. Those little kitchen gnomes, we sold nearly a half million of those things, not to mention all the spin-offs. That's a half-million *lives*—a half-million *households*—that we changed just by thinking up something cool and making it real. These RFID things of Lester's—we'll sign a couple million customers with those. People will change everything about how they live from moment to moment because of something Lester thought up in my junkyard over there."

"Well, there's thirty million of us living in what the social workers call 'marginal housing,'" Francis said, grinning wryly. He had a funny smile that Suzanne had found adorable until he explained that he had an untreated dental abscess that he couldn't afford to get fixed. "So that's a lot of difference you could make."

"Yeah," Perry said. "Yeah, it sure is."

That night, she found herself still blogging and answering emails—they always piled up when she traveled and took a couple of late nights to clear out—after 9 PM, sitting alone in a pool of light in the back corner of Lester's workshop that she had staked out as her office. She yawned and stretched and listened to her old back crackle. She hated feeling old, and late nights made her feel old—feel every extra ounce of fat on her tummy, feel the lines bracketing her mouth and the little bag of skin under her chin.

She stood up and pulled on a light jacket and began to switch off lights and get ready to head home. As she poked her head in Tjan's office, she saw that she wasn't the only one working late.

"Hey, you," she said. "Isn't it time you got going?"

He jumped like he'd been stuck with a pin and gave a little yelp. "Sorry," he said, "didn't hear you."

He had a cardboard box on his desk and had been filling it with his personal effects—little one-off inventions the guys had made for him, personal fetishes and tchotchkes, a framed picture of his kids.

"What's up?"

He sighed and cracked his knuckles. "Might as well tell you now as tomorrow morning. I'm resigning."

She felt a flash of anger and then forced it down and forcibly replaced it with professional distance and curiosity. Mentally she licked her pencil tip and flipped to a blank page in her reporter's notebook.

"Oh yes?"

"I've had another offer, in Westchester County. Westinghouse has spun out its own version of Kodacell and they're looking for a new vice president to run the division. That's me."

"Good job," she said. "Congratulations, Mr. Vice President."

He shook his head. "I emailed Kettlewell half an hour ago. I'm leaving in the morning. I'm going to say goodbye to the guys over breakfast."

"Not much notice," she said.

"Nope," he said, a note of anger creeping into his voice. "My contract lets Kodacell fire me on one day's notice, so I insisted on the right to quit on the same terms. Maybe Kettlewell will get his lawyers to write better boilerplate from here on in."

When she had an angry interview, she habitually changed the subject to something sensitive: angry people often say more than they intend to. She did it instinctively, not really meaning to psyops Tjan, whom she thought of as a friend, but not letting that get in the way of the story. "Westinghouse is doing what, exactly?"

"It'll be as big as Kodacell's operation in a year," he said. "George Westing-house personally funded Tesla's research, you know. The company under-stands funding individual entrepreneurs. I'm going to be training the talent scouts and mentoring the financial people, then turning them loose to sign up entrepreneurs for the Westinghouse network. There's a competitive market for garage inventors now." He laughed. "Go ahead and print that," he said. "Blog it tonight. There's competition now. We're giving two points more equity and charging half a point less on equity than the Kodacell network."

"That's amazing, Tjan. I hope you'll keep in touch with me—I'd love to follow your story."

"Count on it," he said. He laughed. "I'm getting a week off every eight weeks to scout Russia. They've got an incredible culture of entrepreneur-ship."

"Plus you'll get to see your kids," Suzanne said. "That's really good."

"Plus, I'll get to see my kids," he admitted.

"How much money is Westinghouse putting into the project?" she asked, replacing her notional notebook with a real one, pulled from her purse.

"I don't have numbers, but they've shut down the whole appliances divi-sion to clear the budget for it." She nodded—she'd seen news of the layoffs on the wires. Mass demonstrations, people out of work after twenty years' service. "So it's a big budget."

"They must have been impressed with the quarterlies from Kodacell."

Tjan folded down the flaps on his box and drummed his fingers on it, squinting at her. "You're joking, right?"

"What do you mean?"

"Suzanne, they were impressed by *you*. Everyone knows that quarterly numbers are easy to cook—anything less than two annual reports is as likely to be enronning as real fortune making. But *your* dispatches from here—they're what sold them. It's what's convincing *everyone*. Kettlewell said that three quar-ters of his new recruits come on board after reading your descriptions of this place. That's how *I* ended up here."

She shook her head. "That's very flattering, Tjan, but—"

He waved her off and then, surprisingly, came around the desk and hugged her. "But nothing, Suzanne. Kettlewell, Lester, Perry—they're all basically big kids. Full of enthusiasm and invention, but they've got the emotional maturity and sense of scale of hyperactive five-year-olds. You and me, we're grown-ups. People take us seriously. It's easy to get a kid excited, but when a grown-up chimes in you know there's some there there."

Suzanne recovered herself after a second and put away her notepad. "I'm just the person who writes it all down. You people are making it happen."

"In ten years' time, they'll remember you and not us," Tjan said. "You should get Kettlewell to put you on the payroll."

Kettlewell himself turned up the next day. Suzanne had developed an intuitive sense of the flight times from the West Coast and so for a second she couldn't figure out how he could possibly be standing there—nothing in the sky could get him from San Jose to Miami for a 7 AM arrival.

"Private jet," he said, and had the grace to look slightly embarrassed. "Kodak had eight of them and Duracell had five. We've been trying to sell them all off but no one wants a used jet these days, not even Saudi princes or Colombian drug lords."

"So, basically, it was going to waste."

He smiled and looked eighteen—she really did feel like the only grown-up sometimes—and said, " 'Zackly—it's practically environmental. Where's Tjan?"

"Downstairs saying goodbye to the guys, I think."

"OK," he said. "Are you coming?"

She grabbed her notebook and a pen and beat him out the door of her rented condo.

"What's this all about," Tjan said, looking wary. The guys were hangdog and curious-looking, slightly in awe of Kettlewell, who did little to put them at their ease—he was staring intensely at Tjan.

"Exit interview," he said. "Company policy."

Tjan rolled his eyes. "Come on," he said. "I've got a flight to catch in an hour."

"I could give you a lift," Kettlewell said.

"You want to do the exit interview between here and the airport?"

"I could give you a lift to JFK. I've got the jet warmed up and waiting."

Sometimes, Suzanne managed to forget that Kodacell was a multibillion-dollar operation and that Kettlewell was at its helm, but other times the point was very clear.

"Come on," he said, "we'll make a day of it. We can stop on the way and pick up some barbecue to eat on the plane. I'll even let you keep your seat in the reclining position during takeoff and landing. Hell, you can turn your cellphone on—just don't tell the Transport Security Administration!"

Tjan looked cornered, then resigned. "Sounds good to me," he said, and Kettlewell shouldered one of the two huge duffel bags that were sitting by the door.

"Hi, Kettlewell," Perry said.

Kettlewell set down the duffel. "Sorry, sorry. Lester, Perry, it's really good to see you. I'll bring Suzanne back tonight and we'll all go out for dinner, OK?"

Suzanne blinked. "I'm coming along?"

"I sure hope so," Kettlewell said.

Perry and Lester accompanied them down in the elevator.

"Private jet, huh?" Perry said. "Never been in one of those."

Kettlewell told them about his adventures trying to sell off Kodacell's private air force.

"Send one of them our way, then," Lester said.

"Do you fly?" Kettlewell said.

"No," Perry said. "Lester wants to take it apart. Right, Les?"

Lester nodded. "Lots of cool junk in a private jet."

"These things are worth millions, guys," Kettlewell said.

"No, someone *paid* millions for them," Perry said. "They're *worth* whatever you can sell them for."

Kettlewell laughed. "You've had an influence around here, Tjan," he said. Tjan managed a small, tight smile.

Kettlewell had a driver waiting outside of the building who loaded the duffels into the spacious trunk of a spotless dark town car whose doors chunked shut with an expensive sound.

"I want you to know that I'm really not angry at all, OK?" Kettlewell said.

Tjan nodded. He had the look of a man who was steeling himself for a turn in an interrogation chamber. He'd barely said a word since Kettlewell arrived. For his part, Kettlewell appeared oblivious to all of this, though Suzanne was pretty sure that he understood exactly how uncomfortable this was making Tjan.

"The thing is, six months ago, nearly everyone was convinced that I was a fucking moron, that I was about to piss away ten billion dollars of other people's money on a stupid doomed idea. Now they're copying me and poaching my best people. So this is good news for me, though I'm going to have to find a new business manager for those two before they get picked up for turning planes into component pieces."

Suzanne's PDA vibrated whenever the number of online news stories mentioning her or Kodacell or Kettlewell increased or decreased sharply. She used to try to read everything, but it was impossible to keep up—now all she wanted was to keep track of whether the interestingness index was on the uptick or downtick.

It had started to buzz that morning and the pitch had increased steadily until it was actually uncomfortable in her pocket. Irritated, she yanked it out and was about to switch it off when the lead article caught her eye.

KODACELL LOSES TJAN TO WESTINGHOUSE

The byline was Freddy. Feeling like a character in a horror movie who can't resist the compulsion to look under the bed, Suzanne thumbed the PDA's wheel and brought up the whole article.

> Kodacell business manager Tjan Lee Tang, whose adventures we've
> followed through Suzanne Church's gushing, besotted "blog" posts,

She looked away and reflexively reached toward the delete button. The innuendo that she was romantically involved with one or more of the guys had circulated on her blog's message boards and around the diggdots ever since she'd started writing about them. No woman could possibly be writing about this stuff because it was important—she had to be "with the band," a groupie or a whore.

Combine that with Rat-Toothed Freddy's sneering tone and she was instantly sent into heart-thundering rage. She deleted the post and looked out the window. Her pager buzzed some more and she looked down. The same article, being picked up on blogs, on some of the bigger diggdots, and an AP wire.

She forced herself to reopen it.

> has been hired to head up a new business unit on behalf of the
> multinational giant Westinghouse. The appointment stands as more
> proof of Church's power to cloud men's minds with pretty, empty
> words about the half-baked dotcom schemes that have oozed out of
> Silicon Valley and into every empty and dead American suburb.

It was hypnotic, like staring into the eyes of a serpent. Her pulse actually thudded in her ears for a second before she took a few deep breaths and calmed down enough to finish the article, which was just more of the same: nasty personal attacks, sniping, and innuendo. Freddy even managed to imply that she was screwing all of them—and Kettlewell besides.

Kettlewell leaned over her shoulder and read.

"You should send him an email," he said. "That's disgusting. That's not reportage."

"Never get into a pissing match with a skunk," she said. "What Freddy wants is for me to send him mail that he can publish along with more snarky commentary. When the guy you're arguing with controls the venue you're arguing in, you can't possibly win."

"So blog him," Kettlewell said. "Correct the record."

"The record is correct," she said. "It's never been incorrect. I've written an exhaustive record that is there for everyone to see. If people believe this, no amount of correction will help."

Kettlewell made a face like a little boy who'd been told he couldn't have a toy. "That guy is poison," he said. "Those quote marks around 'blog.'"

"Let him add his quote marks," she said. "My daily readership is higher than the *Merc*'s paid circulation this week." It was true. After a short uphill climb from her new URL, she'd accumulated enough readers that the advertising revenue was dwarfing her old salary at the *Merc*, an astonishing happenstance that nevertheless kept her bank account full. She clicked a little. "Besides, look at this, there are three dozen links pointing at this story so far and all of them are critical of him. We don't need to stick up for ourselves—the world will."

Saying it calmed her and now they were at the airport. They cruised into a private gate, away from the militarized gulag that fronted Miami International. A courteous security guard waved them through and the driver confidently piloted the car up to a wheeled jetway beside a cute, stubby little toy jet. On the side, in cursive script, was the plane's name: Suzanne.

She looked accusatorially at Kettlewell.

"It was called that when I bought the company," he said, expressionless but somehow mirthful behind his curved surfer shades. "But I kept it because I liked the private joke."

"Just no one tell Freddy that you've got an airplane with my name on it or we'll never hear the fucking end of it."

She covered her mouth, regretting her language, and Kettlewell laughed, and so did Tjan, and somehow the ice was broken between them.

"No *way* flying this thing is cost-effective," Tjan said. "Your CFO should be kicking your ass."

"It's a little indulgence," Kettlewell said, bounding up the steps and shaking hands with a small, neat woman pilot, an African-American with cornrows peeking out under her smart peaked cap. "Once you've flown in your own bird, you never go back."

"This is a *monstrosity*," Tjan said as he boarded. "What this thing eats up in hangar fees alone would be enough to bankroll three or four teams." He settled into an oversized Barcalounger of a seat and accepted a glass of orange juice that the pilot poured for him. "Thank you, and no offense."

"None taken," she said. "I agree one hundred percent."

"See," Tjan said.

Suzanne took her own seat and her own glass and buckled in and watched the two of them, warming up for the main event, realizing that she'd been brought along as a kind of opening act.

"They paying you more?"

"Yup," Tjan said. "All on the back end. Half a point on every dollar brought in by a team I coach or whose members I mentor."

Kettlewell whistled. "That's a big share," he said.

"If I can make my numbers, I'll take home a million this year."

"You'll make those numbers. Good negotiations. Why didn't you ask us for the same deal?"

"Would you have given it to me?"

"You're a star," Kettlewell said, nodding at Suzanne, whose invisibility to the conversation popped like a bubble. "Thanks to her."

"Thanks, Suzanne," Tjan said.

Suzanne blushed. "Come on, guys."

Tjan shook his head. "She doesn't really understand. It's actually kind of charming."

"We might have matched the offer."

"You guys are first to market. You've got a lot of procedures in place. I wanted to reinvent some wheels."

"We're too *conservative* for you?"

Tjan grinned wickedly. "Oh yes," he said. "I'm going to do business in *Russia.*"

Kettlewell grunted and pounded his orange juice. Around them, the jet's windows flashed white as they broke through the clouds and the ten-thousand-foot bell sounded.

"How the hell are you going to make anything that doesn't collapse under its own weight in Russia?"

"The corruption's a problem, sure," Tjan said. "But it's offset by the entrepreneurship. Some of those cats make the Chinese look lazy and unimaginative. It's a shame that so much of their efforts have been centered on graft, but there's no reason they couldn't be focused on making an honest ruble."

They fell into a discussion of the minutiae of Perry and Lester's businesses, franker than any business discussion she'd ever heard. Tjan talked about the places where they'd screwed up, and places where they'd scored big, and about all the plans he'd made for Westinghouse, the connections he had in Russia. He even talked about his kids and his ex in St. Petersburg, and Kettlewell admitted that he'd known about them already.

For Kettlewell's part, he opened the proverbial kimono wide, telling Tjan about conflicts within the board of directors, poisonous holdovers from the pre-Kodacell days who sabotaged the company from within with petty bureaucracy, even the problems he was having with his family over the long hours they were working. He opened the minibar and cracked a bottle of champagne to toast Tjan's new job, and they mixed it with more orange juice, and then there were bagels and schmear, fresh fruit, power bars, and canned Starbucks coffees with deadly amounts of sugar and caffeine.

When Kettlewell disappeared into the tiny—but marble-appointed—bathroom, Suzanne found herself sitting alone with Tjan, almost knee to knee, light-headed from lack of sleep and champagne and altitude.

"Some trip," she said.

"You're the best," he said, wobbling a little. "You know that? Just the best. The stuff you write about these guys, it makes me want to stand up and salute. You make us all seem so fucking *glorious*. We're going to end up taking over the world because you inspire us so. Maybe I shouldn't tell you this, because you're not very self-conscious about it right now, but Suzanne, you won't believe it because you're so goddamned modest, too. It's what makes your writing so right, so believable—"

Kettlewell stepped out of the bathroom. "Touching down soon," he said, and patted them each on the shoulder as he took his seat. "So that's about it, then," he said, and leaned back and closed his eyes. Suzanne was accustomed to thinking of him as twentysomething, the boyish age of the magazine cover portraits from the start of his career. Now, eyes closed on his private jet, harsh upper atmosphere sun painting his face, his crow's-feet and the deep vertical brackets around his mouth revealed him for someone pushing a youthful forty, kept young by exercise and fun and the animation of his ideas.

"Guess so," Tjan said, slumping. "This has been one of the more memorable experiences of my life, Kettlewell, Suzanne. Not entirely pleasant, but pleasant on the whole. A magical time in the clouds."

"Once you've flown private, you'll never go back to coach," Kettlewell said, smiling, eyes still closed. "You still think my CFO should spank me for not selling this thing?"

"No," Tjan said. "In ten years, if we do our jobs, there won't be five companies on earth that can afford this kind of thing—it'll be like building a cathedral after the Protestant Reformation. While we have the chance, we should keep these things in the sky. But you should give one to Lester and Perry to take apart."

"I was planning to," Kettlewell said. "Thanks."

Suzanne and Kettlewell didn't get off the plane and Tjan didn't look back when they'd landed at JFK. "Should we go into town and get some bialy to bring back to Miami?" Kettlewell said, squinting at the bright day on the tarmac.

"Bring deli to Miami?"

"Right, right," he said. "Forget I asked. Besides, we'd have to charter a chopper to get into Manhattan and back without dying in traffic."

Something about the light through the open hatch or the sound or the smell—something indefinably New York—made her yearn for Miami. The great cities of commerce like New York and San Francisco seemed too real for her, while the suburbs of Florida were a kind of endless summer camp, a dreamtime where anything was possible.

"Let's go," she said. The champagne buzz had crashed and she had a touch of headache. "I'm bushed."

"Me too," Kettlewell said. "I left San Jose last night to get into Miami before Tjan left. Not much sleep. Gonna put my seat back and catch some winks, if that's OK?"

"Good plan," Suzanne said.

Embarrassingly, when fully reclined, they nearly touched, their seats forming something like a double bed. Suzanne lay awake in the hum of the jets for a while, conscious of the breathing human beside her, the first man she'd done anything like share a bed with in at least a year. The last thing she remembered was the ten-thousand-foot bell going off and then she slipped away into sleep.

> Perry thought that they'd sell a million Home Awares in six
> months. Lester thought he was nuts, that number was too high.
>
> "Please," he said, "I *invented* these things but there aren't a
> million roommate households in all of America. We'll sell half
> a million tops, total."

Lester always complained when she quoted him directly in her blog posts, but she thought he secretly enjoyed it.

> Today the boys shipped their millionth unit. It took six weeks.

They'd uncorked a bottle of champagne when unit one million shipped. They hadn't actually shipped it, per se. The manufacturing was spread out across forty different teams all across the country, even a couple of Canadian teams. The RFID printer company had rehired half the workers they'd laid off the year before, and had them all working overtime to meet demand.

> What's exciting about this isn't just the money that these guys
> have made off of it, or the money that Kodacell will return to
> its shareholders, it's the ecosystem that these things have
> enabled. There're at least ten competing commercial systems for
> organizing, tagging, sharing, and describing Home Aware objects.
> Parents love them for their kids. Schoolteachers love them.
> Seniors' homes.

The seniors' homes had been Francis's idea. They'd brought him in to over-see some of the production engineering, along with some of the young braves who ran around the squatter camps. Francis knew which ones were biddable and he kept them to heel. In the evenings, he'd join the guys and Suzanne up on the roof of the workshop on folding chairs, with beers, watching the sweaty sunset.

> They're not the sole supplier. That's what an ecosystem is all
> about, creating value for a lot of players. All this competition
> is great news for you and me, because it's already driven the
> price of Home Aware goods down by 40 percent. That means that
> Lester and Perry are going to have to invent something new, soon,
> before the margin disappears altogether—and that's also good
> news for you and me.

"Are you coming?" Lester had dated a girl for a while, someone he met on Craigslist, but she'd dumped him, and Perry had confided that she'd left him because he didn't live up to the press he'd gotten in Suzanne's column. When he got dumped, he became even touchier about Suzanne, caught at a distance from her that was defined by equal parts of desire and resentment.

"Up in a minute," she said, trying to keep her smile light and noncommittal. Lester was very nice, but there were times when she caught him staring at her like a kicked puppy and it made her uncomfortable. Naturally, this increased his discomfort as well.

On the roof they already had a cooler of beers going and beside it a huge plastic tub of brightly colored machine parts.

"Jet engine," Perry said. The months had put a couple pounds on him and new wrinkles, and given him some gray at the temples, and laugh lines inside his laugh lines. Perry was always laughing at everything around them. ("They fucking *pay me* to do this," he'd told her once, before literally collapsing to the floor, rolling with uncontrollable hysteria). He laughed again.

"Good old Kettlebelly," she said. "Must have broken his heart."

Francis held up a curved piece of cowling. "This thing wasn't going to last anyway. See the distortion here and here? This thing was designed in a virtual wind tunnel and machine-lathed. We tried that a couple times, but the wind-tunnel sims were never detailed enough and the forms that flew well in the machine always died a premature death in the sky. Another two years and he'd have had to have it rebuilt anyway, and the Koreans who built this charge shitloads for parts."

"Too bad," Lester said. "It's pretty. Gorgeous, even." He mimed its curve in the air with a pudgy hand, that elegant swoop.

"Aerospace loves the virtual wind tunnel," Francis said, and glared at the cowling. "You can use evolutionary algorithms in the sim and come up with really efficient designs, in theory. And computers are cheaper than engineers."

"Is that why you were laid off?" Suzanne said.

"I wasn't laid off, girl," he said. He jiggled his lame foot. "I retired at sixty-five and was all set up, but the pension plan went bust. So I missed a month of medical and they cut me off and I ended up uninsured. When the wife took sick, bam, that was it, wiped right out. But I'm not bitter—why should the poor be allowed to live, huh?"

His acolytes, three teenagers in do-rags from the shantytown, laughed and went on to pitching bottle caps off the edge of the roof.

"Stop that, now," he said, "you're getting the junkyard all dirty. Christ, you'd think that they grew up in some kind of zoo." When Francis drank, he got a little mean, a little dark.

"So, kids," Perry said, wandering over to them, hands in pockets. Silhouetted against the setting sun, biceps bulging, muscular chest tapering to his narrow hips, he looked like a Greek statue. "What do you think of the stuff we're building?"

They looked at their toes. " 'S OK," one of them grunted.

"Answer the man," Francis snapped. "Complete sentences, looking up and at him, like you've got a shred of self-respect. Christ, what are you, five years old?"

They shifted uncomfortably. "It's fine," one of them said.

"Would you use it at home?"

One of them snorted. "No, man. My dad steals anything nice we get and sells it."

"Oh," Perry said.

"Fucker broke in the other night and I caught him with my ipod. Nearly took his fucking head off with my cannon before I saw who it was. Fucking juicehead."

"You should have fucked him up," one of the other kids said. "My ma pushed my pops in front of a bus one day to get rid of him, guy broke both his legs and never came back."

Suzanne knew it was meant to shock them, but that didn't take away from its shockingness. In the warm fog of writing and living in Florida, it was easy to forget that these people lived in a squatter camp and were technically criminals, and received no protection from the law.

Perry, though, just squinted into the sun and nodded. "Have you ever tried burglar alarms?"

The kids laughed derisively and Suzanne winced, but Perry was undaunted. "You could be sure that you woke up whenever anyone entered, set up a light and siren to scare them off."

"I want one that fires spears," the one with the juicehead father said.

"Blowtorches," said the one whose mother pushed his father under a bus.

"I want a force field," the third one said, speaking for the first time. "I want something that will keep anyone from coming in, period, so I don't have to sleep one eye up, 'cause I'll be safe."

The other two nodded slowly.

"Damn straight," Francis said.

That was the last time Francis's acolytes joined them on the rooftop. Instead, when they finished work they went home, walking slowly and talking in low murmurs. With just the grown-ups on the roof, it was a lot more subdued.

"What's that smoke?" Lester said, pointing at the black billowing column off to the west, in the sunset's glare.

"House fire," Francis said. "Has to be. Or a big fucking car wreck, maybe."

Perry ran down the stairs and came back up with a pair of high-power binox. "Francis, that's your place," he said after a second's fiddling. He handed the binox to Francis. "Just hit the button and they'll self-stabilize."

"That's my place," Francis said. "Oh, Christ." He'd gone gray and seemed to have sobered up instantly. His lips were wet, his eyes bright.

They drove over at speed, Suzanne wedged into Lester's frankensmartcar, practically under his armpit, and Perry traveling with Francis. Lester still wore the same cologne as her father, and when she opened the window, its smell was replaced by the burning-tires smell of the fire.

They arrived to discover a firetruck parked on the side of the freeway nearest the shantytown. The firefighters were standing soberly beside it, watching the fire rage across the canal.

They rushed for the footbridge and a firefighter blocked their way.

"Sorry, it's not safe," he said. He was Latino, good-looking, like a movie star, bronze skin flickering with copper highlights from the fire.

"I live there," Francis said. "That's my home."

The firefighter looked away. "It's not safe," he said.

"Why aren't you fighting the fire?" Suzanne said.

Francis's head snapped around. "You're not fighting the fire! You're going to let our houses burn!"

A couple more firefighters trickled over. Across the river, the fire had consumed half of the little settlement. Some of the residents were operating a slow and ponderous bucket brigade from the canal, while others ran into the unburned buildings and emerged clutching armloads of belongings, bits of furniture, boxes of photos.

"Sir," the movie star said, "the owner of this property has asked us not to intervene. Since there's no imminent risk to life and no risk of the burn spreading off his property, we can't trespass to put out the fire. Our hands are tied."

"The owner?" Francis spat. "This land is in title dispute. The court case has been under way for twenty years now. What owner?"

The movie star shrugged. "That's all I know, sir."

Across the canal, the fire was spreading, and the bucket brigade was falling back. Suzanne could feel the heat now, like putting your face in the steam from a boiling kettle.

Francis seethed, looking from the firemen and their truck back to the fire. He looked like he was going to pop something, or start shouting, or charge into the flames.

Suzanne grabbed his hand and walked him over to the truck and grabbed the first firefighter she encountered.

"I'm Suzanne Church, from the *San Jose Mercury News,* a McClatchy paper. I'd like to speak to the commanding officer on the scene, please." She hadn't been with the *Merc* for months, but she hadn't been able to bring herself to say, *I'm Suzanne Church with SuzanneChurch.org.* She was pretty sure that no matter how high her readership was and how profitable her ad sales were, the firefighter wouldn't have been galvanized into the action that was invoked when she mentioned the name of a real newspaper.

He hopped to, quickly moving to an older man, tapping him on the shoulder, whispering in his ear. Suzanne squeezed Francis's hand as the fire chief approached them. She extended her hand and talked fast. "Suzanne Church," she said, and took out her notebook, the key prop in any set piece involving a reporter. "I'm told that you are going to let those homes burn because someone representing himself as the titleholder to that property has denied you entry. However, I'm also told that the title to that land is in dispute and has been in the courts for decades. Can you resolve this for me, Chief . . . ?"

"Chief Brian Wannamaker," he said. He was her age, with the leathery skin of a Florida native who spent a lot of time out of doors. "I'm afraid I have no comment for you at this time."

Suzanne kept her face deadpan, and gave Francis's hand a warning squeeze to keep him quiet. He was trembling now. "I see. You can't comment, you can't fight the fire. Is that what you'd like me to write in tomorrow's paper?"

The chief looked at the fire for a moment. Across the canal, the bucket-brigaders were losing worse than ever. He frowned and Suzanne saw that his hands were clenched into fists. "Let me make a call, OK?" Without waiting for an answer, he turned on his heel and stepped behind the fire engine, reaching for his cellphone.

Suzanne strained to hear his conversation, but it was inaudible over the crackle of the fire. When she turned around again, Francis was gone. She caught sight of him again in just a moment, running for the canal, then jumping in and landing badly in the shallow, swampy water. He hobbled across to the opposite bank and began to laboriously climb it.

A second later, Perry followed. Then Lester.

"Chief!" she said, going around the engine and pointing. The chief had the phone clamped to his head still, but when he saw what was going on, he snapped it shut, dropped it in his pocket, and started barking orders.

Now the firefighters *moved,* boiling across the bridge, uncoiling hoses, strapping on tanks and masks. They worked in easy, fluid concert, and it was only seconds before the water and foam hit the flames and the smoke changed to white steam.

The shantytown residents cheered. The fire slowly receded. Perry and Lester had Francis, holding him back from charging into the fray as the fire-fighters executed their clockwork dance.

The steam was hot enough to scald, and Suzanne pulled the collar of her blouse up over her face. Around her were the shantytowners, mothers with small children, old men, and a seemingly endless parade of thug-life teenagers, the boys in miniature cycling shorts and do-rags, the girls in bandeau tops, glitter makeup, and skirts made from overlapping strips of rag, like postapocalyptic hula outfits. Their faces were tight, angry, smudged with smoke and pinkened by the heat.

She saw the one whose father had reportedly been pushed under a bus by his mother, and he grimaced at her. "What we gonna do now?"

"I don't know," she said. "Are you all right? Is your family all right?"

"Don't got nowhere to sleep, nowhere to go," he said. "Don't even have a change of clothes. My moms won't stop crying."

There were tears in his eyes. He was all of fifteen, she realized. He'd seemed much older on the roof. She gathered him into her arms and gave him a hug. He was stiff and awkward at first and then he kind of melted into her, weeping on her shoulder. She stroked his back and murmured reassuringly. Some of the other shantytowners looked at the spectacle, then looked away. Even a couple of his homeboys—whom she'd have bet would have laughed and pointed at this show of weakness—only looked and then passed on. One had tears streaking the smoke smudges on his face.

For someone who isn't good at comforting people, I seem to be doing a lot of it, she thought.

Francis and Lester and Perry found her and Francis gave the boy a gruff hug and told him everything would be fine.

The fire was out now, the firefighters hosing down the last embers, going through the crowd and checking for injuries. A TV news crew had set up and a pretty black reporter in her twenties was doing a stand-up.

"The illegal squatter community has long been identified as a problem area for gang and drug activity by the Broward County sheriff's office. The destruction here seems total, but it's impossible to say whether this spells the end of this encampment, or whether the denizens will rebuild and stay on."

Suzanne burned with shame. That could have been her. When she'd first seen this place, it had been like something out of a documentary on Ethiopia. As she'd come to know it, it had grown homier. The residents built piecemeal, one wall at a time, one window, one poured concrete floor, as they could afford it. None of them had mortgages, but they had neat vegetable gardens and walkways spelled out in white stones with garden gnomes standing guard.

The reporter was staring at her—and naturally so; she'd been staring at the reporter. Glaring at her.

"My RV," Francis said, pointing, distracting her. It was a charred wreck. He went to the melted doors and opened them, stepping back as a puff of smoke rose from the inside. A firefighter spotted it and diverted a stream of water into the interior, soaking Francis and whatever hadn't burned. He turned and shouted something at the firefighter, but he was already hosing down something else.

Inside Francis's trailer, they salvaged a drenched photo album, a few tools, and a lockbox with some of his papers in it. He had backed up his laptop to his watch that morning, so his data was safe. "I kept meaning to scan these in," he said, paging through the photos in the soaked album. "Should have done it."

Night was falling, the mosquitos singing and buzzing. The neat little laneways and homey, patchwork buildings lay in ruins around them.

The shantytowners clustered in little groups or picked through the ruins.

Drivers of passing cars slowed down to rubberneck, and a few shouted filthy, vengeful things at them. Suzanne took pictures of their license plates. She'd publish them when she got home.

A light drizzle fell. Children cried. The swampy sounds of cicadas and frogs and mosquitoes filled the growing dark and then the streetlights flicked on all down the river of highway, painting everything in blue-white mercury glow.

"We've got to get tents up," Francis said. He grabbed a couple of young men and gave them orders, things to look for—fresh water, plastic sheeting, anything with which to erect shelters.

Lester started to help them, and Perry stood with his hands on his hips, next to Suzanne.

"Jesus Christ," he said. "This is a fucking disaster. I mean, these people are used to living rough, but this—" he broke off, waving his hands helplessly. He wiped his palms off on his butt, then grabbed Francis.

"Get them going," he said. "Get them to gather up their stuff and walk them down to our place. We've got space for everyone for now at least."

Francis looked like he was going to say something, then he stopped. He climbed precariously up on the hood of Lester's car and shouted for people to gather round. The boys he bossed around took up the call and it wasn't long before nearly everyone was gathered around them.

"Can everyone hear? This is as loud as I go."

There were murmurs of assent. Suzanne had seen him meet with his people before in the daylight and the good times, seen the respect they afforded to him. He wasn't the leader, per se, but when he spoke, people listened. It was a characteristic she'd encountered in the auto trade and in technology, in the ones the others all gravitated to. Charismatics.

"We've got a place to stay a bit up the road for tonight. It's about a half-hour walk. It's indoors and there's toilets, but maybe not much to make beds out of. Take what you can carry for about a mile, you can come back tomorrow for the rest. You don't have to come, but this isn't going to be any fun tonight."

A woman came forward. She was young, but not young enough to be a homegirl. She had long dark hair and she twisted her hands as she spoke in a soft voice to Francis. "What about our stuff? We can't leave it here tonight. It's all we've got."

Francis nodded. "We need ten people to stand guard in two shifts of five tonight. Young people. You'll get flashlights and phones, coffee and whatever else we can give you. Just keep the rubberneckers out." The rubberneckers were out of earshot. The account they'd get of this would come from the news anchor who'd tell them how dangerous and dirty this place was. They'd never see what Suzanne saw, ten men and women forming up to one side of the crowd. Young braves and homegirls, people her age, their faces solemn.

Francis oversaw the gathering up of belongings. Suzanne had never had a sense of how many people lived in the shantytown but now she could count them as they massed up by the roadside and began to walk: a hundred, a little more than a hundred. More if you counted the surprising number of babies.

Lester conferred briefly with Francis and then Francis tapped three of the old timers and two of the mothers with babes in arms and they crammed into Lester's car and he took off. Suzanne walked by the roadside with the long line of refugees, listening to their murmuring conversation, and in a few minutes, Lester was back to pick up more people, at Francis's discretion.

Perry was beside her now, his eyes a million miles away.

"What now?" she said.

"We put them in the workshop tonight; tomorrow we help them build houses."

"At your place? You're going to let them stay?"

"Why not? We don't use half of that land. The landlord gets his check every month. Hasn't been by in five years. He won't care."

She took a couple more steps. "Perry, I'm going to write about this," she said.

"Oh," he said. They walked further. A small child was crying. "Of course you are. Well, fuck the landlord. I'll sic Kettlewell on him if he squawks."

"What do you think Kettlewell will think about all this?"

"This? Look, this is what I've been saying all along. We need to make products for these people. They're a huge untapped market."

What she wanted to ask was *What would Tjan say about this?* but they didn't talk about Tjan these days. Kettlewell had promised them a new business manager for weeks, but none had appeared. Perry had taken over more and more of the managerial roles, and was getting less and less workshop time in. She could tell it frustrated him. In her discussions with Kettlewell, he'd confided that it had turned out to be harder to find suits than it was finding wildly inventive nerds. Lots of people *wanted* to run businesses, but the number who actually seemed likely to be capable of doing so was only a small fraction.

They could see the junkyard now. Perry pulled out his phone and called his server and touch-toned the codes to turn on all the lights and unlock all the doors.

They lost a couple of kids in the aisles of miraculous junk, and Francis had to send out bigger kids to find them and bring them back, holding the treasures they'd found to their chests. Lester kept going back for more old-timers, more mothers, more stragglers, operating his ferry service until they were all indoors in the workshop.

"This is the place," Francis said. "We'll stay indoors here tonight. Toilets are there and there—orderly lines, no shoving."

"What about food?" asked a man with a small boy sleeping over his shoulder.

"This isn't the Red Cross, Al," Francis snapped. "We'll organize food for ourselves in the morning."

Perry whispered in his ear. Francis shook his head, and Perry whispered some more.

"There will be food in the morning. This is Perry. It's his place. He's going to go to Costco for us when they open."

The crowd cheered and a few of the women hugged him. Some of the men shook his hand. Perry blushed. Suzanne smiled. These people were good people. They'd been through more than Suzanne could imagine. It felt right that she could help them—like making up for every panhandler she'd ignored and every passed-out drunk she'd stepped over.

There were no blankets; there were no beds. The squatters slept on the concrete floor. Young couples spooned under tables. Children snuggled between their parents, or held on to their mothers. As the squatters dossed down and as Suzanne walked past them to get to her car her heart broke a hundred times. She felt like one of those Depression-era photographers walking through an Okie camp, a rending visual at each corner.

Back at her rented condo, she found herself at the foot of her comfortable bed with its thick duvet—she liked keeping the AC turned up enough to snuggle under a blanket—and the four pillows. She was in her jammies, but she couldn't climb in between those sheets.

She couldn't.

And then she was back in her car with all her blankets, sheets, pillows, big towels—even the sofa cushions, which the landlord was not going to be happy about—and speeding back to the workshop.

She let herself in and set about distributing the blankets and pillows and towels, picking out the families, the old people. A woman—apparently able-bodied and young, but skinny—sat up and said, "Hey, where's one for me?" Suzanne recognized the voice. The junkie from the IHOP. Lester's friend. The one who'd grabbed her and cursed her.

She didn't want to give the woman a blanket. She only had two left and there were old people lying on the bare floor.

"Where's one for me?" the woman said more loudly. Some of the sleepers stirred. Some of them sat up.

Suzanne was shaking. Who the hell was she to decide who got a blanket? Did being rude to her at the IHOP disqualify you from getting bedding when your house burned down?

Suzanne gave her a blanket, and she snatched one of the sofa cushions besides.

It's why she's still alive, Suzanne thought. *How she's survived.*

She gave away the last blanket and went home to sleep on her naked bed underneath an old coat, a rolled-up sweater for a pillow. After her shower, she dried herself on T-shirts, having given away all her towels to use as bedding.

The new shantytown went up fast—faster than she'd dreamed possible. The boys helped. Lester downloaded all the information he could find on temporary shelters—building out of mud, out of sandbags, out of corrugated cardboard and sheets of plastic—and they tried them all. Some of the houses had two or more rickety-seeming stories, but they all felt solid enough as she toured them, snapping photos of proud homesteaders standing next to their handiwork.

Little things went missing from the workshops—tools, easily pawned books and keepsakes, Perry's wallet—and they all started locking their desk drawers. There were junkies among the squatters, and desperate people, and immoral people, them too. One day she found that her cute little gold earrings weren't beside her desk lamp, where she'd left them the night before, and she practically burst into tears, feeling set upon on all sides.

She found the earrings later that day, at the bottom of her purse, and that only made things worse. Even though she hadn't voiced a single accusation, she'd accused every one of the squatters in her mind that day. She found herself unable to meet their eyes for the rest of the week.

"I have to write about this," she said to Perry. "This is part of the story." She'd stayed clear of it for a month, but she couldn't go on writing about the successes of the Home Aware without writing about the workforce that was turning out the devices and add-ons by the thousands, all around her, in impromptu factories with impromptu workers.

"Why?" Perry said. He'd been a dervish, filling orders, training people, fighting fires. By nightfall, he was hollow-eyed and snappish. Lester didn't join them on the roof anymore. He liked to hang out with Francis and some of the young men and pitch horseshoes down in the shantytown, or tinker with the composting toilets he'd been installing at strategic crossroads through the town. "Can't you just concentrate on the business?"

"Perry, this *is* the business. Kettlewell hasn't sent a replacement for Tjan and you've filled in and you've turned this place into something like a worker-owned co-op. That's important news—the point of this exercise is to try all the different businesses that are possible and see what works. If you've found something that works, I should write about it. Especially since it's not just solving Kodacell's problem, it's solving the problem for all of those people, too."

Perry drank his beer in sullen silence. "I don't want Kettlewell to get more involved in this. It's going good. Scrutiny could kill it."

"You've got nothing to be embarrassed about here," she said. "There's nothing here that isn't as it should be."

Perry looked at her for a long moment. He was at the end of his fuse, trying to do too much, and she regretted having brought it up. "You do what you have to do," he said.

> The original shantytown was astonishing. Built around a nexus of
> trailers and RVs that didn't look in the least roadworthy, the
> settlers had added dwelling on dwelling to their little patch of
> land. They started with plastic sheeting and poles, and when they
> could afford it, they replaced the sheets, one at a time, with
> bricks or poured concrete and rebar. They thatched their roofs
> with palm leaves, shingles, linoleum, corrugated tin—even
> plywood with flattened beer cans. Some walls were wood. Some had
> windows. Some were made from old car doors, with hand-cranked
> handles to lower them in the day, then roll them up again at
> night when the mosquitoes came out. Most of the settlers slept on
> nets.
>
> A second wave had moved into the settlement just as I arrived,
> and rather than building out—and farther away from their
> neighbors' latrines, water pumps, and mysterious sources of
> electrical power—they built *up*, on top of the existing
> structures, shoring up the walls where necessary. It wasn't
> hurricane-proof, but neither are the cracker-box condos that
> "property owners" occupy. They made contractual arrangements with
> the dwellers of the first stories, paid them rent. A couple with
> second-story rooms opposite one another in one of the narrow
> "streets" consummated their relationship by building a sky bridge
> between their rooms, paying joint rent to two landlords.
>
> The thing these motley houses had in common, all of them, was
> ingenuity and pride of work. They had neat vegetable gardens,
> flower boxes, and fresh paint. They had kids' bikes leaned up
> against their walls, and the smell of good cooking in the air.
> They were homely homes.

>

> Many of the people who lived in these houses worked regular
> service jobs, walking three miles to the nearest city bus stop
> every morning and three miles back every evening. They sent
> their kids to school, faking local addresses with PO boxes. Some
> were retired. Some were just down on their luck.
>
> They helped each other. When something precious was stolen, the
> community pitched in to find the thieves. When one of them
> started a little business selling sodas or sandwiches out of her
> shanty, the others patronized her. When someone needed medical
> care, they chipped in for a taxi to the free clinic, or someone
> with a working car drove them. They were like the neighbors of
> the long-lamented American town, an ideal of civic virtue that is
> so remote in our ancestry as to have become mythical. There were
> eyes on the street here, proud residents who knew what everyone
> was about and saw to it that bad behavior was curbed before it
> could get started.
>
> Somehow, it burned down. The fire department won't investigate,
> because this was an illegal homestead, so they don't much care
> about how the fire started. It took most of the homes, and most
> of their meager possessions. The water got the rest. The fire
> department wouldn't fight the fire at first, because someone at
> city hall said that the land's owner wouldn't let them on the
> property. As it turns out, the owner of that sad strip of land
> between an orange grove and the side of a four-lane highway is
> unknown—a decades-old dispute over title has left it in legal
> limbo that let the squatters settle there. It's suspicious all
> right—various entities had tried to evict the squatters
> before, but the legal hassles left them in happy limbo. What the
> law couldn't accomplish, the fire did.
>
> The story has a happy ending. The boys have moved the squatters
> into their factory, and now they have "live-work" condos that
> look like something Dr. Seuss designed [photo gallery]. Like the
> Central Park shantytown of the last century, these look like they
> were "constructed by crazy poets and distributed by a whirlwind
> that had been drinking," as a press account of the day had it.
>
> Last year, the city completed a new housing project near
> here, and social workers descended on the shantytowners to get
> them to pick up and move to these low-rent high-rises. The
> shantytowners wouldn't go: "It was too expensive," said Mrs X,
> who doesn't want her family back in Oklahoma to know she's
> squatting with her husband and their young daughter. "We can't

> afford *any* rent, not if we want to put food on the table on
> what we earn."
>
> She made the right decision: the housing project is an urban-
> renewal nightmare, filled with crime and junkies, the kind of
> place where little old ladies triple-chain their doors and order
> in groceries that they pay for with direct debit, unwilling to
> keep any cash around.
>
> The squatter village was a shantytown, but it was no slum. It was
> a neighborhood that could be improved. And the boys are doing
> that: having relocated the village to their grounds, they're
> inventing and remixing new techniques for building cheap and
> homey shelter fast. **profile: ten shanties and the technology**
> **inside them**

The response was enormous and passionate. Dozens of readers wrote to tell her that she'd been taken in by these crooks who had stolen the land they squatted. She'd expected that—she'd felt that way herself, when she'd first walked past the shantytown.

But what surprised her more were the message-board posts and emails from homeless people who'd been living in their cars, on the streets, in squatted houses, or in shanties. To read these, you'd think that half her readership was sleeping rough and getting online at libraries, Starbuckses, and stumbled wireless networks that they accessed with antique laptops on street corners.

"Kettlewell's coming down to see this," Perry said.

Her stomach lurched. She'd gotten the boys in trouble. "Is he mad?"

"I couldn't tell—I got voicemail at three AM." Midnight in San Jose, the hour at which Kettlewell got his mad impulses. "He'll be here this afternoon."

"That jet makes it too easy for him to get around," she said, and stretched out her back. Sitting at her desk all morning answering emails and cleaning up some draft posts before blogging them had her in knots. It was practically lunchtime.

"Perry . . ." she began, then trailed off.

"It's all right," he said. "I know why you did it. Christ, we wouldn't be where we are if you hadn't written about us. I'm in no position to tell you to stop now." He swallowed. The month since the shantytowners had moved in had put five years on him. His tan was fading, the wrinkles around his eyes deeper, gray salting his stubbly beard and short hair. "But you'll help me with Kettlewell, right?"

"I'll come along and write down what he says," she said. "That usually helps."

> Kodacell is supposed to be a new way of doing business.
> Decentralized, Net-savvy, really twenty-first century. The
> suck-up tech press and tech-addled bloggers have been trumpeting
> its triumph over all other modes of commerce.
>
> But what does decentralization really mean? On her "blog" this
> week, former journalist Suzanne Church reports that the inmates
> running the flagship Kodacell asylum in suburban Florida have
> invited an entire village of homeless squatters to take up
> residence at their factory premises.
>
> Describing their illegal homesteading as "live-work" condos that
> Dr. Seuss might have designed, Kodacell shill Church goes on to
> describe how this captive, live-in audience has been converted to
> a workforce for Kodacell's most profitable unit ("most
> profitable" is a relative term: to date, this unit has turned a
> profit of about 1.5 million, per the last quarterly report; by
> contrast the old Kodak's most profitable unit made twenty times
> that in its last quarter of operation).
>
> America has a grand tradition of this kind of indentured living:
> the coal barons' company towns of the nineteenth century are the
> original model for this kind of industrial practice in the USA.
> Substandard housing and only one employer in town—that's the
> kind of brave new world that Church's boyfriend Kettlewell has
> created.
>
> A reader writes: "I live near the shantytown that was relocated
> to the Kodacell factory in Florida. It was a dangerous slum full
> of drug dealers. None of the parents in my neighborhood let their
> kids ride their bikes along the road that passed it by—it was
> a haven for all kinds of down-and-out trash."
>
> There you have it, the future of the American workforce:
> down-and-out junkie squatters working for starvation wages.

"Kettlewell, you can't let jerks like Freddy run this company. He's just looking to sell banner space. This is how the Brit rags write—it's all mean-spirited sniping." Suzanne had never seen Kettlewell so frustrated. His surfer good looks were fading fast—he was getting a little paunch on him and his cheeks were sagging off his bones into the beginnings of jowls. His car had pulled up to the end of the driveway and he'd gotten out and walked through the shantytown with the air of a man in a dream. The truckers who pulled in and out all week picking up orders had occasionally had a curious word at the odd little settlement, but for Suzanne it had all but disappeared into her normal experience. Kettlewell made it strange and even a little outrageous, just by his stiff, outraged walk through its streets.

"You think I'm letting *Freddy* drive this decision?" He had spittle flecks on the corners of his mouth. "Christ, Suzanne, you're supposed to be the adult around here."

Perry looked up from the floor in front of him, which he had been staring at intently. Suzanne caught his involuntary glare at Kettlewell before he dropped his eyes again. Lester put a big meaty paw on Perry's shoulder. Kettlewell was oblivious.

"Those people can't stay, all right? The shareholders are baying for blood. The fucking liability—Christ, what if one of those places burns down? What if one of them knifes another one? We're on the hook for everything they do. We could end up being on the hook for a fucking *cholera epidemic.*"

Irrationally, Suzanne burned with anger at Freddy. He had written every venal, bilious word with the hope that it would result in a scene just like this one. And not because he had any substantive objection to what was going on: simply because he had a need to deride that which others hailed. He wasn't afflicting the mighty, though: he was taking on the very meekest, people who had *nothing,* including a means of speaking up for themselves.

Perry looked up. "You've asked me to come up with something new and incredible every three to six months. Well, this is new and incredible. We've built a living lab on our doorstep for exploring an enormous market opportunity to provide low-cost, sustainable technology for use by a substantial segment of the population who have no fixed address. There are millions of American squatters and billions of squatters worldwide. They have money to spend and no one else is trying to get it from them."

Kettlewell thrust his chin forward. "How many millions? How much money do they have to spend? How do you know that any of this will make us a single cent? Where's the market research? Was there any? Or did you just invite a hundred hobos to pitch their tent out front of my factory on the strength of your half-assed guesses?"

Lester held up a hand. "We don't have any market research, Kettlewell, because we don't have a business manager on the team anymore. Perry's been taking that over as well as his regular work, and he's been working himself sick for you. We're flying by the seat of our pants here because you haven't sent us a pilot."

"You need an MBA to tell you not to turn your workplace into a slum?" Kettlewell said. He was boiling. Suzanne very carefully pulled out her pad and wrote this down. It was all she had, but sometimes it was enough.

Kettlewell noticed. "Get out," he said. "I want to talk with these two alone."

"No," Suzanne said. "That's not our deal. I get to document everything. *That's* the deal."

Kettlewell glared at her, and then he deflated. He sagged and took two steps to the chair behind Perry's desk and collapsed into it.

"Put the notebook away, Suzanne, please?"

She silently shook her head at him. He locked eyes with her for a moment, then nodded curtly. She resumed writing.

"Guys, the major shareholders are going to start dumping their stock this week. A couple of pension funds, a merchant bank. It's about ten, fifteen percent of the company. When that happens, our ticker price is going to fall by sixty percent or more."

"They're going to short us because they don't like what we've done here?" Perry said. "Christ, that's ridiculous!"

Kettlewell sighed and put his face in his hands, scrubbed at his eyes. "No, Perry, no. They're doing it because they can't figure out how to value us. Our business units have an industry-high return on investment, but there's not enough of them. We've only signed a thousand teams and we wanted ten thousand, so ninety percent of the money we had to spend is sitting in the bank at garbage interest rates. We need to soak up that money with big projects—the Hoover Dam, Hong Kong Disneyland, the Big Dig. All we've got are little projects."

"So it's not our fault then, is it?" Lester said. Perry was staring out the window.

"No, it's not your fault, but this doesn't help. This is a disaster waiting to turn into a catastrophe."

"Calm down, Landon," Perry said. "Calm down for a sec and listen to me, OK?"

Kettlewell looked at him and sighed. "Go ahead."

"There are more than a billion squatters worldwide. San Francisco has been giving out tents and shopping carts ever since they ran out of shelter beds in the nineties. From Copenhagen to Cape Town, there are more and more people who are going off the grid, often in the middle of cities."

Suzanne nodded. "They farm Detroit, in the ruins of old buildings. Raise crops and sell them. Chickens, too. Even pigs."

"There's something there. These people have money, like I said. They buy and sell in the stream of commerce. They often have to buy at a premium because the services and goods available to them are limited—think of how a homeless person can't take advantage of bulk-packaged perishables because she doesn't have a fridge. They are the spirit of ingenuity, too—they mod their cars, caves, anything they can find to be living quarters. They turn RVs into permanent homes. They know more about tents, sleeping bags, and cardboard than any UN shelter specialist. These people need housing, goods, appliances, you name it. It's what Tjan used to call a greenfield market: no one else knows it's there. You want something you can spend ungodly amounts of money on? This is it. Get every team in the company to come up with products for these people. Soak up every cent they spend. Better us providing them with quality goods at reasonable prices than letting them get ripped off by the profiteers who have a captive market. This plant is a living lab: this is the kind of market intelligence you can't buy, right here. We should set up more of these. Invite squatters all over the country to move onto our grounds, test out our products, help us design, build, and market them. We can recruit traveling salespeople to go door-to-door in the shantytowns and take orders. Shit, man, you talk about the Grameen Bank all the time—why not go into business providing these people with easy microcredit without preying on them the way the banks do? Then we could loan them money to buy things that we sell them that they use to better their lives and earn more money so they can pay us back and buy more things and borrow more money—"

Kettlewell held up a hand. "I like the theory. It's a nice story. But I have to sell this to my board, and they want more than stories: where can I get the research to back this up?"

"We're it," Perry said. "This place, right here. There's no numbers to prove what I'm saying is right because everyone who knows it's right is too busy chasing after it and no one else believes it. But right here, if we're allowed to do this—right here we can prove it. We've got the capital in our account, we're profitable, and we can roll those profits back into more R&D for the future of the company."

Suzanne was writing so fast she was getting a hand cramp. Perry had never given speeches like this, even a month before. Tjan's leaving had hurt them all, but the growth it had precipitated in Perry was stunning.

Kettlewell argued more, but Perry was a steamroller and Suzanne was writing down what everyone said and that kept it all civil, like a silent camera rolling in the corner of the room. No one looked at her, but she was the thing they were conspicuously not looking at.

Francis took the news calmly. "Sound business strategy. Basically, it's what I've been telling you to do all along, so I'm bound to like it."

It took a couple weeks to hive off the Home Aware stuff to some of the other Kodacell business units. Perry flew a bunch, spending days in Minnesota, Oregon, Ohio, and Michigan overseeing the retooling efforts that would let him focus on his new project.

By the time he got back, Lester had retooled their workspace, converting it to four functional areas: communications, shelter, food, and entertainment. "They were Francis's idea," he said. Francis's gimpy leg was bothering him more and more, but he'd overseen the work from a rolling ergonomic office chair. "It's his version of the hierarchy of needs—stuff he knows for sure we can sell."

It was the first time the boys had launched something new without knowing what it was, where they'd started with a niche and decided to fill it instead of starting with an idea and looking for a niche for it.

"You're going to underestimate the research time," Francis said during one of their flip-chart brainstorms, where they had been covering sheet after sheet with ideas for products they could build. "Everyone underestimates research time. Deciding what to make is always harder than making it." He'd been drinking less since he'd gotten involved in the retooling effort, waking earlier, bossing around his young-blood posse to get him paper, bricks, Tinkertoys.

He was right. Suzanne steadily recorded the weeks ticking by as the four competing labs focus-grouped, designed, tested, and scrapped all manner of "tchotchkes for tramps," as Freddy had dubbed it in a spiraling series of ever more bilious columns. But the press was mostly positive: camera crews liked to come by and shoot the compound. One time, the pretty black reporter from the night of the fire came by and said very nice things during her stand-up. Her name was Maria and she was happy to talk shop with Suzanne, endlessly fascinated by a "real" journalist who'd gone permanently slumming on the Internet.

"The problem is that all this stuff is too specialized, it has too many prerequisites," Perry said, staring at a waterproof, cement-impregnated bag that could be filled with a hose, allowed to dry, and used as a self-contained room. "This thing is great for refugees, but it's too one-size-fits-all for squatters. They have to be able to heavily customize everything they use to fit into really specialized niches."

More squatters had arrived to take up residence with them—families, friends, a couple of dodgy drifters—and a third story was going onto the buildings in the camp. They were even more Dr. Seussian than the first round, idiosyncratic structures that had to be built light to avoid crushing the floors below them, hanging out over the narrow streets, corkscrewing like vines seeking sun.

He kept staring, and would have been staring still had he not heard the sirens. Three blue-and-white Broward County sheriff's cars were racing down the access road into their dead mall, sirens howling, lights blazing.

They screeched to a halt at the shantytown's edge and their doors flew open. Four cops moved quickly into the shantytown, while two more worked the radios, sheltering by the cars.

"Jesus Christ," Perry said. He ran for the door, but Suzanne grabbed him.

"Don't run toward armed cops," she said. "Don't do anything that looks threatening. Slow down, Perry."

He took a couple deep breaths. Then he looked around his lab for a while, frantically muttering, "Where the fuck did I put it?"

"Use Home Aware," she said. He shook his head, grimaced, went to a keyboard and typed MEGAPHONE. One of the lab drawers started to throb with a white glow.

He pulled out the megaphone and went to his window.

"ATTENTION, POLICE," he said. "THIS IS THE LEASEHOLDER FOR THIS PROPERTY. WHY ARE YOU RUNNING AROUND WITH YOUR GUNS DRAWN? WHAT IS GOING ON?"

The police at the cars looked toward the workshop, then back to the shantytown, then back to the workshop.

"SERIOUSLY. THIS IS NOT COOL. WHAT ARE YOU DOING HERE?"

One of the cops grabbed the mic for his own loud-hailer. "THIS IS THE BROWARD COUNTY SHERIFF'S DEPARTMENT. WE HAVE RECEIVED INTELLIGENCE THAT AN ARMED FUGITIVE IS ON THESE PREMISES. WE HAVE COME TO RETRIEVE HIM."

"WELL, THAT'S WEIRD. NONE OF THE CHILDREN, CIVILIANS, AND HARDWORKING PEOPLE HERE ARE FUGITIVES AS FAR AS I KNOW. CERTAINLY THERE'S NO ONE ARMED AROUND HERE. WHY DON'T YOU GET BACK IN YOUR CARS AND I'LL COME OUT AND WE'LL RESOLVE THIS LIKE CIVILIZED PEOPLE, OK?"

The cop shook his head and reached for his mic again, and then there were two gunshots, a scream, and a third.

Perry ran for the door and Suzanne chased after him, trying to stop him. The cops at the cars were talking intently into their radios, though it was impossible to know if they were talking to their comrades in the shantytown or to their headquarters. Perry burst out of the factory door and there was another shot and he spun around, staggered back a step, and fell down like a sack of grain. There was blood around his head. Suzanne stuck her hand in her mouth to stifle a scream and stood helplessly in the doorway of the workshop, just a few paces from Perry.

Lester came up behind her and firmly moved her aside. He lumbered deliberately and slowly and fearlessly to Perry's side, knelt beside him, touched
him gently. His face was gray. Perry thrashed softly and Suzanne let out a
sound like a cry, then remembered herself and took out her camera and began to shoot and shoot and shoot: the cops, Lester with Perry like a tragic
Pietà, the shantytowners running back and forth screaming. Snap of the cops
getting out of their cars, guns in hands, snap of them fanning out around the
shantytown, snap of them coming closer and closer, snap of a cop pointing
his gun at Lester, ordering him away from Perry, snap of a cop approaching
her.

"It's live," she said, not looking up from the viewfinder. "Going out live to
my blog. Daily readership half a million. They're watching you now, every
move. Do you understand?"

The officer said, "Put the camera down, ma'am."

She held the camera. "I can't quote the First Amendment from memory,
not exactly, but I know it well enough that I'm not moving this camera. It's
live, you understand—every move is going out live, right now."

The officer stepped back, turned his head, muttered in his mic.

"There's an ambulance coming," he said. "Your friend was shot with a
nonlethal rubber bullet."

"He's bleeding from the head," Lester said. "From the eye."

Suzanne shuddered.

Ambulance sirens in the distance. Lester stroked Perry's hair. Suzanne
took a step back and panned it over Perry's ruined face, bloody and swollen.
The rubber bullet must have taken him either right in the eye or just over it.

"Perry Mason Gibbons was unarmed and posed no threat to sheriff's
deputy badge number 5724"—she zoomed in on it—"when he was shot with
a rubber bullet in the eye. He is unconscious and bloody on the ground in
front of the workshop where he has worked quietly and unassumingly to invent and manufacture new technologies."

The cop knew when to cut his losses. He turned aside and walked back
into the shantytown, leaving Suzanne to turn her camera on Perry, on the
EMTs who evacced him to the ambulance, on the three injured shantytowners who were in the ambulance with him, on the corpse they wheeled out on
his own gurney, one of the newcomers to the shantytown, a man she didn't
recognize.

They operated on Perry all that night, gingerly tweezing fragments of
bone from his shattered left orbit out of his eye and face. Some had floated to
the back of the socket and posed a special risk of brain damage, the doctor explained into her camera.

Lester was a rock, sitting silently in the waiting room, talking calmly and firmly with the cops and over the phone to Kettlewell and the specially impaneled boardroom full of Kodacell lawyers who wanted to micromanage this. Rat-Toothed Freddy filed a column in which he called her a "grandstanding bint," and accused Kodacell of harboring dangerous fugitives. He'd dug up the fact that one of the newcomers to the shantytown—not the one they'd killed, that was a bystander—was wanted for holding up a liquor store with a corkscrew the year before.

Lester unscrewed his earphone and scrubbed at his eyes. Impulsively, she leaned over and gave him a hug. He stiffened up at first but then relaxed and enfolded her in his huge, warm arms. She could barely make her arms meet around his broad, soft back—it was like hugging a giant loaf of bread. She squeezed tighter and he did, too. He was a good hugger.

"You holding in there, kiddo?" she said.

"Yeah," he murmured into her neck. "No." He squeezed tighter. "As well as I need to, anyway."

The doctor pried them apart to tell them that the EEG and fMRI were both negative for any brain damage, and that they'd managed to salvage the eye, probably. Kodacell was springing for all the care he needed, cash money, no dorking around with the fucking HMO, so the doctors had put him through every machine on the premises in a series of farcically expensive tests.

"I hope they sue the cops for the costs," the doctor said. She was Pakistani or Bangladeshi, with a faint accent, and very pretty even with the dark circles under her eyes. "I read your columns," she said, shaking Suzanne's hand. "I admire the work you do," she said, shaking Lester's hand. "I was born in Delhi. We were squatters who were given a deed to our home and then evicted because we couldn't pay the taxes. We had to build again, in the rains, outside of the city, and then again when we were evicted again."

She had two brothers who were working for startups like Kodacell's, but run by other firms: one was backed by McDonald's, the other by the AFL-CIO's investment arm. Suzanne did a little interview with her about her brothers' projects—a bike helmet that had been algorithmically evolved for minimum weight and maximum protection; a smart skylight that deformed itself to follow light based on simple phototropic controllers. The brother working on bike helmets was riding a tiger and could barely keep up with orders; he was consuming about half of the operational capacity of the McDonald's network and climbing fast.

Lester joined in, digging on the details. He'd been following the skylights in blogs and on a list or two, and he'd heard of the doctor's brother, which really tweaked her, she was visibly proud of her family.

"But your work is most important. Things for the homeless. We get them in here sometimes, hurt, off the ambulances. We usually turn them away again. The ones who sell off the highway medians and at the traffic lights." Suzanne had seen them, selling homemade cookies, oranges, flowers, newspapers, plasticky toys, sad or beautiful handicrafts. She had a carved coconut covered in intricate scrimshaw that she'd bought from a little girl who was all skin and bones except for her malnourished pot belly.

"They get hit by cars?"

"Yes," the doctor said. "Deliberately, too. Or beaten up."

Perry was moved out of the operating theater to a recovery room and then to a private room and by then they were ready to collapse, though there was so much email in response to her posts that she ended up pounding on her computer's keyboard all the way home as Lester drove them, squeezing the bridge of his nose to stay awake. She didn't even take her clothes off before collapsing into bed.

"They need the tools to make any other tools," is what Perry said when he returned from the hospital, the side of his head still swaddled in bandages that draped over his injured eye. They'd shaved his head at his insistence, saying that he wasn't going to try to keep his hair clean with all the bandages. It made him look younger, and his fine skull bones stood out through his thin scalp when he finally came home. Before, he'd looked like a outdoorsman engineer. Now he looked like a radical, a pirate.

"They need the tools that will let them build anything else, for free, and use it or sell it." He gestured at the rapid prototyping machines they had, the 3-D printer and scanner setups. "I mean something like that, but I want it to be capable of printing out the parts necessary to assemble another one. Machines that can reproduce themselves."

Francis shifted in his seat. "What are they supposed to do with those?"

"Everything," Perry said, his eye glinting. "Make your kitchen fixtures. Make your shoes and hat. Make your kids' toys—if it's in the stores, it should be a downloadable, too. Make tool chests and tools. Make it and build it and sell it. Make other printers and sell them. Make machines that make the goop we feed into the printers. Teach a man to fish, Francis, teach a man to fucking *fish*. No top-down 'solutions' driven by 'market research'"—his finger-quotes oozed sarcasm—"the thing that we need to do is make these people the authors of their own destiny."

They put up the sign that night: AUTHOR OF YOUR OWN DESTINY, hung over the workshop door. Suzanne trailed after Perry transcribing the rants that spilled out of his mouth as he explained it to Lester and Francis, and then to

Kettlewell when he called, and then to the pretty young black lady from the TV who by now had figured out that there was a real story in her backyard, then to an NPR man on the phone, and then to a CNN crew who drove in from Miami and filmed the shantytown and the workshop like Japanese tourists at Disney World, never having ventured into the skanky, failed-strip-mall suburbs just outside of town.

Francis had a protégé who had a real dab touch with the 3-D printers. The manufacturer, Lester's former employer, had been out of business for two years by then, so all the service on the machines had to be done on the premises. Francis's protégé—the one who claimed his mother had pushed his father under a bus, his name was Jason—watched Lester work on recalcitrant machines silently for a couple days, then started to hand him the tool he needed next without having to be asked. Then he diagnosed a problem that had stumped Lester all morning. Then he suggested an improvement to the feedstock pump that increased the mean time between failures by a couple hours.

"No, man, no, not like that," Jason said to one of the small gang of boys he was bossing. "Gently, or you'll snap it off." The boy snapped it off and Jason pulled another replacement part out of a tub and said, "See, like *this*," and snapped it on. The small gang of boys regarded him with something like awe.

"How come no girls?" Suzanne said as she interviewed him while he took a smoke break. Perry had banned cigarettes from all indoor workshops, nominally to keep flames away from the various industrial chemicals and such, but really just to encourage the shantytowners to give up the habit that they couldn't afford anyway. He'd also leaned on the shantytowners who'd opened up small shops in their houses to keep cigs out of the town, without a lot of success.

"Girls aren't interested in this stuff, lady."

"You think?" There was a time when she would have objected, but it was better to let these guys say it out loud, hear themselves say it.

"No. Maybe where you come from, OK? Don't know. But here girls are different. They do good in school but when they have babies they're done. I mean, hey, it's not like I don't *want* girls on the team, they'd be great. I love girls. They fuckin' *work*, you know. No bullshit, no screwing around. But I know every girl in this place and none of 'em are even interested, OK?"

Suzanne cocked one eyebrow just a little and Jason shifted uncomfortably. He scratched his bare midriff and shuffled. "I do, all of them. Why would they? One girl, a roomful of boys, it'd be gross. They'd act like jerks. There's no way we'd get anything done."

Suzanne lifted her eyebrow one hair higher. He squirmed harder.

"So all right, that's not their fault. But I got enough work, all right? Too much to do without spending time on that. It's not like any girls have *asked* to join up. I'm not keeping them out."

Suzanne jotted a couple of notes, keeping perfectly mum.

"Well, I'd like to have them in the workshop, OK? Maybe I should ask some of them if they'd come. Shit, if I can teach these apes, I can teach a girl. They're smart. Girls'd made this place a little better to work in. Lots of them trying to support their families, so they need the money, too."

There was a girl there by the afternoon. The next day, there were two more. They seemed like quick studies, despite their youth and their lip gloss. Suzanne approved.

Lester stayed long enough to see the first prototype printer-printers running, then he lit out with a duffel bag jammed into the back of his modded Smart car. "Where are you going?" Suzanne said as Perry looked on gloomily. "I'll come and visit you. I want to follow your story." Truth be told, she was sorry to see him go, very sorry. He was such a rock, such an anchor for Perry's new crazy pirate energy and for the madness around them. He hadn't given much notice (not to her—Perry didn't seem that surprised).

"I can't really talk about it," he said. "Nondisclosure."

"So it's a new job," she said. "You're going to work for Tjan?" Tjan's Westinghouse operation was fully rocking. He had fifty teams up the eastern seaboard, ten in the Midwest, and was rumored to have twice as many in Eastern Europe.

He grinned. "Oh, Suzanne, don't try to journalist me." He reached out and hugged her in a cloud of her father's cologne. "You're fantastic, you know that? No, I'm not going to a job. It's a thing that's an amazing opportunity, you know?"

She didn't, but then he was gone and boy did she miss him.

Perry and she went out for dinner in Miami the next night with a PhD candidate from Pepperdine's B-school, eating at the same deco patio that she'd dined at with Tjan. Perry wore a white shirt open to reveal his tangle of wiry chest hair and the waitress couldn't keep her eyes off of him. He had a permanent squint now, and a scar that made his eyebrow into a series of small hills.

"I was just in Greensboro, Miss," the PhD candidate said. He was in his mid-twenties, young and slick, his only nod to academe a small goatee. "I used to spend summers there with my grandpa." He talked fast, flecks of spittle in the corners of his mouth, eyes wide, fork stabbing blindly at the bits of crab cake on his plate. "There wasn't *anything* left there, just a couple gas stations and a 7-Eleven, shit, they'd even closed the Wal-Mart. But now, but

now, it's *alive* again, it's buzzing and hopping. Every empty storefront is full of people playing and tinkering, just a little bit of money in their pockets from a bank or a company or a fund. They're doing the dumbest things, mind you: tooled-leather laptop cases, switchblade knives with thumb drives in the handles, singing and dancing lawn Santas that yodel like hillbillies."

"I'd buy a tooled-leather laptop case," Perry said, swilling a sweaty bottle of beer. He waggled his funny eyebrow and rubbed his fuzzy scalp.

"The rate of employment is something like ninety-five percent, which it hasn't been in like a hundred years. If you're not inventing stuff, you're keeping the books for someone who is, or making sandwiches for them, or driving delivery vehicles around. It's like a tiny, distributed gold rush."

"Or like the New Deal," Suzanne said. That was how she'd come to invite him down, after she'd read his paper coining the term New Work to describe what Perry was up to, comparing it to Roosevelt's public-investment plan that spent America free of the Depression.

"Yeah, exactly, exactly! I've got research that shows that one in five Americans is employed in the New Work industry. Twenty percent!"

Perry's lazy eye opened a little wider. "No way," he said.

"Way," the PhD candidate said. He finished his caipirinha and shook the crushed ice at a passing waiter, who nodded and ambled to the bar to get him a fresh one. "You should get on the road and write about some of these guys," he said to Suzanne. "They need some ink, some phosphors. They're pulling up stakes and moving to the small towns their parents came from, or to abandoned suburbs, and just *doing it*. Bravest fucking thing you've seen in your life."

The PhD candidate stayed out the week, and went home with a suitcase full of the parts necessary to build a 3-D printer that could print out all of the parts necessary to build a 3-D printer.

Lester emailed her from wherever it was he'd gone, and told her about the lovely time he was having. It made her miss him sharply. Perry was hardly ever around for her now, buried in his work, buried with the kids from the shantytown and with Francis. She looked over her last month's blogs and realized that she'd been turning in variations on the same theme for all that time. She knew it was time to pack a duffel bag of her own and go see the bravest fucking thing she'd seen in her life.

"Bye, Perry," she said, stopping by his workbench. He looked up at her and saw the bag and his funny eyebrow wobbled.

"Leaving for good?" he said. He sounded unexpectedly bitter.

"No!" she said. "No! Just a couple weeks. Going to get the rest of the story. But I'll be back, count on it."

He grunted and slumped. He was looking a lot older now, and beaten down. His hair, growing out, was half gray, and he'd gotten gaunt, his cheek-bones and forehead springing out of his face. On impulse, she gave him a hug like the ones she'd shared with Lester. He returned it woodenly at first, then with genuine warmth. "I will be back, you know," she said. "You've got plenty to do here, anyway."

"Yeah," he said. "Course I do."

She kissed him firmly on the cheek and stepped out the door and into her car and drove to Miami International.

Tjan met her at Logan and took her bag. "I'm surprised you had the time to meet me," she said. The months had been good to him, slimming down his potbelly and putting a twinkle in his eye.

"I've got a good organization," he said as they motored away toward Rhode Island, through strip-mall suburbs and past boarded-up chain restaurants. Everywhere there were signs of industry: workshops in old storefronts, roadside stands selling disposable music players, digital whoopee cushions, and so forth. "I barely have to put in an appearance."

Tjan yawned hugely and constantly. "Jet lag," he apologized. "Got back from Russia a couple days ago."

"Did you see your kids?" she said. "How's business there?"

"I saw my kids," he said, and grinned. "They're amazing, you know that? Good kids, unbelievably smart. Real little operators. The older one, Lyenitchka, is running a babysitting service—not babysitting herself, you see, but recruiting other kids to do the sitting for her while she skims a management fee and runs the quality control."

"She's your daughter all right," she said. "So tell me everything about the Westinghouse projects."

She'd been following them, of course, lots of different little startups, each with its own blogs and such. But Tjan was quite fearless about taking her through their profits and losses, and taking notes on it all kept her busy until she reached her hotel. Tjan dropped her off and promised to pick her up the next morning for a VIP tour of the best of his teams, and she went to check in.

She was in the middle of receiving her key when someone grabbed her shoulder and squeezed it. "Suzanne bloody Church! What are you doing here, love?"

The smell of his breath was like a dead thing left to fester. She turned around slowly, not wanting to believe that of all the hotels in rural Rhode Island, she ended up checking in to the same one as Rat-Toothed Freddy.

"Hey, Freddy," she said. Seeing him gave her an atavistic urge to stab him

repeatedly in the throat with the hotel stick pen. He was unshaven, his gawky Adam's apple bobbing up and down, and he swallowed and smiled wetly. "Nice to see you."

"Fantastic to see you, too! I'm here covering a shareholder meeting for Westinghouse. Is that what you're here for, too?"

"No," she said. She knew the meeting was on that week but hadn't planned on attending it. She was done with press conferences, preferring on-the-ground reporting. "Well, nice to see you."

"Oh, do stay for a drink," he said, grinning more widely, exposing those gray teeth in a shark's smile. "Come on—they have a free cocktail hour in this place. I'll have to report you to the journalist's union if you turn down a free drink."

"I don't think 'bloggers' have to worry about the journalist's union," she said, making sarcastic finger-quotes in case he didn't get the message. He still didn't. He laughed instead.

"Oh, love, I'm sure they'll still have you even if you have lapsed away from the one true faith."

"Good night, Freddy," was all she could manage to get out without actually hissing through her teeth.

"OK, good night," he said, moving in to give her a hug. As he loomed toward her, she snapped.

"Freeze, mister. You are not my friend. I do not want to touch you. You have poor personal hygiene and your breath smells like an overflowing camp toilet. You write vicious personal attacks on me and on the people I care about. You are unfair, mean-spirited, and you write badly. The only day I wouldn't piss on you, Freddy, is the day you were on fire. Now get the fuck out of my way before I kick your tiny little testicles up through the roof of your reeking mouth."

She said it quietly, but the desk clerks behind her overheard it anyway and giggled. Freddy's smile only wobbled, but then returned, broader than ever.

"Well said," he said, and gave her a single golf clap. "Sleep well, Suzanne."

She boiled all the way to her room and when she came over hungry, she ordered in room service, not wanting to take the chance that Rat-Toothed Freddy would still be in the lobby.

Tjan met her as she was finishing her coffee in the breakfast room. She hadn't seen Freddy yet.

"I've got five projects slated for you to visit today," Tjan said, sliding into the booth beside her. Funnily, now that he was in the cold Northeast, he was

dressing like a Floridian in blue jeans and a Hawaiian bark-cloth shirt with a bright spatter of pineapples and Oscar Mayer Wienermobiles. Back in Florida, he'd favored unflattering nylon slacks and white shirts with ironed collars.

The projects were fascinating and familiar. The cultural differences that distinguished New England New Work from Florida New Work were small but telling: a lot more woodcraft, in a part of the country where many people had grown up in their grandfathers' woodworking shops. A little more unreflexive kitsch, like the homely kittens and puppies that marched around the reactive, waterproof, smash-proof screens integrated into a bio-monitoring crib.

At the fourth site, she was ambushed by a flying hug. Tjan laughed as she nearly went down under the weight of a strong, young woman who flung her arms around Suzanne's neck. "Holy *crap* it's good to see you!"

Suzanne untangled herself and got a look at her hugger. She had short mousy hair, twinkling blue eyes, and was dressed in overalls and a pretty flowered blouse, scuffed work boots, and stained and torn work gloves. "Uh . . ." she said, then it clicked. "Fiona?"

"Yeah! Didn't Tjan tell you I was here?" The last time she'd seen this woman, she was weeping over pizza and getting ready to give up on life. Now she was practically vibrating.

"Uh, no," she said, shooting a look at Tjan, who was smiling like the Buddha and pretending to inspect a pair of shoes with gyroscopically stabilized retractable wheels in the heels.

"I've been here for months! I went back to Oregon, like you told me to, and then I saw a recruiting ad for Westinghouse and I sent them my CV and then I got a videoconference interview and then, bam, I was on an airplane to Rhode Island!"

Suzanne blinked. *I told you to go back to Oregon?* Well, maybe she had. That was a lifetime ago.

The workshop was another dead mall, this one a horseshoe of storefronts separated by flimsy gyprock. The Westinghousers had cut through the walls with drywall knives to join all the stores together. The air was permeated with the familiar Saran-Wrap-in-a-microwave tang of 3-D printers. The parking lot was given over to some larger apparatus and a fantastical children's jungle gym in the shape of a baroque, spired pirate fortress, with elegantly curved turrets, corkscrew sky bridges, and flying buttresses crusted over with ornate, grotesque gargoyles. Children swarmed over it like ants, screeching with pleasure.

"Well, you're looking really good, Fiona," Suzanne said. *Still not great with people,* she thought. Fiona, though, was indeed looking good, and beaming.

She wasn't wearing the crust of cosmetics and hair-care products she'd affected in the corporate Silicon Valley world. She glowed pink.

"Suzanne," Fiona said, getting serious now, taking her by the shoulders and looking into her eyes. "I can't thank you enough for this. This has saved my life. It gave me something to live for. For the first time in my life, I am doing something I'm proud of. I go to bed every night thankful and happy that I ended up here. Thank you, Suzanne. Thank you."

Suzanne tried not to squirm. Fiona gave her another long hug. "It's all your doing," Suzanne said at last. "I just told you about it. You've made this happen for you, OK?"

"OK," Fiona said, "but I still wouldn't be here if it wasn't for you. I love you, Suzanne."

Ick. Suzanne gave her another perfunctory hug and got the hell out of Dodge.

"What's with the jungle gym?" It really had been something, fun and Martian-looking.

"That's the big one," Tjan said with a big grin. "Most people don't even notice it, they think it's day care or something. Well, that's how it started out, but then some of the sensor people started noodling with jungle-gym components that could tell how often they were played with. They started modding the gym every night, adding variations on the elements that saw the most action, removing the duds. Then the CAD people added an algorithm that would take the sensor data and generate random variations on the same basis. Finally, some of the robotics people got in on the act so that the best of the computer-evolved designs could be instantiated automatically: now it's a self-modifying jungle gym. The kids love it. It is the crack cocaine of jungle gyms, though we won't be using that in the marketing copy, of course."

"Of course," Suzanne said dryly. She'd automatically reached for her notepad and started writing when Tjan started talking. Now, reviewing her notes, she knew that she was going to have to go back and get some photos of this. She asked Tjan about it.

"The robots go all night, you know. Not much sleep if you do that."

No going back to the hotel to see Freddy, what a pity. "I'll grab a couple blankets from the hotel to keep warm," she said.

"Oh, you needn't," he said. "That crew has a set of bleachers with gas heaters for the night crew and their family to watch from. It's pretty gorgeous, if you ask me."

They had a hasty supper of burgers at a drive-through and then went back to the jungle-gym project. Suzanne ensconced herself at someone's vacated desk for a couple hours and caught up on email before finally emerging as the sun was dipping swollen and red behind the mall. She set herself up on the bleachers, and Fiona found her with a thermos of coffee and a flask of whisky. They snuggled under a blanket amid a small crowd of geeks, an outdoor slumber party under the gas heaters' roar.

Gradually, the robots made an appearance. Most of them humped along like inchworms, carrying chunks of new playground apparatus in coils of their long bodies. Some deployed manipulator arms, though they didn't have much by way of hands at their ends. "We just use rare-earth magnets," Fiona said. "Less fiddly than trying to get artificial vision that can accurately grasp the bars."

Tjan nudged her and pointed to a new tower that was going up. The robots were twisting around themselves to form a scaffold, while various of their number crawled higher and higher, snapping modular pieces of high-impact plastic together with *snick* sounds that were audible over the whine of their motors.

Suzanne switched on her camera's night-vision mode and got shooting. "Where did you get all these robots?"

Tjan grinned. "It's an open design—the EPA hired Westinghouse to build these to work on sensing and removing volatile organic compounds on Superfund sites. Because we did the work for the government, we had to agree not to claim any design copyright or patents in the outcome. There's a freaking warehouse full of this stuff at Westinghouse, all kinds of crazy things that Westinghouse abandoned because they weren't proprietary enough and they were worried that they'd have to compete on the open market if they tried to productize them. Suits us just fine, though."

The field was aswarm with glinting metal inchworm robots now, shifting back and forth, boiling and roiling and picking up enormous chunks of climber like cartoon ants carrying away a picnic basket. The playground was being transformed before her eyes, in ways gross and subtle, and it was enchanting to watch.

"Can I go out and have a look?" she said. "I mean, is it safe?"

"Sure," Fiona said. "Of course! Our robots won't harm you; they just nuzzle you and then change direction."

"Still, try to stay out of their way," Tjan said. "Some of that stuff they're moving around is heavy."

So she waded out onto the playground and carefully picked her way through the robot swarm. Some crawled over her toes. A couple twined between her feet and nearly tripped her up, and once she stepped on one and it went still and waited politely for her to step off.

Once in the thick of it all, she switched on her video and began to record through the night filter. Standing there amid the whirl and racket and undulating motion of the jungle gym as it reconfigured itself, she felt like she'd arrived at some posthuman future where the world no longer needed her or her kind. Like humanity's creations had evolved past their inventors.

She was going to have to do a *lot* of writing before bed.

Freddy was checking out in the lobby when Tjan dropped her off at 5 AM. It was impossible to sneak past him, and he gave her a nasty, bucktoothed smile as she passed by him. It distracted her and made the writing come more slowly, but she was a pro and her readers had sent in a lot of kind mail, and there was one from Lester, still away on his mysterious errand but sounding happier than he had in months, positively giddy.

She set the alarm clock so that she could be awake for her next stop, outside of North Carolina's Research Triangle, where some local millionaires had backed a dozen New Work teams.

Another three weeks of this stuff and she'd get to go home—Florida. The condo was home now, and the junkyard. Hot and sticky and inventive and ever-changing. She fell asleep thinking of it and smiling.

It was two weeks more before Lester caught up with her, in Detroit of all places. Going back to the old place hadn't been her idea, she'd been dragged back by impassioned pleas from the local Ford and GM New Work teams, who were second-generation-unemployed, old rust belt families who'd rebooted with money from the companies that had wrung their profit from their ancestors and abandoned them.

The big focus in the rust belt was eradicating the car. Some were building robots that could decommission leaky gas stations and crater out the toxic soil. Some were building car-disassembly plants that reclaimed materials from the old beasts' interiors. Between the Ford and GM teams, with their latest bailout, and those funded by the UAW out of the settlements they'd won from the automakers, Detroit was springing up anew.

Lester emailed her and said that he'd seen on her blog that she was headed to Detroit, and did she want to meet him for dinner, being as he'd be in town, too?

They ate at Devil's Night, a restaurant in one of the reclaimed mansions in Brush Park, a neighborhood of wood-frame buildings that teenagers had all but burned to the ground over several decades' worth of Halloweens. In Detroit, Devil's Night was the pre-Halloween tradition of torching abandoned buildings, and all of Brush Park had been abandoned for years, its handsome houses attractive targets for midnight firebugs.

Reclaiming these buildings was an artisanal practice of urethaning the charred wood and adding clever putty, cement, and glass to preserve the look of a burned-out hulk while restoring structural integrity. One entire floor of the restaurant was missing, having been replaced by polished tempered one-way glass that let upstairs diners look down on the bald spots and cleavage of those eating below.

Suzanne showed up a few minutes late, having gotten lost wandering the streets of a Detroit that had rewritten its map in the decades since she'd left. She was flustered, and not just because she was running late. There was a lingering awkwardness between her and Lester and her elation at seeing him again had an inescapable undercurrent of dread.

When the waiter pointed out her table, she told him he was mistaken. Lester wasn't there, some stranger was: short-haired, burly, with a few days' stubble. He wore a smart blazer and a loose striped cotton shirt underneath. He was beaming at her.

"Suzanne," he said.

Her jaw literally dropped. She realized she was standing with her mouth open and shut it with a snap. "Lester?" she said, wonderingly.

He got up, still smiling, even laughing a little, and gave her a hug. It was Lester all right. That smell was unmistakable, and those big, warm paws he called hands.

When he let go of her, he laughed again. "Oh, Suzanne, I could *not* have asked for any better reaction than this. *Thank you.*" They were drawing stares. Dazedly, she sat down. So did he.

"Lester?" she said again.

"Yes, it's me," he said. "I'll tell you about it over dinner. The waiter wants to take our drink orders."

Theatrically, she ordered a double Scotch. The waiter rattled off the specials and Suzanne picked one at random. So did Lester.

"So," he said, patting his washboard tummy. "You want to know how I got to this in ten weeks, huh?"

"Can I take notes?" Suzanne said, pulling out her pad.

"Oh by all means," he said. "I got a discount on my treatment on the basis that you would end up taking notes."

The clinic was in St. Petersburg, Russia, in a neighborhood filled with Russian dentists who catered to American health tourists who didn't want to pay U.S. prices for crowns. The treatment hadn't originated there: The electro-muscular stimulation and chemical therapy for skin tightening was standard for rich new mothers in Hollywood who wanted to get rid of pregnancy bellies.

The appetite-suppressing hormones had been used in the Mexican pharma industry for years. Stem cells had been an effective substitute for steroids when it came to building muscle in professional athletic circles the world round. Genomic therapy using genes cribbed from hummingbirds boosted metabolism so that the body burned ten thousand calories a day sitting still.

But the St. Petersburg clinic had ripped, mixed, and burned these different procedures to make a single holistic treatment that had dropped Lester from 400 to 175 pounds in ten weeks.

"Is that safe?" she said.

"Everyone asks that," he said, laughing. "Yeah, it's safe if they're monitoring you and standing by with lots of diagnostic equipment. But if you're willing to take slower losses, you can go on a way less intensive regime that won't require supervision. This stuff is the next big gray-market pharma gold. They're violating all kinds of pharma patents, of course, but that's what Cuba and Canada are for, right? Inside of a year, every fat person in America is going to have a bottle of pills in his pocket, and inside of two years, there won't be any fat people."

She shook her head. "You look . . . Lester, you look *incredible.* I'm so proud of you."

He ducked his head. He really did look amazing. Dropping the weight had taken off ten years, and between that and the haircut and the new clothes, he was practically unrecognizable.

"Does Perry know?"

"Yeah," Lester said. "I talked it over with him before I opted for it. Tjan had mentioned it in passing, it was a business his ex-wife was tangled up with through her mafiyeh connections, and once I had researched it online and talked to some people who'd had the treatment, including a couple MDs, I decided to just do it."

It had cost nearly everything he'd made from Kodacell, but it was a small price to pay. He insisted on getting dinner.

Afterward, they strolled through the fragrant evening down Woodward Avenue, past the deco skyscrapers and the plowed fields and community gardens, their livestock pens making soft animal noises.

"It's wonderful to see you again, Lester," she said truthfully. She'd really missed him, even though his participation on her message boards had hardly let up (though it had started coming in at weird hours, something explained by the fact that he'd been in Russia). Walking alongside him, smelling his smell, seeing him only out of the corner of her eye, it was like nothing had changed.

"It's great to see you again, too." Tentatively, he took her hand in his big paw. His hand was warm but not sweaty, and she realized it had been a long time since anyone had held her hand. Heart pounding, she gave his hand a squeeze.

Their conversation and their walk rambled on, with no outward acknowledgment of the contact of hand on hand, but her hand squeezed his softly now and again, or he squeezed hers, and then they were at her hotel. *How did that happen?* she asked herself.

But then they were having a nightcap, and then he was in the elevator with her and then he was at the door of her room, and the blood was roaring in her ears as she stuck her credit card in the reader to open it.

Wait, she tried to say. *Lester, hang on a second,* is what she tried to say, but her tongue was thick in her mouth. He stepped through the door with her, then said, "Uh, I need to use the bathroom."

With relief, she directed him to the small water closet. The room was basic—now that she was her own boss, she wasn't springing for Crowne Plazas and Hiltons, this was practically a coffin—and there was nowhere to sit except the bed. Her laptop was open and there was a lot of email in her inbox, but for once, she didn't care. She was keenly attuned to the water noises coming from behind the door, each new sound making her jump a little. What was he doing in there, inserting a fucking diaphragm?

She heard him work the latch on the door and she put on her best smile. Her stomach was full of butterflies. He smiled back and sat down on the bed next to her, taking her hand again. His hand was moist from being washed, and a little slippery. She didn't mind. Wordlessly, she put her head on his barrel chest. His heart was racing, and so was hers.

Gradually, they leaned back, until they were side by side on the bed, her head still on his chest. Moving like she was in a dream, she lifted her head from his chest and stared into his eyes. They were wide and scared. She kissed him, softly. His lips were trembling and unyielding. She kissed him more insistently, running her hands over his chest and shoulders, putting one leg over him. He closed his eyes and kissed her back. He wasn't bad, but he was scared or nervous and all jittery.

She kissed his throat, breathing in the smell, savoring the rough texture of his three-day beard. Tentatively, he put his hands on her back, stroked her, worked gradually toward her bottom. Then he stopped.

"What's wrong?" she said, propping herself up on her forearms, still straddling him.

She saw that there were tears in his eyes.

"Lester? What's wrong?"

He opened his mouth and then shut it. Tears slid off his face into his ears. She blotted them with a corner of hotel pillow.

She stroked his hair. "Lester?"

He gave out a choked sob and pushed her away. He sat up and put his face in his hands. His back heaved. She stroked his shoulders tentatively.

Finally, he seemed to get himself under control. He sniffled.

"I have to go," he said.

"Lester, what's *wrong*?"

"I can't do this," he said. "I . . ."

"Just tell me," she said. "Whatever it is, tell me."

"You didn't want me before." He said it simply without accusation, but it stung like he'd slapped her in the face.

"Oh, Lester," she said, moving to hug him, but he pushed her away.

"I have to go," he said, drawing himself up to his full height. He was tall, though he'd never seemed it before, but oh, he was tall, six foot four or taller. He filled the room. His eyes were red and swollen, but he put on a smile for her. "Thanks, Suzanne. It was really good to see you again. I'll see you in Florida."

She stood up and moved quickly to him, stood on tiptoe to put her arms around his neck and hug him fiercely. He hugged her back and she kissed him on the cheek.

"I'll see you in Florida," she said.

And then he was gone. She sat on the edge of her bed and waited for tears, but they didn't come. So she picked up her laptop and started to work through her mountain of email.

When she saw him again, he was coming down the drive leading to the shantytown and the factory. She was having tea in the tearoom that opened in a corkscrew spire high above the rest of the shantytown. The lady who operated it called herself Mrs. Torrence, and she was exquisitely antique but by no means frail, and when she worked the ropes on her dumbwaiter to bring up supplies from the loading area on the ground, her biceps stood at attention like Popeye's. There was a rumor that Mrs. Torrence used to be a man, or still was, under her skirts, but Suzanne didn't pay attention to it.

Lester came down the drive grinning and bouncing on the balls of his feet. Perry had evidently been expecting him, for he came racing through the shantytown and pelted down the roadway and threw himself at Lester, grabbing him in a crazy, exuberant, whooping hug. Francis gimped out a moment later and gave him a solemn handshake. She hadn't blogged their meeting in Detroit, so if Francis and Perry knew about Lester's transformation, they'd found out without hearing it from her.

She finished recording the homecoming from Mrs. Torrence's crow's nest, then paid the grinning old bag and took the stairs two at a time, hurrying to catch up with Lester and his crowd.

Lester accepted her hug warmly but distantly, letting go a fraction of a second before she did. She didn't let it get to her. He had drawn a crowd now, with Francis's protégé printer techs in the innermost circle, and he was recounting the story of his transformation. He had them as spellbound as a roomful of Ewoks listening to C-3PO.

"Shit, why don't we sell that stuff?" Jason said. He'd taken a real interest in the business end of their 3-D printer project.

"Too much competition," Lester said. "There are already a dozen shops tooling up to make bathtub versions of the therapy here in America. Hundreds more in Eastern Europe. There just won't be any profit in it by the time we get to market. Getting thin on the cheap's going to be *easy*. Hell, all it takes to do it is the stuff you'd use for a meth lab. You can buy all that in a kit from a catalog."

Jason nodded but looked unconvinced.

Suzanne took Lester's return as her cue to write about his transformation. She snapped more pics of him, added some video. He gave her ten minutes' description of the therapies he'd undergone, and named a price for the therapy that was substantially lower than a couple weeks at a Hollywood fat farm, and far more effective.

The response was amazing. Every TV news crew in the greater Miami area made a pilgrimage to their factory to film Lester working in a tight T-shirt over a 3-D printer, wrangling huge vats of epoxy-mix goop in the sun with sweat beading over his big, straining biceps.

Her message boards exploded. It seemed that a heretofore unsuspected contingent of her growing readership was substantially obese. And they had friends. Lester eventually gave up on posting, just so he could get some work done. They had the printers to the point where they could turn out new printers, but the whole system was temperamental and needed careful nursing. Lester was more interested in what people had to say on the engineering message boards than chatting with the fatties.

The fatties were skeptical and hopeful in equal measures. The big fight was over whether there was anything to this, whether Lester would keep the weight off, whether the new skinny Lester was really Lester, whether he'd undergone surgery or had his stomach stapled. America's wallets had been cleaned out by so many snake-oil peddlers with a "cure" for obesity that no one could believe what they saw, no matter how much they wanted to.

Lord, but it was bringing in the readers, not to mention the advertising dollars. The clearing price for a thousand weight-loss ads targeted to affluent, obese English speakers was over fifty bucks, as compared with her customary CPM of three bucks a thou. Inside of a week, she'd made enough to buy a car. It was weird being her own circulation and ad-sales department, but it wasn't as hard as she'd worried it might be—and it was intensely satisfying to have such a nose-to-tail understanding of the economics of her production.

"You should go," Lester told her as she clicked him through her earnings spreadsheet. "Jesus, this is insane. You know that these fatties actually follow me around on the Net now, asking me questions in message boards about engineering? The board moderators are asking me to post under an assumed name. Madame, your public has spoken. There is a dire need for your skills in St. Petersburg. Go. They have chandeliers in the subways and caviar on tap. All the blini you can eat. Bear steaks."

She shook her head and slurped at the tea he'd brought her. "You're joking. It's all mafiyeh there. Scary stuff. Besides, I'm covering this beat right now, New Work."

"New Work isn't going anywhere, Suzanne. We'll be here when you get back. And this story is one that needs your touch. They're micro-entrepreneurs solving postindustrial problems. It's the same story you've been covering here, but with a different angle. Take that money and buy yourself a business-class ticket to St. Petersburg and spend a couple weeks on the job. You'll clean up. They could use the publicity, too—someone to go and drill down on which clinics are legit and which ones are clip joints. You're perfect for the gig."

"I don't know," she said. She closed her eyes. Taking big chances had gotten her this far and it would take her farther, she knew. The world was your oyster if you could stomach a little risk.

"Yeah," she said. "Yeah, hell yeah. You're totally right, Lester."

"Zasterovyeh!"

"What you said!"

"It's cheers," he said. "You'll need to know that if you're going to make time in Petrograd. Let me go send some email and get you set up. You book a ticket."

And just like that she was off to Russia. Lester insisted that she buy a business-class ticket, and she discovered to her bemusement that British Airways had about three classes above business, presumably with even more exclusive classes reserved to royalty and peers of the realm. She luxuriated in fourteen hours of reclining seats and warm peanuts and in-flight connectivity, running a brief videoconference with Lester just because she could. Tjan had sent her a guide to the hotels and she'd opted for the Pribaltiyskaya, a crumbling Stalin-era four-star of spectacular, Vegas-esque dimensions. The facade revealed the tragedy of the USSR's unrequited love affair with concrete, as did the cracks running up the walls of the lobby.

They checked her in to the hotel with the nosiest questionnaire ever, a two-pager on government stationery that demanded to know her profession, employer, city of birth, details of family, and so forth. An American business-man next to her at the check-in counter saw her puzzling over it. "Just make stuff up," he said. "I always write that I come from 123 Fake Street, Anytown, California, and that I work as a professional paper hanger. They don't check on it, except maybe the mob when they're figuring out who to mug. First time in Russia?"

"It shows, huh?"

"You get used to it," he said. "I come here every month on business. You just need to understand that if it seems ridiculous and too bad to be true, it is. They have lots of rules here, but no one follows 'em. Just ignore any unrea-sonable request and you'll fit right in."

"That's good advice," she said. He was middle-aged, but so was she, and he had nice eyes and no wedding ring.

"Get a whole night's sleep, don't drink the so-called champagne, and don't change money on the streets. Did you bring melatonin and modafinil?"

She stared blankly at him. "Drugs?"

"Sure. One tonight to sleep, one in the morning to wake up, and do it again tomorrow and you'll be un-lagged. No booze or caffeine, either, not for the first couple days. Melatonin's over the counter, even in the States, and modafinil's practically legal. I have extra, here." He dug in his travel bag and came up with some generic Walgreens bottles.

"That's OK," she said, handing her credit card to a pretty young clerk. "Thanks, though."

He shook his head. "It's your funeral," he said. "Jet lag is way worse for you than this stuff. It's over the counter stateside. I don't leave home without it. Anyway, I'm in room 1422. If it's two in the morning and you're staring at the ceiling and regretting it, call me and I'll send some down."

Was he hitting on her? Christ, she was so tired, she could barely see straight. There was no way she was going to need any help getting to sleep. She thanked him again and rolled her suitcase across the cavernous lobby with its gigantic chandeliers and to the elevators.

But sleep didn't come. The network connection cost a fortune—something she hadn't seen in years—and the number of worms and probes bouncing off her firewall was astronomical. The connection was slow and frustrating. Come 2 AM, she was, indeed, staring at the ceiling.

Would you take drugs offered by a stranger in a hotel lobby? They were in a *Walgreens bottle* for chrissakes. How bad could they be? She picked up the house phone on the chipped bedstand and punched his hotel room.

"'Lo?"

"Oh Christ, I woke you up," she said. "I'm sorry."

"'S OK. Lady from check-in, right? Gimme your room number, I'll send up a melatonin now and a modafinil for the morning. No sweatski."

"Uh," she hadn't thought about giving a strange man her room number. In for a penny, in for a pound. "2813," she said. "Thanks."

"Geoff," he said. "It's Geoff. New York—Upper West Side. Work in health products."

"Suzanne," she said. "Florida, lately. I'm a writer."

"Good night, Suzanne. Pills are en route."

"Good night, Geoff. Thanks."

"Tip the porter a euro, or a couple bucks. Don't bother with rubles."

"Oh," she said. It had been a long time since her last visit overseas. She'd forgotten how much minutiae was involved.

He hung up. She put on a robe and waited. The porter took about fifteen minutes, and handed her a little envelope with two pills in it. He was about fifteen, with a bad mustache and bad skin, and bad teeth that he displayed when she handed him a couple of dollar bills.

A minute later, she was back on the phone.

"Which one is which?"

"Little white one is melatonin. That's for now. My bad."

She saw him again in the breakfast room, loading a plate with hard-boiled eggs, potato pancakes, the ubiquitous caviar, salami, and cheeses. In his other hand he balanced a vat of porridge with strawberry jam and enough dried fruit to keep a parrot zoo happy for a month.

"How do you keep your girlish figure if you eat like that?" she said, settling down at his table.

"Ah, that's a professional matter," he said. "And I make it a point never to discuss bizniz before I've had two cups of coffee." He poured himself a cup of decaf. "This is number two."

She picked her way through her cornflakes and fruit salad. "I always feel like I don't get my money's worth out of buffet breakfasts," she said.

"Don't worry," he said. "I'll make up for you." He pounded his coffee and poured another cup. "Humanity returns," he said, rubbing his thighs. "Marthter, the creature waketh!" he said in high Igor.

She laughed.

"You are really into, uh, *substances,* aren't you?" she said.

"I am a firm believer in better living through chemistry," he said. He pounded another coffee. "Ahhh. Coffee and modafinil are an amazing combo."

She'd taken hers that morning when the alarm got her up. She'd been so tired that it actually made her feel nauseated to climb out of bed, but the modafinil was getting her going. She knew a little about the drug, and figured that if the TSA approved it for use by commercial pilots, it couldn't be that bad for you.

"So, my girlish figure. I work for a firm that has partners here in Petersburg who work on cutting-edge pharma products, including some stuff the FDA is dragging its heels on, despite widespread acceptance in many nations, this one included. One of these is a pill that overclocks your metabolism. I've been on it for a year now, and even though I am a stone calorie freak and pack away five or six thousand calories a day, I don't gain an ounce. I actually have to remember to eat enough so that my ribs don't start showing."

Suzanne watched him gobble another thousand calories. "Is it healthy?"

"Compared to what? Being fat? Yes. Running ten miles a day and eating a balanced diet of organic fruit and nuts? No. But when the average American gets the majority of her calories from soda pop, 'healthy' is a pretty loaded term."

It reminded her of that talk with Lester, a lifetime ago in the IHOP. Slowly, she found herself telling him about Lester's story.

"Wait a second, you're Suzanne *Church*? New Work Church? *San Jose Mercury News* Church?"

She blushed. "You can't *possibly* have heard of me," she said.

He rolled his eyes. "Sure. I shoulder-surfed your name off the check-in form and did a background check on you last night just so I could chat you up over breakfast."

It was a joke, but it gave her a funny, creeped-out feeling. "You're kidding?"

"I'm kidding. I've been reading you for freaking *years*. I followed Lester's story in detail. Professional interest. You're the voice of our generation, woman. I'd be a philistine if I didn't read your column."

"You're not making me any less embarrassed, you know." It took an effort of will to keep from squirming.

He laughed hard enough to attract stares. "All right, I *did* spend the night googling you. Better?"

"If that's the alternative, I'll take famous, I suppose," she said.

"You're here writing about the weight-loss clinics, then?"

"Yes," she said. It wasn't a secret, but she hadn't actually gone out of her way to mention it. After all, there might not be any kind of story after all. And somewhere in the back of her mind was the idea that she didn't want to tip off some well-funded newsroom to send out its own investigative team and get her scoop.

"That is fantastic," he said. "That's just, wow, that's the best news I've had all year. You taking an interest in our stuff, it's going to really push it over the edge. You'd think that selling weight loss to Americans would be easy, but not if it involves any kind of travel: eighty percent of those lazy insular fucks don't even have passports. Ha. Don't quote that. Ha."

"Ha," she said. "Don't worry, I won't. Look, how about this, we'll meet in the lobby around nine, after dinner, for a cup of coffee and an interview?" She had gone from intrigued to flattered to creeped out with this guy, and besides, she had her first clinic visit scheduled for ten and it was coming up on nine and who knew what a Russian rush hour looked like?

"Oh. OK. But you've got to let me schedule you for a visit to some of our clinics and plants—just to see what a professional shop we run here. No gold-teeth, shiny-suit places like you'd get if you just picked the top Google AdWord. Really American-standard places, better even, Scandinavian-standard; a lot of our doctors come over from Sweden and Denmark to get out from under the socialist medicine systems there. They run a tight ship, ya shore, you betcha." He delivered this last in a broad Swedish bork-bork-bork.

"Um," she said. "It all depends on scheduling. Let's sort it out tonight, OK?"

"OK," he said. "Can't *wait*." He stood up with her and gave her a long, two-handed handshake. "It's a real honor to meet you, Suzanne. You're one of my real heros, you know that?"

"Um," she said again. "Thanks, Geoff."

He seemed to sense that he'd come on too strong. He looked like he was about to apologize.

"That's really kind of you to say," she said. "It'll be good to catch up to-night."

He brightened. It was easy enough to be kind, after all.

She had the front desk call her a taxi—she'd been repeatedly warned off of gypsy cabs and any vehicle that one procured by means of a wandering tout. She got into the back, had the doorman repeat the directions to Lester's clinic twice to the cabbie, watched him switch on the meter and checked the tariff, then settled in to watch St. Petersburg go flying by.

She switched on her phone and watched it struggle to associate with a Russian network. They were on the road for all of five minutes—long enough to note the looming bulk of the Hermitage and the ripples left by of-ficial cars slicing through the traffic with their blue blinking lights—when her phone went nutso. She looked at it—she had ten texts, half a dozen voice-mails, a dozen new clipped articles, and it was ringing with a number in New York.

She bumped the New York call to voicemail. She didn't recognize the number. Besides, if the world had come to an end while she was asleep, she wanted to know some details before she talked to anyone about it. She paged back through the texts in reverse chronological—the last five were increasingly pan-icked messages from Lester and Perry. Then one from Tjan. Then one from Kettlebelly. They all wanted to discuss "the news," whatever that was. One from her old editor at the *Merc* asking if she was available for comment about "the news." Tjan, too. The first one was from Rat-Toothed Freddy, that snake.

"Kodacell's creditors calling in debts. Share price below one cent. Imminent NAS-DAQ delisting. Comments?"

Her stomach went cold, her breakfast congealed into a hard lump. The clipped articles had quotes from Kettlewell ("We will see to it that all our em-ployees are paid, our creditors are reimbursed, and our shareholders are well-done-by through an orderly wind-down"), Perry ("Fuck it—I was doing this shit before Kodacell, don't expect to stop now"), and Lester ("It was too beautiful and cool to be real, I guess"). Where she was mentioned, it was usually in a snide context that made her out to be a disgraced pitchwoman for a failed movement.

Which she was. Basically.

Her phone rang. Kettlewell.

"Hi, Kettlewell," she said.

"Where have you been?" he said. He sounded really edgy. It was the middle of the night in California.

"I'm in St. Petersburg," she said. "In Russia. I only found out about ten seconds ago. What happened?"

"Oh Christ. Who knows? Cascading failure. Fell short of last quarter's es-timates, which started a slide. Then a couple lawsuits filed. Then some unfa-vorable press. The share price kept falling, and things got worse. Your basic clusterfuck."

"But you guys had great numbers overall—"

"Sure, if you looked at them our way, they were great. If you looked at them the way the Street looks at them, we were in deep shit. Analysts couldn't figure out how to value us. Add a little market chaos and some old score-settling ass-holes, like that fucker Freddy, and it's a wonder we lasted as long as we did. They're already calling us the twenty-first-century Enron."

"Kettlewell," she said, "I lived through a couple of these, and something's not right. When the dotcoms were going under, their CEOs kept telling everyone everything was all right, right up to the last minute. They didn't throw in the towel. They stood like captains on the bridge of sinking ships."

"So?"

"So what's going on here? It sounds like you're whipped. Why aren't you fighting? There were lots of dotcoms that tanked, but a few of those deep-in-denial CEOs pulled it off, restructured, and came out of it alive. Why are you giving up?"

"Suzanne, oh, Suzanne." He laughed, but it wasn't a happy laugh. "You think that this happened overnight? You think that this problem just cropped up yesterday and I tossed in the towel?"

Oh. "Oh."

"Yeah. We've been tanking for months. I've been standing on the bridge of this sinking ship with my biggest smile pasted on for two consecutive quarters now. I've thrown out the most impressive reality distortion field the business world has ever seen. Just because I'm giving up doesn't mean I gave up without a fight."

Suzanne had never been good at condolences. She hated funerals. "Landon, I'm sorry. It must have been very hard—"

"Yeah," he said. "Well, sure. I wanted you to have the scoop on this, but I had to talk to the press once the story broke, you understand."

"I understand," she said. "Scoops aren't that important anyway. I'll tell you what. I'll post a short piece on this right away, just saying, 'Yes, it's true, and I'm getting details.' Then I'll do interviews with you and Lester and Perry and put up something longer in a couple of hours. Does that work?"

He laughed again, no humor in it. "Yeah, that'll be *fine*."

"Sorry, Kettlewell."

"No, no," he said. "No, it's OK."

"Look, I just want to write about this in a way that honors what you've done over the past two years. I've never been present at the birth of anything remotely this important. It deserves to be described well."

It sounded like he might be crying. There was a snuffling sound. "You've been amazing, Suzanne. We couldn't have done it without you. No one could have described it better. Great deeds are irrelevant if no one knows about them or remembers them."

Her phone was beeping. She snuck a peek. It was her old editor. "Listen," she said. "I have to go. There's a call coming in I *have* to take. I can call you right back."

"Don't," he said. "It's OK. I'm busy here anyway. This is a big day." His laugh was like a dog's bark.

"Take care of yourself, Kettlewell," she said. "Don't let the bastards grind you down."

"Nil carborundum illegitimis to you, too."

She clicked over to her editor. "Jimmy," she said. "Long time no speak. Sorry I missed your calls before—I'm in Russia on a story."

"Hello, Suzanne," he said. His voice had an odd, strained quality, or maybe that was just her mood, projecting. "I'm sorry, Suzanne. You've been doing good work. The best work of your career, if you ask me. I follow it closely."

It made her feel a little better. She'd been uncomfortable about the way she and Jimmy had parted ways, but this was vindicating. It emboldened her. "Jimmy, what the hell do I do now?"

"Christ, Suzanne, I don't know. I'll tell you what not to do, though. Off the record."

"Off the record."

"Don't do what I've done. Don't hang grimly onto the last planks from the sinking ship, chronicling the last few struggling, sinking schmucks' demise. It's no fun being the stenographer for the fall of a great empire. Find something else to cover."

The words made her heart sink. Poor Jimmy, stuck there in the *Merc's* once-great newsroom, while the world crumbled around him. It must have been heartbreaking.

"Thanks," she said. "You want an interview?"

"What? No, woman. I'm not a ghoul. I wanted to call and make sure you were all right."

"Jimmy, you're a prince. But I'll be OK. I land on my feet. You've got someone covering this story, so give her my number and have her call me and I'll give her a quote."

"Really, Suzanne—"

"It's *fine*, Jimmy."

"Suzanne," he said. "We don't cover that kind of thing from our newsroom anymore. Just local stuff. National coverage comes from the wires or from the McClatchy national newsroom."

She sucked in air. Could it be possible? Her first thought when Jimmy called was that she'd made a terrible mistake by leaving the *Merc*, but if this was what the paper had come to, she had left just in time, even if her own life raft was sinking, it had kept her afloat for a while.

"The offer still stands, Jimmy. I'll talk to anyone you want to assign."

"You're a sweetheart, Suzanne. What are you in Russia for?"

She told him. Screw scoops, anyway. Not like Jimmy was going to send anyone to *Russia*; he couldn't even afford to dispatch a reporter to Marin County by the sounds of things.

"What a story!" he said. "Man!"

"Yeah," she said. "Yeah, I guess it is."

"You *guess*? Suzanne, this is the single most important issue in practically every American's life—there isn't one in a thousand who doesn't worry end-lessly about his weight."

"Well, I have been getting really good numbers on this." She named the figure. He sucked air between his teeth. "That's what the whole freaking *chain* does on a top story, Suzanne. You're outperforming fifty local papers *combined*."

"Yeah?"

"Hell yeah," he said. "Maybe I should ask you for a job."

When he got off the phone, she spoke to Perry, and then to Lester. Lester said that he wanted to go traveling and see his old friends in Russia and that if she was still around in a couple weeks, maybe he'd see her there. Perry was morose and grimly determined. He was on the verge of shipping his 3-D printers and he was sure he could do it, even if he didn't have the Kodacell network for marketing and logistics. He didn't even seem to register it when she told him that she was going to be spending some time in Russia.

Then she had to go into the clinic and ask intelligent questions and take pictures and record audio and jot notes and pay attention to the small details so that she would be able to write the best account possible.

They dressed well in Russia, in the clinics. Business casual, but well tai-lored and made from good material. The Europeans knew from textiles, and expert tailoring seemed to be in cheap supply here.

She'd have to get someone to run her up a blue blazer and a white shirt and a decent skirt. It would be nice to get back into grown-up clothes after a couple years' worth of Florida casual.

She'd see Geoff after dinner that night, get more detail for the story. There was something big here in the medical tourism angle—not just weight loss but gene therapy, too, and voodoo stem-cell stuff and advanced prostheses and even some crazy performance-enhancement stuff that had kept Russia out of the past Olympics.

She typed her story notes and answered the phone calls. One special call she returned once she was sitting in her room, relaxed, with a cup of coffee from the in-room coffeemaker.

"Hello, Freddy," she said.

"Suzanne, darling!" He sounded like he was breathing hard.

"What can I do for you?"

"Just wanted a quote, love, something for color."

"Oh, I've got a quote for you." She'd given the quote a lot of thought. Living with the squatters had broadened her vocabulary magnificently.

"And those are your good points," she said, taking a sip of coffee. "Goodbye, Freddy."

PART II

The drive from Orlando down to Hollywood got worse every time Sammy took it. The turnpike tolls went up every year and the road-surface quality declined, and the gas prices at the clip joints were heart-attack-inducing. When Sammy started at Disney Imagineering a decade before, the company had covered your actual expenses—just collect the receipts and turn them in for cash back. But since Parks had been spun off into a separate company with its own shareholders, the new austerity measures meant that the bean counters in Burbank set a maximum per-mile reimbursement and never mind the actual expense.

Enough of this competitive intelligence work and Sammy would go broke.

Off the turnpike, it was even worse. The shantytowns multiplied and multiplied. Laundry lines stretched out in the parking lots of former strip malls. Every traffic light clogged with aggressive techno-tchotchke vendors, the squeegee bums of the twenty-first century, with their pornographic animatronic dollies and infinitely varied robot dogs. Disney World still sucked in a fair number of tourists (though not nearly so many as in its golden day), but they were staying away from Miami in droves. The snowbirds had died off in a great demographic spasm over the past decade, and their children lacked the financial wherewithal to even think of overwintering in their parents' now-derelict condos.

The area around the dead Wal-Mart was particularly awful. The shanties here rose three, even four stories into the air, clustered together to make medieval street mazes. Broward County had long since stopped enforcing the property claims of the bankruptcy courts that managed the real-estate interests of the former owners of the fields and malls that had been turned into the new towns.

By the time he pulled into the Wal-Mart's enormous parking lot, the day had heated up, his air-con had conked, and he'd accumulated a comet tail of urchins who wanted to sell him a computer-generated bust of himself in the style of a Roman emperor—they worked on affiliate commission for some 3-D printer jerk in the shanties, and they had a real aggressive pitch, practically flinging their samples at him.

He pushed past them and wandered through the open-air market stalls, a kind of cruel parody of the long-gone Florida flea markets. These gypsies sold fabricated parts that could be modded to make single-shot zip guns and/or bongs and/or illegal-gain wireless antennae. They sold fruit smoothies and suspicious "beef" jerky. They sold bootleg hard copies of Mexican fotonovelas and bound printouts of Japanese fan-produced tentacle-porn comics. It was all damnably eye-catching and intriguing, even though Sammy knew that it was all junk.

Finally, he reached the ticket window in front of the Wal-Mart and slapped down five bucks on the counter. The guy behind the counter was the kind of character that kept the tourists away from Florida: shaven-headed, with one cockeyed eyebrow that looked like a set of hills, a three-day beard, and skin tanned like wrinkled leather.

"Hi again!" Sammy said brightly. Working at Disney taught you to talk happy even when your stomach was crawling—the castmember's grin.

"Back again?" the guy behind the counter laughed. He was missing a canine tooth and it made him look even more sketchy. "Christ, dude, we'll have to invent a season's pass for you."

"Just can't stay away," Sammy said.

"You're not the only one. You're a hell of a customer for the ride, but you haven't got anything on some of the people I get here—people who come practically every day. It's flattering, I tell you."

"You made this, then?"

"Yeah," he said, swelling up with a little pigeon-chested puff of pride. "Me and Lester, over there." He gestured at a fit, graying man sitting on a stool before a small cocktail bar built into a scavenged Orange Julius stand—God knew where these people got all their crap from. He had the look of one of the fatkins, unnaturally thin and muscled and yet somehow lazy, the combination of a ten-kilocalorie diet, zero body fat, and nonsteroidal muscle enhancers. Ten years ago, he would have been a model, but today he was just another ex-tubbalard with a serious food habit. Time was that Disney World was nigh unnavigable from all the powered wheelchairs carting around morbidly obese Americans who couldn't walk from ride to ride, but these days it looked more like an ad for a gymnasium, full of generically buff fatkins in tight-fitting clothes.

"Good work!" he said again in castmemberese. "You should be very proud!"

The proprietor smiled and took a long pull off a straw hooked into the distiller beside him. "Go on, get in there—flatterer!"

Sammy stepped through the glass doors and found himself in an air-conditioned cave of seemingly infinite dimension. The old Wal-Mart had been the size of five football fields, and a cunning arrangement of curtains and baffles managed to convey all that space without revealing its contents. Before him was the ride vehicle, in a single shaft of spotlight.

Gingerly, he stepped into it. The design was familiar—there had been a glut of these things before the fatkins movement took hold, stair-climbing wheelchairs that used gyro-stabilizers to pitch, yaw, stand, and sit in a perpetual controlled fall. The Disney World veterans of their heyday remembered them as failure-prone behemoths that you needed a forklift to budge when they died, but the ride people had done something to improve on the design. These things performed as well as the originals, though they were certainly knockoffs—no*how* were these cats shelling out fifty grand a pop for the real deal.

The upholstered seat puffed clouds of dust into the spotlight's shaft as he settled into the chair and did up his lap belt. The little LCD set into the control panel lit up and started to play the standard video spiel, narrated in grizzled voice-over.

WELCOME TO THE CABINET OF WONDERS

THERE WAS A TIME WHEN AMERICA HELD OUT THE PROMISE OF A NEW WAY OF LIVING AND WORKING. THE NEW WORK BOOM OF THE TEENS WAS A PERIOD OF UNPARALLELED INVENTION, A CAMBRIAN EXPLOSION OF CREATIVITY NOT SEEN SINCE THE TIME OF EDISON—AND UNLIKE EDISON, THE PEOPLE WHO INVENTED THE NEW WORK REVOLUTION WEREN'T RIP-OFF ARTISTS AND FRAUDS.

THEIR MARVELOUS INVENTIONS EMERGED AT THE RATE OF FIVE OR SIX PER WEEK. SOME DANCED, SOME SANG, SOME WERE HELP-MEETS AND SOME WERE MERE JESTERS.

TODAY, NEARLY ALL OF THESE WONDERFUL THINGS HAVE VANISHED WITH THE COLLAPSE OF NEW WORK. THEY'VE ENDED UP BACK IN THE TRASH HEAPS THAT INSPIRED THEM.

HERE IN THE CABINET OF WONDERS, WE ARE PRESERVING THESE

LAST REMNANTS OF THE GOLDEN AGE, A SINGLE BEACON OF LIGHT IN A TIME OF DARKNESS.

AS YOU MOVE THROUGH THE RIDESPACE, PLEASE REMAIN SEATED. HOWEVER, YOU MAY PAUSE YOUR VEHICLE TO GET A CLOSER LOOK BY MOVING THE JOYSTICK TOWARD YOURSELF. PULL THE JOYSTICK UP TO CUE NARRATION ABOUT ANY OBJECT.

MOVE THE JOYSTICK TO THE LEFT, TOWARD THE MINUS-ONE, IF YOU THINK AN ITEM IS UGLY, UNWORTHY, OR MISPLACED. MOVE THE JOYSTICK TO THE RIGHT, TOWARD THE PLUS-ONE, IF YOU THINK AN ITEM IS PARTICULARLY PLEASING. YOUR FEEDBACK WILL BE FACTORED INTO THE CONTINUOUS REARRANGEMENT OF THE CABINET, WHICH TAKES PLACE ON A MINUTE-BY-MINUTE BASIS, DRIVEN BY THE ROBOTS YOU MAY SEE CRAWLING AROUND THE FLOOR OF THE CABINET.

THE RIDE LASTS BETWEEN TEN MINUTES AND AN HOUR, DEPENDING ON HOW OFTEN YOU PAUSE.

PLEASE ENJOY YOURSELF, AND REMEMBER WHEN WE WERE GOLDEN.

This plus-one/minus-one business was new to him. It had been a mere four days since he'd been up here, but like on so many other of his visits, they'd made major rehabs to their ride in the amount of time it would have taken Imagineering to write a memo about the possibility of holding a design-review meeting.

He velcroed his camera's wireless eye to his lapel, tapped the preset to correct for low light and motion, and hit the joystick. The wheelchair stood up with wobbly grace and began to roll forward on two wheels, heeling over precipitously as it cornered into the main space of the ride. The gyros could take it, he knew, but it still thrilled him the way that a fast, out-of-control go-kart did, miles away from the safe rides back in Disney.

The chair screeched around a corner and pulled into the first scene, a diorama littered with cross-sectioned cars. Each one was kitted out with different crazy technologies—dashboard gods that monitored and transmitted traffic heuristics, parallel-parking autopilots, peer-to-peer music-sharing boxes, even an amphibious retrofit on a little hybrid that apparently worked, converting the little Bug into a water Bug.

The chair swooped around each one, pausing while the narration played back reminiscences by the inventors, or sometimes by the owners of the old gizmos. The stories were pithy and sweet and always funny. These were artifacts scavenged from the first days of a better nation that had died aborning.

Then on to the kitchen, and the bathrooms—bathroom after bathroom, with better toilets, better showers, better tubs, better floors, and better lights—bedrooms, kids' rooms. One after another, a hyper-museum.

The decor was miles ahead of where it had been the last time he'd been through. There were lots of weird grace notes, like taxidermied alligators, vintage tourist pennants, chintz lamps, and tiny dioramae of action figures.

He paused in front of a fabric printer surrounded by custom tees and knit caps and 3-D video-game figurines machine-crocheted from bright yarns, and was passed by another chair. In it was a cute woman in her thirties, white-blond shaggy hair luminous in the spotlight over the soft goods. She paused her chair and lovingly reached out to set down a pair of appliquéd shorts with organic LEDs pulsing and swirling around the waistband. "Give it a plus-one, OK? These were my best sellers," she said, smiling a dazzling beach-bunny smile at him. She wheeled away and paused at the next diorama to set down a dollhouse in a child's room diorama.

Wow—they were getting user-generated content in the *ride*. Holy crap.

He finished out the ride with a keen hand on the plus-one/minus-one lever, carefully voting for the best stuff and against the stuff that looked out of place—like a pornographic ceramic bong that someone had left in the midst of a clockwork animatronic jug band made from stitched-together stuffed animals.

Then it was over, and he was debarking in what had been the Wal-Mart's garden center. The new bright sun made him tear up, and he fished out his shades.

"Hey, mister, c'mere, I've got something better than sunglasses for you!" The guy who beckoned him over to a market stall had the look of an aging bangbanger: shaved head, tattoos, ridiculous cycling shorts with some gut hanging over them.

"See these? Polarizing contact lenses—prescription or optically neutral. Everyone in India is into these things, but we make 'em right here in Florida." He lifted a half-sphere of filmy plastic from his case and peeled back his eyelid and popped it in. His whole iris was tinted black, along with most of the whites of his eyes. Geometric shapes like Maori tattoos were rendered in charcoal gray across the lenses. "I can print you up a set in five minutes, ten bucks for plain, twenty if you want them bitmapped."

"I think I'll stick with my shades, thanks," Sammy said.

"C'mon, the ladies love these things. Real conversation starter. Make you look all anime and shit, guy like you can try this kind of thing out for twenty bucks, you know, won't hurt."

"That's all right," Sammy said.

"Just try a pair on, then, how about that. I printed an extra set last

Wednesday and they've only got a shelf life of a week, so these'll only be good for another day. Fresh in a sealed package. You like 'em, you buy a pair at full price, c'mon that's as good as you're going to get."

Before Sammy knew it, he was taking receipt of a sealed plastic packet in hot pink with a perforated strip down one side. "Uh, thanks . . ." he said as he began to tuck it into a pocket. He hated hard sells; he was no good at them, it was why he bought all his cars online now.

"Naw, that's not the deal. You got to try them on; otherwise how can you buy them once you fall in love with 'em? They're safe, man. Go on—it's easy, just like putting in a big contact lens."

Sammy thought about just walking away, but the other vendors were watching him now, and the scrutiny sapped his will. "My hands are too dirty for this," he said. The vendor silently passed him a sealed sterile wipe, grinning.

Knowing he was had, he wiped his hands, tore open the package, took out the lenses, and popped them one at a time into his eyes. He blinked a couple times. The world was solarized and gray, like he was seeing it through a tinted windscreen.

"Oh man, you look bad*ass*," the vendor said. He held up a hand mirror.

Sammy looked. His eyes were shiny black beads, like a mouse's eyes, solid save for a subtle tracery of Mickey Mouse heads at the corners. The trademark infringement made him grin, hard and spitless. He looked ten years younger, like those late-teen hipsters whose parents dragged them to Walt Disney World, who showed up in bangbanger threads and sneered and scratched their groins and made loud remarks about how suckballs it all was. His conservative buzz cut looked more like a retro skinhead thing, and his smooth-shaved, round cheeks made him boyish.

"Those are good for two days tops—your eyes start getting itchy, you just toss 'em. You want a pair that's good for a week, twenty dollah with the Mickeys. I got Donalds and Astro Boys and all kinds of shit, just have a look through my flash book. Some stuff I drew myself, even."

Playing along now, Sammy let himself be led on a tour of the flash book, which featured the kind of art he was accustomed to seeing in tattoo parlor windows: skulls and snakes and scorpions and naked ladies. Mickey Mouse giving the finger, Daisy Duck with a strap-on, Minnie Mouse as a dominatrix. The company offered a bounty for turning in trademark infringers, but somehow he doubted that the company lawyers would be able to send this squatter a cease-and-desist letter.

In the end, he bought one of each of the Disney sets.

"You like the mouse, huh?"

"Sure," he said.

"I never been. Too expensive. This is all the ride I want, right here." He gestured at the dead Wal-Mart.

"You like that, huh?"

"Man, it's cool! I go on that sometimes, just to see what it's turned into. I like that it's always different. And I like that people add their own stuff. It makes me feel, you know . . ."

"What?"

Suddenly, the vendor dropped his hard-case bangbanger facade. "Those were the best days of my life. I was building three-dee printers, making them run. My older brother liked to fix cars, and so did my old man, but who needs a car, where you going to go? The stuff I built, man, it could make *anything*. I don't know why or how it ended, but while it was going, I felt like the king of the goddamned world."

It felt less fun and ironic now. There were tears bright on the vendor's black-bead eyes. He was in his mid-twenties, younger than he'd seemed at first. If he'd been dressed like a suburban homeowner, he would have looked like someone smart and accomplished, with lively features and clever hands. Sammy felt obscurely ashamed.

"Oh," he said. "Well, I spent those years working a straight job, so it didn't really touch me."

"That's your loss, man," the vendor said. The printer behind him was spitting out the last of Sammy's contact lenses, in sealed plastic wrap. The vendor wrapped them up and put them in a brown liquor-store bag.

Sammy plodded through the rest of the market with his paper bag. It was all so depressing. The numbers at Disney World were down, way down, and it was his job to figure out how to bring them up again, without spending too much money. He'd done it before a couple of times, with the live-action role-playing stuff, and with the rebuild of Fantasyland as an ironic goth hangout (being a wholly separate entity from the old Walt Disney Company had its advantages). But to do it a third time—Christ, he had no idea how he'd get there. These weird-ass Wal-Mart squatters had seemed promising, but could you possibly transplant something like this to a high-throughput, professional location-based entertainment product?

The urchins were still in the parking lot with their Roman emperor busts. He held his hands out to ward them off and found himself holding on to a bust of his own head. One of the little rats had gotten a 3-D scan of his head while he was walking by and had made the bust on spec. He looked older in Roman emperor guise than he did in his mind's eye, old and tired, like an emperor in decline.

"Twenty dollah man, twenty, twenty," the kid said. He was about twelve, and still chubby, with long hair that frizzed away from his head in a dandelion halo.

"Ten," Sammy said, clutching his tired head. It was smooth as epoxy resin, and surprisingly light. There was a lot of different goop you could run through those 3-D printers, but whatever they'd used for this, it was feather-weight.

The kid looked shrewd. "Twenty dollah and I get rid of these other kids, OK?"

Sammy laughed. He passed the kid a twenty, taking care to tuck his wallet deep into the inside pocket of his jacket. The kid whistled shrilly and the rest of the kids melted away. The entrepreneur made the twenty disappear, tapped the side of his nose, and took off running back into the market stalls.

It was hot and muggy and Sammy was tired, and the drive back to Orlando was another five hours if the traffic was against him—and these days, every-thing was against him.

Perry's funny eyebrow twitched as he counted out the day's take. This gig was all cream, all profit. His overhead amounted to a couple hundred a month to Jason and his crew to help with the robot and machinery mainte-nance in the Wal-Mart, half that to some of the shantytown girls to dust and sweep after closing, and a retainer to a bangbanger pack that ran security at the ride and in the market. Plus he got the market-stall rents, and so when the day was over, only the first hundred bucks out of the till went into overheads and the rest split even-steven with Lester.

Lester waited impatiently, watching him count twice before splitting the stack. Perry rolled up his take and dropped it into a hidden pocket sewn into his cargo shorts.

"Someday you're going to get lucky and some chick is going to reach down and freak out, buddy," Lester said.

"Better she finds my bankroll than my prostate," Perry said. Lester spent a lot of time thinking about getting lucky, making up for a lifetime of bad luck with girls.

"OK, let's get changed," Lester said. As usual, he was wearing tight-fitting jeans that owed a little debt to the bangbanger cycling shorts, something you would have had to go to a gay bar to see when Perry was in college. His shirt clung to his pecs and was tailored down to his narrow waist. It was a fatkins style, the kind of thing you couldn't wear unless you had a uniquely adver-sarial relationship with your body and metabolism.

"No, Lester, no," Perry said. "I said I'd go on this double date with you, but

I didn't say anything about letting you dress me up for it." The two girls were a pair that Lester had met at a fatkins club in South Beach the week before, and he'd camera-phoned their pic to Perry with a scrawled drunken note about which one was his. They were attractive enough, but the monotonic fatkins devotion to sybaritism was so tiresome. Perry didn't see much point in hooking up with a girl he couldn't have a good technical discussion with.

"Come *on*, it's good stuff, you'll love it."

"If I have to change clothes, I'm not interested." Perry folded his arms. In truth, he wasn't interested, period. He liked his little kingdom there, and he could get everything he needed from burritos to RAM at the market. He had a chest freezer full of bankruptcy-sale organic MREs, for variety.

"Just the shirt then—I had it printed just for you."

Perry raised his funny eyebrow. "Let's see it."

Lester turned to his latest car, a trike with huge, electric blue back tires, and popped the trunk, rummaged, and proudly emerged holding a bright blue Hawaiian print shirt.

"Lester, are those . . . turds?"

"It's transgressivist moderne," Lester said, hopping from foot to foot. "Saw it in the *New York Times,* brought the pic to Gabriela in the market, she cloned it, printed it, and sent it out for stitching—an extra ten buck for same-day service."

"I am *not* wearing a shirt covered in steaming piles of shit, Lester. No, no, no. A googol times no."

Lester laughed. "Christ, I had you going, didn't I? Don't worry, I wouldn't actually have let you go out in public wearing this. But how about *this*?" he said with a flourish, and brought out another shirt. Something stretchy and iridescent, like an oil slick. It was sleeveless. "It'll really work with your biceps and pecs. Also: looks pretty good compared to the turd shirt, doesn't it? Go on, try it on."

"Lester Banks, you are the gayest straight man I know," Perry said. He shucked his sweaty tee and slipped into the shirt. Lester gave him a big thumbs-up. He examined his reflection in the blacked-out glass doors of the Wal-Mart.

"Yeah, OK," he said. "Let's get this over with."

"Your enthusiasm, your best feature," Lester said.

Their dates were two brunettes with deep tans and whole-eye cosmetic contacts that hid their pupils in favor of featureless expanses of white, so they looked like their eyes had rolled back into their heads, or maybe like they were wearing cue balls for glass eyes. Like most of the fatkins girls Perry had met, they dressed to the nines, ate like pigs, drank like fishes, and talked about nothing but biotech.

"So I'm thinking, sure, mitochrondrial lengthening *sounds* like it should work, but if that's so, why have we been screwing around with it for thirty years without accomplishing anything?" His date, Moira, worked at a law office, and she came up to his chest, and it was hard to tell with those eyes, but it seemed like she was totally oblivious to his complete indifference to mitochondria.

He nodded and tried not to look bored. South Beach wasn't what it had once been, or maybe Perry had changed. He used to love to come here to people-watch, but the weirdos of South Beach seemed too precious when compared with the denizens of his own little settlement out on the Hollywood freeway.

"Let's go for a walk on the beach," Lester said, digging out his wallet and rubbing his card over the pay-patch on the table.

"Good idea," Perry said. Anything to get off this patio and away from the insufferable club music thundering out of the speakers pole-mounted directly over their table.

The beach was gorgeous, so there was that. The sunset behind them stained the ocean bloody and the sand was fine and clean. Around their feet, Dade County beachcombers wormed endlessly through the sand, filtering out all the gunk, cig butts, condoms, needles, wrappers, loose change, wedding rings, and forgotten sunglasses. Perry nudged one with his toe and it roombaed away, following its instinct to avoid human contact.

"How do you figure they keep the vags from busting those open for whatever they've got in their bellies?" Perry said, looking over his date's head at Lester, who was holding hands with his girl, carrying her shoes in his free hand.

"Huh? Oh, those things are built like tanks. Have to be to keep the sand out. You need about four hours with an air hammer to bust one open."

"You tried it?"

Lester laughed. "Who, me?"

Now it was Perry's date's turn to be bored. She wandered away toward the boardwalk, with its strip of novelty sellers. Perry followed, because he had a professional interest in the kind of wares they carried. Most of them originated on one of his printers, after all. Plus, it was the gentlemanly thing to do.

"What have we here?" he said as he pulled up alongside her. She was trying on a bracelet of odd, bony beads.

"Ectopic fetuses," she said. "You know, like the Christian fundies use for stem-cell research? You quicken an unfertilized egg in vitro and you get a little ball of fur and bone and skin and stem cells. It can never be a human, so it has no soul, so it's not murder to harvest them."

The vendor, a Turkish teenager with a luxurious mustache, nodded. "Every bead made from naturally occurring fetus bones." He handed one to Perry.

It was dry and fragile in his hand. The bones were warm and porous, and in tortured Elephant Man shapes that he recoiled from atavistically.

"Good price," the Turkish kid said. He had practically no accent at all, and was wearing a Japanese baseball team uniform and spray-on foot coverings. Thoroughly Americanized. "Look here," he said, and gestured at a little corner of his table.

It was covered in roses made from fabric—small and crude, with pin backs. Perry picked one up. It had a certain naive charm. The fabric was some kind of very delicate leather—

"It's skin," his date said. "Fetal skin."

He dropped it. His fingers tingled with the echo of the feeling of the leather. *Jesus I hate biotech.* The rose fluttered past the table to the sandy boardwalk, and the Turkish kid picked it up and blew it clean.

"Sorry," Perry said, sticking his hands in his pockets. His date bought a bracelet and a matching choker made of tiny bones and teeth, and the Turkish kid, leering, helped her fasten the necklace. When they returned to Lester and his date, Perry knew the evening was at a close. The girls played a couple rounds of eye hockey, unreadable behind their lenses, and Perry shrugged apologetically at Lester.

"Well then," Lester said, "it sure has been a nice night." Lester got smooched when they saw the girls off in a pedicab. In the buzz and hum of its flywheel, Perry got a damp and unenthusiastic handshake.

"Win some, lose some," Lester said as the girls rolled away in a flash of muscular calves from the pair of beach-perfect cabbies pedaling the thing.

"You're not angry?" Perry said.

"Nah," Lester said. "I get laid too much as it is. Saps me of my precious bodily fluids. Gotta keep some chi inside, you know?"

Perry raised up his funny eyebrow and made it dance.

"Oh, OK," Lester said. "You got me. I'm meeting mine later, after she drops her friend off."

"I'll get a cab home then, shall I?"

"Take my car," Lester said. "I'll get a ride back in the morning. No way you'll get a taxi to take you to our neighborhood at this hour."

Perry's car had been up on blocks for a month, awaiting his attention to its failing brakes and mushy steering. So it was nice to get behind the wheel of Lester's Big Daddy Roth trike and give it a little gas out on the interstate, the smell of the swamp and biodiesel from the big rigs streaming past the windscreen. The road was dark and treacherous with potholes, but Perry got into the rhythm of it and found he didn't want to go home, quite, so he kept driving, into the night. He told himself that he was scouting dead malls for future expansion, but he had kids who'd video-documented the status of all the likely candidates in the hood, and he kept tabs on his choicest morsels via daily sat photos that he subscribed to in his morning feed.

What the hell was he doing with his life? The Wal-Mart ride was a lark— it had been Lester's idea, but Lester had lost interest and Perry had done most of the work. They weren't quite squatting the Wal-Mart: Perry paid rent to a state commission that collected in escrow for the absentee landlord. It was a fine life, but the days blurred one into the next, directionless. Building the ride had been fun, setting up the market had been fun, but running them— well, he might as well be running a Laundromat for all the mental acuity his current job required.

"You miss it," he said to himself over the whistle of the wind and the hiss of the fat contact-patches on the rear tires. "You want to be back in the shit, inventing stuff, making it all happen."

For the hundredth time, he thought about calling Suzanne Church. He missed her, too, and not just because she made him famous (and now he was no longer famous). She put it all in perspective for him, and egged him on to greater things. She'd been their audience, and they'd all performed for her, back in the golden days.

It was, what, 5 AM in Russia? Or was it two in the afternoon? He had her number on his speed dial, but he never rang it. He didn't know what he'd tell her.

He could call Tjan, or even Kettlebelly, just ring them out of the blue, veterans together shooting the shit. Maybe they could have a Kodacell reunion, and get together to sing the company song, wearing the company T-shirt.

He pulled the car off at a truck stop and bought an ice cream novelty from a vending machine with a robotic claw that scooped the ice cream, mushed it into the cone, then gave it a haircut so that it looked like Astro Boy's head, then extended the cone on a robotic claw. It made him smile. Someone had invented this thing. It could have been him. He knew where you could download vision-system libraries, and force-feedback libraries. He knew where you could get plans for the robotics, and off-the-shelf motors and sensors. Christ, these days he had a good idea where you could get the ice cream wholesale, and which crooked vending-machine interests he'd have to grease to get his stuff into truck stops.

He was thirty-four years old, he was single and childless, and he was eating an ice cream in a deserted truck stop at two in the morning by the side of a freeway in south Florida. He bossed a low-budget tourist attraction and he ran a pirate flea market.

What the hell was he doing with his life?

Getting mugged, that's what.

They came out of the woods near the picnic tables, four bangbangers, but young ones, in their early teens. Two had guns—nothing fancy, just AK-47s run off a computer-controlled mill somewhere in an industrial park. You saw them all over the place, easy as pie to make, but the ammo was a lot harder to come by. So maybe they were unloaded.

Speaking of unloaded. He was about to piss his pants.

"Wallet," one of them said. He had a bad mustache that reminded him of the Turkish kid on the beach. Probably the same hormones that gave kids mustaches gave them bad ideas like selling fetus jewelry or sticking up people by the ice cream machines at late-night truck stops. "Keys," he said. "Phone," he added.

Perry slowly set down the ice cream cone on the lid of the trash can beside him. He'd only eaten one spike off Astro Boy's head.

His vision telescoped down so that he was looking at that kid, at his mustache, at the gun in his hands. He was reaching for his wallet, slowly. He'd need to hitch a ride back to town. Canceling the credit cards would be tough, since he'd stored all the identity-theft passwords and numbers in his phone, which they were about to take off him. And he'd have to cancel the phone, for that matter.

"Do you have an older brother named Jason?" his mouth said, while his hands were still being mugged.

"What?"

"Works a stall by the Wal-Mart ride, selling contact lenses?"

The kid's eyes narrowed. "You don't know me, man. You don't want to know me. Better for your health if you don't know me."

His hands were passing over his phone, his wallet, his keys—Lester's keys. Lester would be glad to have an excuse to build a new car.

"Only I own the Wal-Mart ride, and I've known Jason a long time. I gave him his first job, fixing the printers. You look like him."

The kid's three buddies were beginning their slow fade into the background. The kid was visibly on the horns of a dilemma. The gun wavered. Perry's knees turned to water.

"You're that guy?" the kid said. He peered closer. "Shit, you are."

"Keep it all," Perry said. His mouth wasn't so smart. Knowing who mugged you wasn't good for your health.

"Shit," the kid said. The gun wavered. Wavered.

"Come *on*," one of his buddies said. "Come on, man!"

"I'll be there in a minute," the kid said, his voice flat.

Perry knew he was a dead man.

"I'm really sorry," the kid said, once his friends were out of range.

"Me too," said Perry.

"You won't tell my brother?"

Perry froze. Time dilated. He realized that his fists were clenched so tight that his knuckles hurt. He realized that he had a zit on the back of his neck that was rubbing against his collar. He realized that the kid had a paperback book stuck in the waistband of his bangbanger shorts, which was unusual. It was a fantasy novel. A Conan novel. Wow.

Time snapped back.

"I won't tell your brother," he said. Then he surprised himself, "But you've got to give me back the credit cards and leave the car at the market in the morning."

The kid nodded. Then he seemed to realize he was holding a gun on Perry. He lowered it. "Yeah, that's fair," he said. "Can't use the fucking cards these days anyway."

"Yeah," Perry said. "Well, there's some cash there anyway." He realized he had five hundred bucks in a roll in a hidden pocket in his shorts.

"You get home OK?"

"I'll thumb a ride," Perry said.

"I can call you a taxi," the kid said. "It's not safe to hang around here."

"That's really nice of you," Perry said. "Thanks."

The kid took out a little phone and prodded it for a minute. "On the way," he said. "The guns aren't loaded."

"Oh, well," Perry said. "Good to know."

An awkward silence spread between them. "Look, I'm really sorry," the kid said. "We don't really do this. It's our first night. My brother would really kill me."

"I won't tell him," Perry said. His heart was beating again, not thundering or keeping ominously still. "But you know, this isn't smart. You're going to stick someone up who has bullets and he's gonna shoot you."

"We'll get ammo," the kid said.

"And shoot him? That's only a little better, you know."

"What do you want me to say?" the kid said, looking young and petulant. "I apologized."

"Come by tomorrow with the car and let's talk, all right?"

Lester didn't even notice that his car was missing until the kid drove up with it, and when he asked about it, Perry just raised his funny eyebrow at him. That funny eyebrow, it had the power to cloud men's minds.

"What's your name?" Perry asked the kid, giving him the spare stool by the ticket window. It was after lunchtime, when the punishing heat slowed everyone to a sticky crawl, and the crowd was thin—one or two customers every half hour.

"Glenn," the kid said. In full daylight, he looked older. Perry had noticed that the shantytowners never stopped dressing like teenagers, wearing the fashions of their youths forever, so that a walk through the market was like a tour through the teen fashions of the last thirty years.

"Glenn, you did me a real solid last night."

Glenn squirmed on his stool. "I'm sorry about that—"

"Me too," Perry said. "But not as sorry as I might have been. You said it was your first night. Is that true?"

"Carjacking, sure," the kid said.

"But you get into other shit, don't you? Mugging? Selling a little dope? Something like that?"

"Everyone does that," Glenn said. He looked sullen.

"Maybe," Perry said. "And then a lot of them end up doing a stretch in a work camp. Sometimes they get bit by water moccasins and don't come out. Sometimes, one of the other prisoners hits them over the head with a shovel. Sometimes you just lose three to five years of your life to digging ditches."

Glenn said nothing.

"I'm not trying to tell you how to run your life," Perry said. "But you seem like a decent kid, so I figure there's more in store for you than getting killed or locked up. I know that's pretty normal around here, but you don't have to go that way. Your brother didn't."

"What the fuck do you know about it, anyway?" The kid was up now, body language saying he wanted to get far away, fast.

"I could ask around the market," Perry said, as though the kid hadn't spoken. "Someone here has got to be looking for someone to help out. You could open your own stall."

The kid said, "It's all just selling junk to idiots. What kind of job is that for a man?"

"Selling people stuff they can't be bothered to make for themselves is a time-honored way of making a living. There used to be professional portrait photographers who'd take a pic of your family for money. They were even considered artists. Besides, you don't have to sell stuff you download. You can invent stuff and print that."

"Get over it. Those days are over. No one cares about inventions anymore."

It nailed Perry between the eyes, like a slaughterhouse bolt. "Yeah, yeah," he said. He didn't want to talk to this kid any more than this kid wanted to talk to him. "Well, if I can't talk you out of it, it's your own business. . . ." He started to rearrange his ticket desk.

The kid saw his opportunity for freedom and bolted. He was probably headed for his brother's stall and then the long walk to wherever he planned on spending his day. Everything was a long walk from here, or you could wait for the buses that ran on the hour during business hours.

Perry checked out the car, cleaned out the empties and the roaches and twists from the backseat, then parked it. A couple more people came by to ride his ride, and he took their money.

Lester had just finished his largest-ever flattened-soda-can mechanical computer; it snaked back and forth across the whole of the old Wal-Mart solarium, sheets of pressboard with precision-cut gears mounted on aviation bearings—Francis had helped him with those. All day, he'd been listening to the racket of it grinding through its mighty 0.001 kHz calculations, dumping carloads of M&M's into its output hopper. You programmed it with regulation baseballs, footballs, soccer balls, and wiffleballs: dump them in the input hopper and they would be sorted into the correct chutes to trigger the operations. With a whopping one kilobit of memory, the thing could best any of the early vacuum-tube computers without a single electrical component, and Lester was ready to finally declare victory over the cursed Univac.

Perry let himself be coaxed into the workroom, deputizing Francis to man the ticket desk, and watched admiringly as Lester put the machine through its paces.

"You've done it," Perry said.

"Well, I gotta blog it," Lester said. "Run some benchmarks, really test it out against the old monsters. I'm thinking of using it to brute-force the old Nazi Enigma code. That'll show those dirty Nazi bastards! We'll win the war yet!"

Perry found himself giggling. "You're the best, man," he said to Lester. "It's good that there's at least one sane person around here."

"Don't flatter yourself, Perry."

"I was talking about *you*, Lester."

"Uh-oh," Lester said. He scooped a double handful of brown M&M's up from the output hopper and munched them. "It's not a good sign when you start accusing me of being the grown-up in our partnership. Have some M&M's and tell me about it."

Perry did, unburdening himself to his old pal, his roommate of ten years, the guy he'd gone to war with and started businesses with and collaborated with.

"You're restless, Perry," Lester said. He put nine golf balls, a ping-pong ball, and another nine golf balls in the machine's input hopper. Two and a third seconds later, eighty-one M&M's dropped into the output hopper. "You're just *bored.* You're a maker, and you're running things instead of making things."

"No one cares about made things anymore, Les."

"That's sort of true," Lester said. "I'll allow you that. But it's only sort of true. What you're missing is how much people care about organizations still. That was the really important thing about the New Work: the way we could all come together to execute, without a lot of top-down management. The bangbanger arms dealers, the bioterrorists and fatkins suppliers—they all run on social institutions that we perfected back then. You've got something like that here with your market, a fluid social institution that you couldn't have had ten or fifteen years ago."

"If you say so," Perry said. The M&M's were giving him heartburn. Cheap chocolate didn't really agree with his stomach.

"I do. And so the answer is staring you right in the face: go invent some social institutions. You've got one creeping up here in the ride. There are little blogospheres of fans who coordinate what they're going to bring down and where they're going to put it. Build on that."

"No one's going to haul ass across the country to ride this ride, Les. Get real."

"Course not." Lester beamed at him. "I've got one word for you, man: franchise!"

"Franchise?"

"Build dupes of this thing. Print out anything that's a one of a kind, run them as franchises."

"Won't work," Perry said. "Like you said, this thing works because of the hardcore of volunteer curators who add their own stuff to it—it's always different. Those franchises would all be static, or would diverge. . . . It'd just be boring compared to this."

"Why should they diverge? Why should they be static? You could network them, dude! What happens in one, happens in all. The curators wouldn't just be updating one exhibit, but all of them. Thousands of them. Millions of them. A gigantic physical wiki. Oh, it'd be so very, very, very cool, Perry. A cool *social institution.*"

"Why don't you do it?"

"I'm gonna. But I need someone to run the project. Someone who's good at getting people all pointed in the same direction. You, pal. You're my hero on this stuff."

"You're such a flatterer."

"You love it, baby," Lester said, and fluttered his long eyelashes. "Like the lady said to the stamp collector, philately will get you everywhere."

"Oy," Perry said. "You're fired."

"You can't fire me, I'm a volunteer!"

Lester dropped six golf balls and a heavy medicine ball down the hopper. The machine ground and chattered, then started dropping hundred-loads of M&M's—one hundred, two hundred, three hundred, four hundred, five hundred, six hundred, seven hundred—then some change.

"What operation was that?" Perry said. He'd never seen Lester pull out the medicine ball.

"Figure it out," Lester said.

Perry thought for a moment. Six squared? Six cubed? Log six? "Six *factorial*? My God, you're weird, Les."

"Genius is never appreciated." He scooped up a double handful of brown M&M's. "In your face, von Neumann! Let's see your precious ENIAC top *this!*"

A month later, Perry was clearing security at Miami International, looking awkard in long trousers, closed-sole shoes, and a denim jacket. It was autumn in Boston, and he couldn't show up in flip-flops and a pair of cutoffs. The security guards gave his leathery, lopsided face a hard look. He grinned like a pirate and made his funny eyebrow twitch, a stunt that earned him half an hour behind the screen and a date with Doctor Jellyfinger.

"What, exactly, do you think I've got hidden up there?" he asked as he gripped the railing and tried not to let the illegitimati carborundum.

"It's procedure, sir."

"Well, the doc said my prostate was the size of a guava about a month ago— in your professional opinion, has it shrunk or grown? I mean, while you're up there."

The TSA man didn't like that at all. A minute later, Perry was buckling up and leaving the little room with an exaggerated bowlegged gait. He tipped an imaginary hat at the guard's retreating back and said, "Call me!" in a stagey voice.

It was the last bit of fun he had for the next four hours, crammed in the tin can full of recycled discount air-traveler flatulence and the clatter of fingers on keyboards and the gabble of a hundred phone conversations as the salarymen on the flight stole a few minutes of cramped productivity from the dead travel time.

Touching down in Boston and getting his luggage, he felt like he'd landed on an alien planet. The feeling of disorientation and foreignness was new to Perry. He was used to being supremely comfortable, in control—confident. But he was nervous now, maybe even scared, a little.

He dialed Tjan. "I've got my bags," he said.

"I'll be right around," Tjan said. "Really looking forward to seeing you."

There were more cops than passengers in the arrivals area at Logan, and they watched Tjan warily as he pulled up and swung open a door of his little sports car.

"What the fuck is this, a Porsche?" Perry said as he folded himself awkwardly into the front seat, stepping in through the sunroof, pulling his bag down into his lap after him.

"It's a Lada. I had it imported—they're all over Russia. Evolutionary algorithm used to produce a minimum-materials/maximum-strength chassis. It's nice to see you, Perry."

"It's nice to see you, Tjan," he said. The car was so low to the ground that it felt like he was riding luge. Tjan hammered mercilessly on the gearbox, rocketing them to Cambridge at such speed that Perry barely had time to admire the foliage, except at stoplights.

They were around the campus now, taking a screeching right off Mass Ave. onto a tree-lined street of homely two-story brick houses. Tjan pulled up in front of one and popped the sunroof. The cold air that rushed in was as crisp as an apple, unlike any breath of air to be had in Florida, where there was always a mushiness, a feeling of air that had been filtered through the moist lungs of Florida's teeming fauna.

Perry climbed out of the little Russian sports car and twisted his back and raised his arms over his head until his spine gave and popped and crackled.

Tjan followed, and then he shut down the car with a remote that made it go through an impressive and stylish series of clicks, clunks, and chirps before settling down over its wheels, dropping the chassis to a muffler-scraping centimeter off the ground.

"Come on," he said. "I'll show you your room."

Tjan's porch sagged, with a couple kids' bikes triple-locked to it and an all-covering chalk mosaic over every inch of it. The wood creaked and gave beneath their feet.

The door sprang open and revealed a pretty little girl, nine or ten years old, in blue jeans and a hoodie sweater that went nearly to her ankles, the long sleeves bunched up like beach balls on her forearms. The hood hung down to her butt—it was East Coast bangbanger, as reinterpreted through the malls.

"Daddy!" she said, and put her arms around Tjan's waist, squeezing hard.

He pried her loose and then hoisted her by the armpits up to eye height. "What have you done to your brother?"

"Nothing he didn't deserve," she said, with a smile that showed dimples and made her little nose wrinkle.

Tjan looked over at Perry. "This is my daughter, Lyenitchka, who is about to be locked in the coal cellar until she learns to stop torturing her younger brother. Lyenitchka, this is Perry Gibbons, upon whom you have already made an irreparably bad first impression." He shook her gently Perrywards.

"Hello, Perry," she said, giggling, holding out one hand. She had a faint accent, which made her sound like a tiny, skinny Bond villainess.

He shook gravely. "Nice to meet you," he said.

"You got your kids," Perry said, once she was gone.

"For the school year. Me and the ex, we had a heart-to-heart about the Russian education system and ended up here: I get the kids from September to June, but not Christmases or Easter holidays. She gets them the rest of the time, and takes them to a family dacha in Ukraine, where she assures me there are hardly any mafiyeh kids to influence my darling daughter."

"You must be loving this," Perry said.

Tjan's face went serious. "This is the best thing that's ever happened to me."

"I'm really happy for you, buddy."

They had burgers in the backyard, cooking on an electric grill that was caked with the smoking grease of a summer's worth of outdoor meals. The plastic tablecloth was weighed down with painted rocks and the corners blew up in the freshening autumn winds. Lyenitchka's little brother appeared when the burgers began to spit and smoke on the grill, a seven-year-old in metallic mesh trousers and shirt wrought with the logo of a cartoon Cossack holding a laser sword aloft.

"Sasha, meet Perry." Sasha looked away, then went off to swing on a tire swing hanging from the big tree.

"You've got good kids," Perry said, handing Tjan a beer from the cooler under the picnic table.

"Yup," Tjan said. He flipped the burgers and then looked at both of them. Lyenitchka was pushing her brother on the swing, a little too hard. Tjan smiled and looked back down at his burgers.

Tjan cut the burgers in half and dressed them to his kids' exacting standards. They picked at them, pushed them onto each other's plates and got some into their mouths.

"I've read your briefing on the ride," Tjan said, once his kids had finished and eaten half a package of Chutney Oreos for dessert. "It's pretty weird stuff."

Perry nodded and cracked another beer. The cool air was weirding him out, awakening some atavistic instinct to seek a cave. "Yup, weird as hell. But they love it. Not just the geeks, either, though they eat it up, you should see it. Obsessive doesn't begin to cover it. But the civilians come by the hundreds, too. You should hear them when they come out: 'Jee-zus, I'd forgotten about those dishwasher stackers, they were wicked! Where can I get one of those these days you figger?' The nostalgia's thick enough to cut with a knife."

Tjan nodded. "I've been going over your books, but I can't figure out if you're profitable."

"Sorry, that's me. I'm pretty good at keeping track of numbers, but getting them massaged into a coherent picture—"

"Yeah, I know." Tjan got a faraway look. "How'd you make out on Koda-cell, Perry? Finance-wise?"

"Enough to open the ride, buy a car. Didn't lose anything."

"Ah." Tjan fiddled with his beer. "Listen, I got rich off of Westinghouse. Not fuck-the-service-here-I'm-buying-this-restaurant rich, but rich enough that I never have to work again. I can spend the rest of my life in this yard, flipping burgers, taking care of my kids, and looking at porn."

"Well, you were the suit. Getting rich is what suits do. I'm just a grunt."

Tjan had the good grace to look slightly embarrassed. "Now here's the thing. I don't *have* to work, but, Perry, I have *no idea* what I'm going to do if I don't work. The kids are at school all day. Do you have any idea how much daytime TV sucks? Playing the stock market is completely nuts, it's all gone sideways and upside down. I got an education so I wouldn't *have* to flip burgers for the rest of my life."

"What are you saying, Tjan?"

"I'm saying yes," Tjan said, grinning piratically. "I'm saying that I'll join your little weird-ass hobby business and I'll open another ride here for the Massholes. I'll help you run the franchising op, collect fees, make it profitable."

Perry felt his face tighten.

"What? I thought you'd be happy about this."

"I am," Perry said. "But you're misunderstanding something. These aren't meant to be profitable businesses. I'm done with that. These are art, or community, or something. They're museums. Lester calls them *wunderkammers*— cabinets of wonders. There's no franchising op the way you're talking about it. It's ad hoc. It's a protocol we all agree on, not a business arrangement."

Tjan grunted. "I don't think I understand the difference between an agreed-upon protocol and a business arrangement." He held up his hand to fend off Perry's next remark. "But it doesn't matter. You can let people have the franchise for free. You can claim that you're not letting anyone have anything, that they're letting themselves in for their franchise. It doesn't matter to me.

"But, Perry, here's something you're going to have to understand: it's going to be nearly impossible *not to* make a business out of this. Businesses are great structures for managing big projects. It's like trying to develop the ability to walk without developing a skeleton. Once in a blue moon, you get an octopus, but for the most part, you get skeletons. Skeletons are good shit."

"Tjan, I want you to come on board to help me create an octopus," Perry said.

"I can try," Tjan said, "but it won't be easy. When you do cool stuff, you end up making money."

"Fine," Perry said. "Make money. But keep it to a minimum, OK?"

The next time Perry turned up at Logan, it was colder than the inside of an icebox and shitting down gray snow with the consistency of frozen custard.

"Great weather for an opening," he said, once he'd climbed through the roof of Tjan's car and gotten snow all over the leather upholstery. "Sorry about the car."

"Don't sweat it, the kids are murder on leather. I should trade this thing in on something that's less of a death trap anyway."

Tjan was balder than he'd been in September, and skinnier. He had a three-day beard that further hollowed out his normally round cheeks. The Lada fishtailed a little as they navigated the tunnels back toward Cambridge, the roads slick and icy.

"We scored an excellent location," Tjan said. "I told you that, but check this out." They were right in the middle of a built-up area of Boston, something that felt like a banking district, with impressive towers. It took Perry a minute to figure out what Tjan was pointing at.

"That's the site?" There was a mall on the corner, with a boarded-up derelict Hyatt overtopping it, rising high into the sky. "But it's right in the middle of town!"

"Boston's not Florida," Tjan said. "Lots of people here don't have cars. There were some dead malls out in Worcester and the like, but I got this place for nothing. The owners haven't paid taxes in the ten years since the hotel folded, and the only shops that were left open were a couple of Azerbaijani import-export guys', selling junky stuff from India.

"We gutted the whole second floor and turned the ground-floor food court into a flea market. There's an old tunnel connecting this to the T and I managed to get it reopened, so I expect we'll get some walk-in."

Perry marveled. Tjan had a suit's knack for pulling off the ambitious. Perry had never tried to even rent an apartment in a big city, figuring that any place where land was at a premium was a place where people willing to spend more than him could be found. Give him a ghost mall that was off the GPS grid anytime.

"Have you managed to fill the flea market?" It had taken Perry a long time to fill his, and still he had a couple of dogs—a tarot reader and a bong stall, a guy selling high-pressure spray-paint cans and a discount porn stall that sold naked shovelware by the petabyte.

"Yeah, I got protégés up and down New England. A lot of them settled here after the crash. One place is as good as another, and the housing was wicked cheap once the economy disappeared. They upped stakes and came to Boston as soon as I put the word out. I think everyone's waiting for the next big thing."

"You think?"

"Perry, New Work is the most important thing that ever happened to some of those people. It was the high point of their lives. It was the only time they ever felt useful."

Perry shook his head. "Don't you think that's sad?"

Tjan negotiated a tricky tunnel interchange and got the car pointed to Cambridge. "No, Perry, I don't think it's sad. Jesus Christ, you can't believe that. Why do you think I'm helping you? You and me and all the rest of them, we did something *important*. The world changed. It's continuing to change. Have you stopped to think that one in five American workers picked up and moved somewhere else to do New Work projects? That's one of the largest American resettlements since the Dust Bowl. The average New Work collective shipped more inventions per year than Edison Labs at its peak. In a hundred years, when they remember the centuries that were America's, they'll count this one among them, because of what we made.

"So no, Perry, I don't think it's sad."

"I'm sorry. Sorry, OK? I didn't mean it that way. But it's tragic, isn't it, that the dream ended? That they're all living out there in the boonies, thinking of their glory days?"

"Yes, that *is* sad. But that's why I agreed to do the ride—not to freeze the old projects in amber, but to create a new project that we can all participate in again. These people uprooted their lives to follow us, it's the least we can do to give them something back for that."

Perry stewed on that the rest of the way to Tjan's, staring at the sleet, hand resting against the icy window glass.

Sammy checked in to a Comfort Inn tucked into the thirty-seventh story of the Bank of America building in downtown Boston. The lobby was empty, the security guard's desk unmanned. B of A was in receivership, and not doing so hot at that, as the fact that they had let out their executive floors to a discount business hotel testified.

The room was fine, though—small and windowless, but fine: power, shower, toilet, and bed, all he demanded in a hotel room. He ate the packet of nuts he'd bought at the airport before jumping on the T and then checked his email. He had more of it than he could possibly answer—he didn't think he'd ever had an empty in-box.

But he picked off anything that looked important, including a note from his ex, who was now living in the Keys on a squatter beach and wanted to know if he could loan her a hundred bucks. No sense of how she'd pay him back without work. But Michelle was resourceful and probably good for it. He paypalled it to her, feeling like a sucker for hoping that she might repay it in person. He'd been single since she'd left him the year before and he was lonely and hard up.

He'd landed at two and by the time he was done with all the bullshit, it was after dinnertime and he was hungry as hell. Boston was full of taco wagons and kebab stands that he'd passed on the walk in, and he hustled out onto the street to see if any were still open. He got a huge garlicky kebab and ate it in the lee of a frozen ATM shelter, wolfing it without tasting it.

He went and scouted the location of the new ride. He'd gotten wind of it online—none of his idiot colleagues could be bothered to read the public email lists of the competitors they were supposedly in charge of oppo researching. Shaking loose the budget to get a discount flight to Boston had been a major coup, requiring horse-trading, blackmail, and passive-aggressive gaming of the system. With the ridiculously low per diem and hotel allowance, he'd still go home a couple hundred bucks out of pocket. Why did he even do his job? He should just play by the rules and get nothing done.

And get fired. Or passed up for promotion, which was practically the same thing.

The new ride was in an impressive urban mall. He'd spent his college years in Philly and had passed many a happy day in malls like this one, cruising for girls or camping out on a bench with his books and a smoothie. Unlike the crappy roadside malls of Florida, there had been nothing but the best stores in them, the property values too high to make anything but high-margin, high-turnover, high-ticket shops viable.

So it was especially sad to see this mall turned over to the junky stalls and junkier ride—like a fat, washed-up supermodel sentenced to a talk-show appearance for her shoplifting arrests. He approached the doors with trepidation. He was resolved not to buy anything from the market—no busts or contact lenses—and had stuck his wallet in his front pocket on the way over.

The mall was like a sauna. He shucked his jacket and sweater and hung them over one arm. The whole ground floor had been given over to flimsy market stalls. He skulked among them, trying to simultaneously take note of their contents and avoid their owners' notice.

He came to realize that he needn't skulk. It seemed like half of Boston had turned out—not just young people, either. There were plenty of tweedy academics, big working-class Southie boys with thick accents, recent immigrants with Scandie-chic clothes. They chattered and laughed and mixed freely and ate hot food out of huge cauldrons or off of clever electric grills. The smells made his stomach growl, even though he'd just polished off a kebab the size of his head.

The buzz of the crowd reminded him of something, what was it? A premiere, that was it. When they opened a new ride or area at the Park, there was the same sense of thrilling anticipation, of excitement and eagerness. That made it worse—these people had no business being this excited about something so . . . lowbrow? Cheap? Whatever it was, it wasn't worthy.

They were shopping like fiends. A mother with a baby on her hip pushed past him, her stroller piled high with shopping bags screened with giant, pixelated Belgian pastries. She was laughing and the baby on her hip was laughing, too.

He headed for the escalator, whose treads had been anodized in bright colors, something he'd never seen before. He let it carry him upstairs, but looked down, and so he was nearly at the top before he realized that the guy from the Florida ride was standing there, handing out fliers and staring at Sammy like he knew him from somewhere.

It was too late to avoid him. Sammy put on his best castmember smile. "Hello there!"

The guy grinned and wiggled his eyebrow. "I know you from somewhere," he said slowly.

"From Florida," Sammy said, with an apologetic shrug. "I came up to see the opening."

"No *way!*" The guy had a huge smile now, looked like he was going to hug him. "You're shitting me!"

"What can I say? I'm a fan."

"That's *incredible.* Hey, Tjan, come here and meet this guy. What's your name?"

Sammy tried to think of another name, but drew a blank. "Mickey," he said at last, kicking himself.

"Tjan, this is Mickey. He's a regular on the ride in Florida and he's come up here just to see the opening."

Tjan had short hair and sallow skin, and dressed like an accountant, but his eyes were bright and sharp as they took Sammy in, looking him up and down quickly. "Well that's certainly flattering." He reached into his creased blazer and pulled out a slip of paper. "Have a couple comp tickets then—the least we can do for your loyalty." The paper was festooned with holograms and smart cards and raised bumps containing RFIDs, but Sammy knew that you could buy standard anticounterfeiting stock like it from a mail-order catalog.

"That's mighty generous of you," he said, shaking Tjan's dry, firm hand.

"Our pleasure," the other guy said. "Better get in line, though, or you're gonna be waiting a long, long time." He had a satisfied expression. Sammy saw that what he'd mistaken for a crowd of people was in fact a long, jostling queue stretching all the way around the escalator mezzanine and off one of the mall's side corridors.

Feeling like he'd averted a disaster, Sammy followed the length of the queue until he came to its end. He popped in a headphone and set up his headline reader to text-to-speech his day's news. He'd fallen behind, what with the air travel and all. Most of the stuff in his cache came in from his coworkers, and it was the most insipid crap anyway, but he had to listen to it or he'd be odd man out at the watercooler when he got back.

He listened with half an ear and considered the gigantic crowd stretching away as far as the eye could see. Compared with the reopening of Fantasyland, it was nothing—goths from all over the world had flocked to central Florida for that, Germans and Greeks and Japanese and even some from Mumbai and Russia. They'd filled the park to capacity, thrilled with the delightful perversity of chirpy old Disney World remade as a goth theme park.

But a line this long in Boston, in the dead of winter, for something whose sole attraction was that there was another one like it by a shitty forgotten B road outside of Miami? Christ on an Omnimover.

The line moved, just a little surge, and there was a cheer all down the mall's length. People poured past him, headed for the line's tail, vibrating with excitement. But the line didn't move again for five minutes, then ten. Then another surge, but maybe that was just people crowding together more. Some of the people in line were drinking beers out of paper bags and getting raucous.

"What's going on?" someone hollered from behind him. The cry was taken up, and then the line shuddered and moved forward some. Then nothing.

Thinking, *Screw this,* Sammy got out of line and walked to the front. Tjan was there, working the velvet rope, letting people through in dribs and drabs. He caught sight of Sammy and gave him a solemn nod. "They're all taking too long to ride," he said. "I tell them fifteen minutes max, get back in line if you want to see more, but what can you do?"

Sammy nodded sympathetically. The guy with the funny eyebrow put in an appearance from behind the heavy black curtains. "Send through two more," he said, and grabbed Sammy, tugging him in.

Behind the curtain, it was dim and spotlit, almost identical to Florida, and half a dozen vehicles waited. Sammy slid into one and let the spiel wash over him.

THERE WAS A TIME WHEN AMERICA HELD OUT THE PROMISE OF A NEW WAY OF LIVING AND WORKING. THE NEW WORK BOOM OF THE TEENS WAS A PERIOD OF UNPARALLELED INVENTION, A CAMBRIAN EX-PLOSION OF CREATIVITY NOT SEEN SINCE THE TIME OF EDISON—AND UNLIKE EDISON, THE PEOPLE WHO INVENTED THE NEW WORK REVO-LUTION WEREN'T RIP-OFF ARTISTS AND FRAUDS.

The layout was slightly different due to the support pillars, but as similar to the Florida version as geography allowed. Robots humped underfoot, moving objects, keeping them in sync with the changes in Florida. He'd read on the message boards that Florida would stay open late so that the riders could collaborate with the attendees at the Boston premiere, tweeting back and forth to one another.

The other chairs in the ride crawled around each exhibit, reversing and turning slowly. Riders brought their chairs up alongside one another and conferred in low voices, over the narration from the scenery. He thought he saw a couple making out—a common enough occurrence in dark rides that he'd even exploited a few times when planning out rides that would be likely to attract amorous teenagers. They had a key demographic: too young to leave home, old enough to pay practically anything for a private spot to score some nookie.

The air smelled of 3-D printer, the cheap smell of truck stops where vending machines outputted cheap kids' toys. Here it wasn't cheap, though: here it smelled futuristic, like the first time someone had handed him a printed prop for one of his rides—it had been a head for an updated Small World ride. Then it had smelled like something foreign and new and exciting and frightening, like the first days of a different world.

Smelling that again, remembering the crowds outside waiting to get in, Sammy started to get a sick feeling, the kebab rebounding on him. Moving as if in a dream, he reached down into his lap and drew out a small utility knife. There would be infrared cameras, but he knew from experience that they couldn't see through ride vehicles.

Slowly, he fingered the access panel's underside until he found a loose corner. He snicked out the knife's little blade—he'd brought an entire suitcase just so he could have a checked bag to store this in—and tugged at the cables inside. He sawed at them with small movements, feeling the copper wires inside the insulation give way one strand at a time. The chair moved jerkily, then not at all. He snipped a few more wires just to be sure, then tucked them all away.

"Hey!" he called. "My chair's dead!" He had fetched up in a central pathway where the chairs tried to run cloverleafs around four displays. A couple chairs swerved around him. He thumped the panel dramatically, then stepped out and shook his head. He contrived to step on three robots on the way to another chair.

"Is yours working?" he asked the kid riding in it, all of ten years old and of indefinite gender.

"Yeah," the kid said. It scooted over. "There's room for both of us, get in."

Christ, don't they have stranger danger in the north? He climbed in beside the kid and contrived to slide one sly hand under the panel. Teasing out the wires the second time was easier, even one-handed. He sliced through five large bundles this time before the chair ground to a halt, its gyros whining and rocking it from side to side.

The kid looked at him and frowned. "These things are shit," he said with real vehemence, climbing down and kicking one of its tires, and then kicking a couple of the floor-level robots for good measure. They'd landed in another great breakdown spot: directly in front of a ranked display of ray-gun-shaped appliances and objects. He remembered seeing that one in its nascent stage, back in Florida—just a couple of toy guns, which were presently joined by three more, then there were ten, then fifty, then a high wall of them, striking and charming. The chair's breakdown position neatly blocked the way.

"Guess we'd better walk out," he said. He stepped on a couple more robots, making oops noises. The kid enthusiastically kicked robots out of its way. Chairs swerved around them as other riders tried to navigate. They were approaching the exit when Sammy spotted a charge plate for the robots. They were standard issue for robotic vacuum cleaners and other semiautonomous appliances, and he'd had one in his old apartment. They were supposed to be safe as anything, but a friend's toddler had crawled over to his and shoved a stack of dimes into its recessed jack and one of them had shorted it out in a smoking, fizzing fireworks display.

"You go on ahead, I'm going to tie my shoes."

Sammy bent down beside the charge plate, his back to the kid and the imagined cameras that were capturing his every move, and slipped the stack of coins he'd taken from his pocket into the little slot where the robots inserted their charging stamen.

The ensuing shower of sparks was more dramatic than he'd remembered—maybe it was the darkened room. The kid shrieked and ran for the EXIT sign, and he took off, too, at a good clip. They'd get the ride up and running soon enough, but maybe not tonight, not if they couldn't get the two chairs he'd toasted out of the room.

There were the beginnings of chaos at the exit. There was that Tjan character, giving him an intense look. He tried to head for the down escalator, but Tjan cut him off.

"What's going on in there?"

"Damnedest thing," he said, trying to keep his face composed. "My chair died. Then another one—a little kid was riding in it. Then there was a lot of electrical sparks, and I walked out. Crazy."

Tjan cocked his head. "I hope you're not hurt. We could have a doctor look at you; there are a couple around tonight."

It had never occurred to Sammy that professional types might turn out for a ride like this, but of course it was obvious. There were probably off-duty cops, local politicians, lawyers, and the like.

"I'm fine," he said. "Don't worry about me. Maybe you should send someone in for the people still in there, though?"

"That's being taken care of. I'm just sorry you came all the way from Florida for this kind of disappointment. That's just brutal." Tjan's measuring stare was even more intense.

"Uh, it's OK. I had meetings here this week. This was just a cool bonus."

"Who do you work for, Mickey?"

Shit.

"Insurance company," he said.

"That'd be Norwich Union, then, right? They've got a headquarters here."

Sammy knew how this went. Norwich Union didn't have headquarters here. Or they did. He'd have to outguess Tjan with his answer.

"Are you going to stay open tonight?"

Tjan nodded, though it wasn't clear whether he was nodding because he was answering in the affirmative or because his suspicions had been confirmed.

"Well then, I should be going."

Tjan put out a hand. "Oh, please stay. I'm sure we'll be running soon; you should get a whole ride through."

"No, really, I have to go." He shook off the hand and pelted down the escalator and out into the freezing night. His blood sang in his ears. They probably wouldn't get the ride running that night at all. They probably would send that whole carnival crowd home, disappointed. He'd won some kind of little victory over something.

He'd felt more confident of his victory when he was concerned with the guy with the funny eyebrow—with Perry. He'd seemed little more than a bum, a vag. But this Tjan reminded him of the climbers he'd met through his career at Walt Disney World: keenly observant and fast formulators of strategies. Someone who could add two and two before you'd know that there was such a thing as four.

Sammy walked back to his hotel as quickly as he could, given the icy sidewalks underfoot, and by the time he got to the lobby of the old office tower his face hurt—forehead, cheeks, and nose. He'd booked his return flight for a day later, thinking he'd do more reccies of the new site before writing his report and heading home, but there was no way he was facing down that Tjan guy again.

What had prompted him to sabotage the ride? It was something primeval, something he hadn't been in any real control of. He'd been in some kind of fugue state. But he'd packed the little knife in his suitcase and he'd slipped it into his pocket before leaving the room. So how instinctive could it possibly have been?

He had a vision of the carnival atmosphere in the market stalls outside and knew that even after the ride had broken down, the crowd had lingered, laughing and browsing and enjoying a night's respite from the world and the cold city. The Whos down in Who-ville had gone on singing even after he'd Grinched their ride.

That was it. The ride didn't just make use of user-created content—it *was* user-created content. He could never convince his bosses in Orlando to let him build anything remotely like this, and given enough time, it would surely overtake them. That Tjan—someone like him wouldn't be involved if there wasn't some serious money opportunity on the line.

He'd seen the future that night and he had no place in it.

It only took a week on the Boston ride before they had their third and fourth nodes. The third was outside of San Francisco, in a gigantic ghost mall that was already being used as a flea market. They had two former anchor stores, one of which was being squatted by artists who needed studio space. The other one made a perfect location for a new ride, and the geeks who planned on building it had cut their teeth building elaborate Burning Man confectioneries together, so Perry gave them his blessing.

The fourth was to open in Raleigh, in the Research Triangle, where the strip malls ran one into the next. The soft-spoken, bitingly ironic southerners who proposed it were the daughters of old IBM blue-tie stalwarts, who'd been running a women's tech collective since they realized they couldn't afford college and dropped out together. They wanted to see how much admission they could charge if they let it be known that they would plow their profits into scholarship funds for local women.

Perry couldn't believe that these people wanted to open their own rides, nor that they thought they needed his permission to do so. He was reminded of the glory days of New Work, when every day there were fifty New Work sites with a hundred new gizmos, popping up on the mailing lists, looking for distributors, recruiting, competing, swarming, arguing, forming and reforming. Watching Tjan cut the deals whereby these people were granted permission to open their own editions of the ride felt like that, and weirder still.

"Why do they need our permission? The API's wide open. They can just implement. Are they sheep or something?"

Tjan gave him an old-fashioned look. "They're being polite, Perry—they're giving you face for being the progenitor of the ride."

"I don't like it," Perry said. "I didn't get anyone's permission to include their junk in the ride. When we get a printer to clone something that someone brings here, we don't get their permission. Why the hell is seeking permission considered so polite? Shit, why not send me a letter asking me if I mind receiving an email? Where does it end?"

"They're trying to be nice to you, Perry, that's all."

"Well I don't like it," Perry said. "How about this: from now on when someone asks for permission we tell them no, we don't give out *or* withhold permission for joining the network, but we hope that they'll join it anyway. Maybe put up an FAQ on the site."

"You'll just confuse people."

"I won't be confusing them, man! I'll be educating them!"

"How about if you add a Creative Commons license to it? Some of them are very liberal."

"I don't *want* to license this. You have to *own* something to license it. A license is a way of saying, 'Without this license, you're forbidden to do this.' You don't need a license to click a link and load a webpage—no one has to give you permission to do this and no one could take it away from you. Licensing just gives people even worse ideas about ownership and permission and property!"

"It's your show," Tjan said.

"No it *isn't*! That's the *point*!"

"OK, OK, it's not your show. But we'll do it your way. You are a lovable, cranky weirdo, you know it?"

They did it Perry's way. He was scheduled to go back to Florida a few days later, but he changed his ticket to go out to San Francisco and meet with the crew who were implementing the ride there. One of them taught interaction design at SFSU and brought him in to talk to the students. He wasn't sure what he was going to talk to them about, but when he got there, he found himself telling the story of how he and Lester and Tjan and Suzanne and Kettlebelly had built and lost the New Work movement, without even trying. It was a fun story to tell from start to finish, and they talked through the lunch break and then a group of students took him to a bar in the Mission with a big outdoor patio where he went on telling war stories until the sun had set and he'd drunk so much beer he couldn't tell stories any longer.

They were all ten or fifteen years younger than him, and the girls were pretty and androgynous and the boys were also pretty and androgynous, not that he really swung that way. Still, it was fine being surrounded by the catcalling, joking, bullshitting crowd of young, pretty, flirty people. They hugged him a lot, and two of the prettier girls (who, he later realized, were a lot more interested in each other than him) took him back to a capsule hotel built across three parking spots and poured him into bed and tucked him in.

He had a burrito the size of a football for breakfast, stuffed with shredded pig parts and two kinds of sloppy beans. He washed it down with a quart of a cinnamon-rice drink called horchata that was served ice-cold and did wonders for his hangover.

A couple hours' noodling on his laptop and a couple bags of Tecate later and he was feeling almost human. Early mariachis strolled the street with electric guitars that controlled little tribes of dancing, singing knee-high animatronics, belting out old José Alfredo Jiménez tunes.

It was shaping up to be a good day. His laptop rang and he screwed in his headset and started talking to Tjan.

"Man, this place is excellent," he said. "I had the best night I've had in years last night."

"Well then you'll love this: there's a crew in Madison that want to do the same thing and could use a little guidance. They spoke to me this morning and said they'd be happy to spring for the airfare. Can you make a six o'clock flight at SFO?"

They gave him cheese in Madison and introduced him to the biohackers who were the spiritual progeny of the quirky moment when Madison was one of six places where stem cells could be legally researched. The biohackers gave him the willies. One had gills. One glowed in the dark. One was orange and claimed to photosynthesize.

He got his hosts to bring him to the rathskeller, where they sat down to comedy-sized beers and huge, suspicious steaming wursts.

"Where's your site?"

"We were thinking of building one—there's a lot of farmland around here." Either the speaker was sixteen years old or Perry was getting to be such a drunken old fart that everyone seemed sixteen. He wasn't old enough to shave, anyway. Perry tried to remember his name and couldn't. Jet lag or sleep dep or whatever.

"That's pretty weird. Everywhere else, they're just moving into spaces that have been left vacant."

"We haven't got many of those. All the offices and stuff are being occupied by heavily funded startups."

"Heavily funded startups? In this day and age?"

"Superbabies," the kid said with a shrug. "It's all anyone here thinks about anymore. That and cancer cures. I think superbabies are crazy—imagine being a twenty-year-old superbaby, with two-decade-old technology in your genes. In your germ line! Breeding other obsolete superbabies. Crazy. But the Chinese are investing heavily."

"So no dead malls? Christ, that's like running out of sand or hydrogen or something. Are we still in America?"

The kid laughed. "The campus is building more student housing because none of us can afford the rents around here anymore. But there's lots of farmland, like I said. Won't be a problem to throw up a prefab and put the ride inside it. It'll be like putting up a haunted cornfield at Halloween. Used to do that every year to raise money for the ACLU, back in Nebraska."

"Wow." He wanted to say, *They have the ACLU in Nebraska?* but he knew that wasn't fair. The midwesterners he'd met had generally been kick-ass geeks and hackers, so he had no call to turn his nose up at this kid. "So why do you want to do this?"

The kid grinned. "Because there's got to be a way to do something cool without moving to New York. I like it around here. Don't want to live in some run-down defaulted shit-built condo where the mice are hunchbacked. Like the wide-open spaces. But I don't want to be a farmer or an academic or run a student bar. All that stuff is a dead end, I can see it from here. I mean, who drinks beer anymore? There's much sweeter highs out there in the real world."

Perry looked at his beer. It was in a themed stein with Germano-Gothic gingerbread worked into the finish. It felt like it had been printed from some kind of ceramic-epoxy hybrid. You could get them at traveling carny midways, too.

"I like beer," he said.

"But you're—" The kid broke off.

"Old," Perry said. " 'S OK. You're what, sixteen?"

"Twenty-one," the kid said. "I'm a late bloomer. Devoting resources to more important things than puberty."

Two more kids slid into their booth, a boy and a girl who actually did look twenty-one. "Hey, Luke," the girl said, kissing him on the cheek.

Luke, that was his name. Perry came up with a mnemonic so he wouldn't forget it again—Nebraska baby-faced farm boy, that was like Luke Skywalker. He pictured the kid swinging a lightsaber and knew he'd keep the name for good now.

"This is Perry Gibbons," Luke said. "Perry, this is Hilda and Ernie. Guys, Perry's the guy who built the ride I was telling you about."

Ernie shook his hand. "Man, that's the coolest shit I've ever seen, wow. What the hell are you doing here? I love that stuff. Wow."

Hilda flicked his ear. "Stop drooling, fanboy," she said.

Ernie rubbed his ear. Perry nodded uncertainly.

"Sorry. It's just—well, I'm a big fan is all."

"That's really nice of you," Perry said. He'd met a couple people in Boston and San Francisco who called themselves his fans, and he hadn't known what to say to them, either. Back in the New Work days he'd meet reporters who called themselves fans, but that was just blowing smoke. Now he was meeting people who seemed to really mean it. Not many, thank God.

"He's just like a puppy," Hilda said, pinching Ernie's cheek. "All enthusiasm."

Ernie rubbed his cheek. Luke reached out abruptly and tousled both of their hair. "These two are going to help me build the ride," he said. "Hilda's an amazing fundraiser. Last year she ran the fundraising for a whole walk-in clinic."

"Women's health clinic or something?" Perry asked. He was starting to sober up a little. Hilda was one of those incredible, pneumatic midwestern girls that he'd seen at five-minute intervals since getting off his flight in Madison. He didn't think he'd ever met one like her.

"No," Hilda said. "Metabolic health. Lots of people get the fatkins treatment at puberty, either because their fatkins parents talk them into it or because they hate their baby fat."

Perry shook his head. "Come again?"

"You think eating ten thousand calories a day is easy? It's hell on your digestive system. Not to mention you spend a fortune on food. A lot of people get to college and just switch to high-calorie powdered supplements because they can't afford enough real food to stay healthy, so you've got all these kids sucking down vanilla slurry all day just to keep from starving. We provide counseling and mitigation therapies to kids who want it."

"And when they get out of college—do they get the treatment again?"

"You can't. The mitigation's permanent. People who take it have to go through the rest of their lives taking supplements and eating sensibly and exercising."

"Do they get fat?"

She looked away, then down, then back up at him. "Yes, most of them do. How could they not? Everything around them is geared at people who need to eat five times as much as they do. Even the salads all have protein powder mixed in with them. But it is *possible* to eat right. You've never had the treatment, have you?"

Perry shook his head. "Trick metabolism, though. I can eat like a hog and not put on an ounce."

Hilda reached out and squeezed his bicep. "Really—and I suppose that all that lean muscle there is part of your trick metabolism, too?"

She left her hand where it was.

"OK, I do a fair bit of physical labor, too. But I'm just saying—if they get fat again after they reverse the treatment—"

"There are worse things than being fat."

Her hand still hadn't moved. He looked at Ernie, whom he'd assumed was her boyfriend, to see how he was taking it. Ernie was looking somewhere else, though, across the rathskeller, at the huge TV that was showing competitive multiplayer gaming, apparently some kind of championships. It was as confusing as a hundred air-hockey games being played on the same board, with thousands of zipping, jumping, firing entities and jump cuts so fast that Perry couldn't imagine how you'd make sense of it.

The girl's hand was still on his arm, and it was warm. His mouth was dry but more beer would be a bad idea. "How about some water?" he said, in a bit of a croak.

Luke jumped up to get some, and a silence fell over the table. "So this clinic, how'd you fundraise for it?"

"Papercraft," she said. "I have a lot of friends who are into paper folding and we modded a bunch of patterns. We did really big pieces, too—bed frames, sofas, kitchen tables, chairs—"

"Like actual furniture?"

"Like actual furniture," she said with a solemn nod. "We used huge sheets of paper and treated them with stiffening, waterproofing, and fireproofing agents. We did a frat house's outdoor bar and sauna, with a wind dynamo— I even made a steam engine."

"You made a steam engine out of paper?" He was agog.

"You mean to say that *you're* surprised by building stuff out of unusual materials?"

Perry laughed. "Point taken."

"We just got a couple hundred students to do some folding in their spare time and then sold it on. Everyone on campus needs bookshelves, so we started with those—using accordion-folded arched supports under each shelf. We could paint or print designs on them, too, but a lot of people liked them all-white. Then we did chairs, desks, kitchenette sets, place mats—you name it. I called the designs 'Multiple Origami.'"

Perry sprayed beer out his nose. "That's awesome!" he said, wiping up the mess with a kleenex that she extracted from a folded paper purse. Looking closely, he realized that the white baseball cap she was wearing was also folded out of paper.

She laughed and rummaged some more in her handbag, coming up with a piece of stiff card. Working quickly and nimbly, she gave it a few deft folds along pre-scored lines, and a moment later she was holding a baseball hat that was the twin of the one she was wearing. She leaned over the table and popped it on his head.

Luke came back with the water and set it down between them, pouring out glasses for everyone.

"Smooth lid," he said, touching the bill of Perry's cap.

"Thanks," Perry said, draining his water and pouring another glass. "Well, you people certainly have some pretty cool stuff going on here."

"This is a great town," Luke said expansively, as though he had traveled extensively and settled on Madison, Wisconsin, as a truly international hot spot. "We're going to build a kick-ass ride."

"You going to make it all out of paper?"

"Some of it, anyway," Luke said. "Hilda wouldn't have it any other way, right?"

"This one's your show, Luke," she said. "I'm just a fundraiser."

"Anyone hungry?" Hilda said. "I want to go eat something that doesn't have unidentified organ meat mixed in."

"Go on without me," Ernie said. "I got money on this game."

"Homework," Luke said.

Perry had just eaten, and had planned on spending this night in his room catching up on email. "Yeah, I'm starving," he said. He felt like a high-school kid, but in a good way.

They went out for Ukrainian food, which Perry had never had before, but the crepes and the blood sausage were tasty enough. Mostly, though, he was paying attention to Hilda, who was running down her war stories from the Multiple Origami fundraiser. There were funny ones, sad ones, scary ones, triumphant ones.

Every one of her stories reminded him of one of his own. She was an organizer and so was he and they'd been through practically the same shit. They drank gallons of coffee afterward, getting chucked out when the restaurant closed and migrating to a café on the main drag where they had low tables and sofas, and they never stopped talking.

"You know," Hilda said, stretching and yawning, "it's coming up on four AM."

"No way," he said, but his watch confirmed it. "Christ." He tried to think of a casual way of asking her to sleep with him. For all their talking, they'd hardly touched on romance—or maybe there'd been romance in every word.

"I'll walk you to your hotel," she said.

"Hey, that's really nice of you," he said. His voice sounded fakey and forced in his ears. All of a sudden, he wasn't tired at all, instead his heart was hammering in his chest and his blood sang in his ears.

There was hardly any talk on the way back to the hotel, just the awareness of her steps and his in time with one another over the cold late-winter streets. No traffic at that hour, and hardly a sound from any of the windows they passed. The town was theirs.

At the door to his hotel—another stack of the ubiquitous capsules, these geared to visiting parents—they stopped. They were looking at one another like a couple of googly-eyed kids at the end of a date in a sitcom.

"Um, what's your major?" he said.

"Pure math," she said.

"I think I know what that is," he said. It was freezing out on the street. "Theory, right?"

"Pure math as opposed to applied math," she said. "Do you really care about this?"

"Um," he said. "Well, yes. But not very much."

"I'll come into your hotel room, but we're not having sex, OK?"

"OK," he said.

There was room enough for the two of them in the capsule, but only just. These were prefabbed in bulk and they came in different sizes—in the Midwest they were large, the ones stacked up in San Francisco parking spots were small. Still, he and Hilda were almost in each other's laps, and he could smell her, feel wisps of her hair tickling his ear.

"You're really nice," he said. Late at night, his ability to be flippant evaporated. He was left with simple truths, simply declared. "I like you a lot."

"Well then you'll have to come back to Madison and check in on the ride, won't you?"

"Um," he said. He had a planning meeting with Luke and the rest of his gang the next day, then he was supposed to be headed for Omaha, where Tjan had set up another crew for him to speak to. At this rate, he would get back to Florida sometime in June.

"Perry, you're not a career activist, are you?"

"Nope," he said. "I hadn't really imagined that there was such a thing."

"My parents. Both of them. Here's what being a career activist means: you are on the road most of the time. When you get on the road, you meet people, have intense experiences with them—like going to war or touring with a band. You fall in love a thousand times. And then you leave all those people behind. You get off a plane, turn some strangers into best friends, get on a plane and forget them until you come back into town, and then you take it all back up again.

"If you want to survive this, you've got to love that. You've got to get off a plane, meet people, fall in love with them, treasure every moment, and know that moments are all you have. Then you get on a plane again and you love them forever. Otherwise, every new meeting is sour because you know how soon it will end. It's like starting to say your summer-camp goodbyes before you've even unpacked your duffel bag. You've got to embrace—or at least forget—that every gig will end in a day or two."

Perry took a moment to understand this, swallowed a couple times, then nodded. Lots of people had come in and out of his factory and his ride over the years. Lester came and went. Suzanne was gone. Tjan was gone but was back again. Kettlebelly was no longer in his life at all, a ghost of a memory with a great smile and good cologne. Already he was forgetting the faces in Boston, the faces in San Francisco. Hilda would be a memory in a month.

Hilda patted his hand. "I have friends in practically every city in America. My folks campaigned for stem cells up and down every red state in the country. I even met superman before he died. He knew my name. I spent ten years on the road with them, back and forth. The Bush years, a couple years afterward. You can live this way and you can be happy, but you've got to have right mind.

"What it means is you've got to be able to say things to people you meet, like, 'You're really nice,' and mean it, really mean it. But you've also got to be cool with the fact that really nice people will fall out of your life every week, twice a week, and fall back into it or not. I think you're very nice, too, but we're not gonna be a couple, ever. Even if we slept together tonight, you'd be gone tomorrow night. What you need to ask yourself is whether you want to have friends in every city who are glad to see you when you get off the plane, or ex-girlfriends in every city who might show up with their new boyfriends, or not at all."

"Are you telling me this to explain why we're not going to sleep together? I just figured you were dating that guy, Ernie."

"Ernie's my brother," she said. "And yeah, that's kind of why I'm telling you this. I've never gone on what you might call a date. With my friends, it tends to be more like, you work together, you hang out together, you catch yourself looking into one another's eyes a couple times, then you do a little circling around and then you end up in your bed or their bed having hard, energetic sex and then you sort out some details and then it lasts as long as it lasts. We've done a compressed version of that tonight, and we're up to the sex, and so I thought we should lay some things on the table, you should forgive the expression."

Perry thought back to his double date with Lester. The girl had been pretty and intelligent and would have taken him home if he'd made the least effort. He hadn't, though. This girl was inappropriate in so many ways: young, rooted to a city thousands of miles from home—why had he brought her back to the hotel?

A thought struck him. "Why do you think I'm going to be getting on and off planes for the rest of my life? I've got a home to get to."

"You haven't been reading the message boards, have you?"

"Which message boards?"

"For ride builders. There are projects starting up everywhere. People like what they've heard and what they've seen, and they remember you from the old days and want to get in on the magic you're going to bring. A lot of us know each other anyway, from other joint projects. Everyone's passing the hat to raise your airfare and arguing about who's sofa you're going to stay on."

He'd known that they were there. There were always message boards. But they were just talk—he never bothered to read them. That was Lester's job. He wanted to make stuff, not chatter. "Jesus, when the hell was someone going to tell me?"

"Your guy in Boston, we've been talking to him. He said not to bug you, that you were busy enough as it is."

He did, did he? In the old days, Tjan had been in charge of planning and he'd been in charge of the ideas: in charge of what to plan. Had they come full circle without him noticing? If they had, was that so bad?

"Man, I was really looking forward to spending a couple nights in my own bed."

"Is it much more comfortable than this one?" She thumped the narrow coffin bed, which was surprisingly comfortable, adjustable, heated, and massaging.

He snorted. "OK, I sleep on a futon on the floor back home, but it's the principle of the thing. I just miss home, I guess."

"So go home for a couple days after this stop, or the next one. Charge up your batteries and do your laundry. But I have a feeling that home is going to be your suitcase pretty soon, Perry my dear." Her voice was thick with sleep, her eyes heavy-lidded and bleary.

"You're probably right." He yawned as he spoke. "Hell, I know you're right. You're a real smarty."

"And I'm too tired to go home," she said, "so I'm a smarty who's staying with you."

He was suddenly wide awake, his heart thumping. "Um, OK," he said, trying to sound casual.

He turned back the sheets, then, standing facing into the cramped corner, took off his jeans and shoes and socks, climbing in between the sheets in his underwear and tee. There were undressing noises—exquisite ones—behind him and then she slithered in and snuggled up against him. With a jolt, he realized that her bare breasts were pressed to his back. Her arm came around him and rested on his stomach, which jumped like a spring uncoiling. He felt certain his erection was emitting a faint cherry red glow. Her breath was on his neck.

He thought about casually rolling onto his back so that he could kiss her, but remembered her admonition that they would not be having sex. Her fingertips traced small circles on his stomach. Each time they grazed his navel, his stomach did a flip.

He was totally awake now, and when her lips very softly—so softly he barely felt it—brushed against the base of his skull, he let out a soft moan. Her lips returned, and then her teeth, worrying at the tendons at the back of his neck with increasing roughness, an exquisite pain-pleasure that was electric. He was panting, her hand was flat on his stomach now, gripping him. His erection strained toward it.

Her hips ground against him and she moved her mouth toward his ear, nipping at it, the tip of her tongue touching the whorls there. Her hand was on the move now, sliding over his ribs, her fingertips at his nipple, softly and then harder, giving it an abrupt hard pinch that had some fingernail in it, like a bite from little teeth. He yelped and she giggled in his ear, sending shivers up his spine.

He reached back behind him awkwardly and put his hand on her ass, discovering that she was bare there, too. It was wide and hard, foam rubber over steel, and he kneaded it, digging his fingers in. She groaned in his ear and tugged him onto his back.

As soon as his shoulders hit the narrow bed, she was on him, her elbows on his biceps, pinning him down, her breasts in his face, fragrant and soft. Her hot, bare crotch ground against his underwear. He bit at her tits, hard little bites that made her gasp. He found a stiff nipple and sucked it into his mouth, beating at it with his tongue. She pressed her crotch harder against his, hissed something that might have been *yesssss*.

She straightened up so that she was straddling him and looking imperiously down on him. Her braids swung before her. Her eyes were exultant. Her face was set in an expression of fierce concentration as she rocked on him.

He dug his fingers into her ass again, all the way around, so that they brushed against her labia, her asshole. He pulled at her, dragging her up his body, tugging her vagina toward his mouth. Once she saw what he was after, she knee-walked up the bed in three or four quick steps and then she was on his face. Her smell and her taste and her texture and temperature filled his senses, blotting out the room, blotting out introspection, blotting out everything except for the sweet urgency.

He sucked at her labia before slipping his tongue up her length, letting it tickle her ass, her opening, her clit. In response, she ground against him, planting her opening over his mouth and he tongue-fucked her in hard, fast strokes. She reached back and took hold of his cock, slipping her small, strong hand under the waistband of his boxers and curling it around his rigid shaft, pumping vigorously.

He moaned into her pussy and that set her shuddering. Now he had her clit sucked into his mouth and he was lapping at its engorged length with short strokes. Her thighs were clamped over his ears, but he could still make out her cries, timed with the shuddering of her thighs, the spasmodic grip on his cock.

Abruptly she rolled off of him and the world came back. They hadn't kissed yet. They hadn't said a word. She lay beside him, half on top of him, shuddering and making kittenish sounds. He kissed her softly, then more forcefully. She bit at his lips and his tongue, sucking it into her mouth and chewing at it while her fingernails raked his back.

Her breathing became more regular and she tugged at the waistband of his boxers. He got the message and yanked them off, his cock springing free and rocking slightly, twitching in time with his pulse. She smiled a cat-ate-the-canary grin and went to work kissing his neck, his chest—hard bites on his nipples that made him yelp and arch his back—his stomach, his hips, his pubes, his thighs. The teasing was excruciating and exquisite. Her juices dried on his face, the smell caught in his nose, refreshing his eros with every breath.

Her tongue lapped eagerly at his balls like a cat with a saucer of milk. Long, slow strokes, over his sack, over the skin between his balls and his thighs, over his perineum, tickling his ass as he'd tickled hers. She pulled back and spat out a pube and laughed and dove back in, sucking softly at his sack, then, in one swift motion, taking his cock to the hilt.

He shouted and then moaned and her head bobbed furiously along the length of his shaft, her hand squeezing his balls. It took only moments before he dug his hands hard into the mattress and groaned through clenched teeth and fired spasm after spasm down her throat, her nose in his pubes, his cock down her throat to the base. She refused to let him go, swirling her tongue over the head while he was still supersensitive, making him grunt and twitch and buck involuntarily, all the while her hand caressing his balls, rubbing at his prostate over the spot between his balls and his ass.

Finally she worked her way back up his body, licking her lips and kissing as she went.

"Hello," she said as she buried her face in his throat.

"Wow," he said.

"So if you're going to be able to live in the moment and have no regrets, this is a pretty good place to start. It'd be a hell of a shock if we saw each other twice in the next year—are we going to be able to be friends when we do? Will the fact that I fucked your brains out make things awkward?"

"That's why you jumped me?"

"No, not really. I was horny and you're hot. But that's a good post-facto reason."

"I see. You know, you haven't actually fucked my brains out," he said.

"Yet," she said. She retrieved her backpack from beside the bed, dug around in it, and produced a strip of condoms. "Yet."

He licked his lips in anticipation, and a moment later she was unrolling the condom down his shaft with her talented mouth. He laughed and then took her by the waist and flipped her onto her back. She grabbed her ankles and pulled her legs wide and he dove between her, dragging the still-sensitive tip of his cock up and down the length of her vulva a couple times before sawing it in and out of her opening, sinking to the hilt.

He wanted to fuck her gently but she groaned urgent demands in his ear to pound her harder, making satisfied sounds each time his balls clapped against her ass.

She pushed him off her and turned over, raising her ass in the air, pulling her labia apart and looking over her shoulder at him. They fucked doggy-style then, until his legs trembled and his knees ached, and then she climbed on him and rocked back and forth, grinding her clit against his pubis, pushing him so deep inside her. He mauled her tits and felt the pressure build in his balls. He pulled her to him, thrust wildly, and she hissed dirty encouragement in his ear, begging him to fill her, ordering him to pound her harder. The stimulation in his brain and between his legs was too much to bear and he came, lifting them both off the bed with his spasms.

"Wow," he said.

"Yum," she said.

"Jesus, it's eight AM," he said. "I've got to meet with Luke in three hours."

"So let's take a shower now, and set an alarm for half an hour before he's due," she said. "Got anything to eat?"

"That's what I like about you, Hilda," he said. "Businesslike. Vigorous. Living life to the hilt."

Her dimples were pretty and luminous in the hints of light emerging from under the blinds. "Feed me," she said, and nipped at his earlobe.

In the shoebox-sized fridge, he had a cow-shaped brick of Wisconsin cheddar that he'd been given when he stepped off the plane. They broke chunks off it and ate it in bed, then started in on the bag of soy crispies his hosts in San Francisco had given him. They showered slowly together, scrubbing one another's backs, set an alarm, and sacked out for just a few hours before the alarm roused them.

They dressed like strangers, not embarrassed, just too groggy to take much notice of one another. Perry's muscles ached pleasantly, and there was another ache, dull and faint, even more pleasant, in his balls.

Once they were fully clothed, she grabbed him and gave him a long hug, and a warm kiss that started on his throat and moved to his mouth, with just a hint of tongue at the end.

"You're a good man, Perry Gibbons," she said. "Thanks for a lovely night. Remember what I told you, though: no regrets, no looking back. Be happy about this—don't mope, don't miss me. Go on to your next city and make new friends and have new conversations, and when we see each other again, be my friend without any awkwardness. All right?"

"I get it," he said. He felt slightly irritated. "Only one thing. We weren't going to sleep together."

"You regret it?"

"Of course not," he said. "But it's going to make this injunction of yours hard to understand. I'm not good at anonymous one-night stands."

She raised one eyebrow at him. "Earth to Perry: this wasn't anonymous, and it wasn't a one-night stand. It was an intimate, loving relationship that happened to be compressed into a single day."

"Loving?"

"Sure. If I'd been with you for a month or two, I would have fallen in love. You're just my type. So I think of you as someone I love. That's why I want to make sure you understand what this all means."

"You're a very interesting person," he said.

"I'm smart," she said, and cuddled him again. "You're smart. So be smart about this and it'll be forever sweet."

She left him off at the spot where he was supposed to meet Luke and the rest of his planning team to go over schematics and theory and practice. All of these discussions could happen online—they did, in fact—but there was something about the face-to-face connection. The meeting ran six hours before he was finally saved by his impending flight to Nebraska.

Sleep dep came down on him like a hammer as he checked in for his flight and began the ritual security-clearing buck-and-wing. He missed a cue or two and ended up getting a "detailed hand search" but even that didn't wake him up. He fell asleep in the waiting room and in the plane, in the taxi to his hotel.

But when he dropped down onto his hotel bed, he couldn't sleep. The hotel was the spitting image of the one he'd left in Wisconsin, minus Hilda and the musky smell the two of them had left behind after their roll in the hay.

It had been years since he'd had a regular girlfriend, and he'd never missed it. There had been women, high-libido fatkins girls and random strangers, some who came back for a date or two. But no one who'd meant anything or whom he'd wanted to mean anything. The closest he'd come had been—he sat up with a start and realized that the last woman he'd had any strong feelings for had been Suzanne Church.

Kettlewell emerged from New Work rich. He'd taken home large bonuses every year that Kodacell had experienced growth—a better metric than turning an actual ahem profit—and he'd invested in a diverse portfolio that had everything from soybeans to software in it, along with real estate (oops) and fine art. He believed in the New Work, believed in it with every fiber of his being, but an undiverse portfolio was flat-out irresponsible.

The New Work crash had killed the net worth of a lot of irresponsible people.

Living in the Caymans got boring after a year. The kids hated the international school, scuba diving amazed him by going from endlessly, meditatively fascinating to deadly dull in less than a year. He didn't want to sail. He didn't want to get drunk. He didn't want to join the creepy zillionaires on their sex tours of the Caribbean and wouldn't have even if his wife would have stood for it.

A year after the New Work crash, he filed a 1040 with the IRS and paid them forty million dollars in back taxes and penalties, and repatriated his wealth to an American bank.

Now he lived in a renovated housing project on Potrero Hill in San Francisco, all upscale now with restored, kitschy window bars and vintage linoleum and stucco ceilings. He had four units over two floors, with cleverly knocked-through walls and a spiral staircase. The kids freaking loved the staircase.

Suzanne Church called him from SFO to let him know that she was on her way in, having cleared security and customs after a scant hour. He found himself unaccountably nervous about her now, and realized with a little giggle that he had something like a crush on her. Nothing serious—nothing his wife needed to worry about—but she was smart and funny and attractive and incisive and fearless, and it was a hell of a combination.

The kids were away at school and his wife was having a couple of days camping with the girls in Yosemite, which facts lent a little charge to Suzanne's impending visit. He looked up the AirBART schedule and calculated how long he had until she arrived at the Twenty-fourth Street station, a brisk twenty-minute walk from his place.

Minutes, just minutes. He checked the guest room and then did a quick mirror check. His months in the Caymans had given him a deep tan that he'd kept up despite San Francisco's gray skies. He still looked like a surfer, albeit with just a little daddy paunch—he'd gained more weight through his wife's pregnancies than she had, and only hard, aneurysm-inducing cycling over and around Potrero Hill had knocked it off again. His jeans' neat rows of pockets and Möbius seams were a little outdated, but they looked good on him, as did his Hawaiian print shirt with its machine-screw motif.

Finally he plopped down to read a book and waited for Suzanne, and managed to get through a whole page in the intervening ten minutes.

"Kettlebelly!" she hollered as she came through the door. She took him in a hug that smelled of stale airplane and restless sleep and gave him a thorough squeezing.

She held him at arm's length and they sized each other up. She'd been a well-preserved mid-forties when he'd seen her last, buttoned-down in a California-yoga-addict way. Now she was years older, and her time in Russia had given her a forest of smile lines at the corners of her mouth and eyes. She had a sad, wise turn to her face that he'd never seen there before, like a painted Pietà. Her hands had gone a little wrinkly, her knuckles more prominent, but her fingernails were beautifully manicured and her clothes were stylish, foreign, exotic and European.

She laughed huskily and said, "You haven't changed a bit."

"Ouch," he said. "I'm older and wiser, I'll have you know."

"It doesn't show," she said. "I'm older, but no wiser."

He took her hand and looked at the simple platinum band on her finger. "But you're married now—nothing wises you up faster in my experience."

She looked at her hand. "Oh, that. No. That's just to keep the wolves at bay. Married women aren't the same kinds of targets that single ones are. Give me water, and then a beer, please."

Glad to have something to do, he busied himself in the kitchen while she prowled the place. "I remember when these places were bombed-out, real ghettos."

"What did you mean about being a target?"

"St. Pete's, you know. Lawless state. Everyone's on the make. I had a bodyguard most of the time, but if I wanted to go to a restaurant, I didn't want to have to fend off the dating-service mafiyeh who wanted to offer me the deal of a lifetime on a green-card marriage."

"Jeez."

"It's another world, Landon. You know what the big panic there is this week? A cult of ecstatic evangelical Christians who 'hypnotize' women in the shopping malls and steal their babies to raise as soldiers to the Lord. God knows how much of it is true. These guys don't bathe, and dress in heavy coats with big beards all year round. I mean, freaky, really freaky."

"They hypnotize women?"

"Weird, yeah? And the *driving*! Anyone over the age of fifty who knows how to drive got there by being an apparat in the Soviet days, which means that they learned to drive when the roads were empty. They don't signal, they straddle lanes, they can't park—I mean, they *really* can't park. And drunk! Everyone, all the time! You've never seen the like. Imagine a frat party the next day, with a lot of innocent bystanders, hookers, muggers, and pickpockets."

Landon looked at her. She was animated and vivid, thin—age had brought out her cheekbones and her eyes. Had she had a chin tuck? It was common enough—all the medical tourists loved Russia. Maybe she was just well preserved.

She made a show of sniffing herself. "Phew! I need a shower! Can I borrow your facilities?"

"Sure," he said. "I put clean towels out in the kids' bathroom—upstairs and second on the right."

She came down with her fine hair slicked back over her ears, her face scrubbed and shining. "I'm a new woman," she said. "Let's go somewhere and eat something, OK?"

He took her for pupusas at a Salvadoran place on Goat Hill. They slogged up and down the hills and valleys, taking the steps cut into the steep sides, walking past the Painted Ladies—grand, gaudy Victorian wood-frames—and the wobbly, heavy-canvas bubble houses that had sprung up where the big quake and landslides had washed away parts of the hills.

"I'd forgotten that they had hills like that," she said, greedily guzzling an horchata. Her face was streaked with sweat and flushed—it made her look prettier, younger.

"My son and I walk them every day."

"You drag a little kid up and down that every *day*? Christ, that's child abuse!"

"Well, he poops out after a couple of peaks and I end up carrying him."

"You *carry* him? You must be some kind of superman." She gave his bicep a squeeze, then his thigh, then slapped his butt. "A fine specimen. Your wife's a lucky woman."

He grinned. Having his wife in the conversation made him feel less at risk. *That's right, I'm married and we both know it. This is just fun flirting. Nothing more.*

They bit into their pupusas—stuffed cornmeal dumplings filled with grilled pork and topped with shredded cabbage and hot sauce—and grunted and ate and ordered more.

"What are these called again?"

"Pupusas, from El Salvador."

"Humph. In my day, we ate Mexican burritos the size of a football, and we were grateful."

"No one eats burritos anymore," he said, then covered his mouth, aware of how pretentious that sounded.

"Dahling," she said, "burritos are *so* 2005. You *must* try a pupusa—it's what all the most charming Central American peasants are eating now."

They both laughed and stuffed their faces more. "Well, it was either here or one of the fatkins places with the triple-decker stuffed pizzas, and I figured—"

"They really do that?"

"The fatkins? Yeah—anything to get that magical ten thousand calories any day. It must be the same in Russia, right? I mean, they invented it."

"Maybe for fifteen minutes. But most of them don't bother—they get a little metabolic tweak, not a wide-open throttle like that. Christ, what it must do to your digestive system to process ten thousand calories a day!"

"Chacun à son goût," he said, essaying a Gallic shrug.

She laughed again and they ate some more. "I'm starting to feel human at last."

"Me too."

"It's still mid-afternoon, but my circadian thinks it's two AM. I need to do something to stay awake or I'll be up at four tomorrow morning."

"I have some modafinil," he said.

"Swore 'em off. Let's go for a walk."

They did a little more hill climbing and then headed into the Mission and window-shopped the North African tchotchke emporia that were crowding out the Mexican rodeo shops and hairdressers. The skin drums and rattles were laser-etched with intricate designs—Coca-Cola logos, the UN Access to Essential Medicines Charter, Disney characters. It put them both in mind of the old days of the New Work, and the subject came up again, hesitant at first and then a full-bore reminisce.

Suzanne told him stories of the things that Perry and Lester had done that she'd never dared report on, the ways they'd skirted the law and his orders. He told her a few stories of his own, and they rocked with laughter in the street, staggering like drunks, pounding each other on the back, gripping their knees and stomachs and doubling over to the curious glances of the passersby.

It was fine, that day, Landon thought. Some kind of great sorrow that he'd forgotten he'd carried lifted from him and his chest and shoulders expanded and he breathed easy. What was the sorrow? The death of the New Work. The death of the dotcoms. The death of everything he'd considered important and worthy, its fading into tawdry, cheap nostalgia.

They were sitting in the grass in Dolores Park now, watching the dogs and their people romp among the robot pooper-scoopers. He had his arm around her shoulders, like war buddies on a bender (he told himself) and not like a middle-aged man flirting with a woman he hadn't seen in years.

And then they were lying down, the ache of laughter in their bellies, the sun on their faces, the barks and happy shouts around them. Their hands twined together (but that was friendly, too, Arab men held hands walking down the street as a way of showing friendship).

Now their talk had banked down to coals, throwing off an occasional spark when one or the other would remember some funny anecdote and grunt out a word or two that would set them both to gingerly chuckling. But their hands were tied and their breathing was in sync, and their flanks were touching and it wasn't just friendly.

Abruptly, she shook her hand free and rolled on her side. "Listen, married man, I think that's enough of that."

He felt his face go red. His ears rang. "Suzanne—what—" He was sputtering.

"No harm no foul, but let's keep it friendly, all right."

The spell was broken, and the sorrow came back. He looked for the right thing to say. "God I miss it," he said. "Oh, Suzanne, God, I miss it so much, every day."

Her face fell, too. "Yeah." She looked away. "I really thought we were changing the world."

"We were," he said. "We did."

"Yeah," she said again. "But it didn't matter in the end, did it? Now we're older and our work is forgotten and it's all come to nothing. Petersburg is nice, but who gives a shit? Is that what I'm going to do with the rest of my life, hang around Petersburg blogging about the mafiyeh and medical tourism? Just shoot me now."

"I miss the people. I'd meet ten amazing creative geniuses every day—at least! Then I'd give them money and they'd make amazing stuff happen with it. The closest I come to that now is my kids, watching them learn and build stuff, which is really great, don't get me wrong, but it's nothing like the old days."

"I miss Lester. And Perry. Tjan. The whole gang of them, really." She propped herself up on one elbow and then shocked him by kissing him hard on the cheek. "Thanks, Kettlebelly. Thank you so much for putting me in the middle of all that. You changed my life, that's for sure."

He felt the imprint of her lips glowing on his cheek and grinned. "OK, here's an idea: let's go buy a couple bottles of wine, sit on my patio, get a glow on, and then call Perry and see what he's up to."

"Oh, that's a good one," she said. "That's a *very* good one."

A few hours later, they sat on the horsehair club sofa in Kettlewell's living room and hit a number he'd never taken out of his speed dial. "Hi, this is Perry. Leave a message."

"Perry!" they chorused. They looked at each other, at a loss for what to say next, then dissolved in peals of laughter.

"Perry, it's Suzanne and Kettlebelly. What the hell are you up to? Call us!"

They looked at the phone with renewed hilarity and laughed some more. But by the time the sun was setting over Potrero Hill and Suzanne's jet lag was beating her up again, they'd both descended into their own personal funks. Suzanne went up to the guest room and put herself to bed, not bothering to brush her teeth or even change into her nightie.

Perry touched down in Miami in a near coma, his eyes gummed shut by several days' worth of hangovers chased by drink. Sleep deprivation made him uncoordinated, so he tripped twice deplaning, and his voice was a barely audible rasp, his throat sore with a cold he'd picked up in Texas, or maybe it was Oklahoma.

Lester was waiting beyond the luggage carousels, grinning like a holy fool, tall and broad-shouldered and tanned, dressed in fatkins pimped-out finery, all tight stretch fabrics and glitter.

"Oh man, you look like shit," he said, breaking off from the fatkins girl he'd been chatting up. Perry noticed that he was holding his phone, a sure sign that he'd gotten her number.

"Ten," Perry said, grinning through the snotty rheum of his cold. "Ten rides."

"Ten rides?" Lester said.

"Ten. San Francisco, Austin, Minneapolis, Omaha, Oklahoma City, Madison, Bellingham, Chapel Hill, and—" He faltered. "And—shit. I forget. It's all written down."

Lester took his bag from him and set it down, then crushed him in an enormous, muscular hug that whiffed slightly of the ketosis fumes that all the fatkins exuded.

"You did good, cowboy," he said. "Let's mosey back to the ranch, feed you and put you to bed, s'awright?"

"Can I sleep in?"

"Of course."

"Until April?"

Lester laughed and slipped one of Perry's arms over his shoulders and picked up his suitcase and walked them back through the parking lot to his latest hot rod.

Perry breathed in the hot, wet air as they went, feeling it open his chest and nasal passages. His eyes were at half mast, but the sight of the sickly roadside palms, the wandering vendors on the traffic islands with their net bags full of ipods and vpods—he was home, and his body knew it.

Lester cooked him a huge plate of scrambled eggs with corned beef, pastrami, salami, and cheese, with a mountain of sauerkraut on top. "There you go, fatten you up. You're all skinny and haggard, buddy." Lester was an expert at throwing together high-calorie meals on short order.

Perry stuffed away as much as he could, then collapsed on his old bed with his old sheets and his old pillows, and in seconds he was sleeping the best sleep he'd had in months.

When he woke the next day, his cold had turned into a horrible, wet, crusty thing that practically had his face glued to his pillow. Lester came in, took a good look at him, and came back with a quart of fresh orange juice, a pot of tea, and a stack of dry toast, along with a pack of cold pills.

"Take *all* of this and then come down to the ride when you're ready. I'll hold down the fort for another couple days if that's what it takes."

Perry spent the day in his bathrobe, shuttling between the living room and the sun chairs on the patio, letting the heat bake some of the snot out of his head. Lester's kindness and his cold made him nostalgic for his youth, when his father doted on his illnesses.

Perry's father was a little man. Perry—no giant himself—was taller than the old man by the time he turned thirteen. His father had always reminded him of some clever furry animal, a raccoon or badger. He had tiny hands and his movements were small and precise and careful.

They were mostly cordial and friendly, but distant. His father worked as a CAD/CAM manager in a machine shop, though he'd started out his career as a plain old machinist. Of all the machinists he'd started with at the shop, only he had weathered the transition to the new computerized devices. The others had all lost their jobs or taken early retirement or just quit, but his father had taken to CAD/CAM with total abandon, losing himself in the screens and staggering home bleary after ten or fifteen hours in front of the screen.

But that all changed when Perry took ill. Perry's father loved to play nurse. He'd book off from work and stay home, ferrying gallons of tea and beef broth, flat ginger ale and dry toast, cold tablets and cough syrup. He'd open the windows when it was warm and then run around the house shutting them at the first sign of a cool breeze.

Best of all was what his father would do when Perry got restless: he and Perry would go down to the living room, where the upright piano stood. It had been Perry's grandfather's, and the old man—who'd died before Perry was born—had been a jazz pianist who'd played sessions with everyone from Cab Calloway to Duke Ellington.

"You ready, P?" his father would ask.

Perry always nodded, watching his father sit down at the bench and try a few notes.

Then his father would play, tinkling and then pounding, running up and down the keyboard in an improvised jazz recital that could go for hours, sometimes only ending once Perry's mom came home from work at the framing shop.

Nothing in Perry's life since had the power to capture him the way his father's music did. His fingers danced, literally *danced* on the keys, walking up and down them like a pair of high-kicking legs, making little comedy movements. The little stubby fingers with their tufts of hair on the knuckles, like goat's legs, nimbly prancing and turning.

And then there was the *music*. Perry sometimes played with the piano and he'd figured out that if you hit every other key with three fingers, you got a chord. But Perry's dad almost never made chords: he made anti-chords, sounds that involved those mysterious black keys and clashed in a way that was *precisely* not a chord, that jangled and jarred.

The anti-chords made up anti-tunes. Somewhere in the music there'd be one or more melodies, often the stuff that Perry listened to in his room, but sometimes old jazz and blues standards.

The music would settle into long runs of improvisational noise that wasn't *quite* noise. That was the best stuff, because Perry could never tell if there was a melody in there. Sometimes he'd be sure that he had the know of it, could tell what was coming next, a segue into "Here Comes the Sun" or "Let the Good Times Roll" or "Merrily We Roll Along," but then his father would get to that spot and he'd move into something else, some other latent pattern that was unmistakable in hindsight.

There was a joke his dad liked, "Time flies like an arrow, fruit flies like a banana." This was funny in just that way: you expected one thing, you got something else, and when your expectations fell apart like that, it was pure hilarity. You wanted to clutch your sides and roll on the floor sometimes, it was so funny.

His dad usually closed his eyes while he played, squeezing them shut, letting his mouth hang open slightly. Sometimes he grunted or scatted along with his playing but more often he grunted out something that was kind of the *opposite* of what he was playing, just like sometimes the melody and rhythms he played on the piano were sometimes the opposite of the song he was playing, something that was exactly and perfectly opposite, so you couldn't hear it without hearing the thing it was the opposite of.

The game would end when his dad began to improvise on parts of the piano besides the keys, knocking on it, reaching in to pluck its strings like a harp, rattling Perry's teacup on its saucer just so.

Nothing made him feel better faster. It was a tonic, a fine one, better than pills and tea and toast, daytime TV and flat ginger ale.

As Perry got older, he and the old man had their share of fights over the normal things: girls, partying, school . . . But every time Perry took ill, he was transported back to his boyhood and those amazing piano recitals, his father's stubby fingers doing their comic high kicks and pratfalls on the keys, the grunting anti-song in the back of his throat, those crazy finales with teacups and piano strings.

Now he stared morosely at the empty swimming pool six stories below his balcony, filled with blowing garbage, leaves, and a huge wasps' nest. His father's music was in his ears, distantly now and fading with his cold. He should call the old man, back home in Westchester County, retired now. They talked only rarely these days, three or four times a year on birthdays and anniversaries. No fight had started their silence, only busy lives grown apart.

He should call the old man, but instead he got dressed and went for a jog around the block, trying to get the wet sick wheeze out of his whistling breath, stopping a couple times to blow his nose. The sun was like a blowtorch on his hair, which had grown out of his normal duckling fuzz into something much shaggier. His head baked, the cold baked with it, and by the time he got home and chugged a quart of orange juice, he was feeling fully human again and ready for a shower, street clothes, and a turn at the old ticket window at work.

The queue snaked all the way through the market and out to the street, where the line had a casual, party kind of atmosphere. The market kids were doing a brisk business in popsicles, homemade colas, and clever origami stools and sunbeds made from recycled cardboard. Some of the kids recognized him and waved, then returned to their hustle.

He followed the queue through the stalls. The vendors were happier than the kids, if that was possible, selling stuff as fast as they could set it out. The queue had every conceivable kind of person in it: old and young, hipsters and conservative rawboned southerners, Latina moms with their babies, stone-faced urban homeboys, crackers, and Miami Beach queers in pastel shorts. There were old Jewish couples and smartly turned out European tourists with their funny two-tone shag cuts and the filter masks that they smoked around. There was a no-fooling Korean tour group, of the sort he'd seen now and again in Disney World, led by a smart lady in a sweltering little suit, holding an umbrella over her head.

"Lester, what the *fuck*?" he said, grinning and laughing as he clapped Lester on the shoulder, taking a young mall-goth's five bucks out of a hand whose fingernails were painted with chipped black polish. "What the hell is going on here?"

Lester laughed. "I was saving this for a surprise, buddy. Record crowds—growing every day. There's a lineup in the morning no matter how early I open, and no matter what time I close, I turn people away."

"How'd they all find out about it?"

Lester shrugged. "Word of mouth," he said. "Best advertising you can have. Shit, Perry, you just got back from ten cities where they want to clone this thing—how did *they* find out about it?"

Perry shook his head and marveled at the queue some more. The Korean tour group was coming up on them, and Perry nudged Lester aside and got out his ticket roll, the familiar movements lovely after all that time on the road.

The tour guide put a stack of twenties down on the counter. "I got fifty of 'em," she said. "That's five hundred bucks." She had an American accent, somewhere south of the Mason-Dixon Line. Perry had been expecting a Korean accent, broken English.

Perry riffled the bills. "I'll take your word for it."

She winked at him. "They got off the plane and they were all like, 'Screw Disney, we have one of those in Seoul, what's *new*, what's *American*?' So I took them here. You guys totally rock."

He could have kissed her. His heart took wing. "In you go," he said. "Lester will get you the extra ride vehicles."

"They're all in there already," Lester said. "I've been running the whole fleet for two weeks and I've got ten more on order."

Perry whistled. "You shoulda said," he said, then turned back to the tour guide. "It might be a little bit of a wait."

"Ten, fifteen minutes," Lester said.

"No *problem*," she said. "They'll wait till kingdom come, provided there's good shopping to be had." Indeed the tour group was at the center of a pack of vendor kids hawking busts and tattoos, contacts and action figures, kitchenware and cigarette lighters.

Once she was gone, Lester gave his shoulder another squeeze. "I hired two more kids to bring the ride cars back around to the entrance." When Perry had left, that had been a once-daily chore, something you did before shutting down for the night.

"Holy crap," Perry said, watching the tour group edge toward the entrance, slip inside in ones and twos.

"It's amazing, isn't it?" Lester said. "And wait till you see the ride!"

Perry didn't get a chance to ride until much later that day, once the sun had set and the last market stall had been shut and the last rider had been chased home, when he and Lester slugged back bottles of flat distilled water from their humidity still and sat on the ticket counter to get the weight off their tired feet.

"Now we ride," Lester said. "You're going to *love* this."

The first thing he noticed was that the ride had become a lot less open. When he'd left, there'd been the sense that you were in a giant room—all that dead Wal-Mart—with little exhibits spread around it, like the trade floor at a monster-car show. But now the exhibits had been arranged out of one another's sight lines, and some of the taller pieces had been upended to form baffles. It was much more like a carny haunted-house trade-show floor now.

The car circled slowly in the first "room," which had accumulated a lot of junk that wasn't mad inventions from the heyday of New Work. There was a chipped doll cradle, and a small collection of girls' dolls, a purse spilled on the floor with photos of young girls clowning at a birthday party. He reached for the joystick with irritation and slammed it toward minus one—what the hell was this crap?

Next was a room full of boys' tanks and cars and trading cards, some in careful packages and frames, some lovingly scuffed and beaten up. They were from all eras, and he recognized some of his beloved toys from his own boyhood among the mix. The items were arranged in concentric rings—one of the robots' default patterns for displaying materials—around a writhing tower of juddering, shuddering domestic robots that had piled one atop the other. The vogue for these had been mercifully brief, but it had been intense, and for Perry, the juxtaposition of the cars and the cards, the tanks and the robots made something catch in his throat. There was a statement here about the drive to automate household chores and the simple pleasure of rolling an imaginary tank over the imaginary armies of your imaginary enemies. So, too, something about the collecting urge, the need to get every card in a set, and then to get each in perfect condition, and then to arrange them in perfect order, and then to forget them altogether.

His hand had been jerking the joystick to plus one all this time and now he became consciously aware of this.

The next room had many of the old inventions he remembered, but they were arranged not on gleaming silver tables but mixed in with heaps of clothing, mountains of the brightly colored ubiquitous T-shirts that had gone hand in hand with every New Work invention and crew. Mixed in among them were some vintage tees from the dotcom era, and perched on top of the mountain, staring glassily at him, was a little girl doll that looked familiar; he was almost certain that he'd seen her in the first doll room.

The next room was built out of pieces of the old "kitchen" display, but there was disarray now, dishes in the sink and a plate on the counter with a cigarette butted out in the middle of it. Another plate lay in three pieces on the linoleum before it.

The next room was carpeted with flattened soda tins that crunched under the chair's wheels. In the center of them, a neat workbench with ranked tools.

The ride went on and on, each room utterly different from how he'd left it, but somehow familiar, too. The ride he'd left had celebrated the New Work and the people who'd made it happen, and so did this ride, but this ride was less linear, less about display, more—

"It's a story," he said when he got off.

"I think so, too," Lester said. "It's been getting more and more storylike. The way that doll keeps reappearing. I think that someone had like ten of them and just tossed them out at regular intervals and then the plus-oneing snuck one into every scene."

"It's got scenes! That's what they are, scenes. It's like a Disney ride, one of those dark rides in Fantasyland."

"Except those suck and our ride rocks. It's more like Pirates of the Caribbean."

"Have it your way. Whatever, how freaking weird is that?"

"Not so weird. People see stories like they see faces in clouds. Once we gave them the ability to subtract the stuff that felt wrong and reinforce the stuff that felt right, it was only natural that they'd anthropomorphize the world into a story."

Perry shook his head. "You think?"

"We have this guy, a cultural studies prof, who comes practically every day. He's been telling me all about it. Stories are how we understand the world, and technology is how we choose our stories.

"Check out the Greeks. All those Greek plays, they end with the deus ex machina—the playwright gets tired of writing, so he trots a god out on stage to simply point a finger at the players and make it all better. You can't do that in a story today, but back then, they didn't have the tools to help them observe and record the world, so as far as they could tell, that's how stuff worked!

"Today we understand a little more about the world, so our stories are about people figuring out what's causing their troubles and changing stuff so that those causes go away. Causal stories for a causal universe. Thinking about the world in terms of causes and effects makes you seek out causes and effects—even where there are none. Watch how gamblers play, that weird cargo-cult feeling that the roulette wheel came up black a third time in a row so the next spin will make it red. It's not superstition, it's kind of the *opposite*—it's causality run amok."

"So this is the story that has emerged from our collective unconscious?"

Lester laughed. "That's a little pretentious, I think. It's more like those Japanese crabs."

"Which Japanese crabs?"

"Weren't you there when Tjan was talking about this? Or was that in Russia? Anyway. There are these crabs in Japan, and if they have anything that looks like a face on the backs of their shells, the fishermen throw them back because it's bad luck to eat a crab with a face on its shell. So the crabs with facelike shells have more babies. Which means that gradually, the crabs' shells get more face-like, since all non-facelike shells are eliminated from the gene pool. This leads the fishermen to raise the bar on their selection criteria, so they will eat crabs with shells that are a little facelike, but not *very* facelike. So all the slightly face-like crab shells are eliminated, leaving behind moderately facelike shells. This gets repeated over several generations, and now you've got these crabs that have vivid faces on their shells.

"We let our riders eliminate all the non-storylike elements from the ride, and so what's left behind is more and more storylike."

"But the plus-one / minus-one lever is too crude for this, right? We should give them a pointer or something so they can specify individual elements they don't like."

"You want to encourage this?"

"Don't you?"

Lester nodded vigorously. "Of course I do. I just thought that you'd be a little less enthusiastic about it, you know, because so much of the New Work stuff is being de-emphasized."

"You kidding? This is what the New Work was all about: group creation! I couldn't be happier about it. Seriously—this is so much cooler than anything that I could have built. And now with the network coming online soon—wow. Imagine it. It's going to be so fucking weird, bro."

"Amen," Lester said. He looked at his watch and yelped. "Shit, late for a date! Can you get yourself home?"

"Sure," Perry said. "Brought my wheels. See you later—have a good one."

"She's amazing," Lester said. "Used to weigh nine hundred pounds and was shut in for ten years. Man has she got an imagination on her. She can do this thing—"

Perry put his hands over his ears. "La la la, I'm not listening to you. TMI, Lester. Seriously. Way, way TMI."

Lester shook his head. "You are such a prude, dude."

Perry thought about Hilda for a fleeting moment, and then grinned. "That's me, a total puritan. Go. Be safe."

"Safe, sound, and slippery," Lester said, and got in his car.

Perry looked around at the shuttered market, rooftops glinting in the rosy tropical sunset. Man he'd missed those sunsets. He snorted up damp lungsful of the tropical air and smelled dinners cooking at the shantytown across the street. It was different and bigger and more elaborate every time he visited it, which was always less often than he wished.

There was a good barbecue place there, Dirty Max's, just a hole in the wall with a pit out back and the friendliest people. There was always a mob scene around there, locals greasy from the ribs in their hands, a big bucket overflowing with discarded bones.

Wandering toward it, he was amazed by how much bigger it had grown since his last visit. Most buildings had had two stories, though a few had three. Now almost all had four, leaning drunkenly toward each other across the streets. Power cables, network cables, and clotheslines gave the overhead spaces the look of a carelessly spun spider's web. The new stories were most remarkable because of what Francis had explained to him about the way that additional stories got added: most people rented out or sold the right to build on top of their buildings, and then the new upstairs neighbors in turn sold *their* rights on. Sometimes you'd get a third-story dweller who'd want to build atop two adjacent buildings to make an extra-wide apartment for a big family, and that required negotiating with all of the "owners" of each floor of both buildings.

Just looking at it made his head hurt with all the tangled property and ownership relationships embodied in the high spaces. He heard the easy chatter out the open windows and music and crying babies. Kids ran through the streets, laughing and chasing each other or bouncing balls or playing some kind of networked RPG with their phones that had them peeking around corners, seeing another player and shrieking and running off.

The grill woman at the barbecue joint greeted him by name and the men and women around it made space for him. It was friendly and companionable, and after a moment Francis wandered up with a couple of his protégés. They carried boxes of beer.

"Hey hey," Francis said. "Home again, huh?"

"Home again," Perry said. He wiped rib sauce off his fingers and shook Francis's hand warmly. "God, I've missed this place."

"We missed having you," Francis said. "Big crowds across the way, too. Seems like you hit on something."

Perry shook his head and smiled and ate his ribs. "What's the story around here?"

"Lots and lots," Francis said. "There's a whole Net-community thing happening. Lots of traffic on the AARP message boards from other people setting these up around the country."

"So you've hit on something, too."

"Naw. When it's railroading time, you get railroads. When it's squatter time, you get squats. You know they want to open a 7-Eleven here?"

"No!" Perry laughed and choked on ribs and then guzzled some beer to wash it all down.

Francis put a wrinkled hand over his heart. He still wore his wedding band, Perry saw, despite his wife's being gone for decades. "I swear it. Just there." He pointed to one of the busier corners.

"And?"

"We told them to fuck off," Francis said. "We've got lots of community-owned businesses around here that do everything a 7-Eleven could do for us, without taking the wealth out of our community and sending it to some corporate jack-off. Some soreheads wanted to see how much money we could get out of them, but I just kept telling them—whatever 7-Eleven gives us, it'll only be because they think they can get more *out of us*. They saw reason. Besides, I'm in charge—I always win my arguments."

"You are the most benevolent of dictators," Perry said. He began to work on another beer. Beer tasted better outside in the heat and the barbecue smoke.

"I'm glad someone thinks so," Francis said.

"Oh?"

"The 7-Eleven thing left a lot of people pissed at me. There's plenty around here that don't remember the way it started off. To them, I'm just some alter kocker who's keeping them down."

"Is it serious?" Perry knew that there was the potential for serious, major lawlessness from his little settlement. It wasn't a failing condo complex rented out to Filipina domestics and weird entrepreneurs like him. It was a place where the cops would love an excuse to come in with riot batons (his funny eyebrow twitched) and gas, the kind of place where there almost certainly were a few very bad people living their lives. Miami had bad people, too, but the bad people in Miami weren't his problem.

And the bad people and the potential chaos were what he loved about the place, too. He'd grown up in the kind of place where everything was predictable and safe, and he'd hated every minute of it. The glorious chaos around him was just as he liked it. The woodsmoke curled up his nose, fragrant and all-consuming.

"I don't know anymore. I thought I'd retire and settle down and take up painting. Now I'm basically a mob boss. Not the bad kind, but still. It's a lot of work."

"Pimpin' ain't easy." Perry saw the shocked look on Francis's face and added hastily, "Sorry—not calling you a pimp. It's a song lyric is all."

"We got pimps here now. Whores, too. You name it, we got it. It's still a good place to live—better than Miami, if you ask me—but it could go real animal. Bad, bad animal."

Hard to believe, standing there in the woodsmoke, licking his fingers, drinking his beer. His cold seemed to have been baked out by the steamy, swampy heat.

"Well, Francis, if anyone knows how to keep peace, it's you."

"Social workers come around, say the same thing. But there's people around here with little kids. They worry that the social workers could force them out, take away their children."

It wasn't like Francis to complain like this, it wasn't in his nature, but here it was. The strain of running things was showing on him. Perry wondered if his own strain was showing that way. Did he complain more these days? Maybe he did.

An uncomfortable silence descended upon them. Perry drank his beer morosely. He thought of how ridiculous it was to be morose about the possibility that he was being morose, but there you had it.

Finally his phone rang and saved him from further conversation. He looked at the display and shook his head. It was Kettlewell again. That first voicemail had made him laugh aloud, but when they hadn't called back for a couple days, he'd figured that they had just had a little too much wine and placed the call.

Now they were calling back, and it was still pretty early on the West Coast. Too early for them to have had too much wine, unless they'd really changed.

"Perry Perry Perry!" It was Kettlebelly. He sounded like he might be drunk, or merely punch-drunk with excitement. Perry remembered that he got that way sometimes.

"Kettlewell, how are you doing?"

"I'm here, too, Perry. I cashed in my return ticket."

"Suzanne?"

"Yeah," she said. She, too, sounded punchy, like they'd been having a fit of the giggles just before calling. "Kettlewell's family have taken me in, wayward wanderer that I am."

"You two sound pretty, um, happy."

"We've been having an amazing time," Kettlewell said. His speakerphone made him sound like he was at the bottom of a well. "Mostly reminiscing about you guys. What the hell are you up to? We tried to follow it on the Net, but it's all jumbled. What's this about a *story*?"

"Story?"

"I keep reading about this ride of yours and its story. I couldn't make any sense of it."

"I haven't read any of this, but Lester and I were talking about some stuff to do with stories tonight. I didn't know anyone else was talking about this, though. Where'd you see it?"

"I'll email it to you," Suzanne said. "I was going to blog it tonight anyway."

"So you two are just hanging around San Francisco giggling and walking down memory lane?"

"Well, yeah! It's about time, too. We've all been separated for too long. We want a reunion, Perry."

"A reunion?"

"We want to come down for a visit and see what you're doing and hang out. You wouldn't believe how much fun we've been having, Perry, seriously." Kettlewell sounded like he'd been huffing nitrous or something. "Have *you* been having fun?"

He thought about the question. "Um, kind of?" He told them about his travels, a quick thumbnail sketch, struggling to remember which city he'd been to when, leaving out the crazy sex—which came back to him in a rush, that night with Hilda in the coffin, like a warm hallucination. "On balance, yes. It's been fun."

"Right, so we want to come down and have fun with you and Lester. He's still hanging around, right?"

Lester had told him about the history he had with Suzanne, and there was something in the way she asked after Lester that suggested to Perry that there was still something there.

"You kidding? You'd have to pry us apart with a crowbar."

"See, I told you so," Suzanne said. "This guy thought that Lester might have gotten bored and wandered off."

"Never! Plus anyone who follows his message board traffic and blogs would know that he was right here, minding the shop." And you're reading his blog, aren't you, Suzanne? He didn't need to say it. He could almost hear her blush over the line.

"So how about tomorrow?"

"For what?"

"For us coming to town. I'll bring the wife and kids. We'll rent out a couple hotel rooms and spend a week there. It'll be a blast."

"Tomorrow?"

"We could get the morning flight and be there for breakfast. You got a good hotel? Not a coffin hotel, not with the kids."

Perry's heart beat faster. He did miss these two, and they were so punchy, so gleeful. He'd love to see them. He muted his phone.

"Hey, Francis? That guesthouse down the road, is it still running?"

"Lulu's? Sure. They just built another story and took over the top floor of the place next door."

"Perfect." He unmuted. "How'd you like to stay in a squatter guesthouse in the shantytown?"

"Um," Kettlewell said, but Suzanne laughed.

"Oh hell *yes*," she said. "Get that look off your face, Kettlewell, this is an *adventure*."

"We'd love it," Kettlewell said.

"Great, I'll make you a reservation. How long are you staying?"

"Until we leave," Suzanne said.

"Right," Perry said, and laughed himself. They were different people, these two, from the people he remembered, but they were also old friends. And they were coming to see him tomorrow. "OK, lemme go make your reservations."

Francis walked him over and the landlord fussed over the two of them like they were visiting dignitaries. Perry looked the place over and it was completely charming. He spotted what he thought was probably a hooker and a trick taking a room for the night, but you got that at the Hilton, too.

By the time he got home he was sure that he'd sleep like a log. He could barely keep his eyes open on the drive. But after he climbed into bed and closed his eyes, he found that he couldn't sleep at all. Something about being back in his own room in his own bed felt alien and exciting. He got up and paced the apartment and then Lester came home from his date with the fatkins nympho, full of improbable stories and covered in little hickeys.

"You won't believe who's coming for a visit," Perry said.

"Steve Jobs. He's come down from the lamasery and renounced Buddhism. He wants to give a free computer to every visitor."

"Close," Perry said. "Kettlebelly and Suzanne Church. Coming *tomorrow* for a stay of unspecified duration. It's a reunion. It's a *reunion* you big sono-fabitch! Woot! Woot!" Perry did a little two-step. "A reunion!"

Lester looked confused for a second, and then for another second he looked, what, upset? and then he was grinning and jumping up and down with Perry. "Reunion!"

He felt like he'd barely gotten to sleep when his phone rang. The clock showed 6 AM, and it was Kettlebelly and Suzanne, bleary, jet-lagged, and grouchy from their one-hour postflight security processing.

"We want breakfast," Suzanne said.

"We've gotta open the ride, Suzanne."

"At six in the morning? Come on, you've got hours yet before you have to be at work. How about you and Lester meet us at the IHOP?"

"Jesus," he said.

"Come *on*! Kettlebelly's kids are dying for something to eat and his wife looks like she's ready to eat *him*. It's been years, dude! Get your ass in the shower and down to the International House of Pancakes!"

Lester didn't rouse easy, but Perry knew all the tricks for getting his old pal out of bed, they were practically married after all.

They arrived just in time for the morning rush but Tony greeted them with a smile and sent them straight to the front of the line. Lester ordered his usual ("Bring me three pounds of candy with a side of ground animal parts and potatoes") and they waited nervously for Suzanne and the clan Kettlewell to turn up.

They arrived in a huge bustle of taxis and luggage and two wide-eyed, jet-lagged children hanging off of Kettlewell and Mrs. Kettlewell, whom neither of them had ever met. She was a small, youthful woman in her mid-forties with artfully styled hair and big, abstract chunky silver jewelry. Suzanne had gone all Eurochic, rail-thin and smoking, with quiet, understated dark clothes. Kettlewell had a real daddy belly on him now, a little pot that his daughter thumped rhythmically from her perch on his hip.

"Sit, sit," Perry said to them, getting up to help them stack their luggage at either end of the long table down the middle of the IHOP. Big family groups with tons of luggage were par for the course in Florida, so they didn't really draw much attention beyond mild irritation from the patrons they jostled as they got everyone seated.

Perry was mildly amused to see that Lester and Suzanne ended up sitting next to one another and were already chatting avidly and close up, in soft voices that they had to lean in very tight to hear.

He was next to Mrs. Kettlewell, whose name, it transpired, was Eva—"As in Extra-Vehicular Activity," she said, geeking out with him. Kettlewell was in the bathroom with his daughter and son, and Mrs. Kettlewell—Eva—seemed relieved at the chance for a little adult conversation.

"You must be a very patient woman," Perry said, laughing at all the ticklish noise and motion of their group.

"Oh, that's me all right," Eva said. "Patience is my virtue. And you?"

"Oh, patience is something I value very much in other people," Perry said. It made Eva laugh, which showed off her pretty laugh lines and dimples. He could see how this woman and Kettlewell must complement each other.

She rocked her head from side to side and took a long swig of the coffee that their waiter had distributed around the table, topping up from the carafe he'd left behind. "Thank God for legal stimulants."

"Long flight?"

"Traveling with larvae is always a challenge," she said. "But they dug it hard. You should have seen them at the windows."

"They'd never been on a plane before?"

"I like to go camping," she said with a shrug. "Landon's always on me to take the kids to Hawaii or whatever, but I'm always like, 'Man, you spend half your fucking life in a tin can—why do you want to start your holidays in one? Let's go to Yosemite and get muddy.' I haven't even taken them to Disneyland!"

Perry put the back of his hand to his forehead. "That's heresy around here," he said. "You going to take them to Disney World while you're in Florida? It's a lot bigger, you know—and it's a different division. Really different feel, or so I'm told."

"You kidding? Perry, we came here for *your* ride. It's famous, you know."

"Net.famous, maybe. A little." He felt his cheeks burning. "Well, there will be one in your neck of the woods soon enough." He told her about the Burning Man collective and the plan to build one down the 101, south of San Francisco International.

Kettlebelly returned then with the kids, and he managed to get them into their seats while sucking back a coffee and eating a biscuit from the basket in the center of the table, breaking off bits to shove in the kids' mouths whenever they protested.

"These are some way-tired kids," he said, leaning over to give his wife a kiss. Perry thought he saw Suzanne flick a look at them then, but it might have been his imagination. Suzanne and Lester were off in their own world, after all.

"The plane almost crashed," said the little girl next to Perry. She had a halo of curly hair like a dandelion clock and big solemn dark eyes and a big wet mouth set between apple-round cheeks.

"Did it really?" Perry said. She was seven or eight, he thought, the bossy big sister who'd been giving orders to her little brother from the moment they came through the door.

She nodded solemnly. He looked at Eva, who shrugged.

"Really?" he said.

"Really," she said, nodding vigorously now. "There were terrists on the plane who wanted to blow it up, but the sky marshas stopped them."

"How could you tell they were 'terrists'?"

She clicked her tongue and rolled her eyes. "They were *whispering,*" she said. "Just like on *Captain President and the Freedom Fighters.*" He knew something of this cartoon, mostly because of all the knockoff merch for sale in the market stalls in front of the ride.

"I see," he said. "Well, I'm glad the sky marshas stopped them. Do you want pancakes?"

"I want caramel apple chocolate pancakes with blueberry-banana sauce," she said, rolling one pudgy finger along the description in the glossy menu, beneath an oozing food-porn photo. "And my brother wants a chocolate milk shake and a short stack of happy-face clown waffles with strawberry sauce, but not too many because he's still a baby and can't eat much."

"You'll become as fat as your daddy if you eat like that," Perry said. Eva snorted beside him.

"No," she said. "I'm gonna be a fatkins."

"I see," he said. Eva shook her head.

"It's the goddamned fatkins agitprop games," Eva said. "They come free with everything now—digital cameras, phones, even in cereal boxes. You have to eat a minimum number of calories per level or you starve to death. This one is a champeen."

"I'm nationally ranked," the little girl said, not looking up from the menu.

Perry looked across the table and discovered that Suzanne had covered Lester's hand with hers and that Lester was laughing along with her at something funny. Something about that made him a little freaked out, like Lester was making time with his sister or their mom.

"Suzanne," he said. "What's happening with you these days, anyway?"

"Petersburg is what's happening with me," she said, with a hoarse little chuckle. "Petersburg is like Detroit crossed with Paris. Completely decrepit and decadent. There's a serial killer who's been working the streets for five years there and the biggest obstacle to catching him is that the first cops on the scene let rubberneckers bribe them to take home evidence as souvenirs."

"No way!" Lester said.

"Oh, da, big vay," she said, dropping into a comical Boris and Natasha accent. "Bolshoi vay."

"So why are you there?"

"It's like home for me. It's got enough of Detroit's old brutal, earthy feel, plus enough of Silicon Valley's manic hustle, it just feels right."

"You going to settle in there?"

"Well, put that way, no. I couldn't hack it for the long term. But at this time in my life, it's been just right. But it's good to get back to the States, too. I'm thinking of hanging out here for a couple months. Russia's so cheap, I've got a ton saved up. Might as well blow it before inflation kills it."

"You keep your money in rubles?"

"Hell no—no one uses rubles except tourists. I'm worried about another run of *U.S.* inflation. I mean, have you looked around lately? You're living in a third-world country, buddy."

A waiter came between them, handing out heaping, steaming plates of food. Lester, who'd finished his first breakfast while they waited, had ordered a second breakfast, which arrived along with the rest of them. Mountains of food stacked up on the table, side plates crowding jugs of apple juice and carafes of coffee.

Incredibly, the food kept coming—multiple syrup jugs, plates of hash browns, baskets of biscuits, and bowls of white sausage gravy. Perry hadn't paid much attention when orders were being taken, but from the looks of things, he was eating with a bunch of IHOP virgins, unaccustomed to the astonishing portions to be had there.

He cocked his funny eyebrow at Suzanne, who laughed. "OK, not quite a third-world country. But not a real industrial nation anymore, either. Maybe more like the end days of Rome or something. Drowning in wealth and wallowing in poverty." She forked up a mouthful of hash browns and chased them with coffee. Perry attacked his own plate.

Kettlewell fed the kids, sneaking bites in between, while Eva looked on approvingly. "You're a good man, Landon Kettlewell," she said, slicing up her steak and eggs into small, precise cubes, wielding the knife like an artist.

"You just enjoy your breakfast, my queen," he said, spooning oatmeal with raisins, bananas, granola, and boysenberry jam into the little boy's mouth.

"We got you presents," the little girl said, taking a break from shoveling banana-chocolate caramel apples into her mouth.

"Really?" Perry raised his funny eyebrow and she giggled. He did it again, making it writhe like a snake. She snarfed choco-banana across the table, then scooped it up and put it back in her mouth.

She nodded vigorously. "Dad, give them their presents!"

Kettlewell said, "Someone has to feed your brother, you know."

"I'll do it," she said. She forked up some of his oatmeal and attempted to get it into the little boy's face. "Presents!"

Kettlewell dug through the luggage cluster under the table and came up with an overstuffed diaper bag, then pawed through it for a long time, urged on by his daughter, who kept chanting "Presents! Presents! Presents!" while attempting to feed her little brother. Eva and Lester and Suzanne took up the chant. They were drawing stares from nearby tables, but Perry didn't mind. He was laughing so hard his sides hurt.

Finally Kettlewell held a paper bag aloft triumphantly, then clapped a hand over his daughter's mouth and shushed the rest.

"You guys are really hard to shop for," he said. "What the hell do you get for two guys who not only have everything, but *make* everything?"

Suzanne nodded. "Damned right. We spent a whole day looking for something."

"What is it?"

"Well," Kettlewell said. "We figured that it should be something useful, not decorative. You guys have decorative coming out of your asses. So that left us with tools. We wanted to find you a tool that you didn't have, and that you would appreciate."

Suzanne picked up the story. "I thought we should get you an antique tool, something so well made that it was still usable. But to be useful, it had to be something no one had improved on, and that had in fact been degraded by modern manufacturing techniques.

"At first we looked at old tape measures, but I remembered that you guys were mostly using key-chain laser range finders these days. Screwdrivers, pliers, and hammers were all out—I couldn't find a damned thing that looked any better than what you had around here. The state of the art is genuinely progressing.

"There were a lot of nice old brass spirit levels and hand-lathed plumb bobs but they were more decorative than useful by a damned sight. Great old steel work helmets looked cool, but they weighed about a hundred times what the safety helmets around here weigh.

"We were going to give in and try to bring you guys a big goddamned tube amp, or maybe some Inuit glass knives, but I didn't see you having much of a use for either.

"Which is how we came to give up on tools per se and switched over to leisure—sports tools. There was a much richer vein. Wooden bats, oh yes, and real pigskin footballs that had nice idiosyncratic spin that you'd have to learn to compensate for. But when we found these, we knew we'd hit pay dirt."

188 | CORY DOCTOROW

She picked up Kettlewell's paper sack bulging carry-on with a flourish and unzipped it. A moment later she presented them with two identical packages wrapped in coarse linen paper hand-stamped with Victorian woodcuts of sporting men swinging bats and charging the line with pigskins under their arms.

"Ta-dah!"

The kids echoed it. "These are the best presents," the little girl confided to Perry as he picked delicately at the exquisite paper.

The paper gave way in folds and curls, and then he and Lester both held their treasures aloft.

"Baseball gloves!" Perry said.

"A catcher's mitt and a fielder's glove," Kettlewell said. "You look at that catcher's mitt. 1910!" It was black and bulbous, the leather soft and yielding, with a patina of fine cracks like an old painting. It smelled like oil and leather, an old rich smell like a gentleman's club or an expensive briefcase. Perry tried it on and it molded itself to his hand, snug and comfortable. It practically cried out to have a ball thrown at it.

"And this fielder's glove," Kettlewell went on, pointing at the glove Lester held. It was the more traditional tan color, comically large, like the glove of a cartoon character. It, too, had the look of ancient, well-loved leather, the same mysterious smell of hide and oil. Perry touched it with a finger and it felt like a woman's cheek, smooth and soft. "Rawlings XPG6. The Mickey Mantle. Early 1960s—the ultimate glove."

"You got the whole sales pitch, huh, darling?" Eva said, not unkindly, but Kettlewell flushed and glared at her for a moment.

Perry broke in. "Guys, these are—wow. Incredible."

"They're better than the modern product," Suzanne said. "That's the point. You can't print these or fab these. They're wonderful because they're so well made *and so well used*! The only way to make a glove this good would be to fab it and then give it to several generations of baseball players to love and use for fifty to a hundred years."

Perry turned over the catcher's mitt. Over a hundred years old. This wasn't something to go in a glass case. Suzanne was right: this was a great glove because people had played with it, all the time. It needed to be played with or it would get out of practice.

"I guess we're going to have to buy a baseball," Perry said.

The little girl beside him started bouncing up and down.

"Show him," Suzanne said, and the girl dove under the table and came up with two white, fresh hard balls. Once he fitted one to the pocket of his glove, it felt so perfectly right—like a key in a lock. This pocket had held a lot of balls over the years.

Lester had put a ball in the pocket of his glove, too. He tossed it lightly in the air and caught it, then repeated the trick. The look of visceral satisfaction on his face was unmistakable.

"These are *great* presents, guys," Perry said. "Seriously. Well done."

They all beamed and murmured and then the ball Lester was tossing crashed to the table and broke a pitcher of blueberry syrup, upset a carafe of orange juice, and rolled to a stop in the chocolate mess in front of the little girl, who laughed and laughed and laughed.

"And *that* is why we don't play with balls indoors," Suzanne said, looking as stern as she could while obviously trying very hard not to bust out laughing.

The waiters were accustomed to wiping up spills and Lester was awkwardly helpful. While they were getting everything set to rights again, Perry looked at Eva and saw her lips tightly pursed as she considered her husband. He followed Kettlebelly's gaze and saw that he was watching Suzanne (who was laughingly restraining Lester from doing any more "cleaning") intently. In a flash, Perry thought he had come to understanding. *Oh dear,* he thought.

The kids loved the shantytown. The little girl—Ada, "like the programming language," Eva said—insisted on being set down so she could tread the cracked cement walkways herself, head whipping back and forth to take the crazy leaning buildings in, eyes following the zipping motorbikes and bicycles as they wove in and out of the busy streets. The shantytowners were used to tourists in their midst. A few yardies gave them the hairy eyeball, but then they saw Perry was along and they found something else to pay attention to. That made Perry feel obscurely proud. He'd been absent for months, but even the corner boys knew who he was and didn't want to screw with him.

The guesthouse's landlady greeted them at the door, alerted to their coming by the jungle telegraph. She shook Perry's hand warmly, gave Ada a lollipop, and chucked the little boy (Pascal, "like the programming language," said Eva, with an eye roll) under the chin. Check-in was a lot simpler than at a coffin hotel or a Hilton: just a brief discussion of the available rooms and a quick tour. The Kettlewells opted for the lofty attic, which could fit two three-quarter-width beds and a crib, and overlooked the curving streets from a high vantage; Suzanne took a more quotidian room just below, with lovely tile mosaics made from snipped-out sections of plastic fruit and smashed novelty soda bottles. (The landlady privately assured Perry that her euphemistic "hourly trade" was in a different part of the guesthouse altogether, with its own staircase.)

A few hours later, Perry was alone again, working his ticket counter. The Kettlewells were having naps, Lester and Suzanne had gone off to see some sights, and the crowd for the ride was already large, snaking through the market, thick with vendors and hustling kids trying to pry the visitors loose of their bankrolls.

He felt like doing a carny barker spiel: *Step right up; step right up; this way to the great egress!* But the morning's visitors didn't seem all that frivolous—they were serious-faced and sober.

"Everything OK?" he asked a girl who was riding for at least the second time. She was a midwestern-looking giantess in her early twenties with big white front teeth and broad shoulders, wearing a faded Hoosiers ball cap and a lot of coral jewelry. "I mean, you don't look like you're having a fun time."

"It's the story," she said. "I read about it online and I didn't really believe it, but now I totally see it. But you made it, right? It didn't just . . . *happen*, did it?"

"No, it just happened," Perry said. This girl was a little spooky looking. He put his hand over his heart. "On my honor."

"It can't be," she said. "I mean, the story is like *right there*. Someone must have made it."

"Maybe they did," Perry said. "Maybe a bunch of people thought it would be fun to make a story out of the ride and came by to do it."

"That's probably it," the girl said. "The other thing, that's just ridiculous."

She was gone and on the ride before he could ask her what this meant, and the three bangbangers behind her just wanted tickets, not conversation.

An hour later, she was back.

"I mean the message boards," she said. "Don't you follow your referers? There's a guy in Osceola who says that this is—I don't know—like the story that's inside our collective unconsciousness." Perry restrained a smile at the malapropism. "Anyway a lot of people agree. I don't think so, though. No offense, mister, but I think that this is just a prank or something."

"Something," Perry said. But she rode twice more that day, and she wasn't the only one. It was a day of many repeat riders, and the market-stall people came by to complain that the visitors weren't buying much besides the occasional ice cream or pork cracklin.

Perry shrugged and told them to find something that these people wanted to buy, then. One or two of the miniatures guys got gleams in their eyes and bought tickets for the ride (Perry charged them half price) and Perry knew that by the time the day was out, there'd be souvenir ride-replicas to be had.

Lester and Suzanne came by after lunchtime and Lester relieved him, leaving him to escort Suzanne back to the shantytown and the Kettlewells.

"You two seem to be getting on well," Perry said, jerking his head back at Lester as they walked through the market.

Suzanne looked away. "This is amazing, Perry," she said, waving her hand at the market stalls, a gesture that took in the spires of the shantytown and the ride, too. "You have done something . . . stupendous, you know it? I mean, if you had a slightly different temperament, I'd call this a cult. But it seems like you're not in charge of anything—"

"That's for sure!"

"—even though you're still definitely *leading* things."

"No way—I just go where I'm told. Tjan's leading."

"I spoke to Tjan before we came out, and he points the finger at you. 'I'm just keeping the books and closing the contracts.' That's a direct quote."

"Well maybe no one's leading. Not everything needs a leader, right?"

Suzanne shook her head at him. "There's a leader, sweetie, and it's you. Have a look around. Last I checked, there were three more rides going operational this week, and five more in the next month. Just looking at your speaking calendar gave me a headache—"

"I have a speaking calendar?"

"You do indeed, and it's a busy one. You knew that, though, right?"

Tjan sent him email all the time telling him about this group or that, where he was supposed to go and give a talk, but he'd never seen a calendar. But who had time to look at the website anymore?

"I suppose. I knew I was supposed to get on a plane again in a couple weeks."

"So that's what a leader is—someone who gets people mobilized and moving."

"I met a girl in Madison, Wisconsin, you'd probably get along with." Thinking of Hilda made him smile and feel a little horny, a little wistful. He hadn't gotten fucked in mind and body like that since his twenties.

"Maybe I'll meet her. Is she working on a local ride?"

"You're going to go to the other rides?"

"I got to write about something, Perry. Otherwise my pageviews fall off and I can't pay my rent. This is a story—a big one, and no one else has noticed it yet. That kind of story can turn into the kind of money you buy a house with. I'm speaking from experience here."

"You think?"

She put her hand over her heart. "I'm good at spotting these. Man, you've got a cult on your hands here."

"What?"

"The story people. I've been reading the message boards and blogs. It's where I get all my best tips."

Perry shook his head. Everyone else was more on top of this stuff than him. He was going to have to spend less time hacking the ride and more time reading the interweb, clearly.

"It was all Lester's idea, anyway," he said.

She looked down with an unreadable expression. He hazarded a guess as to what that was about.

"Things are getting tight between you two, huh?"

"Christ it doesn't show that much does it?"

"No," he lied. "I just know Lester is all."

"He's something else," she said.

Suzanne needed some sundries, so he directed her to a little bodega in the back room of one of the houses. He told her he'd meet her at the guesthouse and took a seat in the lobby. He was still beat from the cold and the jet lag, the work and the sheer exhaustion.

On the road he'd had momentum dragging him from one thing to the next, flights to catch, speeches to make. Back at home, confronted with routine, it was like his inertia was disappearing.

Eva Kettlewell thundered down the stairs three at a time with a sound like a barely controlled fall, burst into the lobby, and headed for the door, her back rigid, her arms swinging, her face a picture of rage.

She went out the door like a flash and then stood in the street for a moment before striking out, seemingly at random.

Uh-oh, Perry thought.

Sammy didn't dare go back to the ride for weeks after the debacle in Boston. He'd been spotted by the Chinese guy and the bummy-looking guy who said he'd designed the ride, that much was sure. They probably suspected him of having sabotaged the Boston ride.

But he couldn't stay away. Work was dismal. The other execs at Disney World were all amazingly petty, and always worse so before the quarterly numbers came out. Management liked to chase any kind of bad numbers with a few ritual beheadings.

The new Fantasyland had been a feather in Sammy's cap that had kept him safe from politics for a long time, but not anymore. Now it was getting run-down: cigarette burns, graffiti, and every now and again someone would find a couple having pervy eyeliner sex in the bushes.

He'd loved to work openings in Fantasyland's heyday. He'd stand just past the castle gate and watch the flocking crowds of black-clad, lightly sweating, white-faced goth kids pour through it, blinking in the unnatural light of the morning. A lot of them took drugs and partied all night and then capped it off with an early morning at Fantasyland—Disney had done focus groups, and they'd started selling the chewy things that soothed the clenched jaws brought on by dance drugs.

But now he hated the raven-garbed customers who sallied into his park like they owned the joint. A girl—maybe sixteen—walked past on vinyl platform heels with two gigantic men in their thirties behind her, led on thin black leather leashes. A group of whippet-thin boys in gray dusters with impossibly high sprays of teased electric blue hair followed. Then a group of heavily pierced older women, their faces rattling.

Then it was a river of black, kids in chains and leather, leathery grown-ups who dressed like surly kids. They formed neat queues by their favorite rides—the haunted houses, the graveyard walk-through, the coffin coaster, the river of blood—and puffed cloves through smokeless hookahs. At least he hoped it was cloves.

The castmembers in Sammy's Fantasyland were no better than the guests. They were pierced, dyed, teased, and branded to within an inch of their lives, even gothier than the goths who made the long pilgrimages to ride his unwholesome rides.

The worst of it was that there weren't *enough* of them anymore. The goth scene, which had shown every sign of surging and resurging every five years, seemed finally to be dying. Numbers were down. A couple of goth-themed parks in the area had shuttered, as had the marshy one in New Orleans (admittedly that might have been more to do with the cholera outbreak).

Last month, he'd shut down the goth toddler clothing shop and put its wares on deep online discount. All his little nieces and nephews were getting bat-wing onesies, skull platform booties, and temporary hair dye and tattoos for Christmas. Now he just had to get rid of the other ten million bucks' worth of merch.

"Morning, Death," he said. The kid's real name was Darren Weinberger, but he insisted on being called Death Waits, which, given his eager-to-please demeanor, was funny enough that it had taken Sammy a full year to learn to control his grin when he said it.

"Sammy! Good morning—how're you doing?"

"The numbers stink," Sammy said. "You must have noticed."

Death's grin vanished. "I noticed. Time for a new ride, maybe." No one called them "attractions" anymore—all that old Orwellian Disneyspeak had been abolished. "They love the coaster and the free fall. Thrill rides are always crowd-pleasers."

Death Waits had worked at Disney for three years now, since the age of sixteen, and he had grown up coming to the park, one of the rare Orlando locals. Sammy had come to rely on him for what he thought of as insight into the "goth street." He never said that aloud, because he knew how much it sounded like "whatever you crazy kids are into these days."

But this wasn't helpful. "I *know* that everyone likes thrill rides, but how the hell can you compete with the gypsy coasters?" They set up their coasters by the road and ran them until there was an injury serious enough to draw the law—a week or two at best. You could order the DIY coaster kits from a number of suppliers across the U.S. and Mexico, put them up with cranes and semiskilled labor and wishful thinking, start taking tickets, and when the inevitable catastrophe ensued, you could be packed and on the lam in a couple hours.

"Gypsy coasters? They suck. We've got theming. Our rides are *art*. That stuff is just *engineering*." Death Waits was a good kid, but he was a serious imbiber of the kool-aid. "Maybe try dance parties again?" They'd tried a string of all-night raves, but the fights, drugs, and sex were just too much for the upper management, no matter how much money they brought in.

Sammy shook his head morosely. "I've told you that a company this size can't afford the risks from that sort of thing." A few more goths straggled in. They headed for the walk-through, which probably meant they planned to get high or make out, something he'd given up on trying to prevent. Anything to get the numbers up. He and the security staff had come to an understanding on this and no one was telling his boss or his colleagues.

"I should just bulldoze the whole fucking thing and start over. What comes after goth, anyway? Are ravers back? Hippies? Punks? Chavs?"

Death Waits was staring at him with round eyes. "You wouldn't really—"

He waved at the kid. This was his whole life. "No, Death, no. We're not going to bulldoze this place. You've got a job for life here." It was a lie of such amazing callousness that Sammy felt a twinge of remorse while saying it. Those twinges didn't come often. But Death Waits looked a lot happier once the words were out of his mouth—goths with big candy-apple cheeks were pretty unconvincing gloom-meisters.

Sammy stalked back to the nearest utilidor entrance, over by what had been the Pinocchio Village Haus. He'd turned the redesign over to a designer who'd started out as a lit major and whose admiration for the dark and twisted elements of the original Pinocchio tale by Carlo Collodi shone through. Now it featured murals of donkeys being flensed by fish, hectic Pleasure Island. Hanged Pinocchio on his gibbet dangled over the condiment bar, twitching and thrashing. The smell of stale grease rose from it like a miasma, clashing with the patchouli they pumped out from the underground misters.

Down into the tunnels and then into a golf cart and out to his office. He had time to paw desultorily at the mountain of merchandise samples that had come in over the week since he'd last tackled it—every plaster-skull vendor and silver cross-maker in the world saw him as a ticket to easy street. None had twigged to the fact that they were *reducing* their goth-themed merch these days. Still, going through merch had been his task for three years now and it was a hard habit to break. He liked the lick-and-stick wounds with dancing maggots that were activated by body heat. The skeletal bikers with flocking algorithms that led them into noisy demolition derbies were a great idea, too, since you'd have to buy another set after a couple hours' play.

His desk was throbbing pink, which meant that he was late for something. He slapped at it, read the message that came up, remembered that there was a weekly status meeting for theme leaders that he'd been specifically instructed to attend. He didn't go to these things if he could help it. The time markers who ran Adventureland and Tomorrowland and so on were all boring curatorial types who thought that change was what you gave a sucker back from a ten at a frozen-banana wagon.

The theme leaders met in a sumptuous boardroom that had been themed in the glory years of the unified Walt Disney Company. It had renewable tropical hardwood paneling, a beautiful garden and a koi pond, and an aviary that teemed with chirruping bright birds borrowed from the Animal Kingdom menagerie. The table was a slab of slate with a brushed finish over its pits and shelves; the chairs were so ergonomic that they had zero adjustment controls, because they knew much better than you ever could how to arrange themselves for your maximum comfort.

He was the last one through the door, and they all turned to stare at him. They all dressed for shit, in old-fashioned slacks and high-tech walking shoes, company pocket tees or baseball jerseys. None of them had a haircut that was worth a damn, not even the two women execs who co-ran Main Street. They dressed like the Middle Americans they catered to, or maybe a little better.

Sammy had always been a sharp dresser. He liked shirts that looked like good cotton but had a little stretch built into them so they rested tight at his chest, which was big, and tight at his waist, which was small. He liked jeans in whatever style jeans were being worn in Barcelona that year, which meant black jeans cut very square and wide-legged, ironed stiff without a crease. He had shades that had been designed to make his face look a little vulpine, a trait he'd always known he had. It put people on edge if you looked a little wolfy.

He stopped outside the door of the boardroom and squared his shoulders. He was the youngest person on the board, and he'd always been the biggest, cockiest bastard in the room. He had to remember that if he was going to survive this next hour.

He came through the door and stopped and looked at the people around the table and waited for everyone to notice him. They looked so midwestern and goofy, and he gave them his wolfy smile—hello, little piggies, here to blow your house down.

"Hey, kids," he said, and grabbed the coffee carafe and a mug off the sideboard. He filled his cup, then passed the carafe off, as though every meeting began with the passing-around of the low-grade stimulants. He settled into his seat and looked around expectantly.

"Glad you could make it, Sammy." That was Wiener, who generally chaired the meetings. Theoretically, it was a rotating chairship, but there's a certain kind of person who naturally ends up running every meeting, and Ron Wiener was that kind of person. He co-ran Tomorrowland with three faceless nonentities who had been promoted above their competence due to his inexplicable loyalty to them, and between the four of them, they'd managed to keep Tomorrowland the most embarrassingly badly themed part of the park. "We were just talking about you."

"I love being the subject of conversation," Sammy said. He slurped loudly at his coffee.

"What we were talking about was the utilization numbers from Fantasyland."

Which sucked, Sammy knew. They'd been in free fall for months now, and looking around at those cowlike midwestern faces, Sammy understood that it was time for the knives to come out.

"They suck," Sammy said brightly. "That's why we're about to change things up."

That preempted them. "Can you explain that some?" Wiener said, clicking his pen and squaring up his notepad. These jerks and their paper fetish.

Sammy did his best thinking on his feet and on the move. Confident. Wolfy. You're better than these jerks with their pads and their corn-fed notions. He sucked in a breath and began to pace and use his hands.

"We're going to take out every underutilized ride in the land, effective immediately. Lay off the deadwood employees. We're going to get a couple off-the-shelf thrill rides and give them a solid working-over for theming—build our own ride vehicles, queue areas, and enclosures, big ones, weenies that will draw your eye from outside the main gate. But that's just a stopgap.

"Next I'm going to start focus-grouping the fatkins. They're ready-made for this stuff. All about having fun. Most of those ex-fatties used to pack this place when they were stuck in electric wheelchairs, but now they're too busy"—he stopped himself from saying "fucking"—"having more adult fun to come back, but anyone who can afford fatkins has discretionary income, and we should have a piece of it.

"It's hard to say without research, but I'm willing to bet that these guys will respond strongly to nostalgia. I'm thinking of reinstating the old Fantasyland dark-rides, digging parts out of storage, whatever we haven't auctioned off on the collectibles market, anyway, and cloning the rest, but remaking them with a little, you know, darkness. Like the Pinocchio thing, but more so. Captain Hook's grisly death. Tinker Bell's inherent porniness. What kind of friendship did Snow White have with the dwarfs? You see where I'm going. Ironic—we haven't done ironic in a long time. It's probably due for a comeback."

They stared at him in shocked silence.

"You say you're going to do this when?" Wiener said. He'd want to know so he could get someone senior to intervene.

"You know, research first. We'll shut down the crap rides next week and can the deadwood. Want to commission the research today if I can. Start work on the filler thrill rides next week, too."

He sat down. They continued to boggle.

"You're serious about this?"

"About what? Getting rid of unprofitable stuff? Researching profitable directions? Yes and yes."

There were other routine agenda items, which reminded Sammy of why he didn't come to these meetings. He spent the time surfing readymade coasters and checking the intranet for engineer availability. He was just getting into the HR records to see who he'd have to lay off when they finally wound down and he sauntered out, giving his wolfy grin to all, with a special flash of it for Wiener.

"Death, I'd like a word, please?"

"I'd be delighted." Death talked like someone who'd learned to talk by being a precocious reader. He over-pronounced his words, spoke in complete sentences, and paused at the commas. Sammy knew that speech pattern well, since he'd worked hard to train himself out of it. It was a geek accent, and it made you sound like a smart-ass instead of a sharp operator. You got that way if you grew up trying to talk with a grown-up vocabulary and a child's control of your speech muscles; you learned to hold your chin and cheeks still while you spoke, to give you a little precision boost. That was the geek accent.

"Remember what we talked about this morning?"

"Building a thrill ride?"

"Yes," Sammy said. He'd forgotten that Death Waits had suggested that in the first place. Good—that was a good spin. "I've decided to take your suggestion. Of course, we need to make room for it, so I'm going to shut down some of the crap—you know which ones I mean."

Death Waits was green under his white makeup. "You mean—"

"All the walk-throughs. The coffin coaster, of course. The flying bats. Maybe one or two others. And I'm going to need to make some layoffs, of course. Gotta make room."

"You're going to lay people off? How many people? We're already barely staffed." Death was the official arbiter of shift changing, schedule swapping, and cross-scheduling. If you wanted to take an afternoon off to get your mom out of the hospital or your dad out of jail, he was the one to talk to.

"That's why I'm coming to you. If I shut down six of the rides—" Death gasped. Fantasyland had ten rides in total. "Six of the rides. How many of the senior staffers can I get rid of and still have the warm bodies to keep everything running?" Senior people cost a *lot* more than the teenagers who came through. He could hire six juniors for what Death cost him. Frigging Florida labor laws meant that you had to give cost-of-living raises every year, and it added up.

Death looked like he was going to cry.

"I've got my own estimates," Sammy said. "But I wanted to get a reality check from you, since you're right there, on the ground. I'd hate to leave too much fat on the bone."

He knew what effect this would have on the kid. Death blinked back his tears, put his fist under his chin, and pulled out his phone and started scribbling on it. He had a list of every employee in there and he began to transfer names from it to another place.

"They'll be back, right? To operate the new rides?"

"The ones we don't bring back, we'll get them unemployment counseling. Enroll them in a networking club for the jobless, one of the really good ones. We can get a group rate. A job reference from this place goes a long way, too. They'll be OK."

Death looked at him, a long look. The kid wasn't stupid, Sammy knew. None of these people were stupid, not Wiener, not the kid, not the goths who led each other around Fantasyland on leashes. Not the fatkins who'd soon pack the place. They were none of them stupid. They were just—soft. Unwilling to make the hard choices. Sammy was good at hard choices.

Perry got home that night and walked in on Lester and Suzanne. They were tangled on the living room carpet, mostly naked, and Lester blushed right to his ass cheeks when Perry came through the door.

"Sorry, sorry!" Lester called as he grabbed a sofa cushion and passed it to Suzanne, then got one for himself. Perry averted his eyes and tried not to laugh.

"Jesus, guys, what's wrong with the bedroom?"

"We would've gotten there eventually," Lester said as he helped Suzanne to her feet. Perry pointedly turned to face the wall. "You were supposed to be at dinner with the gang," Lester said.

"Close-up on the ride was crazy. Everything was changing and the printers were out of goop. Lots of action on the network—Boston and San Francisco are introducing a lot of new items to the ride. By the time I got to the guesthouse, the Kettlewells were already putting the kids to bed." He decided not to mention Eva's angry storm-out to Suzanne. No doubt she had already figured out that all was not well in the House of Kettlewell.

Suzanne ahem'd.

"Sorry, sorry," Lester said. "Let's talk about this later, OK? Sorry."

They scurried off to Lester's room and Perry whipped out a computer, put on some short humor videos in shuffle mode, and grabbed a big tub of spare parts he kept around to fiddle with. It could be soothing to take apart and reassemble a complex mechanism, and sometimes you got ideas from it.

Five minutes later, he heard the shower running and then Suzanne came into the living room.

"I'm going to order some food. What do you feel like?"

"Whatever you get, you'll have to order it from one of the fatkins places. It's not practical to feed Lester any other way. Get me a small chicken tikka pizza."

She pored over the stack of menus in the kitchen. "Does Food in Twenty Minutes really deliver in twenty minutes?"

"Usually fifteen. They do most of the prep in the vans and use a lot of predictive math in their routing. There's usually a van within about ten minutes of here, no matter what the traffic. They deliver to traffic jams, too, on scooters."

Suzanne made a face. "I thought *Russia* was weird." She showed the number on the brochure to her phone and then started to order.

Lester came out a minute later, dressed to the nines as always. He was barely capable of entering his bedroom without effecting a wardrobe change.

He gave Perry a slightly pissed off look and Perry shrugged apologetically, though he didn't feel all that bad. Lester's fault.

Christ on a bike, it was weird to think of the two of them together, especially going at it on the living room rug like a couple of horny teens. Suzanne had always been the grown-up in their little family. But that had been back when there was a big company involved. Something about being a piece of a big company made you want to act like you'd always figured grown-ups should act. Once you were a free agent, there wasn't any reason not to embrace your urges.

When the food came, the two of them attacked it like hungry dogs. It was clear that they'd forgotten their embarrassment and were planning another retreat to the bedroom once they'd refueled. Perry left.

"Hey, Francis." Francis was sitting on the second-story balcony of his mayoral house, surveying the electric glow of the shantytown. As usual now, he was alone, without any of his old gang of boys hanging around him. He waved an arm toward Perry and beckoned him inside, buzzing him in with his phone.

Perry tracked up the narrow stairs, wondering how Francis negotiated them with his bad knee and his propensity to have one beer too many.

"What's the good word?"

"Oh, not much," Perry said. He helped himself to a beer. They made it in the shantytown and fortified it with fruits, like a Belgian beer. The resulting suds were strong and sweet. This one was raspberry and it tasted a little pink, like red soda.

"Your friends aren't getting along too good, is what I hear."

"Really." Nothing was much of a secret in this place.

"The little woman's taken a room of her own down the road. My wife did that to me once. Crazy broad. That's their way sometimes. Get so mad they just need to walk away."

"I get that mad, too," Perry said.

"Oh, hell, me too, all the time. But men usually don't have the guts to pack a suitcase and light out. Women have the guts. They're nothing but guts."

Perry cursed. Why hadn't Kettlebelly called him? What was going on? He called Kettlebelly.

"Hi, Perry!"

"Hi, Landon. What's up?"

"Up?"

"Yeah, how are things?"

"Things?"

"Well, I hear Eva took off. That sort of thing. Anything we can talk about?" Kettlewell didn't say anything.

"Should I come over?"

"No," he said. "I'll meet you somewhere. Where?"

Francis wordlessly passed Kettlewell a beer as he stepped onto the terrace. "So?"

"They're in a motel not far from here. The kids love coffins."

Francis opened another beer for himself. "Hard to imagine a kid loved a coffin more than your kids loved this place this afternoon."

"Eva's pretty steamed at me. It just hasn't been very good since I retired. I guess I'm pretty hard to live with all the time."

Perry nodded. "I can see that."

"Thanks," Kettlewell said. "Also." He took a pull off his beer. "Also, I had an affair."

Both men sucked air between their teeth.

"With her best friend."

Perry coughed a little.

"While Eva was pregnant."

"You're still breathing? Patient woman," Francis said.

"She's a good woman," Kettlewell said. "The best. Mother of my children. But it made her a little crazy jealous."

"So what's the plan, Kettlewell? You're a good man with a plan," Perry said.

"I have to give her a night off to cool down and then we'll see. Never any point in doing this while she's hot. Tomorrow morning, it'll come together."

The next morning, Perry found himself desperately embroiled in ordering more goop for the 3-D printers. *Lots more.* The other rides had finally come online in the night, after interminable network screwups and malfing robots and printers and scanners that wouldn't cooperate, but now there were seven rides in the network, seven rides whose riders were rearranging, adding, and subtracting, and there was reconciling to do. The printers hummed and hummed.

"The natives are restless," Lester said, pointing a thumb over his shoulder at the growing queue of would-be riders. "We going to be ready to open soon?"

Perry had fallen into a classic nerd trap of having almost solved a problem and not realizing that the last 3 percent of the solution would take as long as the rest of it put together. Meanwhile, the ride was in a shambles as robots attempted to print and arrange objects to mirror those around the nation.

"Soon, soon," Perry said. He stood up and looked around at the shambles. "I lie. This crap won't be ready for hours yet. Sorry. Fuck it. Open up."

Lester did.

"I know, I know, but that's the deal with the ride. It's got to get in sync. You know we've been working on this for months now. It's just growing pains. Here, I'll give you back your money. You come back tomorrow; it'll all be set to rights."

The angry rider was a regular, one of the people who came by every morning to ride before work. She was gaunt and tall and geeky and talked like an engineer, with the nerd accent.

"What kind of printer?" Lester broke in. Perry hid his snicker with a cough. Lester would get her talking about the ins and outs of her printer, talking shop, and before you knew it she'd be mollified.

Perry sold another ticket, and another.

"Hi again!" It was the creepy guy, the suit who'd shown up in Boston. Tjan had a crazy theory about why he'd left the Boston launch in such a hurry, but who knew?

"Hi there," Perry said. "Long time no see. Back from Boston, huh?"

"For months." The guy was grinning and sweating and didn't look good. He had a fresh bruise on his cheek with a couple of knuckle prints clearly visible. "Can't wait to get back on the ride. It's been too long."

Sammy had been through a rehab and knew how they went. You laid off a bunch of people in one fast, hard big bang. Hired some unemployment coaches for the senior unionized employees, scheduled a couple of "networking events" where they could mingle with other unemployed slobs and pass around homemade business cards.

You needed a Judas goat, someone who'd talk up the rehab to the other employees, whom you could rely on. Death Waits had been his Judas goat for the Fantasyland goth makeover. He'd tirelessly evangelized the idea to his coworkers, had found goth tru-fans who'd blog the hell out of every inch of the rehab, had run every errand, no matter how menial.

But his passion didn't carry over to dismantling the goth rehab. Sammy should have anticipated that, but he had totally failed to do so. He was just so used to thinking of Death Waits as someone who was a never-questioning slave to the park.

"Come on, cheer up! Look at how cool these thrill rides are going to be. Those were your idea, you know. Check out the coffin cars and the little photo op at the end that photoshops all the riders into zombies. That's got to be right up your alley, right? Your friends are going to love this."

Death moped as only a goth could. He performed his duties slowly and unenthusiastically. When Sammy pinned him down with a direct question, he let his bangs fall over his eyes, looked down at his feet, and went silent.

"Come on, what the hell is going on? The fences were supposed to be up this morning!" The plan had been to get the maintenance crews in before rope-drop to fence off the doomed rides so that the dismantling could begin. But when he'd shown up at eight, there was no sign of the fences, no sign of the maintenance crews, and the rides were all fully staffed.

Death looked at his feet. Sammy bubbled with rage. If you couldn't trust your own people, you were lost. There were already enough people around the park looking for a way to wrong-foot him.

"Death, I'm talking to you. For Christ's sake, don't be such a goddamned baby. You shut down the goddamned rides and send those glue sniffers home. I want a wrecking crew here by lunchtime."

Death Waits looked at his feet some more. His floppy black wings of hair covered his face, but from the snuffling noises, Sammy knew there was some crying going on underneath all that hair.

"Suck it up," he said. "Or go home."

Sammy turned on his heel and started for the door, and that was when Death Waits leapt on his back, dragged him to the ground, and started punching him. He wasn't much of a puncher, but he did have a lot of chunky silver skull rings that really stung. He pasted a couple good ones on Sammy before Sammy came to his senses and threw the skinny kid off of him. Strangely, Sammy's anger was dissipated by the actual, physical violence. He had never thrown a punch in his life and he was willing to bet the same was true of Death Waits. There was something almost funny about an actual punch-up.

Death Waits picked himself up and looked at Sammy. The kid's eyeliner was in smears down his cheeks and his hair was standing on end. Sammy shook his head slowly.

"Don't bother cleaning out your locker. I'll have your things sent to you. And don't stop on your way out of the park, either."

He could have called security, but that would have meant sitting there with Death Waits until they arrived. The kid would go and he would never come back. He was disgraced.

And leave he did. Sammy had Death Waits's employee pass deactivated and the contents of his locker—patchouli-reeking black T-shirts and blunt eyeliner pencils—sent by last-class mail to his house. He cut off Death Waits's benefits. He had the deadwood rides shuttered and commenced their destruction, handing over any piece recognizable as coming from a ride to the company's auction department to list online. Anything to add black to his bottom line.

But his cheek throbbed where Death had laid into him, and he'd lost his fire for the new project. Were fatkins a decent-sized market segment? He should have commissioned research on it. But he'd needed to get a plan in the can in time to mollify the executive committee. Plus he knew what his eyes told him every day: the park was full of fatkins, and always had been.

The ghost of Death Waits was everywhere. Sammy had to figure out for himself whom to fire, and how to do it. He didn't really know any of the goth kids that worked the rides these days. Death Waits had hired and led them. There were lots of crying fits and threats, and the kids he didn't fire acted like they were next, and if it hadn't been for the need to keep revenue flowing, Sammy would have canned all of them.

Then he caught wind of what they were all doing with their severance pay: traveling south to Hollywood and riding that goddamned frankenride in the dead Wal-Mart, trying to turn it into goth paradise. Judging from the message boards he surfed, the whole thing had been Death Waits's idea. Goddamn it.

It was Boston all over again. He'd pulled the plug and the machine kept on moving. The hoardings went up and the rides came down, but all his former employees and their weird eyeliner pervert pals all went somewhere else and partied on just the same. His attendance numbers were way down, and the photobloggers posting shots of black clouds of goths at the frankenride made it clear where they'd all gone.

Fine, he thought, *fine. Let's go have a look.*

The guy with the funny eyebrow made him immediately but didn't seem to be suspicious. Maybe they never figured out what he'd done in Boston. The goth kids were busy in the market stalls or hanging around smoking clove and patchouli hookahs and they ignored him as a square and beneath their notice.

The ride had changed a great deal since his last fated visit. He'd heard about The Story, of course—the dark-ride press had reported on it in an editorial that week. But now The Story—which, as he perceived it, was an orderly progression of what seemed to be someone's life unfolding from childhood naïveté to adolescent exuberance to adult cynicism to a nostalgic, elderly delight—was augmented by familiar accoutrements.

There was a robot zombie head from one of the rides he'd torn down yesterday. And here was half the sign from the coffin coaster. A bat-wing bush from the hedge maze. The little bastards had stolen the deconstructed ride debris and brought it here.

By the time he got off the ride, he was grinning ferociously. By tomorrow there'd be copies of all that trademarked ride stuff rolling off the printers in ten cities around the United States. That was a major bit of illegal activity, and he knew where he could find some hungry attack lawyers who'd love to argue about it. He jumped on the ride again and got his camera configured for low-light shooting.

Eva showed up on Perry's doorstep that night after dinner. Lester and Suzanne had gone off to the beach and Perry was alone, updating his inventory of tchotchkes with a camera and an old computer, getting everything stickered with RFIDs.

She had the kids in tow. Ada spotted the two old, lovely baseball mitts on the crowded coffee table and made a beeline for them, putting one over each hand and walking around smacking them together to hear the leathery sound, snooping in drawers, and peering at the business end of an arc welder that Perry hastily snapped up and put on a high shelf, which winked once to let him know that it had tracked the movement and noted the location of the tool.

The little boy, Pascal, rode on his mother's hip. Eva had clearly had a bit of a cry, but had gotten over it. Now she was determined, with her jaw thrust out and her chin uptilted.

"I don't know what to do about him. He's been driving me crazy since he retired. You know he had an affair?"

"He told me."

She laughed. "He tells *everyone*. He's boasting, you know? Whatever. I know why he did it. Midlife crisis. But before that, it was early-adulthood crisis. And adolescent crisis. That guy doesn't know what to do with himself. He's a good man, but he's out of his fucking mind if he's not juggling a hundred balls."

Perry tried out a noncommittal shrug.

"You're his buddy, I know. But you have to see that it's true, right? I love him, I really do, but he's got a self-destructive streak a mile wide. It doesn't matter how much he loves me or the kids, if he's not torturing himself with work, he's got to come up with something else to screw up his life. I thought that we were going to spend the next twenty years raising the kids, doing volunteer work, and traveling. Not much chance of that, though. You saw how he was looking at Suzanne."

"You think he and Suzanne—"

"No, I asked him and he said no. Then I talked to *her* and she told me that she wouldn't ever let something like that happen. Her I believe." She sat down and dandled the little boy until he gurgled contentedly. Perry heard Ada going crazy in the kitchen with a mechanical sphincter he'd been building. "Rides are a lot of fun, Perry. Your ride, it's amazing. But I don't want to ride a ride for the rest of my life, and Landon is a ride that doesn't stop. You can't get off."

Perry was at a loss. "I've never had a relationship that lasted more than six months, Eva. I've got no business giving you advice on this stuff. Kettlewell is pretty amazing, though. It sounds like you've got him pretty wired, right? You know that if he's busy, he's happy, and when he's slack, he's miserable.

Sounds like if you keep him busy, he'll be the kind of guy you want him to be, even if you won't have much time to play with him."

She unholstered a tit and stuck it in the boy's mouth and Perry looked at the carpet. She laughed. "You are such a geek," she said. "OK, fine. I hear what you're saying. So how do I get him busy again? Can you use him around here?"

"Here?" Perry thought about it. "I don't think we need much empire-building around here."

"I thought you'd say that. Perry, what the hell am I going to do?"

There was a tremendous crash from the kitchen, a shriek of surprise, then a small "oops."

"Ada!" Eva called. "What now?"

"I was playing ball in the house," Ada said in the same small voice. "Even though you have told me not to. And I broke something. I should have listened to you."

Eva shook her head. "Plays me like a goddamned cello," she said. "I'm sorry, Perry. We'll pay for whatever it was."

He patted her arm. "You forget who you're talking to. I love fixing stuff. Don't sweat it."

"Whatever—I'll buy you one and you can use it for parts. Ada! What did you break, anyway?"

"Made of seashells, by the toaster. It's twitching."

"Toast-making seashell robot," Perry said. "No sweat—it was due for an overhaul, anyway."

"Christ," she said. "Toast-making *seashell* robot?"

"Kettlewell is why we gave up making that kind of thing," he said.

"Have you seen him?"

"I've seen him."

"How penitent was he?"

He thought back to Kettlewell's long puss on Francis's terrace. "Yeah, pretty penitent. He's pretty worried, I'd say."

She nodded. "All right then. Maybe he's learned a lesson. Ada! Stop breaking things and get your shoes back on!"

"We going back to Daddy?"

"Yes," she said.

"Good," Ada said.

They were barely out the door when Suzanne and Lester came in. They nodded at Perry and disappeared into the bedroom. Ten minutes later, Suzanne stomped out again. She barely looked at Perry as she disappeared into the corridor, slamming the door behind her.

Perry waited five minutes to see if Lester would come out on his own. This happened sometimes with the fatkins girls; love among the fatkins was stormy and unpredictable and Lester seemed to like bragging about the melt-downs they experienced, each one an oddity of sybaritic fatkins culture to boast about.

But Lester didn't come out this time. Perry thought about calling him or sending him an email. Finally, Perry went and knocked at his door.

"Oh, go back to the living room. I'll come out, I'll come out."

Perry went back and moused desultorily at some ride-fan blogs for a while, listening for Lester's door opening. Finally, out he came, long-faced and puffy-eyed.

Perry shook his head. Was everyone miserable tonight?

"Hello, Lester," he said. "Something on your mind?"

He barked a humorless laugh. "With her, I'm still fat."

Perry nodded as though he understood, though he didn't.

"Since fatkins, I've felt like—I don't know—a real person. When I was big, I was invisible and totally asexual. I didn't think about having sex with anyone and no one ever thought about having sex with me. When I felt something for a woman, it was more like a big, romantic love, like I was a beast and she was a beauty and we could enjoy some kind of chaste, spiritual love.

"Fatkins made me . . . whole. A whole person, with a life below my belt as well as above my neck. I know it looks gross and desperate to you, but to me it's a celebration. Every time I get together with a fatkins girl and we're, you know, partying—for both of us it becomes something really intimate. A denial of pain. A fuck-you to the universe that made us so gross and untouchable."

"And with her, you're still fat, huh?"

Lester winced. "Yeah, it's my problem. I guess I really resent her for not wanting me when I was big, though I totally get why she wouldn't have."

"Maybe you're angry that she wants you now."

"Huh." Lester looked at his hands, which he was dry-washing in his lap. "OK, maybe. Why should she want me now? I'm the same person, after all."

"Except that you're whole now."

"Urk." Lester started pacing. "Who broke the toast robot?"

"Kettlewell's daughter, Ada. Eva was over with the kids. She moved out on Kettlebelly." He thought about whether he should tell Lester. What the hell. "She thinks he's in love with Suzanne."

"Jesus," Lester said. "Maybe we should swap. I'll take Eva and he can take Suzanne."

"You're such a pig," Perry said.

"You know us fatkins—fuck, food, and folly."

"So what's going on with you and Suzanne now?"

"She's gone away until I can get naked around her without either bursting into tears or making sarcastic remarks."

Jesus. Crying. Perry couldn't remember when he'd ever seen Lester cry. It was waterworks city these days around here.

"Ah." Perry just wanted this day to be over. He missed Hilda, though he barely knew her. It would have been nice to have someone here at home with him, someone he could cuddle up to in bed and talk this all out with. Maybe he should call Tjan. He hit the button on his computer that made the TV blink the time in Morse code. It was 1 AM. He'd have to be up in six hours to get the ride up and running. Screw all this; he was going to bed. He hadn't even gotten a single email from Hilda since he'd left Madison. Not that he'd sent one to her, of course.

Lester was still snoring when Perry slipped out of the condo, a bulb of juice and a microwavable venison and quail-egg breakfast burrito under his arm. He had a little glove-box microwave and by the time he hit his first red light, the burrito was nuclear hot and ready to eat. He gobbled it one-handed while he made his way to the ride.

There were two cop cars at the end of the driveway leading to the parking lot. Broward County sheriff's deputy black-and-whites, parked horizontally to blockade the drive.

Perry pulled over and got out of his car slowly, keeping his hands in plain sight. The doors of the cruisers opened, too. The deputies already had their mirrorshades on, though the sun was still rising, and they set down their coffees on the hood of the cars.

"This yours?" A deputy said, jerking his thumb over his shoulder at the flea market and the ride.

Perry knew better than to answer any questions. "Can I help you?"

"We're shutting you down, buddy, sorry." The cop was young, Latina, and female, her partner was older, white and male, with the ruddy complexion that Perry associated with old-time Florida cops.

"What's the charge?"

"There's no charge," the male cop said. He sounded like he was angry already and anything Perry said would just make him angrier. "We charge you if we're going to arrest you. We're enforcing an injunction. Now, if you try to get past us, we'll come up with a charge and *then* we'll arrest you."

"Can I see the injunction?"

"Sure, you can go to the courthouse and see the injunction."

"Aren't you supposed to have a copy of it to show to me?"

"Am I?" The cop's grin was mean and impatient.

"Can I go and get some stuff from my office?"

"If you want to get arrested you can." He pulled a dyspeptic face and drank some coffee, then got back into his cruiser.

The other cop had the grace to look faintly embarrassed at her asshole partner, but then she, too, got back in her car.

Perry thought furiously about this. The cop was clearly itching to bust his ass. Maybe he hated the ride, or this duty, or maybe he hated Perry—maybe he was one of the cops who had raided the shantytown all those years before. Perry had taken a pretty big settlement off the county over the shot in his head, and it was a sure bet that a lot of cops had suffered for it and now harbored some enmity for him.

As bad as this was, it was about to get worse. The goth kids who'd been hanging around in droves lately—they didn't seem like the sort with a lot of good instincts when it came to dealing with authority figures. Then there were the flea-market stall owners, who'd be coming over the road to open their shops in an hour or so. This could get really goddamned ugly.

He needed a lawyer, and someone to front for him with the lawyer. He could call Tjan—he would call him, in fact, but not just yet. There were limits to what Tjan could do from Boston, after all.

He got back in his car and peeled across the road to the shantytown and the guesthouse.

"Kettlewell!" He thumped the door. "Come on, Landon, it's me, Perry. It's an emergency."

He heard Eva curse, then heard movement. "Whazzit?"

"Sorry, man, I wouldn't have woken you but it's a real emergency."

"Fire?"

"No. Cops. They've shut down the ride."

Kettlewell opened the door a crack and stared at him with a red-rimmed, hungover eye. "Cops shut down the ride?"

"Yeah, they say there's an injunction."

"Gimme a sec, gotta put some pants on." He closed the door. As Perry listened to the sounds of him getting dressed, he reflected that he'd done Eva the favor she'd been seeking: he'd found something to keep Kettlewell busy.

Kettlewell quizzed him intensely as they drove back across the road to the police cars. He called Tjan and got voicemail, left a brief message, then got out of the car and stood still outside it, waving at the cop cars.

"What?"

The male cop looked even more dyspeptic.

"Hi there! I wondered if I could get you to explain what's going on here so we can open up shop again?"

"We've shut you down to enforce an injunction."

"What injunction is that?"

"A court injunction."

"Which court?"

The cop looked really angry for a second, then he got back in his car and fished around. "Broward County." He sounded aggrieved.

"Is that the injunction there?" Kettlewell said.

"No," the cop said, too quickly. They both knew he was lying, jerking them around.

"Can I see it? Does it have information about who to talk to to get the injunction lifted?" Kettlewell's tone was even, pleasant and very adult. The voice of someone used to being obeyed.

"You'll have to go to the courthouse. They open in a couple hours."

"I'd really like to see it."

"Oh for chrissakes," the female cop said. "Just show it to them, Tom. God." She spat on the ground. Her partner gave her a look, then handed the paper over to Kettlewell, who pored over it intently. Perry shoulder-surfed him and gathered that they were being shut down for infringing Disney Parks Company trademarks. That was weird. You could hardly go ten feet in Florida without tripping over a bootleg Mickey, so why should the market stalls' Mickey designs trigger legal action?

"All right, then," Kettlewell said. "Let's make some phone calls."

They got in the car and drove across the road to the shantytown. There was a teahouse that opened early and they commandeered its window table and spread out their things. Perry called Lester and woke him up. It took two or three tries to get his head around it—Lester couldn't figure out why they'd shut down the market stalls, but once he got that the ride was down, too, he woke up fast and promised to meet them.

Kettlewell's conversation with Tjan was a lot more heated. Perry tried to eavesdrop but couldn't make any sense of it.

"All the rides are down," he said once he'd dropped the phone to bounce a couple times on the tabletop, making the coffees shiver. "Every one of them was shut down by the cops this morning."

"You're shitting me. But they don't all sell the same stuff."

"They were shut down because of Disney trademarks in the ride itself, or so it seems. Now, what are we going to do? Tjan's hired a lawyer for the Boston group and we can hire one for here, but I don't think we're going to be able to hire fixers everywhere that there's a ride. That's going to be really expensive. Disney's filed all the injunctions at the state level—they have an industry association they work through that has cooperating attorneys in every city in the country, so it was easy for them."

"Holy crap."

"Yeah. Who did you piss off, Perry?"

Damned if he knew. He literally couldn't think of a single person who'd want to do this—someone had convinced the Disney company to clobber him like Godzilla going after Tokyo. It just didn't make any sense.

"So what do we do?"

Kettlewell looked at him. "I have no clue, Perry. You aren't a company. You aren't a network of companies. You aren't an industry association. No one can speak for you. You can't lobby or even field a spokesman. I mean, none of that stuff works for you—and that's the only way I know to fight back in court."

"I thought we were immune to this stuff. If there's no one to sue, how can they sue us?"

"If there's no one to sue, there's no one to show up in court and object, either."

"Yeah."

"I don't think we can incorporate you in time to make a difference," Kettlewell said. "So we need to think of something else."

Suzanne slid into the booth beside them. Her hair was tied back and her makeup was spare and severe. She had on European-cut trousers, high like a bolero dancer's, and a loose, flowing white cotton overshirt on top of a luminescent pink tank. Perry couldn't tell whether it was formal or informal, but it looked good and a little intimidatingly foreign. She didn't meet Perry's eye.

"Brief me," she said. She held out her phone and put it in record mode.

Kettlewell ran it down quickly and she nodded, jotting notes.

"So what happens next?"

"Not much we can do," Kettlewell said.

"The riders will be along shortly. Oh, and the merchants." Perry still couldn't catch her eye.

"I'll go take some pictures," she said.

"Be careful," Perry said.

She mugged for him. "Sweetie, I take pictures of the mafiyeh." Then it was all right between them again, somehow.

"Right," Kettlewell said. "How's our time looking?"

"Got thirty minutes until the first of the merchants show up. An hour until the riders start turning up."

"You don't have a lawyer, do you?"

Perry quirked his funny eyebrow.

"Stupid question. OK. Right, I'll make some more calls. Let's get some people out of bed."

"What can I do?"

Kettlewell looked at him. "Huh. Um. This is really my beat now. I suppose you could go keep Suzanne company."

"Gee, thanks."

"Something wrong with Suzanne?"

"Nothing's wrong with Suzanne," he said. "OK, off I go."

He set off on foot. The shantytown had woken up now, people getting ready for the hike to the early buses into places where the few remaining jobs were.

He took his phone out and tossed it from hand to hand. Then he called the number that he'd programmed in all those days ago in Madison but had never bothered to call. He forgot until the ringing started that it was another time zone there—an hour or two earlier. But when Hilda answered, she sounded wide awake.

"Nice of you to call," she said.

"Nice of you to answer." Her voice sent a thrill up his spine.

"We've got cops outside of the ride here," she said. "We've only been live for a week, too."

"They're at every ride," he said. "They shut us down, too."

"Well, what are you going to do about it?"

"What am *I* going to do about it?"

"Sure, this is your thing, Perry. We woke up and discovered the cops this morning and the first thing everyone did was wonder when you'd call with the plan."

"You're kidding. What do I know about cops?"

"What do any of us know about cops? All we know is we built this thing after you came and talked to us about it and now it's been shut down, so we're waiting for you to tell us what to do next."

He groaned and sat down on a curb. "Oh, crap."

Then she sighed heavily at the other end. "OK, Perry, you need to pull it together. We need you now. We need something that explains what's going on, what to do next, and how to do it. There's a lot of energy out here, a lot of people ready to fight. Just point us in the right direction."

"I have a guy who's trying to figure that out right now."

"Perfect. Now you need to set up a conference call with every ride operator so we can talk this over. Get online and post a time and an address. I'll chat it up and make some calls. You make some calls, too. Everyone likes to hear from you. They like to know you're on their side."

"Right," he said, getting back to his feet, turning around to get his computer out of his trunk. "Right. That's totally the right thing to do. I'm on it."

"Good man," she said.

A little pause stretched between them. "So," he said. "How you doing, apart from all this?"

Her laugh was merry. "I thought you'd never ask. I'm looking forward to your next visit, is how I'm doing."

"Really?"

"Of course really."

"You sounded a little pissed at me there, is all." He sounded like a lovesick teenager. "I mean—" He broke off.

"Your ass needed kicking, was all." Pause. "I'm not pissed at you, though. When are you coming for a visit?"

"Got me," he said. "I guess I should, right?" He really sounded like a teenager.

"You need to visit all the sites, check in on how we're doing." Pause. "Plus you should come hang out with me some."

He almost pointed out all her warnings about only having a one-night stand and not missing the people he was away from and so forth, but stayed his tongue. The fact that she wanted him to come for a visit was overshadowing everything, even the looming crisis with the cops.

"It's a deal."

"Deal."

"Well, bye."

"Bye."

He almost said, "You hang up first," but that would have been too much. Instead he just kept the phone at his ear until he heard her click.

Suzanne was pointing and shooting like mad. Perry sat down on the cracked pavement beside her and unfolded his computer and started sending out emails, setting up a conference channel. He gave Suzanne a short version of his talk with Hilda, being careful not to give a hint of his feelings for her.

"She sounds like a sensible girl," Suzanne said. "You should go and pay her another visit."

He blushed and she socked him in the shoulder.

"Take your call," she said. The cops were giving them the hairy eyeball, and Perry screwed in his headset.

The conference channel was filling up. Perry checked off names as reps from all the rides came online. There was a lot of tight, tense chatter, jokes about the fuzz.

"OK," Perry said. "Let's get it started. There's cops blockading every ride, right? Use the poll please." He posted a poll to the conference page and it quickly got to 100 percent green. "So I just found the cops outside of mine, too, and I'm not sure what to do about it. I've got some dough for a lawyer, but I can't afford lawyers for everyone. To make that work, we'd have to fly attorneys to every city with a ride in it, and that's not practical, as I'm sure you can tell."

A half-dozen flags went up in the conference page. "I need someone to play moderator, 'cause I can't talk and mod at the same time. How about you, Hilda?"

"OK," she said. "I'm Hilda Hammersen, from the Madison group. Post one-line summaries of your points and I'll set a speaker order."

The conference page filled up. There was the official back channel at the bottom, where the text was spilling by too fast for Perry to parse, and he knew that there were lots of unofficial back channels in use, too. He covered the mic and sighed. He had nothing to say to these people. He didn't have any answers.

"Right. So who knows what we should do?" The back channel went crazy. Hilda started green-lighting speakers with their flags up.

"Why are you asking us, Perry? You've got to run this." The voice was petulant and Perry saw that it was one of the Boston crew, which made him wonder what Tjan was going to do when he discovered that Perry was doing this.

The page pinkened and then sank into red. The other people on the call clearly thought this was BS, which was a relief to Perry. Hilda cued up the next speaker.

"We could set up information pickets at the gates to each ride hitting people up for donations for our legal defense—get the press to cover it and maybe we could bring in enough to fight all the injunctions."

The pink lightened a little, went back to neutral white, turned a little green. Perry slowed down the back channel a little and skimmed it:

> No way could we bring in enough, that's like thirty grand each I get a couple hundred people here in the morning and that would mean a hundred and fifty bucks each
> No no it's totally doable we can raise that easy just set up some paypals and publicize the shit out of it

The next speaker was talking. "What if we got the maintenance bots to break open the doors and carry the ride outside where everyone can see it?"

Bright red. Dumb idea.

Perry broke in. "I'm worried that when people show up it'll provoke some kind of confrontation with the law. It could get ugly here. How can we keep that cooled out?"

Green.

"That's totally got to be our top priority," Hilda said.

Next speaker. "OK, so the best way to keep people calm is to tell them that there's an alternative to going nuts, which maybe could be raising money for a legal defense."

Greenish. "What about finding pro bono lawyers? What about the ACLU or EFF?"

Greener.

The back channel filled up with URLs and phone numbers and email addresses.

"OK, time's running out here," Perry said. "You guys need to organize a call-around to those orgs and see if they'll help us out. Pass the hat at your rides, try to find lawyers. Everyone keep reporting in all day—especially if you get a win anywhere. I'm going to go take care of things here."

Hilda IMed him: "Good luck, Perry. You'll kick ass."

Perry started to IM back, but a shadow fell across his screen. It was Jason, who ran the contact lens stall. He was staring at the two cop cars quizzically, looking groggy but growing alarmed.

Perry closed his lid and got to his feet. "Morning, Jason." Behind Jason were five or six other vendors. The sellers who lived in the shantytown and could therefore walk to work were always first in. Soon the commuters would start arriving in their beater cars.

"Hey, Perry," Jason said. He was chewing on an unlit cigarette, a disgusting habit that was only marginally less gross than smoking them. He'd tried toothpicks, but nothing would satisfy his oral cravings like a filter-tip. At least he didn't light them. "What's up?"

Perry told him what he knew, which wasn't much. Jason listened carefully, as did the other vendors who arrived. "They're fucking with you, man. The cops, Disney, all of them. Just fucking with you. You go ahead and hire a lawyer to go to court for you and see how far it gets you. They're not playing by any rules, they're not interested in the law you broke or whatever. They just want to fuck with you."

Suzanne appeared over Perry's shoulder.

"I'm Suzanne Church, Jason. I'm a reporter."

"Sure, I know you. You were there when they burned down the old place."

"That was me. I think you're right. They're fucking with you guys. I want to report on that because it might be that exposing it makes it harder to continue. Can I record what you guys say and do?"

Jason grinned and slid the soggy cig from one corner of his mouth to the other and back again. "Sure, that's cool with me." He turned to the other sellers: "You guys don't mind, do you?" They joked and laughed and said no. Perry let out a breath slowly. These guys didn't want a confrontation with the cops—they knew better than him that they couldn't win that one.

Suzanne started interviewing them. The cops got out of their cars and stared at them. The woman cop had her mirrorshades on now, and so the both of them looked hard and eyeless. Perry looked away quickly.

The vendors with cars were pulling them around to the roadside leading up to the ride, unpacking merchandise, and setting it out on their hoods. Vendors from the shantytown headed home and came back with folding tables and blankets. These guys were business people. They weren't going to let the law stand in the way of putting food on the table for their families.

The cops got back into their cars. Kettlewell worked his way cautiously across the freeway, climbing laboriously over the median. He had changed into a smart blazer and slacks, with a crisp white shirt that hid his incipient belly. He looked like the Kettlewell of old, the kind of man used to giving orders and getting respect.

"Hey, man," Perry said. Kettlewell's easy smile was reassuring.

"Perry," he said, throwing an arm around his shoulders and leading him away. "Come here and talk with me."

They stood in the lee of one of the sickly palms that stood by the roadside. The day was coming up hot and Perry's T-shirt stuck to his chest, though Kettlewell seemed dry and in control.

"What's going on, Perry?"

"Well, we did a phoner this morning with all the ride operators. They're going to work on raising money for the defense and getting pro bono lawyers from the EFF or the ACLU or something."

Kettlewell did a double take. "Wait, what? They're going to ask the ACLU? They can't be trusted, Perry. They're *impact litigators*—they'll take cases to make a point, even when it's not in their clients' best interests."

"What could be more in our interests than getting lawyers to fight these bogus injunctions?"

Kettlewell blew out a long breath. "OK, table it. Table it. Here's what I've been pulling together: we've got a shitkicking corporate firm that used to handle the Kodacell business that's sending out a partner to go to the Broward County court this morning to get the injunction lifted. They're doing this as a freebie, but I told them that they could handle the business if we put together all the rides into one entity."

Now it was Perry's turn to boggle. "What kind of entity?"

"We have to incorporate them all, get them all under one umbrella so that we can defend them all in one go. Otherwise there's no way we're going to be able to save them. Without a corporate entity, it's like trying to herd cats. Besides, you need some kind of structure, a formal constitution or something for this thing. You've got a network protocol, and that's it. There's money at stake here—potentially some big money—and you can't run something like that on a handshake. It's too vulnerable. You'll get embezzled or sued into oblivion before you even have a chance to grow. So I've started the paperwork to get everything under one banner."

Perry counted to ten, backwards. "Landon, I'm really thankful that you're helping us out here. You're probably going to save our asses. But you can't put everything under one banner—you can't just declare to these people that their projects are ours—"

"Of course they're yours. They're using your IP, your protocols, your designs. . . . If they don't come on board, you can just threaten to sue them—"

"Landon! Please listen to me. We are not going to effect a hostile takeover of my friends. They are equal owners of everything we do here. And no offense, but if you ever mention suing other projects over our 'IP' "—he made sarcastic finger quotes—"then we're through having any discussions about this. OK?"

Kettlewell snorted air through his nostrils. "My apologies. I didn't realize that this was such a sensitive area for you." Perry boggled at this—lawsuits against ride operators! "But I can get that. Here's the thing, Perry. Without some kind of fast-moving structure you're going to be dead. Even if we repel the boarders this morning, they'll be back tomorrow and the day after. You need something stronger than a bunch of friends who have loose agreements. You need a legal entity that can speak for everyone. Maybe that's a co-op or a charity or something else, but it's got to exist. You may not think you have any say over these other rides, but does everyone else agree? What if you get sued for someone's bad deeds in Minneapolis? What if some ride operator sues *you* to put you out of business?"

Perry's head swam. He hated conversations like this. He didn't have any good answer for Kettlewell's objections, but it was ridiculous. No one from a ride was going to sue him. Or maybe they would, if he got all grabby and went MINE MINE MINE and incorporated everything with him at the top. Hilda said he was the one they all looked to, but that was because he would never try to hijack their projects.

"No."

"No what?"

"No to all of it. We have to defend this thing, but we're not going to do it by trying to tie everyone down to contracts and agreements where I get to control everything. Maybe a co-op is the right way to go, but we can't just declare a co-op and force everyone to be members. We have to get everyone to agree, everyone who's involved, and then they can elect a council or something and work out some kind of uniform agreement. I mean, that's how all the good free software projects work. There's authority, but it's not all unilateral and imperious. I'm not interested in that. I'd rather shut this down than declare myself pope-emperor of ride land."

Kettlewell scrubbed his eyes with his fists. Up close, the lines in his face were deep-sunk, his eyeballs bloodshot and hung over. "You're killing me, you know that? What good is principle going to do when they knock this fucking thing down and slap you with a gigantic lawsuit?"

Perry shrugged. "I really appreciate what you've done, but I'd rather lose it than fuck it up."

They stared at each other for a long time. Cars whizzed past. Perry felt like a big jerk. Kettlewell had done amazing work for him this morning, just out of the goodness of his own heart, and Perry had repaid him by being a stiff-necked dickwad. He felt an overwhelming desire to take it back, just put Kettlewell in charge and let him run the whole show. Just shrug his shoulders and abdicate.

He looked down at the ground and up into the straggly palms, then heaved a sigh.

"Landon, I'm sorry, OK, but that's just how it is. I totally dig that you're saying that we're risking everything by not doing it your way, but from my seat, doing it your way will kill it anyway. So we need a better answer."

Kettlewell scrubbed his eyes some more. "You and my wife sound like you'd get along."

Perry waited for him to go on, but it became clear he had nothing more to say.

Perry went back to the cop cars just as the first gang of goths showed up to take a ride.

PART III

Sammy had filled a cooler and stuck it in the backseat of his car the night before, programmed his coffeemaker, and when his alarm roused him at 3 AM, he hit the road. First he guzzled his thermos of lethal coffee, then reached around in back for bottles of icy distilled water. He kept the windows rolled down and breathed in the swampy, cool morning air, the most promising air of the Florida day, before it all turned to steam and sizzle.

He didn't bother looking for truck stops when he needed to piss, just pulled over on the turnpike's side and let fly. Why not? At that hour, it was just him and the truckers and the tourists with morning flights.

He reached Miami ahead of schedule and had a diner breakfast big enough to kill a lesser man, a real fatkins affair. He got back on the road, groaning from the chow, and made it to the old Wal-Mart just as the merchants were setting up their market on the roadside.

When he'd done the Boston ride, he'd been discouraged that they'd kept on with their Who-ville Xmas even though he'd Grinched away all their fun, but this time he was expecting something like this. Watching these guys sell souvenirs at the funeral for the ride made him feel pretty good this time around: their disloyalty had to be a real morale killer for those ride operators.

The cops were getting twitchy, which made him grin. Twitchy cops were a key ingredient for bad trouble. He reached behind him and pulled an iced coffee from the cooler and cracked it, listening to the hiss as the embedded CO_2 cartridge forced bubbles through it.

Now here came a suit. He looked like a genuine mighty morphin' power broker, which made Sammy worry, because a guy like that hadn't figured into his plans, but look at that; he was having a huge fight with the eyebrow guy and now the eyebrow guy was running away from him.

Getting the lawyers to agree to spring the budget to file in every location where there was a ride had been tricky. Sammy had had to fudge a little on his research, claim that they were bringing in real money, tie it to the drop in numbers in Florida, and generally do a song and dance, but it was all worth it. These guys clearly didn't know whether to shit or go blind.

Now eyebrow man was headed for the cop cars and the entrance, and there, oh yes, there it was. Five cars' worth of goths, lugging bags full of some kind of homemade or scavenged horror memorabilia, pulling up short at the entrance.

They piled out of their cars and started milling around, asking questions. Some approached the cops, who seemed in no mood to chat. The body language could be read at 150 feet:

GOTH: But, officer, I wanna get on this riiiiiide.

COP: You sicken me.

GOTH: All around me is gloom, gloom. Why can't I go on my riiiiiide?

COP: I would like to arrest you and lock you up for being a weird, sexually ambiguous melodramatic who's dumb enough to hang around out of doors, all in black, in *Florida*.

GOTH: Can I take your picture? I'm gonna put it on my blog and then everyone will know what a meanie you are.

COP: Yap yap yap, little bitch. You go on photographing me and mouthing off, see how long it is before you're in cuffs in the back of this car.

SCUMBAG STREET VENDORS: Ha ha ha, look at these goth kids mouthing off to the law, that cop must have minuscule testicles!

COP: Don't make me angry; you wouldn't like me when I'm angry.

EYEBROW GUY: Um, can everyone just be nice? I'd prefer that this all not go up in flames.

SCUMBAGS, GOTHS: Hurr hurr hurr, shuttup; look at those dumb cops, ahahaha.

COPS: Grrrr.

EYEBROW: Oh, shit.

Four more cars pulled up. Now the shoulder was getting really crowded and freeway traffic was slowing to a crawl.

More goths piled out. Family cars approached the snarl, slowed, then sped up again, not wanting to risk the craziness. Maybe some of them would get on the fucking turnpike and drive up to Orlando, where the real fun was.

The four-lane road was down to about a lane and a half, and milling crowds from the shantytown and the arriving cars were clogging what remained of the thoroughfare. Now goths were parking their cars way back at the intersection and walking over, carrying the objects they'd planned to sacrifice to the ride and smoking clove cigarettes.

Sammy saw Death Waits before Death Waits turned his head, and so Sammy had time to duck down before he was spotted. He giggled to himself and chugged his coffee, crouched down below the window.

The situation was heating up now. Lots of people were asking questions of the cops. People trying to drive through got shouted at by the people in the road. Sometimes a goth would slam a fist down on a hood and there'd be a little bit of back and forth. It was a powder keg, and Sammy decided to touch it off.

He swung his car out into the road and hit the horn and revved his engine, driving through the crowd just a hair faster than was safe. People slapped his car as it went by and he just leaned on the horn, ploughing through, scattering people who knocked over vendors' tables and stepped on their wares.

In his rearview, he saw the chaos begin. Someone threw a punch, someone slipped, someone knocked over a table of infringing merch. Wa-hoo! Party time!

He hit the next left, then pointed his car at the freeway. He reached back and snagged another can of coffee and went to work on it. As the can hissed open, he couldn't help himself: he chuckled. Then he laughed—a full, loud belly laugh.

Perry watched it happen as though it were all a dream: The crowds thickening. The cops getting out of their cars and putting their hands on their belts. A distant siren. More people milling around, hanging out in the middle of the road, like idiots, *idiots*. Then that jerk in the car—what the hell was he thinking, he was going to kill someone!

And then it all exploded. There was a knot of fighting bodies over by the tables, and the knot was getting bigger. The cops were running for them, batons out, pepper spray out. Perry shouted something, but he couldn't hear himself. In a second the crowd noises had gone from friendly to an angry roar.

Perry spotted Suzanne watching it all through the viewfinder on her phone, presumably streaming it live, then shouted again, an unheard warning, as a combatant behind her swung wide and clocked her in the head. She went down and he charged for her.

He'd just reached her when a noise went off that dropped him to his knees. It was their antipersonnel sound cannon, which meant that Lester was around here somewhere. The sound was a physical thing; it made his bowels loose and made his head ring like a gong. Thought was impossible. Everything was impossible except curling up and wrapping your hands around your head.

Painfully, he raised his head and opened his eyes. All around him, people were on their knees. The cops, though, had put giant industrial earmuffs on, the kind of thing you saw jackhammer operators wearing. They were moving rapidly toward . . . Lester, who was in a pickup truck with the AP horn stuck in the cargo bed, wired into the cigarette lighter. They had guns drawn and Lester was looking at them wide-eyed, hands in the air.

Their mouths were moving, but whatever they were saying was inaudible. Perry took his phone out of his pocket and aimed it at them. He couldn't move without spooking them and possibly knocking himself out from the sound, but he could rodneyking them as they advanced on Lester. He could practically read Lester's thoughts: *If I move to switch this off, they'll shoot me dead.*

The cops closed on Lester and then the sour old male cop was up in the bed and he had Lester by the collar, throwing him to the ground, pointing his gun. His partner moved quickly and efficiently around the bed, eventually figuring out how to unplug the horn. The silence rang in his head. He couldn't hear anything except a dog-whistle whine from his abused eardrums. Around him, people moved sluggishly, painfully.

He got to his feet as quick as he could and drunk-walked to the truck. Lester was already in plastic cuffs and leg restraints, and the big, dead-eyed cop was watching an armored police bus roll toward them in the eerie silence of their collective deafness.

Perry managed to switch his phone over to streaming, so that it was uploading everything instead of recording it locally. He faded back behind some of the cars for cover and kept rolling as the riot bus disgorged a flying squadron of helmeted cops who began to methodically and savagely grab, cuff, and toss the groaning crowd lying flat on the ground. He wanted to add narration, but he didn't trust himself to whisper, since he couldn't hear his own voice.

A hand came down on his shoulder and he jumped, squeaked, and fell into a defensive pose, waiting for the truncheon to hit him, but it was Suzanne, grim-faced, pointing her own phone. She had a laminated press pass out in her free hand and was holding it up beside her head like a talisman. She pointed off down the road, where some of the goth kids who'd just been arriving when things went down were more ambulatory, having been somewhat shielded from the noise. They were running and being chased by cops. She made a little scooting gesture and Perry understood that she meant he should be following them, getting the video. He sucked in a big breath and nodded once and set off. She gave his hand a firm squeeze and he felt that her palms were slick with sweat.

He kept low and moved slow, keeping the viewfinder up so that he could keep the melee in shot. He hoped like hell that someone watching this online would spring for his bail.

Miraculously, he reached the outlier skirmish without being spotted. He recorded the cops taking the goths down, cuffing them, and hooding one kid who was thrashing like a fish on a hook. It seemed that he would never be spotted. He crept forward, slowly, slowly, trying to feel invisible and unnoticed, trying to project it.

It worked. He was getting incredible footage. He was practically on top of the cops before anyone noticed him. Then there was a shout and a hand grabbed for his phone and the spell was broken. Suddenly his heart was thundering, his pulse pounding in his ears.

He turned on his heel and ran. A mad giggle welled up in his chest. His phone was still streaming, presumably showing wild, nauseous shots of the landscape swinging past as he pumped his arm. He was headed for the ride, for the rear entrance, where he knew he could take cover. He felt the footsteps thud behind him, dimly heard the shouts—but his temporary deafness drowned out the words.

He had his fob out before he reached the doors, and he badged in, banging the fob over the touch plate an instant before slamming into the crash bar and the doors swung open. He waited in agitation for the doors to hiss shut slowly after him, and then it was the gloom of the inside of the ride, dark in his sun-adjusted eyesight.

It was only when the doors shivered behind him that he realized what he'd just done. They'd break in and come and get him, and in the process, they'd destroy the ride, for spite. His eyes were adjusting to the gloom now and he made out the familiar/unfamiliar shapes of the dioramas, now black and lacy with goth memorabilia. This place gave him calm and joy. He would keep them from destroying it.

He set his phone down on the floor, propped against a plaster skull so that the doorway was in the shot. He walked to the door and shouted as loud as he could, his voice inaudible in his own ears. "I'm coming out now!" he shouted. "I'm opening the doors!"

He waited for a two-count, then reached for the lock. He turned it and let the door crash open as two cops in riot visors came through, pepper spray at the fore. He was down on the ground, writhing and clawing at his face in an instant, and the phone caught it all.

All Perry wanted was for someone to cut the plastic cuffs off so he could scrub at his eyes, though he knew that would only make it worse. The riot bus sounded like an orgy, moaning and groaning with dozens of voices every time the bus jounced over a pothole.

Perry was on the floor of the bus, next to a kid—judging from the voice—who cursed steadily the whole way along. One hard jounce made their heads connect and they both cussed, then apologized to one another, then laughed a little.

"My name's Perry." His voice sounded like he was underwater, but he could hear. The pepper spray seemed to have cleared out his sinuses and given him back some of his hearing.

"I'm Death Waits." He said it without any drama. Perry wasn't sure if he'd heard right. He supposed he had. Goth kids.

"Nice to meet you."

"Likewise." Their heads were banged together again. They laughed and cursed.

"Christ my face hurts," Perry said.

"I'm not surprised. You look like a tomato."

"You can see?"

"Lucky me, yup. I got a pretty good couple of whacks on the back and shoulders once I was down, but no gas."

"Lucky you all right."

"I'm more pissed that I lost the tombstone I brought down. It was a real rarity, and it was hard to get, too. I bet it got tromped."

"Tombstone, huh?"

"From the Graveyard Walk at Disney. They tore it down last week."

"And you were bringing it to add it to the ride?"

"Sure—that's where it belongs."

Perry's face still burned, but the pain was lessening. Before it had been like his face was on fire. Now it was like a million fire ants biting him. He tried to put it out of his mind by concentrating on the pain in his wrists where the plastic straps were cutting into him.

"Why?"

There was a long silence. "Has to go somewhere. Better there than in a vault or in the trash."

"How about selling it to a collector?"

"You know, it never occurred to me. It means too much to go to a collector."

"The tombstone means too much?"

"I know it sounds stupid, but it's true. You heard that Disney's tearing out all the goth stuff? Fantasyland meant a lot to some of us."

"You didn't feel like it was, what, co-opting you?"

"Dude, you can buy goth clothes at a chain of mall stores. We're all over the mainstream/nonmainstream fight. If Disney wants to put together a goth homeland, that's all right with me. And that ride, it was the best place to remember it. You know that it got copied over every night to other rides around the country? So all the people who loved the old Disney could be part of the memorial, even if they couldn't come to Florida. We had the idea last week and everyone loved it."

"So you were putting stuff from Disney rides into my ride?"

"Your ride?"

"Well, I built it."

"No fucking way."

"Way." He smiled and that made his face hurt.

"Dude, that is the coolest thing ever. You built that? How did—how do you become the kind of person who can build one of those things? I'm out of work and trying to figure out what to do next."

"Well, you could join one of the co-ops that's building the other rides."

"Sure, I guess. But I want to be the kind of person who invents the idea of making something like that. Did you get an electrical engineering degree or something?"

"Just picked it up as I went along. You could do the same, I'm sure. But hang on a sec—you were putting stuff from Disney rides into my ride?"

"Well, yeah. But it was stuff they'd torn down."

Perry's eyes streamed. This couldn't be a coincidence, stuff from Disney rides showing up in his ride and the cops turning up to enforce a court order Disney got. But he couldn't blame this kid, who sounded like a real puppy dog.

"Wait, you don't think the cops were there because—"

"Probably. No hard feelings, though. I might have done the same in your shoes."

"Oh shit, I am *so sorry*. I didn't think it through at *all*; I can see that now. Of course they'd come after you. They must totally hate you. I used to work there, they just hate anything that takes a Florida tourist dollar. It's why they built the monorail extension to Orlando airport—to make sure that from the moment you get off the plane, you don't spend a nickel on anything that they don't sell you. I used to think it was cool, because they built such great stuff, but then they went after the new Fantasyland—"

"You can't be a citizen of a theme park," Perry said.

The kid barked a laugh. "Man, how true is *that*? You've nailed it, pal."

Perry managed to crack an eye, painfully, and catch a blurry look at the kid: a black Edward Scissorhands dandelion clock of hair, eyeliner, frock coat—but a baby face with cheeks you could probably see from the back of his head. About as threatening as a Smurf. Perry felt a sudden, delayed rush of anger. How *dare* they beat up kids like this "Death Waits"—all he wanted to do was ride a goddamned ride! He wasn't a criminal, wasn't out rolling old ladies or releasing malicious bio-organisms on the beach!

The bus turned a sharp corner and their heads banged together again. They groaned and then the doors were being opened and Perry squeezed his eyes shut again.

Rough hands seized him and marched him into the station house. The crowd susurrations were liquid in his screwed-up ears. He couldn't smell or see, either. He felt like he was in some kind of terrible sensory-deprivation nightmare, and it made him jerky, so whenever a hand took him and guided him to another station in the check-in process (his wallet lifted from his pocket, his cheek swabbed, his fingers pressed against a fingerprint scanner) he flinched involuntarily. The hands grew rougher and more insistent. At one point, someone peeled open his swollen eyelid, a feeling like being stabbed in the eye, and his retina was scanned. He screamed and heard laughter, distant through his throbbing eardrums.

It galvanized him. He forced his eyes open, glaring at the cops around him. Mostly they were Florida crackers, middle-aged guys with dead-eyed expressions of impersonal malevolence. There was a tiny smattering of brown faces and women's faces, but they were but a sprinkling when compared to the dominant somatype of Florida law.

The next time someone grabbed him to shove him toward the next station on this quest, he jerked his arm away and sat down. He'd seen protestors do this before, and knew that it was hard to move a sitting man expeditiously or with dignity. Hands seized him by the arms, and he flailed until he was free, remaining firmly seated. The laughter was turning to anger now. Beside him, someone else sat. Death Waits, looking white-faced and round-eyed. More people hit the floor. A billy club was shoved under his arm, which was then twisted into an agonizing position. He was suddenly ready to give up the fight and go along, but he couldn't get to his feet fast enough. With a sickening *crack*, his arm broke. He had a moment's lucid awareness that a bone had broken in his body, and then the pain was on him and he choked out a shout, then a louder one, and then everything went dark.

As it turned out, his prison infirmary time didn't last long at all. Kettlewell had faded fast from the riot, headed back to the guesthouse, and got the lawyers on the phone. He'd shown them the stream off of Perry's phone and they were in front of a judge before Perry reached the jail.

Perry was led out of the infirmary with his arm in a sling. His face was still painfully swollen, and he'd managed to turn an ankle as well. At least his hearing was coming back.

Kettlewell took Perry's good arm and gave him a soulful hug that embarrassed him. Kettlewell led him outside, to where a big cab was waiting. In it

were the family Kettlewell, Lester, and Suzanne. Lester had a couple bandages taped to his face, and when Suzanne smiled, he saw her lips were stained
red and one of her front teeth had been knocked out.

He managed a brave smile. "Looks like you guys got the full treatment,
huh?"

Suzanne squeezed his hand. "Nothing that can't be fixed." Ada and Pascal
looked goggle-eyed at them. Ada was popping Korean lotus bean–walnut
cakes into her mouth from a greasy paper bag, and she offered them silently
to Perry, who took one just to be polite, but found after the first bite that he
wasn't really hungry after all.

Kettlewell and Perry fought about what to do next, but Kettlewell prevailed. He took them to a private doctor who photographed them and examined them and x-rayed them, documenting everything while Ada Kettlewell
played camerawoman with her phone, videoing it all.

"I don't think suing the police is going to help, Landon," Perry said.
Suzanne nodded vigorously. The three victims were in paper examining
gowns, and the Kettlewells were still in street clothes, which gave them a real
advantage in the self-confidence department.

"It'll help if we cash out a big settlement—it'll bankroll our defense
against the Disney trademark claims. IP lawyers charge more than God per
hour. I got the injunction lifted, but we're still going to have to go to court,
and that's not going to be cheap."

It needled Perry—he didn't like the idea of being embroiled in the legal
system in the first place, and while he could grudgingly admit a certain ele-
gance in using cash settlements from the law to fund their defense in court,
the whole business made him squirm.

Eva sat down beside him. "I can tell this sucks for you, Perry." Ada whispered the word "sucks" and giggled, and Eva rolled her eyes. "But there's fifty
people we *didn't* bail out in there, who are all of them going to have to figure
out their own way through the legal system. You can't run a business if your
customers risk a solid beating and jail time just for showing up."

I don't want to run a business, he thought, but he knew that was petulant.
He was the man with the roll of bills down his pants. "There are fifty people
still in the slam?"

Kettlewell nodded. Suzanne had her camera out and she was recording. It
had been a long time since Perry had really felt the camera's eye on him. It was
one thing to be recorded by some friends for remembrance, but now Suzanne's
camera seemed like the gaze of posterity. He needed to rise to it, he knew.

"Let's get them out. All of them."

Kettlewell raised his eyebrows. "And how do you plan on doing that?"

"We'll charge it to the business," Perry said. Lester chuckled and gave him a thump on the back. "It's a legit expense—these are our *customers* after all."

Kettlewell shook his head at all of them, then he left the doctor's office. He already had his phone stuck to his head and was talking with the lawyer before he got out of earshot.

Perry and Lester and Suzanne and Eva exchanged mischievous glances, grinning with unexpected delight. Pascal, riding on Eva's hip, woke up and started crying and Eva handed him to Lester while she went for the diaper bag.

"Here we go again," Lester said, wrinkling his nose and holding the wailing Pascal at arm's length.

Suzanne got it all with her phone, then she flipped it shut and gave Lester a hard kiss on the cheek.

"Fatherhood would suit you," she said.

He went bright red. "Don't you get any ideas," he said. Suzanne laughed and skipped away, looking all of ten.

Perry felt huge. Larger than life. The adventure was beginning anew, with these good people whom he loved like family. He had the work and the people, and who needed anything more.

It was a feeling that lasted all the way back to the ride.

But then he surveyed the ride itself and found it in utter ruins, far worse than it had been left when he'd been dragged out of it. Every single exhibit was smashed, strewn here and there.

He couldn't believe it. He brought up the clean-up lights, flooding the place, and then he saw what he'd missed at first: the smashed exhibits were not smashed exhibits—they were *replicas* of smashed exhibits. At every ride in the country, police had gone in smashing, and every other ride in the country had faithfully reproduced the damage, dutiful printers churning out replica detritus and dutiful robots placing it with micrometer precision.

He began to laugh and couldn't stop. Lester came in and immediately got the joke and laughed along with him. They managed to stop laughing just long enough to explain it to Suzanne and Kettlewell, who didn't find it nearly as funny as they did. Suzanne took pictures.

Finally he got down to business, opening the change log and rolling the ride back through the revisions, to its unsmashed state. It would take the robots a long time to set everything right again, but at least he didn't have to oversee it.

Instead, he tracked down as many of the market-stall vendors as he could locate in the shantytown and made sure they were all right—they were, though they'd lost some inventory. He comped them all a month's rent and made sure they knew that steps were being taken to keep it from happening again. He knew that they could make nearly as much money selling from a roadside or online, and he wanted to keep them happy. Besides, it wasn't their fault.

He was exhausted and his arm was really starting to gripe him. He found himself stopping in the street every few steps to rub his eyes and force himself on. Francis came on him when he was like that, leaning against the prefab concrete wall of one of the tall, twisty shanties, and he took Perry's car keys away and drove him home. Perry was in too much of a state by the time he got there to think about how Francis would get back—he was already lying in bed before it occurred to him that the old man with the gimpy leg probably walked the ten miles home.

He woke up later that night to sex noises from Lester's room and he recognized Suzanne's voice. Later, he woke again to hear the tail end of another argument between Lester and Suzanne, and then Suzanne storming out of the apartment. *Oh, goody,* he thought. He lay on his back, trying to find sleep again—the clock said 3 AM—and found thoughts of Hilda drifting unbidden into his mind.

It was silly—they'd only spent one night together, and he had to admit that as great as the sex had been, he'd had better with the fatkins gymnasts you could pick up down on South Beach. She was too young for him. She lived in *Wisconsin*. But there were touches in the ride that had originated with her instantiation—he looked over the logs every now and then—and he found himself contemplating them with sentimental smiles.

He fell asleep again and only woke when he rolled over on his bad arm and yelped himself awake. The smell of waffles, bacon, and eggs was strong in the apartment. He couldn't be bothered to figure out how to shower with his cast on, so he pulled on a pair of shorts and let himself into the living room.

Lester was at the stove, cooking up half a pig and pouring maple batter into the waffle iron. He waved a spatula at him and pointed out at the terrace. Perry stepped out and saw Suzanne and Tjan and Tjan's little kids—what were their names? Lyenitchka and the little boy? Man, the whole family was here.

"Your arm is broken," Lyenitchka said, pointing at him.

Perry nodded gravely. "That's true. Want to sign my cast?" He was pretty sure that he had a grease pencil that would mark the surface, though the hospital had sworn that it would shed dirt, ink, and anything else he threw at it.

She nodded vigorously. Tjan looked him over and gave a little wave, then Perry went back into the living room and asked his computer to find the grease pencil.

"Thought you'd be busy in Boston," he said, while Lyenitchka painstakingly spelled out her name, going over the letters to get them to show up dark—the cast surface really didn't want to suck up any tint.

"Boston came out OK. We had lawyers on tap at the start and the vibe was cool. I incorporated there, so it was easier than you guys had it. But some of the others were hit bad, like San Francisco and Madison."

"*Madison?*" Perry was alarmed by how alarmed he sounded.

"Mass arrests. The cops there are real hard cases, with all this antipersonnel gear left over from the stem-cell riots."

Perry jerked and spoiled Lyenitchka's writing. He patted her head and set his arm back down where she could get at it. He groaned.

"They're mostly still in. We're trying to get them bailed out, but the judge at the arraignment set bail pretty high."

"I'll post it," Perry said. "I can put up my savings or something. . . ."

Tjan looked uncomfortable. "Perry, there are two hundred and fifty people in the lockup in Wisconsin. Some of them are going to skip out, it's nearly a certainty. If you bail them all out, you'll go broke. I mean, it's good to see you and I'm sorry you got hurt and all respect, but don't be an idiot."

Perry felt himself go belligerent. His hands went into fists and his broken wing protested. That brought him back to reality. He forced himself to smile.

"There's a girl in Madison. I want to make sure she's OK."

Tjan and Suzanne stared at him for a second. Then Lester clapped him across the back from behind him, startling him and making him squeak. "Big fella!" he crowed. "I should have known."

Perry gave him a mock glare. "*You* have no right to say *anything* on this score." He darted a glance at Suzanne and saw that she was blushing. Tjan took this in and nodded, as though his suspicions had just been confirmed.

"Fair enough," Tjan said. "Let's make some inquiries about the young lady. What's her name?"

"Hilda Hammersen."

Tjan's eyebrows shot up. "Hilda *Hammersen?* From the mailing lists? *That* Hilda?"

Hilda was the queen of the mailing lists—brash, quick, and argumentative, but never the kind of person who started flamewars. Hilda's arguments were hot and fast, and she always won. Perry had watched her admiringly from the sidelines, only weighing in occasionally, but he seemed to remember now that she'd taken Tjan to the cleaners once on an issue of protocol resolution.

"That's the one," Perry said.

"I always pictured her as being about fifty, with a machete between her teeth," Lester said. "No offense."

"Lyenitchka, go get my phone from my bed stand," Perry said, patting the girl on the shoulder. When she got back he went through his photos of Hilda with them.

Lester made a wolf whistle and Suzanne punched him in the shoulder and took the phone away.

"She's very pretty," Suzanne said, disapprovingly. "And very young."

"Oh yes, dating younger people is *so* sleazy," Lester said with a chuckle. Suzanne squirmed and even Perry had to laugh.

"Guys, here it is. I need to spring Hilda, and we need to do something about all those customers and supporters and so on who went to jail today. We need to fight all the injunctions—all of them—and prevent them from recurring."

"And we need to eat breakfast, which is ready," Lester said, gesturing at the table behind him, which was stacked high with waffles, sausages, eggs, toast, and pitchers of juice and carafes of coffee.

Lyenitchka and Sasha looked at each other and ran to the table, taking seats next to one another. The adults followed and soon they were eating. Perry managed a waffle and a sausage, but then he went off to his room. Hilda was in the slam in Madison, and who the hell knew what the antipersonnel stuff the Madison cops used had done to her. He just wanted to get on a fucking plane and *go there.*

Halfway through his shower, he knew that that was what he was going to do. He packed a shoulder bag, took a couple more painkillers, and walked out into the living room.

"Guys, I'm going to Madison. I'll be back in a day or two. We'll work everything out over the phone, OK?"

Lester and Suzanne came over to him. "You going to be OK, buddy?" Lester said.

"I'll be fine," he said.

"We can spring her from here," Tjan said. "We have the Internet, you know."

"I know," Perry said. "You do that, OK? And tell her I'll be there as soon as I can."

The security at the airport went bonkers over him. The perfect storm: a fresh arrest, a suspicious cast, and a ticket bought with cash. He missed the first two flights to Chicago, but by mid-afternoon he was landing at O'Hare and submitting to an interim screening procedure before boarding for Madison. His phone rang in the middle of the screening, and the wrinkly old TSA goon-lady primly informed him that he might as well get that, since once the phone rings, they have to start the procedure over again.

"Tjan," he said.

"They can't spring her today. Tomorrow, though."

He closed his eyes and shut out the TSA goon. She had a huge bouffant of copper hair, and a midwesterner's sense of proportionality when it came to eye shadow and rouge. She was the kind of woman who could call you "honey" and make it sound like "Islamofascist faggot."

"Why not, Tjan?"

There was a pause. "She's in the infirmary and they won't release her until tomorrow."

"Infirmary."

"Nothing serious—she took a knock on the head and they want to hold her for observation."

He pictured a copper's electrified billy club coming down on shining blond hair and felt like throwing up.

"Perry? Buddy. She's OK, really. I had our lawyer visit her in the prison infirmary and she swears she looks great. The lawyer's name is Candice—take a cab to her office from the airport. OK?"

"Why is she in the prison infirmary, Tjan? Why can't she be moved to a real hospital?"

"It's just a liability thing. The police don't want to risk the suit if she goes complicated on them between hospitals."

"Jesus."

"Seriously, she's fine. We've got a good lawyer on the scene."

But Perry had a bad feeling. The TSA goon picked up on it and gave him a little bit of extra attention. Acting nervous or agitated in an airport was a one-way ticket to a cavity search.

But then he was lifting off and headed for Madison, and though the time crawled on the one-hour flight, it was, after all, only an hour. He even napped briefly, though a sky marshal woke him shortly after for a random bag search. His fellow passengers—badly dressed midwesterners and a couple of hipster students—all turned their bags out in the cramped cabin and then got back in their seats for the landing.

Perry had meant to phone in a car reservation at O'Hare, but the extra search had eaten up the time he'd allocated for it, and now all the rental counters were sold out. Reluctantly, he got into a taxi and asked the driver to take him to the office of the lawyers that Tjan had hired.

The cabbie was a young African kid with a shaved head. He had a dent in one temple and more dents in one of his wrists, visible as he let his long hands drape over the steering wheel.

"I know where it is," he said when Perry gave him the address. "That lawyer, she is very good. She helped me with the Homeland Security."

The kid was young, twenty-one or twenty-two, with a studious air, despite his old injuries. He reminded Perry of the shantytowners, people who didn't always get medical attention for their ailments, people who were often missing a tooth or two, who had mysterious lumps from badly set bones or scars or funny eyebrows like his. The midwesterners on the plane had been flawless as action figures, but Perry's friends and this African kid looked like something carved out of coal and chalk.

Perry was one big jitter from the trip and the coffee and the pills for his arm, but he found himself drawn into conversation as they whizzed past the fields and malls, the factories and office parks.

"I'm from Gulu, in Uganda. There has been civil war there for thirty-five years. I studied chemical engineering through the African Virtual University wiki program, and qualified for a Chavez scholarship here in Madison." His accent was light but exotic, the African rolling of the *r*'s, the British-sounding vowel shifts. "But the Homeland Security didn't want to renew my visa last year. They said I had financial irregularities. I was paypalling to a friend in Kampala who withdrew it in shillings and sent it to my family in giros. Homeland Security said that I was *money laundering*. I thought I'd be sent away or put in prison, but Ms. Candice wrote them a letter and they vanished." He snapped his long, knuckly fingers for emphasis.

"Jesus. Well, that's good. She's going to help me get my girlfriend out of jail." Perry realized he'd just called Hilda his girlfriend, which would be news to her, but there it was.

"You don't need to worry. She'll get your friend free."

Perry nodded and tried to close his eyes and relax. He couldn't. What the hell had happened to the world? It had seemed so exciting when his father was bringing home new shapes he'd spun off his CAD/CAM rig. When Perry had started to trade designs with people, to effortlessly find people on the Net who wanted to collaborate with him and vice versa. When Perry had started a business making cool art out of free junk and selling it off an Internet connection that was likewise free.

Free, free, free. No need to talk to a government, or grovel for a curator, or put up with an agent or a boss. He'd just assumed all along that he'd end up living in a world where all those parasites and bullies and middlemen would just blow away in the wind.

But they'd all found jobs in the new world. They weren't needed anymore, but that didn't mean that they went away. Now they were wanding him in airports and suing him for trademark infringement and busting his girlfriend and breaking his arm and giving hassle to this poor African kid who'd taught himself to be an engineer with a ferchrissakes *wiki*.

He dry-swallowed another painkiller and then remembered that taking the pills meant he wouldn't be able to get a drink, which he could sure as shit use.

"My name's Perry," he said.

"Richard," the driver said. "We're almost there, Perry. I wish you the very best of luck."

"You too," he said. The driver shook his hand warmly after getting his luggage out of the trunk, a limp handshake by North American standards, but gentle and friendly nonetheless. His dented wrist flexed oddly as the half-knit bones there moved.

The lawyer's office was not what Perry was expecting. It looked like someone's living room, with a couple of overstuffed sofas, a dozing cat, and the lawyer, Candice, who was a young-looking woman in her mid-twenties. She dressed in jeans and an oversized WSU sweatshirt, with a laptop perched on one knee. She had a friendly, open face, framed with lots of curly brown hair.

"You must be Perry," she said, setting the laptop down and giving him an unexpected hug. "That was from Hilda. I saw her a couple hours ago. She was very adamant that I pass it on to you."

"Nice to meet you," he said, accepting a cup of tea from an insulated jug on a cardboard sideboard. "Hilda is all right?"

"Sit down," the lawyer said.

Perry's stomach turned a somersault. "Hilda's all right?"

"Sit."

Perry sat.

"She was gassed with a neurotoxin that has given her a temporary but severe form of Parkinson's disease. Normally it just renders people immobile, but one in a million has a reaction like this. It's just bad luck that Hilda was one of them."

"She was *gassed*?"

"They all were. There was a hell of a fight, as I understand it. It really looks like it was the cops' fault. Someone told them that there were printed guns in the ride location and they used extreme and disproportionate force."

"I see," Perry said. His blood whooshed in his ears. Printed guns? No frigging way. Sure, ray guns in some of the exhibits. But nothing that fired anything. He felt tears begin to stream down his face. The lawyer moved to his sofa and put her arm around his shoulders.

"She's going to be fine," Candice said. "The Parkinson's is rare, but it goes away in hundred percent of the cases where it occurs. What this means is that we've got an amazing chance of taking a huge bite out of the local law that we can use to fund future defense. Tjan told me that that's the strategy, and I think it's sound. Plus the harder we hit the law today, the more reluctant they'll be to rush off half-cocked the next time someone trumps up a BS trademark claim. It could be much worse, Perry. There's a kid who lost an eye to a rubber bullet."

Perry fisted the tears away. "Let's go get her," he said.

"They say she shouldn't be moved," Candice said.

"What does our doctor say?"

"I phoned a couple MDs this afternoon and got conflicting stories. Everyone agrees that not moving her is safer than moving her, though. The only disagreement is about how dangerous it would be to move her."

"Let's go see her, then."

"That we can do."

Perry had trouble with the search at the prison hospital. His cast and their scanners didn't get along and they couldn't be satisfied with a hand search. For a couple minutes it looked like he was going to be kept out, but Candice—who had changed into a power suit before they left the office—put on a stern voice and demanded to speak to the duty sergeant, and then to his commanding officer, and in ten minutes, they were on the hospital ward, where the metal-railed beds had prisoners handcuffed to them.

"Hilda?" She looked sunken and sick, her face slack and her jaw askew. Her eyes opened and rolled crazily; they focused on him. Her body shook through two waves of tremors before she was able to raise a shaking hand toward him, trailing IV tubes. She was trying to say his name, but it wouldn't come out, just a series of plosive p's.

But then he took her hand and felt its fine warmth, the calluses he remembered from all those months ago, and he felt better. Actually better. Felt some peace for the first time in a long time.

"Hello, Hilda," he said, and he was smiling so broadly his face hurt, and tears were running down his cheeks and dripping off his nose and running into his mouth. She was weeping, too, her head vibrating like a bobble doll. He bent over her and took her head in his hands, burying them in her thick blond hair, and kissed her on the lips. She shook under him, but she kissed him back, he could feel her lips move on his.

They kissed for a long time. He subconsciously took note of the fact that Candice had moved back, giving them some privacy. When the kiss broke, he had an overwhelming desire to tell her he loved her, but they hadn't taken that step yet, and maybe a prison hospital bed wasn't the right place to make pronouncements of love.

"I love you," he said softly, in her ear, kissing the lobe. "I love you, Hilda."

She cried harder, and made choking sobs. He hugged her as hard as he dared. Candice came back and stood by them.

"They think that she'll be better in the morning. She's already much better off than she was just a couple hours ago. Sleep's the only thing for it. They've got her mildly sedated, too."

Hilda smelled like he remembered, the undersmell beneath her shampoo and the chemicals clinging to her hair. It took him back to their night together, and he stroked her cheek.

"I'll stay here," he said.

"I don't think that they're going to let you do that, Perry. This is a prison, not a hospital."

"I'll stay here," he said again. "Just make it happen, OK? We're going to sue them into a smoking hole, right? That's got to give us some leverage. I'll stay here."

She sighed and looked at him for a long time, but he wouldn't take his eyes off of Hilda. His broken arm throbbed and he was out of painkillers. They'd have painkillers here.

Candice went away, and then, a while later, she came back. "Stay here," she said. "I'll come and get you in the morning."

"Thanks," he said. Then he thought that he should say something more, and he turned around, but the lawyer had gone.

He fell asleep holding Hilda's hand with his good hand, and woke up with an unbelievable pain in his broken arm and couldn't find a nurse. He bit down on the pain and spent a long watch that night staring at Hilda, thinking of all she meant to him and how weird it was that she meant so much when they'd had so brief a moment together. They hadn't let him bring his phone in, or he'd have taken a thousand pictures of her face in repose. He nodded off again.

He woke when she did, stirring in her bed. Her movements were still weak and feeble, but they lacked the uncontrolled tremors of the night before. He leaned in for a kiss, not caring about his sour breath or hers.

"Good morning," he said.

"Morning, gorgeous," she said, and took him in a soft, sleepy hug.

Candice sprung them and took them across town to her doctor, a young man who took great care in examining Hilda, explaining patiently which fluids he was drawing and which tests he planned on running on them. Perry had noticed that midwesterners came in two flavors: big Scandinavian Aryans with giant shoulders and easy smiles, and exchange students and immigrants in varying shades of brown, who looked hurt and bent alongside the natives—looked like the people he knew from back home, people who didn't have ready access to medical care or good nutrition in their formative years.

The doctor was Vietnamese, but he was at least a couple generations in, judging by his accent, and he had the same midwestern smile and seemed big and bulky compared with the Vietnamese people Perry knew in Florida. He watched the man peer intently at a screen after taping some electrodes to Hilda's head, and felt like he'd come to some land of Norse giants.

The doctor eventually told Hilda to go home and rest, and she promised she would. Perry and she got into the back of Candice's car and cuddled up to one another, dozing. It wasn't until Perry got back with her to her apartment— every stick of furniture made from clever cardboard—and emptied out his pockets that he remembered to switch his phone on again.

He was down to his boxers and she was in cotton pj's with sexy cowgirls printed on them, and when he powered the phone up, it went bonkers, lighting up like a Christmas tree, vibrating, and making urgent bleats.

"Shit," he said, and began to sort through the alerts while his back and neck muscles tightened. He sat on the edge of the bed and prodded at the phone with his right hand, holding it awkwardly in his left hand, trying to work around the cast. Hilda took the phone and held it for him so he could work more freely, and they both read what was going on.

A second round of lawsuits had been filed that night, and the injunctions had been reinstated. The story about the rides being a source of printed arms and munitions had spread, and in San Francisco the ride had been taken apart by Homeland Security bomb robots that had detonated several key pieces of equipment. Three of the San Francisco ride crew ended up in the hospital after clashes with overreacting cops.

Hilda nodded and took the phone from him and set it down.

"Right, what's the game plan?"

"How should I know?" Perry said. He could hear the whine in his voice. "I just build stuff. Tjan and Candice say that they think we can sue the cops over the brutality and use the money to fund legal defenses, but Disney's denial-of-service attacking us in the courtroom. They're also getting all this destruction dealt to us by the cops."

"You know how you eat an elephant? One bite at a time. Let's break this down into small component pieces and work on solutions to them, then call up the troops and let them know what's going on. I'll get a conference call set up while we chat."

She was still moving slowly and weakly, and he tried to get her to put down her laptop and rest, but she wasn't having any of it.

And so they worked, dividing the problem up into manageable pieces: incorporating a nonprofit co-op, writing the bylaws, getting the word out through the press, reopening the rides, putting together scrapbooks of the carnage wrought.

It all seemed doable once it was reduced to its component parts. Perry put it all online and then conferenced Tjan and Kettlewell in.

"Perry, do you think it's a good idea to tell our enemies how we plan to respond to them?"

Hilda shook her head and put a hand on Perry's good arm to calm him down before he answered Kettlewell. "That's how we do it over on our side. Their side is all about secrecy. Our side trades the advantage of surprise for the advantage of openness. You watch—by tonight we'll have bylaws drafted, press releases, exhaustive documentation. You watch."

On the screen, Lester's face suddenly hove into view, fish-eye distorted by his proximity to the lens. Hilda gave an amused squeak and pulled back.

"So that's Yoko, huh?" Lester said, grinning. "Cute! Listen guys, don't let these suits talk you out of what you're doing. This is the right thing. I'm on all the message boards and stuff and they're all champing to do something for real."

"Yoko?" Hilda said. She raised an adorable eyebrow.

"Just a figure of speech," Lester said. "I'm Lester. You must be Hilda. Perry's told us practically nothing about you, which is probably a sign of something or other."

Hilda regarded Perry with mock coolness. "Oh really?"

"Lester," Perry said. "I love you like a brother. Shut the fuck up already."

Lester made a little whipping motion. Suddenly he was gone from the picture, and they saw Suzanne pulling him away by one ear. Hilda snorted. "I like her," she said. Suzanne gave them a wave and Tjan and Kettlewell came back into frame.

They made their goodbyes and hung up. Now Hilda and Perry were alone, together, in her bedroom, laptops shut, day done—though it was hardly gone noon—and the silence stretched.

"Thanks for coming, Perry," she said.

"I—" He broke off. He didn't know what to say. They had only known each other for a day, only had a one-night stand. She probably thought that he was a giant creep. "I was worried," he said. "Um. You should probably rest up some more, right?"

He got up and headed for the door.

"Where do you think you're going?" she said.

"Figured I'd let you rest," he said with a half-shrug.

"Get in this bed this instant, young man," she said, slapping the bed beside her. "And get those stinky clothes off before you do—I won't have you getting my sheets all covered in your travel grime."

He felt the foolish grin spread across his face and he skinned out of his clothes as fast as he could with his cast on.

They didn't leave the house until suppertime, freshly showered (she'd been a delightful help in scrubbing those spots where the cast impeded access) and changed. Perry took a painkiller after the shower, which kicked in as they went out the door, and the autumn evening was crisp and sharp.

They got as far as the corner before the man approached them. "Perry Gibbons, isn't it?" He had an English accent, and a little potbelly, and a big white bubble jacket and a scarf wound round his throat.

"That's right," Perry said. He looked at the guy. "Do I know you?"

"No, I don't think so. But I've followed you in the press. Quite remarkable."

"Thanks," Perry said. Being recognized—how weird was that. Cool that it happened in front of Hilda. "This is Hilda," he said. She took the man's hand, and he grinned, showing two long, ratlike front teeth.

"Fred," he said. "What an absolute delight running in to you out here, of all places. What are you doing in town?"

"Just visiting with friends," Perry said.

"Wasn't there some kind of dustup at your place in Florida? I saw what they did to the ride here, what a bloody mess."

"Yeah," Perry said. He pointed at his casted arm. "Seemed like a good time to get out of Dodge."

Hilda said, "We're getting some dinner, if you'd like to come along."

"I wouldn't want to intrude."

"No, it's no sweat, we've got a whole bunch of people associated with the ride meeting us. You'd be more than welcome."

"Goodness, that *is* hospitable of you. How can I refuse?"

Luke and Ernie were there with their girlfriends, and there were more kids, midwestern and healthy, even if they weren't necessarily all Scandic, some Vietnamese kids, some Hmong, some desis descended from the H-1B diaspora. They had a gigantic meal in a student place that was heavy on the potatoes and beers the size of your head, which Perry resisted for a couple hours until he figured that he'd metabolized most of the painkiller, and then he started in, getting just short of roaring drunk. He told them war stories, told them about Death Waits, told them about the co-op and the plan to fight back.

"That just doesn't sound right to me," said a friend of Luke's, a law-school grad student who had been bending Perry's ear all night with stories from his law-clinic work defending university students from music-industry lawsuits. "I mean, sure, go after the cops because they roughed you guys up, but how much money do the cops have? You gotta target some fat cash, and for that you want to go after Disney. Abuse of trademark, abuse of process, something like that. The standard's pretty high, but if you can get a judgement, the money is incredible. You could take them to the cleaners."

Perry looked blearily at him. He was young, like all of them, but he had a good rhetorical style that Perry recognized as something born of real confidence. He knew his stuff, or thought he did. He had a strawberry mark on his high forehead that looked like a map of a distant island, and Perry thought that the mark probably threw off the kid's opponents. "So we sue Disney and five years from now we cash in—how does that help us now?"

The kid nodded. "I hoped you'd ask me that. I've been thinking about this a lot lately. Here's what you need to do, dude, here's the fucking thing." The room had grown silent. Everyone leaned closer. Fred poured Perry another beer from the pitcher in the middle of the table. "Here's how you do it. You raise investment capital for it. There's a ton of money in this, a ton. Disney's got deep pockets and you've got a great case.

"But like you say, it'll take ten, fifteen years to get the money out of them. And it'll cost a mil in legal fees on the way. So what you do is, you create an investment syndicate. You can maybe get thirty million out of Disney, plus whatever the jury awards in punitives, and if you keep half of it, you can deliver a fifteen-x return on investment. So go find a millionaire and borrow sixteen million, and turn the defense over to him."

Perry was dumbstruck. "You're joking. How can that possibly work?"

"It's how patent lawsuits work! Some dickhead engineer gets a bogus patent for his doomed startup, and as they're sinking into the mud, some venture capitalist comes and buys the company up just so it can go around and threaten other companies with real businesses for violating the patent. They ask for sums just below what it would cost to get the U.S. Patent and Trademark Office to invalidate the patent, and everyone ponies up. Venture capitalism is the major source of funding for commercial lawsuits these days."

Fred laughed and clapped. "Brilliant! Perry, that's just brilliant. Are you going to do it?"

Perry looked at the table, doodling in the puddles of beer with a fingertip. "I just want to get back to making stuff, you know. This is nuts. Devoting ten years of my life to suing someone?"

"You don't have to do the suing. That's the point. You outsource that. You get the money; someone else does the business stuff." Hilda put her arm around his shoulders. "Give the suits something to occupy themselves with—otherwise they get antsy and stir up trouble."

Perry and Hilda laughed like it was the funniest thing they'd ever heard. Fred and the others joined in, and Perry scrawled a drunken note to Tjan and Kettlewell with the info. The party broke up not long after, amid much chortling and snorting, and they staggered home. Fred gave Perry a warm handshake and treated Hilda to a lingering, sloppy hug until she pushed him off, laughing even harder.

"All right then," Perry said, "home again, home again."

Hilda gave his groin a friendly honk and then made a dash for it, and he gave chase.

———

PHOTO: *A drunken Perry Gibbons gets a how's-your-father from ride bride Hilda Hammersen*

MADISON, WI—Say you managed to inspire some kind of "movement" of techno-utopians who built a network of amusement park rides that guide their visitors through an illustrated history of the last dotcom bubble.

Say that your merry band of unwashed polyamorous info-hippies was overtaken by jackbooted thugs from one of the dinosauric media empires of yesteryear, whose legal machinations resulted in nationwide raids, beatings, gassings, and the total shutdown of your "movement."

What would you do? Sue? Call a press conference? Bail your loyal followers out of the slam?

Get laid, get shitfaced, and let a bunch of students spitball bullshit ideas for fighting back?

If you picked the latter, you're in good company. Last night, Perry Gibbons, soi-disant "founder" of the rideafarian religious cult, was spotted out for drinks and cuddles with a group of twentysomething students in the backwater town of Madison, WI, a place better known for its cheddar than its activism.

While Gibbons regaled the impressionable postadolescents with tales of his derring-do, he avidly noted their strategic suggestions for solving his legal, paramilitary, and technical problems.

One suggestion that drew Gibbons's attention and admiration was to approach venture capitalists and beg them for the capital to sue Disney and then use the settlements from the suits to pay back the VCs.

This mind-croggling Ponzi scheme is the closest thing to a business model we've yet heard of from the chip-addled techno-hippies of the New Work and its post-boom incarnation.

One can only imagine how our Ms. Church will cover this in her fan blog:

breathless admiration for Mr. Gibbons's cunning in soliciting yet more "way out of the box" thinking from the Junior Guevaras of the Great Midwest, no doubt.

Perhaps Gibbons can be afforded a little sympathy, though. His latest encounter with Florida law left him with a broken arm and it may be that the pain medication is primarily responsible for Gibbons's fancy thinking. If that's the case, we can only hope that his young, blond Scandie nursie will carefully minister him back to health (while his comrades rot in gaol around the country).

This organization needs to die before it gets someone killed.

Comments? Write to Freddy at honestfred@techstink.co.uk.

Lester interrupted Suzanne's phone call to break in and announce that he'd run Rat-Toothed Freddy to ground: the reporter had caught the first flight from Madison to Chicago and then gone west to San Jose. The TSA had flagged him as a person of interest and were watching his movements, and a little digging on its website could cause it to disclose Freddy's every airborne movement.

Suzanne relayed this to Perry.

"Don't you go there," she said. "He's gunning for the San Francisco crew, and he's hoping for a confrontation or a denunciation so that he can print it. He gets idées fixes that he worries at like a terrier, going for more bile."

"Is he a psycho? What the hell is his beef with me?"

"I think that he thinks that technology hasn't lived up to its promise and that we should all be demanding better of our tech. So for him, that means that anyone who actually *likes* technology is the enemy, the worst villain, undermining the case for bringing tech up to its true potential."

"Fuck, that is so twisted."

"And given the kind of vile crap he writes, the only readers he has are nutcases who get off on seeing people who are actually creating stuff flayed alive for their failures. They egg him on—ever see one of his letters columns? If he changed to actual reportage, telling the balanced stories of what was going on in the world, they'd jump ship for some other hatemonger. He's a lightning rod for assholes—he's the king of the trolls."

Perry looked away. "What do I do?"

"You could try to starve him. If you don't show your head, he can't report on you, except by making stuff up—and made-up stuff gets boring, even for the kinds of losers who read his stuff."

"But I've got work to do."

"Yeah, yeah you do. Maybe you've just got to take your lumps. Every complex ecosystem has parasites, after all. Maybe you just call up San Francisco and brief them on what to expect from this guy and take it from there."

Once they were off the line, Lester came up behind her and hugged her at the waist, squeezing the little love handles there, reminding her of how long it had been since she'd made it to yoga.

"You think that'll work?"

"Maybe. I've been talking to the *New Journalism Review* about writing a piece on moral responsibility and paid journalism, and if I can bang it out this aft, I bet they'll publish it tomorrow."

"What's that going to do?"

"Well, it'll distract him from Perry, maybe. It might get his employer to take a hard look at what he's writing—I mean that piece is just lies, mischaracterizations, and editorial masquerading as reportage." She put her lid down and paced around the condo, looking at the leaves floating in the pool. "It'll give me some satisfaction."

Lester gave her a hug, and it smelled of the old days and the old Lester, the giant, barrel-chested pre-fatkins Lester. It took her back to a simpler time, when they'd had to worry about commercial competition, not police raids.

She hugged him back. He was all hard muscle and zero body fat underneath his tight shirt. She'd never dated anyone that fit, not even back in high school. It was a little disorienting, and it made her feel especially old and saggy sometimes, though he never seemed to notice.

Speaking of which, she felt his erection pressing against her midriff, and tried to hide her grin. "Gimme a couple hours, all right?"

She dialed the *NJR* editor's number as she slid into her chair and pulled up a text editor. She knew what she planned on writing, but it would help to be able to share an outline with the *NJR* if she was going to get this out in good time. Working with editors was a pain after years of writing for the blog, but sometimes you wanted someone else's imprimatur on your work.

Five hours later, the copy was filed. She rocked back in her chair and stretched her arms high over her head, listening to the crackle of her spine. She'd been half-frozen by the air-conditioning, so she'd turned it off and opened a window, and now the condo was hot and muggy. She stripped down to her underwear and headed for the shower, but before she could make it, she was intercepted by Lester.

He fell on her like a dog on dinner, and hours slipped by as they made the apartment even muggier. Lester's athleticism in the sack was flattering, but sometimes boundless to the point of irritation. She was rescued from it this time by the doorbell.

Lester put on a bathrobe and answered the door, and she heard the sounds of the family Kettlewell spilling in, the kids' little footfalls pounding up and down the corridors. Hurriedly, Suzanne threw on a robe and ducked across the corridor into the bathroom, but not before catching sight of Eva and Landon. Eva's expression was grimly satisfied; Landon looked stricken. Fuck it, anyway. She'd never given him any reason to hope, and he had no business hoping.

Halfway through her shower, she heard someone moving around in the bathroom, and thinking it was Lester, she stuck her head around the curtain, only to find Ada on the pot, little jeans around her ankles. "I hadda make," Ada said, with a shrug.

Christ. What was she doing back here, anyway? She'd missed it all so much from Petersburg. But she hadn't really bargained for this. It was only a matter of time until Tjan showed up, too; surely they'd be wanting a council of war after Freddy's opening salvo.

She waited for the little girl to flush (ouch! hot water!) and got dressed as discreetly as possible.

By the time she got to the balcony where the council of war was under way, the two little girls, Lyenitchka and Ada, had gotten Pascal up on the sofa and were playing dress-up with him, hot-gluing barbie heads to his cheeks and arms and chubby knees, like vacantly staring warts.

"Do you like him?"

"I think he looks wonderful, girls. Is that glue OK for him, though?"

Ada nodded vigorously. "I've been gluing things to my brother with that stuff forever. Dad says it's OK so long as I don't put it in his eyes."

"Your dad's a smart man."

"He's in love with you," Lyenitchka said, and giggled. Ada slugged her in the arm.

"That's supposed to be a secret, stupid," Ada said.

Flustered, Suzanne ducked out onto the patio and shut the door behind her. Eva and Tjan and Kettlewell all turned to look at her.

"Suzanne!" Tjan said. "Nice article."

"Is it up already?"

"Yeah, just a couple minutes ago." Tjan held up his phone. "I've got a watch list for anything to do with Freddy that gets a lot of link love in a short period. Your piece rang the cherries."

She took the phone from him and looked at the list of links that had been found to the *NJR* piece. Three of the diggdots had picked up the story, since they loved to report on anything that made fun of Freddy—he was a frequent savager of their readers' cherished beliefs, after all—and thence it had wormed its way all around the Net. In the time she'd needed to take a shower, her story had been read by about three million people. She felt a twinge of regret for not publishing it on her blog—that would have been some serious advertising coin.

"Well, there you have it."

"What do you suppose he'll come back with?" Kettlewell said, then looked uncomfortably at Eva. She pretended not to notice, and continued to stare at the grimy Hollywood palms, swimming pools, and freeways.

"Something nasty and full of lies, no doubt."

Nerd Groupie Church Finds Fatkins Love with Ride Sidekick

Sources close to the Hollywood, Florida, ride cult have revealed that Suzanne Church, the celebrity blogger who helped inflate the New Work stock bubble, is in the midst of a romantic entanglement with one of the cult's co-founders.

Church recently came out of retirement in St. Petersburg, where she has been producing PR^H^H journalistic accounts of the new generation of Russian experimental plastic surgery butchers.

Church was lured back by the promise of a story about the ride network that was founded by her old pals from the New Work pump-and-dump, Lester Banks and Perry Gibbons. Now on the scene are more familiar faces: Landon Kettlewell, the disgraced former CEO of Kodacell, and Tjan Tang, the former business manager of the Banks/Gibbons scam.

But not long after arriving on the scene, Church fell in with Banks, an early fatkins and stalwart of the New Work movement, a technologist who entranced his fellow engineers with his accounts of the New Work's many "inventions"—prompting one message-board commenter to characterize him as "a cross between Steve Wozniak and the Reverend Sun Myung Moon."

Now, eyewitness accounts have them going at it like shagging marmots, as the bio-enhanced Banks falls on Church's wrinkly carcass half a dozen times a day, apparently consummating a romance that blossomed while Banks was, to put it bluntly, a giant fat bastard. It seems that radical weight loss has put Banks into the category of "blokes that Suzanne Church is willing to play hide the sausage with."

All this would be mere sordid gossip but for the fact that Church is once again glowingly chronicling the adventures of the Florida cultists, playing journalist, without a shred of impartiality or disclosure.

One can only imagine when the other, financial shoe will drop. For wherever Church goes, money isn't far behind: surely there's a financial aspect to this business with the ride.

UPDATE:

Indeed there is: further anonymous tipsterism reveals that papers have been filed to create a "co-operative" structured like a classic Ponzi scheme, in which franchise operators of the ride are expected to pay membership dues further up the ladder. All the romance of Church's accounts will certainly find a fresh batch of suckers—if there's one thing we know about Suzanne Church, it's that she knows how to separate a mark from his money.

––––––––

Lester ran the ride basically on his own that week, missing his workshop and his tinkering, thinking of Suzanne, wishing that Perry was back already. He wasn't exactly a people person, and there were a *lot* of people.

"I brought some stuff," the goth kid said as he paid for his ticket, hefting two huge duffel bags. "That's still OK, right?"

Was it? Damned if Lester knew. The kid had a huge bruise covering half of his face, and Lester thought he recognized him from the showdown— Death Waits, that's what Perry had said.

"Sure, it's fine."

"You're Lester, right?"

Christ, another one.

"Yes, that's me."

"Honest Fred is full of shit. I've been reading your posts since forever. That guy is just jealous because your girlfriend outed him for being such a lying asshole."

"Yeah." Death Waits wasn't the first one to say words to this effect— Suzanne had had that honor—and he wouldn't be the last. But Lester wanted to forget it. He'd liked the moments of fame he'd gained from Suzanne's writing, from his work on the message boards. He'd even had a couple of fanboys show up to do a little interview for their podcast about his mechanical computer. That had been nice. But "blokes that Suzanne Church is willing to play hide the sausage with"—ugh.

Suzanne was holding it together as far as he could tell. But she didn't seem as willing to stick her neck out to broker little peaces between Tjan and Kettlewell anymore, and those two were going at it hammer and tongs now, each convinced that he was in charge. Tjan reasoned that since he actually ran one of the most developed rides in the network, he should be the executive, with Kettlewell as a trusted adviser. Kettlewell clearly felt that he deserved the crown because he'd actually run global businesses, as opposed to Tjan, who was little more than a middle manager.

Neither had said exactly that, but that was only because whenever they headed down that path, Suzanne interposed herself and distracted them.

No one asked Lester or Perry, even though they were the ones who'd invented it all. It was all so fucked up. Why couldn't he just make stuff and do stuff? Why did it always have to turn into a plan for world domination? In Lester's experience, most world-domination plans went sour, while a hefty proportion of modest plans to Make Something Cool actually worked out pretty well, paid the bills, and put food on the table.

The goth kid looked expectantly at him. "I'm a huge fan, you know. I used to work for Disney, and I was always watching what you did to get ideas for new stuff we should do. That's why it's so totally suckballs that they're accusing you of ripping them off—we rip you off all the time."

Lester felt like he was expected to do something with that information—maybe deliver it to some lawyer or whatever. But would it make a difference? He couldn't get any spit in his mouth over legal fights. Christ—legal fights!

"Thanks. You're Death Waits, right? Perry told me about you."

The kid visibly swelled. "Yeah. I could help around here if you wanted, you know. I know a lot about ride operating. I used to train the ride runners at Disney, and I could work any position. If you wanted."

"We're not really hiring—" Lester began.

"I'm not looking for a job. I could just, you know, help. I don't have a job or anything right now."

Lester needed to pee. And he was sick of sitting here taking people's money. And he wanted to go play with his mechanical computer, anyway.

"Lester? Who's the kid taking ticket money?" Suzanne's hug was sweaty and smelled good.

"Look at this," Lester said. He flipped up his magnifying goggles and handed her the soda can. He'd cut away a panel covering the whole front of the can, and inside he'd painstakingly assembled sixty-four flip-flops. He turned the crank on the back of the can slowly, and the correct combination of rods extended from the back of the can, indicating the values represented on the flip-flops within. "It's a sixty-four bit register. We could build a shitkicking Pentium out of a couple million of these."

He turned the crank again. The can smelled of solder and it had a pleasant weight in his hand. The mill beside him hummed, and on his screen, the parts he'd CADded up rotated in wireframe. Suzanne was at his side, and he'd just built something completely teh awesome. He'd taken his shirt off somewhere along the afternoon's lazy, warm way and his skin prickled with a breeze.

He turned to take Suzanne in his arms. God he loved her. He'd been in love with her for years now, and she was his.

"Look at how cool this thing is; just look." He used a tweezer to change the registers again and gave it a little crank. "I got the idea from the old Princeton Institute Electronic Computer Project. All these comp-sci geniuses, von Neumann and Dyson and Gödel, they brought in their kids for the summer to wind all the cores they'd need for their RAM. Millions of these things, wound by the kids of the smartest people in the universe. What a cool way to spend your summer.

"So I thought I'd prototype the next generation of these, a sixty-four-bit version that you could build out of garbage. Get a couple hundred of the local kids in for the summer and get them working. Get them to understand just how these things work—that's the problem with integrated circuits; you can't take them apart and see how they work. How are we going to get another generation of tinkerers unless we get kids interested in how stuff works?"

"Who's the kid taking ticket money?"

"He's a fan, that kid that Perry met in jail. Death Waits. The one who brought in the Disney stuff."

He gradually became aware that Suzanne was rigid and shaking in his arms.

"What's wrong?"

Her face was purple now, her hands clenched into fists. "What's wrong? Lester, what's wrong? You've left a total stranger, who, by his own admission, is a recently terminated employee of a company that is trying to bankrupt you and put you in jail. You've left him in charge of an expensive, important capital investment, and given him the authority to collect money on your behalf. Do you really need to ask me what's wrong?"

He tried to smile. "It's OK, it's OK, he's only—"

"Only what? Only your possible doom? Christ, Perry, you don't even have fucking *insurance* on that business."

Did she just call him Perry? He carefully set down the Coke can and looked at her.

"I'm down here busting my *ass* for you two, fighting cops, letting that shit Freddy smear my name all over the Net, and what the hell are you doing to save yourself? You're in here playing with Coke cans!" She picked it up and shook it. He heard the works inside rattling and flinched toward it. She jerked it out of his reach and threw it, *threw it* hard at the wall. Hundreds of little gears and ratchets and rods spilled out of it.

"Fine, Lester, fine. You go on being an emotional ten-year-old. But stop roping other people into this. You've got people all over the country depending on you and you are just *abdicating* your responsibility to them. I won't be a part of it." She was crying now. Lester had no idea what to say now.

"It's not enough that Perry's off chasing pussy; you've got to pick this moment to take French leave to play with your toys. Christ, the whole bunch of you deserve each other."

Lester knew that he was on the verge of shouting at her, really tearing into her, saying unforgivable things. He'd been there before with other friends, and no good ever came of it. He wanted to tell her that he'd never asked for the responsibility, that he'd lived up to it anyway, that no one had asked her to put her neck on the line and it wasn't fair to blame him for the shit that Freddy was putting her through. He wanted to tell her that if she was in love with Perry, she should be sleeping with Perry, and not him. He wanted to tell her that she had no business reaming him out for doing what he'd always done: sit in his workshop.

He wanted to tell her that she had never once seen him as a sexual being when he was big and fat, but that he had no trouble seeing her as one now that she was getting old and a little saggy, and so where did she get off criticizing his emotional maturity?

He wanted to say all of this, and he wanted to take back his sixty-four-bit register and nurse it back to health. He'd been in a luminous creative fog when he'd built that can, and who knew if he'd be able to reconstruct it?

He wanted to cry, to blubber at her for the monumental unfairness of it all. He stood stiffly up from his workbench and turned on his heel and walked out. He expected Suzanne to call out to him, but she didn't. He didn't care, or at least he didn't want to.

Sammy skipped three consecutive Theme-Leaders' meetings, despite increasingly desperate requests for his presence. The legal team was eating every spare moment he had, and he hadn't been able to get audience research to get busy on his fatkins project. Now he was behind schedule—not surprising, given that he'd pulled his schedule out of his ass to shut up Wiener and Co.—and dealing with lawyers was making him crazy.

And to top it all off, the goddamned rides were back up and running.

So the last thing he wanted was a visit from Wiener.

"They're suing us, you know. They raised *venture capital* to sue us, because we have such deep pockets. You know that, Sammy?"

"I know it, Wiener. People sue us all the time. Venture capitalists have deep pockets, too, you know—when we win, we'll take them to the cleaners. Christ, why am I having this conversation with you? Don't you have something productive to do? Is Tomorrowland so fucking *perfect* that you've come around to help me with my little projects?"

"Someone's a little touchy today," Wiener said, wagging a finger. "I just wanted to see if you wanted some help coming up with a strategy for getting out of this catastrophe, but since you mention it, I *do* have work I could be doing. I'll see you at the next Theme-Leaders' meeting, Sam. Missing three is grounds for disciplinary action, you know."

Sammy sat back in his chair and looked coolly at Wiener. Threats now. Disciplinary action. He kept on his best poker face, looking past Wiener's shoulder (a favorite trick for staring down adversaries—just don't meet their eyes). In his peripheral vision, he saw Wiener wilt, look away, and then turn and leave the room.

He waited until the door had shut, then slumped in his seat and put his face in his hands. God, and shit, and damn. How did it all go so crapola? How did he end up with a theme area that was half-shut, record absenteeism, and even a goddamned *union organizer* just the day before, whom he'd had to have security remove. Florida laws being what they were, it was a rare organizer brave enough to try to come on an employer's actual premises to do his dirty work; no one wanted a two-year rap without parole for criminal trespass and interference with trade. The kid had been young, about the same age as Death Waits and the castmembers, and had clearly been desperate to collect his bounty from SEIU. He'd gone hard, struggling and kicking, shouting slogans at the wide-eyed castmembers and few guests who watched him go away.

Having him taken away had given Sammy a sick feeling. They hadn't had one of those vultures on the premises in three years, and never on Sammy's turf.

What next, what next? How much worse could it get?

"Hi, Sammy." Hackelberg wasn't the head of the legal department, but he was as high up in the shadowy organization as Sammy ever hoped to meet. He was old and leathery, the way that natives to the Sunbelt could be. He loved to affect ice cream suits and had even been known to carry a cane. When he was in casual conversation, he talked "normal"—like a Yankee newscaster. But the more serious he got, the deeper and thicker his drawl got. Sammy never once believed that this was accidental. Hackelberg was as premeditated as they came.

"I was just about to come over and see you," Sammy lied. Whatever problem had brought Hackelberg down to his office, it would be better to seem as though he was already on top of it.

"I expect you were." *Were* came out *wuh*—when the drawl got that far into the swamps that quickly, disaster was on the horizon. Hackelberg let the phrase hang there.

Sammy sweated. He was good at this game, but Hackelberg was better.

Entertainment lawyers were like fucking vampires, evil embodied. He looked down at his desk.

"Sammy. They're coming back after us—" *They-ah comin' back aft-ah us.* "Those ride people. They did what we thought they'd do, incorporating into a single entity that we can sue once and kill for good, but then they did something else. Do you know what they did, Sammy?"

Sammy nodded. "They're countersuing. We knew they'd do that, right?"

"We didn't expect they'd raise a war chest like the one they've pulled together. They have a *business plan* built around suing us for the next fifteen years, Sammy. They're practically ready to float an IPO. Have you seen this?" He handed Sammy a hardcopy of a chic little investment newsletter that was so expensive to subscribe to that he'd suspected until now that it might just be a rumor.

How Do You Get Rid(e) of a Billion?

The Kodacell experiment recognized one fundamental truth: it's easy to turn ten thousand into two hundred thousand but much harder to turn ten million into two hundred million. Scaling an investment up to gigascale is so hard it's nearly impossible.

But a new paradigm in investment that's unfolding around us might actually solve the problem: venture-financed litigation. Twenty or thirty million sunk into litigation can bankrupt a twenty-billion-dollar firm, transferring to the investors whatever assets remain after legal fees.

It sounds crazy, and only time will tell whether it proves to be sustainable. But the founder of the strategy, Landon Kettlewell, has struck gold for his investors more than once—witness the legendary rise and fall of Kodacell, the entity that emerged from the merger of Kodak and Duracell. Investors in the first two rounds and the IPO on Kodacell brought home 30X returns in three years (of course, investors who stayed in too long came away with nothing).

Meanwhile, Kodacell's bid to take down Disney Parks looks good—the legal analysis of the vexatious litigation and unfair-competition charges have legal scholars arguing and adding up the zeros. Most damning is the number of former Disney Parks employees (or "castmembers" in the treacly dialect of the Magic Kingdom) who've posted information about the company's long-term plan to sabotage Kettlewell's clients.

Likewise fascinating is the question of whether the jury will be able to distinguish between Disney Parks, whose corporate citizenship is actually pretty good, from Disney Products, whose record has been tainted by a string of disastrous child-labor, safety, and design flaws (astute readers will be thinking of the "flammable pajamas" flap of last year, and CEO Robert Montague's memorable words, "Parents who can't keep their kids away from matches have no business complaining about *our* irresponsibility"). Punitive jury awards are a wild card in this kind of litigation, but given the trends in recent years, things look bad for Disney Parks.

Bottom line: should your portfolio include a litigation-investment component? Yes, unequivocally. While risky and slow to mature, litigation investments promise a staggering return on investment not seen in decades. A million or two carefully placed with the right litigation fund could pay off enough to make it all worthwhile. This is creative destruction at its finest: the old dinosaurs like Disney Parks are like rich seams of locked-away capital begging to be liquidated and put to work at nimbler firms.

How can you tell if you've got the right fund? Come back next week, when we'll have a Q&A with a litigation specialist at Credit Suisse.

"There's litigation specialists at Credit Suisse?"

He was big, Hackelberg, though he often gave the impression of being smaller through his habitual slouch. But when he pulled himself up, it was like a string in the center of the top of his head was holding him erect, like he was hovering off the ground, like he was about to leap across the desk and go for your throat. His lower jaw rocked from side to side.

"They are now, Sammy. Every investment bank has one, including the one that the chairman of our board is a majority shareholder in."

Sammy swallowed. "But they've got just as deep pockets as we do—can't we just fight these battles out and take the money off of them when we win?"

"If we win."

Sammy saw his opportunity to shift the blame. "If we've been acting on good legal advice, why wouldn't we win?"

Hackelberg inhaled slowly, his chest filling and filling until his ice cream suit looked like it might pop. His jaw clicked from side to side. But he didn't say anything. Sammy tried to meet that cool gaze, but he couldn't outstare the man. The silence stretched. Sammy got the message: this was not a problem that originated in the legal department. This was a problem that originated with him.

He looked away. "How do we solve this?"

"We need to raise the cost of litigation, Samuel. The only reason this is viable is that it's cost-effective to sue us. When we raise the cost of litigation, we reduce its profitability."

"How do we raise the cost of litigation?"

"You have a fertile imagination, Sammy. I have no doubt that you will be able to conceive of innumerable means of accomplishing this goal."

"I see."

"I hope you do. I really hope you do. Because we have an alternative to raising the cost of litigation."

"Yes?"

"We could sacrifice an employee or two."

Sammy picked up his water glass and discovered that it was empty. He turned away from his desk to refill it from his filter and when he turned back, the lawyer had gone. His mouth was dry as cotton and his hands were shaking.

Raise the cost of litigation, huh?

He grabbed his laptop. There were ways to establish anonymous email accounts, but he didn't know them. Figuring that out would take up the rest of the afternoon, he realized as he called up a couple of FAQs.

In the course of a career as varied and ambitious as Sammy's, it was often the case that you ran across an email address for someone you never planned on contacting, but you never knew, and a wise planner makes space for lots of outlier contingencies.

Sammy hadn't written down these email addresses. He'd committed them to memory.

Death Waits was living the dream. He took people's money and directed them to the ride's entrance, making them feel welcome, talking ride trivia. Some of his pals spotted him at the desk and enviously demanded to know how he came to be sitting on the other side of the wicket, and he told them the incredible story of the fatkins who'd simply handed over the reins.

This, this was how you ran a ride. None of that artificial gloopy sweetness that defined the Disney experience: instead, you got a personal, informal, human-scale experience. Chat people up, find out their hopes and dreams, make admiring noises at the artifacts they'd brought to add to the ride, kibitz about where they might place them. . . .

Around him, the bark of the vendors. One of them, an old lady in a blinding white sundress, came by to ask him if he wanted anything from the coffee cart.

There had been a time, those first days when they'd rebuilt Fantasyland, when he'd really felt like he was part of the magic. No, The Magic, with capital letters. Something about the shared experience of going to a place with people and having an experience with them, that was special. It must be why people went to church. Not that Disney had been a religion for him, exactly. But when he watched the park he'd grown up attending take on the trappings that adorned his favorite clubs, his favorite movies and games—man, it had been a piece of magic.

And to be a part of it. To be an altar boy, if not a priest, in that magical cathedral they'd all built together in Orlando!

But it hadn't been real. He could see that now.

At Disney, Death Waits had been a customer, and then an employee ("castmember"—he corrected himself reflexively). What he wanted, though, was to be a *citizen*. A citizen of The Magic—which wasn't a Magic Kingdom, since kingdoms didn't have citizens, they had subjects.

He started to worry about whether he was going to get a lunch break by about two, and by three he was starving. Luckily that's when Lester came back. He thanked Death profusely, which was nice, but he didn't ask Death to come back the next day.

"Um, when can I come back and do this some more?"

"You *want* to do this?"

"I told you that this morning—I love it. I'm good at it, too."

Lester appeared to think it over. "I don't know, man. I kind of put you in the hot-seat today, but I don't really have the authority to do it. I could get into trouble—"

Death waved him off. "Don't sweat it, then," he said with as much chirp as he could muster, which was precious fucking little. He felt like his heart was breaking. It was worse than when he'd finally asked out a coworker who'd worked the Pinocchio Village Haus and she had looked so horrified that he'd made a joke out of it, worried about a sexual harassment complaint.

Lester clearly caught some of that, for he thought some more and then waved his hands. "Screw her anyway. Meet me here at ten tomorrow. You're in."

Death wasn't sure he'd heard him right. "You're kidding."

"No, man, you want it; you got it. You're good at it, like you said."

"Holy—thanks. Thank you so much. I mean it. Thank you!" He made himself stop blithering. "Nice to meet you," he said finally. "Have a great evening!" Yowch. He was speaking castmemberese. *Nice one, Darren.*

He'd saved enough out of his wages from his first year at Disney to buy a little Shell electric two-seater, and then he'd gone way into debt buying kits to mod it to look like a Big Daddy Roth coffin dragster. The car sat alone at the edge of the lot. Around him, a slow procession of stall operators, with their arms full, headed for the freeway and across to the shantytown.

Meanwhile, he nursed his embarrassment and tried to take comfort in the attention that his gleaming, modded car evinced. He loved the decorative spoilers, the huge rear tires, the shining muffler pipes running alongside the bulging running boards. He stepped in and gripped the bat-shaped gearshift, adjusted the headstone-shaped headrest, and got rolling. It was a long drive back home to Melbourne, and he was reeling from the day's events. He wished he'd gotten someone to snap a pic of him at the counter. Shit.

He pulled off at a filling station after a couple hours. He needed a piss and something with guarana if he was going to make it the rest of the way home. It was all shut down, but the Automat was still open. He stood before the giant, wall-sized glassed-in refrigerator and dithered over the energy drinks. There were chocolate ones, salty ones, colas and cream sodas, but a friend had texted him a picture of a semi-legal yogurt smoothie with taurine and modafinil that sounded really good.

He spotted it and reached to tap on the glass and order it just as the fat guy came up beside him. Fat guys were rare in the era of fatkins; it was practically a fashion statement to be chunky, but this guy wasn't fashionable. He had onion breath that Death could smell even before he opened his mouth, and he was wearing a greasy windbreaker and baggy jeans. He had a comb-over and needed a shave.

"What the hell are you supposed to be?"

"I'm not anything," Death Waits said. He was used to shitkickers and tourists gawping at his shock of black hair with its viridian green highlights, his white face paint and eyeliner, his contact lenses that made his whole eyes into zombie-white cue balls. You just had to ignore them.

"You don't look like nothing to me. You look like something. Something you'd dress up a six-year-old as for Halloween. I mean, what the fuck?" He was talking quietly and without rancor, but he had a vibe like a basher. He must have arrived at the deserted rest stop while Death Waits was having a piss.

Death Waits looked around for a security cam. These rest stops always had a license-plate cam at the entrance and a couple of anti-stickup cams around the cashier. He spotted the camera. Someone had hung a baseball hat over its lens.

He felt his balls draw up toward his abdomen and his breathing quicken. This guy was going to fucking mug him. Shit shit shit. Maybe take his *car*.

"OK," Death said, "nice talking to you." He tried to step around the guy, but he sidestepped to block Death's path, then put a hand on Death's shoulder—it was strong. Death had been mugged once before, but the guy hadn't touched him; he'd just told him, fast and mean, to hand over his wallet and phone and then had split.

"I'm not done," the guy said.

"Look, take my wallet, I don't want any trouble." Apart from two glorious sucker punches at Sammy, Death had never thrown a punch, not since he'd flunked out of karate lessons at the local strip mall when he was twelve.

He liked to dance and he could run a couple miles without getting winded, but he'd seen enough real fights to know that it was better to get away than to try to strike out if you didn't know what you were doing.

"You don't want any trouble, huh?"

Death held out his wallet. He could cancel the cards. Losing the cash would hurt now that he didn't have a day job, but it was better than losing his teeth.

The guy smiled. His onion breath was terrible.

"*I* want trouble." Without any preamble or windup, the guy took hold of the earring that Death wore in his tragus, the little knob of cartilage on the inside of his ear, and briskly tore it out of Death's head.

It was so sudden, the pain didn't come at once. What came first was a numb feeling, the blood draining out of his cheeks and the color draining out of the world, and his brain double- and triple-checking what had just happened. *Did someone just tear a piece out of my ear? Tear? Ear?*

Then the pain roared in, all of his senses leaping to keen awareness before maxing out completely. He heard a crashing sound like the surf, smelled something burning, a light appeared before his eyes, an acrid taste flooded his mouth, and his ear felt like there was a hot coal nestled in it, charring the flesh.

With pain came the plan: *get the fuck out of there.* He took a step back and turned to run, but there was something tangled in his feet—the guy had bridged the distance between them quickly, very quickly, and had hooked a foot around his ankle. He was going to fall over. He landed in a runner's crouch and tried to start running, but a boot caught him in the butt, like an old-timey comedy moment, and he went sprawling, his chin smacking into the pavement, his teeth clacking together with a sound that echoed in his head.

"Get the fuck up," the guy said. He was panting a little, sounding excited. That sound was the scariest thing so far. This guy wanted to kill him. He could hear that. He was some kind of truck-stop murderer.

Death's fingers were encrusted in heavy silver rings—stylized skulls, a staring eyeball, a coffin-shaped poisoner's ring that he sometimes kept artificial sweetener in, an ankh, an alien head with insectile eyes—and he balled his hands into fists, thinking of everything he'd ever read about throwing a punch without breaking your knuckles. *Get close. Keep your fist tight, thumb outside. Don't wind up or he'll see it coming.*

He slowly turned over. The guy's eyes were in shadow. His belly heaved with each excited pant. From this angle, Death could see the guy had a gigantic boner.

The thought of what that might bode sent him into overdrive. He couldn't afford to let this guy beat him up.

He backed up to the rail that lined the walkway and pulled himself upright. He cowered in on himself as much as he could, hoping that the guy would close with him, so he could get in one good punch. He muttered indistinctly, softly, hoping to make the man lean in. His ring-encrusted hands gripped the railings.

The guy took a step toward him. His lips were wet, his eyes shone. He had a hand in his pocket and Death realized that getting his attacker close in wouldn't be smart if he had a knife.

The hand came out. It was pudgy and stub-fingered, and the fingernails were all gnawed down to the quick. Death looked at it. Spray can. Pepper spray? Mace? He didn't wait to find out. He launched himself off the railing at the fat man, going for his wet, whistling cave of a mouth.

The man nodded as he came for him and let him paste one on him. Death's rings drew blood on the fat cheek and rocked the guy's head back a bit. The man stepped back and armed away the blood with his sleeve. Death was running for his car, hand digging into his pocket for his phone. He managed to get the phone out and his hand on the door handle before the fat man caught up, breathing heavily, air whistling through his nose.

He punched Death in the mouth in a vastly superior rendition of Death's sole brave blow, a punch so hard Death's neck made a crackling sound as his head rocked away, slamming off the car's frame, ringing like a gong. Death began to slide down the car's door, and only managed to turn his face slightly when the man sprayed him with his little aerosol can.

Mace. Death's breath stopped in his lungs and his face felt as if he'd plunged it into boiling oil. His eyes felt worse, like dirty fingers were sandpapering over his eyeballs. He choked and fell over and heard the man laugh.

Then a boot caught him in the stomach and while he was doubled over, it came down again on his skinny shin. The sound of the bone breaking was loud enough to be heard over the roaring of the blood in his ears. He managed to suck in a lungful of air and scream it out, and the boot connected with his mouth, kicking him hard and making him bite his tongue. Blood filled his mouth.

A rough hand seized him by the hair and the rasping breath was in his ears.

"You should just shut the fuck up about Disney on the fucking Internet; you know that, kid?"

The man slammed his head against the pavement.

"Just. Shut. The. Fuck. Up." Bang, bang, bang. Death thought he'd lose consciousness soon—he'd had no idea that pain could be this intense. But he didn't lose consciousness for a long, long time. And the pain could be a lot more intense, as it turned out.

Sammy didn't want the writer meeting him at his office. His organization had lots of people who'd been loyal to the old gothy park and even to Death Waits. They plotted against him. They wrote about him on the fucking Internet, reporting on what he'd eaten for lunch and who'd shouted at him in his office and how the numbers were declining and how none of the design crews wanted to work on his new rides.

The writer couldn't come to the office—couldn't come within miles of the park. In fact, if Sammy had had his way, they would have done this all by phone, but when he'd emailed the writer, he'd said that he was in Florida already and would be happy to come and meet up.

Of course he was in Florida—he was covering the ride.

The trick was to find a place where no one, but no one, from work would go. That meant going as touristy as possible—something overpriced and kitschy.

Camelot was just the place. It had once been a demolition derby stadium, and then had done turns as a skate park, a dance club, and a discount wicker furniture outlet. Now it was Orlando's number two Arthurian-themed dining experience, catering to package-holiday consolidators who needed somewhere to fill the gullets of their busloads of tourists. Watching men in armor joust at low speed on glue-factory nags took care of an evening's worth of entertainment, too.

Sammy parked between two giant air-conditioned tour coaches, then made his way to the entrance. He'd told the guy what he looked like, and the guy had responded with an obvious publicity shot that made him look like Puck from a boys'-school performance of *A Midsummer Night's Dream*—unruly hair, mischievous grin.

When he turned up, though, he was ten years older, a cigarette jammed in the yellowing, crooked stumps of his teeth. He needed a shower and there was egg on the front of his denim jacket.

"I'm Sammy," Sammy said. "You must be Freddy."

Freddy spat the cigarette to one side and shook with him. The writer's palms were clammy and wet.

"Pleasure to meet you," Freddy said. "Camelot, huh?"

"Taste of home for you, I expect," Sammy said. "Tallyho. Pip-pip."

Freddy scrunched his face up in an elaborate sneer. "You are joking, right?"

"I'm joking. If I wanted to give you a taste of home, I'd have invited you to the Rose and Crown Pub in Epcot: 'Have a jolly ol' good time at the Rose and Crown!' "

"Still joking, I trust?"

"Still joking," Sammy said. "This place does a decent roast beef, and it's private enough."

"Private in the sense of full of screaming stupid tourists stuffing their faces?"

"Exactly." Sammy took a step toward the automatic doors.

"Before we go in, though," Freddy said. "Before we go in. Why are you talking to me at all, Mr. Disney Parks Executive?"

He was ready for this one. "I figured that sooner or later you'd want to know more about this end of the story that you've been covering. I figured it was in my employer's best interest to see to it that you got my version."

The reporter's grin was wet and mean. "I thought it was something like that. You understand that I'm going to write this the way I see it, not the way you spin it, right?"

Sammy put a hand on his heart. "Of course. I never would have asked anything less of you."

The reporter nodded and stepped inside the air-conditioned, horsey-smelling depths of Camelot. The greeter had acne and a pair of tights that showed off his skinny knock-knees. He took off his great peaked cap with its long plume and made a stiff little bow. "Greetings, milords, to Camelot. Yon feast awaits, and our brave knights stand ready to do battle for their honor and your amusement."

Freddy rolled his eyes at Sammy, but Sammy made a little scooting gesture and handed the greeter their tickets, which were ringside. If he was going to go to a place like Camelot, he could at least get the best seats in the house.

They settled in and let the serving wench—whose fancy contact lenses, piercings, and electric blue ponytails were seriously off-theme—take their roast beef orders and serve them gigantic pewter tankards of "ale"; Bud Light, and the logo was stamped into the sides of the tankards.

"Tell me your story, then," Freddy said. The tourists around them were noisy and already a little drunk, their conversation loud, to be heard over the looping soundtrack of ren-faire polka music.

"Well, I don't know how much you know about the new Disney Parks organization. A lot of people think of us as being just another subsidiary of the Mouse, like back in the old days. But since the IPO, we're our own company. We license some trademarks from Disney and operate rides based on them, but we also aggressively license from other parties—Warners, Universal, Nintendo. Even the French comic-book publisher responsible for Asterix. That means that we get a lot of people coming in and out of the organization, contractors or consultants working on designing a single ride or show.

"That creates a lot of opportunities for corporate espionage. Knowing what properties we're considering licensing gives the competition a chance to get there ahead of us, to land an exclusive deal that sets us back on square one. It's ugly stuff—they call it 'competitive intelligence' but it's just spying, plain old spying.

"All of our employees have been contacted, one time or another, by someone with an offer—get me a uniform, or a pic of the design roughs, or a recording of the soundtrack, or a copy of the contracts, and I'll make it worth your while. From street sweepers to senior execs, the money is just sitting there, waiting for us to pick it up."

The wench brought them their gigantic pewter plates of roast beef, Yorkshire pudding, parsnips, and a mountain of french fries, presumably to appease the middle-American appetites of the more unadventurous diners.

Freddy sliced off a throat-plugging lump of beef and skewered it on his fork.

"You're going to tell me that the temptation overwhelmed one of your employees, yes?" He shoved the entire lump into his mouth and began to masticate it, cheeks pouched out, looking like a kid with a mouthful of bubble gum.

"Precisely. Our competitors don't want to compete with us on a level playing field. They are, more than anything, imitators. They take the stuff that we carefully build, based on extensive research, design, and testing, and they clone it for parking-lot amusement rides. There's no attention to detail. There's no attention to safety! It's all cowboys and gypsies."

Freddy kept chewing, but he dug in the pockets of his sports coat and came up with a small stubby notebook and a ballpoint. He jotted some notes, shielding the pad with his body.

"And these crass imitators enter into our story how?" Freddy asked around his beef.

"You know about these New Work people—they call themselves 'remixers' but that's just a smoke screen. They like to cloak themselves in some postmodern, Creative Commons legitimacy, but when it comes down to it, they made their fortune off the intellectual property of others, uncompensated use of designs and technologies that others had invested in and created.

"So when they made a ride, it wasn't much of much. Like some kind of dusty Commie museum, old trophies from their last campaign. But somewhere along the way, they hooked up with one of these brokers who specializes in sneaking our secrets out of the park and into the hands of our competitors and quick as that, they were profitable—nationally franchised, even." He stopped to quaff his Bud Light and surreptitiously checked out the journalist to see how much of this he was buying. Impossible to say. He was still masticating a cheekful of rare roast, juice overflowing the corners of his mouth. But his hand moved over his pad and he made an impatient go-on gesture with his head, swallowing some of his payload.

"We fired some of the people responsible for the breaches, but there will be more. With fifty thousand castmembers—"

The writer snorted a laugh at the Disney-speak and choked a little, washing down the last of his mouthful with a chug of beer.

"—fifty thousand *employees* it's inevitable that they'll find more. These ex-employees, meanwhile, have moved to the last refuge of the scoundrel: Internet message boards, petulant tweets, and whiny blogs, where they're busily running us down. We can't win, but at least we can stanch the bleeding. That's why we've brought our lawsuits, and why we'll bring the next round."

The journalist's hand moved some more; then he turned a fresh page. "I see; I see. Yes, all fascinating, really. But what about these countersuits?"

"More posturing. Pirates love to put on aggrieved airs. These guys ripped us off and got caught at it, and now they want to sue us for their trouble. You know how countersuits work: they're just a bid to get a fast settlement: 'Well, I did something bad but so did you. Why don't we shake hands and call it a day?' "

"Uh-huh. So you're telling me that these intellectual-property pirates made a fortune knocking off your rides and that they're only countersuing you to get a settlement out of you, huh?"

"That's it in a nutshell. I wanted to sit down with you, on background, and just give you our side of things, the story you won't get from the press releases. I know you're the only one trying to really get at the story behind the story with these people."

Freddy had finished his entire roast and was working his way through the fries and limp Yorkshire pudding. He waved vigorously at their serving wench and hollered, "More here, love!" and quaffed his beer.

Sammy dug into his cold dinner and speared up a forkful, waiting for Freddy to finish swallowing.

"Well, that's a very neat little story, Mr. Disney Executive off the record on background." Sammy felt a vivid twinge of anxiety. Freddy's eyes glittered in the torchlight. "Very neat indeed.

"Let me tell you one of my own. When I was a young man, before I took up the pen, I worked a series of completely rubbish jobs. I cleaned toilets; I drove a taxi; I stocked grocery shelves. You may ask how this qualified me to write about the technology industry. Lots of people have, in fact, asked that.

"I'll tell you why it qualifies me. It qualifies me because unlike all the ivory-tower bloggers, rich and comfortable geeks whose masturbatory rants about Apple not honoring their warranties are what passes for corporate criticism online, I've been there. I'm not from a rich family; I didn't get to go to the best schools; no one put a PC in my bedroom when I was six. I worked for an honest living before I gave up honest work to write.

"As much as the Internet circle jerk disgusts me, it's not a patch on the businesses themselves. You Disney people with your minimum wage and all the sexual harassment, you can eat labor policies in your nice right-to-work state; you get away with murder. Anyone who criticizes you does so on your own terms: Is Disney exploiting its workers too much? Is it being too aggressive in policing its intellectual property? Should it be nicer about it?

"I'm the writer who doesn't watch your corporations on your own terms. I don't care if another business is unfairly competing with your business. I care that your business is unfair to the world. That it aggressively exploits children to get their parents to spend money they don't have on junk they don't need. I care that your workers can't unionize, make shit wages, and get fired when they complain or when you need to flex your power a little.

"I grew up without any power at all. When I was working for a living, I had no say at all in my destiny. It didn't matter how much shit a boss wanted to shovel on me; all I could do was stand and take it. Now I've got some power, and I plan on using it to setting things to rights."

Sammy chewed his roast long past the point that it was ready to swallow. The fact that he'd made an error was readily apparent from the start of Freddy's little speech, but with each passing minute, the depth of his error grew. He'd really fucked up. He felt like throwing up. This guy was going to fuck him, he could tell.

Freddy smiled and quaffed and wiped at his beard with the embroidered napkin. "Oh, look—the jousting's about to start," he said. Knights in armor on horseback circled the arena, lances held high. The crowd applauded and an announcer came on the PA to tell them each knight's name, referring them to a program printed on their place mats. Sammy pretended to be interested while Freddy cheered them on, that same look of unholy glee plain on his face.

The knights formed up around the ring and their pimply squires came out of the gate and tended to them. There was a squire and knight right in front of them, and the squire tipped his hat to them. Freddy handed the kid a ten-dollar bill. Sammy never tipped live performers; he hated buskers and panhandlers. It all reminded him of stuffing a stripper's G-string. He liked his media a little more impersonal than that. But Freddy was looking at him, so with a weak little smile, he handed the squire the smallest thing in his wallet—a twenty.

The jousting began. It was terrible. The "knights" couldn't ride worth a damn, their "lances" missed one another by farcical margins, and their "falls" were so obviously staged that even the chubby ten-year-old beside him was clearly unimpressed.

"Got to go to the bathroom," he said into Freddy's ear. In leaning over, he contrived to get a look at the reporter's notebook. It was covered in obscene doodles of Mickey Mouse with a huge erection, Minnie dangling from a noose. There wasn't a single word written on it. What little blood was left in Sammy's head drained into his feet, which were leaden and uncoordinated on the long trip to the filthy toilets.

He splashed cold water on his face in the sink, and then headed back toward his seat. He never made it. From the top of the stairs leading down to ringside, he saw Freddy quaffing more ale and flirting with the wench. The thunder of horse hooves and the soundtrack of cinematic music drowned out all sounds, but nothing masked the stink of the manure falling from the horses, half of which were panicking (the other half appeared to be drugged).

This was a mistake. He thought Freddy was a gossip reporter who liked juicy stories. Turned out he was also one of those tedious anticorporate types who would happily hang Sammy out to dry. Time to cut his losses.

He turned on his heel and headed for the door. The doorman was having a cigarette with a guy in a sports coat who was wearing a MANAGER badge on his lapel.

"Leaving so soon? The show's only just getting started!" The manager was sweating under his sports coat. He had a thin mustache and badly dyed chestnut hair cut like a lego character's.

"Not interested," Sammy said. "All the off-theme stuff distracted me. Nose rings. Blue hair. Cigarettes." The doorman guiltily flicked his cigarette into the parking lot. Sammy felt a little better.

"I'm sorry to hear that, sir," the manager said. He was prematurely gray under the dye job, for he couldn't have been more than thirty-five. Thirty-five years old and working a dead-end job like this—Sammy was thirty-five. This is where he might end up if his screwups came back to haunt him. "Would you like a comment card?"

"No," Sammy said. "Any outfit that can't figure out clean toilets and decent theming on its own can't benefit from my advice." The doorman flushed and looked away, but the manager's smile stayed fixed and calm. Maybe he was drugged, like the horses. It bothered Sammy. "Christ, how long until this place gets turned into a roller derby again?"

"Would you like a refund, sir?" the manager asked. He looked out at the parking lot. Sammy followed his gaze, looking above the cars, and realized, suddenly, that he was standing in a cool tropical evening. The sky had gone the color of a ripe plum, with proud palms silhouetted against it. The wind made them sway. A few clouds scudded across the moon's luminous face, and the smell of citrus and the hum of insects and the calls of night birds were vivid on the evening air.

He'd been about to say something cutting to the manager, one last attempt to make the man miserable, but he couldn't be bothered. He had a nice screened-in porch behind his house, with a hammock. He'd sat in it on nights like this, years ago. Now all he wanted to do was sit in it again.

"Good night," he said, and headed for his car.

Perry's cast *stank*. It had started to go a little skunky on the second day, but after a week it was like he had a dead animal stuck to his shoulder. A rotting dead animal. A rotting, itchy dead animal.

"I don't think you're supposed to be doing this on your own," Hilda said, as he sawed awkwardly at it with the utility knife. It was made of something a lot tougher than the fiberglass one he'd had when he broke his leg falling off the roof as a kid (he'd been up there scouting out glider possibilities).

"So you do it," he said, handing her the knife. He couldn't stand the smell for one second longer.

"Uh-uh, not me, pal. No way that thing is supposed to come off anytime soon. If you're going to cripple yourself, you're going to have to do it on your own."

He made a rude sound. "Fuck hospitals, fuck doctors, and fuck this fucking cast. My arm barely hurts these days. We can splint it once I get this off; that'll immobilize it. They told me I'd need this for *six weeks*. I can't wear this for six weeks. I'll go nuts."

"You'll go lame if you take it off. Your poor mother, you must have driven her nuts."

He slipped and cut himself and winced, but tried not to let her know, because that's exactly what she'd predicted would happen. After a couple days together, she'd become an expert at predicting exactly which of his escapades would end in disaster. It was a little spooky.

Blood oozed out from under the cast and slicked his hand.

"Right, off to the hospital. I told you you'd get this thing wet if you got in the shower. I told you that it would stink and rot and itch if you did. I told you to let me give you a sponge bath."

"I'm not insured."

"We'll go to the free clinic."

Defeated, he let her lead him to her car.

She helped him buckle in, wrinkling her nose. "What's wrong, baby?" she said, looking at his face. "What are you moping about?"

"It's just the cast," he said, looking away.

She grabbed him by the chin and turned him to face her. "Look, don't do that. Do *not* do that. If something's bothering you, we're going to talk about it. I didn't sign up to fall in love with the strong, silent type. You've been sulking all day; now what's it about?"

He smiled in spite of himself. "All right, I give in. I miss home. They're all in the middle of it, running the ride and stuff, and I'm here." He felt a moment's worry that she'd be offended. "Not that I don't love being here with you, but I'm feeling guilty—"

"OK, I get it. Of course you feel guilty. It's your project, it's in trouble, and you're not taking care of it. Christ, Perry, is that all? I would have been disappointed if this wasn't worrying you. Let's go to Florida, then."

"What?"

She kissed the tip of his nose. "Take me to Florida. Let's meet your friends."

"But . . ." Were they moving in together or something? He was totally smitten with this girl, but that was *fast*. Even for Perry. "Don't you need to be here?"

"They can live without me. It's not like I'm proposing to move in with you. I'll come back here after a while. But I'm only doing two classes this term and they're both offered by distance ed. Let's just go."

"When?"

"After the hospital. You need a new cast, stinkmeister. Roll down your window a little, OK? Whew!"

The doctors warned him to let the new cast set overnight before subjecting it to the rigors of a TSA examination, so they spent one more night at Hilda's place. Perry spent it going over the mailing-list traffic and blog posts, confirming the plane tickets, ordering a car to meet them at the Miami airport. He finally managed to collapse into bed at 3 AM, and Hilda grabbed him, dragged him to her, and spooned him tightly.

"Don't worry, baby. Your friends and I will get along great."

He hadn't realized that he'd been worrying about this, but once she pointed it out, it was obvious. "You're not worried?"

She ran her hands over his furry chest and tummy. "No, of course not. Your friends will love me or I'll have them killed. More to the point, they'll love me because you love me and I love you and they love you, too."

"What does Ernie think of me?" he said, thinking of her brother for the first time since they'd hooked up all those months ago.

"Oh, hum," she said. He stiffened. "No, it's OK," she said, rubbing his tummy some more. It tickled. "He's glad I'm with someone I care about, and he loves the ride. He's just, you know. Protective of his big sister."

"What's he worried about?"

"Just what you'd expect. We live thousands of miles apart. You're ten years older than me. You've been getting into the kind of trouble that attracts armed cops. Wouldn't you be protective if you were my bro?"

"I was an only child, but sure, OK, I see that."

"It's nothing," she said. "Really. Bring him a nice souvenir from Florida when we come back to Madison, take him out for a couple beers, and it'll all be great."

"So we're cool? All the families are in agreement? All the stars are in alignment? Everything is hunky and/or dory?"

"Perry Gibbons, I love you dearly. You love me. We've got a cause to fight for, and it's a just one with many brave comrades fighting alongside of us. What could possibly go wrong?"

"What could possibly go wrong?" Perry said. He drew in a breath to start talking.

"It was rhetorical, goofball. It's also three in the morning. Sleep, for tomorrow we fly."

Lester didn't want to open the ride, but someone had to. Someone had to, and it wasn't Perry, who was off with his midwestern honey. Lester would have loved to sleep in and spend the day in his workshop rebuilding his sixty-four-bit registers—he'd had some good ideas for improving on the initial design, and he still had the CAD files, which were the hard part anyway.

He walked slowly across the parking lot, the sunrise in his eyes, a cup of coffee steaming in his hand. He'd almost gone to the fatkins bars the night before—he'd almost gone ten, fifteen times, every time he thought of Suzanne storming out of his lab, but he'd stayed home with the TV and waited for her to show up or call or post something to her blog or turn up on IM, and when none of those things had happened by 4 AM, he tumbled into bed and slept for three hours, until his alarm went off again.

Blearily, he sat himself down behind the counter, greeted some of the hawkers coming across the road, and readied his ticket roll.

The first customers arrived just before nine—an East Indian family driving a car with Texas plates. Dad wore khaki board shorts and a tank top and leather sandals, Mom was in a beautiful silk sari, and the kids looked like mall bangbangers in designer versions of the stuff the wild kids in the shantytown went around in.

They came out of the ride ten minutes later and asked for their money back.

"There's nothing in there," the dad said, almost apologetically. "It's empty. I don't think it's supposed to be empty, is it?"

Lester put the roll of tickets into his pocket and stepped into the Wal-Mart. His eyes took a second to adjust to the dark after the brightness of the rising Florida sun. When they were fully adjusted, though, he could see that the tourist was right. Busy robots had torn down all the exhibits and scenes, leaving nothing behind but swarming crowds of bots on the floor, dragging things offstage. The smell of the printers was hot and thick.

Lester gave the man his money back.

"Sorry, man, I don't know what's going on. This kind of thing should be impossible. It was all there last night."

The man patted him on the shoulder. "It's all right. I'm an engineer—I know all about crashes. It just needs some debugging, I'm sure."

Lester got out a computer and started picking through the logs. This kind of failure really should be impossible. Without manual oversight, the bots weren't supposed to change more than 5 percent of the ride in response to another ride's changes. If all the other rides had torn themselves down, it might have happened, but they hadn't, had they?

No, they hadn't. A quick check of the logs showed that none of the changes had come from Madison, or San Francisco, or Boston, or Westchester, or any of the other ride sites.

Either his robots had crashed or someone had hacked the system. He rebooted the system and rolled it back to the state from the night before and watched the robots begin to bring the props back from offstage.

How the hell could it have happened? He dumped the logs and began to sift through them. He kept getting interrupted by riders who wanted to know when the ride would come back up, but he didn't know, the robots' estimates were oscillating wildly between ten minutes and ten hours. He finally broke off to write up a little quarter-page flier about it and printed out a couple hundred of them on some neon yellow paper stock he had lying around, along with a jumbo version that he taped over the price list.

It wasn't enough. Belligerent riders who'd traveled for hours to see the ride wanted a human explanation, and they pestered him ceaselessly. All the hawkers felt like they deserved more information than the rubes, and they pestered him even more. All he wanted to do was write some regexps that would help him figure out what was wrong so he could fix it.

He wished that Death kid would show up already. He was supposed to be helping out from now on and he seemed like the kind of person who would happily jaw with the marks until the end of time.

Eventually he gave up. He set the sign explaining what had happened (or rather, not explaining, since he didn't fucking know yet) in the middle of the counter, bolted it down with a couple of lock bolts, and retreated to the ride's interior and locked the smoked-glass doors behind him.

Once he had some peace and quiet, it took him only a few minutes to see where the changes had originated. He verified the info three times, not because he wasn't sure, but because he couldn't tell if this was good news or bad news. He read some blogs and discovered lots of other ride operators were chasing this down, but none of them had figured it out yet.

Grinning hugely, he composed a hasty post and CCed it to a bunch of mailing lists, then went out to find Kettlebelly and Tjan.

He found them in the guesthouse, sitting down to a working breakfast, with Eva and the kids at the end of the table. Tjan's little girl was trying to feed Pascal, but not doing a great job of it; Tjan's son sat on his father's lap, picking at his clown-face pancakes.

"Morning, guys!"

Suzanne narrowed her eyes and looked away. The table fell quiet—even the kids sensed that something was up. "Who's watching the ride, Lester?" Tjan asked, quietly.

"It's shut," he said cheerfully.

"*Shut?*" Tjan spoke loudly enough that everyone jumped a little. Lyenitchka accidentally stabbed Pascal with the spoon and he started to wail. Suzanne stood up from the table and walked quickly out of the guesthouse, holding on to her phone as a kind of thin pretense of having to take a call. Lester chose to ignore her.

Lester held his hands out placatingly. "It's OK—it's just down for a couple hours. I had to reset it after what happened last night."

Lester waited.

"All right," Eva said, "I'll bite. What happened last night?"

"Brazil came online!" Lester said. "Like twenty rides opened there. But they got their protocol implementation a little wrong, so when I showed up, the whole ride had been zeroed out. I'm sure I can help them get it right; in the meantime I've got the ride resetting itself and I've blackholed their changes temporarily." He grinned sunnily. "How fucking cool is that? Brazil!"

They smiled weakly back. "I don't think I understand, Lester," Kettlewell said. "Brazil? We don't have any agreements with anyone in Brazil."

"We have agreements with everyone in Brazil!" Lester said. "We've got an open protocol and a server that anyone can connect to. That's an agreement; that's all a protocol is."

Kettlewell shook his head. "You're saying that all anyone needed to do to reprogram our ride—"

"—was to connect to it and send some changes. Trust is assumed in the system."

"Trust is *assumed*? You haven't changed this?"

Lester took a step back. "No, I haven't changed it. The whole system is open—that's the point. We can't just start requiring logins to get on the network. The whole thing would collapse—it'd be like putting locks on the bathroom and then taking the only key for yourself. We just can't do it."

Kettlewell looked like he was going to explode. Tjan put a hand on his arm. Slowly, Kettlewell sat back down. Tjan took a sip of his coffee.

"Lester, can you walk me through this one more time?"

Lester rocked back and forth a little. They were all watching him now, except for Suzanne, who was fuming somewhere or getting ready to go home to Russia, or something.

"We have a published protocol for describing changes to the ride—it's built on Git3D's system for marking up and syncing three-dee models of objects; it's what we used all through the Kodacell days for collaboration. The way you get a ride online is to sync up with our version server and then instantiate a copy. Then any changes you make get synced back and we instantiate them. Everyone stays in sync, give or take a couple hours."

"But you had passwords on the Subversion server for objects, right?"

"Yeah, but we didn't design this one to take passwords. It's a lot more ad hoc—we wanted to be sure that people we didn't know could get in and play."

Kettlewell put his face in his hands and groaned.

Tjan rolled his eyes. "I think what Kettlewell's trying to say is that things have changed since those carefree days—we're in a spot now where if Disney or someone else who hated us wanted to attack us, this would be a prime way of doing it."

Lester nodded. "Yeah, I figured that. Openness always costs something. But we get a lot of benefits out of openness, too. The way it works now is that no one ride can change more than five percent of the status quo within twenty-four hours without a manual approval. The problem was that the Brazilians opened, like, *fifty* rides at the same time, and each of them zeroed out and tried to sync that, and between them they did way more than a hundred percent. It'd be pretty easy to set things up so that no more than five percent can be changed, period, within a twenty-four-hour period, without manual approval."

"If you can do that, why not set every change to require approval?" Kettlewell said.

"Well, for starters, because we'd end up spending all our time clicking OK for five-centimeter adjustments to prop positioning. But more importantly, it's because the system is all about community—we're not in charge; we're just part of the network."

Kettlewell made a sour face and muttered something. Tjan patted his arm again. "You guys *are* in charge, as much as you'd like not to be. You're the ones facing the legal hassles; you're the ones who invented it."

"We didn't, really," Lester said. "This was a real standing-on-the-shoulders-of-giants project. We made use of a bunch of stuff that was on the shelf already, put it together, and then other people helped us refine it and get it working well. We're just part of the group, like I keep saying." He had a thought. "Besides, if we were in charge, Brazil wouldn't have been able to zero us out.

"You guys are being really weird and suit-y about this, you know? I've fixed the problem: no one can take us down like this again. It just won't happen. I've put the fix on the version server for the codebase, so everyone else can deploy it if they want to. The problem's solved. We'll be shut for an hour or two, but who cares? You're missing the big picture: Brazil opened fifty rides *yesterday*! I mean, it sucks that we didn't notice until it screwed us up, but Brazil's got it all online. Who's next? China? India?"

"Russia?" Kettlewell said, looking at the door that Suzanne had left by. He was clearly trying to needle Lester.

Lester ignored him. "I'd love to go to Brazil and check out how they've done it. I speak a little Portuguese, even—enough to say, 'Are you eighteen yet?' anyway."

"You're *weird*," Lyenitchka said. Ada giggled and said, "Weird!"

Eva shook her head. "The kids have got a point," she said. "You people are all a little weird. Why are you fighting? Tjan, Landon, you came here to manage the business side of things, and that's what you're doing. Lester, you're in charge of the creative and technical stuff, and that's what you're doing. Without Lester, you two wouldn't have any business to run. Without these guys, you'd be in jail or something by now. Make peace, because you're on the same side. I've got enough children to look after here."

Kettlewell snapped a nod at her. "Right as ever, darling. OK, I apologize, all right?"

"Me too," Lester said. "I was kidding about going to Brazil—at least while Perry's still away."

"He's coming home," Tjan said. "He called me this morning. He's bringing the girl, too."

"Yoko!" Lester said, and grinned. "OK, someone should get online and find out how all the other rides are coping with this. I'm sure they're going nutso out there."

"You do that," Kettlewell said. "We've got another call with the lawyers in ten minutes."

"How's all that going?"

"Let me put it this way," Kettlewell said, and for a second he was back in his glory days, slick and formidable, a shark. "I liquidated my shares in Disney this morning. They're down fifty points since the NYSE opened. You wait until Tokyo wakes up; they're going to bail and bail and bail."

Lester smiled back. "OK, well that's good, then."

He hunkered down with a laptop and got his homebrew wireless rig up and running—a card would have been cheaper, but his rig gave him lots of robustness against malicious interference, multipath and plain old attenuation—and got his headline reader running.

He set to reading the posts and dispelling the popups that tried to call his attention to this or that. His filters had lots to tell him about, and the areas of his screen designated for different interests were starting to pinken as they accumulated greater urgency.

He waved them away and concentrated on getting through to all the ride maintainers who had questions about his patches. But there was one pink area that wouldn't go. It was his serendipity zone, where things that didn't match his filters but had lots of interestingness—comments and reposts from people he paid attention to—and some confluence with his keywords turned up.

Impatiently, he waved it up, and a page made of bits of LiveJournals and news reports and photo streams assembled itself.

His eye fell first on the photos. But for the shock of black and neon green hair, he wouldn't have recognized the kid in the pictures as Death Waits. His face was a ruin. His nose was a bloody rose; his eyes were both swollen shut. One ear was ruined—apparently he'd been dragged some distance with that side of his head on the ground. His cheeks were pulpy and bruised. Then he clicked through to the photos from where they'd found Death, before they'd cleaned him up in the ambulance, and he had to turn his head away and breathe deeply. Both legs and both arms were clearly broken, with at least one compound fracture. His crotch—Jesus. Lester looked away again, then quickly closed the window.

He switched to text accounts from Death's friends who'd been to see him in the hospital. He would live, but he might not walk again. He was lucid, and he was telling stories about the man who'd beaten him—

You should just shut the fuck up about Disney on the fucking Internet; you know that, kid?

Lester got up and went to find Kettlewell and Tjan and Suzanne—oh, especially Suzanne—again. He didn't think for one second that Death would have invented that. In fact, it was just the sort of brave thing that the gutsy little kid might have had the balls to report on.

Every step he took, he saw that ruin of a face, the compound fracture, the luminous blood around his groin. He made it halfway to the guesthouse before he found himself leaning against a shanty, throwing up. Tears and bile streaming down his face, chest heaving, Lester decided that this wasn't about fun anymore. Lester came to understand what it meant to be responsible for people's lives. When he stood up and wiped his face on the tail of his tight, glittering shirt, he was a different person.

He was sweating in the suffocating afternoon heat, and his re-casted arm was on fire. Hilda had shown him the article about Death Waits while they were being screened for their connection at O'Hare. The TSA guy had been swabbing his cast with a black-powder residue detector, and as Perry had read the story, he'd let out an involuntary yelp and a jump that sent him back for a full round of tertiary screening. No date with Dr. Jellyfinger, though it was a close thing.

Hilda was deep in her own phone, probing ferociously at it, occasionally picking it up and talking into it, then poking at it some more. Neither of them looked out the windows much, though in his mind, Perry had rehearsed this homecoming as a kind of tour of his territory, picking out which absurd landmarks he'd point out, which funny stories he'd tell, pausing to nuzzle Hilda's throat.

But by the time he'd absorbed the mailing-list traffic and done a couple phoners with the people back in Madison—particularly Ernie, who was freaking about Death Waits and calling for tight physical security for all their people—they were pulling in at the ride. The cabbie, a Turk, wasn't very cool about the neighborhood, and he kept slowing down on the side of the road and offering to let them out there, and Perry kept insisting that he take them all the way.

"No, you can't just drop me here, man. For the tenth time, I've got a fucking *cast* on my *broken arm*. I'm not carrying my suitcase a mile from here. I live there. It's safe. God, it's not like I'm asking you to take me to a war zone."

He didn't want to tip the guy, but he did. The cabbie was just trying to play it safe. Lots of people tried to play it safe. It didn't make them assholes, even if it did make them ineffectual and useless.

While Perry tipped him, Hilda pulled the suitcase out of the cab's trunk, and she'd barely had time to shut the lid when the driver roared off like he was trying to outrun a sniper.

Perry grimaced. This was supposed to be a triumphant homecoming. He was supposed to be showing off his toys, all he'd wrought, to this girl. The town was all around them and they were about to charge in without even pausing to consider its Dr. Seuss wonderment.

"Wait a sec," Perry said. He took her hand. "See that? That was the first shanty they built. Five stories now." The building was made of prefab concrete for the first couple stories, then successively lighter materials, with the roof shack made of bamboo. "The designs are experimental, from the Army Corps of Engineers mostly, but they say they'll stand a force-five hurricane." He grimaced again. "Probably not the bamboo one, of course."

"Of course," Hilda said. "What's that one?" She'd picked up on his mood; she knew he wanted to show her around before they ended up embroiled in ride politics and work again."

"You've got a good eye, my dear. That's the finest BBQ on the continent. See how the walls are a little sooty looking? That's carbonized ambrosia, a mix of fat and spice and hickory that you could scrape off and bottle as perfume."

"Eww."

"You haven't tried Lemarr's ribs yet," he said, and goosed her. She squeaked and punched him in the shoulder. He showed her the tuckshops, the kids playing, the tutor's place, the day-care center, the workshops, taking her on a grand-circle tour of this place he'd help conjure into existence.

"Now there's someone I haven't seen in far too long," Francis said. He'd aged something fierce in the last year, booze making his face subside into a mess of wrinkles and pouches and broken blood vessels. He gave Perry a hard hug that smelled of booze, and it wasn't even lunchtime.

"Francis, meet Hilda Hammersen; Hilda, meet Francis Clammer: aerospace engineer and gentleman of leisure."

He took her hand and feinted a kiss at it, and Hilda good-naturedly rolled her eyes at this.

"What do you think of our lovely little settlement, then, Ms. Hammersen?"

"It's like something out of a fairy tale," she said. "You hear stories about Christiania and how good and peaceful it all was, but whenever you see squatters on TV, it's always crack houses and drive-bys. You've really got something here."

Francis nodded. "We get a bad rap, but we're no different really from any other place where people take pride in what they own. I built my place, with my two hands. If Jimmy Carter had been there with Habitat for Humanity, we would have gotten no end of good press. Because we did it without a dead ex-president on the scene, we're crooks. Perry tell you about what the law does around here?"

Perry nodded. "Yeah. She knows."

Francis patted his cast. "Nice hardware, buddy. So when some Bible-thumping do-gooder gives you a leg up, you're a folk hero. Help yourself, you're a CHUD. It's the same with you people and your ride. If you had the backing of a giant corporation with claws sunk deep into kids' brains, you'd be every package-tour operator's wet dream. Build it yourself in the guts of a dead shopping center, and you're some kind of slimy underclass."

"Maybe that's true," said Hilda, "but it's not necessarily true. Back in Madison, the locals love us; they think we do great stuff. After the law came after us, they came by with food and money and helped us rebuild. Scrappy activists get a lot of love in this country, too. Not everyone wants a big corporation to spoon-feed them."

"Off in hippie college towns you'll always find people with enough brains to realize that their neighbors aren't the boogieman. But there ain't so many hippie college towns these days. I wish you two luck, but I think you'd be nuts to walk out the door in the morning expecting anything better than a kick in the teeth."

That made Perry think of Death Waits, and the sense of urgency came back to him. "OK, we have to go now," he said. "Thanks, Francis."

"Nice to meet you, young woman," he said, and when he smiled, it was a painful thing, all pouches and wrinkles and sags, and he gimped away with his limp more pronounced than ever.

They tracked down the crew at the teahouse's big table. Everyone roared greetings at them when they came through the door, a proper homecoming, but when Perry counted heads, he realized that there was no one watching the ride.

"Guys, who's running the ride?"

They told him about Brazil then, and Hilda listened with her head cocked, her face animated with surprise, dismay, then delight. "You say there are *fifty* rides open?"

"All at once," Lester said. "All in one go."

"Holy mother of poo," Hilda breathed. Perry couldn't bring himself to say *anything*. He couldn't even imagine Brazil in his head—jungles? beaches? He knew nothing about the country. They'd built *fifty* rides, without even making contact with him. He and Lester had designed the protocol to be open because they thought it would make it easier for others to copy what they'd done, but he'd never thought—

It was like vertigo, that feeling.

"So you're Yoko, huh?" Lester said finally. It made everyone smile, but the tension was still there. Something big had just happened, bigger than any of them, bigger than the beating that had been laid on Death Waits, bigger than anything Perry had ever done. From his mind to a nation on another continent—

"You're the sidekick, huh?" Hilda said.

Lester laughed. "Touché. It's very nice to meet you and thank you for bringing him back home. We were starting to miss him, though God alone knows why."

"I plan on keeping him," she said, giving his bicep a squeeze. It brought Perry back to them. The little girls were staring at Hilda with saucer eyes. It made him realize that except for Suzanne and Eva, their whole little band was boys, all boys.

"Well, I'm home now," he said. He knelt down and showed the girls his cast. "I got a new one," he said. "They had to throw the old one out. So I need your help decorating this. Do you think you could do the job?"

Lyenitchka looked critically at the surface. "I think we could do the gig," she said. "What do you think, partner?"

Tjan snorted out his nose, but she was so solemn that the rest kept quiet. Ada matched Lyenitchka's critical posture and then nodded authoritatively. "Sure thing, partner."

"It's a date," Perry said. "We're gonna head home and put down our suit-cases and come back and open the ride if it's ready. It's time Lester got some time off. I'm sure Suzanne will appreciate having him back again."

Another silence fell over the group, tense as a piano wire. Perry looked from Lester to Suzanne and saw in a second what was up. He had time to notice that his first emotional response was to be intrigued, not sorry or scared. Only after a moment did he have the reaction he thought he should have—a mixture of sadness for his friend and irritation that they had yet another thing to deal with in the middle of a hundred other crises.

Hilda broke the tension—"It was great to meet you all. Dinner tonight, right?"

"Absolutely," Kettlewell said, seizing on this. "Leave it to us—we'll book someplace just great and have a great dinner to welcome you guys back."

Eva took his arm. "That's right," she said. "I'll get the girls to pick it out." The little girls jumped up and down with excitement at this, and the baby brothers caught their excitement and made happy kid screeches that got everyone smiling again.

Perry gave Lester a solemn, supportive hug, kissed Suzanne and Eva on the cheeks (Suzanne smelled good, something like sandalwood), shook hands with Tjan and Kettlewell, and tousled all four kids before lighting out for the ride, gasping out a breath as they stepped into the open air.

Death Waits regained consciousness several times over the next week, aware each time that he was waking up in a hospital bed on a crowded ward, that he'd woken here before, and that he hurt and couldn't remember much after the beating had started.

But after a week or so, he found himself awake and aware—he still hurt all over, a dull and distant stoned ache that he could tell was being kept at bay by powerful painkillers. There was someone waiting for him.

"Hello, Darren," the man said. "I'm an attorney working for your friends at the ride. My name is Tom Levine. We're suing Disney and we wanted to gather some evidence from you."

Death didn't like being called Darren, and he didn't want to talk to this dork. He'd woken up with a profound sense of anger, remembering the dead-eyed guy shouting about Disney while bouncing his head off the ground, knowing that Sammy had done this, wanting nothing more than to get ahold of Sammy and, and . . . That's where he ran out of imagination. He was perfectly happy drawing medieval-style torture chambers and vampires in his sketch book, but he didn't actually have much stomach for, you know, *violence.*

Per se.

"Can we do this some other time?" His mouth hurt. He'd lost four teeth and had bitten his tongue hard enough to need stitches. He could barely understand his own words.

"I wish we could, but time is of the essence here. You've heard that we're bringing a suit against Disney, right?"

"No," Death said.

"Must have come up while you were out. Anyway, we are, for unfair competition. We've got a shot at cleaning them out, taking them for every cent. We're going through the pretrial motions now and there's been a motion to summarily exclude any evidence related to your beating from the proceedings. We think that's BS. It's clear from what you've told your friends that they wanted to shut you up because you were making them look bad. So what we need is more information from you about what this guy said to you, and what you'd posted before, and anything anyone at Disney said to you while you were working there."

"You know that that guy said he was beating me up because I talked about this stuff in the first place?"

The lawyer waved a hand. "There's no way they'll come after you now. They look like total assholes for doing this. They're scared stupid. Now, I'm going to want to formally depose you later, but this is a pre-deposition interview just to get clear on everything."

The guy leaned forward and suddenly Death Waits had a bone-deep conviction that the guy was about to punch him. He gave a little squeak and shrank away, then cried out again as every inch of his body awoke in hot agony, a feeling like grating bones beneath his skin.

"Woah, take it easy there, champ," the lawyer said.

Death Waits held back tears. The guy wasn't going to hit him, but just the movement in his direction had scared him like he'd leapt out holding an ax. The magnitude of his own brokenness began to sink in and now he could barely hold back the tears.

"Look, the guys who run the ride have told me that I have to get this from you as soon as I can. If we're going to keep the ride safe and nail the bastards who did this to you, I need to do this. If I had my way, I wouldn't bug you, but I've got my orders, OK?"

Death snuffled back the tears. The back of his throat felt like it had been sanded with a rusty file. "Water," he croaked.

The lawyer shook his head. "Sorry buddy, just the IV, I'm afraid. The nurses were very specific. Let's start, OK, and then we'll be done before you know it."

Defeated, Death closed his eyes. "Start," he said, his voice like something made from soft tar left too long in the sun.

Sammy knew he was a dead man. The only thing keeping him alive was legal's reluctance to read the Net. Hackelberg had a couple of juniors who kept watch lists running on hot subjects, but they liked to print them out and mark them up, and that meant that they lagged a day or two behind the blogosphere.

The Death Waits thing was a freaking disaster. The guy was just supposed to put a scare into him, not cripple him for life. Every time Sammy thought about what would happen when the Death Waits thing percolated up to him, he got gooseflesh.

Damn that idiot thug anyway. Sammy had been very clear. The guy who knew the guy who knew the guy had been reassuring on the phone when Sammy put in the order—sure, sure, nothing too rough, just a little shoving around.

And what's worse is the idiot kid hadn't gotten the hint. Sammy didn't get it. If a stranger beat him half to death and told him to stop hanging out in message boards, well, the message boards would go. Damned right they would.

And with Freddy, there was a shoe waiting to drop. Freddy wouldn't report on their interview, he was pretty sure of that. "Off the record" means something, even to "journalists" like Honest Freddy. But Freddy wasn't going to be nice to him in follow-ups, that much was sure. And if—when!—Freddy got wind of the Death Waits situation . . .

He began to hyperventilate.

"I'm going to go check on the construction," he said to his personal assistant, a new girl they'd sent up when his last one had defected to work for Wiener (Wiener!) after Sammy'd shouted at her for putting through a press call from some blogger who wanted to know when Fantasyland would be reopening.

It had been a mistake to shut down Fantasyland just to get the other managers off his back. Sure the rides were sick dogs, but there had been life in them still. Construction sites don't bring in visitors, and the numbers for the park were down and everyone was looking at him. Never mind that the only reason the numbers had been as high as they were was that Sammy had saved everyone's ass when he'd done the goth rehab. Never mind that the real reason that numbers were down was that no one else in management had the guts to keep the park moving and improving.

He slowed his step on Main Street, USA, and forced himself to pay attention to his surroundings. The stores on Main Street had been co-opted into helping him dump all the superfluous goth merchandise, and it was in their windows and visible through their doors. The fatkins pizza stands and ice cream wagons were doing a brisk trade around the castle roundabout. The crowd was predominantly veering to the left, toward Adventureland and Frontierland and Liberty Square, while the right side of the plaza, which held the gateways to Fantasyland and Tomorrowland, was conspicuously sparse. He'd known that his numbers were down, but standing in the crowd's flow, he could feel it.

He cleared the castle and stood for a moment at the brink of Fantasyland. It should be impossible to stand here at one in the afternoon—there should be busy rushes of people pushing past to get on the rides and to eat and to buy stuff, but now there were just a few kids in eyeliner puffing cloves in smokeless hookahs and a wasteland of hoardings painted a shade Imagineering called "go-away green" for its ability to make the eye slide right past it.

He'd left the two big coasters open, and they had decent queues, but that was it. No one was in the stores, and no one was bothering with the zombie maze. Clouds of dust and loud destruction noises rose over the hoardings, and he slipped into a staff door and threaded his way onto one of the sites, pausing to pick up a safety helmet with mouse ears.

At least these crews were efficient. He'd long ago impressed on the department that hired construction contractors the necessity of decommissioning old rides with extreme care so as to preserve as much of the collectible value of the finishings and trim as possible. It was a little weird—Disney customers howled like stuck pigs when you shut down their rides, then fought for the chance to spend fortunes buying up the dismembered corpses of their favored amusements.

He watched some Cuban kids carefully melting the hot glue that had held the skull trim elements to the pillar of the Día de los Muertos facade, setting them atop a large pile of other trim—scythes, hooded figures, tombstones—with a layer of aerogel beneath to keep the garniture from scratching. The whole area behind the hoardings was like this—rides in pieces, towers of fiberglass detritus sandwiched between layers of aerogel.

They'd done this before, when he'd taken Fantasyland down, and he'd fretted every moment about how long the teardown was taking. There were exciting new plans lurking in the wings then, waiting to leap onstage and take shape. He'd had some of the ride components fabricated by a contractor in Kissimmee, but large chunks of the construction had to take place onsite. The advantage had been his: cheap fabricators, new materials, easy collaboration between remote contractors and his people on-site. No one had ever executed new rides as fast and as well as he had. The things had basically built themselves.

Now the competition was using the same tech, and it was a fucking disaster for him. Worse and worse: he had no plans for what was to come afterward. He'd thought that he'd just grab some of the audience research people, throw together a fatkins focus group or two, and give Imagineering two weeks to come up with some designs they could put up fast. He knew from past experience that design expanded to fill the time available to it, and that the best stuff usually emerged in the first ten days anyway, and after that it was all committee groupthink.

But no one from audience research wanted to return his calls, no one from Imagineering was willing to work for him, and no one wanted to visit a section of the park that was dominated by construction hoardings and demolition dust.

What the hell was happening at the Miami ride, anyway? He could follow it online, run the 3-D flythroughs of the ride as it stood, even download and print his own versions of the ride objects, but none of that told him what it *felt like* to get on the ride, to be in its clanking bowels, surrounded by other riders, pointing and marveling and laughing at the scenes and motion.

Rides were things that you had to ride to understand. Describing a ride was like talking about a movie—so abstract and remote. Like talking about sex versus having sex.

Sammy loved rides. Or he used to, anyway. So much more than films, so much more than books—so immersive and human, and the whole crowd thing, all the other people waiting to ride it or just getting off it. It had started with coasters—doesn't every kid love coasters?—but he'd ended up a connoisseur, a gourmand who loved every species of ride, from thrill rides to monorails, carousels to dark rides.

There'd been a time when he'd ridden every ride in the park once a week, and every ride in every nearby park once a month. That had been years before. Now he sat in an office and made important decisions and he was lucky if he made it onto a ride once a week.

Not that it mattered anymore. He'd screwed up so bad that it was only a matter of time until he ended up on the breadline. Or in jail.

He realized he was staring glumly at the demolition, and pulled himself upright, sucked in a few breaths, mentally kicked himself in the ass, and told himself to stop feeling sorry for himself.

A young woman pried loose another resin skull finial and added it to the pile, placed another sheet of aerogel on top of it.

People loved these little tchotchkes. They had a relationship with Disney Parks that made them want to come again and again, to own a piece of the place. They came for visits and then they visited in their hearts and they came back to bring their hearts home. It was an extremely profitable dynamic.

That's what those ride people up in the Wal-Mart were making their hay on—anyone could replicate the ride in their backyard. You didn't have to fly from Madison to Miami to have a little refresher experience. It was right there, at the end of the road.

If only there was some way to put his rides, his park, right there in the riders' homes, in their literal backyards. Being able to look at the webcams and take a 3-D fly-through was one thing, but it wasn't the physical, visceral experience of being there.

The maintenance crew had finished all the trim and now they were going after the props and animatronics. They never used to sell these off, because manufacturing the guts of a robot was too finicky to do any more than you had to—it was far better to repurpose them, like the America Sings geese that had all their skin removed and found a new home as smart-talking robots in the preshow for the old Star Tours.

But now it all could be printed to order, fabbed, and shipped in. They weren't even doing their own machining at Imagineering anymore—that was all mail-order fulfillment. Just email a 3-D drawing to a shop and you'd have as many as you wanted the next day, FedEx guaranteed. Sammy's lips drew back from his teeth as he considered the possibility that the Wal-Mart ride people had ordered their parts from the same suppliers. Christ on a bike, what a mess.

And there, in the pit of despair, at the bottom of his downward arc, Sammy was hit by a bolt of inspiration:

Put Disney into people's living rooms! Put printers into their homes that decorated a corner of their rooms with a replica of a different ride every day. You could put it on a coffee table, or scale it up to fill your basement rumpus room. You could have a magic room that was a piece of the park, a souvenir that never let go of Disney, there in your home. The people who were willing to spend a fortune on printed skull finials would cream for this! It would be like actually living there, in the park. It would be Imagineering Eye for the Fan Guy.

He could think of a hundred ways to turn this into money. Give away the printers and sell subscriptions to the refresh. Sell the printers and give away the refreshes. Charge sponsors to modify the plans and target different product placements to different users. The possibilities were endless. Best of all, it would extend the reach of Disney Parks further than the stupid ride could ever go—it would be there, on the coffee table, in the rumpus room, in your school gym or at your summer place.

He loved it. Loved it! He actually laughed aloud. What a *great* idea! Sure he was in trouble—big trouble. But if he could get this thing going—and it would go, *fast*—then Hackelberg would get his back. The lawyer didn't give a shit if Sammy lived or died, but he would do anything to protect the company's interests.

Sure, no one from Imagineering had been willing to help him design new rides. They had all the new ride design projects they could use. Audience research, too. But this was new, *new new,* not old new, and new was always appealing to a certain kind of novelty junkie in engineering. He'd find help for this, and then he'd pull together a business plan, and a time line, and a critical path, and he'd start executing. He wanted a prototype out the door in a week. Christ, it couldn't be that hard—those Wal-Mart ride assholes had published the full schematics for their toys already. He could just rip them off. Turn-about is fair play, after all.

Hilda left Perry after a couple hours working the ticket booth together. She wanted to go for a shower and a bit of an explore, and it was a secret re-lief to both of them to get some time apart after all that time living in each other's pockets. They were intimate strangers still, not yet attuned to each other's moods and needs for privacy, and a little separation was welcome.

Welcome, too, was Perry's old post there at the ticket counter, like Lucy's lemonade stand in *Peanuts*. The riders came on thick; a surprising number of them knew his name and wanted to know how his arm was. They were all watching the drama unfold online. They knew about the Brazilian rides com-ing online and the patch Lester had run. They all felt a proprietary interest in this thing. It made him feel good, but a little weird. He could deal with having friends, and customers, but fans?

When he got off work, he wandered over to the shantytown with a bunch of the vendors, to have a customary after-work beer and plate of ribs. He was about to get his phone out and find Hilda when he spotted her, gnawing on a greasy bone with Suzanne and Eva.

"Well, *hello!*" he said, delighted, skipping around the barbecue pit to col-lect a greasy kiss from Hilda, and more chaste but equally greasy pecks on the cheek from Suzanne and Eva. "Looks like you've found the best place in town!"

"We thought we'd show her around," Suzanne said. She and Eva had po-sitioned each other on either side of Hilda, using her as a buffer, but it was great to see that they were on something like speaking terms. Perry had no doubt that Suzanne hadn't led Kettlewell on (they all had crushes on her, he knew it), but that didn't mean that Eva wouldn't resent her anyway. If their positions were reversed, he would have had a hard time controlling his jeal-ousy.

"They've been wonderful," Hilda said, offering him a rib. He introduced her to the market-stall sellers who'd come over with him and there was more greasy handshaking and hugging, and the proprietor of the joint started handing around more ribs, more beers, and someone brought out a set of speakers and suction-cupped their induction-surfaces to a nearby wall, and Perry dropped one of his earbuds into them and set it to shuffle and they had music.

Kids ran past them in shrieking hordes, playing some kind of big game that they'd all been obsessed with. Perry saw that Ada and Lyenitchka were with them, clutching brightly colored mobiles and trying to read their screens while running away from another gang of kids who were clearly "it," taking exaggerated care not to run into invisible obstacles indicated on the screens.

"It was great to get back into the saddle," Perry said, digging into some ribs, getting sauce on his fingers. "I had no idea how much I'd been missing it."

Hilda nodded. "I could tell, anyway. You're a junkie for it. You're like the ones who show up all googly-eyed about the 'story' that's supposedly in there. You act like that's a holy box."

Suzanne nodded solemnly. "She's right. The two of you, you and Lester, you're so into that thing; you're the biggest fanboys in the world. You know what they call it, the fans, when they get together to chat about the stuff they love? Drooling. As in, 'Did you see the drool I posted this morning about the new girl's bedroom scene?' You drool like no one's business when you talk about that thing. It's a holy thing for you."

"You guys sound like you've been comparing notes," Perry said, making his funny eyebrow dance.

Eva arched one of her fine, high eyebrows in response. In some ways, she was the most beautiful of all of them, the most self-assured and poised. "Of course we were, sonny. Your young lady here needed to know that you aren't an ax murderer." The women's camaraderie was almost palpable. Suzanne and Eva had clearly patched up whatever differences they'd had, which was probably bad news for Kettlewell.

"Where is Lester, anyway?" He hadn't planned on asking, but Suzanne's mention of his name led him to believe he could probably get away with it.

"He's talking to Brazil," Suzanne said. "It's all he's done, all day long."

Talking to Brazil. Wow. Perry'd thought of Brazil as a kind of abstract thing, fifty rogue nodes on the network that had necessitated a hurried software patch. Not as a bunch of people. But of course, there they were, in Brazil, real people by the dozens, maybe even hundreds, building rides.

"He doesn't speak Spanish, though," Perry said.

"Neither do they, dork," Hilda said, giving him an elbow in the ribs. "Portuguese."

"They all speak some English and he's using automated translation stuff for the hard concepts."

"Does that work? I mean, any time I've tried to translate a webpage in Japanese or Hebrew, it's kind of read like noun noun noun noun verb noun random."

Suzanne shook her head. "That's how most of the world experiences most of the Net, Perry. Anglos are just about the only people on earth who don't read the Net in languages other than their own."

"Well, good for Lester then," he said.

Suzanne made a sour face that let him know that whatever peace prevailed between her and Lester, it was fragile. "Good for him," she said.

"Where are the boys?"

"Landon and Tjan have them," Eva said. "They've been holed up with your lawyers, going over strategy with them. When I walked out, they were trying to get the firm's partners to take shares in the corporation that owns the settlement in lieu of cash up front."

"Man, that's all too weird for me," Perry said. "I wish we could just run this thing like a business: make stuff people want to give us money for, collect the money, and spend it."

"You are such a nerd fatalist," Suzanne said. "Getting involved in the more abstract elements of commerce doesn't make you into a suit. If you don't participate and take an interest, you'll always be outcompeted by those who do."

"Bull," Perry said. "They can get a court to order us to make pi equal to three, or to ensure that other people don't make Mickey heads in their rides, or that our riders don't think of Disney when they get into one of our chairs, but they'll never be able to enforce it."

Suzanne suddenly whirled on him. "Perry Gibbons, you aren't that stupid, so stop acting like you are." She touched his cast. "Look at this thing on your arm. Your superior technology can *not* make inferior laws irrelevant. You're assuming that the machinery of state is unwilling to completely shut you down in order to make you comply with some minor law. You're totally wrong. They'll come after you and break your head."

Perry rocked back on his heels. He was suddenly furious, even if somewhere in his heart of hearts he knew that she was right and he was mostly angry at being shown up in front of Hilda. "I've been hearing that all my life, Suzanne. I don't buy it. Look, it just keeps getting cheaper and easier to make something like what we've built. To get a printer, to get goop, to make stuff, to download stuff, to message and IM with people who'll help you make stuff. To learn how to make it. Look, the world is getting better because we're getting better at routing around the bullies. We can play their game, or we can invent a new game.

"I refuse to be sucked into playing their game. If we play their game, we end up just like them."

Suzanne shook her head sadly. "It's a good thing you've got Tjan and Kettlewell around then, to do the dirty work. I just hope you can spare them a little pity from atop your moral high ground."

She took Eva by the arm and led her away, leaving Perry, shaking, with Hilda.

"Bitch," he said, kicking the ground. He balled his hands into fists and then quickly relaxed them as his broken arm ground and twinged from the sudden tensing.

Hilda took him by the arm. "You two clearly have a *lot* of history."

He took a couple deep breaths. "She was so out of line there. What the hell, anyway? Why should I have to—" He stopped. He could tell when he was repeating himself.

"I don't think that she would be telling you that stuff if she didn't think you needed to hear it."

"You sound like you're on her side. I thought you were a fiery young revolutionary. You think we should all put on suits and incorporate?"

"I think that if you've got skilled people willing to help you, you owe it to them to value their contribution. I've heard you complain about 'suits' twenty times in the past week. Two of those suits are on your side. They're putting themselves on the line, just like you. Hell, they're doing the shit work while you get to do all the inventing and fly around the country and get laid by hot groupies."

She kissed his cheek, trying to make a joke of it, but she'd really hurt his feelings. He felt like weeping. It was all out of his control. His destiny was not his to master.

"OK, let's go apologize to Kettlewell and Tjan."

She laughed, but he'd only been halfway kidding. What he really wanted to do was have a big old dinner at home with Lester, just the two of them in front of the TV, eating Lester's fatkins cuisine, planning a new invention. He was tired of all these people. Even Suzanne was an outsider. It had just been him and Lester in the old days, and those had been the best days.

Hilda put her arm around his shoulders and nuzzled his neck. "Poor Perry," she said. "Everyone picks on him."

He smiled in spite of himself.

"Come on, sulkypants, let's go find Lester and he can call me 'Yoko' some more. That always cheers you up."

It was two weeks before Death Waits could sit up and prod at a key-board with his broken hands. Some of his pals brought a laptop around and they commandeered a spare dining tray to keep it on—Death's lap was in no shape to support anything heavy with sharp corners.

The first day, he was reduced to tears of frustration within minutes of starting. He couldn't use the shift key, couldn't really use the mouse—and the meds made it hard to concentrate and remember what he'd done.

But there were people on the other end of that computer, human friends whom he could communicate with if only he could relearn to use this tool that he'd lived with since he was old enough to sit up on his own.

So laboriously, peck by peck, key by key, he learned to use it again. The machine had a mode for disabled people, for *cripples,* and once he hit on this, it went faster. The mode tried to learn from him, learn his tremors and mis-keys, his errors and cursing, and so emerge something that was uniquely his interface. It was a kind of a game to watch the computer try to guess what was meant by his mashed keystrokes and spastic pointer movements—he turned on the webcam, aimed it at his eye, and switched it to retinal scanner mode, giving it control of the pointer, then watched in amusement as the wild leaping of the cursor every time a needle or a broken bone shifted inside his body was becalmed into a graceful, normalized curve.

It was humiliating to be a high-tech cripple, and the better the technology worked, the more prone it was to reducing him to tears. He might be like this for the rest of his life. He might never walk without a limp again. Might never dance. Might never be able to reach for and lift objects again. He'd never find a woman, never have a family, never have grandkids.

But this was offset by the real people with their real chatter. He obses-sively flew through the Brazilian mode, strange and wonderful but nowhere near what he loved from "his" variation on the ride. He could roll through all the different changes he'd made with his friends to the ride in Florida, and he became subtly attuned to which elements were wrong and which were right.

It was on one of these flythroughs that he encountered The Story, leaping out of the ride so vividly that he yelped like he'd flexed his IV into a nerve again.

There it was—irrefutable and indefinable. When you rode through there was an escalating tension, a sense of people who belonged to these exhibits going through hard changes, growing up and out.

Once he'd seen it, he couldn't un-see it. When he and his pals had started to add their own stuff to the ride, the story people had been giant pains in the ass, accusing them of something they called "narricide"—destroying the frag-ile story that humanity had laid bare there.

Now that he'd seen it, too, he wanted to protect it. But he could see by skimming forward and back through the change log and trying different fly-throughs that the story wasn't being undermined by the goth stuff they were bringing in; it was being enhanced. It was telling the story he knew, of grow-ing up with an indefinable need to be *different,* to reject the mainstream and to embrace this subculture and aesthetic.

It was the story of his tribe and subspecies and it got realer the more he played it. God, how could he have *missed it*? It made him want to cry, though that might have been the meds. Some of it made him want to laugh, too.

He tried, laboriously, to compose a message-board post that expressed what he was feeling, but every attempt came out sounding like those story mystics he'd battled. He understood now why they'd sounded so hippy-trippy.

So he rode the ride, virtually, again and again, spotting the grace notes and the sly wit and the wrenching emotion that the collective intelligence of all those riders had created. Discovered? It was like the story was there all along, lurking like the statue inside a block of marble.

Oh, it was wonderful. He was ruined, maybe forever, but it was wonderful. And he'd been a part of it.

He went back to writing that message-board post. He'd be laid up in that bed for a long time yet. He had time to rewrite.

If You Can't Beat Them, Rip Them Off

A new initiative from the troubled Disney Parks corporation shows how a little imagination can catapult an ambitious exec to the top of the corporate ladder.

Word has it that Samuel R. D. Page, the Vice President for Fantasyland (I assure you, I am NOT making that up), has been kicked upstairs to Senior Vice President for Remote Delivery of Park Experience (I'm not making that up, either). Insiders in the company tell us that "Remote Delivery of Park Experience" is a plan to convince us to give The Mouse a piece of our homes, which will be constantly refreshed via a robot three-dimensional printer with miniatures of the Disney park.

If this sounds familiar, it should. It's a pale imitation of the no-less-ridiculous (if slightly less evil) "rides" movement pioneered by Perry Gibbons and Lester Banks, previously the antiheroes of the New Work pump-and-dump scandal.

Imitation is meant to be the sincerest form of flattery, and if so, Gibbons and his cultists must be blushing fire-engine red.

This is cheap irony, Disney-style. After all, it's only been a month since the company launched ten separate lawsuits against various incarnations of the ride for trademark violation, and it's now trying to duck the punishing countersuits that have risen up in their wake.

Most ironic of all, word has it that Page was responsible for both ends of this: the lawsuits against the ride and the decision to turn his company into purveyors of cheap knockoffs of the ride.

Page is best known among Park aficionados for having had the "foresight" to gut the children's "Fantasyland" district in Walt Disney World and replace it with a jumped-up version of Hot Topic, a goth-themed area that drew down the nation's eyeliner supply to dangerously low levels.

It was apparently that sort of "way-out-of-the-box" "genius" that led Page to his latest round of disasters: the lawsuits, an abortive rebuilding of Fantasyland, and now this "Remote Delivery" scam.

What's next? The Mouse has already shipped Disney Dollars, an abortive home-wares line, a disastrous fine-art chain, and overseen the collapse of the collectible cel-art market. With "visionaries" like Page at the helm, the company can't help but notch up more "successes."

Death was deep into the story now. The Brazilians had forked off their own ride—they'd had their own New Work culture, too, centered in the favelas, so they had different stories to tell. Some of the ride operators imported a few of their scenes, tentatively, and some of the ride fans were recreating the Brazil scenes on their own passes through the ride.

It was all in there, if you knew where to look for it, and the best part was, no one had written it. It had written itself. The collective judgement of people who rode through had turned chaos into coherence.

Or had it? The message boards were rife with speculation that The Story had been planted by someone—maybe the ride's creators, maybe some clan of riders—who'd inserted it deliberately. These discussions bordered on the metaphysical: what was an "organic" ride decision? It made Death Waits's head swim.

The thing that was really doing his head in, though, was the Disney stuff. Sammy—he couldn't even think of Sammy without a sick feeling in his stomach, crashing waves of nausea that transcended even his narcotic haze— Sammy was making these grotesque parodies of the ride. He was pushing them out to the world's living rooms. Even the deleted rides from the glory days of the goth Fantasyland, in time-limited miniature. If he'd still been at Disney Parks, he would have loved this idea. It was just what he loved, the knowledge that he was sharing experience with his people around the world, part of a tribe, even if he couldn't see them.

Now, in the era of the ride, he could see how dumb this was. How thin and shallow and commercial. Why should they have to pay some giant evil corporation to convene their community?

He kept trying to write about The Story, kept failing. It wouldn't come. But Sammy—he knew what he wanted to say about Sammy. He typed until they sedated him, and then typed some more when he woke up. He had old emails to refer to. He pasted them in.

After three days of doing this, the lawyer came back. Tom Levine was dressed in a stern suit with narrow lapels and a tie pierced with some kind of frat pin. He wasn't much older than Death, but he made Death feel like a little kid.

"I need to talk to you about your Internet activity," he said, sitting down beside him. He'd brought along a saltwater taffy assortment bought from the roadside, cut into double-helix molecules and other odd biological forms—an amoeba, a skeleton.

"OK?" Death said. They'd switched him to something new for the pain that day, and given him a rocker switch he could use to drizzle it into his IV when it got bad. He'd hit it just before the lawyer came to see him and now he couldn't concentrate much. Plus he wasn't used to talking. Writing online was better. He could write something, save it, go back and reread it later and clean it up if it turned out he'd gone off on a stoned ramble.

"You know we're engaged in some very high-stakes litigation here, right, Darren?"

He hated it when people called him Darren.

"Death," he said. His toothless lisp was pathetic, like an old wino's.

"Death, OK. This high-stakes litigation needs a maximum of caution and control. This is a fifteen-year journey that ends when we've broken the back of the company that did this to you. It ends when we take them for every cent, bankrupt their executives, take their summer homes, freeze their accounts. You understand that?"

Death hadn't really understood that. It sounded pretty tiring. Exhausting. Fifteen years. He was only nineteen now. He'd be thirty-four, and that was only if the lawyer was estimating correctly.

"Oh," he said.

"Well, not that you're going to have to take part in fifteen years' worth of this. It's likely we'll be done with your part in a year, tops. But the point is that when you go online and post material that's potentially harmful to this case—"

Death closed his eyes. He'd posted the wrong thing. This had been a major deal when he was at Disney, what he was and wasn't allowed to post about—though in practice, he'd posted about everything, sticking the private stuff in private discussions.

"Look, you can't write about the case, or anything involved with it; that's what it comes down to. If you write about that stuff and you say the wrong thing, you could blow this whole suit. They'd get away clean."

Death shook his head. Not write about it at *all*?

"No," he said. "No."

"I'm not asking you, Death. I can get a court order if I have to. This is serious—it's not some funny little game. There are billions on the line here. One wrong word, one wrong post and *pfft*, it's all over. And nothing in email, either—it's likely everything you write is going to go through discovery. Don't write anything personal in any of your mail—nothing you wouldn't want in a court record."

"I can't do that," Death said. He sounded like a fucking retard, between talking through his mashed mouth and talking through the tears. "I can't. I live in email."

"Well, now you'll have a reason to go outside. This isn't up for negotiation. When I was here last, I thought I made the seriousness of this case clear to you. I'm frankly amazed that you were immature and irresponsible enough to write what I've read."

"I can't—" Death said.

The lawyer purpled. He didn't look like a happy-go-lucky tanned preppie anymore. He looked Dad-scary, like one of those fathers in Disney who was about to seriously lose his shit and haul off and smack a whiny kid. Death's own Pawpaw, who'd stood in for his father, had gone red like that whenever he "mouthed off," a sin that could be committed even without opening his mouth. He had an instinctive curl-up-and-hide reaction to it, and the lawyer seemed to sense this, looming over him. He felt like he was about to be eaten.

"You listen to me, *Darren*—this is not the kind of thing you fuck up. This isn't something *I'm* going to fuck up. I win my cases and you're not going to change that. There's too much at stake here for you to blow it all with your childish, selfish—"

He seemed to catch himself then, and he snorted a hot breath through his nose that blew over Death's face. "Listen, there's a lot on the line here. More money than you or I are worth. I'm trying to help you out here. Whatever you write, whatever you say, it's going to be very closely scrutinized. From now on, you should treat every piece of information that emanates from your fingertips as likely to be covered on the evening news and repeated to everyone you've ever met. No matter how private you think you're being, it'll come out. It's not pretty, and I know you didn't ask for it, but you're here, and there's nothing you can do to change that."

He left then, embarrassed at losing his temper, embarrassed at Death's meek silence. Death poked at his laptop some. He thought about writing down more notes, but that was probably in the same category.

He closed his eyes and now, *now* he felt the extent of his injuries, felt them truly for the first time since he'd woken up in this hospital. There were deep, grinding pains in his legs—both knees broken, a fracture in the left thigh. His ribs hurt every time he breathed. His face was a ruin; his mouth felt like he had twisted lumps of hamburger glued to his torn lips. His dick—well, they'd catheterized him, but that didn't account for the feelings down there. He'd been kicked repeatedly and viciously, and they told him that the reconstructive surgeries—surgeries, plural—would take some time, and nothing was certain until they were done.

He'd managed to pretend that his body wasn't there for so long as he was able to poke at the computer. Now it came back to him. He had the painkiller rocker switch and the pain wasn't any worse than what passed for normal, but he had an idea that if he hit it enough times, he'd be able to get away from his body for a while again.

He tried it.

Hilda and Lester sat uncomfortably on the sofa next to each other. Perry had hoped they'd hit it off, but it was clear after Lester tried his Yoko joke again that the chemistry wasn't there. Now they were having a rare moment of all-look-same-screen, the TV switched on like in an old comedy, no one looking at their own laptop.

The tension was thick, and Perry was sick of it.

He reached for his computer and asked it to find him the baseball gloves. Two of the drawers on the living room walls glowed pink. He fetched the gloves down, tossed one to Lester, and picked up his ball.

"Come on," he said. "TV is historically accurate, but it's not very social."

Lester got up from the sofa, a slow smile spreading on his face, and Hilda followed a minute later. Outside, by the cracked pool, it was coming on slow twilight and that magic, tropical blood-orange sky like a swirl of sorbet.

Lester and Perry each put on their gloves. Perry'd worn his now and again, but had never had a real game of catch with it. Lester lobbed an easy toss to him and when it smacked his glove, it felt so *right,* the sound and the vibration and the fine cloud of dust that rose up from the mitt's pocket, Christ, it was like a sacrament.

He couldn't lob the ball back, because of his busted wing, so he handed the ball to Hilda. "You're my designated right arm," he said. She smiled and chucked the ball back to Lester.

They played until the twilight deepened to velvety warm dark and humming bugs and starlight. Each time he caught a ball, something left Perry, some pain long held in his chest evanesced into the night air. His catching arm, stiff from being twisted by the weight of the cast on his other arm, unlimbered and became fluid. His mind was becalmed.

None of them talked, though they sometimes laughed when a ball went wild, and both Perry and Hilda went "ooh," when Lester made a jump-catch that nearly tumbled him into the dry pool.

Perry hadn't played a game of catch since he was a kid. Catch wasn't his dad's strong suit, and he and his friends had liked video games better than tossing a ball, which was pretty dull by comparison.

But that night it was magic, and when it got to full dark and they could barely see the ball except as a second moon hurtling white through the air, they kept tossing it a few more times before Perry dropped it into the pocket of his baggy shorts. "Let's get a drink," he said.

Lester came over and gave him a big, bearish hug. Then Hilda joined them. "You stink," Lester said. "Seriously, dude. Like the ass of a dead bear."

That broke them up and set them to laughing together, a giggling fit that left them gasping, Lester on all fours. Perry's arm forgot to hurt and he moved to kiss Hilda on the cheek and instead she turned her head to kiss him full on the lips, a real juicy, steamy one that made his earwax melt.

"Drinks," Hilda said, breaking the kiss.

They went upstairs, holding the mitts, and had a beer together on the patio, talking softly about nothing in particular, and then Lester hugged them good night and then they all went to bed, and Perry put his face into the hair at the back of Hilda's neck and told her he loved her, and Hilda snuggled up to him and they fell asleep.

A Game of Catch

Pop quiz: Your empire is crumbling around your ears. Your supporters are hospitalized by jackboot thugs for sticking up for you.

The lawsuits are mounting and fly-by-night MBAs have determined to use your nonprofit, info-hippie ride project to get right by embarking on twenty years of litigation.

What do you do?

Well, if you're like Perry Gibbons, Lester Banks, and Hilda Hammersen, you go out into the backyard and throw a ball around for a while; then you have a big cuddle and head inside.

The pictures shown here were captured by a neighbor of the cult leaders last night, at their palatial condos in Hollywood, Florida.

The three are ringleaders of the loose-knit organization that manages the "rides" that dot ten cities in America and are present in fifty cities in Brazil. Their project came to national attention when Disney brought suit against them, securing injunctions against the rides that resulted in riots and bloodshed.

One supporter of the group, the outspoken "Death Waits," a former Disney employee, has been hospitalized for over a week following a savage beating that he claims resulted from his Internet posting about the unhealthy obsession Disney executive Samuel R. D. Page (see previous coverage) bore for the ride.

Everyone needs to unwind now and then, but sources at the hospital where Death Waits lies abed say that he has had no visits from the cult leaders since he took his beating in their service.

No doubt these three have more important things to do—like play catch.

Suzanne said, "Look, you can't let crazy people set your agenda. If you want to visit this Death kid, you should. If you don't, you shouldn't. But don't let Freddy psyops you into doing something you don't want to do. Maybe he does have a rat in your building. Maybe he's got a rat at the hospital. Maybe, though, he just scored some stills off a flickr stream, maybe he's watching new photos with some face-recognition stuff."

Perry looked up from his screen, still scowling. "People do that?"

"Sure—stalkerware! I use it myself, just to see what photos of me are showing up online. I scour every photo feed published for anything that appears to be a photo of me. Most of it's from blogjects, CCTV cameras, and crap like that. You should see what it's like on days I go to London—you can get photographed eight hundred times a day there without trying. So yeah, if I was Freddy and I wanted to screw with you, I'd be watching every image feed for your pic, and mine, and Lester's. We just need to assume that that's going on. But look at what he actually reported on: you went out and played catch and then hugged after your game. It's not like he caught you cornholing gators while smoking spliffs rolled in C-notes."

"What does that guy have against us, anyway?"

Suzanne sighed. "Well, at first I think it was that *I* liked you, and that you were trying to do something consistent with what he thought everyone should be doing. After all, if anyone were to follow his exhortations, they'd have to be dumb enough to be taking him seriously, and for that they deserve all possible disapprobation.

"These days, though, he hates you for two reasons. The first is that you failed, which means that you've got to have some kind of moral deficiency. The second is that we keep pulling his pants down in public, which makes him even angrier, since pulling down people's pants is *his* job.

"I know it's armchair psychology, but I think that Freddy just doesn't like himself very much. At the end of the day, people who are secure and happy don't act like this."

Perry's scowl deepened. "I'd like to kick him in the fucking balls," he said. "Why can't he just let us be? We've got enough frigging problems."

"I just want to go and visit this kid," Lester said, and they were back where they started.

"But we know that this Freddy guy has an informant in the hospital; he about says as much in this article. If we go there, he wins," Perry said.

Hilda and Lester just looked at him. Finally he smiled and relented. "OK, Freddy isn't going to run my life. If it's the right thing to visit this kid, it's the right thing. Let's do it."

"We'll go after the ride shuts tonight," Lester said. "All of us. I'll buy him a fruit basket and bring him a mini." The minis were Lester's latest mechanical computers, built inside of sardine cans, made of miniaturized, printed, high-impact alloys. They could add and subtract numbers up to ten, using a hand crank on the side, registering their output on a binary display of little windows that were covered and uncovered by tiny shutters. He'd built his first the day before, using designs supplied by some of his people in Brazil and tweaking them to his liking.

The day was as close to a normal day on the ride as Perry could imagine. The crowd was heavy from the moment he opened, and he had to go back into the depths and kick things back into shape a couple times, and one of the chairs shut down, and two of the merchants had a dispute that degenerated into a brawl. Just another day running a roadside attraction in Florida.

Lester spelled him for the end of the day; then they counted the take and said good night to the merchants and all piled into one of Lester's cars and headed for the hospital.

"You liking Florida?" Lester called over the seat as they inched forward in the commuter traffic on the way into Melbourne.

"It's hot; I like that," Hilda said.

"You didn't mention the awesome aesthetics," Lester said.

Suzanne rolled her eyes. "Ticky-tacky chic," she said.

"I love it here," Lester said. "That contrast between crass, overdeveloped, cheap, nasty strip malls and unspoiled tropical beauty. It's gorgeous *and* it tickles my funny bone."

Hilda squinted out the window as though she were trying to see what Lester saw, like someone staring at a random-dot stereogram in a mall store, trying to make the 3-D image pop out.

"If you say so," she said. "I don't find much attractive about human settlement, though. If it needs to be there, it should just be invisible as possible. We fundamentally live in ugly boxes, and efforts to make them pretty never do anything for me except call attention to how ugly they are. I kinda wish that

everything was built to disappear as much as possible so we could concentrate on the loveliness of the world."

"You get that in Madison?" Lester said.

"Nope," she said. "I've never seen any place designed the way I'd design
one. Maybe I'll do that someday."

Perry loved her just then, for that. The casual "oh, yeah, the world isn't
arranged to my satisfaction, maybe I'll rearrange it someday."

The duty nurse was a bored Eastern European who gave them a half-
hearted hard time about having too many people visit Death Waits all at once,
but who melted when Suzanne gave her a little talk in Russian.

"What was that all about?" Perry whispered to her as they made their way
along the sour-smelling ward.

"Told her we would keep it down—and complimented her on her mani-
cure."

Lester shook his head. "I haven't been in a place like this in so long. The
fatkins places are nothing like it."

Hilda snorted. "More upscale, I take it?" Lester and Hilda hadn't really
talked about the fatkins thing, but Perry suddenly remembered the vehemence with which Hilda had denounced the kids who were talked into
fatkins treatments in their teens and wondered if she and Lester should be
clearing the air.

"Not really—but more functional. More about, I don't know, pursuing
your hobby. Less about showing up in an emergency."

Hilda snorted again and they were at Death's room. They walked past his
roommates, an old lady with her teeth out, sleeping with her jaw sagging
down, and a man in a body cast hammering on a video-game controller and
staring fixedly at the screen at the foot of his bed.

Then they came upon Death Waits. Perry had only seen him briefly, and
in bad shape even then, but now he was a wreck, something from a horror
movie or an atrocity photo. Perry swallowed hard as he took in the boy's
wracked, skinny body, the casts, the sunken eyes, the shaved head, the caved-
in face and torn ears.

He was fixedly watching TV, which seemed to be showing a golf show.
His thumb was poised over a rocker switch connected to the IV in his arm.

Death looked at them with dull eyes at first, not recognizing them for a
moment. Then he did, and his eyes welled up with tears. They streamed
down his face and his chin and lips quivered, and then he opened his mouth
and started to bawl like a baby.

Perry was paralyzed—transfixed by this crying wreck. Lester, too, and
Suzanne. They all took a minute step backward, but Hilda pushed past them

and took his hand and stroked his hair and went *"shhh, shhh."* His bawling become more uncontrolled, louder, and his two roommates complained, calling to him to shut up, and Suzanne moved back and drew the curtains around each of their beds. Strangely, this silenced them.

Gradually, Death's cries became softer, and then he snuffled and snorted and Hilda gave him a kleenex from her purse. He wiped his face and blew his nose and squeezed the kleenex tight in his hand. He opened his mouth, shut it, opened and shut it.

Then, in a whisper, he told them his story. The man in the parking lot and his erection. The hospital. Posting on the message boards.

The lawyer.

"What?" Perry said, loud enough that they all jumped and Death Waits flinched pathetically in his hospital bed. Hilda squeezed his arm hard. "Sorry, sorry," Perry muttered. "But this lawyer, what did he say to you?"

Perry listened for a time. Death Waits spoke in a low monotone, pausing frequently to draw in shuddering breaths that were almost sobs.

"Fucking *bastards,*" Perry said. "Evil, corporate, immoral, sleazy—"

Hilda squeezed his arm again. "Shh," she said. "Take it easy. You're upsetting him."

Perry was so angry he could barely see, barely think. He was trembling, and they were all staring at him, but he couldn't stop. Death had shrunk back into himself, squeezed his eyes shut.

"I'll be back in a minute," Perry said. He felt like he was suffocating. He walked out of the room so fast it was practically a jog, then pounded on the elevator buttons, waited ten seconds and gave up and ran down ten flights of stairs. He got outside into the coolness of the hazy night and sucked in huge lungsful of wet air, his heart hammering in his chest.

He had his phone in his hand and he had scrolled to Kettlewell's number, but he kept himself from dialing it. He was in no shape to discuss this with Kettlewell. He wanted witnesses there when he did it, to keep him from doing something stupid.

He went back inside. The security guards watched him closely, but he forced himself to smile and act calm and they didn't stop him from boarding the elevator.

"I'm sorry," he said to all of them. "I'm sorry," he said to Death Waits. "Let me make something very, very clear: you are free to use the Internet as much as you want. You are free to tell your story to anyone you want to tell it to. Even if it screws up my case, you're free to do that. You've given up enough for me already."

Death looked at him with watery eyes. "Really?" he said. It came out in a hoarse whisper.

Perry moved the breakfast tray that covered Death's laptop, then opened the laptop and positioned it where Death could reach it. "It's all yours, buddy. Whatever you want to say, say it. Let your freak flag fly."

Death cried again then, silent tears slipping down his hollow cheeks. Perry got him some kleenex from the bathroom and he blew his nose and wiped his face and grinned at them all, a toothless, wet, ruined smile that made Perry's heart lurch. Jesus, Jesus, Jesus. What the hell was he doing? This kid—he would never get the life he'd had back.

"Thank you, thank you, thank you," Death said.

"Please don't be grateful to me," Perry said. "We owe you the thanks around here. Remember that. We haven't done you any favors. All the favors around here have come from you."

"Any lawyer shows up here again representing me, I want you to email me."

In the car back, no one said anything until they were within sight of the shantytown. "Kettlewell isn't going to like this," Suzanne said.

"Yeah, I expect not," Perry said. "He can go fuck himself."

Imagineering sent the prototype up to Sammy as soon as it was ready, the actual engineers who'd been working on it shlepping it into his office.

He'd been careful to cultivate their friendship through the weeks of production, taking them out for beers and delicately letting them know that they were just the sort of people who really understood what Disney Parks was about, not like those philistines who comprised the rest of the management layer at Disney. He learned their kids' names and forwarded jokes to them by email. He dropped by their break room and let them beat him at pinball on their gigantic, bizarre, multiboard homebrew machine, letting them know just how cool said machine was.

Now it was paying off. Judging from the device he was looking at, a bread-box-sized, go-away-green, round-shouldered, smooth box that it took two of them to carry in.

"Watch this," one of them said. He knocked a complicated pattern on the box's top and a hidden hatch opened out of the side, yawning out and forming a miniature staircase from halfway down the box's surface to the ground. There was soft music playing inside the box, a jazzy, uptempo, futuristic version of "When You Wish upon a Star."

A little man appeared in the doorway. He looked like he was made of pipe cleaners, and he took the stairs in three wobbling strides. He ignored them as he lurched around the box's perimeter until he came to a far corner; then another hatch slid away and the little man reached inside and tugged out the plug and the end of the power cord. He hugged the plug to his chest and began to wander around Sammy's desk, clearly looking for an electrical outlet.

"It's a random-walk search algorithm," one of the Imagineers said. "Watch this." After a couple of circuits of Sammy's desk the little robot went to the edge and jumped, hanging on to the power cable, which unspooled slowly from the box like a belay line, gently lowering the man to the ground. A few minutes later, he had found the electrical outlet and plugged in the box.

The music inside stilled and a fanfare began. The trumpeting reached a joyous peak—"It's found a network connection"—and then subsided into marching-band music. There was a smell like Saran Wrap in the microwave. A moment later, another pipe-cleaner man emerged from the box, lugging a chunk of plastic that looked like the base of a rocket in an old-timey science-fiction movie.

The first pipe-cleaner man was shinnying up the power cable. He crested the desktop and joined his brother in ferrying out more parts. Each one snapped into the previous one with a lego-like *click*. Taking shape on the desktop in slow stages, the original, 1955 Tomorrowland, complete with the rocket to the moon, the Clock of the World and—

"Dairy Farmers of America Present the Cow of Tomorrow?" Sammy said, peering at the little brass plaque on the matchbox-sized diorama, which showed a cow with an IV in her hock, watching a video of a pasture. "You're kidding me."

"No!" one Imagineer said. "It's all for real—the archives have all these tight, high-rez three-dee models of all the rides the park's ever seen. This is totally historically accurate."

The Kaiser Aluminum Hall of Fame. The Monsanto Hall of Chemistry. Thimble Drome Flight Circle, with tiny flying miniature airplanes.

"Holy crap," Sammy said. "People *paid* to see these things?"

"Go on," the other Imagineer said. "Take the roof off the Hall of Chemistry."

Sammy did, and was treated to a tiny, incredibly detailed 3-D model of the hall's interior exhibits, complete with tiny people in 1950s garb, marveling at the truly crappy exhibits.

"We print to twelve hundred dpi with these. We can put pupils on the eyeballs at that rez."

The pieces were still trundling out. Sammy picked up the Monsanto Hall of Chemistry and turned it over and over in his hands, looking at the minute detail, admiring the way all the pieces snapped together.

"It's kind of brittle," the first Imagineer said. He took it from Sammy and gave it a squeeze and it cracked with a noise like an office chair rolling over a sheet of bubble wrap. The pieces fell to the desk.

A pipe-cleaner man happened upon a shard after a moment and hugged it to his chest, then toddled back into the box with it.

"There's a little optical scanner in there—it'll figure out which bit this piece came from and print another one. Total construction of this model takes about two hours."

"You built this entire thing from scratch in three weeks?"

The Imagineers laughed. "No, no—no way! No, almost all the code and designs came off the Net. Most of this stuff was developed by New Work startups back in the day, or by those ride weirdos down in Hollywood. We just shoved it all into this box and added the models for some of our old rides from the archives. This was easy, man—easy!"

Sammy's head swam. Easy! This thing was undeniably supercool. He wanted one. Everyone was going to want one!

"You can print these as big as you want, too—if we gave it enough time, space, and feedstock, it'd run these buildings at full size."

The miniature Tomorrowland was nearly done. It was all brave, sad white curves, like the set of a remake of *Rollerball*, and featured tiny people in 1950s clothes, sundresses and salaryman hats, black-rimmed glasses and Scout uniforms for the boys.

Sammy goggled at it. He moved the little people around, lifted off the lids.

"Man, I'd seen the three-D models and flythroughs, but they're nothing compared to actually seeing it, owning it. People will want libraries of these things. Whole rooms devoted to them."

"Um," one of the Imagineers said. Sammy knew his name, but he'd forgotten it. He had a whole complicated scheme for remembering people's names by making up stories about them, but it was a lot of work. "Well, about that. This feedstock is very fast-setting, but it doesn't really weather well. Even if you stored it in a dark, humidity-controlled room, it'd start to delaminate and fall to pieces within a month or two. Leave it in the living room in direct sunlight and it'll crumble within a couple days."

Sammy pursed his lips and thought for a while. "Please, please tell me that there's something proprietary we can require in the feedstock that can make us into the sole supplier of consumables for this thing."

"Maybe? We could certainly tag the goop with something proprietary and hunt for it when we do the build, refuse to run on anyone else's goop. Of course, that won't be hard to defeat—"

"We'll sue anyone who tries it," Sammy said. "Oh, boys, you've outdone yourselves. Seriously. If I could give you a raise, I would. As it is, take something home from the architectural salvage lot and sell it on eBay. It's as close to a bonus as this fucking company's going to pay any of us."

They looked at him quizzically, with some alarm and he smiled and spread his hands. "Ha-ha, only serious boys. Really—take some stuff home. You've earned it. Try and grab something from the ride system itself, that's got the highest book value."

They left behind a slim folder with production notes and estimates, suppliers who would be likely to bid on a job like this. He'd need a marketing plan, too—but this was farther than he ever thought he'd get. He could show this to legal and to the board, and yes, to Wiener and the rest of the useless committee. He could get everyone lined up behind this and working on it. Hell, if he spun it right they'd all be fighting to have their pet projects instantiated with it.

He fiddled with a couple of overnight shippers' sites for a while, trying to figure out what it would cost to sell these in the Parks and have them waiting on the marks' doorsteps when they got back home. There were lots of little details like that, but ultimately, this was good and clean—it would extend the Parks' reach right into the living rooms of their customers, giving them a new reason to think of the Parks every day.

Kettlewell and Tjan looked up when Perry banged through the door of the teahouse they'd turned into their de facto headquarters.

Perry had gone through mad and back to calm on the ride home, but as he drew closer to the teahouse, passing the people in the streets, the people living their lives without lawyers or bullshit, his anger came back. He'd even stopped outside the teahouse and breathed deeply, but his heart was pounding and his hands kept balling into fists and sometimes, man, sometimes you've just got to go for it.

He got to the table and grabbed the papers there and tossed them over his shoulder.

"You're fired," he said. "Pack up and go, I want you out by morning. You're done here. You don't represent the ride and you never will. Get lost." He didn't know he was going to say it until he said it, but it felt right. This was what he was feeling—*his* project had been stolen and bad things were being done in *his* name and it was going to stop, right now.

Tjan and Kettlewell got to their feet and looked at him, faces blank with shock. Kettlewell recovered first. "Perry, let's sit down and do an exit interview, all right? That's traditional."

Perry was shaking with anger now. These two friends of his, they'd fucking screwed him—committed their dirty work in his name. But Kettlewell was holding a chair out to him and the others in the teahouse were staring and he thought about Eva and the kids and the baseball gloves, and he sat down.

He squeezed his thighs hard with his clenching hands, drew in a deep breath, and recited what Death Waits had told him in an even, wooden voice.

"So that's it. I don't know if you instructed the lawyers to do this or only just distanced yourself enough from them to let them do this on their own. The point is that the way you're running this campaign is victimizing people who believe in us, making life worse for people who already got a shitty, shitty deal on our account. I won't have it."

Kettlewell and Tjan looked at each other. They'd both stayed poker-faced through Perry's accusation, and now Kettlewell made a little go-ahead gesture at Tjan.

"There's no excuse for what that lawyer did. We didn't authorize it, we didn't know it had happened, and we wouldn't have permitted it if we had. In a suit like this, there are a lot of moving parts and there's no way to keep track of all of them all of the time. You don't know what every ride operator in the world is up to; you don't even know where all the rides in the world *are*. That's in the nature of a decentralized business.

"But here's the thing: the lawyer was at least partly right. Everything that kid blogs, emails, and says will potentially end up in the public record. Like it or not, that kid can no longer consider himself to have a private life, not until the court case is up. Neither can you or I, for that matter. That's in the nature of a lawsuit—and it's not something any of us can change at this point."

Perry heard him as from a great distance, through the whooshing of the blood in his ears. He couldn't think of anything to say to that.

Tjan and Kettlewell looked at each other.

"So even if we're 'fired,'" Tjan said at last, making sarcastic finger-quotes, "this problem won't go away. We've floated the syndicate and given control of the legal case to them. If you try to ditch it, you're going to have to contend with *their* lawsuits, too."

"I didn't—" Perry started. But he had; he'd signed all kinds of papers: first, papers that incorporated the ride-runners' co-op and, second, papers that gave legal representation over to the syndicate.

"Perry, I'm the chairman of the Boston ride collective. I'm their rep on the co-op's board. You can't fire me. You didn't hire me. They did. So stop breathing through your nose like a locomotive and calm down. None of us wanted that lawyer to go after that kid."

He knew they were making sense but he didn't want to care. He'd ended up in this place because these supposed pals of his had screwed up.

He knew that he was going to end up making up with them, going to end up getting deeper into this. He knew that this was how good people did shitty things: one tiny rotten compromise at a time. Well, he wasn't going to go there.

"Tomorrow morning," he said. "Gone. We can figure out by email how to have a smooth transition, but no more of this. Not on my head. Not on my account."

He stalked away, which is what he should have done in the first place. Fuck being reasonable. Reasonable sucked.

Death found out about the Disney-in-a-Box printers seconds after they were announced. He'd been tuning his feed watchers to give him news about the Disney Parks for nearly a decade, and this little PR item on the Disney Parks newswire rang all the cherries on his filters, flagging the item red and rocketing it to the top of his news playlist, making all the icons on the sides of his screen bounce with delight.

The announcement made him want to throw up. They were totally ripping off the rides, and he knew for a fact that most of the 3-D meshes of the old yesterland rides and even the contemporary ones were fan-made, so those'd be ripped off, too.

And the worst part was, he could feel himself getting excited. This was just the kind of thing that would have given him major fanboy drool as recently as a month ago.

He just stared angrily at his screen. Being angry made the painkillers wear off, so the madder he got the more he hurt. He could nail the rocker switch and dose himself with more of whatever the painkiller plugged into his IV was today, but since Perry and Lester and their girlfriends (had that other one been Suzanne Church? It sure looked like her) had told him he could use his laptop again, he'd stayed off the juice as much as possible. The computer could make him forget he hurt.

He looked at the clock. It was 4 AM. The blinds on the ward were shut most of the time, and he kept to his own schedule, napping and then surfing, then nodding off and then surfing some more. The hospital staff just left his food on the table beside him if he was asleep when it arrived, though they woke him for his sponge baths and to stick fresh needles in his arms, which were filled with bruisey collapsed veins.

There was no one he could tell about this. Sure, there were chat rooms with 24/7 chatter from Disney freaks, but he didn't much want to chat with them. Some of his friends would still be up and tweaking, but Christ, who wanted to IM with a speed freak at four in the morning? His typing was down to less than thirty wpm, and he couldn't keep it up for long. What he really wanted was to talk to someone about this.

He really wanted to talk to Perry about this. He should send him an email, but he had the inkling of an idea and he didn't want to put it in writing, because it was a deliciously naughty idea.

It was dumb to even think about phoning him, he barely knew him, and no one liked to get calls at 4 AM. Besides—he'd checked—Perry's number was unlisted.

From: deathw@deathwait.er
To: pgibbons@hollywood.ride
Subject: What's your phone number?

Perry, I know that it's presumptuous, but I'd really like to talk to you V2V about something important that I'd prefer not to put in writing. I don't have any right to impose on you, especially not after you've already done me the kindness of coming to see me in the hospital, but I hope you'll send me your number anyway. Alternatively, please call me on my enum—1800DEATHWAITS-GGFSAH.

Your admirer,
Death Waits

It was five minutes later when his laptop rang. It was unnaturally loud on the ward, and he heard his roommates stir when the tone played. He didn't have a headset—Christ, he was an idiot. Wait, there was one, dangling from the TV. No mic, but at least he could pair it with his laptop for sound. He stabbed at the mute button and reached for the headset and slipped it on. Then he held the computer close to his face and whispered "Hello?" into its little mic. His voice was a croak, his ruined mouth distorting the word. Why had he decided to call this guy? He was such an idiot.

"This is Perry Gibbons. Is that Death Waits?"

"Yes, sorry, I don't have a mic. Can you hear me OK?"

"If I turn the volume all the way up I can."

There was an awkward silence. Death tried to think of how to begin.

"What's on your mind, Death?"

"I didn't expect you to be awake at this hour."

"I had a rough night," Perry said. It occurred to Death that he was talking to one of his heros, a man who had come to visit him in the hospital that day. He grew even more tongue-tied.

"What happened?"

"Nothing important," Perry said, and swallowed, and Death suddenly understood that Perry had had a rough night because of *him*, because of what *he'd* told Perry. It made him want to cry.

"I'm sorry," Death said.

"What's on your mind, Death?" Perry said again.

Death told him what he'd found, about the Disney printers. He read Perry the URLs so he could look them up.

"OK, that's interesting," Perry said. Death could tell he didn't really think it was that interesting.

"I haven't told you my idea yet." He groped for the words. His mouth had gone dry. "OK, so Disney's going to ship these things to tons of people's houses, they'll sell them cheap at the parks and mail them as freebies to Magic Kingdom Club gold-card holders. So in a week or two, there's going to be just, you know, tons of these across the country."

"Right."

"So here's my idea: what if you could get them to build non-Disney stuff? What if you could send them plans for stuff from the rides? What if you could just download your friends' designs? What if this was opened wide."

Perry chuckled on the other end of the line, then laughed, full-throated and full of merriment. "I like the way you think, kid," he said, once he'd caught his breath.

And then this amazing thing happened. Perry Gibbons *brainstormed* with him about the kinds of designs they could push out to these things. It was like some kind of awesome dream come true. Perry was treating him like a peer, loving his ideas, keying off of them.

Then a dismal thought struck him. "Wait though, wait. They're using their own goop for the printers. Every design we print makes them richer."

Perry laughed again, really merry. "Oh, that kind of thing never works. They've been trying to tie feedstock to printers since the inkjet days. We go through that like wet kleenex."

"Isn't that illegal?"

"Who the fuck knows? It shouldn't be. I don't care about illegal anymore. Legal gets you lawyers. Come on, dude—what's the point of being all into some anti-authoritarian subculture if you spend all your time sucking up to the authorities?"

Death laughed, which actually hurt quite a bit. It was the first laugh he'd had since he'd ended up in the hospital, maybe the first one since he'd been fired from Disney World, and as much as it hurt, it felt good, too, like a band being loosened from around his broken ribs.

His roommates stirred and one of them must have pushed the nurse call

button, because shortly thereafter, the formidable Ukrainian nurse came in
and savagely told him off for disturbing the ward at five in the morning. Perry
heard and said his goodbyes, like they were old pals who'd chatted too long,
and Death Waits rang off and fell into a light doze, grinning like a maniac.

Hilda eyed Perry curiously. "That sounded like an interesting conver-
sation," she said. She was wearing a long T-shirt of his that didn't really cover
much, and she looked delicious in it. It was all he could do to keep from grabbing her and tossing her on the bed—of course, the cast meant that he couldn't
really do that. And Hilda wasn't exactly smiling, either.

"Sorry, I didn't mean to wake you up," he said.

"It wasn't the talking that did it; it was you not being there in the first
place. Gave me the toss-and-turns."

She came over to him then, the lean muscles in her legs flexing as she
crossed the living room. She took his laptop away and set it down on the coffee table, then took off his headset. He was wearing nothing but boxers, and
she reached down and gave his dick a companionable honk before sitting
down next to him and giving him a kiss on the cheek, the throat, and the lips.

"So, Perry," she said, looking into his eyes. "What the fuck are you doing
sitting in the living room at five AM talking to your computer? And why didn't
you come to bed last night? I'm not going to be hanging out in Florida for the
rest of my life. I woulda thought you'd want to maximize your Hilda time
while you've got the chance."

She smiled to let him know she was kidding around, but she was right, of
course.

"I'm an idiot, Hilda. I fired Tjan and Kettlewell, told them to get lost."

"I don't know why you think that's such a bad idea. You need business
people, probably, but it doesn't need to be those guys. Sometimes you can
have too much history with someone to work with him. Besides, anything
can be unsaid. You can change your mind in a week or a month. Those guys
aren't doing anything special. They'd come back to you if you asked 'em.
You're Perry motherfuckin' Gibbons. You rule, dude."

"You're a very nice person, Hilda Hammersen. But those guys are running our legal defense, which we're going to need, because I'm about to do
something semi-illegal that's bound to get us sued again by the same pack of
assholes as last time."

"Disney?" She snorted. "Have you ever read up on the history of the Disney Company? The old one, the one Walt founded? Walt Disney wasn't just a
racist creep; he was also a mad inventor. He kept coming up with these cool
high-tech ways of making cartoons—sticking real people in them, putting

them in color, adding sync sound. People loved it all, but it drove him out of business. It was all too expensive.

"So he recruited his brother, Roy Disney, who was just a banker, to run the business. Roy turned the business around, watching the income and the outgo. But all this came at a price: Roy wanted to tell Walt how to run the business. More to the point, he wanted to tell Walt that he couldn't just spend millions from the company coffers on weird-ass R&D projects, especially not when the company was still figuring out how to exploit the *last* R&D project Walt had chased. But it was Walt's company, and he'd overrule Roy, and Roy would promise that it was going to put them in the poorhouse and then he'd figure out how to make another million off of Walt's vision, because that's what the money guy is supposed to do.

"Then after the war, Walt went to Roy and said, 'Give me seventeen million dollars. I'm going to build a theme park. And Roy said, 'You can't have it and what's a theme park?' Walt threatened to fire Roy, the way he always had, and Roy pointed out that Disney was now a *public* company with shareholders who weren't going to let Walt cowboy around and piss away their money on his toys."

"So how'd he get Disneyland built?"

"He quit. He started his own company, WED, for Walter Elias Disney. He poached all the geniuses away from the studios and turned them into his 'Imagineers' and cashed in his life-insurance policy and raised his own dough and built the park, and then made Roy buy the company back from him. I'm guessing that that felt pretty good."

"It sounds like it must've," Perry said. He was feeling thoughtful, and buzzed from the sleepless night, and jazzed from his conversation with Death Waits. He had an idea that they could push designs out to the printers that were like the Disney designs, but weird and kinky and subversive and a little disturbing.

"I can understand why you'd be nervous about ditching your suits, but they're just that, suits. At some level, they're all interchangeable, mercenary parts. You want someone to watch the bottom line, but not someone who'll run the show. If that's not these guys, hey, that's cool. Find a couple more suits and run them."

"Jesus, you really *are* Yoko, aren't you?" Lester was wearing his boxers and a bleary grin, standing in the living room's doorway, where Hilda had stood a minute before. It was past 6 AM now, and there were waking up sounds through the whole condo, toilets flushing, a car starting down in the parking lot.

"Good morning, Lester," Hilda said. She smiled when she said it, no offense taken, all good, all good.

"You fired who now, Perry?" Lester dug a pint of chocolate ice cream out of the freezer and attacked it with a self-heating ceramic spoon that he'd designed specifically for this purpose.

"I got rid of Kettlewell and Tjan," Perry said. He was blushing. "I would have talked to you about it, but you were with Suzanne. I had to do it, though. I had to."

"I hate what happened to Death Waits. I hate that we've got some of the blame for it. But, Perry, Tjan and Kettlewell are part of our outfit. It's their show, too. You can't just go shit-canning them. Not just morally, either. Legally. Those guys own a piece of this thing and they're keeping the lawyers at bay, too. They're managing all the evil shit so we don't have to. I don't want to be in charge of the evil, and neither do you, and hiring a new suit isn't going to be easy. They're all predatory; they all have delusions of grandeur."

"You two have the acumen to hire better representation than those two," Hilda said. "You're experienced now, and you've founded a movement that plenty of people would kill to be a part of. You just need better management structure: an executive you can overrule whenever you need to. A lackey, not a boss."

Lester acted as though he hadn't heard her. "I'm being pretty mellow about this, buddy. I'm not making a big deal out of the fact that you did this without consulting me, because I know how rough it must have been to discover that this wickedness had gone down in our name, and I might have done the same. But it's the cold light of day now and it's time to go over there together and have a chat with Tjan and Kettlewell and talk this over and sort it out. We can't afford to burn all this to the ground and start over now."

Perry knew it was reasonable, but screw reasonable. Reasonable was how good people ended up doing wrong. Sometimes you had to be unreasonable.

"Lester, they violated our trust. It was their responsibility to do this thing and do it right. They didn't do that. They didn't look closely at this thing, so that they wouldn't have to put the brakes on if it turned out to be dirty. Which do you think those two would rather have happen: we run a cool project that everyone loves, or we run a lawsuit that makes ten billion dollars for their investors? They're playing a different game from us and their victory condition isn't ours. I don't want to be reasonable. I want to do the right thing. You and me could have sold out a thousand times over the years and made money instead of doing good, but we didn't. We didn't because it's better to be right than to be reasonable and rich. You say we can't afford to get rid of those two. I say we can't afford not to."

"You need to get a good night's sleep, buddy," Lester said. He was blowing through his nose, a sure sign that he was angry. It made Perry's hackles go up—he and Lester didn't fight much but when they did, hoo-boy. "You need to mellow out and see that what you're talking about is abandoning our friends, Kettlewell and Tjan, to make our own egos feel a little better. You need to see that we're risking everything, risking spending our lives in court and losing everything we've ever built."

A Zen-like calm descended on Perry. Hilda was right. Suits were everywhere, and you could choose your own. You didn't need to let the Roy Disneys of the world call the shots.

"I'm sorry you feel that way, Lester. I hear everything you're saying, but you know what; it's going to be my way. I understand that what I want to do is risky, but there's no way I can go on doing what I'm doing and letting things get worse and worse. Making a little compromise here and there is how you end up selling out everything that's important. We're going to find other business managers and we're going to work with them to make a smooth transition. Maybe we'll all come out of this friends later on. They want to do something different from what I want to do is all."

This wasn't calming Lester down at all. "Perry, this isn't your project to do what you want with. This belongs to a lot of us. I did most of the work in there."

"You did, buddy. I get that. If you want to stick with them, that's how it'll go. No hard feelings. I'll go off and do my own thing, run my own ride. People who want to connect to my network; no sweat, they can do it. That's cool. We'll still be friends. You can work with Kettlewell and Tjan." Perry could hardly believe these words were coming out of his mouth. They'd been buddies forever, inseparable.

Hilda took his hand silently.

Lester looked at him with increasing incredulity. "You don't mean that."

"Lester, if we split, it would break my heart. There wouldn't be a day that went by from now to the end of time that I didn't regret it. But if we keep going down this path, it's going to cost me my soul. I'd rather be broke than evil." Oh, it felt so *good* to be saying this. To finally affirm through deed and word that he was a good person who would put ethics before greed, before comfort even.

Lester looked at Hilda for a moment. "Hilda, this is probably something that Perry and I should talk about alone, if you don't mind."

"*I* mind, Lester. There's nothing you can't say in front of her."

Lester apparently had nothing to say to that, and the silence made Perry uncomfortable. Lester had tears in his eyes, and that hit Perry in the chest like a spear. His friend didn't cry often.

He crossed the room and hugged Lester. Lester was wooden and unyielding.

"Please, Lester. Please. I hate to make you choose, but you have to choose.

We're on the same side. We've always been on the same side. Neither of us are the kind of people who send lawyers after kids in hospital. Never. I want to make it good again. We can have the kind of gig where we do the right thing and the cool thing. Come on, Lester. Please."

He let go of Lester. Lester turned on his heel and walked back into his bedroom. Perry knew that that meant he'd won. He smiled at Hilda and hugged her. She was a lot more fun to hug than Lester.

Sammy was at his desk looking over the production prototype for the Disney-in-a-Box® units that Imagineering had dropped off that morning when his phone rang. Not his desk phone—his cellular phone, with the call-return number blocked.

"Hello?" he said. Not many people had this number—he didn't like getting interrupted by the phone. People who needed to talk to him could talk to his secretary first.

"Hi, Sammy. Have I caught you at a bad time?" He could hear the sneer in the voice and then he could see the face that went with the sneer: Freddy. Shit. He'd given the reporter his number back when they were arranging their disastrous face-to-face.

"It's not a good time, Freddy," he said. "If you call my secretary—"

"I just need a moment of your time, sir. For a quote. For a story about the ride response to your printers—your Disney-in-a-Box Circle-R, Tee-Em, Circle-C."

Sammy felt his guts tense up. Of course those ride assholes would have known about the printers. That's what press releases were for. Somewhere on their message boards he was sure that there was some discussion of them. He hadn't had time to look for it, though, and he didn't want to use the Disney Parks competitive intel people on this stuff, because after the Death Waits debacle (debacle on debacle, ack, he could be such a fuck-up) he didn't want to have any train of intel-gathering on the group pointing back to him.

"I'm not familiar with any response," Sammy said. "I'm afraid I can't comment—"

"Oh, it'll only take a moment to explain it," Freddy said, and then launched into a high-speed explanation before Sammy could object. They were delivering their own 3-D models for the printers, and had even gotten hold of one of the test units Disney had passed out last week. They claimed to have reverse-engineered the goop that it ran on, so that anyone's goop could print to it.

"So, what I'm looking for is a quote from Disney on this. Do you condone this? Did you anticipate it? What if someone prints an AK-47 with it?"

"No one's going to print a working AK-47 with this," Sammy said. "It's too brittle. AK-47 manufacturing is already sadly in great profusion across our inner cities, anyway. As to the rest of it—" He closed his eyes and took a couple of deep breaths. "As to the rest of it, that would be something you'd have to speak to one of my legal colleagues about. Would you like me to put you through to them?"

Freddy laughed. "Oh come on, Sammy. A little something on background, no attribution? You going to sue them? Have them beaten up?"

Sammy felt his face go white. "I'm sure I don't know what you're talking about—"

"Word has it that the Death Waits kid came up with this. He used to be your protégé, no? And I hear that Kettlewell and Tjan have been kicked out of the organization—no one around to call the lawyers out on their behalf. Seems like a golden opportunity to strike."

Sammy seethed. He'd been concentrating on making new stuff, great stuff. Competitive stuff, to be sure, but in the end, the reason for making the Disney-in-a-Box devices had been to make them, make them as cool as he could imagine. To plus them and re-plus them, in the old slang of Walt Disney, making the thing because the thing could be made and the world would be a more fun place once it was.

Now here was this troll egging him on to go to war again with those ride shitheads, to spend his energies destroying instead of creating. The worst part? It was all his fault. He'd brought his own destruction: the reporter, Death Waits, even the lawsuit. All the result of his bad planning and dumb decisions. God, he was a total fuck-up.

Disney-in-a-Box sat on his desk, humming faintly—not humming like a fridge hums, but actually humming in a baritone hum, humming a medley of magic-users' songs from Disney movies, like a living thing. Every once in a while it would clear its throat and mutter and even snore a little. There would be happy rustles and whispered conversations from within the guts of the thing. It was plussed all the way to hell and back. It had been easy, as more and more Imagineers had come up with cool features to add to the firmware, contributing them to the versioning system, and he'd been able to choose from among them and pick the best of the lot, making a device that rivaled Walt's 1955 Disneyland itself for originality, excitement, and cool.

"I'll just say you declined to comment, then?"

Asshole.

"You write whatever you need to write, Freddy," he said. A hatch opened a tiny bit on the top of the cube and a pair of eyes peered out, then it slammed shut and there was a round of convincing giggles and scurrying from within the box. This could be huge, if Sammy didn't fuck it up by worrying too much about what someone else was up to.

"Oh, and one other thing: it looks like the Death Waits kid is going to be discharged from the hospital this week."

He wasn't ready to leave the hospital. For starters, he couldn't walk yet, and there were still times when he could barely remember where he was, and there was the problem of the catheter. But the insurance company and the hospital had concurred that he'd had all the treatment he needed—even if his doctor hadn't been able to look him in the eye when this was explained—and it was time for him to go home. Go away. Go anywhere.

He'd put it all in his LJ, the conversation as best he could remember it, the way it made him feel. The conversation he'd had with Perry and the idea he'd had for pwning Disney-in-a-Box. He didn't even know if his apartment was still there—he hadn't been back in weeks and the rent was overdue.

And the comments came flooding in. First a couple dozen from his friends, then hundreds, then thousands. Raging fights—some people accused him of being a fakester sock puppet aimed at gathering sympathy or donations (!)—side conversations, philosophical arguments.

Buried in there, offers from real world and online friends to meet him at the hospital, to get him home, to take care of him. It was unbelievable. There was a small fortune—half a year's wages at his old job—waiting in his paypal, and if this was all to be believed, there was a cadre of people waiting just outside that door to meet him.

The nurse who came to get him looked rattled. "Your friends are here," she said in her Boris-and-Natasha accent, and gave him a disapproving look as she disconnected his hoses and pipes so swiftly he didn't have time to register the pain he felt. She pulled on a pair of Salvation Army underpants—the first pair he'd worn in weeks—and a pair of new, dark blue jeans and a Rotary picnic T-shirt dated three years before. The shirt was a small and it still hung from him like a tent.

"You will use canes?" she asked. He'd had some physiotherapy that week and he could take one or two doddering steps on crutches, but canes? No way.

"I can't," he said, picturing himself sprawled on the polished concrete floor, with what was left of his face bashed in from the fall.

"Wheelchair," she said to someone in the hall, and an orderly came in pushing a chair with a squeaky wheel—though the chair itself was a pretty good one, at least as good as the ones they rented at Disney, which were nearly indestructible. He let the nurse transfer him to it with her strong hands in his armpits and under his knees. A bag containing his laptop and a few cards and things that had shown up at the hospital was dumped into his lap and he clutched it to himself as he was wheeled to the end of the corridor and around the corner, where the nurse's station, the elevators, the common area, and his *fans* were.

They weren't just his pals, though there were a few of them there, but also a big crowd of people he'd never met, didn't recognize. There were goths, skinny and pale and draped in black, but they were outnumbered by the subculture civilians, normal-looking, slightly hippieish, old and young. When he hove into sight, they burst into a wild cheer. The orderly stopped pushing his chair and the nurse rushed forward to shush them sternly, but it barely dampened the calls. There were wolf whistles, cheers, calls, disorganized chants, and then two very pretty girls—he hadn't thought about "pretty" anything in a long, long time— unfurled a banner that said DEATH WAITS in glittery hand-drawn letters, with a lit- tle skull dotting the *i* in WAITS.

The nurse read the banner and reached to tear it out of their hands, but they folded it back. She came over to him and hissed in his ear, something about getting security to get rid of these people if they were bothering him, and he realized that she thought DEATH WAITS was a *threat* and that made him laugh so hard he choked, and she flounced off in a deeply Slavic huff.

And then he was among his welcoming party, and it *was* a party—there were cake and clove cigarettes in smoke-savers and cans of licorice coffee, and everyone wanted to talk with him and take their pictures with him, and the two pretty girls took turns making up his face, highlighting his scars to make him fit for a Bela Lugosi role. They were called Lacey and Tracey, and they were sisters who went to the ride every day, they said breathlessly, and they'd seen the story he'd described, seen it with their own eyes, and it was some- thing that was as personal as the twin language they'd developed to commu- nicate with one another when they were little girls.

His old friends surrounded him: guys who marveled at his recovery, girls who kissed his cheek and messed up Tracey and Lacey's makeup. Some of them had new tattoos to show him—one girl had gotten a full-leg piece showing scenes from the ride, and she slyly pulled her skirt all the way up, all the way up, to show him where it all started.

Security showed up and threw them all out into the street, where the heat was oppressive and wet, but the air was fresh and full of smells that weren't sickness or medicine, which made Death Waits feel like he could get up and dance. Effervescent citrus and biodiesel fumes, moist vegetation and the hum of lazy high-noon bugs.

"Now, it's all arranged," one of the straight-looking ones told him. He'd figured out that these were the pure story people, who'd read his descriptions and concluded that he'd seen something more than anyone else. They all wanted a chance to talk to him but didn't seem too put out that he was spending most of his time with his old mates. "Don't worry about a thing." Car after car appeared, taking away more of the party. "Here you go."

Another car pulled up, an all-electric kneeling number with a huge cargo space. They wheeled the chair right into it, and then two of the story hippies helped him transfer into the seat. "My mom was in a wheelchair for ten years before she passed," a hippie told him. He was older and looked like an English teacher Death Waits had quite liked in grade ten. He strapped Death Waits in like a pro and off they went.

They were ten minutes into Melbourne traffic—Death marveling at buildings, signs, people, in every color, without the oppressive white-and-gore colors of everything in the hospital—when the English teacher dude looked shyly at Death.

"You think it's real—The Story, I mean—don't you?"

Death thought about this for a second. He'd been very focused on the Disney-in-a-Box printers for the past week, which felt like an eternity to him, but he remembered his obsession with the story fondly. It required a kind of floaty non-concentration to really see it, a meditative state he'd found easy to attain with all the painkillers.

"It's real," he said.

The English teacher and two of his friends seemed to relax a little. "We think so, too."

They pulled up to his condo—how'd they know where he lived?—and parked right next to his car! He could see where the tow had kind of fucked up the rear bumper, but other than that, it was just as he remembered it, and it looked like someone had given it a wash, too. The English teacher put his car in park and came around to open his door just as the rest of the welcoming party came out of his building, pushing—

A stair-climbing wheelchair, the same kind that they used in the ride. Death laughed aloud with delight when he saw it rolling toward him, handling the curb easily, hardly a bump, and the two pretty girls, Tracey and Lacey, transferred him into it, and both contrived to brush their breasts and jasmine-scented hair across his cheeks as they did so, and he felt the first stirrings in his ruined groin that he'd felt since before his beating.

He laughed like a wild man, and they all laughed with him and someone put a clove cigarette between his lips and he drew on it, coughed a little, and then had another drag before he rolled into the elevator.

The girls put him to bed hours later. His apartment had been spotless and he had every confidence that it would be spotless again come nighttime. The party had spent the rest of the day and most of the night talking about the story that they'd seen in the ride, where they'd seen it, what it meant. There was a lot of debate about whether they had any business rating things now that the story had shown itself to them. The story was the product of unconscious effort, and it should be left to unconscious effort.

But the counterargument was that they had a duty to garden the story, or possibly to sharpen its telling, or to protect it from people who couldn't see it or wouldn't see it.

At first Death didn't know what to make of all this talk. At first he found it funny and more than a little weird to be taking the story this seriously. It was beautiful, but it was an accidental beauty. The ride was the important thing, the story was its effect.

But these people convinced him that they were right, that the story *had* to be important. After all, it had inspired all of them, hadn't it? The ride was just technology—the story was what the ride was *for*.

His head swam with it.

"We've got to protect it," he said finally, after listening to the argument, after eating the food with which they'd filled his fridge, after talking intensely with Tracey (or possibly Lacey) about their parents' unthinking blandness, after letting the English teacher guy (whose name was Jim) take him to the toilet, after letting his old goth pals play some music some mutual friends had just mixed.

"We've got to protect it and sharpen it. The story wants to get out and there will be those who can't see it." He didn't care that his speech was mangled by his fucked-up face. He'd seen his face in the mirror and Tracey and Lacey had done a nice job in making it up—he looked like a latter-day Marilyn Manson, his twisted mouth a ghoulish smear. The doctors had talked about giving him another series of surgeries to fix his lip, a set of implanted dentures to replace the missing teeth, had even mentioned that there were specialist clinics where he could get a new set budded and grown right out of his own gums. That had been back when the mysterious forces of the lawsuit and the ride were paying his bills.

Now he contemplated his face in the mirror and told himself he'd get used to this; he'd come to like it; it would be a trademark. It would make him gothier than goth, for life, always an outsider, always one of the weird ones, like the old-timers who'd come to Disney with their teenaged, eye-rolling kids. Goths' kids were never goths, it seemed—more like bangbangers or jocky-looking peak-performance types, or hippies or gippies or dippies or tippies or whatever. But their parents were still proudly flying their freak flags, weird to the grave.

"We'll let everyone know about it," he said, thinking not of *everyone* but of all the cool subculture kids he'd grown up with and worshipped and been rejected by and dated and loved and hated, "and we'll make it part of *every-one*'s story. We'll protect it, guys. Of course we'll protect it."

That settled the argument. Death hadn't expected that. Since when did he get the last word on any subject? Since now. They were following his lead.

And then the girls put him to bed, shyly helping him undress, each of them leaning over him to kiss him good night. Tracey's kiss was sisterly, on the cheek, her spicy perfume and her jet black hair caressing him. Lacey's kiss was anything but sisterly. She mashed her breasts to his chest and thrust her tongue into his mouth, keeping her silver eyes open and staring deep into his, her fingers working busily in his hair.

She broke the kiss off with a gasp and a giggle. She traced the ruin of his mouth with a fingertip, breathing heavily, and let it slide lower, down his chest. He found himself actually *hard*, the first pleasurable sensation he'd had in his dick since that fateful night. From the corridor came an impatient cough—Tracey, waiting for Lacey to get going.

Lacey rolled her eyes and giggled again and then slid her hand the rest of the way down, briefly holding his dick and then encircling his balls with her fingers before kissing him again on the twist of his lips and backing out of the room, whispering, "Sleep well; see you in the morning."

Death lay awake and staring at the ceiling for a long time after they had gone. The English teacher dude had left him with a bedpan for the night and many of them had promised to return in rotations indefinitely during the days, helping him out with dressing and shopping and getting him in and out of his marvelous chair.

He stared and stared at that ceiling, and then he reached for his laptop, there beside the bed, the same place it had lived when he was in the hospital. He fired it up and went straight to today's flythroughs of the ride and ran through them from different angles—facing backward and sideways, looking down and looking up, noting all the elements that felt like *story* and all the ones that didn't, wishing he had his plus-one/minus-one joystick with him to carve out the story he was seeing.

Lester wouldn't work the ride anymore, so Perry took it on his own. Hilda was in town buying groceries—his chest freezer of gourmet surplus food had blown its compressor and the contents had spoiled in a mess of venison and sour blueberry sauce and duck pancakes—and he stood alone. Normally he loved this, being the carnival barker at the middle of the three-ring circus of fans, tourists, and hawkers, but today his cast itched, he hadn't slept enough, and there were lawyers chasing him. Lots of lawyers.

A caravan of cars pulled into the lot like a Tim Burton version of a funeral, a long train of funnycar hearses with jacked-up rear wheels and leaning chimney pots, gargoyles, and black bunting, with superbright black-light LEDs giving them a commercially eldritch glow. Mixed in were some straight cars, and they came and came and came, car on car. The hawkers got out more stuff, spread it out further, and waited while the caravan maneuvered itself into parking spots, spilling out into the street.

Riders got out of the cars, mostly super-skinny goths—a line of special low-calorie vegan versions of Victorian organ-meat delicacies had turned a mom-and-pop café in Portland, Oregon, into a Fortune 500 company a few years before—in elaborate DIY costumery. It shimmered darkly, petticoats and toppers, bodices and big stompy boots, and trousers cut off in ribbons at the knees.

The riders converged on one of the straight cars, a beige minivan, and crowded around it. A moment later, they were moving toward Perry's ticket-taking stand. The crowd parted as they approached and Perry saw whom they'd been clustered around. It was a skinny goth kid in a wheelchair like the ones they kept in the ride—they'd get that every now and again, a guest in his own chair, just needing a little wireless +1/−1 box. His hair was shaggy and black with green highlights stuck out like an anime cosplayer's. He was white as Wonder Bread, with something funny about his mouth. His legs were in casts that had been wrapped with black gauze, and a pair of black pointy shoes had been slid over his toes, tipped with elaborate silver curlicues.

The chair zipped forward and Perry recognized him in a flash: Death Waits! He felt his mouth drop open and he shut it and came around the stand.

"No way!" he said, and grabbed Death's hand, encrusted in chunky silver jewelry, a different stylized animal skull on each finger. Death's ruined mouth pulled up in a kind of smile.

"Nice to see you," he said, limply squeezing Perry's hand. "It was very kind of you to visit me in the hospital."

Perry thought of all the things that had happened since then and wondered how much of it, if any, Death had a right to know about. He leaned in close, conscious of all the observers. "I'm out of the lawsuit. We are. Me and Lester. Fired those guys." Behind his reflective contacts, Death's eyes widened a touch.

He slumped a little. "Because of me?"

Perry thought some. "Not exactly. But in a way. It wasn't us."

Death smiled. "Thank you."

Perry straightened up. "Looks like you brought down a good crowd," he said. "Lots of friends!"

Death nodded. "Lots of friends these days," he said. An attractive young woman came over and squeezed his shoulder.

They were such a funny bunch in their DIY goth frocks, micro-manufactured customized boots, their elaborate tattoos and implants and piercings, but for all that, cuddly and earnest with the shadows visible of the geeks they'd been. Perry felt he was smiling so broadly it almost hurt.

"Rides are on me, gang," he said. "In you go. Your money's no good here. Any friend of Death Waits rides for free today."

They cheered and patted him on the back as they went through, and Death Waits looked like he'd grown three inches in his wheelchair, and the pretty girl kissed Perry's cheek as she went by, and Death Waits had a smile so big you could hardly tell there was anything wrong with his mouth.

They rode it through six times in a row, and as they came back around for another go and another, they talked intently about the story, the story, the story. Perry knew about the story; he'd seen it, and he and Lester had talked it over now and again, but he was still constantly amazed by its ability to inspire riders.

Paying customers slipped in and out, too, and seemed to catch some of the infectious intensity of the story group. They went away in pairs, talking about the story, and shopped the market stalls for a while before coming back to ride again, to look for more story.

They'd never named the ride. It had always been "the ride." Not even a capital R. For a second, Perry wondered if they'd end up calling it "The Story" in the end.

Perry got his Disney-in-a-Box through a circuitous route, getting one of the hawkers' brothers to order it to a PO box in Miami, to which Perry would drive down to pick it up and take it back.

Lester roused himself from the apartment when Perry told him it had arrived. Lester and Suzanne had been AWOL for days, sleeping in until Perry left, coming back after Perry came back, until it felt like they were just travelers staying in the same hotel.

He hadn't heard a peep from Kettlewell or Tjan, either. He guessed that they were off figuring things out with their money people. The network of ride operators had taken the news with equanimity—Hilda had helped him write the message so that it kind of implied that everything was under control and moving along nicely.

But when Perry emailed Lester to say he was going to drive down to the PO box the next morning before opening the ride, Lester emailed back in minutes volunteering to come with him.

He had coffee ready by the time Perry got out of the shower. It was still o-dark-hundred outside, the sun not yet risen, and they hardly spoke as they got into the car, but soon they were on the open road.

"Kettlewell and Tjan aren't going to sue you," Lester said. There it was, all in a short sentence: *I've been talking to them. I've been figuring out if I'm with you or with them. I've been saving your ass. I've been deciding to be on your side.*

"Good news," Perry said. "That would have really sucked."

Perry waited the rest of the drive for Lester to say something, but he didn't. It was a long drive.

The whole way back, Lester talked about the Disney-in-a-Box. There'd been some alien autopsy videos of them posted online already, engineers taking them to bits, making guesses about what they did and how. Lester had watched the videos avidly and he held his own opinions, and he was eager to get at the box and find answers for himself. It was the size of an ice chest, too big to fit on his lap, but he kept looking over his shoulder at it.

The box art, a glossy pic of two children staring goggle-eyed at a box from which Disneoid marvels were erupting, looked a little like that of the Make Your Own Monster toy Perry'd had as a boy. It actually made his heart skip a beat the way that that old toy had. Really, wasn't that every kid's dream? A machine that created wonders from dull feedstock?

They got back to the ride long before it was due to open and Perry asked Lester if he wanted to get a second breakfast in the tearoom in the shanty-town, but Lester begged off, heading for his workshop to get to grips with the Box.

So Perry waited alone for the ride to open, standing at his familiar spot behind the counter. The hawkers came and nodded hello to him. A customer showed up. Another. Perry took their money.

The ticket counter smelled of sticky beverages spilled and left to bake in the heat, a sour-sweet smell like bile. His chair was an uncomfortable bar stool he'd gotten from a kitchen-surplus place, happy for the bargain. He'd logged a lot of hours in that chair. It had wreaked havoc on his lower spine and tenderized his ass.

He and Lester had started this as a lark, but now it was a movement, and not one that was good for his mental health. He didn't want to be sitting on that stool. He might as well be working in a liquor store—the skill set was the same.

Hilda broke his reverie by calling his phone. "Hey, gorgeous," she said. She bounded out of bed fully formed, without any intervening stages of pre-coffee, invertebrate, pre-shower, and Homo erectus. He could hear that she was ready to catch the world by the ankle and chew her way up its leg.

"Hey," he said.

"Uh-oh. Mr. Badvibes is back. You and Lester fight in the car?"

"Naw," he said. "That was fine. Just . . ." He told her about the smell and the stool and working at a liquor store.

"Get one of those home slices running the market stalls to take over the counter, and take me to the beach, then. It's been weeks and I still haven't seen the ocean. I'm beginning to think it's an urban legend."

So that's what he did. Hilda drove up in a bikini that made his jaw drop, and bought a pair of polarizing contacts from Jason, and Perry turned the till over to one of the more trustworthy vendors, and they hit the road.

Hilda nuzzled him and prodded him all the way to the beach, kissing him at the red lights. The sky was blue and clear as far as the eye could see in all directions, and they bought a bag of oranges, a newspaper, beach blankets, sunblock, a picnic lunch, and a book of replica vintage luggage stickers from hawkers at various stop points.

They unpacked the trunk in the parking garage and stepped out into the bright day, and that's when they noticed the wind. It was blowing so hard it took Hilda's sarong off as soon as she stepped out onto the street. Perry barely had time to snatch the cloth out of the air. The wind howled.

They looked up and saw the palm trees bending like drawn bows, the hot dog vendors and shave-ice carts and the jewelry hawkers hurriedly piling everything into their cars.

"Guess the beach is canceled," Hilda said, pointing out over the ocean. There, on the horizon, was a wall of black cloud, scudding rapidly toward them in the raging wind. "Shoulda checked the weather."

The wind whipped up stinging clouds of sand and debris. It gusted hard and actually blew Hilda into Perry. He caught her and they both laughed nervously.

"Is this a hurricane?" she asked, joking, not joking, tension in her voice.

"Probably not." He was thinking of Hurricane Wilma, though, the year he'd moved to Florida. No one had predicted Wilma, which had been a tropical storm miles off the coast until it wasn't, until it was smashing a fifty-kilometer-wide path of destruction from Key West to Kissimmee. He'd been working a straight job as a structural engineer for a condo developer, and he'd seen what a good blow could do to the condos of Florida, which were built mostly from dreams, promises, spit, and kleenex.

Wilma had left cars stuck in trees, trees stuck in houses, and it had blown just like this when it hit. There was a crackle in the air, and the sighing of the wind turned to groans, seeming to come from everywhere at once—the buildings were moaning in their bones as the winds buffeted them.

"We have to get out of here," Perry said. "Now."

They got up to the second story of the parking garage when the whole building moaned and shuddered beneath them, like a tremor. They froze on the stairwell. Somewhere in the garage, something crashed into something else with a sound like thunder, and then it was echoed with an actual thunder crack, a sound like a hundred rifles fired in unison.

Hilda looked at him. "No way. Not further up. Not in this building."

He agreed. They pelted down the street and into the first sleeting showers coming out of a sky that was now dirty gray and low. A sandwich board advertising energy beverages spun through the air like a razor-edged frisbee, trailing a length of clothesline that had tethered it to the front of some beachside café. On the beach across the road, beachcomber robots burrowed into the sand, trying to get safe from the wind, but were foiled again and again, rolled around like potato bugs into the street, into the sea, into the buildings. They seizured like dying things. Perry felt an irrational urge to rescue them.

"High ground," Hilda said, pointing away from the beach. "High ground and find a basement. Just like a twister."

A sheet of water lifted off the surface of the sea and swept across the road at them, soaking them to the skin, followed by a sheet of sand that coated them from head to toe. It was all the encouragement they needed. They ran.

They ran, but the streets were running with rain now and more debris was rolling past them. They got up one block and sloshed across the road. They made it halfway up the next block, past a coffee shop and a surf shop in low-slung buildings, and the wind literally lifted them off their feet and slammed them to the ground. Perry grabbed Hilda and dragged her into an alley behind the surf shop. There were dumpsters there, and a recessed doorway, and they squeezed past a dumpster and into the doorway.

Now in the lee, they realized how loud the storm had been. Their ears rang with it, and rang again with another thunderclap. Their chests heaved and they shivered, grabbing each other. The doorway stank of piss and the crackling ozone around them.

"This place, holy fuck, it's about to lift off and fly away," Hilda said, panting. Perry's unbroken arm throbbed and he looked down to see a ragged cut running the length of his forearm. From the dumpster?

"It's a big storm," Perry said. "They come through now and again. Sometimes they blow away."

"What do they blow away? Trailers? Apartment buildings?" They were both spitting sand and Perry's arm oozed blood.

"Sometimes!" Perry said. They huddled together and listened to the wind lashing at the buildings around them. The dumpster blocking their doorway groaned, and then it actually slid a few inches. Water coursed down the alley before them, with debris caught in it: branches, trash, then an electric motorcycle, scratching against the road as it rattled through the river.

They watched it pass without speaking, then both of them screamed and scrambled back as a hissing, soaked house cat scrambled over the dumpster, landing practically in their laps, clawing at them with hysterical viciousness.

"Fuck!" Hilda said as it caught hold of her thumb with its teeth. She pushed at its face ineffectually, hissing with pain, and Perry finally worked a thumb into the hinge of its jaw and forced it open. The cat sprang away, clawing up his face, leaping back onto the dumpster.

Hilda's thumb was punctured many times, already running free with blood. "I'm going to need rabies shots," she said. "But I'll live."

They cuddled, in the blood and the mud, and watched the river swell and run with more odd debris: clothes and coolers, beer bottles and a laptop, cartons of milk and someone's purse. A small palm tree. A mailbox. Finally, the river began to wane, the rain to falter.

"Was that it?" Hilda said.

"Maybe," Perry said. He breathed in the moist air. His arms throbbed— one broken, the other torn open. The rain was petering out fast now, and looking up, he could see blue sky peeking through the dirty, heavy clouds, which were scudding away as fast as they'd rolled in.

"Next time, we check the weather before we go to the beach," he said.

She laughed and leaned against him and he yelped as she came into contact with his hurt arm. "We got to get you to a hospital," she said. "Get that looked at."

"You too," he said, pointing at her thumb. It was all so weird and remote now, as they walked through the Miami streets, back toward the garage. Other shocked people wandered the streets, weirdly friendly, smiling at them like they all shared a secret.

The beachfront was in shambles, covered in blown trash and mud, uprooted trees and fallen leaves, broken glass and rolled cars. Perry hit the car radio before they pulled out of the garage. An announcer reported that Tropical Storm Henry had gone about three miles inland before petering out to a mere sun shower, along with news about the freeways and hospitals being equally jammed.

"Huh," Perry said. "Well, what do we do now?"

"Let's find a hotel room," Hilda said. "Have showers, get something to eat."

It was a weird and funny idea, and Perry liked it. He'd never played tourist in Florida, but what better place to do so? They gathered their snacks from the back of the car and used the first aid kit in the trunk to tape themselves up.

They tried to reach Lester but no one answered. "He's probably at the ride," Perry said. "Or balls-deep in reverse-engineering the Disney Box thing. OK, let's find a hotel room."

Everything on the beach was fully booked, but as they continued inland for a couple blocks, they came upon coffin hotels stacked four or five capsules high, painted gay Miami deco pastels, installed in rows in old storefronts or stuck in street parking spots, their silvered windows looking out over the deserted boulevards.

"Should we?" Perry said, gesturing at them.

"If we can get an empty one? Damn right—these things are going to be in serious demand in pretty short order."

Stepping into the coffin hotel transported Perry back to his days on the road, his days staying at coffin hotel after coffin hotel, to his first night with Hilda, in Madison. One look at Hilda told him she felt the same. They washed each other slowly, as though they were underwater, cleaning out one another's wounds, sluicing away the caked-on mud and grime blown deep into their ears and the creases of their skin, nestled against their scalps.

They lay down in bed, naked, together, spooned against one another. "You're a good man, Perry Gibbons," Hilda said, snuggling against him, hand moving in slow circles on his tummy.

They slept that way and got back on the road long past dark, driving the blasted freeway slowly, moving around the broken glass and blown-out tires that remained.

The path of the hurricane followed the coast straight to Hollywood, a line of smashed trees and car wrecks and blown-off roofs that made the nighttime drive even more disorienting.

They went straight back to the condo, but Lester wasn't there. Worry nagged at Perry. "Take me to the ride?" he said, after he'd paced the apartment a few times.

Hilda looked up from the sofa, where she had collapsed the instant they came through the door, arm flung over her face. "You're shitting me," she said. "It's nearly midnight, and we've been in a hurricane."

Perry squirmed. "I've got a bad feeling, OK? And I can't drive myself." He flapped his busted arm at her.

Hilda looked at him, her eyes narrowed. "Look, don't be a jerk, OK? Lester's a big boy. He's probably just out with Suzanne. He'd have called you if there'd been a problem."

He looked at her, bewildered by the ferocity of her response. "OK, I'll call a cab," he said, trying for a middle ground.

She jumped up from the couch. "Whatever. Fine. Let me get my keys. Jesus."

He had no idea how he'd angered her, but it was clear that he had, and the last thing he wanted was to get into a car with her, but he couldn't think of a way of saying that without escalating things.

So they drove in white-lipped silence to the ride, Hilda tense with anger, Perry tense with worry, both of them touchy as cats, neither saying a word.

But when they pulled up to the ride, they both let out a gasp. It was lit with rigged floodlights and car headlights, and it was swarming with people. As they drew closer, they saw that the market stalls were strewn across the parking lot, in smashed pieces. As they drew closer still, they saw that the ride itself was staring eyeless at them, window glass smashed.

Perry was out of the car even before it stopped rolling, Hilda shouting something after him. Lester was just on the other side of the ride entrance, wearing a paper mask and rubber boots, wading in three-inch deep, scummy water.

Perry splashed to a halt. "Holy shit," he breathed. The ride was lit with glow sticks, waterproof lamps, and LED torches, and the lights reflected crazily from the still water that filled it as far as the eye could see, way out into the gloom.

Lester looked up at him. His face was lined and exhausted, and it gleamed with sweat. "Storm broke out all the windows and trashed the roof, then flooded us out. It did a real number on the market, too." His voice was dead.

Perry was wordless. Bits of the ride exhibits floated in the water, along with the corpses of the robots.

"No drainage," Lester said. "The code says drainage, but there's none here. I never noticed it before. I'm going to rig a pump, but my workshop's pretty much toast." Lester's workshop had been in the old garden center at the side of the ride. It was all glass. "We had some pretty amazing winds."

Perry felt like he should be showing off his wound to prove that he hadn't been fucking off while the disaster was under way, but he couldn't bring himself to do so. "We got caught in it in Miami," he said.

"Wondered where you were. The kid who was minding the shop just cut and run when the storm rolled in."

"He did? Christ, what an irresponsible asshole. I'll break his neck."

A slimy raft of kitchen gnomes—their second business venture—floated past silently in the harsh watery light. The smell was almost unbearable.

"It wasn't his job—" Lester's voice cracked on *job*, and he breathed deeply. "It wasn't his job, Perry. It was your job. You're running around, having a good time with your girlfriend, firing lawyers—" He stopped and breathed again. "You know that they're going to sue us, right? They're going to turn us into a smoking ruin because you fired them, and what the fuck are you going to do about that? Whose job is that?"

"I thought you said they weren't going to sue," Perry said. It came out in an embarrassed mumble. Lester had never talked to him like this. Never.

"Kettlewell and Tjan aren't going to sue," Lester said. "The lawyers you fired, the venture capitalists who backed them? They're going to turn us into paste."

"What would you have preferred?" Hilda said. She'd was standing in the doorway, away from the flood, watching them intently. Her eyes were raccoon-bagged, but she was rigid with anger. Perry could hardly look at her. "Would you have preferred to have those fuckers go around destroying the lives of your supporters in order to enrich a few pig assholes?"

Lester just looked at her.

"Well?"

"Shut up, Yoko," he said. "We're having a private conversation here."

Perry's jaw dropped, and Hilda was already in motion, sloshing into the water in her sandals. She smacked Lester across the cheek, a crack that echoed back over the water and walls.

Lester brought his hand up to his reddening face. "Are you done?" he said, his voice hard.

Hilda looked at Perry. Lester looked at Perry. Perry looked at the water.

"I'll meet you by the car," Perry said. It came out in a mumble. They held for a moment, the three of them, then Hilda walked out again, leaving Lester and Perry looking at one another.

"I'm sorry," Perry said.

"About Hilda? About the lawsuits? About skipping out?"

"About everything," he said. "Let's fix this up, OK?"

"The ride? I don't even know if I want to. Why bother? It'll cost a fortune to get it online, and they'll only shut it down again with the lawsuit. Why bother."

"So we won't fix the ride. Let's fix us."

"Why bother," Lester said, and it came out in the same mumble.

The watery sounds of the room and the smell and the harsh reflected rippling light made Perry want to leave. "Lester—" he began.

Lester shook his head. "There's nothing more we can do tonight, anyway. I'll rent a pump in the morning."

"I'll do it," Perry said. "You work on the Disney-in-a-Box thing."

Lester laughed, a bitter sound. "Yeah, OK, buddy. Sure."

Out in the parking lot, the hawkers were putting their stalls back together as best they could. The shantytown was lit up and Perry wondered how it had held together. Pretty good, is what he guessed—they met and exceeded county code on all of those plans.

Hilda honked the horn at him. She was fuming behind the wheel and they drove in silence. He felt numb and wrung out and he didn't know what to say to her. He lay awake in bed that night waiting to hear Lester come home, but he didn't.

Sammy loved his morning meetings. They all came to his office, all the different park execs, creatives, and emissaries from the old partner companies that had spun off to make movies and merch and educational materials. They all came each day to talk to him about the next day's Disney-in-a-Box build. They all came to beg him to think about adding in something from their franchises and cantons to the next installment.

There were over a million DiaBs in the field now, and they weren't even trying to keep up with orders anymore. Sammy loved looking at the online auction sites to see what the boxes were going for—he knew that some of his people had siphoned off a carload or two of the things to e-tail out the back door. He loved that. Nothing was a better barometer of your success than having made something other people cared enough about to steal.

He loved his morning meetings, and he conducted them with the flair of a benevolent emperor. He'd gotten a bigger office—technically it was a boardroom for DiaB strategy, but Sammy *was* the DiaB strategy. He'd outfitted it with fan photos of their DiaB shrines in their homes, with kids watching enthralled as the day's model was assembled before their eyes. The hypnotic fascination in their eyes was unmistakable. Disney was the focus of their daily lives, and all they wanted was more, more, more. He could push out five models a day, ten, and they'd go nuts for them.

But he wouldn't. He was too cunning. One model a day was all. Leave them wanting more. Never breathe a hint of what the next day's model would be—oh, how he loved to watch the blogs and the chatter as the models self-assembled, the heated, time-bound fights over what the day's model was going to be.

"Good morning, Ron," he said. Wiener had been lobbying to get a Main Street build into the models for weeks now, and Sammy was taking great pleasure in denying it to him without shutting down all hope. Getting Ron Wiener to grovel before him every morning was better than a cup of coffee.

"I've been thinking about what you said, and you're right," Wiener said. He always started the meeting by telling Sammy how right he was to reject his last idea. "The flagpole and marching-band scene would have too many pieces. House cats would knock it over. We need something more unitary, more visually striking. So here's what I've been thinking: what about the fire engine?"

Sammy raised an indulgent eyebrow.

"Kids *love* fire trucks. All the colors are in the printer's gamut—I checked. We could create a Mickey-and-friends fire crew to position around it, a little barn for it."

"The only thing I liked about fire trucks when I was a kid was that the word started with 'f' and ended with 'uck.'" Sammy smiled when he said it and waited for Wiener to fake hilarity, too. The others in the room—other park execs, some of their licensing partners, a few advertisers—laughed as well. Officially, this was a "brainstorming session," but everyone knew that it was all about getting the nod from Sammy.

Wiener laughed dutifully and slunk away. More supplicants came forward.

"How about this?" She was very cute—dressed in smart, dark clothes that were more Lower East Side than Orlando. She smelled good, too—one of the new colognes that hinted at free monomers, like hot plastic or a new-bought tire. Cat-slanted green eyes completed the package.

"What you got there?" She was from an ad agency, someone Disney Parks had done business with at some point. Agencies had been sending their people to these meetings, too, trying to get a co-branding coup for one of their clients.

"It's a series of three, telling a little story. Beginning, middle, and end. The first one is a family sitting down to breakfast, and you can see, it's the same old crap, boring microwave omelets and breakfast puddings. Mom's bored, dad's more bored, and sis and brother here are secretly dumping theirs onto mom's and dad's plates. All this stuff is run using the same printers, so it looks very realistic."

It did indeed. Sammy hadn't thought about it, but he supposed it was only natural that the omelets were printed—how else could General Mills get that uniformity? He should talk to some of the people in food services about getting some of that tech to work at the parks.

"So in part two, they're setting up the kitchen around this mystery box—one part Easy-Bake lightbulb oven, one part Tardis. You know what that is?"

Sammy grinned. "Why yes, I believe I do." Their eyes met in a fierce look of mutual recognition. "It's a breakfast printer, isn't it?" The other supplicants in the room sucked in a collective breath. Some chuckled nervously.

"It's about moving the apparatus to the edge. Bridging the last mile. Why not? This one will do waffles, breakfast cereals, bagels and baked goods, small cakes. New designs every day—something for mom and dad, something for the kids, something for the sullen teens. We're already doing this at the regional plants and distributorships, on much larger scales. But getting our stuff into consumers' homes, getting them *subscribed* to our food—"

Sammy held up a hand. "I see," he said. "And our people are already primed for home-printing experiences. They're right in your sweet spot."

"Part three, Junior and little sis are going cuckoo for Cocoa Puffs, but these things are shaped *like them,* with their portraits on each sugar lump. Mom and Dad are eating très sophistiqué croissants and delicate cakes. Look at Rover here, with his own cat-shaped dog biscuit. See how happy they all are?"

Sammy nodded. "Shouldn't this all be under nondisclosure?" he said.

"Probably, but what are you gonna do? You guys are pretty good at keeping secrets, and if you decide to shaft us by selling out to one of our competitors, we're probably dead, anyway. I'll be able to ship out half a million units in the first week, then we can ramp production if need be—lots of little parts-and-assembly subcontractors will take the work if we offer."

Sammy liked the way she talked. Like someone who didn't need to spend a lot of time screwing around, planning, like someone who could just make it happen.

"You're launching when?"

"Three days after you start running this campaign," she said, without batting an eyelash.

"My name's Sammy," he said. "How's Thursday?"

"Launch on Sunday?" She shook her head. "It's tricky, Sunday launches. Gotta pay everyone scale and a half." She gave him a wink. "What the hell, it's not my money." She stuck out her hand. She was wearing a couple of nice chunky obsidian rings in abstract curvy shapes, looking a little porny in their suggestion of breasts and thighs. He shook her hand and it was warm and dry and strong.

"Well, that's this week taken care of," Sammy said, and pointedly cleared the whiteboard surface running the length of the table. The others groaned and got up and filed out. The woman stayed behind.

"Dinah," she said. She handed him a card and he noted the agency. Dallas-based, not New York, but he could tell she was a transplant.

"You got any breakfast plans?" It was hardly gone 9 AM—Sammy liked to get these meetings started early. "I normally get something sent in, but your little prototypes there . . ."

She laughed. It was a pretty laugh. She was a couple years older than him, and she wore it well. "Do I have breakfast plans? Sammy, my boy, I'm nothing *but* breakfast plans! I have a launch on Sunday, remember?"

"Heh. Oh yeah."

"I'm on the next flight to DFW," she said. "I've got a cab waiting to take me to the airport."

"I wonder if you and I need to talk over some details," Sammy said.

"Only if you want to do it in the taxi."

"I was thinking we could do it on the plane," he said.

"You're going to buy a ticket?"

"On my plane," he said. They'd given him use of one of the company jets when he started really ramping production on the DiaBs.

"Oh yes, I think that can be arranged," she said. "It's Sammy, right?"

"Right," he said. They left the building and had an altogether lovely flight to Dallas. Very productive.

Lester hadn't left Suzanne's apartment in days. She'd rented a place in the shantytown—bemused at the idea of paying rent to a squatter, but pleased to have a place of her own now that Lester and Perry's apartment had become so tense.

Technically, he was working on the Disney printers, which she found interesting in an abstract way. They had a working one and a couple of disassembled ones, and watching the working one do its thing was fascinating for a day or two, but then it was just a 3-D TV with one channel, broadcasting one frame per day.

She dutifully wrote about it, though, and about Perry's ongoing efforts to reopen the ride. She got the sense from him that he was heading for flat-ass broke. Lester and he had always been casual about money, but buying all new robots, more printers, replacement windows, fixing the roof—none of it was cheap. And with the market in pieces, he wasn't getting any rent.

She looked over Lester's shoulder for the fiftieth time. "How's it going?"

"Don't write about this, OK?"

He'd never said that to her.

"I'll embargo it until you ship."

He grunted. "Fine, I guess. OK, well, I've got it running on generic goop, that part was easy. I can also load my own designs, but that requires physical access to the thing, in order to load new firmware. They don't make it easy, which is weird. It's like they don't plan on updating it once it's in the field—maybe they just plan on replacing them at regular intervals."

"Why's the firmware matter to you?"

"Well, that's where it stores information about where to get the day's de-signs. If we're going to push our own designs to it, we need to give people an easy way to tell it to tune in to our feed, and the best way to do that is to change the firmware. The alternative would be, oh, I don't know, putting an-other machine upstream of it to trick it into thinking that it's accessing their site when it's really going to ours. That means getting people to configure an-other machine—no one but a few hardcore geeks will want to do that."

Suzanne nodded. She wondered if "a few hardcore geeks" summed up the total audience for this project in any event. She didn't mention it, though. Lester's brow was so furrowed you could lose a dime in the crease above his nose.

"Well, I'm sure you'll get it," she said.

"Yeah. It's just a matter of getting at the boot loader. I could totally do this if I could get at the boot loader."

Suzanne knew what a boot loader was, just barely. The thing that chose which OS to load when you turned it on. She wondered if every daring, sexy technology project started like this, a cranky hacker muttering angrily about boot loaders.

Suzanne missed Russia. She'd had a good life there covering the biotech scene. Those hackers were a lot scarier than Lester and Perry, but they were still lovable and fascinating in their own way. Better than the Ford and GM execs she used to have to cozy up to.

She'd liked the manic hustle of Russia, the glamour and the squalor. She'd bought a time-share dacha that she could spend weekends at, and the expats in Petersburg had rollicking parties and dinners where they took apart the day's experiences on Planet Petrograd.

"I'm going out, Lester," she said. Lester looked up from the DiaB and blinked a few times, then seemed to rewind the conversation.

"Hey," he said. "Oh, hey. Sorry, Suzanne. I'm just—I'm trying to work in-stead of think these days. Thinking just makes me angry. I don't know what to do—" He broke off and thumped the side of the printer.

"How's Perry getting on with rebuilding?"

"He's getting on," Lester said. "As far as I know. I read that the Death Waits kid and his people had come by to help. Whatever that means."

"He freaks me out," Suzanne said. "I mean, I feel terrible for him, and he seemed nice enough in the hospital. But all those people—the way they fol-low him around. It's just weird. Like the charismatic cults back home." She realized she'd just called Russia "home" and it made her frown. Just how long was she going to stay here with these people, anyway?

Lester hadn't noticed. "I guess they all feel sorry for him. And they like what he has to say about stories. I just can't get a lot of spit in my mouth over the ride these days, though. It feels like something we did and completed and should move on from."

Suzanne didn't have anything to say, and Lester wasn't particularly expecting anything; he was giving off a palpable let-me-work vibe, so she let herself out of the apartment—her apartment!—and headed out into the shantytown. On the way to the ride, she passed the little teahouse where Kettlewell and Tjan had done their scheming and she suddenly felt very, very old. The only grown-up on-site.

She was about to cross the freeway to the ride when her phone rang. She looked at the face and then nearly dropped it. Freddy was calling her.

"Hello, Suzanne," he said. The gloat in his voice was unmistakable. He had something really slimy up his sleeve.

"How can I help you?"

"I'm calling for comment on a story," he said. "It's my understanding that your lad, Perry, pitched a tantie and fired the business managers of the ride, and has told the lawyers representing him against Disney that he intends to drop the suit."

"Is there a question in there?"

"Oh, there are many questions in there, my darling. For starters, I wondered how it could possibly be true if you haven't written about it on your little 'blog.'" Even over the phone, she could hear the sarcastic quotes. "You seem to be quite comprehensive in documenting the undertakings of your friends down there in Florida."

"Are you asking me to comment on why I haven't commented?"

"For starters."

"Have you approached Perry for a comment?"

"I'm afraid he was rather abrupt. And I couldn't reach his Valkyrie of the Midwest, either. So I'm left calling on you, Suzanne. Any comment?"

Suzanne stared across the road at the ride. She'd been gassed there, chased by armed men, watched a war there.

"The ride doesn't have much formal decision-making process," she said finally. "That means that words like 'fired' don't really apply here. The boys might have a disagreement about the best way to proceed, but if that's the case, you'll have to talk to them about it."

"Are you saying that you don't know if your boyfriend's best friend is fighting with his business partners? Don't you all live together?"

"I'm saying that if you want to find out what Lester and Perry are doing, you'll have to ask Lester and Perry."

"And the living-together thing?"

"We don't live together," she said. It was technically true.

"Really?" Freddy said.

"Do we have a bad connection?"

"You don't live together?"

"No."

"Where do you live then?"

"My place," she said. "Have your informants been misinforming you? I hope you haven't been paying for your information, Freddy. I suppose you don't, though. I suppose there's no end of cranks who really enjoy spiteful gossip and are more than happy to email you whatever fantasies they concoct."

Freddy tsked. "And you don't know what's happened to Kettlewell and Tjan?"

"Have you asked them?"

"I will," he said. "But since you're the ranking reporter on the scene."

"I'm just a blogger, Freddy. A busy blogger. Good afternoon."

The call left her shaking, though she was proud of how calm she'd kept her voice. What a goddamned troll. And she was going to have to write about this now.

There were ladders leaned up against the edge of the ride, and a motley crew of roofers and glaziers on them and on the roof, working to replace the gaping holes the storm had left. The workers mostly wore black and had dyed hair and lots of metal flashing from their ears and faces as they worked. A couple had stripped to the waist, revealing full-back tattoos or even more piercings and subcutaneous implants, like armor running over their spines and shoulder blades. A couple of boom boxes blasted out grinding, incoherent music with a lot of electronic screams.

Around the ride, the market stalls were coming back, rebuilt from a tower of fresh-sawed lumber stacked in the parking lot. This was a lot more efficient, with gangs of vendors quickly sawing the lumber to standard sizes, slapping each one with a positional sensor, then watching the sensor's lights to tell them when it was properly lined up with its mates, and then slipping on corner clips that held it all together. Suzanne watched as a whole market stall came together this way, in the space of five minutes, before the vendors moved on to their next stall. It was like a high-tech version of an Amish barn-raising, performed by bandanna-clad sketchy hawkers instead of bearded technophobes.

She found Perry inside, leaning over a printer, tinkering with its guts, LED torches clipped to the temples of his glasses. He was hampered by having only one good arm, and he pressed her into service passing him tools for a good fifteen minutes before he straightened up and really looked at her.

"You come down to help out?"

"To write about it, actually."

The room was a hive of activity. A lot of goth kids of various ages and degrees of freakiness, a few of the squatter kids, some people she recognized from the second coming of Death Waits. She couldn't see Death Waits, though.

"Well, that's good." He powered up the printer and the air filled with the familiar smell of Saran Wrap in a microwave. She had an eerie flashback to her first visit to this place, when they'd showed her how they could print mutated, Warhol-ized barbie heads. "How's Lester getting on with cracking that printer?"

Why don't you ask him yourself? She didn't say it. She didn't know why Lester had come to her place after the flood instead of going home, why he stiffened up and sniffed when she mentioned Perry's name, why he looked away when she mentioned Hilda.

"Something about firmware."

He straightened his back more, making it pop, and gave her his devilish grin, the one where his wonky eyebrow went up and down. "It's always firmware," he said, and laughed a little. Maybe they were both remembering those old days, the Boogie Woogie Elmos.

"Looks like you've got a lot of help," Suzanne said, getting out a little steno pad and a pen.

Perry nodded at it, and she was struck by how many times they'd stood like this, a few feet apart, her pen poised over her pad. She'd chronicled so much of this man's life.

"They're good people, these folks. Some of them have some carpentry or electronics experience, the rest are willing to learn. It's going faster than I thought it would. Lots of support from out in the world, too—people sending in cash to help with replacement parts."

"Have you heard from Kettlewell or Tjan?"

The light went out of his face. "No," he said.

"How about from the lawyers?"

"No comment," he said. It didn't sound like a joke.

"Come on, Perry. People are starting to ask questions. Someone's going to write about this. Do you want your side told or not?"

"Not," he said, and disappeared back into the guts of the printer.

She stared at his back for a long while before turning on her heel, muttering, "Fuck," and walking back out into the sunshine. There'd been a musty smell in the ride, but out here it was the Florida smell of citrus and car fumes, and sweat from the people around her, working hard, trying to wrest a living from the world.

She walked back across the freeway to the shantytown and ran into Hilda coming the other way. The younger woman gave her a cool look and then looked away, and crossed.

That was just about enough, Suzanne thought. Enough playtime with the kids. Time to go find some grown-ups. She wasn't here for her health. If Lester didn't want to hang out with her, if Perry had had enough of her, it was time to go do something else.

She went back to her room, where Lester was still working on his DiaB project. She took out her suitcase and packed with the efficiency of long experience. Lester didn't notice, not even when she took the blouse she'd handwashed and hung to dry on the back of his chair, folded it, and put it in her suitcase and zipped it shut.

She looked at his back working over the bench for a long time. He had a six-pack of chocolate pudding beside him, and a wastebasket overflowing with food wrappers and boxes. He shifted in his seat and let out a soft fart.

She left. She paid the landlady through the end of the week. She could send Lester an email later.

The cab took her to Miami. It wasn't until she got to the airport that she realized she had no idea where she was going. Boston? San Francisco? Petersburg? She opened her laptop and began to price out last-minute tickets. The rush of travelers moved around her and she was jostled many times.

The standby sites gave her a thousand options—Miami to JFK to Heathrow to Petersburg, Miami to Frankfurt to Moscow to Petersburg, Miami to Dallas to San Francisco. . . . The permutations were overwhelming, especially since she wasn't sure where she wanted to be.

Then she heard something homey and familiar: a large group of Russian tourists walking past, talking loudly in Russian, complaining about the long flight, the bad food, and the incompetence of their tour operator. She smiled to see the old men with their high-waisted pants and the old women with their bouffant hair.

She couldn't help but eavesdrop—at their volume, she would have been hard-pressed *not* to listen in. A little boy and girl tore ass around the airport, under the disapproving glares from DHS goons, and they screamed as they ran, "Disney World! Disney World! Disney World!"

She'd never been—she'd been to a couple of the kitschy Gulag parks in Russia, and she'd grown up with Six Flags coaster parks and Ontario Place and the CNE in Toronto, not far from Detroit. But she'd never been to The Big One, the place that even now managed to dominate the world's consciousness of theme parks.

She asked her standby sites to find her a room in a Disney hotel instead, looking for an inclusive rate that would get her onto the rides and pay for her meals. These were advertised at roadside kiosks at one-hundred-yard intervals on every freeway in Florida, so she suspected they were the best deal going.

A moment of browsing showed her that she'd guessed wrong. A week in Disney cost a heart-stopping sum of money—the equivalent of six month's rent in Petersburg. How did all these Russians afford this trip? What the hell compelled people to part with these sums?

She was going to have to find out. It was research. Plus she needed a vacation.

She booked in, bought a bullet-train ticket, and grabbed the handle of her suitcase. She examined her welcome package as she waited for the train. She was staying at something called the Polynesian Resort hotel, and the brochure showed a ticky-tacky tiki-themed set of longhouses set on an ersatz white-sand beach, with a crew of Mexican and Cuban domestic workers in leis, Hawaiian shirts, and lavalavas waving and smiling. Her package included a complimentary luau—the pictures made it clear this was nothing like the tourist luaus she'd attended in Maui. On top of that, she was entitled to a "character breakfast" with a wage slave in an overheated plush costume, and an hour with a "resort counselor" who'd help her plan her trip for maximal fun.

The bullet train came and took on the passengers, families bouncing with anticipation, joking and laughing in every language spoken. These people had just come through a U.S. Customs checkpoint and they were acting like the world was a fine place. She decided there must be something to this Disney business.

Death Waits waited, and waited and waited for the ride to come back online. He split his days between hanging out at home, writing about the story, running the flythroughs from the other rides, watching what was happening in Brazil, answering his fan mail; the rest of the time he spent with his new friends down at the site of the ride, encouraging them to pitch in and help Perry and Lester to get the thing back up and running. Fast, please. It was driving him bonkers not to be able to ride any longer. After everything he'd been through, he deserved a ride.

His friends were wonderful. Wonderful! Lacey especially. She was a nurse and a goddess of mercy. The money that flooded into his paypals whenever his friends let it be known that he needed more covered all his expenses. He never wanted for companionship, conversation, helpmeets, or respect. It was a wonderful life.

If only the ride would come online.

He woke next to Lacey, asleep still, her hair spread out across the pillow in a fall of shiny black with blue highlights—she'd given him a matching dye job a few days before and they looked like a matched set now. He let his hands lazily trace her soft skin, the outlines of her tattoos, her implants and piercings. He felt a stirring between his legs.

Lacey yawned and woke and kissed him. "Good morning, my handsome man," she said.

"Good morning, my beautiful woman. What's the plan for today?"

"Whatever you want," she said.

"Breakfast, then down to the ride," he said. "I'll do my email and writing there today."

"Something before breakfast?" she asked, with a lopsided smile that was adorable.

"Oh yes, please," he said, his voice breathy.

The smell at the Wal-Mart was overpowering. It was one part sharp mold, one part industrial disinfectant, a citrus smell that made your eyes water and your sinuses burn.

"I've rented some big blowers," Perry said. "They'll help air the place out. If that doesn't work, I might have to resurface the floor, which would be rough—it could take a week to get that done properly."

"A week?" Death said. Jesus. No way. Not another week. He didn't know it for sure, but he had a feeling that a lot of these people would stop showing up eventually if there was no ride for them to geek out over. He sure would.

"You smell that? We can't close the doors and the windows and leave it like this."

Death's people, standing around them, listening in, nodded. It was true. You'd melt people's lungs if you shut them up with these fumes.

"How can I help?" Death said. It was his constant mantra with Perry. Sometimes he didn't think Perry liked him very much, and it was good to keep on reminding him that Death and his buddies were here to be part of the solution. That Perry needed them.

"The roof is just about done, the robots are back online. The dividers should be done today. I've got the chairs stripped down for routine maintenance—I could use a couple people for that."

"What's Lester working on?" Death said.

"You'd have to ask him."

Death hadn't seen Lester in days, which was weird. He hoped Lester didn't dislike him. He worried a lot about whether people liked him these days. He'd thought that Sammy liked him, after all.

"Where is he?"

"Don't know."

Perry put dark glasses on.

Death Waits took the hint. "Come on," he said to Lacey, who patted him on the hand as he lifted up in his chair and rolled out to the van. "Let's just call him."

" 'Lo?"

"It's Death Waits. We're down at the ride, but there's not much to do around here. I thought maybe we could help you with whatever you were working on?"

"What do you know about what I'm working on?" Lester said.

"Um. Nothing."

"So how do you know you want to help?"

Death Waits closed his eyes. He wanted to help these two. They'd made something important; didn't they know that?

"What are you working on?"

"Nothing," Lester said.

"Come on," Death said. "Come on. We just want to pitch in. I love you guys. You changed my life. Let me contribute."

Lester snorted. "Cross the road, go straight for two hundred yards, turn left at the house with the César Chávez mural, and I'll meet you there."

"You mean go into the—" Death didn't know what it was called. He always tried not to look at it when he came to the ride. That slum across the road. He knew it was somehow connected with the ride, but in the same way that the administrative buildings at Disney were connected with the parks. The big difference was that Disney's extraneous buildings were shielded from view by berms and painted go-away green. The weird town across the road was *right there.*

"Yeah, across the road into the shantytown."

"OK," Death said. "See you soon." He hung up and patted Lacey's hand. "We're going over there," he said, pointing into the shantytown.

"Is it safe?"

He shrugged. "I guess so." He loved his chair, loved how tall it made him, loved how it turned him into a half-ton cyborg who could raise up on his rear wheels and rock back and forth like a triffid. Now he felt very vulnerable—a crippled cyborg whose apparatus cost a small fortune, about to go into a neighborhood full of people who were technically homeless.

"Should we drive?"

"I think we can make it across," he said. Traffic was light, though the cars that bombed past were doing ninety or more. He started to gather up a few more of his people but reconsidered. It was a little scary to be going into the town, but he couldn't afford to freak out Lester by showing up with an entourage.

The guardrail shielding the town had been bent down and flattened and the chair wheeled over it easily, with hardly a bump. As they crossed this border, they crossed over to another world. There were cooking smells—barbecue and Cuban spices—and a little hint of septic tank or compost heap. The buildings didn't make any sense to Death's eye; they curved or sloped or twisted or leaned and seemed to be made of equal parts prefab cement and aluminum and scrap lumber, laundry lines, power lines, and graffiti.

Death was used to drawing stares, even before he became a cyborg with a beautiful woman beside him, but this was different. There were eyes everywhere. Little kids playing in the street—hadn't these people heard of stranger danger—stopped to stare at him with big shoe-button eyes. Faces peered out of windows from the ground on up to the third story. Voices whispered and called.

Lacey gave them her sunniest smile and even waved at the little kids, and Death tried nodding at some of the homeys staring at him from the window of what looked like a little diner.

Death hadn't known what to expect from this little town, but he certainly hadn't pictured so many little shops. He realized that he thought of shops as being somehow civilized—tax paying, license-bearing entities with commercial relationships with suppliers, with cash registers and employees. Not lawless and wild.

But every ground floor seemed to have at least a small shop, advertised with bright OLED pixel-boards that showed rotating enticements—PRODUCTOS DE DOMINICA, BEAUTIFUL FOR LADIES, OFERTA!!!, FANTASY NAILS. He passed twenty different shops in as many steps, some of them seemingly nothing more than a counter recessed into the wall, with a young man sitting behind it, grinning at them.

Lacey stopped at one and bought them cans of coffee and small Mexican pastries dusted with cinnamon. He watched a hundred pairs of eyes watch Lacey as she drew out her purse and paid. At first he thought of the danger, but then he realized that if anyone was to mug them, it would be in full sight of all these people.

It was a funny thought. He'd grown up in sparse suburbs where you'd never see anyone walking or standing on the sidewalks or their porches. Even though it was a "nice" neighborhood, there were muggings and even killings at regular, horrific intervals. Walking there felt like taking your life into your hands.

Here, in this crowded place with a human density like a Disney park, it felt somehow safer. Weird.

They came to what had to be the César Chávez mural—a Mexican in a cowboy hat standing like a preacher on the tailgate of a truck, surrounded by more Mexicans, farmer types in cotton shirts and blue jeans and cowboy hats. They turned left and rounded a corner into a little cul-de-sac with a confusion of hopscotches chalked onto the ground, ringed by parked bicycles and scooters. Lester stood among them, eating a churro in a piece of wax paper.

"You seem to be recovering quickly," he said, sizing up Death in his chair. "Good to see it." He seemed a little distant, which Death chalked up to being interrupted.

"It's great to see you again," Death said. "My friends and I have been coming by the ride every day, helping out however we can, but we never see you there, so I thought I'd call you."

"You'd call me."

"To see if we could help," Death said. "With whatever you're doing."

"Come in," Lester said. He gestured behind him and Death noticed for the first time the small sign that said HOTEL ROTHSCHILD, with a stately peacock behind it.

The door was a little narrow for his rolling chair. He managed to get it in with a little back-and-forth, but once inside, he was stymied by the narrow staircase leading up to the upper floors. The lobby—such as it was—was completely filled by him, Lacey, and Lester, and even if the chair could have squeezed up the stairs, it couldn't have cornered to get there.

Lester looked embarrassed. "Sorry, I didn't think of that. Um. OK, I could rig a winch and hoist the chair up if you want. We'd have to belt you in, but it's doable. There are masts for pulleys on the top floor—it's how they get the beds into the upper stories."

"I can get up on canes," Death Waits said. "Is it safe to leave my chair outside, though?"

Lester's eyebrows went up. "Well of course—sure it is." Death felt weird for having asked. He backed the chair out and locked the transmission, feeling silly. Who was going to hot-wire a wheelchair? He was such a dork. Lacey handed him his canes and he stood gingerly. He'd been making his way to the bathroom and back on canes all week, but he hadn't tried stairs yet. He hoped Lester wasn't too many floors up.

Lester turned out to be on the third floor, and by the time they reached it, Death Waits was dripping sweat and his eyeliner had run into his eyes. Lacey dabbed at him with her gauzy scarf and fussed over him. Death caught Lester looking at the two of them with a little smirk, so he pushed Lacey away and steadied his breathing with an effort.

"OK," he said. "All done."

"Great," Lester said. "This is what I'm working on. You talked to Perry about it before, right? The Disney-in-a-Box printers. Well, I've cracked it. We can load our own firmware onto it—just stick it on a network with a PC, and the PC will find it and update it. Then it becomes an open box—it'll accept anyone's goop. You can send it your own plans."

Death hadn't seen a DiaB in person yet. Beholding it and knowing that he was the reason that Lester and Perry were experimenting with it in the first place made him feel a sense of excitement he hadn't felt since the goth rehab of Fantasyland began.

"So how does this tie in to the ride?" Death asked. "I was thinking of building rides in miniature, but at that scale, will it really impress people? No, I don't think so.

"So instead I was thinking that we could just push out details from the ride, little tabletop-sized miniatures showing a piece every day. Maybe whatever was newest. And you could have multiple feeds, you know, like an experimental trunk for objects that people in one region liked—"

Lester was shaking his head and holding up his hands. "Woah, wait a second. No, no, no—" Death was used to having his friends hang on his every word when he was talking about ideas for the ride and the story, so this brought him up short. He reminded himself who he was talking to.

"Sorry," he said. "Got ahead of myself."

"Look," Lester said, prodding at the printer. "This thing is its own thing. We're about more than the ride here. I know you really like it, and that's very cool, but there's no way that everything I do from now on is going to be about that fucking thing. It was a lark; it's cool; it's got its own momentum. But these boxes are going to be their own thing. I want to show people how to take control of the stuff in their living rooms, not advertise my little commercial project to them."

Death couldn't make sense out of this. It sounded like Lester didn't *like* the ride. How was that possible? "I don't get it," he said at last. Lester was making him look like an idiot in front of Lacey, too. He didn't like how this was going at all.

Lester picked up a screwdriver. "You see this? It's a tool. You can pick it up and you can unscrew stuff or screw stuff in. You can use the handle for a hammer. You can use the blade to open paint cans. You can throw it away, loan it out, or paint it purple and frame it." He thumped the printer. "This thing is a tool, too, but it's not *your* tool. It belongs to someone else—Disney. It isn't interested in listening to you or obeying you. It doesn't want to give you more control over your life.

"This thing reminds me of life before fatkins. It was my very own personal body, but it wasn't under my control. What's the word the academics use? 'Agency.' I didn't have any agency. It didn't matter what I did, I was just this fat thing that my brain had to lug around behind it, listening to its never-ending complaints and aches and pains.

"If you don't control your life, you're miserable. Think of the people who don't get to run their own lives: prisoners, reform-school kids, mental patients. There's something inherently awful about living like that. Autonomy makes us happy."

He thumped the top of the printer again. "So here's this stupid thing, which Disney gives you for free. It looks like a tool, like a thing that you use to better your life, but in reality, it's a tool that Disney uses to control your life. You can't program it. You can't change the channel. It doesn't even have an *off switch*. That's what gets me exercised. I want to redesign this thing so it gets converted from something that controls to something that gives you control."

Lester's eyes shone. Death hurt from head to toe, from the climb and the aftermath of the beating, and the life he'd lived. Lester was telling him that the ride wasn't important to him anymore, that he'd be doing this other thing with the printer next, and then something else, and then something else. He felt a great, unexpected upwelling of bitterness at the thought.

"So what about the ride?"

"The ride? I told you. I'm done with it. It's time to do the next thing. You said you wanted to help out, right?"

"With the ride," Death said patiently, with the manner of someone talking to a child.

Lester turned his back on Death.

"I'm done with the ride," Lester said. "I don't want to waste your time." It was clear he meant, *You're wasting my time.* He bent over the printer.

Lacey looked daggers at his shoulders, then turned to help Death down the stairs. His canes clattered on the narrow staircase, and it was all he could do to keep from crying.

Suzanne rode the bullet train from Miami airport in air-conditioned amusement, watching the Mickey-shaped hang-straps rock back and forth. She'd bought herself a Mickey waffle and a bucket-sized Diet Coke in the dining car and fended off the offers of plush animatronic toys that were clearly descended from Boogie Woogie Elmo.

Now she watched the kids tear ass up and down the train, or sit mesmerized by the videos and interactives set up at the ends of the cars. The train was really slick, and judging from the brochure she found in the seat pocket, there was another one from the Orlando airport. These things were like chutes leading from the luggage carousel straight into the parks. Disney had figured out how to make sure that every penny spent by its tourists went straight into its coffers.

The voice-over announcements as they pulled into the station were in English, Chinese, Spanish, Farsi, and Russian—in that order—and displayed on the porters' red coats with brass buttons were name badges with the flags of many nations, denoting the languages they spoke. They wore mouse ears, and Suzanne—a veteran of innumerable hotels—could not dissuade one from taking her suitcase.

He brought her to a coach station and saw her aboard a bus marked for the Polynesian, decorated with tiki lamps, bamboo, and palm fronds (she touched one and discovered that it was vinyl). He refused her tip as they saw her aboard, and then stood and waved her off with his white gloves and giant white smile. She had to chuckle as she pulled away, amazed at how effective these little touches were. She felt her muscles loosening, little involuntary chuckles rising in her throat. The coach was full of parents and children from all over the world, grinning and laughing and hugging and talking excitedly about the day ahead of them.

The coach let them off to a group of Hawaiian-shirt-clad staff who shouted "Aloha!" at them as they debarked, and picked up their luggage with swift, cheerful, relentless efficiency. Her check-in was so painless she wasn't sure it was over until a nice young lady who looked Chechen picked up her bag for her and urged her out to the grounds, which were green and lush, like nothing she'd seen since landing in Florida. She was surrounded by the hotel structures, longhouses decorated with Polynesian masks and stalked by leggy ibises and chirping tropical birds. Before her was a white sand beach fronting an artificial lake ringed with other luxury hotels: a gigantic 1970s Soviet A-frame building and a gingerbread-choked Victorian hotel. The lake was ringed with a monorail track and plied by handsome paddle-wheel ferryboats.

She stared gape-jawed at this until the bellhop gently tugged at her elbow, giving her a dazzling smile.

Her room was the kind of thing you'd see Lucy and Ricky checking in to on their honeymoon in an old *I Love Lucy* episode—wicker ceiling fans, bamboo furniture, a huge hot tub shaped like a seashell. Outside, a little terrace looking over the lake, with a pair of cockatoos looking quizzically at her. The bellhop waved at them and they cawed at her and flew off. Suzanne must have made a disappointed noise, because the bellhop patted her on the arm and said, "Don't worry, we feed them here; they come back all the time. Greedy birdies!"

She tipped the bellhop five bucks once she'd been given the grand tour of the room—a tame Internet connection that was "kid-friendly" and a likewise censored video-on-demand service, delivery pizza or sushi, information on park hours, including the dazzling array of extras she could purchase. It turned out that resort guests were eligible to purchase priority passes for boarding rides ahead of the plebes, and for entering parks early and staying late. This made Suzanne feel right at home—it was very Russian in its approach: the more you spent, the better your time was.

She bought it all: all the fast passes and priority cards, all of it loaded into a grinning Mickey on a lanyard, a wireless pendant that would take care of her everywhere she went in the park, letting her spend money like water.

Thus girded, she consulted with her bellhop some more and laid out an itinerary. Once she'd showered she found she didn't want to wear any of her European tailored shorts and blouses. She wanted to disappear into the Great American Mass. The hotel gift shop provided her with a barkcloth Hawaiian shirt decorated with tessellated Disney trademarks and a big pair of loose shorts, and once she donned them, she saw that she could be anyone now, any tourist in the park. A pair of cheap sunglasses completed the look and she paid for it all by waving her Mickey necklace at the register, spending money like water.

She passed the rest of the day at the Magic Kingdom, taking a ferry from the hotel's pier to the Victorian wrought-iron docks on the other side of the little artificial lake. As she cleared the turnstiles into Main Street, USA, her heart quickened. Kids rushed past her, chased by their parents' laughing calls to slow down. Balloon sellers and old-fashioned popcorn machines jostled for space in the crowd, and a brass band was marching down the street in straw boaters and red striped jackets, playing a Sousa march.

She ambled up the road, peering in the adorable little shop windows, like the shops in a fancy casino, all themed artificial facades that were, in back, all one shop, linked through the length of the street.

She reached the castle before she realized it, and saw that it was shorter than it had appeared. Turning around and looking back down Main Street, she saw that the trees lining the sides of the street had been trimmed so they got progressively larger from the gates to the castle, creating a kind of false perspective line. She laughed now, amused by the accomplishment of the little trompe l'oeil.

She squeezed past the hordes of Asian tourists taking precisely the same picture of the castle, one after another, a phenomenon she'd observed at other famous landmarks. For some Japanese shutterbugs, the holiday photo experience was as formal as the Stations of the Cross, with each picture of each landmark rigidly prescribed by custom and unwritten law.

Now she was under the castle and headed for what her map assured her was Fantasyland. Just as she cleared the archway, she remembered her conversations with that Death Waits kid about Fantasyland: this was the part that had been made over as a goth area, and then remade as the Happiest Construction Site on Earth.

And so it was. The contrast was stark. From fairy castle to green-painted construction sidings. From smiling, well turned out "castmembers" to construction workers with butt-crack-itis and grouchy expressions. Fantasyland was like an ugly scar on the blemish-free face of a barbie doll.

She liked it.

Something about all that artifice, all that cunning work to cover up all the bodies a company like Disney would have buried under its manicured Main Street—it had given her a low-level, tooth-grinding headache, a kind of anger at the falseness of it all. Here, she could see the bodies as they buried them.

Out came her camera and she went on the prowl, photographing and photographing, seeking high ground from which to catch snaps over the siding. She'd look at the satellite pics of this spot later.

Now she knew what her next project would be: she would document this scar. She'd dig up the bodies.

Just for completeness's sake, she went on some of the rides. Her superfancy pass let her sail past the long lines of bored kids, angry dads, exhausted moms. She captured their expressions with her camera.

The rides were all right. She was sick of rides, truth be told. As an art form, they were wildly overrated. Some of them made her sick and some of them were like mildly interesting trips through someone's collection of action figures in a dark room. The Disney rides didn't even let you drive, like Lester's ride did, and you didn't get to vote on them.

By the time the sun had gone down, she was ready to go back to the room and start writing. She wanted to get all this down, the beauty and the terror, the commerce lurking underneath the friendly facade. As the day lengthened into night, there were more and more screaming children, more angry parents. She caught parents smacking kids, once, twice, got her camera out, caught three more.

They sent a big pupu platter up to her room with a dish of poi and a hollow pineapple filled with rum. She took her computer out onto her lanai and looked out over the lake. An ibis came by and demanded some of her dinner scraps. She obliged it and it gave her a cold look, as if determining whether she'd be good for dessert, then flew off.

She began to write.

Something had changed between Kettlewell and Eva since they'd left Florida with the kids. It wasn't just the legal hassles, though there were plenty of those. They'd gone to Florida with a second chance—a chance for him to be a mover again, a chance for her to have a husband who was happy with his life again.

Now he found himself sneaking past her when she was in the living room, and they slept back to back in bed with as much room between them as possible.

Ada missed Lyenitchka and spent all her time in her bedroom IMing her friend or going questing with her in their favorite game, which involved barbies, balrogs, and buying outfits. Pascal missed all the attention he had received as the designated mascot of the two little girls.

It was not a high point in the history of the Kettlewell clan.

"Hello?"

"Landon Kettlewell?"

"Hello, Freddy," he said.

"My fame precedes me," the journalist said. Kettlewell could hear the grin in his voice. That voice was unmistakable—Kettlewell had heard it in the occassional harassing voicemail that Suzanne forwarded on.

"How are you?"

"Oh, I'm very well, sir, and kind of you to ask, yes indeed. I hear you're not doing so well, though?"

"I can't complain."

"I wish you would, though." You could tell, Freddy thought he was a funny son of a bitch. "Seriously, Mr. Kettlewell. I'm calling to follow up on the story of the litigation that Perry Gibbons and Lester Banks are facing for unilaterally canceling the arrangement you'd made to finance their litigation. I'm hoping that you'll give me a quote that might put this into perspective. Is the defense off? Will Gibbons and Banks be sued? Are you a party to the suit?"

"Freddy?"

"Yes, Mr. Kettlewell."

"I am not a child, nor am I a fool, nor am I a sucker. I'm also not a hothead. You can't goad me into saying something. You can't trick me into saying something. I haven't hung up on you yet, but I will unless you can give me a single good reason to believe that any good could possibly come out of talking to you."

"I'm going to write this story and publish it today. I can either write that you declined to comment or I can write down whatever comment you might have on the matter. You tell me which is fairer?"

"Goodbye, Freddy."

"Wait, wait! Just wait."

Kettlewell liked the pleading note in Freddy's voice.

"What is it, Freddy?"

"Can I get you to comment on the general idea of litigation investment? A lot of people followed your lead in seeking out litigation investment opportunities. There's lots of money tied up in it these days. Do incidents like the one in Florida mean that litigation investment is a dead strategy?"

"Of course not," Kettlewell snapped. He shouldn't be talking to this man, but the question drove him bonkers. He'd invented litigation investment. "Those big old companies have two common characteristics: they've accumulated more assets than they know what to do with, and they've got poisonous, monopolistic cultures that reward executives who break the law to help the company turn a buck. None of that's changed, and so long as that's all true, there will be little companies with legit gripes against big companies that can be used as investment vehicles for unlocking all that dead Fortune 100 capital and putting it to work."

"But aren't Fortune 100 companies investing in litigation funds?"

Kettlewell suppressed a nasty laugh. "Yeah, so what?"

"Well, if this is about destroying Fortune 100 companies—"

"It's about wringing positive social value out of the courts and out of investment. The way it used to work, there were only two possible outcomes when a big company did something rotten: either they'd get away scot-free or they'd make some lawyers very, very rich. Litigation funds fix that. They socialize the cost of bringing big companies to heel, and they free up the capital that these big companies have accumulated."

"But when a big company invests in destroying another big company—"

"Sometimes you get a forest where a few trees end up winning; they form a canopy that keeps all the sunlight from reaching the floor. Now, this is stable for forests, but stability is the *last* thing you want in a market. Just look at what happens when one of those big trees falls over: whoosh! A million kinds of life are spawned on the floor, fighting for the light that tree had hogged for itself. In a market, when you topple a company that's come to complacently control some part of the ecosystem, you free up that niche for new innovators."

"And why is that better than stability? Don't the workers at these companies deserve the security that comes from their employers' survival?"

"Oh come on, Freddy. Stop beating that drum. If you're an employee and you want to get a good deal out of an employer, you're better off if you've got fifty companies you could work for than just one."

"So you're saying that if you destroy Disney with your lawsuit, the fifty thousand people who work at Walt Disney World will be able to, what, work for those little rides like your friends have built?"

"They'll find lots of work, Freddy. If we make it possible for anyone to open an innovative little ride without worrying about getting clobbered by a big old monopolist. You like big corporations so much?"

"Yes, but it's not little innovative startups that invest in these funds, is it?"

"It's they who benefit once the fund takes up their cause."

"And how's that working out for the ride people you're meant to be helping out? They rejected you, didn't they?"

Kettlewell really hated Freddy, he realized. Not just a little—he had a deep and genuine loathing. "Oh, for fuck's sake. You don't like little companies. You don't like big companies. You don't like workers' co-ops. What do you want us to do, Freddy? You want us to just curl up under a rock and die? You sit there and make up your funny names for things, you make your snarky little commentaries, but how much good have *you* done for the world, you complaining, sniping little troll?"

The line got very quiet. "Can I quote you?"

"You certainly can," Kettlewell huffed. In for a penny, in for a pound. "You can print that, and you can kiss my ass."

"Thank you, Mr. Kettlewell," Freddy said. "I'll certainly take the suggestion under advisement."

Kettlewell stood in his home office and stared at the four walls. Upstairs, Pascal was crying. He did that a lot lately. Kettlewell breathed deeply and tried to chill out.

Someone was knocking at his door, though. He answered it tentatively. The kid he found there was well scrubbed, black, in his twenties, and smiling amiably.

"Landon Kettlewell?"

"Who's suing me?" Kettlewell could spot a process server a mile away.

The guy shrugged and made a little you-got-me smile. "Couldn't say, sir," he said, and handed Kettlewell the envelope, holding it so that the header was clearly visible to the camera set into the lapel of his shirt.

"You want me to sign something?" Kettlewell said.

"It's all right, sir," the kid said and pointed at the camera. "It's all caught on video."

"Oh, right," Kettlewell said. "Want a cup of water? Coffee?"

"I expect you're going to be too busy to entertain, sir," the kid said, and ticked a little salute off his forehead. "But you seem like a nice guy. Good luck with it all."

Kettlewell watched him go, then closed the door and walked back to his office, opening the envelope and scanning it. No surprises there—the shareholders in the investment syndicate that had backed Lester and Perry were suing him for making false representations about his ability to speak for them.

Tjan called him a minute later.

"They got you too, huh?" Kettlewell said.

"Just left. Wish I could say it was unexpected."

"Wish I could say I blamed them," Kettlewell said.

"Hey, you should see what the ride's been doing this week since Florida went down," Tjan said. "It's totally mutated. I think it's mostly coming from the Midwest, though those Brazilians seem to keep on logging in somehow, too."

"How many rides are there in South America, anyways?"

"Brazilians of them!" Tjan said with a mirthless chuckle. "Impossible to say. They've got some kind of variant on the protocol that lets a bunch of them share one network address. I think some of them aren't even physical rides, just virtual flythroughs. Some are directly linked; some do a kind of mash-up between their current norms and other rides' current norms. It's pretty weird."

Kettlewell paced. "Well, at least someone's having a good time."

"They're going to nail us to the wall," Tjan said. "Both of us. Probably the individual ride operators, too. They're out for blood."

"It's not like they even lost much money."

"They didn't need to—they feel like they lost the money they might have won from Disney."

"But that was twenty years away, and highly speculative."

Tjan sighed heavily on the other end of the phone. "Landon, you're a very, very good finance person. The best I've ever met, but you really need to understand that even the most speculative investor is mostly speculating about how he's going to spend all the money you're about to make him. If investors didn't count their chickens before they hatched, you'd never raise a cent."

"Yeah," Kettlewell said. He knew it, but he couldn't soak it in. He'd won and lost so many fortunes—his own and others'—that he'd learned to take it all in stride. Not everyone else was so sanguine.

"So what do we do about it? I don't much want to lose everything."

"You could always go back to Russia," Kettlewell said, suddenly feeling short-tempered. Why did he always have to come up with the plan? "Sorry. You know what the lawyers are going to tell us."

"Yeah. Sue Perry and Lester."

"And we told Lester we wouldn't do that. It was probably a mistake to do this at all, you know."

"No, don't say that. The idea was a really good one. You might have saved their asses if they'd played along."

"And if I'd kept the lawyers on a shorter leash."

They both sat in glum silence.

"How about if we defend ourselves by producing evidence that they re-neged on a deal we'd made in good faith? Then the bastards can sue Perry and Lester and we'll still be keeping our promise."

Kettlewell tried to picture Perry in a courtroom. He'd never been the most even-keeled dude, and since he'd been shot and had his arm broken and been gassed, he was almost pathological.

"I've got a better idea," he said, growing excited as it unfolded in his mind. He had that burning sensation he got sometimes when he knew he was having a real doozy. "How about if we approach each of the individual ride co-ops and see if they'll join the lawsuit separately from the umbrella org? Play it right and we'll have the lawsuit back on, without having to get our asses handed to us and without having to destroy Perry and Lester!"

Tjan laughed. "That's—that's . . . Wow! Genius. Yeah, OK, right! The Boston group is in, I'll tell you that much. I'm sure we can get half a dozen more in, too. Especially if we can get Perry to agree not to block it, which I'm sure he'll do after I have a little talk with him. This'll work!"

"Sometimes the threat of total legal destruction can have a wonderful, clarifying effect on one's mind," Kettlewell said drily. "How're the kids?"

"Lyenitchka is in a sulk. She wants to go back to Florida and she wants to see Ada some more. Plus she's upset that we never made it to Disney World."

Kettlewell flopped down on his couch. "Have you seen Suzanne's blog lately?"

Tjan laughed. "Yeah. Man, she's giving it to them with both barrels. Makes me feel sorry for 'em."

"Um, you *do* know that we're suing them for everything they've got, right?"

"Well, yes. But that's just money. Suzanne's going to take their balls."

They exchanged some more niceties and promised that they'd get to-gether face-to-face real soon and Kettlewell hung up. From behind him, he heard someone fidgeting.

"Kids, you know you aren't supposed to come into my office."

"Sounds like things have gotten started up again." It wasn't the kids, it was Eva. He sat up. She was standing with her arms folded in the doorway of his office, staring at him.

"Yeah," he said, mumbling a little. She was really beautiful, his wife, and she put up with a hell of a lot. He felt obscurely ashamed of the way that he'd treated her. He wished he could stand up and give her a warm hug. He couldn't.

Instead, she sat beside him. "Sounds like you'll be busy."

"Oh, I just need to get all the individual co-ops on board, talk to the lawyers, get the investors off my back. Have a shareholders' meeting. It'll be fine."

Her smile was little and sad. "I'm going, Landon," she said.

The blood drained from his face. She'd left him plenty, over the years. He'd deserved it. But it had always been white-hot, in the middle of a fight, and it had always ended with some kind of reconciliation. This time, it had the feeling of something planned and executed in cold blood.

He sat up and folded his hands in his lap. He didn't know what else to do.

Her smile wilted. "It's not going to work, you and me. I can't live like this, lurching from crisis to crisis. I love you too much to watch that happen. I hate what it turns me into. You're only happy when you're miserable, you know that? I can't do that forever. We'll be part of each other's lives forever, but I can't be Mrs. Stressbunny forever."

None of this was new. She'd shouted variations on this at him at many times in their relationship. The difference was that now she wasn't shouting. She was calm, assured, sad but not crying. Behind her in the hallway, he saw that she'd packed her suitcase, and the little suitcases the kids used when they traveled together.

"Where will you go?"

"I'm going to stay with Lucy, from college. She's living down the peninsula in Mountain View. She's got room for the kids."

He felt like raging at her, promising her a bitter divorce and custody suit, but he couldn't do it. She was completely right, after all. Even though his first impulse was to argue, he couldn't do it just then.

So she left, and Kettlewell was alone in his nice apartment with his phone and his computer and his lawsuits and his mind fizzing with ideas.

The last thing Sammy wanted was a fight. Dinah's promo was making major bank for the company—and he was taking more and more meetings in Texas with Dinah, which was a hell of a perk. They'd shipped two million of the DiaBs, and were projecting ten million in the first quarter. Park admission was soaring and the revenue from the advertising was going to cover the entire cost of the next rev of the DiaBs, which would be better, faster, smaller, and cheaper.

That business with Death Waits and the new Fantasyland and the ride—what did it matter now? He'd been so focused on the details that he'd lost track of the big picture. Walt Disney had made his empire by figuring out how to do the next thing, not wasting his energy on how to protect the last thing. It had all been a mistake, a dumb mistake, and now he was back on track. From all appearances, the lawsuits were on the verge of blowing away anyway. Fantasyland—he'd turned that over to Wiener, of all people, and he was actually doing some good stuff there. Really running with the idea of restoring it as a nostalgia site aimed squarely at fatkins, with lots of food and romantic kiddie rides that no kid would want to ride in the age of the break-neck coaster.

The last thing he wanted was a fight. What he wanted was to make ass-loads of money for the company, remake himself as a power in the organization.

But he was about to have a fight.

Hackelberg came into his office unannounced. Sammy had some of the Imagineers in, showing him prototypes of the next model, which was being designed for more reliable shipping and easier packing. Hackelberg was carrying his cane today, wearing his ice cream suit, and was flushed a deep, angry red that seemed to boil up from his collar.

One look from his blazing eyes was enough to send the Imagineers scurrying. They didn't even take their prototype with them. Hackelberg closed the door behind them.

"Hello, Samuel," he said.

"Nice to see you. Can I offer you a glass of water? Iced tea?"

Hackelberg waved the offers away. "They're using your boxes to print their own designs," he said.

"What?"

"Those freaks with their homemade ride. They've just published a system for printing their own objects on your boxes."

Sammy rewound the conversations he'd had with the infosec people in Imagineering about what countermeasures they'd come up with, what they were proof against. He was pissed that he was finding out about this from Hackelberg. If Lester and Perry were hacking the DiaBs, they would be talking about it nonstop, running their mouths on the Internet. Back when he was his own competitive intelligence specialist, he would have known about this project the second it began. Now he was trying to find a competitive intelligence person who knew his ass from his elbow, so far without success.

"Well, that's regrettable, obviously, but so long as we're still selling the consumables . . ." The goop was a huge profit-maker for the company. They bought it in bulk, added a proprietary, precisely mixed chemical that the printer could check for in its hoppers, and sold it to the DiaB users for a 2,000 percent markup. If you tried to substitute a competitor's goop, the machine would reject it. They shipped out new DiaBs with only half a load of goop, so that the first purchase would come fast. It was making more money, week on week, than popcorn.

"The crack they're distributing also disables the checking for the water-mark. You can use any generic goop in them."

Sammy shook his head and restrained himself from thumping his hand down on the desk. He wanted to scream.

"We're not suing them, are we?"

"Do you think that's wise, Samuel?"

"I'm no legal expert. You tell me. Maybe we can take stronger counter-measures with the next generation—" He gestured at the prototype on his desk.

"And abandon the two million units we've shipped to date?"

Sammy thought about it. Those families might hang on to their original two million forever, or until they wore out. Maybe he should be building them to fall apart after six months of use, to force updates.

"It's just so unfair. They're ripping us off. We spent the money on those units so that we could send our message out. What the hell is wrong with those people? Are they compulsive? Do they *have* to destroy every money-making business?"

Hackelberg sat back. "Samuel, I think it's time we dealt with them."

Sammy's mind was still off on the strategies for keeping Lester and Perry at bay, though. Sure, a six-month obsolescence curve would do it. Or they could just charge money for the DiaBs, now that people were starting to understand what they were for. Hell, they could just make the most compelling stuff for a DiaB to print and maybe that would be enough.

Hackelberg tapped the tip of his cane once, sharply. Sammy came back to the conversation. "So that's settled. Filing suit today. We're going to do a discovery on them that'll split them open from asshole to throat. No more of this chickenshit police stuff—we're going to figure out every source of income these bastards have; we're going to take away their computers; we're going down to their ISPs and getting their emails and instant messages.

"And as we've seen, they're going to retaliate. That's fine. We're not treating these people as a couple of punk pirates who go down at the first sign of trouble. Not anymore. We know that these people are the competition. We're going to make an example of them. They're the first ones to attack on this front, but they won't be the last. We're vulnerable, Samuel, but we can contain that vulnerability with enough deterrent."

Hackelberg seemed to be expecting something of Sammy, but Sammy was damned if he knew what it was. "OK," he said lamely.

Hackelberg's smile was like a jack-o'-lantern's. "That means that we've got to be prepared for their discovery on *us*. I need to know every single detail of this DiaB project, including the things I'd find if I went through your phone records and your email. Because they *will* be going through them. They'll be putting you and your operation under the microscope."

Sammy restrained his groan. "I'll have it for you," he said. "Give me a day or two."

He saw Hackelberg out of his office as quickly as he could, then shut the door. Hackelberg wanted everything, and that meant *everything*, including his playmates from the advertising industry—everything. He was becoming the kind of executive who emitted strategic intelligence, rather than the kind who gathered it. That wouldn't do. That wasn't the natural order of things.

He sat down at his computer. Someone had to do the competitive intelligence work around here and it looked like it would have to be him.

What the World Can Learn from Disney
Suzanne Church

It's easy to dismiss Disney. They make more lawsuits than rides these days. They have a reputation for Pollyannaish chirpiness. Their corporate communications veer from Corporate Passive Voice Third Person to a syrupy, condescending kiddie-speak that's calculated to drive children into a frenzy of parent-nagging screeches.

But if you haven't been to a Disney park in a while, you don't know what you're missing. I've been in Walt Disney World for a week now, and I'm here to tell you, it's pretty good. No, it's better than that—it's *amazing*.

You've probably heard about the attention to detail: the roofline over Fantasyland features sagging Georgian tiles, crazy chimneys, and subtly animated gargoyles (left over from a previous, goth-ier incarnation of this part of the park). You don't see this unless you raise your eyes above the busy, intriguing facades that front the rides, above the masterfully painted signage, and higher still. In other words, unless you're someone like me, looking for details, you won't spot them. They're there as pure gold plating; they're there because someone who took pride in his work *put them there*.

It tells you something about the people behind the scenes here. People who care about their jobs work here. It's easy to forget that when you're thinking about Disney, a company whose reputation these days has more to do with whom they sue than with what they make.

But oh, what they make. There's a safari park here, something like a zoo but without that stuff that makes you feel like you're participating in some terrible exercise that strips noble animals of their dignity for our amusement. Instead, the animals here roam free, near their hairless monkey cousins, separated from them by water features, camouflaged ditches, simulated ancient ruins **more details**.

That's just one of six parks, each subdivided into six or seven "lands," each land with its own unique charm, culture, and customs. That's not counting the outlying areas: two new towns, golf courses, a velodrome, a preserved marshland that you can tour in a skiff with a local naturist. In these days of cheap fabrication, it's easy to forget what you can do with several billion dollars and the kind of hubris that leads you to dredge lakes, erect papier-mâché mountains, and create your own toy mass-transit system.

Of course, Disney Parks are no strangers to small scale fabrication. See their tiny, clever Disney-in-a-Box devices, which I have chronicled here from the other side. On the one hand, these things are networked volumetric printers, but on the other, they are superb category-busters that have achieved an entirely justifiable—yet still staggering—market penetration in just a few months.

I came here ready to be bored and disgusted and fleeced of every nickel. I am disappointed. The parks are tremendous at separating people from money, it's true. They've structured each promenade and stroll so that even a walk to the bathroom can create a "Mommy, Daddy, Want It NOW!" situation. For such a happy place, there certainly are a lot of weepy children and frustrated parents.

But it's hard to fault Disney for being a business that makes a lot of money. That's the point, after all. And it can't be cheap to keep the tens of thousands of "castmembers" (yes, they really do call them that, even when they're earning minimum wage and work jobs with all the glamour of a bathroom attendant) hanging around, picking up litter and confronting every new "guest" with eerily convincing cheer.

As for "bored" and "disgusted"—not yet. Bored—it's impossible to imagine such a thing. For starters, the world's middle classes have converged here in a sort of bourgeois UN, and you can get a lot of pleasure out of watching a Chinese "little emperor" with doting parents in tow making friends with a tiny perfect Russian mafiyeh princess whose parents flick nervously at their nicotine inhalers and scout the building facades for hidden cameras.

Of course, if people-watching isn't your thing, there are the rides themselves, which make art out of the shoe-box diorama. There are luaus, indoor scuba diving with live sharks, and an island of genuinely sleazy nightclubs where you can get propositioned for some improbable acts that are hardly family-friendly. These last appear to be largely populated by the "castmembers" seeking a little after-work action.

Disgusted? I think if I were a parent, there'd be parts of the experience that drove me nuts. But once you get to know the rhythm of the place, you start to see that there are navigable pathways that don't lead through any commercial areas—fantastic adventure playgrounds, nature hikes, petting zoos, horseback rides, sports training. And for every kid who's having a blood-sugar meltdown after consuming half a quart of high-fructose lube slathered on a cinnamon bun, there's another who is standing open-mouthed with complete bodily wonder at some stupendous spectacle, clearly forming neuronal connections of a sort that will create the permanent predisposition to an appreciation of spectacle, wonder and beauty.

This is the kind of place where you have to love the sin and hate the sinner. The company may sue and resort to dirty tricks, but it's also chock-full of real artists making real art.

If you haven't been for a visit, you should. Honestly. Oh, by all means, also go somewhere unspoiled (if you can find it). Go camping. Go to one of the rides I've written so much about. But if you want to see the bright side of what billions can do—the stuff you never get from outside the walls of this fortress of fun—buy a ticket.

The barman at Suzanne's hotel started building her a Lapu Lapu as she came up the stairs. The drink involved a hollow pineapple, overproof rum, and an umbrella, and she'd concluded that it contained the perfect dosage of liquid CNS depressant to unwind her after a day of battle at the parks. That day she'd spent following around the troupes of role-playing actors at Disney's Hollywood Studios: a cast of a hundred costumed players who acted out a series of interlocking comedies set in the black-and-white days of Hollywood. They were fearlessly cheeky, grabbing audience members and conscripting them into their plays.

Now she was footsore and there was still a nighttime at Epcot in her future. The barman passed her the pineapple and she thumped her lanyard against the bar twice—once to pay for the drink and once to give him a generous tip. He was gay as a goose, but fun to look at, and he flirted with her for kicks.

"Gentleman caller for you, Suzanne," he said, tilting his head. "You temptress."

She looked in the direction indicated and took in the man sitting on the bar stool. He didn't have the look of a harried dad and he was too old to be a love-flushed honeymooner. In sensible tropical-weight slacks and a western shirt, he was impossible to place. He smiled and gave her a little wave.

"What?"

"He came in an hour ago and asked for you."

She looked back at the man. "What's your take on him?"

"I think he works here. He didn't pay with an employee card, but he acted like it."

"OK," she said, "send out a search party if I'm not back in an hour."

"Go get him, tiger," the barman said, giving her hand a squeeze.

She carried her pineapple with her and drifted down the bar.

"Hello there," she said.

"Ms. Church," the man said. He had a disarming, confident smile. "My name is Sammy Page."

She knew the name, of course. The face, too, now that she thought about it. He offered her his hand. She didn't take it. He put it down, then wiped it on his trouser leg.

"Are you having a good time?"

"A lovely time, thank you." She sipped her drink and wished it was a little more serious and intimidating. It's hard to do frosty when you're holding a rum-filled pineapple with a paper parasol.

His smile faltered. "I read your article. I can't believe I missed it. I mean, you've been here for six days and I just figured it out today? I'm a pretty incompetent villain."

She let a little smile slip out at that. "Well, it's a big Internet."

"But I *love* your stuff. I've been reading it since, well, back when I lived in the Valley. I used to get the *Merc* actually delivered on paper."

"You are a walking fossil, aren't you?"

He bobbed his head. "So it comes down to this. I've been very distracted with making things besides lawsuits lately, as you know. I've been putting my energy into doing stuff, not preventing stuff. It's been refreshing."

She grubbed in her pocket and came up with a little steno book and a pencil. "Do you mind if I take notes?"

He gulped. "Can this all be on background?"

She hefted her notebook. "No," she said finally. "If there's anything that needs publishing, I'm going to have to publish it. I can respect the fact that you're speaking to me with candor, but frankly, Mr. Page, you haven't earned the privilege of speaking on background."

He sipped at his drink—a more grown-up highball, with a lone ice cube in it, maybe a Scotch and soda. "OK, right. Well, then, on the record, but candorously. I loved your article. I love your work in general. I'm really glad to have you here, because I think we make great stuff and we're making more of it than ever. Your latest post was right on the money—we care about our work here. That's how we got to where we are."

"But you devote a lot of your resources to other projects here, don't you? I've heard about you, Mr. Page. I've interviewed Death Waits." He winced and she scribbled a note, leaving him on tenterhooks while she wrote. Something cold and angry had hold of her writing arm. "I've interviewed him and heard what he has to say about this place, what you have done."

"My hands aren't the cleanest," he said. "But I'm trying to atone." He swallowed. The barman was looking at them. "Look, can I take you for a walk, maybe? Someplace more private?"

She thought about it. "Let me get changed," she said. "Meet you in the lobby in ten."

She swapped her tennis shoes for walking sandals and put on a clean shirt and long slacks, then draped a scarf over her shoulders like a shawl. Outside, the sunset was painting the lagoon bloody. She was just about to rush back down to the lobby when she stopped and called Lester, her fingers moving of their own volition.

"Hey, you," he said. "Still having fun in Mauschwitz?"

"It keeps getting weirder here, let me tell you," she said. She told him about Sammy showing up, wanting to talk with her.

"Ooh, I'm jealous," Lester said. "He's my archrival, after all."

"I hadn't thought of it that way. He *is* kind of cute—"

"Hey!"

"In a slimy, sharky way. Don't worry, Lester. I miss you, you know?"

"Really?"

"Really. I think I'm about done here. I'm going to come home soon."

There was a long pause, then a snuffling sound. She realized he was crying. He slurped. "Sorry. That's great, babe. I missed you."

"I—I missed you, too. Listen, I've got to go meet this guy."

"Go, go. Call me after dinner and tell me how it goes. Meanwhile, I'm going to go violate the DiaB some more."

"Channel it—that's right."

"Right on."

Sammy met her in the lobby. "I thought we could go for a walk around the lake," he said. "There's a trail that goes all the way around. It's pretty private."

She looked at the lake. At twelve o'clock, the main gates of the Magic Kingdom; at three, the retro A-frame Contemporary hotel; at nine, the wedding-cake Grand Floridian Resort.

"Lead on," she said. He led her out onto the artificial white-sand beach and around, and a moment later they were on a pathway paved with octagonal tiles, each engraved with the name of a family and a year.

"I really liked your article."

"You said that."

They walked a while longer. "It reminded me of why I came here. I worked for startups, and they were fun, but they were ephemeral. No one expected something on the Web to last for half a century. Maybe the brand survives, but who knows? I mean, who remembers Yahoo! anymore? But for sure, anything you built then would be gone in a year or two, a decade tops.

"But here . . ." He waved his hands. They were coming around the bend for the Contemporary now, and she could see it in all its absurd glory. It had been kept up so that it looked like it might have been erected yesterday, but the towering white A-frame structure with the monorail running through its midriff was clearly of another era. It was like a museum piece, or a bit of artillery on the field at a Civil War reenactment.

"I see."

"It's about the grandiosity, the permanence. The belief in doing something—anything—that will endure."

"You didn't need to bring me someplace private to tell me that."

"No, I didn't." He swallowed. "It's hard because I want to tell you something that will compromise me if I say it."

"And I won't let you off the hook by promising to keep it confidential."

"Exactly."

"Well, you're on the horns of a dilemma then, aren't you?" The sun was nearly set now, and stones at their feet glittered from beneath, sprinkled with twinkling lights. It made the evening, scented with tropical flowers and the clean smell of the lake, even more lovely. A cool breeze fluffed her hair.

He groaned. She had to admit it, she was enjoying this. Was it any less than this man deserved?

"Let me try this again. I have some information that, if I pass it on to you, could save your friends down in Hollywood from terrible harm. I can only give you this information on the condition that you take great pains to keep me from being identified as the source."

They'd come to the Magic Kingdom now. Behind them, the main gates loomed, and a pufferbelly choo-choo train blew its whistle as it pulled out of the station. Happy, exhausted children ran across the plaza, heading for the ferry docks and the monorail ramps. The stones beneath her feet glittered with rainbow light, and tropical birds called to each other from the Pirates of the Caribbean Adventure Island in the middle of the lake.

"Hum," she said. The families laughed and jostled each other. "Hum. OK, one time only. This one is off the record."

Sammy looked around nervously. "Keep walking," he said. "Let's get past here and back into the private spots."

But it's the crowds that put me in a generous mood. She didn't say it. She'd give him this one. What harm could it do? If it was something she had to publish, she could get it from another source.

"They're going to sue your friends."

"So what else is new?"

"No, personally. They're going to the mattresses. Every trumped-up charge they can think of. But the point here isn't to get the cops to raid them, it's to serve discovery on every single communication, every document, every file. Open up everything. Root through every email until they find something to hang them with."

"You say 'they'—aren't *you* 'they'?"

It was too dark to see his face now, but she could tell the question made him uncomfortable.

"No. Not anymore." He swallowed and looked out at the lake. "Look, I'm doing something now—something . . . *amazing*. The DiaB, it's breaking new ground. We're putting three-D printers into every house in America. What your friend Lester is doing, it's actually *helping* us. We're inventing a whole new—"

"Business?"

"No, not just a business. A world. It's what the New Work was missing—a three-D printer in every living room. A killer app. There were personal computers and geeks for years before the spreadsheet came along. Then there was a reason to put one in every house. Then we got the Internet, the whole software industry. A new world. That's where we're headed. It's all I want to do. I don't want to spend the rest of my life suing people. I want to *do stuff.*"

He kicked at the rushes that grew beside the trail. "I want to be remembered for that. I want *that* to be my place in the history books—not a bunch of lawsuits."

Suzanne walked along beside him in silence for a time. "OK, so what do you want me to do about it?"

"I thought that if—" He shut up. "Look, I tried this once before. I told that Freddy bastard everything in the hopes that he'd come onto my side and help me out. He screwed me. I'm not saying you're Freddy, but—"

Suzanne stopped walking. "What do you want from me, sir? You have hardly been a friend to me and mine. It's true that you've made something very fine, but it's also true that you helped sabotage something every bit as fine. You're painting yourself as the victim of some mysterious 'them.' But as near as I can work out, the only difference between you and 'them' is that you're having a little disagreement with them. I don't like to be used as part of your corporate head games and power struggles."

"Fine," he said. "Fine. I deserve that. I deserve no better. Fine. Well, I tried."

Suzanne refused to soften. Grown men sulking did not inspire any sympathy in her. Whatever he wanted to tell her, it wasn't worth going into his debt.

He gave a shuddering sigh. "Well, I've taken you away from your evening of fun. Can I make it up to you? Would you like to come with me on some of my favorite rides?"

This surprised her a little, but when she thought about it, she couldn't see why not. "Sure," she said.

Taking a guest around Disney World was like programming a playlist for a date or a car trip. Sammy had done it three or four times for people he was trying to win over (mostly women he was trying to screw) and he refined his technique every time.

So he took her to the Carousel of Progress. It was the oldest untouched ride in the park, a replica of the one that Walt himself had built for GE at the 1964 World's Fair. There had been attempts to update it over the years, but they'd all been ripped out and the show restored to its mid-sixties glory.

It was a revolving theater where robots danced and sang and talked through the American Century, from the last days of the coal stove up to the dawn of the space age. It had a goofy, catchy song, cornball jokes, and he relished playing guide and telling his charges about the time that the revolving theater had trapped a careless castmember in its carousel and crushed her to death. That juxtaposition of sunny, goofy American corporate optimism and the macabre realities of operating a park where a gang of half-literate minimum-wage workers spent their days shoveling the world's rich children into modified threshing machines—it was delicious.

Suzanne's body language told him the whole story from the second she sat down, arms folded, a barely contained smirk on her lips. The lights played over the GE logo, which had acquired an even more anachronistic luster since the last time he'd been. Now that GE had been delisted from the NYSE, it was only a matter of time before they yanked the sponsorship, but for now, it made the ride seem like it was part time-machine. Transported back to the corporate Pleistocene, when giant dinocorps thundered over the plains.

The theater rotated to the first batch of singing, wise-cracking robots. Her eyebrows shot up and she shook her head bemusedly. Out came the second batch, the third—now they were in the fabulous forties and the Andrews Sisters played while grandma and grandpa robot watched a bulging fish-eye TV and sister got vibrated by an electric slimming belt. The jokes got worse, the catchy jingle—"There's a great big beautiful tomorrow, shining at the end of every daaaaay!"—got repeated with more vigor.

"It's like an American robot performance of *Triumph of the Will*," she whispered to him, and he cracked up. They were the only two in the theater. It was never full, and he himself had taken part in spitball exercises brainstorming replacements, but institutionally, Disney Parks couldn't bring itself to shut it down. There was always some excuse—rabid fans, historical interest, competing priorities—but it came down to the fact that no one wanted to bring the ax down on the robot family.

The final segment now, the whole family enjoying a futuristic Christmas with a high-tech kitchen whose voice-activated stove went haywire. All the robots were on stage for the segment, and they exhorted the audience to sing and clap along. Sammy gave in and clapped, and a second later, Suzanne did, too, laughing at the silliness of it all. When the house lights came up and the bored—but unsquashed—castmember spieled them out of the ride, Sammy had a bounce in his step and the song in his head.

"That was *terrible!*" Suzanne said.

"Isn't it great?"

"God, I'll never get that song out of my head." They moved through the flashing lights of Tomorrowland.

"Look at that—no line on Space Mountain," Sammy said, pointing.

So they rode Space Mountain—twice. Then they caught the fireworks. Then Sammy took her over to Tom Sawyer Island on a maintenance boat and they sat up in the tree house and watched as the park heaved and thronged, danced and ran, laughed and chattered.

"Hear the rustling?"

"Yeah, what is that, rabbits or something?"

"Giant rats." Sammy grinned in the dark. "Giant, feral rats."

"Come on, you're joking."

"Cross my heart. We drain the lake every now and then and they migrate to the island. No predators. Lots of dropped french fries—it's ratopia here. They get as big as cats. Bold little fuckers, too. No one likes to be here alone at night."

"What about us?"

"We're together."

The rustling grew louder and they held their breath. A bold rat like a raccoon picked its way across the path below them. Then two more. Suzanne shivered and Sammy did, too. They were huge, feral, menacing.

"Want to go?"

"Hell *yes,*" she said. She fumbled in her purse and came out with a bright little torch that shone like a beacon. You weren't supposed to use bright lights on the island after hours while the rest of the park was open, but Sammy was glad of it.

Back on the mainland, they rode Big Thunder Mountain and moseyed over to the new, half-rebuilt Fantasyland. The zombie maze was still open, and they got lost in it amid the groans, animatronic shamblers, and giggling kids running through the hedges.

Something happened in the maze. Between entering it and leaving it, they lost their cares. Instead of talking about the park and Hackelberg, they talked about ways of getting out of the maze, talked about which zombie was coming next, about the best zombie movies they'd ever seen, about memorable Halloweens. As they neared the exit, they started to strategize about the best ride to go on next. Suzanne had done the Haunted Mansion twice when she first arrived and now—

"Come on, it's such a cliché," Sammy said. "Anyone can be a Haunted Mansion fan. It's like being a Mickey fan. It takes real character to be a Goofy fan."

"You're a Goofy fan, I take it?"

"Indeed. And I'm also a Jungle Cruise man."

"More corny jokes?"

" 'We've been *dying* to have you'—talk about cornball humor."

They rode both. The park was closing, and all around them, people were streaming away from the rides. No lines at all, not even in front of the roller coasters, not even in front of Dumbo, not even in front of the ultraviolent fly-over of the world of the zombies (née Peter Pan's Flight, and a perennial favorite).

"You know, I haven't just *enjoyed* the park like this in years." He was wearing a huge foam Goofy hat that danced and bobbed on his head, trying to do little pas de deux with the other Goofy hats in the vicinity. It also let out the occasional chuckle and snatch of song.

"Shut up," Suzanne said. "Don't talk about magic. Live magic."

They closed the park, letting themselves get herded off of Main Street along with the last stragglers. He looked over his shoulder as they moved through the arches under the train station. The night crew was moving through the empty Main Street, hosing down the streets, sweeping, scrubbing. As he watched, the work lights came on, throwing the whole thing into near-daylight illumination, making it seem less like an enchanted wonderland and more like a movie set, an artifice. A sham.

It was one in the morning and he was exhausted. And Hackelberg was going to sue.

"Suzanne," he said. "Forget off-the-record, on-the-record, whatever. I'm going to tell you something and if it gets me fired, so be it. The guy who is running this action against you is Augustus Hackelberg, the vice president of legal affairs at Disney Parks. He would be hellaciously freaked out if you knew that, but it would be even more dramatic if you mentioned to him that he oversaw a program to reduce preventative maintenance and put aside a budget for settling lawsuits with people the rides injure."

"Sammy, what do you want me to do, blackmail him?"

"I don't know—sure. Why not? You could call him and say, 'I hear you're working on this lawsuit, but don't you think it's hypocritical when you've been doing all this bad stuff—' "

"I don't blackmail people."

"Fine. Tell your friends, then. Tell some lawyers. That could work."

"Sammy, I think we're going to have to fight this suit on its merits, not on the basis of some sneaky intel. I appreciate the risk you're putting yourself to—"

"We ripped off some of Lester's code for the DiaB." He blurted it out, not believing he was hearing himself say it. "I didn't know it at the time. The libraries were on the Net and my guys were in a hurry, and they just imported it into the build and left it there—they rewrote it with the second shipment, but we put out a million units running a library Lester wrote for volumetric imaging. It was under some crazy viral open-source license and we were supposed to publish all our modifications, and we never did."

Suzanne threw her head back and laughed, long and hard. Sammy found himself laughing along with her.

"OK," she said. "OK. That's a good one. I'll tell Lester about it. Maybe he'll want to use it. Maybe he'll want to sue."

Sammy wanted to ask her if she'd keep his name out of it, but he couldn't ask. He'd gone to Hackelberg with the info as soon as he'd found out and they'd agreed to keep it quiet. The Imagineers responsible had had a very firm talking to, and had privately admitted to a curious and aghast Sammy over beers that everyone everywhere did this all the time, that it was so normal as to be completely unremarkable. He was pretty sure that a judge wouldn't see it that way.

Suzanne surprised him by giving him a strong, warm hug. "You're not the worst guy in the world, Sammy Page," she said. "Thanks for showing me around your park."

Kettlewell had been almost pathetic in his interest in helping Lester out. Lester got the impression that he'd been sitting around his apartment, moping, ever since Eva had taken the kids and gone. As Lester unspooled the story for him—Suzanne wouldn't tell him how she'd found this out, and he knew better than to ask—Kettlewell grew more and more excited. By the time Lester was through, he was practically slobbering into the phone.

"Oh, oh, oh, this is going to be a *fun* phoner," he said.

"You'll do it, then? Even after everything?"

"Does Perry know you've called me?"

Lester swallowed. "No," he said. "I don't talk to Perry much these days."

Kettlewell sighed. "What the hell am I going to do with you two?"

"I'm sorry," Lester said.

"Don't be sorry. Be happy. Someone should be happy around here."

Herve Guignol chaired the executive committee. Sammy had known him for years. They'd come east together from San Jose, where Guignol had run the entertainment side of eBay. They'd been recruited by Disney Parks at the same time, during the hostile takeover and breakup, and they'd had their share of nights out, golf games, and stupid movies together.

But when Guignol was wearing his chairman's hat, it was like he was a different person. The boardroom was filled with huge, ergonomic chairs, the center of the table lined with bottles of imported water and trays of fanciful canapés in the shapes of Disney characters. Sammy sat to Guignol's left and Hackelberg sat to his right.

Guignol brought the meeting to order and the rest of the committee stopped chatting and checking email and looked expectant. At the touch of a button, the door swung shut with an authoritative clunk and shutters slid down over the window.

"Welcome, and thank you for attending on such short notice. You know Augustus Hackelberg; he has something to present to you."

Hackelberg climbed to his feet and looked out at them. He didn't look good.

"An issue has arisen—" Sammy loved the third-person passive voice that dominated corporate meetings. Like the issue had arisen all on its own, spontaneously. "A decision that was taken has come back to bite us." He explained about the DiaBs and the code, laying it out more or less as it happened, though of course he downplayed his involvement in advising Sammy to go ahead and ship.

The committee asked a few intense questions, none directed at Sammy, who kept quiet, though he instinctively wanted to defend his record. They took a break after an hour, and Sammy found himself in a corner with Guignol.

"What do you think?" Sammy asked him.

Guignol grimaced. "I think we're pretty screwed. Someone is going to have to take a fall for this, you know. It's going to cost us a fortune."

Sammy nodded. "Well, unless we just settle with them," he said. "You know—we drop the suit we just filed and they drop theirs. . . ." He had hoped that this would come out on its own, but it was clear that Hackelberg wasn't going to offer it up himself. He was too in love with the idea of getting his hands on Perry and Lester.

Guignol rocked his head from side to side. "You think they'd go for it?"

Sammy dropped his voice to a whisper and turned away from the rest of the room to confound any lip-readers. "I think they've *offered* to do that."

Guignol cut his eyes over to Hackelberg, and Sammy nodded, imperceptibly.

Guignol moved away, leaving Sammy to eat a Mickey head built from chunks of salmon and hamachi. Guignol moved among the committee, talking to a few members. Sammy recognized the behavior—consolidating power. Hard to remember that this was the guy he'd played savage, high-stakes games of putt-putt golf with.

The meeting reconvened. No one looked at Sammy. They all looked at Hackelberg.

"What about trying to settle the suit?" Guignol said.

Hackelberg flushed. "I don't know if that's possible—"

"What about if we offer to settle in exchange for dropping the suit we've just filed?"

Hackelberg's hands squeezed the side of the table. "I don't think that that would be a wise course of action. This is the opportunity we've been waiting for—the chance to crack them wide open and see what's going on inside. Discover just what they've taken from us and how. Out them for all their bad acts."

Guignol nodded. "OK, that's true. Now, as I understand it, every DiaB we shipped with this Banks person's code on it is a separate act of infringement. We shipped a million of them. What's the potential liability per unit?"

"Courts usually award—"

Guignol knocked quietly on the table. "What's the *potential liability*—what's the size of the bill a court *could* hand down, if a jury was involved? If, say, this became part of someone's litigation portfolio."

Hackelberg looked away. "It's up to five hundred thousand per separate act of infringement."

Guignol nodded. "So, we're looking at a ceiling on the liability at five hundred billion dollars, then?"

"Technically, yes. But—"

"I propose that we offer a settlement, quid pro quo with this Banks person. We drop our suit if he indemnifies us from damages for his."

"Seconded," said someone at the table. Things were picking up steam. Sammy bit the inside of his cheek to keep his smile in check.

"Wait," Hackelberg said. "Gentlemen and lady, please. While it's true that damages can technically run to five hundred thousand dollars per infringement, that simply isn't done. Not to entities like this firm. Listen, we *wrote* that law so we could sue people who took from *us*. It won't be used against us. We will face, at worst, a few hundred dollars per act of infringement. Still a sizable sum of money, but in the final analysis—"

"Thank you," Guignol said. "All in favor of offering a settlement?"

It was unanimous—except for Hackelberg.

Sammy got his rematch with Hackelberg when the quarterly financials came out. It was all that black ink, making him giddy.

"I don't want to be disrespectful," he said, knowing that in Hackelberg's books, there could be nothing more disrespectful than challenging him. "But we need to confront some business realities here."

Hackelberg's office was nothing like Sammy had expected—not a southern gentleman's study lined with hunting trophies and framed ancestral photos. It was as spare as the office of a temp, almost empty save for a highly functional desk, built-in bookcases lined with law books, and a straight-backed chair. It was ascetic, severe, and it was more intimidating than any dark-wood den could hope to be.

Hackelberg's heavy eyelids drooped a little, the corners of his eyes going down with them. It was like staring down a gator. Sammy resisted the urge to look away.

"The numbers don't lie. DiaB is making us a fortune, and most of it's coming from the platform, not the goop and not the increased visitor numbers. We're making money because other people are figuring out ways to use our stuff. It's our fastest-growing revenue source and if it continues, we're going to end up being a DiaB company with a side business in theme parks.

"That's the good news. The bad news is that these characters in the ghost mall have us in their crosshairs. They're prying us open faster than we can lock ourselves down. But here's another way of looking at it: every time they add another feature to the DiaB, they make owning a DiaB more attractive, which makes it easier for us to sell access to the platform to advertisers."

Hackelberg held up his hands. "Samuel, I think I've heard enough. Your job is to figure out new businesses for us to diversify into. My job is to contain our liability and protect our brand and investors. It sounds a lot to me like you're saying that you want me to leave off doing my job so that you can do yours."

Sammy squirmed. "No, that's not it at all. We both want to protect the business. I'm not saying that you need to give these guys a free ride. What I'm saying is, suing these guys is *not* good for our business. It costs us money, goodwill—it distracts us from doing our jobs."

Hackelberg leaned back and looked coolly into Sammy's eyes. "What are you proposing as an alternative, then?"

The idea had come to Sammy in the shower one morning, as he mentally calculated the size of his coming quarterly bonus. A great idea. Out-of-the-box thinking. The right answer to the question that no one had thought to ask. It had seemed so *perfect* then. Now, though—

"I think we should buy them out."

Hackelberg's thin, mirthless grin made his balls shrivel up.

Sammy held up his hands. "Here, look at this. I drew up some figures. What they're earning. What we earn from them. Growth estimates over the next five quarters. It's not just some random idea I had in the shower. This makes *sense*." He passed over a sheaf of papers, replete with pie charts.

Hackelberg set it down in the center of his desk, perfectly square to the corners. He flipped through the first five pages, then squared the stack up again.

"You've done a lot of work here, Samuel. I can really see that."

He got up from his straight-backed chair, lifted Sammy's papers between his thumb and forefinger, and crossed to the wall. There was a shredder there, its maw a wide rectangle, the kind of thing that you can stick entire hardcover books (or hard drives) into. Calmly, Hackelberg fed Sammy's paper into the shredder, fastidiously holding the paper-clipped corner between thumb and forefinger, then dropping the corner in once the rest had been digested.

"I won't ask you for your computer," he said, settling back into his chair. "But I expect that you will back up your other data and then send the hard drive to IT to be permanently erased. I don't want any record of this, period. I want this done by the end of business today."

Sammy's mouth hung open. He shut it. Then he opened it again.

Abruptly, Hackelberg stood, knocking his chair to the ground behind him.

"Not one word, do you understand me? Not one solitary word, you god-damned idiot! We're in the middle of being sued by these people. I *know* you know this, since it's your fault that it's happening. I know that you know that the stakes are the *entire* company. Now, say a jury were to discover that we were considering buying these assholes out? Say a jury were to decide that our litigation was a base stratagem to lower the asking price for their, their 'company' "—the word dripped with sarcasm—"what do you suppose would happen? If you had the sense of a five-year-old, you'd have known better than to do this. Good Christ, Page, I should have security escort you to the gate.

"Turn on your heel and go weep in the corridor. Don't stand in my office for one more second. Get your computer to IT by two PM. I will check. That goes for anyone you worked with on this, anyone who has a copy of this in-formation. Now, leave." Sammy stood rooted in place. "LEAVE, you ridicu-lous little dog's pizzle, get out of my sight!"

Sammy drew in a deep breath. He thought about saying something like, *You can't talk to me like that,* but it was very likely that Hackelberg could talk to him just like that. He felt light-headed and a little sick, and he backed slowly out of the office.

Standing in the corridor, he began to shake. He pounded the elevator but-ton, and felt the eyes of Hackelberg's severe secretary burning into his back. Abruptly, he turned away and yanked open the staircase door so hard it smashed into the wall with a loud bang. He took the stairs in a rush of des-perate claustrophobia, wanting more than anything to get outside, to breathe in the fresh air.

He stumbled on the way down, falling a couple of steps and smashing into the wall on the landing. He stood pressed against the wall, the cold cin-der block on his cheek, which felt like it might be bruised. The pain was enough to bring him back to his senses.

This is ridiculous. He had the right answer. Hackelberg was wrong. Hackelberg didn't run the company. Yes, it was hard to get anything done without his sign-off, but it wasn't impossible. Going behind Hackelberg's back to the executive committee could cost him his job, of course.

Of course.

Sammy realized that he didn't actually *care* if he lost his job. Oh, the thought made his chest constrict and thoughts of living in a refrigerator box materialize in his mind's eye, but beyond that, he really didn't care. It was such a goddamned roller-coaster ride—Sammy smiled grimly at the metaphor. You guess right, you end up on top. You guess wrong, you bottom out. He spent half his career lording it over the poor guessers and the other half panicking about a bad guess he'd made. He thought of Perry and Lester, thought of that night in Boston. He'd killed their ride and the party had gone on all the same. They had something, in that crazy shantytown, something pure and happy, some camaraderie that he'd always assumed he'd get someday, but that had never materialized.

If this was his dream job, how much worse would unemployment really be?

He would go to the executive committee. He would not erase his numbers. He set off for his office, moving quickly, purposefully, head up. A last stand, how exciting; why not?

He piloted the little golf cart down the back road and was nearly at his building's door when he spotted the security detail. Three of them, in lightweight Disney cop uniforms, wearing ranger hats and looking around alertly. Hackelberg must have sent them there to make sure that he followed through with deleting his data.

He stopped the golf cart abruptly and reversed out of the driveway before the guards spotted him. He needed to get his files somewhere that Hackelberg wouldn't be able to retrieve them. He zipped down the service roads, thinking furiously.

The answer occurred to him in the form of a road sign for the Polynesian hotel. He turned up its drive and parked the golf cart. As he stepped out, he removed his employee badge and untucked his shirt. Now he was just another sweaty fresh-arrived tourist, Dad coming in to rendezvous with Mom and the kids, back from some banal meeting that delayed his arrival, hasn't even had time to change into a T-shirt.

He headed straight for the sundries store and bought a postage-paid Walt Disney World postcard with a little magnetic patch mounted on one corner. You filled up the memory with a couple hours' worth of video and as many photos as you wanted and mailed it off. The pixelated display on the front played a slide show of the images—at least once a year, some honeymoon couple would miss this fact and throw a couple racy bedroom shots in the mix, to the perennial delight of the mail room.

He hastily wrote some banalities about the great time he and the kids were having in Disney World, then he opened his computer and looked up the address that the Church woman had checked in under. He addressed it, simply, to "Suzanne," to further throw off the scent; then he slipped it into a mail slot with a prayer to the gods of journalist shield laws.

He walked as calmly as he could back to his golf cart, clipping on his employee badge and tucking his shirt back in. Then he motored calmly to his office building. The Disney cops were sweating under the midday sun.

"Mr. Page?"

"Yes," he said.

"I'm to take your computer to IT, sir."

"I don't think so," Sammy said, with perfect calm. "I think we'll GO up to my office and call a meeting of the executive committee instead."

The security guard was young, Latino, and skinny. His short back and sides left his scalp exposed to the sun. He took his hat off and mopped his forehead with a handkerchief, exposing a line of acne where his hatband irritated the skin. It made Sammy feel sorry for the kid—especially considering that Sammy earned more than twenty times the kid's salary.

"This really isn't your job, I know," Sammy said, wondering where all this sympathy for the laboring classes had come from, anyway. "I don't want to make it hard for you. We'll go inside. You can hang on to the computer. We'll talk to some people. If they tell you to go ahead, you go ahead. Otherwise, we go see them, all right?"

He held his computer out to the kid, who took it.

"Let's go up to my office now," he said.

The kid shook his head. "I'm supposed to take this—"

"I know, I know. But we have a deal." The kid looked like he would head out anyway. "And there are backups in my office, so you need to come and get those, too."

That did it. The kid looked a little grateful as they went inside, where the air-conditioning was blowing icy cold.

"You should have waited in the lobby, Luis," Sammy said, reading the kid's name off his badge. "You must be boiled."

"I had instructions," Luis said.

Sammy made a face. "They don't sound like very reasonable instructions. All the more reason to sort this out, right?"

Sammy had his secretary get Luis a bottle of cold water and a little plate of grapes and berries out of the stash he kept for his visitors, then he called Guignol from his desk phone.

"It's Sammy. I need to call an emergency meeting of the exec committee," he said without preamble.

"This is about Hackelberg, isn't it?"

"He's already called you?"

"He was very persuasive."

"I can be persuasive, too. Give me a chance."

"You know what will happen if you push this?"

"I might save the company."

"You might," Guignol said. "And you might—"

"I know," Sammy said. "What the hell, it's only a career."

"You can't keep your data—Hackelberg is right about that."

"I can send all the backups and my computer to your office right now."

"I was under the impression that they were all on their way to IT for disposal."

"Not yet. There's a security castmember in my office with me named Luis. If you want to call dispatch and have them direct him to bring this stuff to you instead—"

"Sammy, do you understand what you're doing here?"

Sammy suppressed a mad giggle. "I do," he said. "I understand exactly what I'm doing. I want to help you all understand that, too."

"I'm calling security dispatch now."

A moment later, Luis's phone rang and the kid listened intently, nodding unconsciously. Once he'd hung up, Sammy passed him his backups, hardcopy, and computer. "Let's go," he said.

"Right," Luis said, and led the way.

It was a short ride to the casting-office building, where Guignol had his office. The wind felt terrific on his face, drying his sweat. It had been a long day.

When they pulled up, Sammy let Luis lead the way again, badging in behind him, following him up to the seventh-floor boardroom at the end of the Gold Coast where the most senior offices were.

Guignol met them at the door and took the materials from Luis, then ushered Sammy in. Sammy caught Luis's eye, and Luis surprised him by winking and slipping him a surreptitious thumbs-up, making Sammy feel like they shared a secret.

There were eight on the executive committee, but they traveled a lot. Sammy had expected to see no more than four. There were two. And Hackelberg, of course. The lawyer was the picture of saurian calm.

Sammy sat down at the table and helped himself to a glass of water, watching a ring pool on the table's polished and waxed wooden surface.

"Samuel," Hackelberg said, shaking his head. "I hoped it wouldn't come to this."

Sammy took a deep breath, looking for that don't-give-a-shit calm that had suffused him before. It was there still, not as potent, but there. He drew upon it.

"Let's put this to the committee, shall we? I mean, we already know how we feel."

"That won't be necessary," Hackelberg said. "The committee has already voted on this."

Sammy closed his eyes and rubbed the bridge of his nose. He looked at Hackelberg, who was smiling grimly, a mean grin that went all the way to the corners of his eyes.

Sammy looked around at Guignol and the committee members. They wouldn't meet his eye. Guignol gestured Luis into the room and handed him Sammy's computer, papers, and backups. He leaned in and spoke quietly to him. Luis turned and left.

Guignol cleared his throat. "There's nothing else to discuss, then," he said. "Thank you all for coming."

In his heart, Sammy had known this was coming. Hackelberg would beat him to the committee—never let him present his side. Watching the lawyer get up stiffly and leave with slow, dignified steps, Sammy had a moment's intuition about what it must be like to be that man—possessed of a kind of cold, furious power that came from telling everyone that not obeying you to the letter would put them in terrible danger. He knew that line of reasoning: it was the same one he got from the TSA at the airport before they bent him over and greased him up. *You* can't understand the grave danger we all face. You must obey me, for only I can keep it at bay.

He waited for the rest of the committee to file out. None of them would meet his eye. Then it was just him and Guignol. Sammy raised his eyebrows and spread out his hands, miming *What happens now?*

"You won't be able to get anything productive done until IT gets through with your computer. Take some time off. Call up Dinah and see if she wants to grab some holiday time."

"We split," Sammy said. He drank his water and stood up. "I've just got one question before I go."

Guignol winced but stood his ground. "Go ahead," he said.

"Don't you want to know what the numbers looked like?"

"It's not my job to overrule legal—"

"We'll get to that in a second. It's not the question. The question is, don't you *want to know?*"

Guignol sighed. "You know I want to know. Of course I want to know. This isn't about me and what I want, though. It's about making sure we don't endanger the shareholders—"

"So ignoring this path, sticking our heads in the sand, that's *good* for the shareholders?"

"No, of course it's not good for the shareholders. But it's better than endangering the whole company—"

Sammy nodded. "Well, how about if we both take some time off and drive down to Hollywood. It'd do us some good."

"Sammy, I've got a job to do—"

"Yeah, but without your computer . . ."

Guignol looked at him. "What did you do?"

"It's not what I did. It's what I might have done. I'm going to be a good boy and give Hackelberg a list of everyone I might have emailed about this. All those people are losing their computers to the big magnet at IT."

"But you never emailed me about this—"

"You sure? I might have. It's the kind of thing I might have done. Maybe your spam filter ate it. You never know. That's what IT's for."

Guignol looked angry for a moment, then laughed. "You are such a shithead. Fuck that lawyer asshole anyway. What are you driving these days?"

"Just bought a new Dell Luminux," Sammy said, grinning back. "Ragtop."

"When do we leave?"

"I'll pick you up at six AM tomorrow. Beat the morning traffic."

Suzanne was getting sick of breakfast in bed. It was hard to imagine that such a thing was possible, but there it was. Lester stole out from between the covers before 7 AM every day, and then, half an hour later, he was back with a laden tray, something new every day. She'd had steaks, burritos, waffles, homemade granola, fruit salad with Greek yogurt, and today there were eggs Benedict with fresh-squeezed grapefruit juice. The tray always came with a French press of fresh-ground Kona coffee, a cloth napkin, and her computer, so she could read the news.

In theory, this was a warm ritual that ensured that they had quality time together every day, no matter what. In practice, Lester was so anxious about the food and whether she was enjoying it that she couldn't really enjoy it. Plus, she wasn't a fatkins, so three-thousand-calorie breakfasts weren't good for her.

Most of all, it was the pressure to be a happy couple, to have cemented over the old hurts and started anew. She felt it every moment, when Lester climbed into the shower with her and soaped her back, when he brought home flowers, and when he climbed into bed with her in the morning to eat breakfast with her.

She picked at her caviar and blini glumly and poked at her computer. Beside her, Lester hoovered up three thousand calories' worth of fried dough and clattered one-handed on his machine.

"This is delicious, babe, thanks," she said, with as much sincerity as she could muster. It was really generous and nice of him to do this. She was just a bitter old woman who couldn't be happy no matter what was going on in her life.

There was voicemail on her computer, which was unusual. Most people sent her email. This originated from a pay phone on the Florida Turnpike.

"Ms. Church, this is—ah, this is a person whom you recently had the acquaintance of, while on your holidays. I have a confidential matter to discuss with you. I'm traveling to your location with a colleague today and should arrive mid-morning. I hope you can make some time to meet with me."

She listened to it twice. Lester leaned over.

"What's that all about?"

"You're not going to believe it. I think it's that Disney guy, the guy I told you about. The one Death used to work for."

"He's coming *here*?"

"Apparently."

"Woah. Don't tell Perry."

"You think?"

"He'd tear that guy's throat out with his teeth." Lester took a bite of blini. "I might help."

Suzanne thought about Sammy. He hadn't been the sort of person she could be friends with, but she'd known plenty of his kind in her day, and he was hardly the worst of the lot. He barely rated above average on the corporate psychopath meter. Somewhere in there, there was a real personality. She'd seen it.

"Well, then I guess I'd better meet with him alone."

"It sounds like he wants a doctor-patient meeting anyway."

"Or confessor-penitent."

"You think he'll leak you something."

"That's a pretty good working theory when it comes to this kind of call."

Lester ate thoughtfully, then reached over and hit a key on her computer, replaying the call.

"He sounds, what, giddy?"

"That's right; he does, doesn't he. Maybe it's good news."

Lester laughed and took away her dishes, and when he came back in, he was naked, stripped and ready for the shower. He was a very handsome man, and he had a devilish grin as he whisked the blanket off of her.

He stopped at the foot of the bed and stared at her, his grin quirking in a way she recognized instantly. She didn't have to look down to know that he was getting hard. In the mirror of his eyes, she was beautiful. She could see it plainly. When she looked into the real mirror at the foot of the bed, draped with gauzy sun-scarves and crusted around the edges with kitschy tourist magnets Lester brought home, she saw a saggy, middle-aged woman with cottage-cheese cellulite and saddlebags.

Lester had slept with more fatkins girls than she could count, women made into doll-like mannequins by surgery and chemical enhancements, women who read sex manuals in public places and boasted about their Kegel weight–lifting scores.

But when he looked at her like that, she knew that she was the most beautiful woman he'd ever loved, that he would do anything for her. That he loved her as much as he could ever love anyone.

What the hell was I complaining about? she thought as he fell on her like a starving man.

She met Sammy in their favorite tearoom, the one perched like a crow's nest four stories up a corkscrew building, whose supplies came up on a series of dumbwaiters and winches that shrouded its balconies like vines.

She staked out the best table, the one with the panoramic view of the whole shantytown, and ordered a plate of the tiny shortbread cakes that were the house specialty, along with a gigantic mug of nonfat decaf cappuccino.

Sammy came up the steps red-faced and sweaty, wearing a Hawaiian shirt and Bermuda shorts, like some kind of tourist. Or like he was on holidays? Behind him came a younger man, with severe little designer glasses, dressed in the conventional polo-shirt-and-slacks uniform of the corporate exec on a non-suit day.

Suzanne sprinkled an ironic wave at them and gestured to the mismatched schoolroom chairs at her table. The waitress—Shayna—came over with two glasses of water and a paper-napkin dispenser. The men thanked her and mopped their faces and drank their water.

"Good drive?"

Sammy nodded. His friend looked nervous, like he was wondering what might have been swimming in his water glass. "This is some place."

"We like it here."

"Is there, you know, a bathroom?" the companion asked.

"Through there." Suzanne pointed.

"How do you deal with the sewage around here?"

"Sewage? Mr. Page, sewage is *solved*. We feed it into our generators and the waste heat runs our condenser purifiers. There was talk of building one big one for the whole town, but that required way too much coordination and, anyway, Perry was convinced that having central points of failure would be begging for a disaster. I wrote a series on it. If you'd like I can send you the links."

The Disney exec made some noises and ate some shortbread, peered at the chalkboard menu and ordered some Thai iced tea.

"Look, Ms. Church—Suzanne—thank you for seeing me. I would have understood completely if you'd told me to go fuck myself."

Suzanne smiled and made a go-on gesture.

"Before my friend comes back from the bathroom, before we meet up with anyone from your side, I just want you to know this. What you've done, it's changed the world. I wouldn't be here today if it wasn't for you."

He had every appearance of being completely sincere. He was a little road-crazed and windblown today, not like she remembered him from Orlando. What the hell had happened to him? What was he here for?

His friend came back and Sammy said, "I ordered you a Thai iced tea. This is Suzanne Church, the writer. Ms. Church, this is Herve Guignol, co-director of the Florida regional division of Disney Parks."

Guignol was more put-together and standoffish than Sammy. He shook her hand and made executive-sounding grunts at her. He was young, and clearly into playing the role of exec. He reminded Suzanne of fresh Silicon Valley millionaires who could go from pizza-slinging hackers to suit-wearing biz-droids who bullshitted knowledgeably about EBITDA overnight.

What the hell are you two here for?

"Mr. Page—"

"Sammy, call me Sammy, please. Did you get my postcard?"

"That was from you?" She'd not been able to make heads or tails of it when it arrived in the mail the day before and she'd chucked it out as part of some viral marketing campaign she didn't want to get infected by.

"You got it?"

"I threw it out."

Sammy went slightly green.

"But it'll still be in the trash," she said. "Lester never takes it out, and I haven't."

"Um, can we go and get it now, all the same?"

"What's on it?"

Sammy and Guignol exchanged a long look. "Let's pretend that I gave you a long run-up to this. Let's pretend that we spent a lot of time with me impressing on you that this is confidential, and not for publication. Let's pretend that I charmed you and made sure you understood how much respect I have for you and your friends here—"

"I get it," Suzanne said, trying not to laugh. *Not for publication*—really!

"OK, let's pretend all that. Now I'll tell you: what's on that postcard is the financials for a Disney Parks buyout of your friends' entire operation here. DiaBolical, the ride, all of it."

Suzanne had been expecting a lot of things, but this wasn't one of them. It was loopy. Daffy. Not just weird, but inconceivable. As though he'd said, "I sent you our plans to carve your portrait on the moon's surface with a green laser." But she was a pro. She kept her face still and neutral, and calmly swallowed her cappuccino.

"I see."

"And there are—there are people at Disney who feel like this idea is so dangerous that it doesn't even warrant discussion. That it should be suppressed."

Guignol cleared his throat. "That's the consensus," he said.

"And normally, I'd say, hey, sure, the consensus. That's great. But I'll tell you, I drew up these numbers because I was curious, I'm a curious guy. I like to think laterally, try stuff that might seem silly at first. See where it goes. I've had pretty good instincts."

Guignol and Suzanne snorted at the same time.

"And an imperfect record," Sammy said. Suzanne didn't want to like him, but there was something forthright about him that she couldn't help warming to. There was no subtlety or scheming in this guy. Whatever he wanted, you could see it right on his face. Maybe he was a psycho, but he wasn't a sneak.

"So I ran these numbers for my own amusement, to see what they would look like. Assume that your boys want, say, thirty times gross annual revenue for a buyout. Say that this settles our lawsuit—not theirs, just ours, so we don't have to pay for the trademark suit to go forward. Assume that they generate one DiaBolical-scale idea every six months—" Suzanne found herself nodding along, especially at this last one. "Well, you make those assumptions and you know what comes out of it?"

Suzanne let the numbers dance behind her own eyelids. She'd followed all the relevant financials closely for years, so closely that they were as familiar as her monthly take-home and mortgage payments had been, back when she had a straight job and a straight life.

"Well, you'd make Lester and Perry *very* wealthy," she said. "After they vested out, they'd be able to live off the interest alone."

Sammy nodded judiciously. His sidekick looked alarmed. "Yup. And for us?"

"Well, assuming your last quarterly statement was accurate—"

"We were a little conservative," Sammy said. The other man nodded reflexively.

You were very conservative, she thought. *DiaB's making you a fortune and you didn't want to advertise that to the competition.*

"Assuming that, well, you guys earn back your investment in, what, eighteen months?"

"I figure a year. But eighteen months would be good."

"If you vest the guys out over three years, that means—"

"One hundred percent ROI, plus or minus two hundred percent," Sammy said. "For less money than we'll end up spending on our end of the lawsuit."

Guignol was goggling at them both. Sammy drank his Thai iced tea, slurping noisily. He signaled for another one.

"And you sent me these financials on a postcard?"

"There was some question about whether they'd be erased before I could show them to anyone, and I knew there was no way I'd be given the chance to re-create them independently. It seemed prudent to have a backup copy."

"A backup copy in my hands?"

"Well, at least I knew you wouldn't give it up without a fight." Sammy shrugged and offered her a sunny smile.

"We'd better go rescue that postcard from the basket before Lester develops a domestic instinct and takes out the trash, then," Suzanne said, pushing away from the table. Shayna brought the bill and Sammy paid it, overtipping by a factor of ten, which endeared him further to Suzanne. She couldn't abide rich people who stiffed on the tip.

Suzanne walked them through the shantytown, watching their reactions closely. She liked to take new people here. She'd witnessed its birth and growth, then gone away during its adolescence, and now she got to enjoy its maturity. Crowds of kids ran screeching and playing through the streets, adults nodded at them from their windows, wires and plumbing and antennas crowded the skies above them. The walls shimmered with murals and graffiti and mosaics.

Sammy treated it like he had his theme park, seeming to take in every detail with a connoisseur's eye; Guignol was more nervous, clearly feeling unsafe amid the cheerful lawlessness. They came upon Francis and a gang of his kids, building bicycles out of stiffened fabric and strong monofilament recycled from packing crates.

"Ms. Church," Francis said gravely. He'd given up drinking, maybe for good, and he was clear-eyed and charming in his engineer's coveralls. The kids—boys *and* girls, Suzanne noted approvingly—continued to work over the bikes, but they were clearly watching what Francis was up to.

"Francis, please meet Sammy and his colleague, Herve. They're here for a story I'm working on. Gentlemen, Francis is the closest thing we have to a mayor around here."

Francis shook hands all around, but Sammy's attention was riveted on the bicycles.

Francis picked one up with two fingers and handed it to him. "Like it? We got the design from a shop in Liberia, but we made our own local improvements. The trick is getting the stiffener to stay liquid long enough to get the fabric stretched out in the right proportion."

Sammy took the frame from him and spun it in one hand like a baton. "And the wheels?"

"Mostly we do solids, which stay in true longer. We use the carbon stiffener on a precut round of canvas or denim, then fit a standard tire. They go out of true after a while. You just apply some solvent to them and they go soft again and you re-true them with a compass and a pair of tailor's shears, then re-stiffen them. You get maybe five years of hard riding out of a wheel that way."

Sammy's eyes were round as saucers. He took one of the proffered wheels and spun it between opposing fingertips. Then, grinning, he picked up another wheel and the bike-frame and began to *juggle* them, one-two-three, hoop-la! Francis looked amused, rather than pissed—giving up drink had softened his temper. His kids stopped working and laughed. Sammy laughed, too. He transferred the wheels to his left hand, then tossed the frame high in the air, spun around and caught it and then handed it all back to Francis. The kids clapped and he took a bow.

"I didn't know you had it in you," Guignol said, patting him on the shoulder.

Sammy, sweating and grinning like a fool, said, "Yeah, it's not something I get a lot of chances to do around the office. But did you see that? It was light enough to juggle! I mean, how exciting is all this?" He swept his arm around his head. "Between the sewage and the manufacturing and all these kids—" He broke off. "What do you do about education, Suzanne?"

"Lots of kids bus into the local schools, or ride. But lots more homeschool these days. We don't get a very high caliber of public school around here."

"Might that have something to do with all the residents who don't pay property tax?" Guignol said pointedly.

Suzanne nodded. "I'm sure it does," she said. "But it has more to do with the overall quality of public education in this state. Forty-seventh in the nation for funding."

They were at her and Lester's place now. She led them through the front door and picked up the trash can next to the little table where she sorted the mail after picking it up from her PO box at a little strip mall down the road.

There was the postcard. She handed it silently to Sammy, who held it for a moment, then reluctantly passed it to Guignol. "You'd better hang on to it," he said, and she sensed that there was something bigger going on there.

"Now we go see Lester," Suzanne said.

He was behind the building in his little workshop, hacking DiaBolical. There were five different DiaBs running around him, chugging and humming. The smell of goop and fuser and heat filled the room, and an air conditioner like a jet engine labored to keep things cool. Still, it was a few degrees warmer inside than out.

"Lester," Suzanne shouted over the air-conditioner din, "we have visitors."

Lester straightened up from his keyboard and wiped his palms and turned to face them. He knew who they were, based on his earlier conversation with Suzanne, but he also clearly recognized Sammy.

"You!" he said. "You work for Disney?"

Sammy blushed and looked away.

Lester turned to Suzanne. "This guy used to come up, what, twice, three times a week."

Sammy nodded and mumbled something. Lester reached out and snapped off the AC, filling the room with eerie silence and stifling heat. "What was that?"

"I'm a great believer in competitive intelligence."

"You work for Disney?"

"They both work for Disney, Lester," Suzanne said. "This is Sammy and Herve." *Herve doesn't do much talking,* she mentally added, *but he seems to be in charge.*

"That's right," Sammy said, seeming to come to himself at last. "And it's an honor to formally meet you at last. I run the DiaB program. I see you're a fan. I've read quite a bit about you, of course, thanks to Ms. Church here."

Lester's hands closed and opened, closed and opened. "You were, what, you were sneaking around here?"

"Have I mentioned that I'm a great fan of *your work*? Not just the ride, either. This DiaBolical, well, it's—"

"What are you doing here?"

Suzanne had expected something like this. Lester wasn't like Perry; he wouldn't go off the deep end with this guy, but he wasn't going to be his best buddy, either. Still, someone needed to intervene before this melted down altogether.

"Lester," she said, putting her hand on his warm shoulder. "Do you want to show these guys what you're working on?"

He blew air through his nose a couple times, then settled down. He even smiled.

"This one," he said, pointing to a DiaBolical, "I've got it running an experimental firmware that lets it print out hollow components. They're a lot lighter and they don't last as long. But they're also way less consumptive on goop. You get about ten times as much printing out of them."

Suzanne noted that this bit of news turned both of the Disney execs a little green. They made a lot of money selling goop, she knew.

"This one," Lester continued, patting a DiaB that was open to the elements, its imps lounging in its guts, "we mix some serious epoxy in with it, some carbon fibers. The printouts are practically indestructible. There are some kids around here who've been using it to print parts for bicycles—"

"Those were printed on *this*?" Sammy said.

"We ran into Francis and his gang," Suzanne explained.

Lester nodded. "Yeah, it's not perfect, though. The epoxy clogs up the works and the imps really don't like it. I only get two or three days out of a printer after I convert it. I'm working on changing the mix to fix that, though."

"After all," Guignol noted sourly, "it's not as if you have to pay for new DiaBs when you break one."

Lester smiled nastily at him. "Exactly," he said. "We've got a great research subsidy around here."

Guignol looked away, lips pursed.

"This one," Lester said, choosing not to notice, "this one is the realization of an age-old project." He pointed to the table next to it, where its imps were carefully fitting together some very fine parts.

Sammy leaned in close, inspecting their work. After a second, he hissed like a teakettle, then slapped his knee.

Now Lester's smile was more genuine. He loved it when people appreciated his work. "You figured it out?"

"You're printing DiaBs!"

"Not the whole thing," Lester said. "A lot of the logic needs an FPGA burner. And we can't do some of the conductive elements, either. But yeah, about ninety percent of the DiaB can be printed in a DiaB."

Suzanne hadn't heard about this one, though she remembered earlier attempts, back in the golden New Work days, the dream of self-replicating machines. Now she looked close, leaning in next to Sammy, so close she could feel his warm breath. There was something, well, *spooky* about the imps building a machine using another one of the machines.

"It's, what, it's like it's alive, and reproducing itself," Sammy said.

"Don't tell me this never occurred to you," Lester said.

"Honestly? No. It never did. Mr. Banks, you have a uniquely twisted, fucked-up imagination, and I say that with the warmest admiration."

Guignol leaned in, too, staring at it.

"It's so obvious now that I see it," he said.

"Yeah, all the really great ideas are like that," Lester said.

Sammy straightened up and shook Lester's hand. "Thank you for the tour, Lester. You have managed to simultaneously impress and depress me. You are one sharp motherfucker."

Lester preened and Suzanne suppressed a giggle.

Sammy held his hand up like he was being sworn in. "I'm dead serious, man. This is amazing. I mean, we manage some pretty out-of-the-box thinking at Disney, right? We may not be as nimble as some little whacked out co-op, but for who we are—I think we do a good job.

"But you, man, you blow us out of the water. This stuff is just *crazy*, like it came down from Mars. Like it's from the future." He shook his head. "It's humbling, you know."

Guignol looked more thoughtful than he had to this point. He and Lester stared at Sammy, wearing similar expressions of bemusement.

"Let's go into the apartment," Suzanne said. "We can sit down and have a chat."

They trooped up the stairs together. Guignol expressed admiration for the weird junk-sculptures that adorned each landing, made by a local craftswoman and installed by the landlord. They sat around the living room and Lester poured iced coffee out of a pitcher in the fridge, dropping in ice cubes molded to look like legos.

They rattled their drinks and looked uncomfortably at one another. Suzanne longed to whip out her computer and take notes, or at least a pad, or a camera, but she restrained herself. Guignol looked significantly at Sammy.

"Lester, I'm just going to say it. Would you sell your business to us? The ride, DiaBolical, all of it? We could make you a very, very rich man. You and Perry. You would have the freedom to go on doing what you're doing, but we'd put it in our production chain, mass-market the hell out of it, get it into places you've never seen. At its peak, New Work—which you were only a small part of, remember—touched twenty percent of Americans. *Ninety percent* of Americans have been to a Disney park. We're a bigger tourist draw than *all of Great Britain*. We can give your ideas legs."

Lester began to chuckle, then laugh, then he was doubled over, thumping his thighs. Suzanne shook her head. In just a few short moments, she'd gotten used to the idea, and it was growing on her.

Guignol looked grim. "It's not a firm offer—it's a chance to open a dialogue, a negotiation. Talk the possibility over. A good negotiation is one where we both start by saying what we want and work it over until we get to the point where we're left with what we both need."

Lester wiped tears from his eyes. "I don't think that you grasp the absurdity of this situation, fellas. For starters, Perry will never go for it. I mean *never*." Suzanne wondered about that. And wondered whether it mattered. The two had hardly said a word to each other in months.

"What's more, the rest of the rides will never, never, *never* go in for it. That's also for sure.

"Finally, what the fuck are you talking about? Me go to work for you? Us go to work for you? What will you do—stick Mickey in the ride? He's already in the ride, every now and again, as you well know. You going to move me up to Orlando?"

Sammy waggled his head from side to side. "I have a deep appreciation for how weird this is, Lester. To tell you the truth, I haven't thought much about your ride or this little town. As far as I'm concerned, we could just buy it and then turn around and sell it back to the residents for one dollar—we wouldn't want to own or operate any of this stuff, the liability is too huge. Likewise the other rides. We don't care about what you did *yesterday*—we care about what you're going to do tomorrow.

"Listen, you're a smart guy. You make stuff that we can't dream of, that we lack the institutional imagination to dream of. We need *that*. What the hell is the point of fighting you, suing you, when we can put you on the payroll? And you know what? Even if we throw an idiotic sum of money at you, even if you never make anything for us, we're still ahead of the game if you stop making stuff *against* us.

"I'm putting my cards on the table here. I know your partner is going to be even harder to convince, too. None of this is going to be easy. I don't care about easy. I care about what's right. I'm sick of being in charge of sabotaging people who make awesome stuff. Aren't you sick of being sabotaged? Wouldn't you like to come work someplace where we'll shovel money and resources at your projects and keep the wolves at bay?"

Suzanne was impressed. This wasn't the same guy Rat-Toothed Freddy had savaged. It wasn't the same guy that Death Waits had described. He had come a long way. Even Guignol—whom, she suspected, needed to be sold on the idea almost as much as Lester—was nodding along by the end of it.

Lester wasn't, though: "You're wasting your time, mister. That's all there is to it. I am not going to go and work for"—a giggle escaped his lips—"Disney. It's just—"

Sammy held his hands up in partial surrender. "OK, OK. I won't push you today. Think about it. Talk it over with your buddy. I'm a patient guy." Guignol snorted. "I don't want to lean on you here."

They took their leave, though Suzanne found out later that they'd taken a spin around the ride before leaving. Everyone went on the ride.

Lester shook his head at the door behind them.

"Can you believe that?"

Suzanne smiled and squeezed his hand. "You're funny about this, you know that? Normally, when you encounter a new idea, you like to play with it, think it through, see what you can make of it. With this, you're not even willing to noodle with it."

"You can't seriously think that this is a good idea—"

"I don't know. It's not the dumbest idea I've ever heard. Become a millionaire, get to do whatever you want? It'll sure make an interesting story."

He goggled at her.

"Kidding," she said, thinking, *It would indeed make an interesting story, though.* "But where are you going from here? Are you going to stay here forever?"

"Perry would never go for it—" Lester said, then stopped.

"You and Perry, Lester, how long do you think that's going to last?"

"Don't you go all Yoko on me, Suzanne. We've got one of those around here already—"

"I don't like this Yoko joke, Lester. I never did. Hilda doesn't want to drive Perry away from you. She wants to make the rides work. And it sounds like that's what Perry wants, too. What's wrong with them doing that? Especially if you can get them a ton of money to support it?"

Lester stared at her, openmouthed. "Honey—"

"Think about it, Lester. Your most important virtue is your expansive imagination. Use it."

She watched this sink in. It did sink in. Lester listened to her, which surprised her every now and again. Most relationships seemed to be negotiations, or possibly competitions. With Lester it was a conversation.

She gave him a hug that seemed to go on forever.

Sammy was glad he was driving. The mood Guignol was in, he'd have wrecked the car. "That was *not* the plan, Sammy," he said. "The plan was to get the data, talk it over—"

"The first casualty of any battle is the battle plan," Sammy said, threading them through the press of tourist buses and commuter cars.

"I thought the first casualty was the truth."

They'd spent too long at the ride, then gotten stuck in the afternoon rush hour out of Miami. "That too. Look, I'm proposing to spend a tenth of the profits from the DiaB on this venture. In any other circumstance, I would do it with a *purchase order*. The only reason it's a big deal is—"

"That it carries enough legal liability to destroy the company. Sammy, didn't you listen to Hackelberg?"

"The reason I still work at Disney is that it's the kind of company where the lawyers don't *always* set the agenda."

Guignol drummed his hands on the dashboard. Sammy pulled over and gassed up. At the next pump was a minivan with Kansas plates. Dad was a dumpy Korean guy, Mom was a dumpy white midwesterner with a country-and-western denim jacket, and the backseat was filled with vibrating children, two girls and a boy. The kids were screaming and fighting, the girls trying to draw on the boy's face with candy-flavored lipstick and kiddie mascara, the boy squirming mightily and lashing out at them with his gameboy.

Dad and Mom were having their own heated discussion as Dad gassed up; Sammy eavesdropped enough to hear that they were fighting over Dad's choice of taking the toll roads instead of the cheaper, slower alternative route. The kids were shouting so loud, though—

"You keep that up and we're not going to Disney World!"

It was the magic sentence, the litmus test for Disney's currency. As it rose and fell, so did the efficacy of the threat. If Sammy could, he'd take a video of the result every time this was uttered.

The kids looked at Dad and shrugged. "Who cares?" the eldest sister said, and grabbed the boy again.

Sammy turned to Guignol and waggled his eyebrows. Once he was back in the car, he said, "You know, it's risky doing anything. But riskiest of all is doing nothing."

Guignol shook his head and pulled out his computer.

He spent a lot of time looking at the numbers while Sammy fought traffic. Finally he closed his computer, put his head back and shut his eyes. Sammy drove on.

"You think this'll work?" Guignol said.

"Which part?

"You think if you buy these guys out—"

"Oh, that part. Sure, yeah, slam dunk. They're cheap. Like I say, we could make back the whole nut just by settling the lawsuit. The hard part is going to be convincing them to sell."

"And Hackelberg."

"That's your job, not mine."

Guignol slid the seat back so it was flat as a bed. "Wake me when we hit Orlando."

It took IT three days to get Sammy his computer back. His secretary managed best she could, but he wasn't able to do much without it.

When he got it back at last, he eagerly downloaded his backlog of mail. It beggared the imagination. Even after auto-filtering it, there were hundreds of new messages, things he had to pay real attention to. When he was dealing with this stuff in little spurts every few minutes, all day long, it didn't seem like much, but it sure piled up.

He enlisted his secretary to help him with sorting and responding. After an hour she forwarded one back to him with a bold red flag.

It was from Freddy. He got an instant headache, the feeling halfway between a migraine and the feeling after you bang your head against the corner of a table.

> Sammy, I'm disappointed in you. I thought we were friends. Why do I have to learn about your bizarre plan to buy out Gibbons and Banks from strangers. I do hope you'll give me a comment on the story?

He'd left the financials with Guignol, who had been discreetly showing them around to the rest of the executive committee in closed door, off-site meetings. One of them must have blabbed, though—or maybe it was a leak at Lester's end.

He tasted his lunch and bile as his stomach twisted. It wasn't fair. He had a real chance of making this happen—and it would be a source of genuine good for all concerned.

He got halfway through calling Guignol's number, then put the phone down. He didn't know who to call. He'd put himself in an unwinnable position. As he contemplated the article that Freddy would probably write, he realized that he would almost certainly lose his job over this, too. Maybe end up on the wrong end of a lawsuit. Man, that seemed to be his natural state at Disney. Maybe he was in the wrong job.

He groaned and thumped himself on the forehead. All he wanted to do was have good ideas and make them happen.

Basically, he wanted to be Lester.

Then he knew who he had to call.

"Ms. Church?"

"We're back to that, huh? That's probably not a good sign."

"Suzanne then."

"Sammy, you sound like you're about to pop a testicle. Spit it out."

"Do you think I could get a job with Lester?"

"You're not joking, are you?"

"Freddy found out about the buyout offer."

"Oh."

"Yeah."

"So I'm gonna be in search of employment. All I ever wanted to do was come up with cool ideas and execute them—"

"Shush now. Freddy found out about this, huh? Not surprising. He's got a knack for it. It's just about his only virtue."

"Urgh."

"However, it's also his greatest failing. I've given this a lot of thought, since my last run-in with Rat-Toothed Freddy."

"You call him that to his face?"

"Not yet. But I look forward to it. Tell you what, give me an hour to talk to some people here, and I'll get back to you."

An hour? "An hour?"

"He'll keep you squirming for at least that long. He loves to make people squirm. It's good journalism—shakes loose some new developments."

"An hour?"

"Have you got a choice?"

"An hour, then."

Suzanne didn't knock on Lester's door. Lester would fall into place, once Perry was in.

She found him working the ride, Hilda back in the maintenance bay, tweaking some of the robots. His arm was out of the cast, but it was noticeably thinner than his good, left arm, weak and pale and flabby.

"Hello, Suzanne." He was formal, like he always was these days, and it saddened her, but she pressed on.

"Perry, we need to shut down for a while, it's urgent."

"Suzanne, this is a busy time, we just can't shut down—"

She thumped her hand on his lemonade-stand counter. "Cut it out, Perry. I have never been an alarmist, you know that. I understand intimately what it means to shut this place down. Look, I know that things haven't been so good between us, between *any* of us, for a long time. But I am your dear friend, and you are mine, no matter what's going on at this second, and I'm telling you that you need to shut this down and we need to talk. Do it, Perry."

He gave her a long, considering look.

"Please?"

He looked at the little queue of four or five people, pretending not to eavesdrop, waiting their turn.

"Sorry, folks, you heard the lady. Family emergency. Um, here—" He rummaged under the counter, came up with scraps of paper. "Mrs. Torrence's tearoom across the street—they make the best cappuccino in the hood, and the pastries are all baked fresh. On me, OK?"

"Come on," Suzanne said. "Time's short."

She accompanied him to the maintenance bay and they pulled the doors shut behind them. Hilda looked up from her robot, wiping her hands on her shorts. She was really lovely, and the look on her face when she saw Perry was pure adoration. Suzanne's heart welled up for the two of them, such a perfect picture of young love.

Then Hilda saw Suzanne, and her expression grew guarded, tense. Perry took Hilda's hand.

"What's this about, Suzanne?" he said.

"Let me give this to you in one shot, OK?" They nodded. She ran it down for them. Sammy and Guignol, the postcard, and the funny circumstances of their visit—the phone call.

"So here's the thing. He wants to buy you guys out. He doesn't want the ride or the town. He just wants—I don't know—the *creativity*. The PR win. He wants peace. And the real news is, he's over a barrel. Freddy's forcing his hand. If we can make that problem go away, we can ask for *anything*."

Hilda's jaw hung slack. "You have to be kidding—"

Perry shushed her. "Suzanne, why are you here? Why aren't you talking to Lester about this? Why hasn't Lester talked to me about this? I mean, just what the fuck is going on?"

She winced. "I didn't talk to Lester because I thought he'd be easier to sell on this than you are. This is a golden opportunity and I thought that you would be conflicted as hell about it and I thought if I talked to you first, we could get past that. I don't really have a dog in this fight, except that I want all parties to end up not hating each other. That's where you're headed now—you're melting down in slow motion. How long since you and Lester had a conversation together, let alone a real meal? How long since we all sat around and laughed? Every good thing comes to some kind of end, and then the really good things come to a beginning again.

"You two *were* the New Work. Lots of people got blisteringly rich off of

New Work, but not you. Here's a chance for you to get what you deserve for a change. You solve this—and you *can* solve it, and not just for you, but for that Death kid. You can get him justice that the courts will take fifteen years to deliver."

Perry scowled. "I don't care about money—"

"Yes, that's admirable. I have one other thing: I've been saving it for last, waiting to see if you'd come up with it on your own."

"What?"

"Why is time of the essence?"

"Because Freddy's going to out this dirtball—"

"And how do we solve that?"

Hilda grinned. "Oh, this part I like."

Suzanne laughed. "Yeah."

"What?" Perry said.

"Freddy's good at intelligence gathering, but he's not so good at distinguishing truth from fiction. In my view, this presents a fascinating opportunity. Depending on what we leak to him and how, we can turn him into—"

"A laughingstock?"

"A puddle of deliquesced organ meat."

Perry began to laugh. "You're saying you think that we should do this deal for *spite*?"

"Yeah, that's the size of it," Suzanne said.

"I love it," he said.

Hilda laughed, too. Suzanne extended her hand to Perry and he shook it. Then she shook with Hilda.

"Let's go find Lester."

By the time the call came, Sammy was ready to explode. He got in a golf cart and headed to the Animal Kingdom Lodge, which backed onto the safari park portion of the Animal Kingdom. He snuck himself onto the roof of the grand hotel, which had a commanding view of the artificial savanna. He watched a family of giraffes graze, using the zoom on his phone to resolve the hypnotic patterns of the little calf. It calmed him. But the sound of his phone ringing startled him so much he nearly did a half-gainer off the roof. Heart hammering, he answered it.

"Is this Sammy?"

"Yes," he said.

"Landon Kettlewell," the voice on the other side said. Sammy knew the name, of course. But he hadn't been expecting a call from him.

"Hello, Mr. Kettlewell."

"The boys have asked me to negotiate this deal for them. It makes sense—it'll be hard to make this happen without my contributions. I hope you agree."

"It does make sense," Sammy said noncommittally. This wasn't the best day of his life. The giraffes were moving off, but a flock of cranes was wheeling overhead in quiet splendor.

"I'll tell you where we're at. We're going to do a deal with you, a fair one. But a condition of the deal is that we are going to destroy Freddy."

"What?"

"We're going to leak him bad intel on the deal. Lots of it. Give him a whole story. Wait until he publishes it, and then—"

Sammy sat down on the roof. This was going to be a long conversation.

Perry ground his teeth and squeezed his beer. The idea of doing this in a big group had seemed like a good idea. Dirty Max's was certainly full of camaraderie, the smell of roasting meat and the chatter of nearly a hundred voices. He heard Hilda laughing at something Lester said to her, and there were Kettlewell and his kids, fingers and faces sticky with sauce.

Lester had set up the projector and they'd hung sheets over one of the murals for a screen, and brought out a bunch of wireless speakers that they'd scattered around the courtyard. It looked, smelled, sounded, and tasted like a carnival.

But Perry couldn't meet anyone's eye. He just wanted to go home and get under the covers. They were about to destroy Freddy, which had also seemed like a hell of a lark at the time, but now—

"Perry." It was Sammy, up from Orlando, wearing the classic Mickey-gives-the-finger bootleg tee.

"Can you get fired for that?" Perry pointed.

Sammy shook his head. "Actually, it's official. I had them produced last year—they're a big seller. If you can't beat 'em . . . Here—" He dug in the backpack he carried and pulled out another. "You look like a large, right?"

Perry took it from him, held it up. Shrugging, he put down his beer and skinned his tee, then pulled on the Mickey-flips-the-bird. He looked down at his chest. "It's a statement."

"Have you and Lester given any thought to where you're going to relocate, after?"

Perry drew in a deep breath. "I think Lester wants to come to Orlando. But I'm going to go to Wisconsin. Madison."

"You're what now?"

Perry hadn't said anything about this to anyone except Hilda. Something about this Disney exec, it made him want to spill the beans. "I can't go along with this. I'm going to bow out. Do something new. I've been in this shithole for what feels like my whole life now."

Sammy looked poleaxed. "Perry, that wasn't the deal—"

"Yeah, I know. But think about this: do you want me there if I hate it, resent it? Besides, it's a little late in the day to back out."

Sammy reeled. "Christ almighty. Well, at least you're not going to end up my employee."

Francis—who had an uncanny knack for figuring out the right moment to step into a conversation—sidled over. "Nice shirt, Perry."

"Francis, this is Sammy." Francis had a bottle of water and a plate of ribs, so he extended a friendly elbow.

"We've met—showed him the bicycle factory."

Sammy visibly calmed himself. "That's right, you did. Amazing, just amazing."

"All this is on Sammy," Perry said, pointing at the huge barbecue smoker, the crowds of sticky-fingered gorgers. "He's the Disney guy."

"Hence the shirts, huh?"

"Exactly."

"So what's the rumpus, exactly?" Francis asked. "It's all been hush-hush around here for a solid week."

"I think we're about to find out," Perry said, nodding at the gigantic screen, which rippled in the sultry Florida night breeze, obscured by blowing clouds of fragrant smoke. It was lit up now, showing CNNfn, two pan-racial anchors talking silently into the night.

The speakers popped to life and gradually the crowd noises dimmed. People moved toward the screen, all except Francis and Perry and Sammy, who hung back, silently watching the screen.

"—guest on the show is Freddy Niedbalski, a technology reporter for the notorious British technology publication *Tech Stink*. Freddy has agreed to come on *Countdown* to break a story that will go live on *Tech Stink*'s website in about ten minutes." The camera zoomed out to show Freddy, sitting beside the anchor desk in an armchair. His paunch was more pronounced than it had been when Perry had seen him in Madison, and there was something wrong with his makeup, a color mismatch that made him look like he'd slathered himself with Man-Tan. Still, he was grinning evilly and looking like he could barely contain himself.

"Thank you, Tania-Luz, it's a pleasure."

"Now, take us through the story. You've been covering it for a long time, haven't you?"

"Oh yes. This is about the so-called New Work cult, and its aftermath. I've broken a series of scandals involving these characters over the years—weird sex, funny money, sweatshop labor. These are the people who spent all that money in the New Work bubble, and then went on to found an honest-to-God slum that they characterized as a 'living laboratory' "—out came the sarcastic finger-quotes—"but, as near as anyone can work out, was more of a human-subject experiment gone mad. They pulled off these bizarre stunts with the help of some of the largest investment funds on the planet."

Perry looked around at the revelers. They were chortling, pointing at each other, mugging for the camera. Freddy's words made Perry uncomfortable—maybe there was something to what he said. But there was Francis, unofficial mayor of the shantytown, smiling along with the rest. They hadn't been perfect, but they'd left the world a better place than they'd found it.

"There are many personalities in this story, but tonight's installment has two main players: a venture capitalist named Landon Kettlewell and a Disney Parks senior vice president called Sammy Page. Technically, these two hate each other's guts—" Sammy and Kettlewell toasted each other through the barbecue smoke. "But they've been chumming up to one another lately as they brokered an improbable deal to shaft everyone else in the sordid mess."

"A deal that you've got details on for us tonight?"

"Exactly. My sources have turned up reliable memos and other intelligence indicating that the investors behind the shantytown are about to *take over Disney Parks*. It all stems from a lawsuit that was brought on behalf of a syndicate of operators of bizarre, trademark-infringing rides that were raided off the backs of complaints from Disney Parks. These raids, and a subsequent and very suspicious beating of an ex–Disney Park employee, led to the creation of an investment syndicate to fund a monster lawsuit against Disney Parks, one that could take the company down.

"The investment syndicate found an unlikely ally in the person of Sammy Page, the senior VP from Disney Parks, who worked with them to push through a plan where they would settle the lawsuit in exchange for a controlling interest in Disney Parks."

The anchors looked suitably impressed. Around the screen, the partiers had gone quiet, even the kids, mesmerized by Freddy's giant head, eyes rolling with irony and mean humor.

"And that's just for starters. The deal required securing the cooperation of the beaten-up ex-Disney employee, who goes by the name of 'Death Waits'—no, really!—and *he* required that he be made a vice president of the new company as well, running the Fantasyland section of the Florida park. In the new structure, the two founders of the New Work scam, Perry Gibbons and Lester Banks, are to oversee the Disneyfication of the activist rides around the country, selling out their comrades, who signed over control of their volunteer-built enterprises as part of the earlier lawsuit."

The male anchor shook his head. "If this is true, it's the strangest turn in American corporate history."

"Oh yes," Freddy said. "These people are like some kind of poison, a disease that affects the judgement of all those around them—"

"If it's true," the male anchor continued, as if Freddy hadn't spoken. "But is it? Our next guest denies all of this, and claims that Mr. Niedbalski has his facts all wrong. Tjan Lee Tang is the chairman of Massachusetts Ride Theorists, a nonprofit that operates three of the spin-off rides in New England. He is in our Boston studios. Welcome, Mr. Tang."

Freddy's expression was priceless: a mixture of raw terror and contempt. He tried to cover it, but only succeeded in looking constipated. On the other half of the split screen, Tjan beamed sunnily at them.

"Hi there!" he said. "Greetings from the blustery Northeast."

"Mr. Tang, you've heard what our guest has to say about the latest developments in the extraordinary story of the rides you helped create. Do you have any comment?"

"I certainly do. Freddy, old buddy, you've been had. Whomever your leak was in Disney, he was putting you on. There is not one single word of truth to anything you had to say." He grinned wickedly. "So what else is new?"

Freddy opened his mouth and Tjan held up one hand. "No, wait, let me finish. I know it's your schtick to come after us this way, you've been at it for years. I think it's because you have an unrequited crush on Suzanne Church.

"Here's what's really happening. Lester Banks and Perry Gibbons have taken jobs with Disney Parks as part of a straightforward deal. They're going to do research and development there, and Disney is settling its ongoing lawsuit with us with a seventy-million-dollar cash settlement. Half goes to the investors. Some of the remainder will go to buy the underlying titles to the shantytown and put them in a trust to be managed by a cooperative of residents. The rest is going into another trust that will be disbursed in grants to people operating rides around the country. There's a nonmonetary part of the deal, too: all rides get a perpetual, worldwide license on all Disney trademarks for use in the rides."

The announcers smiled and nodded.

"We think this is a pretty good win. The rides go on. The shantytown goes on. Lester and Perry get to do great work in a heavily resourced lab environment."

Tania-Luz turned to Freddy. "It seems that your story is in dispute. Do you have further comment?"

Freddy squirmed. A streak of sweat cut through his pancake makeup as the camera came in for a close-up. "Well, if this is true, I'd want to know why Disney would make such a generous offer—"

"Generous?" Tjan said. He snorted. "We were asking for *eight billion* in punitive damages. They got off easy!"

Freddy acted like he hadn't heard. "Unless the terms of this so-called deal are published and subject to scrutiny—"

"We posted them about five minutes ago. You could have just asked us, you know."

Freddy's eyes bugged out. "We have no way of knowing whether what this man is saying is true—"

"Actually, you do. Like I say, it's all online. The deals are signed. Securities filings and everything."

Freddy got up out of his seat. *"Would you shut up and let me finish?"* he screamed.

"Sorry, sorry," Tjan said with a chuckle. He was enjoying this way too much. "Go on."

"And what about Death Waits? He's been a pawn all along in this game you've played with other people's lives. What happens to him as you all get rich?"

Tjan shrugged. "He got a large cash settlement, too. He seemed pretty happy about it—"

Freddy was shaking. "You can't just sell off your lawsuit—"

"We were looking to get compensated for bad acts. We got compensated for them, and we did it without tying up the public courts. Everybody wins." He cocked his head. "Except you, of course."

"This was a fucking ambush," Freddy said, pointing his fingers at the two coiffed and groomed anchors, who shied away dramatically, making him look even crazier. He stormed off the stage, cursing, every word transmitted by his still-running wireless mic. He shouted at an invisible security guard to get out of his way. Then they heard him make a phone call, presumably to his editor, shouting at him to kill the article, nearly weeping in frustration. The anchors and Tjan pasted on unconvincing poker faces, but around the barbecue pit, it was all howls of laughter, which turned to shrieks when Freddy finally figured out that he was still on a live mic.

Perry and Sammy locked eyes and grinned. Perry ticked a little salute off his forehead at Sammy and hefted his tee. Then he turned on his heel and walked off into the night, the fragrant smell of the barbecue smoke and the sound of the party behind him.

He parked his car at home and trudged up the stairs. Hilda had packed her suitcase that morning. He had a lot more than a suitcase's worth of stuff around the apartment, but as he threw a few T-shirts—including his new fake bootleg Mickey tee—and some underwear in a bag, he suddenly realized that he didn't care about any of it.

Then he happened upon the baseball glove. The cloud of old-leather smell it emitted when he picked it up made tears spring into his eyes. He hadn't cried through any of this process, though, and he wasn't about to start now. He wiped his eyes with his forearm and reverently set the glove into his bag and shut it. He carried both bags downstairs and put them in the trunk, then he drove to just a little ways north of the ride and called Hilda to let her know he was ready to go.

She didn't say a word when she got in the car, and neither did he, all the way to Miami airport. He took his frisking and secondary screening in stoic silence, and once they were seated on the Chicago flight, he put his head down on Hilda's shoulder and she stroked his hair until he fell asleep.

epilogue

Lester was in his workshop when Perry came to see him. He had the yoga mat out and he was going through the slow exercises that his physiotherapist had assigned to him, stretching his crumbling bones and shrinking muscles, trying to keep it all together. He'd fired three physios, but Suzanne kept finding him new ones, and (because she loved him) prettier ones.

He was down on all fours, his ass stuck way up in the air, when Perry came through the door. He looked back through his ankles and squinted at the upside-down world. Perry's expression was carefully neutral, the same upside down as it would be right-side up. He grunted and went down to his knees, which crackled like popcorn.

"That doesn't sound good," Perry remarked mildly.

"Funny man," Lester said. "Get over here and help me up, will you?"

Perry went down in a crouch before him. There was something funny about his eye, the whole side of his head. He smelled a little sweaty and a little gamy, but the face was the one Lester knew so well. Perry held out his strong, leathery hands, and after a moment, Lester grasped them and let Perry drag him to his feet.

They stood facing one another for an uncomfortable moment, hands clasped together. Then Perry flung his arms wide and shouted, "Here I am!"

Lester laughed and embraced his old friend, not seen or heard from these last fifteen years.

Lester's workshop had a sofa where he entertained visitors and took his afternoon nap. Normally, he'd use his cane to cross from his workbench to the sofa, but seeing Perry threw him for such a loop that he completely forgot until he was a pace or two away from it and then he found himself flailing for support as his hips started to give way. Perry caught him under the shoulders and propped him up. Lester felt a rush of shame color his cheeks.

"Steady there, cowboy," Perry said.

"Sorry, sorry," Lester muttered.

Perry lowered him to the sofa, then looked around. "You got anything to drink? Water? I didn't really expect the bus would take as long as it did."

"You're taking the bus around Burbank?" Lester said. "Christ, Perry, this is Los Angeles. Even homeless people drive cars."

Perry looked away and shook his head. "The bus is cheaper." Lester pursed his lips. "You got anything to drink?"

"In the fridge," Lester said, pointing to a set of nested clay-pot evaporative coolers. Perry grinned at the jury-rigged cooler and rummaged around in its mouth for a while. "Anything, you know, buzzy? Guarana? Caffeine, even?"

Lester gave an apologetic shrug. "Not me, not anymore. Nothing goes into my body without oversight by a team of very expensive nutritionists."

"You don't look so bad," Perry said. "Maybe a little skinny—"

Lester cut him off. "Not bad like the people you see on TV, huh? Not bad like the dying ones." The fatkins had overwhelmed the nation's hospitals in successive waves of sickened disintegrating skeletons whose brittle bones and ruined joints had outstripped anyone's ability to cope with them. The only thing that kept the crisis from boiling over entirely was the fast mortality that followed on the first symptoms—difficulty digesting, persistent stiffness. Once you couldn't keep down high-calorie slurry, you just starved to death.

"Not like them," Perry agreed. He had a bit of limp, Lester saw, and his old broken arm hung slightly stiff at his side.

"I'm doing OK," Lester said. "You wouldn't believe the medical bills, of course."

"Don't let Freddy know you've got the sickness," Perry said. "He'd love that story—'fatkins pioneer pays the price' "

"Freddy! Man, I haven't thought of that shitheel in—Christ, a decade, at least. Is he still alive?"

Perry shrugged. "Might be. I'd think that if he'd keeled over someone would have asked me to pitch in to charter a bus to go piss on his grave."

Lester laughed hard, so hard he hurt his chest and had to sag back into the sofa, doing deep yoga breathing until his ribs felt better.

Perry sat down opposite him on the sofa with a bottle of Lester's special thrice-distilled flat water in a torpedo-shaped bottle. "Suzanne?" he asked.

"Good," Lester said. "Spends about half her time here and half on the road. Writing, still."

"What's she on to now?"

"Cooking, if you can believe it. Molecular gastronomy—food hackers who use centrifuges to clarify their consommé. She says she's never eaten better. Last week it was some kid who'd written a genetic algorithm to evolve custom printable molecules that can bridge two unharmonious flavors to make them taste good together—like, what do you need to add to chocolate and sardines to make them freakin' delicious?"

"Is there such a molecule?"

"Suzanne says there is. She said that they misted it into her face with a vaporizer while she ate a sardine on a slab of dark chocolate and it tasted better than anything she'd ever had before."

"OK, that's just wrong," Perry said. The two of them were grinning at each other like fools.

Lester couldn't believe how good it felt to be in the same room as Perry again after all these years. His old friend was much older than the last time they'd seen each other. There was a lot of gray in his short hair, and his hairline was a lot higher up his forehead. His knuckles were swollen and wrinkled, and his face had deep lines, making him look carved. He had the leathery skin of a roadside homeless person, and there were little scars all over his arms and a few on his throat.

"How's Hilda?" Lester asked.

Perry looked away. "That's a name I haven't heard in a while," he said.

"Yowch. Sorry."

"No, that's OK. I get email blasts from her every now and again. She's chipper and scrappy as always. Fighting the good fight. Fatkins stuff again—same as when I met her. Funny how that fight never gets old."

"Hardy har har," Lester said.

"OK, we're even," Perry said. "One-one in the faux-pas masters' tournament."

They chatted about inconsequentialities for a while, stories about Lester's life as the closeted genius at Disney Labs, Perry's life on the road, getting itinerant and seasonal work at little micro-factories.

"Don't they recognize you?"

"Me? Naw, it's been a long time since I got recognized. I'm just the guy, you know, he's handy, keeps to himself. Probably going to be moving on soon. Good with money, always has a quiet suggestion for tweaking an idea to make it return a little higher on the investment."

"That's you, all right. All except the 'keeps to himself' part."

"A little older, a little wiser. Better to keep your mouth shut and be thought a fool than to open it and remove all doubt."

"Thank you, Mister Twain. You and Huck been on the river a while, then?"

"No Huck," he said. His smile got sad, heartbreakingly sad. This wasn't the Perry Lester knew. Lester wasn't the same person, either. They were both broken. Perry was alone, though—gregarious Perry, always making friends. Alone.

"So, how long are you staying?"

"I'm just passing through, buddy. I woke up in Burbank this morning and I thought, 'Shit, Lester's in Burbank; I should say hello.' But I got places to go."

"Come on, man, stay a while. We've got a guest cottage out back, a little mother-in-law apartment. There are fruit trees, too."

"Living the dream, huh?" He sounded unexpectedly bitter.

Lester was embarrassed for his wealth. Disney had thrown so much stock at him in the beginning, and Suzanne had sold most of it and wisely invested it in a bunch of micro-funds; add to that the money she was raking in from the affiliate sites her Junior Woodchucks—kid reporters she'd trained and set up in business—ran, and they never had to worry about a thing.

"Well, apart from dying. And working here." As soon as the words were out of his mouth, he wished he could take them back. He never let on that he wasn't happy at the Mouse, and the dying thing—well, Suzanne and he liked to pretend that medical science would cure what it had brought.

Perry, though, he just nodded as if his suspicions were confirmed. "Must be hard on Suzanne."

Now that was hitting the nail on the head. "You always were a perceptive son of a bitch."

"She never said fatkins was good for you. She just reported the story. The people who blame her—"

This was the elephant in the room whenever Lester and Suzanne talked about his health. Between the two of them, they'd popularized fatkins, sent millions winging to Russia for the clinics, fueled the creation of the clinics in the United States and Mexico.

But they never spoke of it. Never. Now Perry was talking about it, still talking:

"—the FDA, the doctors. That's what we pay them for. The way I see it, you're a victim, their victim."

Lester couldn't say anything. Words stoppered themselves up in his mouth like a cork. Finally, he managed to choke out, "Change the subject, OK?"

Perry looked down. "Sorry. I'm out of practice with people."

"I hope you'll stay with us," he said, thinking, *I hope you leave soon and never come back.*

"You miss it, huh?"

"Sometimes."

"You said working here—"

"Working here. They said that they wanted me to come in and help them turn the place around, help them reinvent themselves. Be nimble. Shake things up. But it's like wrestling a tar baby. You push; you get stuck. You argue for something better and they tell you to write a report, then no one reads the report. You try to get an experimental service running and no one will recon-figure the firewall. Turn the place around?" He snorted. "It's like turning around a battleship by tapping it on the nose with a toothpick."

"I hate working with assholes."

"They're not assholes, that's the thing, Perry. They're some really smart people. They're nice. We have them over for dinner. They're fun to eat lunch with. The thing is, *every single one of them feels the same way I do.* They *all* have cool shit they want to do, but they can't do it."

"Why?"

"It's like an emergent property. Once you get a lot of people under one roof, the emergent property seems to be crap. No matter how great the people are, no matter how wonderful their individual ideas are, the net effect is shit."

"Reminds me of reliability calculation. Like if you take two components that are ninety percent reliable and use them in a design, the outcome is ninety percent of ninety percent—eighty-one percent. Keep adding ninety percent reliable components and you'll have something that explodes before you get it out of the factory.

"Maybe people are like that. If you're ninety percent non-bogus and ten percent bogus, and you work with someone else who's ninety percent non-bogus, you end up with a team that's eighty-one percent non-bogus."

"I like that model. It makes intuitive sense. But fuck me, it's depressing. It says that all we do is magnify each other's flaws."

"Well, maybe that's the case. Maybe flaws are multiplicative."

"So what are virtues?"

"Additive, maybe. A shallower curve."

"That'd be an interesting research project, if you could come up with some quantitative measurements."

"So what do you do around here all day?"

Lester blushed.

"What?"

"I'm building bigger mechanical computers, mostly. I print them out us-ing the new volumetrics and have research assistants assemble them. There's something soothing about them. I have an Apple][+ clone running entirely on physical gates made out of extruded plastic skulls. It takes up an entire building out on one of the lots, and when you play Pong on it, the sound of the jaws clacking is like listening to corpse beetles skeletonizing an elephant."

"I think I'd like to see that," Perry said, laughing a little.

"That can be arranged," Lester said.

They were like gears that had once emerged from a mill with perfectly precise teeth, gears that could mesh and spin against each other, transferring energy.

They were like gears that had been ill-used in machines, apart from each other, until their precise teeth had been chipped and bent, so that they no longer meshed.

They were like gears, connected to one another and mismatched, clunking and skipping, but running still, running still.

Perry and Lester rode in the back of the company car, the driver an old Armenian who'd fled Azerbaijan, whom Lester introduced as Kapriel. It seemed that Lester and Kapriel were old friends, which made sense, since Lester couldn't drive himself, and in Los Angeles, you didn't go anywhere except by car. The relationship between a man and his driver would be necessarily intimate.

Perry couldn't bring himself to feel envious of Lester having a chauffeured car, though it was clear that Lester was embarrassed by the luxury. It was too much like an invalid's subsidy to feel excessive.

"Kap," Lester said, stirring in the nest of paper and parts and empty health-food packages that he'd made of the backseat.

Kapriel looked over his shoulder at them. "Home now?" He barely had an accent, but when he turned his head, Perry saw that one ear had been badly mangled, leaving behind a misshapen fist of scar.

"No," Lester said. "Let's eat out tonight. How about Musso and Frank's?"

"Ms. Suzanne says—"

"We don't need to tell her," Lester said.

Perry spoke in a low voice, "Lester, I don't need anything special. Don't make yourself sick—"

"Perry, buddy, shut the fuck up, OK? I can have a steak and a beer and a big-ass dessert every now and again. Purified medicated fatkins chow gets old. My colon isn't going to fall out of my asshole in terror if I send a cheeseburger down there."

They parked behind Musso and Frank and let the valet park the town car. Kapriel went over to the Walk of Fame to take pictures of the robotic movie stars doing acrobatic busking acts, and they went into the dark cave of the restaurant, all dark wood, dark carpets, pictures of movie stars on the walls.

The maître d' gave them a look, tilted his head, looked again. Calmly, Lester produced a hundred-dollar bill and slid it across the podium.

"We'd like Orson Welles's table, please," he said.

The maître d'—an elderly, elegant Mexican with a precise spade beard—nodded affably. "Give me five minutes, gentlemen. Would you care to have a drink in the bar?"

They sat at the long counter and Perry ordered a Scotch and soda. Lester ordered water, then switched his order to beer, then nonalcoholic beer, then beer again. "Sorry," he said to the waitress. "Just having an indecisive kind of night, I guess."

Perry tried to figure out if Lester had been showing off with the C-note, and decided that he hadn't been. He'd just gone native in L.A., and a hundred for the maître d' when you're in a hurry can't be much for a senior exec.

Lester sipped gingerly at his beer. "I like this place," he said, waving the bottle at the celebrity caricatures lining the walls. "It's perfect Hollyweird kitsch. Celebrities who usually eat out in some ultramodern place come here. They come because they've always come—to sit in Orson Welles's booth."

"How's the food?"

"Depends on what you order. The good stuff is great. You down for steaks?"

"I'm down for whatever," Perry said. Lester was in his medium here, letting the waiter unfold his napkin and lay it over his lap without taking any special notice of the old man.

The food was delicious, and they even got to glimpse a celebrity, though neither Perry nor Lester knew who the young woman was, nor what she was famous for. She was surrounded by children who came over from other tables seeking autographs, and more than one patron snapped a semi-subtle photo of her.

"Poor girl," Perry said with feeling.

"It's a career decision here. You decide to become famous because you want that kind of life. Sometimes you even kid yourself that it'll last forever—that in thirty years, they'll come into Musso and Frank's and ask for Miss Whatshername's table. Anyone who wants to know what stardom looks like can find out—and no one becomes a star by accident."

"You think?" Perry said. "I mean, we were celebs, kind of, for a while there—"

"Are you saying that that happened by accident?"

"I never set out to get famous—"

"You took part in a national movement, Perry. You practically *founded* it. What did you think was going to happen—"

"You're saying that we were just attention whores—"

"No, Perry, no. We weren't *just* attention whores. We were attention whores *and* we built and ran cool shit. There's nothing wrong with being an attention whore. It's an attention economy. If you're going to be a working stiff, you should pick a decent currency to get paid in. But you can't sit there and tell me that it didn't feel good, didn't feel *great* to have all those people looking up to us, following us into battle, throwing themselves at us—"

Perry held up his hands. His friend was looking more alive than he had at any time since Perry had been ushered into his workshop. He sat up straight, and the old glint of mischief and good humor was in his eye.

"I surrender, buddy, you're right." They ordered desserts, heavy "diplomat puddings"—bread pudding made with cake and cherries—and Lester dug in, after making Perry swear not to breathe a word of it to Suzanne. He ate with such visible pleasure that Perry felt like a voyeur.

"How long did you say you were in town for?"

"I'm just passing through," Perry said. He had only planned on maybe seeing Lester long enough for lunch or something. Now it seemed a foregone conclusion that he'd be put up in the "guest cottage." He thought about getting back on the road. There was a little gang in Oregon that made novelty school supplies; they were always ramping up for their busy season at this time of year. They were good people to work for.

"Come on, where you got to be? Stay a week. I'll put you on the payroll as a consultant. You can give lunch-hour talks to the R&D team, whatever you want."

"Lester, you just got through telling me how much you hate your job—"

"That's the beauty of contracting—you don't stick around long enough to hate it, and you never have to worry about the org chart. Come on, pal—"

"I'll think about it."

Lester fell asleep on the car ride home, and Kapriel didn't mind if Perry didn't want to chat, so he just rolled his windows down and watched the L.A. lights scream past as they hit the premium lanes on the crosstown freeways, heading to Lester's place in Topanga Canyon. When they arrived, Lester roused himself heavily, clutched his stomach, then raced for the house. Kapriel shook his head and rolled his eyes, then showed Perry to the front door and shook his hand.

In the morning, he prowled Lester and Suzanne's place like a burglar. The guesthouse had once served as Lester's workshop and it had the telltale leavings of a busy inventor—drawers and tubs of parts, a moldy coffee cup in a desk drawer, pens and toys and unread postal spam in piles. What it didn't have was a kitchen, so Perry helped himself to the key that Lester had left him with the night before and wandered around the big house, looking for the kitchen.

It turned out to be on the second floor, a bit of weird architectural design that was characteristic of the place, which had started as a shack in the hills on several acres of land and then grown and grown as successive generations of owners had added extensions, seismic retrofitting, and new floors.

Perry found the pantries filled with high-tech MREs, each nutritionally balanced and fortified in ways calculated to make Lester as healthy as possible. Finally, he found a small cupboard clearly devoted to Suzanne's eating, with boxes of breakfast cereal and, way in the back, a little bag of Oreos. He munched thoughtfully on the cookies while drinking more of the flat, thrice-distilled water.

He heard Lester totter into a bathroom on the floor above, and called, "Good morning," up a narrow, winding staircase.

Lester groaned back at him, a sound that Perry hadn't heard in years, that theatrical oh-my-shit-it's-another-day sound.

He clomped down the stairs with his cane, wearing a pair of boxer shorts and rubber slippers. He was gaunt, the hair on his sunken chest gone wiry gray, and the skin around his torso sagged. From the neck down, he looked a hundred years old. Perry looked away.

"Morning, bro," Lester said, and took a vacuum-sealed pouch out of a medical white box over the sink, tore it open, added purified water, and put it in the microwave. The smell was like wet cardboard in a dumpster. Perry wrinkled his nose.

"Tastes better than it smells. Or looks," Lester said. "Very easy on the digestion. Which I need. Never let me pig out like that again, OK?"

He collapsed heavily into a stool and closed his sunken eyes. Without opening them, he said, "So, are you in?"

"Am I in?"

"You going to come on board as my consultant?"

"You were serious about that, huh?"

"Perry, they can't fire me. If I quit, I lose my health bennies, which means I'll be broke in a month. Which puts us at an impasse. I'm past feeling guilty about doing nothing much all day long, but that doesn't mean I'm not bored."

"You make it sound so attractive."

"You got something better to do?"

"I'm in."

Suzanne came home a week later and found them sitting up in the living room. They'd pushed all the furniture up against the walls and covered the floor with board-game boards, laid edge to edge or overlapping. They had tokens, cards, and money from several of the games laid out around the rims of the games.

"What the blistering fuck?" she said good-naturedly. Lester had told her that Perry was around, so she'd been prepared for something odd, but this was pretty amazing, even so. Lester held up a hand for silence and rolled two dice. They skittered across the floor, one of them slipping through the heating grating.

"Three points," Perry said. "One for not going into the grating, two for going into the grating."

"I thought we said it was two points for not going into the grating, and one for dropping it?"

"Let's call it 1.5 points for each."

"Gentlemen," Suzanne said, "I believe I asked a question? To wit: 'What the blistering fuck?' "

"Calvinball," Lester said. "Like in the old Calvin and Hobbes strips. The rules are, the rules can never be the same twice."

"And you're supposed to wear a mask," Perry said. "But we kept stepping on the pieces."

"No peripheral vision," Lester said.

"Caucus race!" Perry yelled, and took a lap around the world. Lester struggled to his feet, then flopped back down.

"I disbelieve," he said, taking up two ten-sided dice and rolling them. "Eighty-seven," he said.

"Fine," Perry said. He picked up a Battleship board and said, "B-seven," and then he said, "What's the score, anyway?"

"Orange to seven," Lester said.

"Who's orange?"

"You are."

"Shit. OK, let's take a break."

Suzanne tried to hold in her laughter, but she couldn't. She ended up doubled over, tears streaming down her face. When she straightened up, Lester hobbled to her and gave her a surprisingly strong welcome-home hug. He smelled like Lester, like the man she'd shared her bed with all these years.

Perry held out his hand to her and she yanked him into a long, hard hug.

"It's good to have you back, Perry," she said, once she'd kissed both his cheeks.

"It's fantastic to see you, Suzanne," he said. He was thinner than she remembered, with snow on the roof, but he was still handsome as a pirate.

"We missed you. Tell me everything you've been up to."

"It's not interesting," he said. "Really."

"I find that difficult to believe."

So he told them stories from the road, and they were interesting in a kind of microcosm sort of way. Stories about interesting characters he'd met, improbable meals he'd eaten, bad working conditions, memorable rides hitched.

"So that's it?" Suzanne said. "That's what you've done?"

"It's what I do," he said.

"And you're happy?"

"I'm not sad," he said.

She shook her head involuntarily. Perry stiffened.

"What's wrong with not sad?"

"There's nothing wrong with it, Perry. I'm—" she faltered, searched for the words. "Remember when I first met you, met both of you, in that ghost mall? You weren't just happy; you were hysterical. Remember the Boogie Woogie Elmos? The car they drove?"

Perry looked away. "Yeah," he said softly. There was a hitch in his voice.

"All I'm saying is, it doesn't have to be this way. You could—"

"Could what?" he said. He sounded angry, but she thought that he was just upset. "I could go work for Disney, sit in a workshop all day making crap no one cares about? Be the wage slave for the end of my days, a caged monkey for some corporate sultan's zoo?" The phrase was Lester's, and Suzanne knew then that Perry and Lester had been talking about it.

Lester, leaning heavily against her on the sofa (they'd pushed it back into the room, moving aside pieces of the Calvinball game), made a warning sound and gave her knee a squeeze. Aha, definitely territory they'd covered before then.

"You two have some of the finest entrepreneurial instincts I've ever encountered," she said. Perry snorted.

"What's more, I've never seen you happier than you were back when I first met you, making stuff for the sheer joy of it and selling it to collectors. Do you know how many collectors would pony up for an original Gibbons/Banks today? You two could just do that forever—"

"Lester's medical—"

"Lester's medical nothing. You two get together on this, you could make so much money, we could buy Lester his own hospital." *Besides, Lester won't last long no matter what happens.* She didn't say it, but there it was. She'd come to grips with the reality years ago, when his symptoms first appeared—when *all* the fatkins' symptoms began to appear. Now she could think of it without getting that hitch in her chest that she'd gotten at first. Now she could go away for a week to work on a story without weeping every night, then drying her eyes and calling Lester to make sure he was still alive.

"I'm not saying you need to do this to the exclusion of everything else, or forever"—*there is no forever for Lester*—"but you two would have to be insane not to try it. Look at this board-game thing you've done—"

"Calvinball," Perry said.

"Calvinball. Right. You were made for this. You two make each other better. Perry, let's be honest here. You don't have anything better to do."

She held her breath. It had been years since she'd spoken to Perry, years since she'd had the right to say things like that to him. Once upon a time, she wouldn't have thought twice, but now—

"Let me sleep on it," Perry said.

Which meant no, of course. Perry didn't sleep on things. He decided to do things. Sometimes he decided wrong, but he'd never had trouble deciding.

That night, Lester rubbed her back, the way he always did when she came back from the road, using the hand cream she kept on her end table. His hands had once been so *strong,* mechanic's hands, stubby-fingered pistons he could drive tirelessly into the knots in her back. Now they smoothed and petted, a rub, not a massage. Every time she came home, it was gentler, somehow more loving. But she missed her massages. Sometimes she thought she should tell him not to bother anymore, but she was afraid of what it would mean to end this ritual—and how many more rituals would end in its wake.

It was the briefest backrub yet and then he slid under the covers with her. She held him for a long time, spooning him from behind, her face in the nape of his neck, kissing his collar bone the way he liked, and he moaned softly.

"I love you, Suzanne," he said.

"What brought that on?"

"It's just good to have you home," he said.

"You seem to have been taking pretty good care of yourself while I was away, getting in some Perry time."

"I took him to Musso and Frank's," he said. "I ate like a pig."

"And you paid the price, didn't you?"

"Yeah. For days."

"Serves you right. That Perry is *such* a bad influence on my boy."

"I'll miss him."

"You think he'll go, then?"

"You know he will."

"Oh, honey."

"Some wounds don't heal," he said. "I guess."

"I'm sure it's not that," Suzanne said. "He loves you. I bet this is the best week he's had in years."

"So why wouldn't he want to stay?" Lester's voice came out in the petulant near sob she had only ever heard when he was in extreme physical pain. It was a voice she heard more and more often lately.

"Maybe he's just afraid of himself. He's been on the run for a long time. You have to ask yourself, what's he running from? It seems to me that he's spent his whole life trying to avoid having to look himself in the eye."

Lester sighed and she squeezed him tight. "How'd we get so screwed up?"

"Oh, baby," she said, "we're not screwed up. We're just people who want to do things, big things. Any time you want to make a difference, you face the possibility that you'll, you know, make a difference. It's a consequence of doing things with consequences."

"Gak," he said. "You always get so Zen-koan when you're on the road."

"Gives me time to reflect. Were you reading?"

"Was I reading? Suzanne, I read your posts whenever I feel lonely. It's kind of like having you home with me."

"You're sweet."

"Did you really eat sardines on sorbet toast?"

"Don't knock it. It's better than it sounds. Lots better."

"You can keep it."

"Listen to Mr. Musso and Frank's—boy, you've got no business criticizing anyone else's food choices."

He heaved a happy sigh. "I love you, Suzanne Church."

"You're a good man, Lester Banks."

Perry met them at the breakfast table the next morning as Suzanne was fiddling with the espresso machine, steaming soy milk for her latte. He wore a pair of Lester's sloppy drawstring pants and a T-shirt for a motorcycle shop in Kansas City that was spotted with old motor-oil stains.

"Bom dia," he said, and chucked Lester on the shoulder. He was carrying himself with a certain stiffness, and Suzanne thought, *Here it comes; he's going to say goodbye. Perry Gibbons, you bastard.*

"Morning," Lester said, brittle and chipper.

Perry dug around on Suzanne's non-medicated food shelf for a while and came up with a bagel for the toaster and a jar of peanut butter. No one said anything while he dug around for the big bread knife, found the cutting board, toasted the bagel, spread peanut butter, and took a bite. Suzanne and

Lester just continued to eat, in uncomfortable silence. *Tell him,* Suzanne urged silently. *Get it over with, damn you.*

"I'm in," Perry said, around a mouthful of bagel, looking away.

Suzanne saw that he had purple bags under his eyes, like he hadn't slept a wink all night.

"I'm staying. If you'll have me. Let's make some stuff."

He put the bagel down and swallowed. He looked back at Lester, and the two old comrades locked eyes for a long moment.

Lester smiled. "All right!" He danced a shuffling step, mindful of his sore hips. "All right, buddy, *fuckin' A!* Yeah!"

Suzanne tried to fade then, to back out of the room and let them do their thing, but Lester caught her arm and drew her into an embrace, tugging on her arm with a strength she'd forgotten he had.

He gave her a hard kiss. "I love you, Suzanne Church," he said. "You're my savior."

Perry made a happy sound behind her.

"I love you, too, Lester," she said, squeezing his skinny, brittle back.

Lester let go of her and she turned to face Perry. Tears pricked his eyes, and she found that she was crying, too. She gave him a hug, and felt the ways that his body had changed since she'd last held him, back in Florida, back in some forgotten time. He was thicker, but still solid, and he smelled the same. She put her lips close to his ear and whispered, "You're a good man, Perry Gibbons."

Lester gave his notice that morning. Though it was 8 PM in Tehran when Lester called, Sammy was at his desk.

"Why are you telling me this, Lester?"

"It says in my contract that I have to give my notice to you, specifically."

"Why the hell did I put that there?" Sammy's voice sounded far away—not just in Iran. It sounded like he had traveled through time, too.

"Politics, I think," he said.

"Hard to remember. Probably wanted to be sure that someone like Wiener wouldn't convince you to quit, switch companies, and hire you again."

"Not much risk of that now," Lester said. "Let's face it, Sammy, I don't actually do anything for the company."

"Nope. That's right. We're not very good at making use of people like you."

"Nope."

"Well, email me your paperwork and I'll shove it around. How much notice are you supposed to give?"

"Three months'."

"Yowch. Whatever. Just pack up and go home. Gardening leave."

It had been two years since Lester'd had any contact with Sammy, but it was clear that running Iranian ops had mellowed him out. Harder to get into trouble with women there, anyway.

"How's Iran treating you?"

"The Middle East operation is something else, boy. You'd like it here. The postwar towns all look like your squatter city—the craziest buildings you ever saw. They love the DiaBs, though—we get the most fantastic designs through the fan channels. . . ." He trailed off. Then, with a note of suspicion: "What are you going to do now?"

Ah. No sense in faking it. "Perry and I are going to go into business together. Making kinetic sculptures. Like the old days."

"No *way*! Perry *Gibbons*? You two are back together? Christ, we're all doomed." He was laughing. "Sculptures—like that toast robot? And he wants to go into *business*? I thought he was some kind of Commie."

Lester had a rush of remembrance, the emotional memory of how much he'd hated this man and everything he stood for. What had happened to him over the years that he counted this sneak, this thug, as his colleague? What had he sold when he sold out?

"Perry Gibbons," Lester said, and drew in a breath. "Perry Gibbons is the sharpest entrepreneur I've ever met. He can't *help* but make businesses. He's an artist who anticipates the market a year ahead of the curve. He could be a rich man a hundred times over if he chose. Commie? Page, you're not fit to keep his books."

The line went quiet, the eerie silence of a Net connection with no packets routing on it. "Goodbye, Lester," Sammy said at length.

Lester wanted to apologize. He wanted *not* to want to apologize. He swallowed the apology and disconnected the line.

When it was time for bed, Suzanne shut her lid and put the computer down beside the sofa. She stepped carefully around the pieces of the Calvin-ball game that still covered the living room floor and stepped into a pair of slippers. She slid open the back door and hit the switch for the yard's flood-light. The last thing she wanted to do was trip into the pool.

She picked her way carefully down the flagstones that led to the work-shop, where the lights burned merrily in the night. There was no moon to-night, and the stars were laid out like a bag of synthetic diamonds arrayed on a piece of black velour in a street-market stall.

She peered through the window before she went around to the door, the journalist in her wanting to fix an image of the moment in her mind be-fore she moved in and disturbed it. That was the problem with being a reporter—everything changed the instant you started reporting on it. By now, there wasn't a person alive who didn't know what it meant to be in the presence of a reporter. She was a roving Panopticon.

The scene inside the workshop was eerie. Perry and Lester stood next to each other, cheek by jowl, hunched over something on the workbench. Perry had a computer open in front of him, and he was typing, Lester holding something out of sight.

How many times had she seen this tableau? How many afternoons had she spent in the workshop in Florida, watching them hack a robot, build a sculpture, turn out the latest toy for Tjan's amusement, Kettlewell's enrichment? The postures were identical—though their bodies had changed, the hair thinner and grayer. Like someone had frozen one of those innocent moments in time for a decade, then retouched it with wizening makeup and hair dye.

She must have made a noise, because Lester looked up—or maybe it was just the uncanny, semi-psychic bond between an old married couple. He grinned at her like he was ten years old and she grinned back and went around to the door.

"Hello, boys," she said. They straightened up, both of them unconsciously cradling their lower backs, and she suppressed a grin. *My little boys, all grown up.*

"Darling!" Lester said. "Come here, have a look!"

He put his arm over her shoulders and walked her to the bench, leaning on her a little.

It was in pieces, but she could see where it was going: a pair of familiar boxy shapes, two of Lester's mechanical computers, their cola-can registers spilling away in a long daisy chain of worm gears and rotating shafts. One figure was big and round-shouldered like a vintage refrigerator. The other was cockeyed, half its gears set higher than the other half. Each had a single, stark mechanical arm extended before it, and at the end of each arm was a familiar cracked and fragrant baseball glove.

Lester put a ball into one of the gloves and Perry hammered away at the keyboard. Very, very slowly, the slope-shouldered robot drew its mechanical arm back—"We used one of the open-source prosthestic plans," Lester whispered in the tense moment. Then it lobbed a soft underhand toss to the lopsided one.

The ball arced through the air and the other bot repositioned its arm in a series of clattering jerks. It seemed to Suzanne that the ball would miss the glove and bounce off of the robot's carapace, and she winced. Then, at the very last second, the robot repositioned its arm with one more fast jerk, and the ball fell into the pocket.

A moment later, the lopsided bot—Perry, it was Perry, that was easy to see—tossed the ball to the round-shouldered one, who was clearly her Lester, as she'd first known him. Lester-bot caught the ball with a similar series of jerks and returned the volley.

It was magic to watch the robots play their game of catch. Suzanne was mesmerized, mouth open. Lester squeezed her shoulder with uncontained excitement.

The Lester-bot lobbed one to Perry-bot, but Perry-bot flubbed the toss. The ball made a resounding gong sound as it bounced off of Perry-bot's carapace, and Perry-bot wobbled.

Suzanne winced, but Lester and Perry both dissolved in gales of laughter. She watched the Perry-bot try to get itself reoriented, aligning its torso to face Lester-bot, and she saw that it *was* funny, very funny, like a particularly great cartoon.

"They do that on purpose?"

"Not exactly—but there's no way they're going to be perfect, so we built in a bunch of stuff that would make it funnier when it happened. It is now officially a feature, not a bug." Perry glowed with pride.

"Isn't it bad for them to get beaned with a baseball?" she asked as Lester carefully handed the ball to Perry-bot, who lobbed it to Lester-bot again.

"Well, yeah. But it's kind of an artistic statement," Perry said, looking away from them both. "About the way that friendships always wear you down, like upper and lower molars grinding away at each other."

Lester squeezed her again. "Over time, they'll knock each other apart."

Tears pricked at Suzanne's eyes. She blinked them away. "Guys, this is great." Her voice cracked, but she didn't care. Lester squeezed her tighter.

"Come to bed soon, hon," she said to Lester. "I'm going away again tomorrow afternoon—New York, a restaurant opening."

"I'll be right up," Lester said, and kissed the top of her head. She'd forgotten that he was that tall. He didn't stand all the way up.

She went to bed, but she couldn't sleep. She crossed to the window and drew back the curtain and looked out at the backyard—the scummy swimming pool she kept forgetting to do something about, the heavy grapefruit and lemon trees, the shed. Perry stood on the shed's stoop, looking up at the night sky. She pulled the curtains around herself an instant before he looked up at her.

Their eyes met and he nodded slowly.

"Thank you," she mouthed silently.

He blew her a kiss, stuck out a foot, and then bowed slightly over his outstretched leg.

She let the curtain fall back into place and went back to bed. Lester climbed into bed with her a few minutes later and spooned up against her back, his face buried in her neck.

She fell asleep almost instantly.

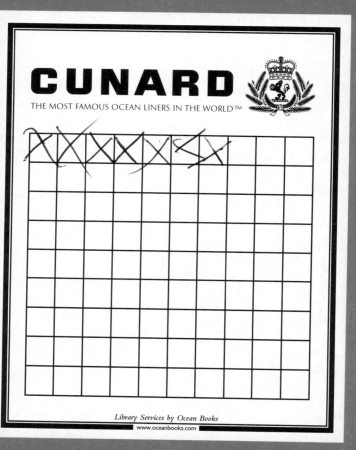